W9-BHY-400

ANTHONY TROLLOPE

was born in 1815 in London. His father eventually failed both as barrister and as gentleman farmer. His mother, Frances Trollope, became a popular author, whose literary labors saved the family from financial ruin. Trollope's youth was miserably unhappy, as were his early years as a clerk in the London General Post Office. At the age of twenty-six he was promoted to surveyor's clerk in Ireland, a development he was to call the first good fortune of his life. He later became a postal surveyor, first in Ireland and then in England; he retired from the Post Office only in 1867.

He began writing novels in Ireland in the 1840s, but his first critical success came with *The Warden* in 1855, followed by the even greater success of *Barchester Towers* in 1857. Thereafter his career blossomed. As early as 1859 a reviewer for *The Times* said Trollope was "at the top of the tree." By the 1860s another reviewer called him "almost a national institution." The novels that brought him this enormous popularity were chiefly the Chronicles of Barsetshire, which included not only *The Warden* and *Barchester Towers* but *Doctor Thorne* (1858), *Framley Parsonage* (1861), *The Small House at Allington* (1864), and *The Last Chronicle of Barset* (1867).

Before the Barchester series was completed he began a sequence of political stories called the Palliser Novels: *Can You Forgive Her?* (1864), *Phineas Finn* (1869), *The Eustace Diamonds* (1873), *Phineas Redux* (1874), *The Prime Minister* (1876), and *The Duke's Children* (1880). The Barsetshire and Palliser novels are considered the two finest series of connected stories in English fiction. Among his other novels the most highly regarded are *Orley Farm* (1862) and *The Way We Live Now* (1875). All of Trollope's fiction is characterized by gentle humor, remarkable social realism, and, even today, an extraordinary readability. Trollope was one of the most prolific of literary artists, writing seventy books, including forty-seven novels. He died in 1882.

ANTAM CLASSIC·A BANTAM CLASSIC·A BANTAM CLASSIC·A BANTAM CLASSIC·A BANTAM CLASSIC·A B

Bantam Classics
Ask your bookseller for these other British Classics

BEOWULF AND OTHER OLD ENGLISH POEMS
   Translated by Constance B. Hieatt
THE CANTERBURY TALES by Geoffrey Chaucer
ROBINSON CRUSOE by Daniel Defoe
GULLIVER'S TRAVELS AND OTHER WRITINGS by Jonathan Swift
PRIDE AND PREJUDICE by Jane Austen
EMMA by Jane Austen
SENSE AND SENSIBILITY by Jane Austen
MANSFIELD PARK by Jane Austen
PERSUASION by Jane Austen
FRANKENSTEIN by Mary Shelley
JANE EYRE by Charlotte Brontë
WUTHERING HEIGHTS by Emily Brontë
DAVID COPPERFIELD by Charles Dickens
GREAT EXPECTATIONS by Charles Dickens
HARD TIMES by Charles Dickens
OLIVER TWIST by Charles Dickens
A TALE OF TWO CITIES by Charles Dickens
NICHOLAS NICKLEBY by Charles Dickens
BLEAK HOUSE by Charles Dickens
THE PICKWICK PAPERS by Charles Dickens
A CHRISTMAS CAROL by Charles Dickens
BARCHESTER TOWERS and THE WARDEN by Anthony Trollope
SILAS MARNER by George Eliot
FAR FROM THE MADDING CROWD by Thomas Hardy
TESS OF THE D'URBERVILLES by Thomas Hardy
JUDE THE OBSCURE by Thomas Hardy
THE MAYOR OF CASTERBRIDGE by Thomas Hardy
THE RETURN OF THE NATIVE by Thomas Hardy
HEART OF DARKNESS and THE SECRET SHARER
   by Joseph Conrad
LORD JIM by Joseph Conrad
THE SECRET AGENT by Joseph Conrad
DR. JEKYLL AND MR. HYDE by Robert Louis Stevenson
TREASURE ISLAND by Robert Louis Stevenson
KIDNAPPED by Robert Louis Stevenson
DRACULA by Bram Stoker
CAPTAINS COURAGEOUS by Rudyard Kipling
KIM by Rudyard Kipling
ALICE'S ADVENTURES IN WONDERLAND and THROUGH THE
   LOOKING-GLASS by Lewis Carroll
THE MOONSTONE by Wilkie Collins
THE PICTURE OF DORIAN GRAY AND OTHER WRITINGS
   by Oscar Wilde
THE TIME MACHINE by H. G. Wells
THE INVISIBLE MAN by H. G. Wells
THE WIND IN THE WILLOWS by Kenneth Grahame
LADY CHATTERLEY'S LOVER by D. H. Lawrence

Barchester Towers
and
The Warden
by Anthony Trollope

Introduction by N. John Hall

BANTAM BOOKS
TORONTO · NEW YORK · LONDON · SYDNEY · AUCKLAND

BARCHESTER TOWERS and THE WARDEN
A Bantam Classic Book / October 1984

PRINTING HISTORY

The text of The Warden *is based on the first edition, published in 1855 by Longman, Brown, Green, and Longmans, London. The text of* Barchester Towers *is based on the first edition, published in 1857 by Longman, Brown, Green, Longmans, & Roberts, London. Obvious errors have been corrected, and punctuation has been brought into conformity with modern usage.*

Cover art: "Sunday Morning, The Walk from the Church" (detail), by Richard Redgrave, 1846, from an English private collection. Photograph courtesy of the Maas Gallery, London.

All rights reserved.
Introduction copyright © 1984 by N. John Hall.
The copyrighted portions of this book may not be reproduced in whole or in part, by mimeograph or any other means, without permission. For information address: Bantam Books, Inc.

ISBN 0-553-21181-1

Published simultaneously in the United States and Canada

Bantam Books are published by Bantam Books, Inc. Its trademark, consisting of the words "Bantam Books" and the portrayal of a rooster, is Registered in U.S. Patent and Trademark Office and in other countries. Marca Registrada. Bantam Books, Inc., 666 Fifth Avenue, New York, New York 10103.

PRINTED IN THE UNITED STATES OF AMERICA

O   0 9 8 7 6 5 4 3 2 1

Contents

BARCHESTER TOWERS

Volume One

Volume Two

Volume Three

Introduction
by N. John Hall

Barchester Towers, Trollope's most widely read book, and *The Warden,* the short novel to which it is the sequel, together form a kind of touchstone to his works. They are the books recommended to the new reader of Trollope and the books to which the experienced reader of Trollope returns again and again.

The Warden (1855) and *Barchester Towers* (1857) were the first two novels of what eventually became the six Chronicles of Barsetshire, the others being *Doctor Thorne* (1858), *Framley Parsonage* (1861), *The Small House at Allington* (1864), and *The Last Chronicle of Barset* (1867). These are generally regarded as the finest sequence of novels in English—rivaled perhaps only by Trollope's later series of six books, the Palliser Novels. Trollope himself, like most of his readers, was partial to the earlier series. He came to have a positive love for Barset and its inhabitants, the "new shire" he had added to England: "I had it all in my mind—its roads and railroads, its towns and parishes, its members of Parliament, and the different hunts which rode over it. I knew all the great lords and their castles, the squires and their parks, the rectors and their churches. . . . Throughout these stories there has been no name given to a fictitious site which does not represent to me a spot of which I know all the accessories, as though I had lived and wandered there."

But it was not only in imagination that Trollope lived and wandered in his "dear county" of Barset: the origins of *The Warden* and *Barchester Towers* and of the whole series lay in an assignment he received as a postal official in August 1851. At the time he was a surveyor's clerk in the southern district of Ireland, where his work in reorganizing the rural post had been so successful that he was sent to perform the same services in the southwest of England, an area that included Devonshire, Cornwall, Somersetshire, and parts of Dorsetshire, Oxfordshire, Wiltshire, Gloucestershire, Worcestershire, and Herefordshire. The object was to arrange delivery to every residence in the district, and Trollope, who tackled all work with extraordinary energy, admitted to amusement at the "passion" he put into his effort to cover the country with rural letter-carriers. He contrived to combine this work, which he did on horseback, with another of his passions, that for hunting, and dressed in red coat, boots, and breeches, he would swoop down upon country postmasters, demanding to know how every letter in their office was delivered. Similarly attired, he would startle farmers, parsons, and lone country residents and their wives with abrupt questions as to how they got their letters. He visited almost every house in the district. His work enabled him to see, as he put it, "a considerable portion of Great Britain, with a minuteness which few have enjoyed."

His time was so taken up that he could not get on with his writing career; he had published three novels while living in Ireland, two set in Ireland and one historical novel of revolutionary France. Today the Irish novels, especially the first, are considered quite good, but the public had not caught on, and Trollope's literary career had so far been a failure. Still, he hoped to return to novel writing, and one evening in late May 1852, he visited Salisbury and resolved to do so: "whilst wandering there on a midsummer evening round the purlieus of the cathedral I conceived the story of *The Warden*,—from whence came that series of novels of which Barchester, with its bishops, deans, and archdeacon, was the central site."

Trollope tells us that he "thought much" about the story, and a little more than a year later, on 29 July 1853, at Tenbury in Herefordshire, he began to write the novel, called at first *The Precentor*. At this time he was able to write no more than the first chapter, and then he was recalled to Ireland, as acting surveyor and later as surveyor of the northern counties. Trollope would miss the work in England, to which he had become so attached. But in his two years he had learned a great deal about the southwest, that section of the country that even today, in spite of tremendous change, is still in many ways the most rural, agricultural, and "picturesque" part of England. The city of Barchester draws upon Winchester, Salisbury, Wells, and other cathedral cities; the county of Barset, which he later claimed was largely Somerset, drew on various counties of the west country.

Trollope, back in Ireland, with his headquarters at Belfast, was so absorbed in his new assignment that he did not recommence the novel until the end of 1853 and did not finish it until 10 October 1854. After having thought about it for one and a

half years, he took ten months to write it, a quick enough pace
for most writers but slow by Trollope's later standards (when he
would complete a short novel of this length in six weeks, or two
months at most if pressed by other work). Trollope sent the
manuscript to London publisher William Longman, whose reader,
Joseph Cauvin, a little-known writer and translator, returned a
glowing report. He seems egregiously to have misread the "main
interest" of the story, placing it in John Bold's internal conflict
between love and duty. But he liked the "well drawn and
happily distinguished" characters; he liked the "vein of quiet
humour and (good natured) satire" throughout; one passage he
thought "too strong," probably that in Chapter II of Archdeacon
Grantly in bed with his wife discussing Bold's affection for
Eleanor Harding. Cauvin predicted "a large sale" for the book,
and it was published by Longman on 5 January 1855.

The Warden was not a financial success: Trollope received
payments of £9 8s. 8d. for 1855 and £10 15s. 1d. for 1856.
Stonebreaking, he remarked, would have been more remunerative.
On the other hand, the book had fair critical success. As Trollope
later put it, "The novel-reading world did not go mad about *The
Warden;* but I soon felt that it had not failed as the others had
failed. . . . and I could discover that people around me knew
that I had written a book." All the reviewers were impressed
with the characters of the warden, the archdeacon, and the
bishop. All called the book "clever," although some, like the
Spectator, complained that "the object of the writer is not
clear." But generally the reviews were favorable. *The Leader*
innocently said that *The Warden* "certainly promises well for the
author's future, if he gives us more books."

Only six weeks after the publication of *The Warden,* Trollope
wrote to his publisher inquiring about its sale. He had, he told
Longman, from the first intended a sequel to the story, and if
The Warden seemed successful, he would have the manuscript of
the new novel in the publisher's hands by May. Longman's reply
was discouraging, and Trollope interrupted *Barchester Towers,*
of which he had written some eighty-five manuscript pages.
Evidently anxious to come before the public in a big way,
Trollope decided to turn his hand to nonfiction. He wrote a book
of social criticism, a general survey of English institutions called
The New Zealander. This he submitted to Longman by the end
of March, but Longman's reader strongly advised against
publication. Cauvin found the work "both in style and matter
. . . a most feeble imitation" of Carlyle's *Latter-Day Pamphlets.*

He could scarcely believe that the book was by the author of *The Warden*.

Trollope spent more than a year revising the text of *The New Zealander*, though there is no record of his having again submitted the manuscript for consideration, and the book remained unpublished during his lifetime. Doubtless he also did a good deal of "thinking about" *Barchester Towers*. Post office work continued apace, and it was not until 12 May 1856 that he resumed the novel. At this time he determined to work more systematically and more industriously at novel writing. His production of four novels and one (unpublished) play over a dozen years was hardly slight, especially for someone engaged fulltime in other arduous employment. But when he again took up *Barchester Towers* he began keeping a working diary of his books in which he made daily entries of the number of pages he had written "so that if at any time I have slipped into idleness for a day or two, the record of that idleness has been there, staring me in the face." He set a goal of 40 manuscript pages per week; occasionally he slipped to as few as 20 pages per week; at other times he pushed himself to as many as 119 pages. Later, when in November 1859 he was transferred to England and settled at Waltham Cross outside London, he arranged for his groom to wake him early every day so that he might be at his desk by 5:30, writing for three hours, with his watch before him, keeping himself to 250 words every fifteen minutes.

This kind of regularity was not easy with the traveling his postal work required of him in Ireland, and as he was writing *Barchester Towers* he decided to put to better use the many hours he had to pass in railway carriages. Formerly he had used this time reading—though Carlyle later told him that a man while traveling ought not to read but rather "sit still and label his thoughts"—but now he rigged up a "tablet" and found after a few days' practice that he could write as quickly in a railway car as he could at his desk. In this fashion he wrote the greater part of *Barchester Towers*.

Trollope finished the three-volume novel on 9 November 1856, having written it at a pace nearly five times faster than that at which he had produced *The Warden*. He submitted the manuscript to Longman, and on 8 December Cauvin sent the publisher a mixed report. On the whole he considered it inferior to *The Warden;* he disliked the "vulgarity" of the bishop and his wife; he thought Signora Neroni a "great blot on the work"; his strongest objection was to sexual explicitness—the examples he gave are "Mrs. Proudie's Reception" and "A Love Scene"; he thought the novel could be reduced to one volume. Nonetheless, he found to book "far from . . . uninteresting," with parts of it "on the level with the best morsels of contemporary novelists." His only shrewd observation concerned Trollope's "facility in the execution that makes you fancy that the author is playing with his reader, showing how easy it is for him to write a novel in three volumes"; certainly if anything characterizes Trollope's style, it is effortlessness. Trollope told Longman he was willing to negotiate the objectionable passages, though he doubted he could have "in utter ignorance committed a volume of indecencies." He insisted, "Of course [Signora Neroni] is intended to appear as indifferent to all moralities and decent behaviour— but such a character may I think be drawn without offence if her vice be made not attractive." He flatly refused to reduce the novel to two volumes—Longman wisely had not endorsed his reader's suggestion of reduction to one volume. Then there was some wrangling about terms. Trollope felt in a stronger position: *The Warden*, however modest its money earnings, had had a good press; moreover, the sequel was three times as long, and length was a major consideration in Victorian publishing. Trollope said that if Longman did not think the novel worth a £100 advance he would withdraw it. When Longman agreed to pay the money, Trollope went through his manuscript and complied with some objections and rejected others. (Unfortunately the manuscript has not survived, and we have not *Barchester Towers* in its original form.) At the last moment "foul breathing" had to come out and "fat stomach" had to be changed to "deep chest." Trollope refused the publisher's suggestion that he alter the title or add a subtitle: "I do not wish the bishop male or female to be considered the chief character in the book. I was puzzled for a title but the one I took at last is at least inoffensive and easy of pronunciation."

The book appeared in May 1857 and met almost unanimous praise from the critics. *The Leader* said *"The Warden* was a remarkable book; *Barchester Towers* is more remarkable." George Meredith in *The Westminster Review* wrote that *Barchester Towers* was "decidedly the cleverest novel of the season" and recommended that any reader who had not read Trollope get the book and its "dashing predecessor" immediately. Trollope himself was much more modest, saying that *Barchester Towers*, like *The Warden*, "achieved no great reputation, but it was one of the novels which novel readers were called upon to read." After the publication of *Barchester Towers*, Trollope's career took off. He liked to measure his success in pounds paid for his novels, and by that scale we find him receiving £250 for *The Three Clerks* (1858), £400 each for *Doctor Thorne* (1858) and for *The Bertrams* (1859), £600 for *Castle Richmond* (1860), and £1000 for *Framley Parsonage* (1861). This last was another important milestone in his career: the novel appeared serially in the new *Cornhill Magazine* and gave his already considerable popularity a spectacular boost. He became, as one reviewer remarked, "almost a national institution." Thenceforth he commanded on average £3000 for a long novel until a decline began in the 1870s that eventually reduced this figure to about £1800. Trollope's *Autobiography* lays much stress on remuneration for literary work. He says bluntly that he wrote his books for money. But he confessed privately in his letters that he most assuredly would have written novels even without pay, and that his only fear for heaven was that novels would not be wanted there. Moreover, in the midst of all the talk in the *Autobiography* about writing for money he inserted one very revealing passage: "I wished from the beginning to be something more than a clerk in the Post Office. To be known as somebody,—to be Anthony Trollope if it be no more—is very much to me."

To understand the depth of his ambition one should recall Trollope's painful childhood and youth, as recounted in the first three chapters of the *Autobiography*. He was the son of a demanding, eccentric father and a well-meaning but apparently neglectful mother who later became a famous author and who, Trollope says, did not think him clever enough to write a novel. He was a poor boy at rich boys' schools (Harrow and Winchester), a social outcast, sullen and continually miserable. His early career as junior clerk in the London General Post Office was also unhappy, and he wrote of his first twenty-six years: "In truth I was wretched,—sometimes almost unto death, and have often cursed the hour in which I was born. There had clung to me a feeling that I have been looked upon always as an evil, an encumbrance, a useless thing,—as a creature of whom those connected with him had to be ashamed." In 1841, at age twenty-six, he was transferred to Ireland as a surveyor's clerk, a development he was to call "the first good fortune of my life." In Ireland he began writing novels. When in late 1854 he became a surveyor, he was almost forty, and only during the next two years, with the publication of *The Warden* and *Barchester Towers*, did he succeed in making a name for himself in literature. Thereafter he was astonishingly prolific, producing forty-seven novels and some seventy books in all, an accomplishment that is one of the marvels of literary history. It has frequently been said that he wrote more good novels than any other writer in the language.

It is essential for understanding the wide appeal of *The Warden* and *Barchester Towers* to realize that although the novels are about clergymen, Trollope deals with their social and economic lives, not their religious lives. *Barchester Towers* does touch upon the controversy between High Church (Roman Catholic influence via the Oxford Movement, with emphasis upon apostolic succession, church tradition, and liturgy) and Low Church (evangelical influence, with emphasis on literal interpretation of the Scriptures, Sabbath observance, and simplicity of worship), but his real concern is always with his characters as human beings. Warden Harding ("warden" here means ecclesiastical superintendent over a home for old people), Archdeacon Grantly, the bishops, Mr. Slope, and Mr. Arabin might just as well have been barristers or military men. But Trollope began the series by taking as his subject the reform of ecclesiastical abuses in a cathedral town, and the characters followed as a matter of course. He himself said that no one could have had less reason for writing about clergymen. He claimed never to have lived in a cathedral city, except London, and to have had no knowledge of any "close" (the cathedral precinct). Archdeacon Grantly, he said, was "the simple result of an effort of my moral consciousness. It was such as that in my opinion, that an archdeacon should be . . . and lo! an archdeacon was produced who has been declared by competent authorities to be a real archdeacon down to the very ground. And yet, as far as I can remember, I had not then ever spoken to an archdeacon."

In *The Warden* Trollope chose to deal simultaneously with two evils: the misuse by the Church of charitable endowments (a subject that had been much in the news, most notably at Rochester and Winchester) and the "undeserved severity" of newspapers toward clergymen who had been given well-salaried positions at charitable institutions. As Trollope said, "When a man is appointed to a place . . . it is seldom that he will be the first to find out that his services are overpaid." Trollope explained that he could have described a red-nosed, bloated parson conspicuously neglecting all his duties, or a devoted, hardworking ill-paid clergyman subjected to the abuse of the daily press. But instead he put a good man, Harding, in a bad position, that of receiving high pay for little work. Trollope later said his attempt to treat both problems was "altogether wrong," a view

repudiated today, when most readers appreciate the novel's delicate balance. Unlike *The Warden, Barchester Towers* really had
no specific "purpose." But if the sequel is the better novel, it is
not for that reason so much as for Trollope's having apparently
learned from the reviews of the first novel to indulge in less satire:
the attack on Carlyle as Dr. Pessimist Anticant and on Dickens as
Mr. Popular Sentiment had been called "a mistake"; that on three
well-known bishops in the three sons of Archdeacon Grantly had
been labeled "[only] now and then amusing." Although one
reviewer admired the sketch of *The Times* as the *Jupiter,* another
said that this was "not managed in good taste." Even more important, *Barchester Towers* is a longer novel, the traditional Victorian
"three decker," a form in which Trollope was more at home.

But both books abound in the things that delight lovers of
Trollope. There is the unquestionable "realism"—that most troublesome of terms about which little need be said here except that
readers recognize his world as genuine or solid or "real." Vir-
ginia Woolf claimed that "We believe in Barchester as we do in
the reality of our own weekly bills"; we get, she said, from
Trollope's novels "the same sort of refreshment and delight that
we get from seeing something actually happen in the street
below." Henry James declared that Trollope's "great, inestimable merit was a complete appreciation of the usual."

Trollope's "realism" manifests itself in many ways. Almost
any snippet of dialogue, for example, rings true. Take this instance
of a passage of arms between Dr. Stanhope and his son Bertie:

> "Yes, sir, tomorrow," said the doctor. "You shall
> leave this house tomorrow."
> "Very well, sir. Will the 4:30 train be soon enough?"
> "You may go how and when and where you please,
> so that you leave my house tomorrow. You have dis-
> graced me, sir; you have disgraced yourself, and me,
> and your sisters."
> "I am glad at least, sir, that I have not disgraced my
> mother," said Bertie.

Trollope's dialogue—which some critics have called the most
realistic in English fiction—forms the basis for many of his
great "scenes," those marvelous verbal showdowns among characters for which Trollope prepares us so patiently. His excellence in
dialogue also underlies the suitabilty of Trollope for dramatic
adaptation. Think, for example, of the stage possibilities of the

confrontation of Mrs. Proudie and Mr. Slope before the bishop in Chapter XXVI of *Barchester Towers*, or of the havoc wrought by the Stanhopes at Mrs. Proudie's reception in Chapter XI.

Another well-remarked aspect of Trollope's fiction is his accuracy in social detail, something that has been admired by critics, even hostile ones, from the first. One thinks, for example, of Archdeacon Grantly's contempt for a round dining table, his view that there was "something democratic and parvenue in a round table. He imagined that dissenters and calico-printers chiefly used them"; or of the great problem for Miss Thorne at her *fête champêtre* of devising ways of separating the gentry and others—the "quality" to be given breakfast, the nonquality dinner, in carefully distinguished areas of the garden—and the special difficulty presented by Mrs. Lookaloft, the wife of a tenant farmer, who manages to cross that "dreadful line" to associate with the gentry; or of the narrator's remark that the English habit of a man offering each arm to two ladies at the same time was one that "foreigners regard as an approach to bigamy, a sort of incipient Mormonism."

Other readers find impressive and "real" Trollope's sympathy for all his characters: in *Barchester Towers*, Mrs. Proudie, unattractive a person as she is, has her virtues: her championing of Mr. Quiverful, for example, can be seen as at least partially influenced by humane motives. As for the somewhat two-dimensional Mr. Slope, even of him it can be said that he believed in his religion, "hardly palatable, uncharitable as it was."

On the other hand, many readers take special enjoyment in the Trollopian narrator, always at the reader's elbow, participating so fully in the business of telling the story, a presence that in some ways seems the very antithesis of "realism." A famous instance of this authorial "intervention" occurs in *Barchester Towers:* the heroine is being courted by two unsatisfactory suitors, and the narrator, less than a third of the way through the story, breaks in and says, "But let the gentle-hearted reader be under no apprehension whatsoever. It is not destined that Eleanor Bold should marry Mr. Slope or Bertie Stanhope." The narrator then says that he won't conceal until the end of the third volume the fate of his heroine and goes so far as to invite the reader to look through the last pages of the book, suggesting that "the story shall have lost none of its interest." Henry James, for all his high regard for Trollope's fiction, said that Trollope took "suicidal satisfaction in reminding the reader that the story he was telling was only, after all, a make-believe." For James these "little slaps at credulity" were as startling and shocking as if the historian Macaulay were to hint that William of Orange was a myth. But for many the narrator's presence is one of Trollope's major strengths: W. P. Ker remarked of the Eleanor Bold passage that "this confidence does not mean that the spectator knows all the story beforehand. It means that what is going on is comedy." And Chauncey Brewster Tinker said the special quality that makes Trollope's novels so warm and readable arises from the reader's "association with the author himself, a man worldly-wise, yet kindly and, above all, fair-minded. . . . Not even Henry Fielding associates with his readers on more agreeable terms."

It was James, too, who made the classic objection to Trollope's use of fantastic names, physicians called Fillgrave and Rerechild, social climbers called Lookalofts. The name Quiverful, for a man with fourteen children ("fourteen of them *living*," as Mrs. Quiverful urges), is too appropriate to be realistic—even to those unfamiliar nowadays with the passage from the Psalms about children being like arrows that bless the man who has filled his quiver with them. "We can believe in the name," wrote James, "and we can believe in the children; but we cannot manage the combination." Still, such names, which Trollope reserved for minor characters, have an ancient and respected tradition in both the English drama and the English novel, and Trollope believed these little jokes would not spoil the story any more than did his presence.

Critics have had trouble tying down Trollope's precise excellence. Perhaps this is why until recently they have generally been less enthusiastic about him than have the so-called "general reader" and fellow novelists. Trollope has always had a wide readership, as publishers' records prove, and he has long been a favorite with professional writers, from Hawthorne and James to Beerbohm and C. P. Snow. It is only of late that the academic world has caught up with Trollope, and within the past seven or eight years scholars have published more on him than on any of the other great Victorian novelists. But the secret of Trollope's art still remains at least partly a mystery; doubtless it lies in some complex mixture of all those elements that very different critics admire in him: the "photographic realism" and solidity of his depicted society, the verisimilitude of dialogue, the sympathy with which his characters are treated, the skillful management of authorial voice, the omnipresence of humor, the dramatization of the undramatic, the lucidity of style, and the avoidance of the excesses of other Victorian novelists, especialy sentimentality and melodrama. In the end, the single most important element in

Trollope's fiction, as he himself said, is "characterization," an old-fashioned but surely still valid notion. For Trollope this was the essence of the novel. Plot was relatively unimportant ("I am not sure," he wrote, "that the construction of a perfected plot has been at any period within my power"). Of course he needed a story to tell, and he needed a physical and social setting—and his time in the west country served him well in this regard. But most important, he had to "live with his characters," a practice that had its origins in his youthful daydreaming, in which he would carry on a tale in his head "for weeks, for months . . . from year to year." That such daydreaming was dangerous he admitted, but he doubted he would ever have written a novel had he not indulged in it. For the adult Trollope this "castle building" was at the heart of his manner of writing a novel: he would live mentally with his characters, "crying at their grief, laughing at their absurdities, and thoroughly enjoying their joy. I have been impregnated with my own creations till it has been my only excitement to sit with the pen in hand."

Trollope's aim was to make his characters "speaking, moving, living, human creatures." He had to establish "intimacy" with his characters: "They must be with [the novelist] as he lies down to sleep, and as he wakes from his dreams. He must learn to hate them and to love them. He must argue with them, quarrel with them, forgive them, and even submit to them." From this kind of intimacy came a character like Mr. Harding, the glory of *The Warden* and in a way the center of the entire Barsetshire series. Henry James called *The Warden* "a delightful tale, and a signal instance of Trollope's habit of offering us the spectacle of a character. A motive more delicate, more slender, as well as more charming, could scarcely be conceived. It is simply the history of an old man's conscience." The story is the tale of the gradual awakening of that conscience until this shy, retiring man, happy in relative obscurity, manages to fly in the face of his own apparent interests and against those of his order and of his family; this he does, as he says, on "very little but an inward and unguided conviction of my own."

Harding is a fine example of what Trollope especially hoped to effect in his creations, namely growth and change: "On the last day of each month recorded, every person in [a] novel should be another month older than on the first." That much Trollope did as well as anyone who ever wrote English novels. And in the case of many Barsetshire characters Trollope continues their growth through various books. Unfortunately we never again hear of the Stanhope children, Bertie and Signora Neroni; perhaps they were too critical of the "dear county" for his liking. But Mr. Harding, the archdeacon and his wife, Mrs. Proudie and her henpecked husband the bishop, these we meet many times in future novels. Two of Grantly's children will grow into important characters. And that unnamed curate down in Cornwall, the adviser who so helped Arabin, will emerge in *Framley Parsonage* as Josiah Crawley, and in *The Last Chronicle of Barset* he will become perhaps the greatest of Trollope's characters. When the series closed with that novel, reviewers protested their dismay: The *Spectator* quoted a reader as saying "What am I to do without ever meeting Archdeacon Grantly? He was one of my best and most intimate friends." The *London Review* expressed "gentle melancholy" and, paraphrasing Trollope's words, said, "To us, as well as to him, Barset has long been a real county, and its city a real city; and the spires and towers have been before our eyes, and the voices of the people are known to our ears, and the pavements of the city are familiar to our footsteps."

Not only did Trollope close the series with *The Last Chronicle,* but in that novel he brought about the death of two of his best-known characters. Old Mr. Harding was so full of years that his dying was in the course of nature and not unexpected; the scene of his death is one of the most poignant in all of Victorian fiction. But Mrs. Proudie's sudden death from heart failure was a different matter. Trollope explained, in the *Autobiography,* how in the drawing room of the Athenaeum Club he overheard two clergymen discussing *The Last Chronicle* as it appeared serially: "The gravamen of the complaint lay in the fact that I reintroduced the same characters so often!" And when one of them "fell foul of Mrs. Proudie . . . I got up, and standing between them, I acknowledged myself to be the culprit. 'As to Mrs. Proudie,' I said, 'I will go home and kill her before the week is over.' And so I did." He wrote that he later regretted the deed. Mrs. Oliphant, in a review in *Blackwood's Magazine,* complained that Trollope was guilty of "murder, or manslaughter at the least."

But this is to get too far ahead of the reader. The gentle, bright, sunny opening of the series was as good as anything Trollope ever did. *Barchester Towers* remains his most popular novel, and it is far better when read in conjunction with *The Warden.* There is almost no end to Trollope—he wrote so very much. But the place to begin reading Trollope, or to begin rereading him, is with *The Warden* and *Barchester Towers.*

Barchester Towers
and
The Warden

THE WARDEN

I

Hiram's Hospital

The Rev. Septimus Harding was, a few years since, a beneficed clergyman residing in the cathedral town of——; let us call it Barchester. Were we to name Wells or Salisbury, Exeter, Hereford, or Gloucester, it might be presumed that something personal was intended; and as this tale will refer mainly to the cathedral dignitaries of the town in question, we are anxious that no personality may be suspected. Let us presume that Barchester is a quiet town in the West of England, more remarkable for the beauty of its cathedral and the antiquity of its monuments, than for any commercial prosperity; that the west end of Barchester is the cathedral close, and that the aristocracy of Barchester are the bishop, dean, and canons, with their respective wives and daughters.

Early in life Mr. Harding found himself located at Barchester. A fine voice and a taste for sacred music had decided the position in which he was to exercise his calling, and for many years he performed the easy but not highly paid duties of a minor canon. At the age of forty a small living in the close vicinity of the town increased both his work and his income, and at the age of fifty he became precentor of the cathedral.

Mr. Harding had married early in life, and was the father of two daughters. The eldest, Susan, was born soon after his marriage; the other, Eleanor, not till ten years later. At the time at which we introduce him to our readers he was living as precentor at Barchester with his youngest daughter, then twenty-four years of age; having been many years a widower, and having married his eldest daughter to a son of the bishop, a very short time before his installation to the office of precentor.

Scandal at Barchester affirmed that had it not been for the

3

beauty of his daughter, Mr. Harding would have remained a minor canon; but here probably Scandal lied, as she so often does; for even as a minor canon no one had been more popular among his reverend brethren in the close than Mr. Harding; and Scandal, before she had reprobated Mr. Harding for being made precentor by his friend the bishop, had loudly blamed the bishop for having so long omitted to do something for his friend Mr. Harding. Be this as it may, Susan Harding, some twelve years since, had married the Rev. Dr. Theophilus Grantly, son of the bishop, archdeacon of Barchester, and rector of Plumstead Episcopi, and her father became, a few months later, precentor of Barchester Cathedral, that office being, as is not usual, in the bishop's gift.

Now there are peculiar circumstances connected with the precentorship which must be explained. In the year 1434 there died at Barchester one John Hiram, who had made money in the town as a wool stapler, and in his will he left the house in which he died and certain meadows and closes near the town, still called Hiram's Butts, and Hiram's Patch, for the support of twelve superannuated wool-carders, all of whom should have been born and bred and spent their days in Barchester; he also appointed that an almshouse should be built for their abode, with a fitting residence for a warden, which warden was also to receive a certain sum annually out of the rents of the said butts and patches. He, moreover, willed, having had a soul alive to harmony, that the precentor of the cathedral should have the option of being also warden of the almshouse, if the bishop in each case approved.

From that day to this the charity had gone on and prospered—at least, the charity had gone on, and the estates had prospered. Wool-carding in Barchester there was no longer any; so the bishop, dean, and warden, who took it in turn to put in the old men, generally appointed some hangers-on of their own; worn-out gardeners, decrepit grave-diggers, or octogenarian sextons, who thankfully received a comfortable lodging and one shilling and fourpence a day, such being the stipend to which, under the will of John Hiram, they were declared to be entitled. Formerly, indeed—that is, till within some fifty years of the present time—they received but sixpence a day, and their breakfast and dinner was found them at a common table by the warden, such an arrangement being in stricter conformity with the absolute wording of old Hiram's will: but this was thought to be inconvenient, and to suit the tastes of neither warden nor bedesmen, and the daily one shilling and fourpence was substituted with the common consent of all parties, including the bishop and the corporation of Barchester.

Such was the condition of Hiram's twelve old men when Mr. Harding was appointed warden; but if they may be considered as well-to-do in the world according to their condition, the happy warden was much more so. The patches and butts which, in John Hiram's time, produced hay or fed cows, were now covered with rows of houses; the value of the property had gradually increased from year to year and century to century, and was now presumed by those who knew anything about it, to bring in a very nice income; and by some who knew nothing about it, to have increased to an almost fabulous extent.

The property was farmed by a gentleman in Barchester, who also acted as the bishop's steward—a man whose father and grandfather had been stewards to the bishops of Barchester, and farmers of John Hiram's estate. The Chadwicks had earned a good name in Barchester; they had lived respected by bishops, deans, canons, and precentors; they had been buried in the precincts of the cathedral; they had never been known as griping, hard men, but had always lived comfortably, maintained a good house, and held a high position in Barchester society. The present Mr. Chadwick was a worthy scion of a worthy stock, and the tenants living on the butts and patches, as well as those on the wide episcopal domains of the see, were well pleased to have to do with so worthy and liberal a steward.

For many, many years—records hardly tell how many, probably from the time when Hiram's wishes had been first fully carried out—the proceeds of the estate had been paid by the steward or farmer to the warden, and by him divided among the bedesmen; after which division he paid himself such sums as became his due. Times had been when the poor warden got nothing but his bare house, for the patches had been subject to floods, and the land of Barchester butts was said to be unproductive; and in these hard times the warden was hardly able to make out the daily dole for his twelve dependents. But by degrees things mended; the patches were drained, and cottages began to rise upon the butts, and the wardens, with fairness enough, repaid themselves for the evil days gone by. In bad times the poor men had had their due, and therefore in good times they could expect no more. In this manner the income of the warden had increased; the picturesque house attached to the hospital had been enlarged and adorned, and the office had become one of the most coveted of the snug clerical sinecures attached to our church. It was now wholly in the bishop's gift, and though the dean and chapter, in former days, made a stand on the subject, they had thought it more conducive to their honour to have a rich precentor appointed by the bishop, than a poor one appointed by themselves. The stipend of the precentor of Barchester was eighty pounds a year. The income arising from the wardenship of the hospital was eight hundred, besides the value of the house.

Murmurs, very slight murmurs, had been heard in Barchester— few indeed, and far between—that the proceeds of John Hiram's property had not been fairly divided: but they can hardly be said to have been of such a nature as to have caused uneasiness to any one: still the thing had been whispered, and Mr. Harding had heard it. Such was his character in Barchester, so universal was his popularity, that the very fact of his appointment would have quieted louder whispers than those which had been heard; but Mr. Harding was an open-handed, just-minded man, and feeling that there might be truth in what had been said, he had, on his instalment, declared his intention of adding twopence a day to each man's pittance, making a sum of sixty-two pounds eleven shillings and fourpence, which he was to pay out of his own pocket. In doing so, however, he distinctly and repeatedly observed to the men, that though he promised for himself, he could not promise for his successors, and that the extra twopence could only be looked on as a gift from himself, and not from the trust. The bedesmen, however, were most of them older than Mr. Harding, and were quite satisfied with the security on which their extra income was based.

This munificence on the part of Mr. Harding had not been unopposed. Mr. Chadwick had mildly but seriously dissuaded him from it; and his strong-minded son-in-law, the archdeacon, the man of whom alone Mr. Harding stood in awe, had urgently, nay, vehemently, opposed so impolitic a concession; but the warden had made known his intention to the hospital before the archdeacon had been able to interfere, and the deed was done.

Hiram's Hospital, as the retreat is called, is a picturesque building enough, and shows the correct taste with which the ecclesiastical architects of those days were imbued. It stands on the banks of the little river, which flows nearly round the cathedral close, being on the side furthest from the town. The London road crosses the river by a pretty one-arched bridge, and, looking from this bridge, the stranger will see the windows of the old men's rooms, each pair of windows separated by a small buttress. A broad gravel walk runs between the building and the river, which is always trim and cared for; and at the end of the walk, under the parapet of the approach to the bridge, is a large and well-worn seat, on which, in mild weather, three or four of Hiram's bedesmen are sure to be seen seated. Beyond this row of buttresses, and further from the bridge, and also further from the water which here suddenly bends, are the pretty oriel windows of Mr. Harding's house, and his well-mown lawn. The entrance to the hospital is from the London road, and is made through a ponderous gateway under a heavy stone arch, unnecessary, one would suppose, at any time, for the protection of twelve old men, but greatly conducive to the good appearance of Hiram's charity. On passing through this portal, never closed to any one from 6 A.M. till 10 P.M., and never open afterwards, except on application to a huge, intricately hung mediæval bell, the handle of which no uninitiated intruder can possibly find, the six doors of the old men's abodes are seen, and beyond them is a slight iron screen, through which the more happy portion of the Barchester élite pass into the Elysium of Mr. Harding's dwelling.

Mr. Harding is a small man, now verging on sixty years but bearing few of the signs of age; his hair is rather grizzled, though not grey; his eye is very mild, but clear and bright, though the double glasses which are held swinging from his hand, unless when fixed upon his nose, show that time has told upon his sight; his hands are delicately white, and both hands and feet are small; he always wears a black frock coat, black knee-breeches, and black gaiters, and somewhat scandalises some of his more hyperclerical brethren by a black neck-handkerchief.

Mr. Harding's warmest admirers cannot say that he was ever an industrious man; the circumstances of his life have not called on him to be so; and yet he can hardly be called an idler. Since his appointment to his precentorship, he has published, with all possible additions of vellum, typography, and gilding, a collection of our ancient church music, with some correct dissertations on Purcell, Crotch, and Nares. He has greatly improved the choir of Barchester, which, under his dominion, now rivals that of any cathedral in England. He has taken something more than his fair share in the cathedral services, and has played the violoncello daily to such audiences as he could collect, or, *faute de mieux*, to no audience at all.

We must mention one other peculiarity of Mr. Harding. As we have before stated, he has an income of eight hundred a year, and has no family but his one daughter; and yet he is never quite at ease in money matters. The vellum and gilding of Harding's *Church Music* cost more than any one knows except the author, the publisher, and the Rev. Theophilus Grantly, who allows none of his father-in-law's extravagances to escape him. Then he is generous to his daughter, for whose service he keeps a small carriage and pair of ponies. He is, indeed, generous to all, but especially to the twelve old men who are in a peculiar manner under his care. No doubt with such an income Mr. Harding should be above the world, as the saying is; but, at any rate, he is not above Archdeacon Theophilus Grantly, for he is always more or less in debt to his son-in-law, who has, to a certain extent, assumed the arrangement of the precentor's pecuniary affairs.

II

The Barchester Reformer

Mr. Harding has been now precentor of Barchester for ten years; and, alas, the murmurs respecting the proceeds of Hiram's estate are again becoming audible. It is not that any one begrudges to Mr. Harding the income which he enjoys, and the comfortable place which so well becomes him; but such matters have begun to be talked of in various parts of England. Eager pushing politicians have asserted in the House of Commons, with very telling indignation, that the grasping priests of the Church of England are gorged with the wealth which the charity of former times has left for the solace of the aged, or the education of the young. The well-known case of the Hospital of St. Cross has even come before the law courts of the country, and the struggles of Mr. Whiston, at Rochester, have met with sympathy and support. Men are beginning to say that these things must be looked into.

Mr. Harding, whose conscience in the matter is clear, and who has never felt that he had received a pound from Hiram's will to which he was not entitled, has naturally taken the part of the church in talking over these matters with his friend, the bishop, and his son-in-law, the archdeacon. The archdeacon, indeed, Dr. Grantly, has been somewhat loud in the matter. He is a personal friend of the dignitaries of the Rochester Chapter, and has written letters in the public press on the subject of that turbulent Dr. Whiston, which, his admirers think, must well nigh set the question at rest. It is also known at Oxford that he is the author of the pamphlet signed "Sacerdos" on the subject of the Earl of Guildford and St. Cross, in which it is so clearly argued that the manners of the present times do not admit of a literal adhesion to the very words of the founder's will, but that the interests of the church for which the founder was so deeply concerned are best consulted in enabling its bishops to reward those shining lights whose services have been most signally serviceable to Christianity. In answer to this, it is asserted that Henry de Blois, founder of St. Cross, was not greatly interested in the welfare of the reformed church, and that the masters of St. Cross, for many years past, cannot be called shining lights in the service of Christianity; it is, however, stoutly maintained, and no doubt felt, by all the archdeacon's friends, that his logic is conclusive, and has not, in fact, been answered.

With such a tower of strength to back both his arguments and his conscience, it may be imagined that Mr. Harding has never felt any compunction as to receiving his quarterly sum of two hundred pounds. Indeed, the subject has never presented itself to his mind in that shape. He has talked not unfrequently, and heard very much about the wills of old founders and the incomes arising from their estates, during the last year or two; he did even, at one moment, feel a doubt (since expelled by his son-in-law's logic) as to whether Lord Guildford was clearly entitled to receive so enormous an income as he does from the revenues of St. Cross; but that he himself was overpaid with his modest eight hundred pounds;—he who, out of that, voluntarily gave up sixty-two pounds eleven shillings and fourpence a year to his twelve old neighbours;—he who, for the money, does his precentor's work as no precentor has done it before, since Barchester Cathedral was built;—such an idea has never sullied his quiet, or disturbed his conscience.

Nevertheless, Mr. Harding is becoming uneasy at the rumour which he knows to prevail in Barchester on the subject. He is aware that, at any rate, two of his old men have been heard to say, that if every one had his own, they might each have their hundred pounds a year, and live like gentlemen, instead of a beggarly one shilling and sixpence a day; and that they had slender cause to be thankful for a miserable dole of twopence, when Mr. Harding and Mr. Chadwick, between them, ran away with thousands of pounds which good old John Hiram never intended for the life of them. It is the ingratitude of this which stings Mr. Harding. One of this discontented pair, Abel Handy, was put into the hospital by himself; he had been a stone-mason in Barchester, and had broken his thigh by a fall from a scaffolding, while employed about the cathedral; and Mr. Harding had given him the first vacancy in the hospital after the occurrence, although Dr. Grantly had been very anxious to put into it an insufferable clerk of his at Plumstead Episcopi, who had lost all his teeth, and whom the archdeacon hardly knew how to get rid of by other means. Dr. Grantly has not forgotten to remind Mr. Harding how well satisfied with his one and sixpence a day old Joe Mutters would have been, and how injudicious it was on the part of Mr. Harding to allow a radical from the town to get into the concern. Probably Dr. Grantly forgot, at the moment, that the charity was intended for broken-down journeymen of Barchester.

There is living at Barchester, a young man, a surgeon, named John Bold, and both Mr. Harding and Dr. Grantly are well aware that to him is owing the pestilent rebellious feeling which has shown itself in the hospital; yes, and the renewal, too, of that disagreeable talk about Hiram's estates which is now again prevalent in Barchester. Nevertheless, Mr. Harding and Mr. Bold are acquainted with each other; we may say, are friends, considering the great disparity in their years. Dr. Grantly, however, has a holy horror of the impious demagogue, as on one occasion he called Bold, when speaking of him to the precentor; and being a more prudent far-seeing man than Mr. Harding, and possessed of a stronger head, he already perceives that this John Bold will work great trouble in Barchester. He considers that he is to be regarded as an enemy, and thinks that he should not be admitted into the camp on anything like friendly terms. As John Bold will occupy much of our attention, we must endeavour to explain who he is, and why he takes the part of John Hiram's bedesmen.

John Bold is a young surgeon, who passed many of his boyish years at Barchester. His father was a physician in the city of London, where he made a moderate fortune, which he invested in houses in that city. The Dragon of Wantly inn and posting-house belonged to him, also four shops in the High Street, and a moiety of the new row of genteel villas (so called in the advertisements), built outside the town just beyond Hiram's Hospital. To one of these Dr. Bold retired to spend the evening of his life, and to die; and here his son John spent his holidays, and afterwards his Christmas vacation when he went from school to study surgery in the London hospitals. Just as John Bold was entitled to write himself surgeon and apothecary, old Dr. Bold died, leaving his Barchester property to his son, and a certain sum in the three per cents, to his daughter Mary, who is some four or five years older than her brother.

John Bold determined to settle himself at Barchester, and look after his own property, as well as the bones and bodies of such of his neighbours as would call upon him for assistance in their troubles. He therefore put up a large brass plate with "John Bold, Surgeon," on it, to the great disgust of the nine practitioners who were already trying to get a living out of the bishop, dean, and canons; and began house-keeping with the aid of his sister. At this time he was not more than twenty-four years old; and though he has now been three years in Barchester, we have not heard that he has done much harm to the nine worthy practitioners. Indeed, their dread of him has died away; for in three years he has not taken three fees.

Nevertheless, John Bold is a clever man, and would, with practice, be a clever surgeon; but he has got quite into another line of life. Having enough to live on, he has not been forced to work for bread; he has declined to subject himself to what he calls the drudgery of the profession, by which, I believe, he means the general work of a practising surgeon; and has found other employment. He frequently binds up the bruises and sets the limbs of such of the poorer classes as profess his way of thinking—but this he does for love. Now I will not say that the archdeacon is strictly correct in stigmatising John Bold as a demagogue, for I hardly know how extreme must be a man's opinions before he can be justly so called; but Bold is a strong reformer. His passion is the reform of all abuses; state abuses, church abuses, corporation abuses (he has got himself elected a town councillor of Barchester, and has so worried three consecutive mayors, that it became somewhat difficult to find a fourth), abuses in medical practice, and general abuses in the world at large. Bold is thoroughly sincere in his patriotic endeavours to mend mankind, and there is something to be admired in the energy with which he devotes himself to remedying evil and stopping injustice; but I fear that he is too much imbued with the idea that he has a special mission for reforming. It would be well if one so young had a little more diffidence himself, and more trust in the honest purposes of others—if he could be brought to believe that old customs need not necessarily be evil, and that changes may possibly be dangerous; but no, Bold has all the ardour and all the self-assurance of a Danton, and hurls his anathemas against time-honoured practices with the violence of a French Jacobin.

No wonder that Dr. Grantly should regard Bold as a fire-brand, falling, as he has done, almost in the centre of the quiet ancient close of Barchester Cathedral. Dr. Grantly would have him avoided as the plague; but the old Doctor and Mr. Harding were fast friends. Young Johnny Bold used to play as a boy on Mr. Harding's lawn; he has many a time won the precentor's heart by listening with rapt attention to his sacred strains; and since those days, to tell the truth at once, he has nearly won another heart within the same walls.

Eleanor Harding has not plighted her troth to John Bold, nor has she, perhaps, owned to herself how dear to her the young reformer is; but she cannot endure that any one should speak harshly of him. She does not dare to defend him when her brother-in-law is so loud against him; for she, like her father, is somewhat afraid of Dr. Grantly; but she is beginning greatly to dislike the archdeacon. She persuades her father that it would be both unjust and injudicious to banish his young friend because of his politics; she cares little to go to houses where she will not meet him, and, in fact, she is in love.

Nor is there any good reason why Eleanor Harding should not love John Bold. He has all those qualities which are likely to touch a girl's heart. He is brave, eager, and amusing; well-made and good-looking; young and enterprising; his character is in all respects good; he has sufficient income to support a wife; he is her father's friend; and, above all, he is in love with her; then why should not Eleanor Harding be attached to John Bold?

Dr. Grantly, who has as many eyes as Argus, and has long seen how the wind blows in that direction, thinks there are various strong reasons why this should not be so. He has not thought it wise as yet to speak to his father-in-law on the subject, for he knows how foolishly indulgent is Mr. Harding in every-thing that concerns his daughter; but he has discussed the matter with his all-trusted helpmate, within that sacred recess formed by the clerical bed-curtains at Plumstead Episcopi.

How much sweet solace, how much valued counsel has our archdeacon received within that sainted enclosure! 'Tis there alone that he unbends, and comes down from his high church pedestal to the level of a mortal man. In the world Dr. Grantly never lays aside that demeanour which so well becomes him. He has all the dignity of an ancient saint with the sleekness of a modern bishop; he is always the same; he is always the archdeacon; unlike Homer, he never nods. Even with his father-in-law, even with the bishop and dean, he maintains that sonorous tone and lofty deportment which strikes awe into the young hearts of Barchester, and absolutely cows the whole parish of Plumstead Episcopi. 'Tis only when he has exchanged that ever-new shovel hat for a tasselled nightcap, and those shining black habiliments for his accustomed *robe de nuit,* that Dr. Grantly talks, and looks, and thinks like an ordinary man.

Many of us have often thought how severe a trial of faith must this be to the wives of our great church dignitaries. To us these men are personifications of St. Paul; their very gait is a speaking sermon; their clean and sombre apparel exacts from us faith and submission, and the cardinal virtues seem to hover round their sacred hats. A dean or archbishop, in the garb of his order, is sure of our reverence, and a well-got-up bishop fills our very souls with awe. But how can this feeling be perpetuated in the bosoms of those who see the bishops without their aprons, and the archdeacons ever in a lower state of dishabille?

Do we not all know some reverend, all but sacred, personage before whom our tongue ceases to be loud and our step to be elastic? But were we once to see him stretch himself beneath the bed-clothes, yawn widely, and bury his face upon his pillow, we could chatter before him as glibly as before a doctor or a lawyer. From some such cause, doubtless, it arose that our archdeacon listened to the counsels of his wife, though he considered himself entitled to give counsel to every other being whom he met.

"My dear," he said, as he adjusted the copious folds of his nightcap, "there was that John Bold at your father's again today. I must say your father is very imprudent."

"He is imprudent—he always was," replied Mrs. Grantly, speaking from under the comfortable bed-clothes. "There's nothing new in that."

"No, my dear, there's nothing new—I know that; but, at the present juncture of affairs, such imprudence is—is—I'll tell you what, my dear, if he does not take care what he's about, John Bold will be off with Eleanor.''

"I think he will, whether papa takes care or no; and why not?"

"Why not!" almost screamed the archdeacon, giving so rough a pull at his nightcap as almost to bring it over his nose; "why not!—that pestilent, interfering upstart, John Bold—the most vulgar young person I ever met! Do you know that he is meddling with your father's affairs in a most uncalled-for— most——" And being at a loss for an epithet sufficiently injurious, he finished his expressions of horror by muttering, "Good heavens!" in a manner that had been found very efficacious in clerical meetings of the diocese. He must for the moment have forgotten where he was.

"As to his vulgarity, archdeacon" (Mrs. Grantly had never assumed a more familiar term than this in addressing her husband), "I don't agree with you. Not that I like Mr. Bold—he is a great deal too conceited for me; but then Eleanor does, and it would be the best thing in the world for papa if they were to marry. Bold would never trouble himself about Hiram's Hospital if he were papa's son-in-law." And the lady turned herself round under the bed-clothes, in a manner to which the doctor was well accustomed, and which told him, as plainly as words, that as far as she was concerned the subject was over for that night.

"Good heavens!" murmured the doctor again—he was evidently much put beside himself.

Dr. Grantly is by no means a bad man; he is exactly the man which such an education as his was most likely to form; his intellect being sufficient for such a place in the world, but not sufficient to put him in advance of it. He performs with a rigid constancy such of the duties of a parish clergyman as are, to his thinking, above the sphere of his curate, but it is as an archdeacon that he shines.

We believe, as a general rule, that either a bishop or his archdeacons have sinecures: where a bishop works, archdeacons have but little to do, and *vice versa*. In the diocese of Barchester the Archdeacon of Barchester does the work. In that capacity he is diligent, authoritative, and, as his friends particularly boast, judicious. His great fault is an overbearing assurance of the virtues and claims of his order, and his great foible is an equally strong confidence in the dignity of his own manner and the eloquence of his own words. He is a moral man, believing the precepts which he teaches, and believing also that he acts up to them; though we cannot say that he would give his coat to the man who took his cloak, or that he is prepared to forgive his brother even seven times. He is severe enough in exacting his dues, considering that any laxity in this respect would endanger the security of the church; and, could he have his way, he would consign to darkness and perdition, not only every individual reformer, but every committee and every commission that would even dare to ask a question respecting the appropriation of church revenues.

"They are church revenues: the laity admit it. Surely the church is able to administer her own revenues." 'Twas thus he was accustomed to argue, when the sacrilegious doings of Lord John Russell and others were discussed either at Barchester or at Oxford.

It was no wonder that Dr. Grantly did not like John Bold, and that his wife's suggestion that he should become closely connected with such a man dismayed him. To give him his due, the archdeacon never wanted courage; he was quite willing to meet his enemy on any field and with any weapon. He had that belief in his own arguments that he felt sure of success, could he only be sure of a fair fight on the part of his adversary. He had no idea that John Bold could really prove that the income of the hospital was malappropriated; why then, should peace be sought for on such base terms? What! bribe an unbelieving enemy of the church with the sister-in-law of one dignitary and the daughter of another—with a young lady whose connections with the diocese and chapter of Barchester were so close as to give her an undeniable claim to a husband endowed with some of its sacred wealth! When Dr. Grantly talks of unbelieving enemies, he does not mean to imply want of belief in the doctrines of the church, but an equally dangerous scepticism as to its purity in money matters.

Mrs. Grantly is not usually deaf to the claims of the high order to which she belongs. She and her husband rarely disagree as to the tone with which the church should be defended; how singular, then, that in such a case as this she should be willing to succumb! The archdeacon again murmurs "Good heavens!" as he lays himself beside her, but he does so in a voice audible only to himself, and he' repeats it till sleep relieves him from deep thought.

Mr. Harding himself has seen no reason why his daughter should not love John Bold. He has not been unobservant of her feelings, and perhaps his deepest regret at the part which he fears

Bold is about to take regarding the hospital arises from the dread
that he may be separated from his daughter, or that she may be
separated from the man she loves. He has never spoken to
Eleanor about her lover; he is the last man in the world to allude
to such a subject unconsulted, even with his own daughter; and
had he considered that he had ground to disapprove of Bold, he
would have removed her, or forbidden him his house; but he saw
no such ground. He would probably have preferred a second
clerical son-in-law, for Mr. Harding, also, is attached to his
order; and, failing in that, he would at any rate have wished that
so near a connection should have thought alike with him on
church matters. He would not, however, reject the man his
daughter loved because he differed on such subjects with himself.

Hitherto Bold had taken no steps in the matter in any way
annoying to Mr. Harding personally. Some months since, after a
severe battle, which cost him not a little money, he gained a
victory over a certain old turnpike woman in the neighbourhood,
of whose charges another old woman had complained to him. He
got the act of Parliament relating to the trust, found that his
protégée had been wrongly taxed, rode through the gate himself,
paying the toll, then brought an action against the gate-keeper,
and proved that all people coming up a certain by-lane, and
going down a certain other by-lane, were toll free. The fame of
his success spread widely abroad, and he began to be looked on
as the upholder of the rights of the poor of Barchester. Not long
after this success, he heard from different quarters that Hiram's
bedesmen were treated as paupers, whereas the property to which
they were, in effect, heirs was very large; and he was instigated
by the lawyer whom he had employed in the case of the turnpike
to call upon Mr. Chadwick for a statement as to the funds of the
estate.

Bold had often expressed his indignation at the malappro-
priation of church funds in general, in the hearing of his friend
the precentor; but the conversation had never referred to anything
at Barchester; and when Finney, the attorney, induced him to
interfere with the affairs of the hospital, it was against Mr.
Chadwick that his efforts were to be directed. Bold soon found
that if he interfered with Mr. Chadwick as steward, he must also
interfere with Mr. Harding as warden; and though he regretted
the situation in which this would place him, he was not the man
to flinch from his undertaking from personal motives.

As soon as he had determined to take the matter in hand, he
set about his work with his usual energy. He got a copy of John

Hiram's will, of the wording of which he made himself perfectly master. He ascertained the extent of the property, and as nearly as he could the value of it; and made out a schedule of what he was informed was the present distribution of its income. Armed with these particulars, he called on Mr. Chadwick, having given that gentleman notice of his visit; and asked him for a statement of the income and expenditure of the hospital for the last twenty-five years.

This was of course refused, Mr. Chadwick alleging that he had no authority for making public the concerns of a property in managing which he was only a paid servant.

"And who is competent to give you that authority, Mr. Chadwick?" asked Bold.

"Only those who employ me, Mr. Bold," said the steward.

"And who are those, Mr. Chadwick?" demanded Bold.

Mr. Chadwick begged to say that if these inquiries were made merely out of curiosity, he must decline answering them: if Mr. Bold had any ulterior proceeding in view, perhaps it would be desirable that any necessary information should be sought for in a professional way by a professional man. Mr. Chadwick's attorneys were Messrs. Cox and Cumming, of Lincoln's Inn. Mr. Bold took down the address of Cox and Cumming, remarked that the weather was cold for the time of the year, and wished Mr. Chadwick good-morning. Mr. Chadwick said it was cold for June, and bowed him out.

He at once went to his lawyer, Finney. Now, Bold was not very fond of his attorney, but, as he said, he merely wanted a man who knew the forms of law, and who would do what he was told for his money. He had no idea of putting himself in the hands of a lawyer. He wanted law from a lawyer as he did a coat from a tailor, because he could not make it so well himself; and he thought Finney the fittest man in Barchester for his purpose. In one respect, at any rate, he was right: Finney was humility itself.

Finney advised an instant letter to Cox and Cumming, mindful of his six-and-eightpence. "Slap at them at once, Mr. Bold. Demand categorically and explicitly a full statement of the affairs of the hospital."

"Suppose I were to see Mr. Harding first," suggested Bold.

"Yes, yes, by all means," said the acquiescing Finney; "though, perhaps, as Mr. Harding is no man of business, it may lead—lead to some little difficulties; but perhaps you're right, Mr. Bold, I don't think seeing Mr. Harding can do any harm." Finney saw from the expression of his client's face that he intended to have his own way.

III

The Bishop of Barchester

Bold at once repaired to the hospital. The day was now far advanced, but he knew that Mr. Harding dined in the summer at four, that Eleanor was accustomed to drive in the evening, and that he might therefore probably find Mr. Harding alone. It was between seven and eight when he reached the slight iron gate leading into the precentor's garden, and though, as Mr. Chadwick observed, the day had been cold for June, the evening was mild, and soft, and sweet. The little gate was open. As he raised the latch he heard the notes of Mr. Harding's violoncello from the far end of the garden, and, advancing before the house and across the lawn, he found him playing: and not without an audience. The musician was seated in a garden-chair just within the summer-house, so as to allow the violoncello which he held between his knees to rest upon the dry stone flooring; before him stood a rough music desk, on which was open a page of that dear sacred book, that much-laboured and much-loved volume of church music, which had cost so many guineas; and around sat, and lay, and stood, and leaned, ten of the twelve old men who dwelt with him beneath old John Hiram's roof. The two reformers were not there. I will not say that in their hearts they were conscious of any wrong done or to be done to their mild warden, but latterly they had kept aloof from him, and his music was no longer to their taste.

It was amusing to see the positions, and eager listening faces of these well-to-do old men. I will not say that they all appreciated the music which they heard, but they were intent on appearing to do so; pleased at being where they were, they were determined, as far as in them lay, to give pleasure in return; and they were not unsuccessful. It gladdened the precentor's heart to think that the old bedesmen whom he loved so well admired the strains which were to him so full of almost ecstatic joy; and he used to boast that such was the air of the hospital, as to make it a precinct specially fit for the worship of St. Cecilia.

Immediately before him, on the extreme corner of the bench which ran round the summer-house, sat one old man, with his handkerchief smoothly lain upon his knees, who did enjoy the moment, or acted enjoyment well. He was one on whose large frame many years, for he was over eighty, had made small havoc,—he was still an upright, burly, handsome figure, with an open, ponderous brow, round which clung a few, though very few, thin grey locks. The coarse black gown of the hospital, the breeches, and bluckled shoes became him well; and as he sat with his hands folded on his staff, and his chin resting on his hands, he was such a listener as most musicians would be glad to welcome.

This man was certainly the pride of the hospital. It had always been the custom that one should be selected as being to some extent in authority over the others; and though Mr. Bunce, for such was his name, and so he was always designated by his inferior brethren, had no greater emoluments than they, he had assumed, and well knew how to maintain, the dignity of his elevation. The precentor delighted to call him his sub-warden, and was not ashamed, occasionally, when no other guest was there, to bid him sit down by the same parlour fire, and drink the full glass of port which was placed near him. Bunce never went without the second glass, but no entreaty ever made him take a third.

"Well, well, Mr. Harding; you're too good, much too good," he'd always say, as the second glass was filled; but when that was drunk, and the half hour over, Bunce stood erect, and with a benediction which his patron valued, retired to his own abode. He knew the world too well to risk the comfort of such halcyon moments, by prolonging them till they were disagreeable.

Mr. Bunce, as may be imagined, was most strongly opposed to innovation. Not even Dr. Grantly had a more holy horror of those who would interfere in the affairs of the hospital; he was every inch a churchman, and though he was not very fond of Dr. Grantly personally, that arose from there not being

room in the hospital for two people so much alike as the doctor
and himself, rather than from any dissimilarity in feeling. Mr.
Bunce was inclined to think that the warden and himself could
manage the hospital without further assistance; and that, though
the bishop was the constitutional visitor, and as such entitled to
special reverence from all connected with John Hiram's will,
John Hiram never intended that his affairs should be interfered
with by an archdeacon.

At the present moment, however, these cares were off his
mind, and he was looking at his warden, as though he thought
the music heavenly, and the musician hardly less so.

As Bold walked silently over the lawn, Mr. Harding did not
at first perceive him, and continued to draw his bow slowly
across the plaintive wires; but he soon found from his audience
that some stranger was there, and looking up, began to welcome
his young friend with frank hospitality.

"Pray, Mr. Harding; pray don't let me disturb you," said
Bold; "you know how fond I am of sacred music."

"Oh! it's nothing," said the precentor, shutting up the book
and then opening it again as he saw the delightfully imploring
look of his old friend Bunce. Oh, Bunce, Bunce, Bunce, I fear
that after all thou art but a flatterer. "Well, I'll just finish it then;
it's a favourite little bit of Bishop's; and then, Mr. Bold, we'll
have a stroll and a chat till Eleanor comes in and gives us tea."
And so Bold sat down on the soft turf to listen, or rather to think
how, after such sweet harmony, he might best introduce a theme
of so much discord, to disturb the peace of him who was so
ready to welcome him kindly.

Bold thought that the performance was soon over, for he
felt that he had a somewhat difficult task, and he almost regretted the final leave-taking of the last of the old men, slow as they
were in going through their adieus.

Bold's heart was in his mouth, as the precentor made some
ordinary but kind remark as to the friendliness of the visit.

"One evening call," said he, "is worth ten in the morning.
It's all formality in the morning; real social talk never begins till
after dinner. That's why I dine early, so as to get as much as I
can of it."

"Quite true, Mr. Harding," said the other; "but I fear I've
reversed the order of things, and I owe you much apology for
troubling you on business at such an hour; but it is on business
that I have called just now."

Mr. Harding looked blank and annoyed; there was something in the tone of the young man's voice which told him that the interview was intended to be disagreeable, and he shrank back at finding his kindly greeting so repulsed.

"I wish to speak to you about the hospital," continued Bold.

"Well, well, anything I can tell you I shall be most happy——"

"It's about the accounts."

"Then, my dear fellow, I can tell you nothing, for I'm as ignorant as a child. All I know is, that they pay me £800 a year. Go to Chadwick, he knows all about the accounts; and now tell me, will poor Mary Jones ever get the use of her limb again?"

"Well, I think she will, if she's careful; but, Mr. Harding, I hope you won't object to discuss with me what I have to say about the hospital."

Mr. Harding gave a deep, long-drawn sigh. He did object, very strongly object, to discuss any such subject with John Bold; but he had not the business tact of Mr. Chadwick, and did not know how to relieve himself from the coming evil; he sighed sadly, but made no answer.

"I have the greatest regard for you, Mr. Harding," continued Bold; "the truest respect, the most sincere——"

"Thank ye, thank ye, Mr. Bold," interjaculated the precentor somewhat impatiently; "I'm much obliged, but never mind that; I'm as likely to be in the wrong as another man—quite as likely."

"But, Mr. Harding, I must express what I feel, lest you should think there is personal enmity in what I'm going to do."

"Personal enmity! Going to do! Why, you're not going to cut my throat, nor put me into the Ecclesiastical Court——"

Bold tried to laugh, but he couldn't. He was quite in earnest, and determined in his course, and couldn't make a joke of it. He walked on awhile in silence before he recommenced his attack, during which Mr. Harding, who had still the bow in his hand, played rapidly on an imaginary violoncello. "I fear there is reason to think that John Hiram's will is not carried out to the letter, Mr. Harding," said the young man at last; "and I have been asked to see into it."

"Very well, I've no objection on earth; and now we need not say another word about it."

"Only one word more, Mr. Harding. Chadwick has referred me to Cox and Cumming, and I think it my duty to apply to them for some statement about the hospital. In what I do I may appear to be interfering with you, and I hope you will forgive me for doing so.''

"Mr. Bold,'' said the other, stopping, and speaking with some solemnity, ''if you act justly, say nothing in this matter but the truth, and use no unfair weapons in carrying out your purposes, I shall have nothing to forgive. I presume you think I am not entitled to the income I receive from the hospital, and that others are entitled to it. Whatever some may do, I shall never attribute to you base motives because you hold an opinion opposed to my own and adverse to my interests: pray do what you consider to be your duty; I can give you no assistance, neither will I offer you any obstacle. Let me, however, suggest to you, that you can in no wise forward your views nor I mine, by any discussion between us. Here comes Eleanor and the ponies, and we'll go into tea.''

Bold, however, felt that he could not sit down at ease with Mr. Harding and his daughter after what had passed, and therefore excused himself with much awkward apology; and merely raising his hat and bowing as he passed Eleanor and the pony chair, left her in disappointed amazement at his departure.

Mr. Harding's demeanour certainly impressed Bold with a full conviction that the warden felt that he stood on strong grounds, and almost made him think that he was about to interfere without due warrant in the private affairs of a just and honourable man; but Mr. Harding himself was anything but satisfied with his own view of the case.

In the first place, he wished for Eleanor's sake to think well of Bold and to like him, and yet he could not but feel disgusted at the arrogance of his conduct. What right had he to say that John Hiram's will was not fairly carried out? But then the question would arise within his heart, Was that will fairly acted on? Did John Hiram mean that the warden of his hospital should receive considerably more out of the legacy than all the twelve old men together for whose behoof the hospital was built? Could it be possible that John Bold was right, and that the reverend warden of the hospital had been for the last ten years and more the unjust recipient of an income legally and equitably belonging to others? What if it should be proved before the light of day that he, whose life had been so happy, so quiet, so respected, had absorbed £800 to which he had no title, and which he could never repay? I do not say that he feared that such was really the case; but the first shade of doubt now fell across his mind, and from this evening, for many a long, long day, our good, kind loving warden was neither happy nor at ease.

Thoughts of this kind, these first moments of much misery, oppressed Mr. Harding as he sat sipping his tea, absent and ill at ease. Poor Eleanor felt that all was not right, but her ideas as to the cause of the evening's discomfort did not go beyond her lover, and his sudden and uncivil departure. She thought there must have been some quarrel between Bold and her father, and she was half angry with both, though she did not attempt to explain to herself why she was so.

Mr. Harding thought long and deeply over these things, both before he went to bed and after it, as he lay awake, questioning within himself the validity of his claim to the income which he enjoyed. It seemed clear at any rate that, however unfortunate he might be at having been placed in such a position, no one could say that he ought either to have refused the appointment first, or to have rejected the income afterwards. All the world—meaning the ecclesiastical world as confined to the English church—knew that the wardenship of the Barchester Hospital was a snug sinecure, but no one had ever been blamed for accepting it. To how much blame, however, would he have been open had he rejected it! How mad would he have been thought had he declared, when the situation was vacant and offered to him, that he had scruples as to receiving £800 a year from John Hiram's property, and that he had rather some stranger should possess it! How would Dr. Grantly have shaken his wise head, and have consulted with his friends in the close as to some decent retreat for the coming insanity of the poor minor canon! If he was right in accepting the place, it was clear to him also that he would be wrong in rejecting any part of the income attached to it. The patronage was a valuable appanage of the bishopric; and surely it would not be his duty to lessen the value of that preferment which had been bestowed on himself; surely he was bound to stand by his order.

But somehow these arguments, though they seemed logical, were not satisfactory. Was John Hiram's will fairly carried out? that was the true question: and if not, was it not his especial duty to see that this was done—his especial duty, whatever injury it might do to his order—however ill such duty might be received by his patron and his friends? At the idea of his friends, his mind turned unhappily to his son-in-law. He knew well how strongly he would be supported by Dr. Grantly, if he could bring himself to put his case into the archdeacon's hands and to allow him to fight the battle; but he knew also that he would find no sympathy there for his doubts, no friendly feeling, no inward comfort. Dr. Grantly would be ready enough to take up his cudgel against all comers on behalf of the church militant, but he would do so on the distasteful ground of the church's infallibility. Such a contest would give no comfort to Mr. Harding's doubts. He was not so anxious to prove himself right, as to be so.

I have said before that Dr. Grantly was the working man of the diocese, and that his father the bishop was somewhat inclined to an idle life. So it was; but the bishop, though he had never been an active man, was one whose qualities had rendered him dear to all who knew him. He was the very opposite to his son; he was a bland and a kind old man, opposed by every feeling to authoritative demonstrations and episcopal ostentation. It was perhaps well for him, in his situation, that his son had early in life been able to do that which he could not well do when he was younger, and which he could not have done at all now that he was over seventy. The bishop knew how to entertain the clergy of his diocese, to talk easy small-talk with the rectors' wives, and put curates at their ease; but it required the strong hand of the archdeacon to deal with such as were refractory either in their doctrines or their lives.

The bishop and Mr. Harding loved each other warmly. They had grown old together, and had together spent many, many years in clerical pursuits and clerical conversation. When one of them was a bishop and the other only a minor canon they were even then much together; but since their children had married, and Mr. Harding had become warden and precentor, they were all in all to each other. I will not say that they managed the diocese between them, but they spent much time in discussing the man who did, and in forming little plans to mitigate his wrath against church delinquents, and soften his aspirations for church dominion.

Mr. Harding determined to open his mind, and confess his doubts to his old friend; and to him he went on the morning after John Bold's uncourteous visit.

Up to this period no rumour of these cruel proceedings against the hospital had reached the bishop's ears. He had doubtless heard that men existed who questioned his right to present to a sinecure of £800 a year, as he had heard from time to time of some special immorality or disgraceful disturbance in the usually decent and quiet city of Barchester: but all he did, and all he was called on to do, on such occasions, was to shake his head, and to beg his son, the great dictator, to see that no harm happened to the church.

It was a long story that Mr. Harding had to tell before he made the bishop comprehend his own view of the case; but we need not follow him through the tale. At first the bishop counselled but one step, recommended but one remedy, had but one medicine in his whole pharmacopœia strong enough to touch so grave a disorder—he prescribed the archdeacon. "Refer him to the archdeacon," he repeated, as Mr. Harding spoke of Bold and his visit. "The archdeacon will set you quite right about that," he kindly said, when his friend spoke with hesitation of the justness of his cause. "No man has got up all that so well as the archdeacon"; but the dose, though large, failed to quiet the patient; indeed it almost produced nausea.

"But, bishop," said he, "did you ever read John Hiram's will?"

The bishop thought probably he had, thirty-five years ago, when first instituted to his see, but could not state positively: however, he very well knew that he had the absolute right to present to the wardenship, and that the income of the warden had been regularly settled.

"But, bishop, the question is, who has the power to settle it? If, as this young man says, the will provides that the proceeds of the property are to be divided into shares, who has the power to alter these provisions?" The bishop had an indistinct idea that they altered themselves by the lapse of years; that a kind of ecclesiastical statute of limitation barred the rights of the twelve bedesmen to any increase of income arising from the increased value of property. He said something about tradition; more of the many learned men who by their practice had confirmed the present arrangement; then went at some length into the propriety of maintaining the due difference in rank and income between a beneficed clergyman and certain poor old men who were dependent on charity; and concluded his argument by another reference to the archdeacon.

The precentor sat thoughtfully gazing at the fire, and listening to the good-natured reasoning of his friend. What the bishop said had a sort of comfort in it, but it was not a sustaining comfort. It made Mr. Harding feel that many others—indeed, all others of his own order—would think him right; but it failed to prove to him that he truly was so.

"Bishop," said he, at last, after both had sat silent for a while, "I should deceive you and myself too, if I did not tell

you that I am very unhappy about this. Suppose that I cannot
bring myself to agree with Dr. Grantly!—that I find, after inquiry,
that the young man is right, and that I am wrong—what then?''

The two old men were sitting near each other—so near that
the bishop was able to lay his hand upon the other's knee, and he
did so with a gentle pressure. Mr. Harding well knew what that
pressure meant. The bishop had no further argument to adduce;
he could not fight for the cause as his son would do; he could not
prove all the precentor's doubts to be groundless; but he could
sympathise with his friend, and he did so; and Mr. Harding felt
that he had received that for which he came. There was another
period of silence, after which the bishop asked, with a degree of
irritable energy very unusual with him, whether this ''pestilent
intruder'' (meaning John Bold) had any friends in Barchester.

Mr. Harding had fully made up his mind to tell the bishop
everything; to speak of his daughter's love, as well as his own
troubles; to talk of John Bold in his double capacity of future
son-in-law and present enemy; and though he felt it to be sufficiently disagreeable, now was his time to do it.

''He is very intimate at my own house, bishop.'' The
bishop stared. He was not so far gone in orthodoxy and church
militancy as his son, but still he could not bring himself to
understand how so declared an enemy of the establishment could
be admitted on terms of intimacy into the house, not only of so
firm a pillar as Mr. Harding, but one so much injured as the
warden of the hospital.

''Indeed, I like Mr. Bold much, personally,'' continued the
disinterested victim; ''and to tell you the 'truth' ''—he hesitated
as he brought out the dreadful tidings—''I have sometimes thought
it not improbable that he would be my second son-in-law.'' The
bishop did not whistle: we believe that they lose the power of
doing so on being consecrated; and that in these days one might
as easily meet a corrupt judge as a whistling bishop; but he
looked as though he would have done so, but for his apron.

What a brother-in-law for the archdeacon! what an alliance
for Barchester close! what a connection for even the episcopal
palace! The bishop, in his simple mind, felt no doubt that John
Bold, had he so much power, would shut up all cathedrals, and
probably all parish churches; distribute all tithes among Methodists,
Baptists, and other savage tribes; utterly annihilate the sacred
bench, and make shovel hats and lawn sleeves as illegal as
cowls, sandals, and sackcloth! Here was a nice man to be

initiated into the comfortable arcana of ecclesiastical snuggeries; one who doubted the integrity of parsons, and probably disbelieved the Trinity!

Mr. Harding saw what an effect his communication had made, and almost repented the openness of his disclosure; he, however, did what he could to moderate the grief of his friend and patron. "I do not say that there is any engagement between them. Had there been, Eleanor would have told me; I know her well enough to be assured that she would have done so; but I see that they are fond of each other; and as a man and a father, I have had no objection to urge against their intimacy."

"But, Mr. Harding," said the bishop, "how are you to oppose him, if he is your son-in-law?"

"I don't mean to oppose him; it is he who opposes me; if anything is to be done in defence, I suppose Chadwick will do it. I suppose——"

"Oh, the archdeacon will see to that: were the young man twice his brother-in-law, the archdeacon will never be deterred from doing what he feels to be right."

Mr. Harding reminded the bishop that the archdeacon and the reformer were not yet brothers, and very probably never would be; exacted from him a promise that Eleanor's name should not be mentioned in any discussion between the father bishop and son archdeacon respecting the hospital; and then took his departure, leaving his poor old friend bewildered, amazed, and confounded.

IV

Hiram's Bedesmen

The parties most interested in the movement which is about to set Barchester by the ears were not the foremost to discuss the merit of the question, as is often the case; but when the bishop, the archdeacon, the warden, the steward, and Messrs. Cox and Cumming, were all busy with the matter, each in his own way, it is not to be supposed that Hiram's bedesmen themselves were altogether passive spectators. Finney, the attorney, had been among them, asking sly questions, and raising immoderate hopes, creating a party hostile to the warden, and establishing a corps in the enemy's camp, as he figuratively calls it to himself. Poor old men: whoever may be righted or wronged by this inquiry, they at any rate will assuredly be only injured; to them it can only be an unmixed evil. How can their lot be improved? all their wants are supplied; every comfort is administered; they have warm houses, good clothes, plentiful diet, and rest after a life of labour; and above all, that treasure so inestimable in declining years, a true and kind friend to listen to their sorrows, watch over their sickness, and administer comfort as regards this world, and the world to come!

John Bold sometimes thinks of this, when he is talking loudly of the rights of the bedesmen, whom he has taken under his protection; but he quiets the suggestion within his breast with the high-sounding name of justice: "Fiat justitia ruat cœlum." These old men should, by rights, have one hundred pounds a year instead of one shilling and sixpence a day, and the warden should have two hundred or three hundred pounds instead of eight hundred pounds. What is unjust must be wrong; what is wrong should be righted; and if he declined the task, who else would do it?

"Each one of you is clearly entitled to one hundred pounds a year by common law": such had been the important whisper made by Finney into the ears of Abel Handy, and by him retailed to his eleven brethren.

Too much must not be expected from the flesh and blood even of John Hiram's bedesmen, and the positive promise of one hundred a year to each of the twelve old men had its way with most of them. The great Bunce was not to be wiled away, and was upheld in his orthodoxy by two adherents. Abel Handy, who was the leader of the aspirants after wealth, had, alas, a stronger following. No less than five of the twelve soon believed that his views were just, making with their leader a moiety of the hospital. The other three, volatile unstable minds, vacillated between the two chieftains, now led away by the hope of gold, now anxious to propitiate the powers that still existed.

It had been proposed to address a petition to the bishop as visitor, praying his lordship to see justice done to the legal recipients of John Hiram's charity, and to send copies of this petition and of the reply it would elicit to all the leading London papers, and thereby to obtain notoriety for the subject. This it was thought would pave the way for ulterior legal proceedings. It would have been a great thing to have had the signatures and marks of all the twelve injured legatees; but this was impossible: Bunce would have cut his hand off sooner than have signed it. It was then suggested by Finney that if even eleven could be induced to sanction the document, the one obstinate recusant might have been represented as unfit to judge on such a question—in fact, as being *non compos mentis*—and the petition would have been taken as representing the feeling of the men. But this could not be done: Bunce's friends were as firm as himself, and as yet only six crosses adorned the document. It was the more provoking, as Bunce himself could write his name legibly, and one of those three doubting souls had for years boasted of like power, and possessed, indeed, a Bible, in which he was proud to show his name written by himself some thirty years ago—"Job Skulpit"; but it was thought that Job Skulpit, having forgotten his scholarship, on that account recoiled from the petition, and that the other doubters would follow as he led them. A petition signed by half the hospital would have but a poor effect.

It was in Skulpit's room that the petition was now lying, waiting such additional signatures as Abel Handy, by his eloquence, could obtain for it. The six marks it bore were duly attested, thus:

his	his	his
Abel + Handy,	Greg^y + Moody,	Mathew + Spriggs,
mark	mark	mark

etc., and places were duly designated in pencil for those brethren who were now expected to join: for Skulpit alone was left a spot on which his genuine signature might be written in fair clerk-like style. Handy had brought in the document, and spread it out on the small deal table, and was now standing by it persuasive and eager. Moody had followed with an inkhorn, carefully left behind by Finney; and Spriggs bore aloft, as though it were a sword, a well-worn ink-black pen, which from time to time he endeavoured to thrust into Skulpit's unwilling hand.

With the learned man were his two abettors in indecision, William Gazy and Jonathan Crumple. If ever the petition were to be forwarded, now was the time, so said Mr. Finney; and great was the anxiety on the part of those whose one hundred pounds a year, as they believed, mainly depended on the document in question.

"To be kept out of all that money," as the avaricious Moody had muttered to his friend Handy, "by an old fool saying that he can write his own name like his betters!"

"Well, Job," said Handy, trying to impart to his own sour, ill-omened visage a smile of approbation, in which he greatly failed; "so you're ready now, Mr. Finney says; here's the place, d'ye see,"—and he put his huge brown finger down on the dirty paper,—"name or mark, it's all one. Come along, old boy; if so be we're to have the spending of this money, why the sooner the better—that's my maxim."

"To be sure," said Moody. "We a'n't none of us so young; we can't stay waiting for old Catgut no longer."

It was thus these miscreants named our excellent friend. The nickname he could easily have forgiven, but the allusion to the divine source of all his melodious joy would have irritated even him. Let us hope he never knew the insult.

"Only think, old Billy Gazy," said Spriggs, who rejoiced in greater youth than his brethren, but having fallen into a fire when drunk, had had one eye burnt out, one cheek burnt through, and one arm nearly burnt off, and who, therefore, in regard to personal appearance, was not the most prepossessing of men, "a hundred a year, and all to spend; only think, old Billy Gazy"; and he gave a hideous grin that showed off his misfortunes to their full extent.

Old Billy Gazy was not alive to much enthusiasm. Even these golden prospects did not arouse him to do more than rub his poor old bleared eyes with the cuff of his bedesman's gown, and gently mutter; "He didn't know, not he; he didn't know."

"But you'd know, Jonathan," continued Spriggs, turning to the other friend of Skulpit's, who was sitting on a stool by the table, gazing vacantly at the petition. Jonathan Crumple was a meek, mild man, who had known better days; his means had been wasted by bad children, who had made his life wretched till he had been received into the hospital, of which he had not long been a member. Since that day he had known neither sorrow nor trouble, and this attempt to fill him with new hope was, indeed, a cruelty.

"A hundred a year's a nice thing, for sartain, neighbour Spriggs," said he. "I once had nigh to that myself, but it didn't

do me no good." And he gave a low sigh, as he thought of the
children of his own loins who had robbed him.

"And shall have again, Joe," said Handy; "and will have
some one to keep it right and tight for you this time."

Crumple sighed again—he had learned the impotency of
worldly wealth, and would have been satisfied, if left untempted,
to have remained happy with one and sixpence a day.

"Come, Skulpit," repeated Handy, getting impatient, "you're
not going to go along with old Bunce in helping that parson to
rob us all. Take the pen, man, and right yourself. Well," he
added, seeing that Skulpit still doubted, "to see a man as is
afraid to stand by hisself is, to my thinking, the meanest thing as
is."

"Sink them all for parsons, says I," growled Moody; "hungry
beggars, as never thinks their bellies full till they have robbed all
and everything!"

"Who's to harm you, man?" argued Spriggs. "Let them
look never so black at you, they can't get you put out when
you're once in—no, not old Catgut, with Calves to help him!" I
am sorry to say the archdeacon himself was designated by this
scurrilous allusion to his nether person.

"A hundred a year to win, and nothing to lose," continued
Handy. "My eyes! Well, how a man's to doubt about sich a bit
of cheese as that passes me—but some men is timorous—some
men is born with no pluck in them—some men is cowed at the
very first sight of a gentleman's coat and waistcoat."

Oh, Mr. Harding, if you had but taken the archdeacon's
advice in that disputed case, when Joe Mutters was this ungrateful demagogue's rival candidate!

"Afraid of a parson," growled Moody, with a look of
ineffable scorn. "I tell ye what I'd be afraid of—I'd be afraid of
not getting nothing from 'em but just what I could take by might
and right—that's the most I'd be afraid on of any parson of 'em
all."

"But," said Skulpit, apologetically. "Mr. Harding's not so
bad—he did give us twopence a day, didn't he now?"

"Twopence a day!" exclaimed Spriggs with scorn, opening
awfully the red cavern of his lost eye.

"Twopence a day!" muttered Moody with a curse; "sink
his twopence!"

"Twopence a day!" exclaimed Handy; "and I'm to go, hat
in hand, and thank a chap for twopence a day, when he owes me
a hundred pounds a year: no, thank ye; that may do for you,

but it won't for me. Come, I say, Skulpit, are you a going to put your mark to this here paper, or are you not?''

Skulpit looked round in wretched indecision to his two friends. "What d'ye think, Bill Gazy?" said he.

But Bill Gazy couldn't think. He made a noise like the bleating of an old sheep, which was intended to express the agony of his doubt, and again muttered that "he didn't know."

"Take hold, you old cripple," said Handy, thrusting the pen into poor Billy's hand: "there, so—ugh! you old fool, you've been and smeared it all—there—that'll do for you—that's as good as the best name as ever was written": and a big blotch of ink was presumed to represent Billy Gazy's acquiescence.

"Now, Jonathan," said Handy, turning to Crumple.

"A hundred a year's a nice thing, for sartain," again argued Crumple. "Well, neighbour Skulpit, how's it to be?"

"Oh, please yourself," said Skulpit; "please yourself, and you'll please me."

The pen was thrust into Crumple's hand, and a faint, wandering, meaningless sign was made, betokening such sanction and authority as Jonathan Crumple was able to convey.

"Come, Job," said Handy, softened by success, "don't let 'em have to say that old Bunce has a man like you under his thumb—a man that always holds his head in the hospital as high as Bunce himself, though you're never axed to drink wine, and sneak, and tell lies about your betters as he does."

Skulpit held the pen, and made little flourishes with it in the air, but still hesitated.

"And if you'll be said by me," continued Handy, "you'll not write your name to it at all, but just put your mark like the others,"—the cloud began to clear from Skulpit's brow:—"we all know you can do it if you like, but maybe you wouldn't like to seem uppish, you know."

"Well, the mark would be best," said Skulpit: "One name and the rest marks wouldn't look well, would it?"

"The worst in the world," said Handy; "there—there"; and stooping over the petition, the learned clerk made a huge cross on the place left for his signature.

"That's the game," said Handy, triumphantly pocketing the petition; "we're all in a boat now, that is, the nine of us; and as for old Bunce, and his cronies, they may——" But as he was hobbling off to the door, with a crutch on one side and a stick on the other, he was met by Bunce himself.

"Well, Handy, and what may old Bunce do?" said the grey-haired, upright senior.

Handy muttered something, and was departing; but he was stopped in the doorway by the huge frame of the new comer.

"You've been doing no good here, Abel Handy," said he, " 'tis plain to see that; and 'tisn't much good, I'm thinking, you ever do."

"I mind my own business, Master Bunce," muttered the other, "and do you do the same. It ain't nothing to you what I does—and your spying and poking here won't do no good nor yet no harm."

"I suppose then, Job," continued Bunce, not noticing his opponent, "if the truth must out, you've stuck your name to that petition of theirs at last."

Skulpit looked as though he were about to sink into the ground with shame.

"What is it to you what he signs?" said Handy. "I suppose if we all wants to ax for our own, we needn't ax leave of you first, Mr. Bunce, big a man as you are; and as to your sneaking in here, into Job's room when he's busy, and where you're not wanted——"

"I've knowed Job Skulpit, man and boy, sixty years," said Bunce, looking at the man of whom he spoke, "and that's ever since the day he was born. I knowed the mother that bore him, when she and I were little wee things, picking daisies together in the close yonder; and I've lived under the same roof with him more nor ten years; and after that I may come into his room without axing leave, and yet no sneaking neither."

"So you can, Mr. Bunce," said Skulpit; "so you can, any hour, day or night."

"And I'm free also to tell him my mind," continued Bunce, looking at the one man and addressing the other; "and I tell him now that he's done a foolish and a wrong thing. He's turned his back upon one who is his best friend; and is playing the game of others, who care nothing for him, whether he be poor or rich, well or ill, alive or dead. A hundred a year? Are the lot of you soft enough to think that if a hundred a year be to be given, it's the likes of you that will get it?"—and he pointed to Billy Gazy, Spriggs, and Crumple. "Did any of us ever do anything worth half the money? Was it to make gentlemen of us we were brought in here, when all the world turned against us, and we couldn't longer earn our daily bread? A'n't you all as rich in your ways as he in his?"—and the orator pointed to the side on which the warden lived. "A'n't you getting all you hoped for, ay, and more than you hoped for? Wouldn't each of you have given the dearest limb of his body to secure that which now makes you so unthankful?"

"We wants what John Hiram left us," said Handy. "We wants what's ourn by law; it don't matter what we expected. What's ourn by law should be ourn, and by goles we'll have it."

"Law!" said Bunce, with all the scorn he knew how to command—"law! Did ye ever know a poor man yet was the better for law, or for a lawyer? Will Mr. Finney ever be as good to you, Job, as that man has been? Will he see to you when you're sick, and comfort you when you're wretched? Will he——"

"No, nor give you port wine, old boy, on cold winter nights! he won't do that, will he?" asked Handy; and laughing at the severity of his own wit, he and his colleagues retired, carrying with them, however, the now powerful petition.

There is no help for spilt milk; and Mr. Bunce could only retire to his own room, disgusted at the frailty of human nature— Job Skulpit scratched his head—Jonathan Crumple again remarked, that, "for sartain sure a hundred a year was very nice"—and Billy Gazy again rubbed his eyes, and lowly muttered that "he didn't know."

V

Dr. Grantly Visits the Hospital

Though doubt and hesitation disturbed the rest of our poor warden, no such weakness perplexed the nobler breast of his son-in-law. As the indomitable cock preparing for the combat sharpens his spurs, shakes his feathers, and erects his comb, so did the archdeacon arrange his weapons for the coming war, without misgiving and without fear. That he was fully confident of the justice of his cause let no one doubt. Many a man can fight his battle with good courage, but with a doubting conscience. Such was not the case with Dr. Grantly. He did not believe in the Gospel with more assurance than he did in the sacred justice of all ecclesiastical revenues. When he put his shoulder to the wheel to defend the income of the present and future precentors of Barchester, he was animated by as strong a sense of a holy cause, as that which gives courage to a missionary in Africa, or enables a sister of mercy to give up the pleasures of the world for the wards of a hospital. He was about to defend the holy of holies from the touch of the profane; to guard the citadel of his church from the most rampant of its enemies; to put on his good armour in the best of fights; and secure, if possible, the comforts of his creed for coming generations of ecclesiastical dignitaries. Such a work required no ordinary vigour; and the archdeacon was, therefore, extraordinarily vigorous. It demanded a buoyant courage, and a heart happy in its toil; and the archdeacon's heart was happy, and his courage was buoyant.

He knew that he would not be able to animate his father-in-law with feelings like his own, but this did not much disturb him. He preferred to bear the brunt of the battle alone, and did not doubt that the warden would resign himself into his hands with passive submission.

"Well, Mr. Chadwick," he said, walking into the steward's office a day or two after the signing of the petition as commemorated in the last chapter: "anything from Cox and Cumming this morning?" Mr. Chadwick handed him a letter; which he read, stroking the tight-gaitered calf of his right leg as he did so. Messrs. Cox and Cumming merely said that they had as yet received no notice from the adversaries; that they could recommend no preliminary steps; but that should any proceeding really be taken by the bedesmen, it would be expedient to consult that very eminent Queen's Counsel, Sir Abraham Haphazard.

"I quite agree with them," said Dr. Grantly, refolding the letter. "I perfectly agree with them. Haphazard is no doubt the best man; a thorough churchman, a sound conservative, and in every respect the best man we could get—he's in the house, too, which is a great thing."

Mr. Chadwick quite agreed.

"You remember how completely he put down that scoundrel Horseman about the Bishop of Beverley's income; how completely he set them all adrift in the earl's case." Since the question of St. Cross had been mooted by the public, one noble lord had become *"the earl,"* par excellence, in the doctor's

estimation. "How he silenced that fellow at Rochester. Of course
we must have Haphazard; and I'll tell you what, Mr. Chadwick,
we must take care to be in time, or the other party will forestall
us."

With all his admiration for Sir Abraham, the doctor seemed
to think it not impossible that that great man might be induced to
lend his gigantic powers to the side of the church's enemies.

Having settled this point to his satisfaction, the doctor
stepped down to the hospital, to learn how matters were going on
there; and as he walked across the hallowed close, and looked
up at the ravens who cawed with a peculiar reverence as he
wended his way, he thought with increased acerbity of those
whose impiety would venture to disturb the goodly grace of
cathedral institutions.

And who has not felt the same? We believe that Mr.
Horseman himself would relent, and the spirit of Sir Benjamin
Hall give way, were those great reformers to allow themselves to
stroll by moonlight round the towers of some of our ancient
churches. Who would not feel charity for a prebendary, when
walking the quiet length of that long aisle at Winchester, looking
at those decent houses, that trim grassplat, and feeling, as one
must, the solemn, orderly comfort of the spot! Who could be
hard upon a dean while wandering round the sweet close of
Hereford, and owning that in that precinct, tone and colour,
design and form, solemn tower and storied window, are all in
unison, and all perfect! Who could lie basking in the cloisters of
Salisbury, and gaze on Jewel's library and that unequalled spire,
without feeling that bishops should sometimes be rich!

The tone of our archdeacon's mind must not astonish us; it
has been the growth of centuries of church ascendancy; and
though some fungi now disfigure the tree, though there be much
dead wood, for how much good fruit have not we to be thankful?
Who, without remorse, can batter down the dead branches of an
old oak, now useless, but, ah! still so beautiful, or drag out the
fragments of the ancient forest, without feeling that they sheltered the younger plants, to which they are now summoned to
give way in a tone so peremptory and so harsh?

The archdeacon, with all his virtues, was not a man of
delicate feeling; and after having made his morning salutations in
the warden's drawing-room, he did not scruple to commence an
attack on "pestilent" John Bold in the presence of Miss Harding,
though he rightly guessed that that lady was not indifferent to the
name of his enemy.

"Nelly, my dear, fetch me my spectacles from the back room," said her father, anxious to save both her blushes and her feelings.

Eleanor brought the spectacles, while her father was trying, in ambiguous phrases, to explain to her too-practical brother-in-law that it might be as well not to say anything about Bold before her, and then retreated. Nothing had been explained to her about Bold and the hospital; but, with a woman's instinct, she knew that things were going wrong.

"We must soon be doing something," commenced the archdeacon, wiping his brows with a large, bright-coloured handkerchief, for he had felt busy, and had walked quick, and it was a broiling summer's day. "Of course you have heard of the petition?"

Mr. Harding owned, somewhat unwillingly, that he had heard of it.

"Well,"—the archdeacon looked for some expressions of opinion, but none coming, he continued—"We must be doing something, you know; we mustn't allow these people to cut the ground from under us while we sit looking on." The archdeacon, who was a practical man, allowed himself the use of every-day expressive modes of speech when among his closest intimates, though no one could soar into a more intricate labyrinth of refined phraseology when the church was the subject, and his lower brethren were his auditors.

The warden still looked mutely in his face, making the slightest possible passes with an imaginary fiddle bow, and stopping, as he did so, sundry imaginary strings with the fingers of his other hand. 'Twas his constant consolation in conversational troubles. While these vexed him sorely, the passes would be short and slow, and the upper hand would not be seen to work; nay the strings on which it operated would sometimes lie concealed in the musician's pocket, and the instrument on which he played would be beneath his chair; but as his spirit warmed to the subject—as his trusting heart, looking to the bottom of that which vexed him, would see its clear way out,—he would rise to a higher melody, sweep the unseen strings with a bolder hand, and swiftly fingering the cords from his neck, down along his waistcoat, and up again to his very ear, create an ecstatic strain of perfect music, audible to himself and to St. Cecilia, and not without effect.

"I quite agree with Cox and Cumming," continued the archdeacon. "They say we must secure Sir Abraham Haphazard.

I shall not have the slightest fear in leaving the case in Sir Abraham's hands.''

The warden played the slowest and saddest of tunes. It was but a dirge on one string.

''I think Sir Abraham will not be long in letting Master Bold know what he's about. I fancy I hear Sir Abraham cross-questioning him at the Common Pleas.''

The warden thought of his income being thus discussed, his modest life, his daily habits, and his easy work; and nothing issued from that single cord, but a low wail of sorrow. ''I suppose they've sent this petition up to my father.'' The warden didn't know; he imagined they would do so this very day.

''What I can't understand is, how you let them do it, with such a command as you have in the place, or should have with such a man as Bunce. I cannot understand why you let them do it.''

''Do what?'' asked the warden.

''Why, listen to this fellow Bold, and that other low pettifogger, Finney—and get up this petition too. Why didn't you tell Bunce to destroy the petition?''

''That would have been hardly wise,'' said the warden.

''Wise—yes, it would have been very wise if they'd done it among themselves. I must go up to the palace and answer it now, I suppose. It's a very short answer they'll get, I can tell you.''

''But why shouldn't they petition, doctor?''

''Why shouldn't they!'' responded the archdeacon, in a loud brazen voice, as though all the men in the hospital were expected to hear him through the walls; ''why shouldn't they? I'll let them know why they shouldn't: by the bye, warden, I'd like to say a few words to them all together.''

The warden's mind misgave him, and even for a moment he forgot to play. He by no means wished to delegate his son-in-law his place and authority of warden; he had expressly determined not to interfere in any step which the men might wish to take in the matter under dispute; he was most anxious neither to accuse them nor to defend himself. All these things he was aware the archdeacon would do in his behalf, and that not in the mildest manner; and yet he knew not how to refuse the permission requested.

''I'd so much sooner remain quiet in the matter,'' said he, in an apologetic voice.

"Quiet!" said the archdeacon, still speaking with his brazen trumpet; "do you wish to be ruined in quiet?"

"Why, if I am to be ruined, certainly."

"Nonsense, warden; I tell you something must be done—we must act; just let me ring the bell, and send the men word that I'll speak to them in the quad."

Mr. Harding knew not how to resist, and the disagreeable order was given. The quad, as it was familiarly called, was a small quadrangle, open on one side to the river, and surrounded on the others by the high wall of Mr. Harding's garden, by one gable end of Mr. Harding's house, and by the end of the row of buildings which formed the residences of the bedesmen. It was flagged all round, and the centre was stoned; small stone gutters ran from the four corners of the square to a grating in the centre; and attached to the end of Mr. Harding's house was a conduit with four cocks covered over from the weather, at which the old men got their water, and very generally performed their morning toilet. It was a quiet, sombre place, shaded over by the trees of the warden's garden. On the side towards the river, there stood a row of stone seats, on which the old men would sit and gaze at the little fish, as they flitted by in the running stream. On the other side of the river was a rich, green meadow, running up to and joining the deanery, and as little open to the public as the garden of the dean itself. Nothing, therefore, could be more private than the quad of the hospital; and it was there that the archdeacon determined to convey to them his sense of their refractory proceedings.

The servant soon brought in word that the men were assembled in the quad, and the archdeacon, big with his purpose, rose to address them.

"Well, warden, of course you're coming," said he, seeing that Mr. Harding did not prepare to follow him.

"I wish you'd excuse me," said Mr. Harding.

"For heaven's sake, don't let us have division in the camp," replied the archdeacon: "let us have a long pull and a strong pull, but above all a pull all together; come, warden, come; don't be afraid of your duty."

Mr. Harding was afraid; he was afraid that he was being led to do that which was not his duty: he was not, however, strong enough to resist, so he got up and followed his son-in-law.

The old men were assembled in groups in the quadrangle—eleven of them at least, for poor old Johnny Bell was bedridden, and couldn't come; he had, however, put his mark to the petition,

as one of Handy's earliest followers. 'Tis true he could not move
from the bed where he lay; 'tis true he had no friend on earth,
but those whom the hospital contained; and of those the warden
and his daughter were the most constant and most appreciated;
'tis true that every thing was administered to him which his
failing body could require, or which his faint appetite could
enjoy; but still his dull eye had glistened for a moment at the
idea of possessing a hundred pounds a year "to his own cheek,"
as Abel Handy had eloquently expressed it; and poor old Johnny
Bell had greedily put his mark to the petition.

When the two clergymen appeared, they all uncovered their
heads. Handy was slow to do it, and hesitated; but the black coat
and waistcoat, of which he had spoken so irreverently in Skulpit's
room, had its effect even on him, and he too doffed his hat.
Bunce, advancing before the others, bowed lowly to the
archdeacon, and with affectionate reverence expressed his wish,
that the warden and Miss Eleanor were quite well; "and the
doctor's lady," he added, turning to the archdeacon, "and the
children at Plumstead, and my lord"; and having made his
speech, he also retired among the others, and took his place with
the rest upon the stone benches.

As the archdeacon stood up to make his speech, erect in the
middle of that little square, he looked like an ecclesiastical statue
placed there, as a fitting impersonation of the church militant
here on earth; his shovel hat, large, new, and well-pronounced, a
churchman's hat in every inch, declared the profession as plainly
as does the Quaker's broad brim; his heavy eyebrows, large open
eyes, and full mouth and chin expressed the solidity of his order;
the broad chest, amply covered with fine cloth, told how well to
do was its estate; one hand ensconced within his pocket, evinced
the practical hold which our mother church keeps on her temporal possessions; and the other, loose for action, was ready to
fight if need be in her defence; and, below these, the decorous
breeches, and neat black gaiters showing so admirably that well-
turned leg, betokened the decency, the outward beauty and grace
of our church establishment.

"Now, my men," he began, when he had settled himself
well in his position; "I want to say a few words to you. Your
good friend, the warden here, and myself, and my lord the
bishop, on whose behalf I wish to speak to you, would all be
very sorry, very sorry indeed, that you should have any just
ground of complaint. Any just ground of complaint on your part
would be removed at once by the warden, or by his lordship, or

by me on his behalf, without the necessity of any petition on your part." Here the orator stopped for a moment, expecting that some little murmurs of applause would show that the weakest of the men were beginning to give way; but no such murmurs came. Bunce, himself, even sat with closed lips, mute and unsatisfactory. "Without the necessity of any petition at all," he repeated. "I'm told you have addressed a petition to my lord." He paused for a reply from the men, and after a while, Handy plucked up courage and said, "Yes, we has."

"You have addressed a petition to my lord, in which, as I am informed, you express an opinion that you do not receive from Hiram's estate all that is your due." Here most of the men expressed their assent. "Now what is it you ask for? What is it you want that you haven't got here? What is it——"

"A hundred a year," muttered old Moody, with a voice as if it came out of the ground.

"A hundred a year!" ejaculated the archdeacon militant, defying the impudence of these claimants with one hand stretched out and closed, while with the other he tightly grasped, and secured within his breeches pocket, that symbol of the church's wealth which his own loose half-crowns not unaptly represented. "A hundred a year! Why, my men, you must be mad; and you talk about John Hiram's will! When John Hiram built a hospital for worn-out old men, worn-out old labouring men, infirm old men past their work, cripples, blind, bed-ridden, and such like, do you think he meant to make gentlemen of them? Do you think John Hiram intended to give a hundred a year to old single men, who earned perhaps two shillings or half-a-crown a day for themselves and families in the best of their time? No, my men, I'll tell you what John Hiram meant: he meant that twelve poor old worn-out labourers, men who could no longer support themselves, who had no friends to support them, who must starve and perish miserably if not protected by the hand of charity; he meant that twelve such men as these should come in here in their poverty and wretchedness, and find within these walls shelter and food before their death, and a little leisure to make their peace with God. That was what John Hiram meant: you have not read John Hiram's will, and I doubt whether those wicked men who are advising you have done so. I have; I know what his will was; and I tell you that that was his will, and that that was his intention."

Not a sound came from the eleven bedesmen, as they sat listening to what, according to the archdeacon, was their intended estate. They grimly stared upon his burly figure, but did not then express, by word or sign, the anger and disgust to which such language was sure to give rise.

"Now let me ask you," he continued: "do you think you are worse off than John Hiram intended to make you? Have you not shelter, and food, and leisure? Have you not much more? Have you not every indulgence which you are capable of enjoying? Have you not twice better food, twice a better bed, ten times more money in your pocket than you were ever able to earn for yourselves before you were lucky enough to get into this place? And now you send a petition to the bishop, asking for a hundred pounds a year! I tell you what, my friends; you are deluded, and made fools of by wicked men who are acting for their own ends. You will never get a hundred pence a year more than what you have now: it is very possible that you may get less; it is very possible that my lord the bishop, and your warden, may make changes——"

"No, no, no," interrupted Mr. Harding, who had been listening with indescribable misery to the tirade of his son-in-law; "no, my friends. I want no changes—at least no changes that shall make you worse off than you now are, as long as you and I live together."

"God bless you, Mr. Harding," said Bunce; and "God bless you, Mr. Harding, God bless you, sir: we know you was always our friend," was exclaimed by enough of the men to make it appear that the sentiment was general.

The archdeacon had been interrupted in his speech before he had quite finished it; but he felt that he could not recommence with dignity after this little ebullition, and he led the way back into the garden, followed by his father-in-law.

"Well," said he, as soon as he found himself within the cool retreat of the warden's garden; "I think I spoke to them plainly." And he wiped the perspiration from his brow; for making a speech under a broiling midday sun in summer, in a full suit of thick black cloth, is warm work.

"Yes, you were plain enough," replied the warden, in a tone which did not express approbation.

"And that's everything," said the other, who was clearly well satisfied with himself; "that's everything: with those sort of people one must be plain, or one will not be understood. Now, I think they did understand me—I think they knew what I meant."

The warden agreed. He certainly thought they had understood to the full what had been said to them.

"They know pretty well what they have to expect from us; they know how we shall meet any refractory spirit on their part; they know that we are not afraid of them. And now I'll just step into Chadwick's, and tell him what I've done; and then I'll go up to the palace, and answer this petition of theirs.''

The warden's mind was very full—full nearly to overcharging itself; and had it done so—had he allowed himself to speak the thoughts which were working within him, he would indeed have astonished the archdeacon by the reprobation he would have expressed as to the proceeding of which he had been so unwilling a witness. But different feelings kept him silent; he was as yet afraid of differing from his son-in-law—he was anxious beyond measure to avoid even a semblance of rupture with any of his order, and was painfully fearful of having to come to an open quarrel with any person on any subject. His life had hitherto been so quiet, so free from strife; his little early troubles had required nothing but passive fortitude; his subsequent prosperity had never forced upon him any active cares—had never brought him into disagreeable contact with any one. He felt that he would give almost anything—much more than he knew he ought to do—to relieve himself from the storm which he feared was coming. It was so hard that the pleasant waters of his little stream should be disturbed and muddied by rough hands; that his quiet paths should be made a battlefield; that the unobtrusive corner of the world which had been allotted to him, as though by Providence, should be invaded and desecrated, and all within it made miserable and unsound.

Money he had none to give; the knack of putting guineas together had never belonged to him; but how willingly, with what a foolish easiness, with what happy alacrity, would he have abandoned the half of his income for all time to come, could he by so doing have quietly dispelled the clouds that were gathering over him—could he have thus compromised the matter between the reformer and the conservative, between his possible son-in-law, Bold, and his positive son-in-law, the archdeacon.

And this compromise would not have been made from any prudential motive of saving what would yet remain, for Mr. Harding still felt little doubt but he should be left for life in quiet possession of the good things he had, if he chose to retain them. No; he would have done so from the sheer love of quiet, and from a horror of being made the subject of public talk. He had very often been moved to pity—to that inward weeping of the heart for others' woes; but none had he ever pitied more than that old lord, whose almost fabulous wealth, drawn from his church preferments, had become the subject of so much opprobrium, of such public scorn; that wretched clerical octogenarian Crœsus, whom men would not allow to die in peace—whom all the world united to decry and to abhor.

Was he to suffer such a fate? Was his humble name to be bandied in men's mouths, as the gormandiser of the resources of the poor, as of one who had filched from the charity of other ages wealth which had been intended to relieve the old and the infirm? Was he to be gibbeted in the press, to become a byword for oppression, to be named as an example of the greed of the English church? Should it ever be said that he had robbed those old men, whom he so truly and so tenderly loved in his heart of hearts? As he slowly paced, hour after hour, under those noble lime-trees turning these sad thoughts within him he became all but fixed in his resolve that some great step must be taken to relieve him from the risk of so terrible a fate.

In the meanwhile the archdeacon with contented mind and unruffled spirit went about his business. He said a word or two to Mr. Chadwick, and then finding, as he expected, the petition lying in his father's library, he wrote a short answer to the men, in which he told them that they had no evils to redress, but rather great mercies for which to be thankful; and having seen the bishop sign it, he got into his brougham and returned home to Mrs. Grantly, and Plumstead Episcopi.

VI

The Warden's Tea Party

After much painful doubting, on one thing only could Mr. Harding resolve. He determined that at any rate he would take no offence, and that he would make this question no cause of quarrel either with Bold or with the bedesmen. In furtherance of this resolution, he himself wrote a note to Mr. Bold, the same afternoon, inviting him to meet a few friends and hear some music on an evening named in the next week. Had not this little party been promised to Eleanor, in his present state of mind he would probably have avoided such gaiety; but the promise had been given, the invitations were to be written, and when Eleanor consulted her father on the subject, she was not ill pleased to hear him say, ''Oh, I was thinking of Bold, so I took it into my head to write to him myself, but you must write to his sister.''

Mary Bold was older than her brother, and, at the time of our story, was just over thirty. She was not an unattractive young woman, though by no means beautiful. Her great merit was the kindliness of her disposition. She was not very clever, nor very animated, nor had she apparently the energy of her brother; but she was guided by a high principle of right and wrong; her temper was sweet, and her faults were fewer in number than her virtues. Those who casually met Mary Bold thought little of her; but those who knew her well loved her well, and the longer they knew her the more they loved her. Among those who were fondest of her was Eleanor Harding; and though Eleanor had never openly talked to her of her brother, each understood the other's feelings about him. The brother and sister were sitting together when the two notes were brought in.

''How odd,'' said Mary, ''that they should send two notes. Well, if Mr. Harding becomes fashionable, the world is going to change.''

Her brother understood immediately the nature and intention of the peace-offering; but it was not so easy for him to behave well in the matter, as it was for Mr. Harding. It is much less difficult for the sufferer to be generous than for the oppressor. John Bold felt that he could not go to the warden's party: he never loved Eleanor better than he did now; he had never so strongly felt how anxious he was to make her his wife as now, when so many obstacles to his doing so appeared in view. Yet here was her father himself, as it were, clearing away those very obstacles, and still he felt that he could not go to the house any more as an open friend.

As he sat thinking of these things with the note in his hand, his sister was waiting for his decision.

''Well,'' she said, ''I suppose we must write separate answers, and both say we shall be very happy.''

''You'll go, of course, Mary,'' said he; to which she readily assented. "I cannot," he continued, looking serious and gloomy. "I wish I could, with all my heart."

"And why not, John?" said she. She had as yet heard nothing of the new-found abuse which her brother was about to reform—at least nothing which connected it with her brother's name.

He sat thinking for awhile till he determined that it would be best to tell her at once what it was that he was about: it must be done sooner or later.

"I fear I cannot go to Mr. Harding's house any more as a friend, just at present."

"Oh, John! Why not? Ah, you've quarrelled with Eleanor!"

"No, indeed," said he; "I've no quarrel with her as yet."

"What is it, John?" said she, looking at him with an anxious, loving face, for she knew well how much of his heart was there in that house which he said he could no longer enter.

"Why," said he at last, "I've taken up the case of these twelve old men of Hiram's Hospital, and of course that brings me into contact with Mr. Harding. I may have to oppose him, interfere with him, perhaps injure him."

Mary looked at him steadily for some time before she committed herself to reply, and then merely asked him what he meant to do for the old men.

"Why, it's a long story, and I don't know that I can make you understand it. John Hiram made a will, and left his property in charity for certain poor old men, and the proceeds, instead of going to the benefit of these men, goes chiefly into the pocket of the warden and the bishop's steward."

"And you mean to take away from Mr. Harding his share of it?"

"I don't know what I mean yet. I mean to inquire about it. I mean to see who is entitled to this property. I mean to see, if I can, that justice be done to the poor of the city of Barchester generally, who are, in fact, the legatees under the will. I mean, in short, to put the matter right, if I can."

"And why are you to do this, John?"

"You might ask the same question of anybody else," said he; "and according to that the duty of righting these poor men would belong to nobody. If we are to act on that principle, the weak are never to be protected, injustice is never to be opposed, and no one is to struggle for the poor!" And Bold began to comfort himself in the warmth of his own virtue.

"But is there no one to do this but you, who have known

Mr. Harding so long? Surely, John, as a friend, as a young friend, so much younger than Mr. Harding——''

"That's woman's logic, all over, Mary. What has age to do with it? Another man might plead that he was too old; and as to his friendship, if the thing itself be right, private motives should never be allowed to interfere. Because I esteem Mr. Harding, is that a reason that I should neglect a duty which I owe to these old men? or should I give up a work which my conscience tells me is a good one, because I regret the loss of his society?''

"And Eleanor, John?'' said the sister, looking timidly into her brother's face.

"Eleanor, that is, Miss Harding, if she thinks fit—that is, if her father—or, rather, if she—or, indeed, he—if they find it necessary—— but there is no necessity now to talk about Eleanor Harding; but this I will say, that if she has the kind of spirit for which I give her credit, she will not condemn me for doing what I think to be a duty.'' And Bold consoled himself with the consolation of a Roman.

Mary sat silent for awhile, till at last her brother reminded her that the notes must be answered, and she got up, and placed her desk before her, took out her pen and paper, wrote on it slowly—

Pakenham Villas,
Tuesday Morning.

My dear Eleanor
    I——

and then stopped, and looked at her brother.

"Well, Mary, why don't you write it?''

"Oh, John,'' said she, "dear John, pray think better of this.''

"Think better of what?'' said he.

"Of this about the hospital—of all this about Mr. Harding—of what you say about those old men. Nothing can call upon you—no duty can require you to set yourself against your oldest, your best friend. Oh, John, think of Eleanor. You'll break her heart and your own.''

"Nonsense, Mary; Miss Harding's heart is as safe as yours.''

"Pray, pray, for my sake, John, give it up. You know how dearly you love her.'' And she came and knelt before him on the rug. "Pray give it up. You are going to make yourself, and her, and her father miserable: you are going to make us all miserable. And for what? For a dream of justice. You will never make those twelve men happier than they now are.''

"You don't understand it, my dear girl,'' said he, smoothing her hair with his hand.

"I do understand it, John. I understand that this is a chimera—a dream that you have got. I know well that no duty can require you to do this mad—this suicidal thing. I know you love Eleanor Harding with all your heart, and I tell you now that she loves you as well. If there was a plain, a positive duty before you, I would be the last to bid you neglect it for any woman's love; but this—— oh, think again, before you do anything to make it necessary that you and Mr. Harding should be at variance.'' He did not answer, as she knelt there, leaning on his knees, but by his face she thought that he was inclined to yield. "At any rate let me say that you will go to this party. At any rate do not break with them while your mind is in doubt.'' And she got up, hoping to conclude her note in the way she desired.

"My mind is not in doubt,'' at last he said, rising. "I could never respect myself again were I to give way now, because Eleanor Harding is beautiful. I do love her: I would give a hand to hear her tell me what you have said, speaking on her behalf; but I cannot for her sake go back from the task which I have commenced. I hope she may hereafter acknowledge and respect my motives, but I cannot now go as a guest to her father's house.'' And the Barchester Brutus went out to fortify his own resolution by meditations on his own virtue.

Poor Mary Bold sat down, and sadly finished her note, saying that she would herself attend the party but that her brother was unavoidably prevented from doing so. I fear that she did not admire as she should have done the self-devotion of his singular virtue.

The party went off as such parties do. There were fat old ladies in fine silk dresses, and slim young ladies, in gauzy muslin frocks; old gentlemen stood up with their backs to the empty fire-place, looking by no means so comfortable as they would have done in their own armchairs at home; and young gentlemen, rather stiff about the neck, clustered near the door, not as yet sufficiently in courage to attack the muslin frocks, who awaited the battle, drawn up in a semicircular array. The warden endeavoured to induce a charge, but failed signally, not having the tact of a general; his daughter did what she could to comfort the forces under her command, who took in refreshing rations of cake and tea, and patiently looked for the coming engagement: but she herself, Eleanor, had no spirit for the work; the only enemy whose lance she cared to encounter was not there, and she and others were somewhat dull.

Loud above all voices was heard the clear sonorous tones of the archdeacon as he dilated to brother parsons of the danger of the church, of the fearful rumours of mad reforms even at Oxford, and of the damnable heresies of Dr. Whiston.

Soon, however, sweeter sounds began timidly to make themselves audible. Little movements were made in a quarter notable for round stools and music stands. Wax candles were arranged in sconces, big books were brought from hidden recesses, and the work of the evening commenced.

How often were those pegs twisted and retwisted before our friend found that he had twisted them enough; how many discordant scrapes gave promise of the coming harmony. How much the muslin fluttered and crumpled before Eleanor and another nymph were duly seated at the piano; how closely did that tall Apollo pack himself against the wall, with his flute, long as himself, extending high over the heads of his pretty neighbours; into how small a corner crept that round and florid little minor canon, and there with skill amazing found room to tune his accustomed fiddle!

And now the crash begins: away they go in full flow of harmony together—up hill and down dale—now louder and louder, then lower and lower; now loud, as though stirring the battle; then low, as though mourning the slain. In all, through all, and above all, is heard the violoncello. Ah, not for nothing were those pegs so twisted and retwisted—listen, listen! Now alone that saddest of instruments tells its touching tale. Silent, and in awe, stand fiddle, flute, and piano, to hear the sorrows of their wailing brother. 'Tis but for a moment: before the melancholy of those low notes had been fully realised, again comes the full force of all the band—down go the pedals, away rush twenty fingers scouring over the bass notes with all the impetus of passion. Apollo blows till his stiff neckcloth is no better than a rope, and the minor canon works with both arms till he falls in a syncope of exhaustion against the wall.

How comes it that now, when all should be silent, when courtesy, if not taste, should make men listen—how is it at this moment the black-coated corps leave their retreat and begin skirmishing? One by one they creep forth, and fire off little guns timidly, and without precision. Ah, my men, efforts such as these will take no cities, even though the enemy should be never so open to assault. At length a more deadly artillery is brought to bear; slowly, but with effect, the advance is made; the muslin ranks are broken, and fall into confusion; the formidable array of chairs gives way; the battle is no longer between opposing regiments, but hand to hand, and foot to foot with single combatants, as in the glorious days of old, when fighting was really noble. In corners, and under the shadow of curtains, behind sofas and half hidden by doors, in retiring windows, and sheltered by hanging tapestry, are blows given and returned, fatal, incurable, dealing death.

Apart from this another combat arises, more sober and more serious. The archdeacon is engaged against two prebendaries, a pursy full-blown rector assisting him, in all the perils and all the enjoyments of short whist. With solemn energy do they watch the shuffled pack, and, all-expectant, eye the coming trump. With what anxious nicety do they arrange their cards, jealous of each other's eyes! Why is that lean doctor so slow—cadaverous man with hollow jaw and sunken eye, ill beseeming the richness of his mother church! Ah, why so slow, thou meagre doctor? See how the archdeacon, speechless in his agony, deposits on the board his cards, and looks to heaven or to the ceiling for support. Hark, how he sighs, as with thumbs in his waistcoat pocket he seems to signify that the end of such torment is not yet even nigh at hand! Vain is the hope, if hope there be, to disturb that meagre doctor. With care precise he places every card, weighs well the value of each mighty ace, each guarded king, and comfort-giving queen; speculates on knave and ten, counts all his suits, and sets his price upon the whole. At length a card is led, and quick three others fall upon the board. The little doctor leads again, while with lustrous eye his partner absorbs the trick. Now thrice has this been done—thrice has constant fortune favoured the brace of prebendaries, ere the archdeacon rouses himself to the battle; but at the fourth assault he pins to the earth a prostrate king, laying low his crown and sceptre, bushy beard, and lowering brow, with a poor deuce.

"As David did Goliath," says the archdeacon, pushing over the four cards to his partner. And then a trump is led, then another trump; then a king—and then an ace—and then a long ten, which brings down from the meagre doctor his only remaining tower of strength—his cherished queen of trumps.

"What, no second club?" says the archdeacon to his partner.

"Only one club," mutters from his inmost stomach the pursy rector, who sits there red-faced, silent, impervious, careful, a safe but not a brilliant ally.

But the archdeacon cares not for many clubs, or for none. He dashes out his remaining cards with a speed most annoying to his antagonists, pushes over to them some four cards as their allotted portion, shoves the remainder across the table to the red-faced rector; calls out "two by cards and two by honours, and the odd trick last time," marks a treble under the candlestick, and has dealt round the second pack before the meagre doctor has calculated his losses.

And so went off the warden's party, and men and women arranging shawls and shoes declared how pleasant it had been; and Mrs. Goodenough, the red-faced rector's wife, pressing the warden's hand, declared she had never enjoyed herself better; which showed how little pleasure she allowed herself in this world, as she had sat the whole evening through in the same chair without occupation, not speaking, and unspoken to. And Matilda Johnson, when she allowed young Dickson of the bank to fasten her cloak round her neck, thought that two hundred pounds a year and a little cottage would really do for happiness; besides, he was sure to be manager some day. And Apollo, folding his flute into his pocket, felt that he had acquitted himself with honour; and the archdeacon pleasantly jingled his gains; but the meagre doctor went off without much audible speech, muttering ever and anon as he went, "three and thirty points," "three and thirty points!"

And so they all were gone, and Mr. Harding was left alone with his daughter.

What had passed between Eleanor Harding and Mary Bold need not be told. It is indeed a matter of thankfulness that neither the historian nor the novelist hears all that is said by their heroes or heroines, or how would three volumes or twenty suffice! In the present case so little of this sort have I overheard, that I live in hopes of finishing my work within 300 pages, and of completing that pleasant task—a novel in one volume; but something had passed between them, and as the warden blew out the wax candles, and put his instrument into its case, his daughter stood sad and thoughtful by the empty fire-place, determined to speak to her father, but irresolute as to what she would say.

"Well, Eleanor," said he, "are you for bed?"

"Yes," said she, moving, "I suppose so; but papa—— Mr. Bold was not here to-night; do you know why not?"

"He was asked; I wrote to him myself," said the warden.

"But do you know why he did not come, papa?"

"Well, Eleanor, I could guess; but it's no use guessing at such things, my dear. What makes you look so earnest about it?"

"Oh, papa, do tell me," she exclaimed, throwing her arms round him, and looking into his face; "what is it he is going to do? What is it all about? Is there any—any—any—" she didn't well know what word to use—"any danger?"

"Danger, my dear, what sort of danger?"

"Danger to you, danger of trouble, and of loss, and of——. Oh, papa, why haven't you told me of all this before?"

Mr. Harding was not the man to judge harshly of any one, much less of the daughter whom he now loved better than any living creature; but still he did judge her wrongly at this moment. He knew that she loved John Bold; he fully sympathised in her affection; day after day he thought more of the matter, and, with the tender care of a loving father, tried to arrange in his own mind how matters might be so managed that his daughter's heart should not be made the sacrifice to the dispute which was likely to exist between him and Bold. Now, when she spoke to him for the first time on the subject, it was natural that he should think more of her than of himself, and that he should imagine that her own cares, and not his, were troubling her.

He stood silent before her awhile, as she gazed up into his face, and then kissing her forehead he placed her on the sofa.

"Tell me, Nelly," he said (he only called her Nelly in his kindest, softest, sweetest moods, and yet all his moods were kind and sweet), "tell me, Nelly, do you like Mr. Bold—much?"

She was quite taken aback by the question. I will not say that she had forgotten herself, and her own love in thinking about John Bold, and while conversing with Mary: she certainly had not done so. She had been sick at heart to think that a man of whom she could not but own to herself that she loved him, of whose regard she had been so proud, that such a man should turn against her father to ruin him. She had felt her vanity hurt, that his affection for her had not kept him from such a course; had he really cared for her, he would not have risked her love by such an outrage. But her main fear had been for her father, and when she spoke of danger, it was of danger to him and not to herself.

She was taken aback by the question altogether: "Do I like him, papa?"

"Yes, Nelly, do you like him? Why shouldn't you like

him? but that's a poor word—do you love him?'' She sat still in his arms without answering him. She certainly had not prepared herself for an avowal of affection, intending, as she had done, to abuse John Bold herself, and to hear her father do so also. ''Come, my love,'' said he, ''let us make a clean breast of it: do you tell me what concerns yourself, and I will tell you what concerns me and the hospital.''

And then, without waiting for an answer, he described to her, as he best could, the accusation that was made about Hiram's will; the claims which the old men put forward; what he considered the strength and what the weakness of his own position; the course which Bold had taken, and that which he presumed he was about to take; and then by degrees, without further question, he presumed on the fact of Eleanor's love, and spoke of that love as a feeling which he could in no way disapprove: he apologised for Bold, excused what he was doing; nay, praised him for his energy and intentions; made much of his good qualities, and harped on none of his foibles; then, reminding his daughter how late it was, and comforting her with much assurance which he hardly felt himself, he sent her to her room, with flowing eyes and a full heart.

When Mr. Harding met his daughter at breakfast the next morning, there was no further discussion on the matter, nor was the subject mentioned between them for some days. Soon after the party Mary Bold called at the hospital, but there were various persons in the drawing-room at the time, and she therefore said nothing about her brother. On the day following, John Bold met Miss Harding in one of the quiet, sombre, shaded walks of the close. He was most anxious to see her, but unwilling to call at the warden's house, and had in truth waylaid her in her private haunts.

''My sister tells me,'' said he, abruptly hurrying on with his premeditated speech, ''my sister tells me that you had a delightful party the other evening. I was so sorry I could not be there.''

''We were all sorry,'' said Eleanor, with dignified composure.

''I believe, Miss Harding, you understood why, at this moment——'' And Bold hesitated, muttered, stopped, commenced his explanation again, and again broke down.

Eleanor would not help him in the least.

''I think my sister explained to you, Miss Harding?''

''Pray don't apologise, Mr. Bold; my father will, I am sure, always be glad to see you, if you like to come to the house now as formerly; nothing has occurred to alter his feelings: of your own views you are, of course, the best judge.''

"Your father is all that is kind and generous; he always was so; but you, Miss Harding, yourself——I hope you will not judge me harshly, because——"

"Mr. Bold," said she, "you may be sure of one thing; I shall always judge my father to be right, and those who oppose him I shall judge to be wrong. If those who do not know him oppose him, I shall have charity enough to believe that they are wrong, through error of judgment; but should I see him attacked by those who ought to know him, and to love him, and revere him, of such I shall be constrained to form a different opinion." And then curtseying low she sailed on, leaving her lover in anything but a happy state of mind.

VII

The Jupiter

Though Eleanor Harding rode off from John Bold on a high horse, it must not be supposed that her heart was so elate as her demeanour. In the first place, she had a natural repugnance to losing her lover; and in the next, she was not quite so sure that she was in the right as she pretended to be. Her father had told her, and that now repeatedly, that Bold was doing nothing unjust or ungenerous; and why then should she rebuke him, and throw him off, when she felt herself so ill able to bear his loss?—but such is human nature, and young-lady-nature especially. As she walked off from him beneath the shady elms of the close, her look, her tone, every motion and gesture of her body, belied her heart; she would have given the world to have taken him by the hand, to have reasoned with him, persuaded him, cajoled him, coaxed him out of his project; to have overcome him with all her female artillery, and to have redeemed her father at the cost of herself; but pride would not let her do this, and she left him without a look of love or a word of kindness.

Had Bold been judging of another lover and of another lady; he might have understood all this as well as we do; but in matters of love men do not see clearly in their own affairs. They say that faint heart never won fair lady; and it is amazing to me how fair ladies are won, so faint are often men's hearts! Were it not for the kindness of their nature, that seeing the weakness of our courage they will occasionally descend from their impregnable fortresses, and themselves aid us in effecting their own defeat, too often would they escape unconquered if not unscathed, and free of body if not of heart.

Poor Bold crept off quite crestfallen; he felt that as regarded Eleanor Harding his fate was sealed, unless he could consent to give up a task to which he had pledged himself and which indeed it would not be easy for him to give up. Lawyers were engaged, and the question had to a certain extent been taken up by the public; besides, how could a high-spirited girl like Eleanor Harding really learn to love a man for neglecting a duty which he assumed! Could she allow her affection to be purchased at the cost of his own self-respect?

As regarded the issue of his attempt at reformation in the hospital, Bold had no reason hitherto to be discontented with his success. All Barchester was by the ears about it. The bishop, the archdeacon, the warden, the steward, and several other clerical allies, had daily meetings, discussing their tactics, and preparing for the great attack. Sir Abraham Haphazard had been consulted, but his opinion was not yet received: copies of Hiram's will, copies of warden's journals, copies of leases, copies of accounts, copies of everything that could be copied, and of some that could not, had been sent to him; and the case was assuming most creditable dimensions. But, above all, it had been mentioned in the daily *Jupiter*. That all-powerful organ of the press, in one of its leading thunderbolts launched at St. Cross, had thus remarked: "Another case, of smaller dimensions indeed, but of similar import, is now likely to come under public notice. We are informed that the warden or master of an old almshouse attached to Barchester Cathedral is in receipt of twenty-five times the annual income appointed for him by the will of the founder, while the sum yearly expended on the absolute purposes of the charity has always remained fixed. In other words, the legatees under the founder's will have received no advantage from the increase in the value of the property during the last four centuries, such increase having been absorbed by the so-called warden. It is impossible to conceive a case of greater injustice. It is no answer to say that some six or nine or twelve old men receive as much of the goods of this world as such old men require. On what foundation, moral or divine, traditional or legal, is grounded the warden's claim to the large income he receives for doing nothing? The contentment of these almsmen, if content they be, can give him no title to this wealth! Does he ever ask himself, when he stretches wide his clerical palm to receive the pay of some dozen of the working clergy, for what service he is so remunerated? Does his conscience ever entertain the question of his right to such subsidies? Or is it possible that the subject never so presents itself to his mind; that he has received for many years, and intends, should God spare him, to receive for years to come these fruits of the industrious piety of past ages, indifferent as to any right on his own part, or of any injustice to others! We must express an opinion that nowhere but in the Church of England, and only there among its priests, could such a state of moral indifference be found."

I must for the present leave my readers to imagine the state of Mr. Harding's mind after reading the above article. They say that forty thousand copies of the *Jupiter* are daily sold, and that each copy is read by five persons at the least. Two hundred thousand readers then would hear this accusation against him; two hundred thousand hearts would swell with indignation at the griping injustice, the barefaced robbery of the warden of Barchester Hospital! And how was he to answer this? How was he to open his inmost heart to this multitude, to these thousands, the educated, the polished, the picked men of his own country; how show them that he was no robber, no avaricious, lazy priest scrambling for gold, but a retiring, humble-spirited man, who had innocently taken what had innocently been offered to him?

"Write to the *Jupiter*," suggested the bishop.

"Yes," said the archdeacon, more worldly wise than his father, "yes, and be smothered with ridicule; tossed over and over again with scorn; shaken this way and that, as a rat in the mouth of a practised terrier. You will leave out some word or letter in your answer, and the ignorance of the cathedral clergy will be harped upon; you will make some small mistake, which will be a falsehood, or some admission, which will be self-condemnation; you will find yourself to have been vulgar, ill-tempered, irreverend, and illiterate, and the chances are ten to one, but that being a clergyman, you will have been guilty of blasphemy! A man may have the best of causes, the best of talents, and the best of tempers; he may write as well as Addison, or as strongly as Junius; but even with all this he cannot successfully answer, when attacked by the *Jupiter*. In such matters it is omnipotent. What the Czar is in Russia, or the mob in America, that the *Jupiter* is in England. Answer such an article! No, warden; whatever you do, don't do that. We were to look for this sort of thing, you know; but we need not draw down on our heads more of it than is necessary."

The article in the *Jupiter*, while it so greatly harassed our poor warden, was an immense triumph to some of the opposite party. Sorry as Bold was to see Mr. Harding attacked so personally, it still gave him a feeling of elation to find his cause taken up by so powerful an advocate: and as to Finney, the attorney, he was beside himself. What! to be engaged in the same cause and on the same side with the *Jupiter;* to have the views he had recommended seconded, and furthered, and battled for by the *Jupiter*! Perhaps to have his own name mentioned as that of the learned gentleman whose efforts had been so successful on behalf of the poor of Barchester! He might be examined before committees of the House of Commons, with heaven knows how much a day for his personal expenses—he might be engaged for years on such a suit! There was no end to the glorious golden dreams which this leader in the *Jupiter* produced in the soaring mind of Finney.

And the old bedesmen, they also heard of this article, and had a glimmering, indistinct idea of the marvellous advocate which had now taken up their cause. Abel Handy limped hither and thither through the rooms, repeating all that he understood to have been printed, with some additions of his own which he thought should have been added. He told them how the *Jupiter* had declared that their warden was no better than a robber, and that what the *Jupiter* said was acknowledged by the world to be true. How the *Jupiter* had affirmed that each one of them— "each one of us, Jonathan Crumple, think of that!"—had a clear right to a hundred a year; and that if the *Jupiter* had said so, it was better than a decision of the Lord Chancellor: and then he carried about the paper, supplied by Mr. Finney, which, though none of them could read it, still afforded in its very touch and aspect positive corroboration of what was told them; and Jonathan Crumple pondered deeply over his returning wealth; and Job Skulpit saw how right he had been in signing the petition, and said so many scores of times; and Spriggs leered fearfully with his one eye; and Moody, as he more nearly approached the coming golden age, hated more deeply than ever those who still kept possession of what he so coveted. Even Billy Gazy and poor bed-ridden Bell became active and uneasy, and the great Bunce stood apart with lowering brow, with deep grief seated in his heart, for he perceived that evil days were coming.

It had been decided, the archdeacon advising, that no remonstrance, explanation, or defence should be addressed from the Barchester conclave to the editor of the *Jupiter;* but hitherto that was the only decision to which they had come.

Sir Abraham Haphazard was deeply engaged in preparing a bill for the mortification of papists, to be called the "Convent Custody Bill," the purport of which was to enable any Protestant clergyman over fifty years of age to search any nun whom he suspected of being in possession of treasonable papers or jesuitical symbols; and as there were to be a hundred and thirty-seven clauses in the bill, each clause containing a separate thorn for the side of the papist, and as it was known the bill would be fought inch by inch, by fifty maddened Irishmen, the due construction and adequate dovetailing of it did consume much of Sir Abraham's time. The bill had all its desired effect. Of course it never passed into law; but it so completely divided the ranks of the Irish members, who had bound themselves together to force on the ministry a bill for compelling all men to drink Irish whisky, and all women to wear Irish poplins, that for the remainder of the session the Great Poplin and Whisky League was utterly harmless.

Thus it happened that Sir Abraham's opinion was not at once forthcoming, and the uncertainty, the expectation, and suffering of the folk of Barchester was maintained at a high pitch.

VIII

Plumstead Episcopi

The reader must now be requested to visit the rectory of Plumstead Episcopi; and as it is as yet still early morning, to ascend again with us into the bedroom of the archdeacon. The mistress of the mansion was at her toilet; on which we will not dwell with profane eyes, but proceed into a small inner room, where the doctor dressed and kept his boots and sermons; and here we will take our stand, premising that the door of the room was so open as to admit of a conversation between our reverend Adam and his valued Eve.

"It's all your own fault, archdeacon," said the latter. "I told you from the beginning how it would end, and papa has no one to thank but you."

"Good gracious, my dear," said the doctor, appearing at the door of his dressing-room, with his face and head enveloped in the rough towel which he was violently using; "how can you say so? I am doing my very best."

"I wish you had never done so much," said the lady, interrupting him. "If you'd just have let John Bold come and go there, as he and papa liked, he and Eleanor would have been married by this time, and we should not have heard one word about all this affair."

"But, my dear——"

"Oh, it's all very well, archdeacon; and of course you're right; I don't for a moment think you'll ever admit that you could be wrong; but the fact is, you've brought this young man down upon papa by huffing him as you have done."

"But, my love——"

"And all because you didn't like John Bold for a brother-in-law. How is she ever to do better? papa hasn't got a shilling; and though Eleanor is well enough, she has not at all a taking style of beauty. I'm sure I don't know how she's to do better than marry John Bold; or as well indeed," added the anxious sister, giving the last twist to her last shoe-string.

Dr. Grantly felt keenly the injustice of this attack; but what could he say? He certainly had huffed John Bold; he certainly had objected to him as a brother-in-law, and a very few months ago the very idea had excited his wrath: but now matters were changed; John Bold had shown his power, and, though he was as odious as ever to the archdeacon, power is always respected, and the reverend dignitary began to think that such an alliance might not have been imprudent. Nevertheless, his motto was still "no surrender"; he would still fight it out; he believed confidently in Oxford, in the bench of bishops, in Sir Abraham Haphazard, and in himself; and it was only when alone with his wife that doubts of defeat ever beset him. He once more tried to communicate this confidence to Mrs. Grantly, and for the twentieth time began to tell her of Sir Abraham.

"Oh, Sir Abraham!" she said, collecting all her house keys into her basket before she descended; "Sir Abraham won't get Eleanor a husband; Sir Abraham won't get papa another income when he has been worreted out of the hospital. Mark what I tell you, archdeacon: while you and Sir Abraham are fighting, papa will lose his preferment; and what will you do then with him and Eleanor on your hands? besides, who's to pay Sir Abraham? I suppose he won't take the case up for nothing? And so the lady descended to family worship among her children and servants, the pattern of a good and prudent wife.

Dr. Grantly was blessed with a happy, thriving family. There were, first, three boys, now at home from school for the holidays. They were called, respectively, Charles James, Henry, and Samuel. The two younger (there were five in all) were girls; the elder, Florinda, bore the name of the Archbishop of York's wife, whose godchild she was: and the younger had been christened Grizzel, after a sister of the Archbishop of Canterbury. The boys were all clever, and gave good promise of being well able to meet the cares and trials of the world; and yet they were not alike in their dispositions, and each had his individual character, and each his separate admirers among the doctor's friends.

Charles James was an exact and careful boy; he never committed himself; he well knew how much was expected from the eldest son of the Archdeacon of Barchester, and was therefore mindful not to mix too freely with other boys. He had not the great talents of his younger brothers, but he exceeded them in judgment and propriety of demeanour; his fault, if he had one, was an over-attention to words instead of things; there was a thought too much *finesse* about him, and, as even his father sometimes told him, he was too fond of a compromise.

The second was the archdeacon's favourite son, and Henry was indeed a brilliant boy. The versatility of his genius was surprising, and the visitors at Plumstead Episcopi were often amazed at the marvellous manner in which he would, when called on, adapt his capacity to apparently most uncongenial pursuits. He appeared once before a large circle as Luther the reformer, and delighted them with the perfect manner in which he assumed the character; and within three days he again astonished them by acting the part of a Capuchin friar to the very life. For this last exploit his father gave him a golden guinea, and his brothers said the reward had been promised beforehand in the event of the performance being successful. He was also sent on a tour into Devonshire; a treat which the lad was most anxious of enjoying. His father's friends there, however, did not appreciate his talents, and sad accounts were sent home of the perversity of his nature. He was a most courageous lad, game to the backbone.

It was soon known, both at home, where he lived, and within some miles of Barchester Cathedral, and also at Westminster, where he was at school, that young Henry could box well and would never own himself beat; other boys would fight while they had a leg to stand on, but he would fight with no leg at all. Those backing him would sometimes think him crushed by the weight of blows and faint with loss of blood, and his friends would endeavour to withdraw him from the contest; but no, Henry never gave in, was never weary of the battle. The ring was the only element in which he seemed to enjoy himself; and while other boys were happy in the number of their friends, he rejoiced most in the multitude of his foes.

His relations could not but admire his pluck, but they sometimes were forced to regret that he was inclined to be a bully; and those not so partial to him as his father was, observed with pain that, though he could fawn to the masters and the archdeacon's friends, he was imperious and masterful to the servants and the poor.

But perhaps Samuel was the general favourite; and dear little Soapy, as he was familiarly called, was as engaging a child as ever fond mother petted. He was soft and gentle in his manners, and attractive in his speech; the tone of his voice was melody, and every action was a grace; unlike his brothers, he was courteous to all, he was affable to the lowly, and meek even to the very scullery maid. He was a boy of great promise, minding his books and delighting the hearts of his masters. His brothers, however, were not particularly fond of him; they would complain to their mother that Soapy's civility all meant something; they thought that his voice was too often listened to at Plumstead Episcopi, and evidently feared that, as he grew up, he would have more weight in the house than either of them; there was, therefore, a sort of agreement among them to put young Soapy down. This, however, was not so easy to be done; Samuel, though young, was sharp; he could not assume the stiff decorum of Charles James, nor could he fight like Henry; but he was a perfect master of his own weapons, and contrived, in the teeth of both of them, to hold the place which he had assumed. Henry declared that he was a false, cunning creature; and Charles James, though he always spoke of him as his dear brother Samuel, was not slow to say a word against him when opportunity offered. To speak the truth, Samuel was a cunning boy, and those even who loved him best could not but own that for one so young he was too adroit in choosing his words, and too skilled in modulating his voice.

The two little girls Florinda and Grizzel were nice little girls enough, but they did not possess the strong sterling qualities of their brothers; their voices were not often heard at Plumstead Episcopi; they were bashful and timid by nature, slow to speak before company even when asked to do so; and though they looked very nice in their clean white muslin frocks and pink sashes, they were but little noticed by the archdeacon's visitors.

Whatever of submissive humility may have appeared in the gait and visage of the archdeacon during his colloquy with his wife in the sanctum of their dressing-rooms was dispelled as he entered his breakfast-parlour with erect head and powerful step. In the presence of a third person he assumed the lord and master; and that wise and talented lady too well knew the man to whom her lot for life was bound, to stretch her authority beyond the point at which it would be borne. Strangers at Plumstead Episcopi, when they saw the imperious brow with which he commanded silence from the large circle of visitors, children, and servants who came together in the morning to hear him read the word of God, and watched how meekly that wife seated herself behind her basket of keys with a little girl on each side, as she caught that commanding glance; strangers, I say, seeing this, could little guess that some fifteen minutes since she had stoutly held her ground against him, hardly allowing him to open his mouth in his own defence. But such is the tact and talent of women!

And now let us observe the well-furnished breakfast-parlour at Plumstead Episcopi, and the comfortable air of all the belongings of the rectory. Comfortable they certainly were, but neither gorgeous nor even grand; indeed, considering the money that had been spent there, the eye and taste might have been better served; there was an air of heaviness about the rooms which might have been avoided without any sacrifice of propriety; colours might have been better chosen and lights more perfectly diffused; but perhaps in doing so the thorough clerical aspect of the whole might have been somewhat marred; at any rate, it was not without ample consideration that those thick, dark, costly carpets were put down; those embossed, but sombre papers hung up; those heavy curtains draped so as to half exclude the light of the sun: nor were these old-fashioned chairs bought at a price far exceeding that now given for more modern goods, without a purpose. The breakfast-service on the table was equally costly and equally plain; the apparent object had been to spend money without obtaining brilliancy or splendour. The urn was of thick and solid silver, as were also the tea-pot, coffee-pot, cream-ewer, and sugar-bowl; the cups were old, dim dragon china, worth about a pound apiece, but very despicable in the eyes of the uninitiated. The silver forks were so heavy as to be disagreeable to the hand, and the bread-basket was of a weight really formidable to any but robust persons. The tea consumed was the very best, the coffee the very blackest, the cream the very thickest; there was dry toast and buttered toast, muffins and crumpets; hot bread and cold bread, white bread and brown bread, home-made bread and bakers' bread, wheaten bread and oaten bread; and if there be other breads than these, they were there; there were eggs in napkins, and crispy bits of bacon under silver covers; and there were little fishes in a little box, and devilled kidneys frizzling on a hot-water dish; which, by-the-by, were placed closely contiguous to the plate of the worthy archdeacon himself. Over and above this, on a snow-white napkin, spread upon the sideboard, was a huge ham and a huge sirloin; the latter having laden the dinner table on the previous evening. Such was the ordinary fare at Plumstead Episcopi.

And yet I have never found the rectory a pleasant house. The fact that man shall not live by bread alone seemed to be somewhat forgotten; and noble as was the appearance of the host, and sweet and good-natured as was the face of the hostess, talented as were the children, and excellent as were the viands and the wines, in spite of these attractions, I generally found the rectory somewhat dull. After breakfast the archdeacon would retire, of course to his clerical persuits. Mrs. Grantly, I presume, inspected her kitchen, though she had a first-rate housekeeper, with sixty pounds a year; and attended to the lessons of Florinda and Grizzel, though she had an excellent governess with thirty pounds a year: but at any rate she disappeared: and I never could make companions of the boys. Charles James, though he always looked as though there was something in him, never seemed to have much to say; and what he did say he would always unsay the next minute. He told me once that he considered cricket, on the whole, to be a gentleman-like game for boys, provided they would play without running about; and that fives, also, was a seemly game, so that those who played it never heated themselves. Henry once quarrelled with me for taking his sister Grizzel's part in a contest between them as to the best mode of using a watering-pot for the garden flowers; and from that day to this he has not spoken to me, though he speaks at me often enough. For half an hour or so I certainly did like Sammy's gentle speeches; but one gets tired of honey, and I found that he preferred the more admiring listeners whom he met in the kitchen-garden and back precincts of the establishment; besides, I think I once caught Sammy fibbing.

On the whole, therefore, I found the rectory a dull house, though it must be admitted that everything there was of the very best.

After breakfast, on the morning of which we are writing, the archdeacon, as usual, retired to his study, intimating that he was going to be very busy, but that he would see Mr. Chadwick if he called. On entering this sacred room he carefully opened the paper case on which he was wont to compose his favourite sermons, and spread on it a fair sheet of paper and one partly written on; he then placed his inkstand, looked at his pen, and folded his blotting paper; having done so, he got up again from his seat, stood with his back to the fire-place, and yawned comfortably, stretching out vastly his huge arms and opening his burly chest. He then walked across the room and locked the door; and having so prepared himself, he threw himself into his easy chair, took from a secret drawer beneath his table a volume of Rabelais, and began to amuse himself with the witty mischief of Panurge; and so passed the archdeacon's morning on that day.

He was left undisturbed at his studies for an hour or two, when a knock came to the door, and Mr. Chadwick was announced. Rabelais retired into the secret drawer, the easy chair seemed knowingly to betake itself off, and when the archdeacon quickly undid his bolt, he was discovered by the steward working, as usual, for that church of which he was so useful a pillar. Mr. Chadwick had just come from London, and was, therefore, known to be the bearer of important news.

"We've got Sir Abraham's opinion at last," said Mr. Chadwick, as he seated himself.

"Well, well, well!" exclaimed the archdeacon impatiently.

"Oh, it's as long as my arm," said the other; "it can't be told in a word, but you can read it"; and he handed him a copy, in heaven knows how many spun-out folios, of the opinion which the attorney-general had managed to cram on the back and sides of the case as originally submitted to him.

"The upshot is," said Chadwick, "that there's a screw loose in their case, and we had better do nothing. They are proceeding against Mr. Harding and myself, and Sir Abraham holds that, under the wording of the will and subsequent arrangements legally sanctioned, Mr. Harding and I are only paid servants. The defendants should have been either the Corporation of Barchester, or possibly the chapter or your father."

"W—hoo!" said the archdeacon; "so Master Bold is on the wrong scent, is he?"

"That's Sir Abraham's opinion; but any scent almost would be a wrong scent. Sir Abraham thinks that if they'd taken the corporation, or the chapter, we could have baffled them. The bishop, he thinks, would be the surest shot; but even there we could plead that the bishop is only visitor, and that he has never made himself a consenting party to the performance of other duties."

"That's quite clear," said the archdeacon.

"Not quite so clear," said the other. "You see the will says, 'My lord, the bishop, being graciously pleased to see that due justice be done.' Now, it may be a question whether, in accepting and administering the patronage, your father has not accepted also the other duties assigned. It is doubtful, however; but even if they hit that nail—and they are far off from that yet—the point is so nice, as Sir Abraham says, that you would force them into fifteen thousand pounds' cost before they could bring it to an issue! and where's that sum of money to come from?"

The archdeacon rubbed his hands with delight; he had never

doubted the justice of his case, but he had begun to have some
dread of unjust success on the part of his enemies. It was
delightful to him thus to hear that their cause was surrounded
with such rocks and shoals; such causes of shipwreck unseen by
the landsman's eye, but visible enough to the keen eyes of
practical law mariners. How wrong his wife was to wish that
Bold should marry Eleanor! Bold! why, if he should be ass
enough to persevere, he would be a beggar before he knew
whom he was at law with!

"That's excellent, Chadwick—that's excellent! I told you
Sir Abraham was the man for us"; and he put down on the table
the copy of the opinion, and patted it fondly.

"Don't you let that be seen, though, archdeacon."

"Who?—I!—not for worlds," said the doctor.

"People will talk, you know, archdeacon."

"Of course, of course," said the doctor.

"Because, if that gets abroad, it would teach them how to
fight their own battle."

"Quite true," said the doctor.

"No one here in Barchester ought to see that but you and I,
archdeacon."

"No, no, certainly no one else," said the archdeacon,
pleased with the closeness of the confidence; "no one else
shall."

"Mrs. Grantly is very interested in the matter, I know,"
said Mr. Chadwick.

Did the archdeacon wink, or did he not? I am inclined to
think he did not quite wink; but that without such, perhaps,
unseemly gesture he communicated to Mr. Chadwick, with the
corner of his eye, intimation that, deep as was Mrs. Grantly's
interest in the matter, it should not procure for her a perusal of
that document; and at the same time he partly opened the small
drawer, above spoken of, deposited the paper on the volume of
Rabelais, and showed to Mr. Chadwick the nature of the key
which guarded these hidden treasures. The careful steward then
expressed himself contented. Ah! vain man! he could fasten up
his Rabelais, and other things secret, with all the skill of Bramah
or of Chubb; but where could he fasten up the key which solved
these mechanical mysteries? It is probable to us that the contents
of no drawer in that house were unknown to its mistress, and we
think, moreover, that she was entitled to all such knowledge.

"But," said Mr. Chadwick, "we must, of course, tell your

father and Mr. Harding so much of Sir Abraham's opinion as
will satisfy them that the matter is doing well.''

"Oh, certainly—yes, of course,'' said the doctor.

"You had better let them know that Sir Abraham is of
opinion that there is no case at any rate against Mr. Harding; and
that as the action is worded at present, it must fall to the ground;
they must be nonsuited if they carry it on; you had better tell Mr.
Harding, that Sir Abraham is clearly of opinion that he is only a
servant, and as such not liable—or if you like it, I'll see Mr.
Harding myself.''

"Oh, I must see him to-morrow, and my father too, and I'll
explain to them exactly so much,—you won't go before lunch,
Mr. Chadwick: well, if you will, you must, for I know your time
is precious''; and he shook hands with the diocesan steward, and
bowed him out.

The archdeacon had again recourse to his drawer, and twice
read through the essence of Sir Abraham Haphazard's law-
enlightened and law-bewildered brains. It was very clear that to
Sir Abraham, the justice of the old men's claim or the justice of
Mr. Harding's defence were ideas that had never presented
themselves. A legal victory over an opposing party was the
service for which Sir Abraham was, as he imagined, to be paid;
and that he, according to his lights, had diligently laboured to
achieve, and with probable hope of success. Of the intense desire
which Mr. Harding felt to be assured on fit authority that he was
wronging no man, that he was entitled in true equity to his
income, that he might sleep at night without pangs of conscience,
that he was no robber, no spoiler of the poor; that he and all the
world might be openly convinced that he was not the man which
the *Jupiter* had described him to be; of such longings on the part
of Mr. Harding, Sir Abraham was entirely ignorant; nor, indeed,
could it be looked on as part of his business to gratify such
desires. Such was not the system on which his battles were
fought, and victories gained. Success was his object, and he was
generally successful. He conquered his enemies by their weakness rather than by his own strength, and it had been found
almost impossible to make up a case in which Sir Abraham, as
an antagonist, would not find a flaw.

The archdeacon was delighted with the closeness of the
reasoning. To do him justice, it was not a selfish triumph that he
desired; he would personally lose nothing by defeat, or at least
what he might lose did not actuate him; but neither was it love of
justice which made him so anxious, nor even mainly solicitude

for his father-in-law. He was fighting a part of a never-ending battle against a never-conquered foe—that of the church against its enemies.

He knew Mr. Harding could not pay all the expense of these doings; for these long opinions of Sir Abraham's, these causes to be pleaded, these speeches to be made, these various courts through which the case was, he presumed, to be dragged. He knew that he and his father must at least bear the heavier portion of this tremendous cost; but to do the archdeacon justice, he did not recoil from this. He was a man fond of obtaining money, greedy of a large income, but open-handed enough in expending it, and it was a triumph to him to foresee the success of this measure, although he might be called on to pay so dearly for it himself.

IX

The Conference

On the following morning the archdeacon was with his father betimes, and a note was sent down to the warden begging his attendance at the palace. Dr. Grantly, as he cogitated on the matter, leaning back in his brougham as he journeyed into Barchester, felt that it would be difficult to communicate his own satisfaction either to his father or his father-in-law. He wanted success on his own side and discomfiture on that of his enemies. The bishop wanted peace on the subject; a settled peace if possible, but peace at any rate till the short remainder of his own days had spun itself out. Mr. Harding required, not only success and peace, but he also demanded that he might stand justified before the world.

The bishop, however, was comparatively easy to deal with; and before the arrival of the other, the dutiful son had persuaded his father that all was going on well, and then the warden arrived.

It was Mr. Harding's wont, whenever he spent a morning at the palace, to seat himself immediately at the bishop's elbow, the bishop occupying a huge armchair fitted up with candlesticks, a reading table, a drawer, and other paraphernalia, the position of which chair was never moved, summer or winter; and when, as was usual, the archdeacon was there also, he confronted the two elders, who thus were enabled to fight the battle against him together; and together submit to defeat, for such was their constant fate.

Our warden now took his accustomed place, having greeted his son-in-law as he entered, and then affectionately inquired after his friend's health. There was a gentleness about the bishop to which the soft womanly affection of Mr. Harding particularly endeared itself, and it was quaint to see how the two mild old priests pressed each other's hands, and smiled and made little signs of love.

"Sir Abraham's opinion has come at last," began the archdeacon. Mr. Harding had heard so much, and was most anxious to know the result.

"It is quite favourable," said the bishop, pressing his friend's arm. "I am so glad."

Mr. Harding looked at the mighty bearer of the important news for confirmation of these glad tidings.

"Yes," said the archdeacon; "Sir Abraham has given most minute attention to the case; indeed, I knew he would—most minute attention; and his opinion is—and as to his opinion on such a subject being correct, no one who knows Sir Abraham's character can doubt—his opinion is, that they haven't got a leg to stand on."

"But as how, archdeacon?"

"Why, in the first place:—but you're no lawyer, warden, and I doubt you won't understand it; the gist of the matter is this:—under Hiram's will two paid guardians have been selected for the hospital; the law will say two paid servants, and you and I won't quarrel with the name."

"At any rate I will not if I am one of the servants," said Mr. Harding. "A rose, you know——"

"Yes, yes," said the archdeacon, impatient of poetry at such a time. "Well, two paid servants, we'll say; one to look after the men, and the other to look after the money. You and Chadwick are these two servants, and whether either of you be paid too much, or too little, more or less in fact than the founder willed, it's as clear as daylight that no one can fall foul of either of you for receiving an allotted stipend.''

"That does seem clear,'' said the bishop, who had winced visibly at the words servants and stipend, which, however, appeared to have caused no uneasiness to the archdeacon.

"Quite clear,'' said he, "and very satisfactory. In point of fact, it being necessary to select such servants for the use of the hospital, the pay to be given to them must depend on the rate of pay for such services, according to their market value at the period in question; and those who manage the hospital must be the only judges of this.''

"And who does manage the hospital?'' asked the warden.

"Oh, let them find that out; that's another question: the action is brought against you and Chadwick; that's your defence, and a perfect and full defence it is. Now that I think very satisfactory.''

"Well,'' said the bishop, looking inquiringly up into his friend's face, who sat silent awhile, and apparently not so well satisfied.

"And conclusive,'' continued the archdeacon; "if they press it to a jury, which they won't do, no twelve men in England will take five minutes to decide against them.''

"But according to that,'' said Mr. Harding, ".I might as well have sixteen hundred a year as eight, if the managers choose to allot it to me; and as I am one of the managers, if not the chief manager, myself, that can hardly be a just arrangement.''

"Oh, well; all that's nothing to the question. The question is, whether this intruding fellow, and a lot of cheating attorneys and pestilent dissenters, are to interfere with an arrangement which every one knows is essentially just and serviceable to the church. Pray don't let us be splitting hairs, and that amongst ourselves, or there'll never be an end of the cause or the cost.''

Mr. Harding again sat silent for awhile, during which the bishop once and again pressed his arm, and looked in his face to see if he could catch a gleam of a contented and eased mind; but there was no such gleam, and the poor warden continued playing sad dirges on invisible stringed instruments in all manner of positions: he was ruminating in his mind on this opinion of Sir Abraham, looking to it wearily and earnestly for satisfaction, but finding none. At last he said, "Did you see the opinion, archdeacon?''

The archdeacon said he had not—that was to say, he had—

that was, he had not seen the opinion itself; he had seen what had been called a copy, but he could not say whether of a whole or part; nor could he say that what he had seen were the *ipsissima verba* of the great man himself; but what he had seen contained exactly the decision which he had announced, and which he again declared to be to his mind extremely satisfactory.

"I should like to see the opinion," said the warden; "that is, a copy of it."

"Well, I suppose you can if you make a point of it; but I don't see the use myself; of course it is essential that the purport of it should not be known, and it is therefore unadvisable to multiply copies."

"Why should it not be known?" asked the warden.

"What a question for a man to ask!" said the archdeacon, throwing up his hands in token of his surprise; "but it is like you—a child is not more innocent than you are in matters of business. Can't you see that if we tell them that no action will lie against you, but that one may possibly lie against some other person or persons, that we shall be putting weapons into their hands, and be teaching them how to cut our own throats?"

The warden again sat silent, and the bishop again looked at him wistfully: "The only thing we have now to do," continued the archdeacon, "is to remain quiet, hold our peace, and let them play their own game as they please."

"We are not to make known then," said the warden, "that we have consulted the attorney-general, and that we are advised by him that the founder's will is fully and fairly carried out."

"God bless my soul!" said the archdeacon, "how odd it is that you will not see that all we are to do is to do nothing: why should we say anything about the founder's will? We are in possession; and we know that they are not in a position to put us out; surely that is enough for the present."

Mr. Harding rose from his seat and paced thoughtfully up and down the library, the bishop the while watching him painfully at every turn, and the archdeacon continuing to pour forth his convictions that the affair was in a state to satisfy any prudent mind.

"And the *Jupiter*?" said the warden, stopping suddenly.

"Oh! the *Jupiter*," answered the other. "The *Jupiter* can break no bones. You must bear with that; there is much, of course, which it is our bounden duty to bear; it cannot be all roses for us here," and the archdeacon looked exceedingly moral; "besides, the matter is too trivial, of too little general interest to

be mentioned again in the *Jupiter*, unless we stir up the subject."
And the archdeacon again looked exceedingly knowing and worldly
wise.

The warden continued his walk; the hard and stinging words
of that newspaper article, each one of which had thrust a thorn as
it were into his inmost soul, were fresh in his memory; he had
read it more than once, word by word, and what was worse, he
fancied it was as well known to every one as to himself. Was he
to be looked on as the unjust griping priest he had been there
described? Was he to be pointed at as the consumer of the bread
of the poor, and to be allowed no means of refuting such
charges, of clearing his begrimed name, of standing innocent in
the world, as hitherto he had stood? Was he to bear all this, to
receive as usual his now hated income, and be known as one of
those greedy priests who by their rapacity have brought disgrace
on their church? and why? Why should he bear all this? why
should he die, for he felt that he could not live, under such a
weight of obloquy? As he paced up and down the room he
resolved in his misery and enthusiasm that he could with pleasure,
if he were allowed, give up his place, abandon his pleasant
home, leave the hospital, and live poorly, happily, and with an
unsullied name, on the small remainder of his means.

He was a man somewhat shy of speaking of himself, even
before those who knew him best, and whom he loved the most;
but at last it burst forth from him, and with a somewhat jerking
eloquence he declared that he could not, would not, bear this
misery any longer.

"If it can be proved," said he at last, "that I have a just
and honest right to this, as God well knows I always deemed I
had; if this salary or stipend be really my due, I am not less
anxious than another to retain it. I have the well-being of my
child to look to. I am too old to miss without some pain the
comforts to which I have been used; and I am, as others are,
anxious to prove to the world that I have been right, and to
uphold the place I have held; but I cannot do it at such a cost as
this. I cannot bear this. Could you tell me to do so?" And he
appealed, almost in tears, to the bishop, who had left his chair,
and was now leaning on the warden's arm as he stood on the
further side of the table facing the archdeacon. "Could you tell
me to sit there at ease, indifferent, and satisfied, while such
things as these are said loudly of me in the world?"

The bishop could feel for him and sympathise with him, but
he could not advise him, he could only say, "No, no, you shall

be asked to do nothing that is painful; you shall do just what your heart tells you to be right; you shall do whatever you think best yourself. Theophilus, don't advise him, pray don't advise the warden to do anything which is painful.''

But the archdeacon, though he could not sympathise, could advise; and he saw that the time had come when it behoved him to do so in a somewhat peremptory manner.

''Why, my lord,'' he said, speaking to his father: and when he called his father ''my lord,'' the good old bishop shook in his shoes, for he knew that an evil time was coming. ''Why, my lord, there are two ways of giving advice: there is advice that may be good for the present day; and there is advice that may be good for days to come: now I cannot bring myself to give the former, if it be incompatible with the other.''

''No, no, no, I suppose not,'' said the bishop, reseating himself, and shading his face with his hands. Mr. Harding sat down with his back to the further wall, playing to himself some air fitted for so calamitous an occasion, and the archdeacon said out his say standing, with his back to the empty fireplace.

''It is not to be supposed but that much pain will spring out of this unnecessarily raised question. We must all have foreseen that, and the matter has in no wise gone on worse than we expected; but it will be weak, yes, and wicked also, to abandon the cause and own ourselves wrong, because the inquiry is painful. It is not only ourselves we have to look to; to a certain extent the interest of the church is in our keeping. Should it be found that one after another of those who hold preferment abandoned it whenever it might be attacked, is it not plain that such attacks would be renewed till nothing was left us? and, that if so deserted, the Church of England must fall to the ground altogether? If this be true of many, it is true of one. Were you, accused as you now are, to throw up the wardenship, and to relinquish the preferment which is your property, with the vain object of proving yourself disinterested, you would fail in that object, you would inflict a desperate blow on your brother clergymen, you would encourage every cantankerous dissenter in England to make a similar charge against some source of clerical revenue, and you would do your best to dishearten those who are most anxious to defend you and uphold your position. I can fancy nothing more weak, or more wrong. It is not that you think that there is any justice in these charges, or that you doubt your own right to the wardenship: you are convinced of your own honesty, and yet would yield to them through cowardice.''

"Cowardice!" said the bishop, expostulating. Mr. Harding sat unmoved, gazing on his son-in-law.

"Well; would it not be cowardice? would he not do so because he is afraid to endure the evil things which will be falsely spoken of him? Would that not be cowardice? And now let us see the extent of the evil which you dread. The *Jupiter* publishes an article which a great many, no doubt, will read; but of those who understand the subject how many will believe the *Jupiter*? Every one knows what its object is: it has taken up the case against Lord Guildford and against the Dean of Rochester, and that against half a dozen bishops; and does not every one know that it would take up any case of the kind, right or wrong, false or true, with known justice or known injustice, if by doing so it could further its own views? Does not all the world know this of the *Jupiter*? Who that really knows you will think the worse of you for what the *Jupiter* says? And why care for those who do not know you? I will say nothing of your own comfort, but I do say that you could not be justified in throwing up, in a fit of passion, for such it would be, the only maintenance that Eleanor has; and if you did so, if you really did vacate the wardenship, and submit to ruin, what would that profit you? If you have no future right to the income, you have had no past right to it; and the very fact of your abandoning your position would create a demand for repayment of that which you have already received and spent."

The poor warden groaned as he sat perfectly still, looking up at the hard-hearted orator who thus tormented him, and the bishop echoed the sound faintly from behind his hands; but the archdeacon cared little for such signs of weakness, and completed his exhortation.

"But let us suppose the office to be left vacant, and that your own troubles concerning it were over; would that satisfy you? Are your only aspirations in the matter confined to yourself and family? I know they are not. I know you are as anxious as any of us for the church to which we belong; and what a grievous blow would such an act of apostasy give her? You owe it to the church of which you are a member and a minister, to bear with this affliction, however severe it may be: you owe it to my father, who instituted you, to support his rights: you owe it to those who preceded you to assert the legality of their position: you owe it to those who are to come after you, to maintain uninjured for them that which you received uninjured from others; and you owe to us all the unflinching assistance of perfect brotherhood in this matter, so that upholding one another we may support our great cause without blushing and without disgrace.''

And so the archdeacon ceased, and stood self-satisfied, watching the effect of his spoken wisdom.

The warden felt himself, to a certain extent, stifled; he would have given the world to get himself out into the open air without speaking to, or noticing those who were in the room with him; but this was impossible. He could not leave without saying something, and he felt himself confounded by the archdeacon's eloquence. There was a heavy, unfeeling, unanswerable truth in what he had said; there was so much practical, but odious common sense in it, that he neither knew how to assent or to differ. If it were necessary for him to suffer, he felt he could endure without complaint and without cowardice, providing that he was self-satisfied of the justice of his own cause. What he could not endure was, that he should be accused by others, and not acquitted by himself. Doubting, as he had begun to doubt, the justice of his own position in the hospital, he knew that his own self-confidence would not be restored because Mr. Bold had been in error as to some legal form; nor could he be satisfied to escape, because, through some legal fiction, he who received the greatest benefit from the hospital might be considered only as one of its servants.

The archdeacon's speech had silenced him—stupefied him— annihilated him; anything but satisfied him. With the bishop it fared not much better. He did not discern clearly how things were, but he saw enough to know that a battle was to be prepared for; a battle that would destroy his few remaining comforts, and bring him with sorrow to the grave.

The warden still sat, and still looked at the archdeacon, till his thoughts fixed themselves wholly on the means of escape from his present position, and he felt like a bird fascinated by gazing on a snake.

"I hope you agree with me," said the archdeacon at last, breaking the dread silence; "my lord, I hope you agree with me."

Oh, what a sigh the bishop gave! "My lord, I hope you agree with me," again repeated the merciless tyrant.

"Yes, I suppose so," groaned the poor old man, slowly.

"And you, warden?"

Mr. Harding was now stirred to action—he must speak and move, so he got up and took one turn before he answered.

"Do not press me for an answer just at present; I will do nothing lightly in the matter, and of whatever I do I will give you and the bishop notice." And so without another word he took his leave, escaping quickly through the palace hall, and down the lofty steps, nor did he breathe freely till he found himself alone under the huge elms of the silent close. Here he walked long and slowly, thinking on his case with a troubled air, and trying in vain to confute the archdeacon's argument. He then went home, resolved to bear it all—ignominy, suspense, disgrace, self-doubt, and heart-burning—and to do as those would have him, who he still believed were most fit and most able to counsel him aright.

X

Tribulation

Mr. Harding was a sadder man than he had ever yet been when he returned to his own house. He had been wretched enough on that well-remembered morning when he was forced to expose before his son-in-law the publisher's account for ushering into the world his dear book of sacred music; when after making such payments as he could do unassisted, he found that he was a debtor of more than three hundred pounds; but his sufferings then were as nothing to his present misery;—then he had done wrong, and he knew it, and was able to resolve that he would not sin in like manner again; but now he could make no resolution, and comfort himself by no promises of firmness. He had been forced to think that his lot had placed him in a false position, and he was about to maintain that position against the opinion of the world and against his own convictions.

He had read with pity, amounting almost to horror, the strictures which had appeared from time to time against the Earl of Guildford as master of St. Cross, and the invectives that had been heaped on rich diocesan dignitaries and overgrown sinecure pluralists. In judging of them, he judged leniently; the whole bias of his profession had taught him to think that they were more sinned against than sinning, and that the animosity with which they had been pursued was venomous and unjust; but he had not the less regarded their plight as most miserable. His hair had stood on end and his flesh had crept as he read the things which had been written; he had wondered how men could live under such a load of disgrace; how they could face their fellow-creatures while their names were bandied about so injuriously and so publicly—and now this lot was to be his—he, that shy, retiring man, who had so comforted himself in the hidden obscurity of his lot, who had so enjoyed the unassuming warmth of his own little corner, he was now to be dragged forth into the glaring day, and gibbeted before ferocious multitudes. He entered his own house a crestfallen, humiliated man, without a hope of overcoming the wretchedness which affected him.

He wandered into the drawing-room where was his daughter; but he could not speak to her now, so he left it, and went into the book-room. He was not quick enough to escape Eleanor's glance, or to prevent her from seeing that he was disturbed; and in a little while she followed him. She found him seated in his accustomed chair with no book open before him, no pen ready in his hand, no ill-shapen notes of blotted music lying before him as was usual, none of those hospital accounts with which he was so precise and yet so unmethodical: he was doing nothing, thinking of nothing, looking at nothing; he was merely suffering.

"Leave me, Eleanor, my dear," he said; "leave me, my darling, for a few minutes, for I am busy."

Eleanor saw well how it was, but she did leave him, and glided silently back to her drawing-room. When he had sat a while, thus alone and unoccupied, he got up to walk again—he could make more of his thoughts walking than sitting, and was creeping out into his garden, when he met Bunce on the threshold.

"Well, Bunce," said he, in a tone that for him was sharp, "what is it? do you want me?"

"I was only coming to ask after your reverence," said the old bedesman, touching his hat; "and to inquire about the news from London," he added after a pause.

The warden winced, and put his hand to his forehead and felt bewildered.

"Attorney Finney has been there this morning," continued Bunce, "and by his looks I guess he is not so well pleased as he once was, and it has got abroad somehow that the archdeacon has had down great news from London, and Handy and Moody are both as black as devils. And I hope,'' said the man, trying to assume a cheery tone, ''that things are looking up, and that there'll be an end soon to all this stuff which bothers your reverence so sorely?''

''Well, I wish there may be, Bunce.''

''But about the news, your reverence?'' said the old man, almost whispering.

Mr. Harding walked on, and shook his head impatiently. Poor Bunce little knew how he was tormenting his patron.

''If there was anything to cheer you, I should be so glad to know it,'' said he, with a tone of affection which the warden in all his misery could not resist.

He stopped, and took both the old man's hands in his. ''My friend,'' said he, ''my dear old friend, there is nothing; there is no news to cheer me—God's will be done'': and two small hot tears broke away from his eyes and stole down his furrowed cheeks.

''Then God's will be done,'' said the other solemnly; ''but they told me that there was good news from London, and I came to wish your reverence joy; but God's will be done,'' and so the warden again walked on, and the bedesman, looking wistfully after him and receiving no encouragement to follow, returned sadly to his own abode.

For a couple of hours the warden remained thus in the garden, now walking, now standing motionless on the turf, and then, as his legs got weary, sitting unconsciously on the garden seats, and then walking again. And Eleanor, hidden behind the muslin curtains of the window, watched him through the trees as he now came in sight, and then again was concealed by the turnings of the walk; and thus the time passed away till five, when the warden crept back to the house and prepared for dinner.

It was but a sorry meal. The demure parlour-maid, as she handed the dishes and changed the plates, saw that all was not right, and was more demure than ever: neither father nor daughter could eat, and the hateful food was soon cleared away, and the bottle of port placed upon the table.

''Would you like Bunce to come in, papa?'' said Eleanor, thinking that the company of the old man might lighten his sorrow.

''No, my dear, thank you, not to-day; but are not you going

out, Eleanor, this lovely afternoon? don't stay in for me, my dear."

"I thought you seemed so sad, papa."

"Sad," said he, irritated; "well, people must all have their share of sadness here; I am not more exempt than another: but kiss me, dearest, and go now; I will, if possible, be more sociable when you return."

And Eleanor was again banished from her father's sorrow. Ah! her desire now was not to find him happy, but to be allowed to share his sorrows; not to force him to be sociable, but to persuade him to be trustful.

She put on her bonnet as desired, and went up to Mary Bold; this was now her daily haunt, for John Bold was up in London among lawyers and church reformers, diving deep into other questions than that of the wardenship of Barchester; supplying information to one member of Parliament, and dining with another; subscribing to funds for the abolition of clerical incomes, and seconding at that great national meeting at the Crown and Anchor a resolution to the effect, that no clergyman of the Church of England, be he who he might, should have more than a thousand a year, and none less than two hundred and fifty. His speech on this occasion was short, for fifteen had to speak, and the room was hired for two hours only, at the expiration of which the Quakers and Mr. Cobden were to make use of it for an appeal to the public in aid of the Emperor of Russia; but it was sharp and effective; at least he was told so by a companion with whom he now lived much, and on whom he greatly depended— one Tom Towers, a very leading genius, and supposed to have high employment on the staff of the *Jupiter*.

So Eleanor, as was now her wont, went up to Mary Bold, and Mary listened kindly, while the daughter spoke much of her father, and, perhaps kinder still, found a listener in Eleanor, while she spoke about her brother. In the meantime the warden sat alone, leaning on the arm of his chair; he had poured out a glass of wine, but had done so merely from habit, for he left it untouched; there he sat gazing at the open window, and thinking, if he can be said to have thought, of the happiness of his past life. All manner of past delights came before his mind, which at the time he had enjoyed without considering them; his easy days, his absence of all kind of hard work, his pleasant shady home, those twelve old neighbours whose welfare till now had been the source of so much pleasant care, the excellence of his children, the friendship of the dear old bishop, the solemn grandeur of those vaulted aisles, through which he loved to hear his own voice pealing; and then that friend of friends, that choice ally that had never deserted him, that eloquent companion that would always, when asked, discourse such pleasant music, that violoncello of his—ah, how happy he had been! but it was over now; his easy days and absence of work had been the crime which brought on him his tribulation; his shady home was pleasant no longer; maybe it was no longer his; the old neighbours, whose welfare had been so desired by him, were his enemies; his daughter was as wretched as himself; and even the bishop was made miserable by his position. He could never again lift up his voice boldly as he had hitherto done among his brethren, for he felt that he was disgraced; and he feared even to touch his bow, for he knew how grievous a sound of wailing, how piteous a lamentation, it would produce.

He was still sitting in the same chair and the same posture, having hardly moved a limb for two hours, when Eleanor came back to tea, and succeeded in bringing him with her into the drawing-room.

The tea seemed as comfortless as the dinner, though the warden, who had hitherto eaten nothing all day, devoured the plateful of bread and butter, unconscious of what he was doing.

Eleanor had made up her mind to force him to talk to her, but she hardly knew how to commence: she must wait till the urn was gone, till the servant would no longer be coming in and out.

At last everything was gone, and the drawing-room door was permanently closed; then Eleanor, getting up and going round to her father, put her arm round his neck, and said, "Papa, won't you tell me what it is?"

"What what is, my dear?"

"This new sorrow that torments you; I know you are unhappy, papa."

"New sorrow! it's no new sorrow, my dear; we have all our cares sometimes"; and he tried to smile, but it was a ghastly failure; "but I shouldn't be so dull a companion; come, we'll have some music."

"No, papa, not to-night—it would only trouble you tonight"; and she sat upon his knee, as she sometimes would in their gayest moods, and with her arm round his neck, she said: "Papa, I will not leave you till you talk to me; oh, if you only knew how much good it would do to you, to tell me of it all."

The father kissed his daughter, and pressed her to his heart;

but still he said nothing: it was so hard to him to speak of his own sorrows; he was so shy a man even with his own child!

"Oh, papa, do tell me what it is; I know it is about the hospital, and what they are doing up in London, and what that cruel newspaper has said; but if there be such cause for sorrow, let us be sorrowful together; we are all in all to each other now: dear, dear papa, do speak to me."

Mr. Harding could not well speak now, for the warm tears were running down his cheeks like rain in May, but he held his child close to his heart, and squeezed her hand as a lover might, and she kissed his forehead and his wet cheeks, and lay upon his bosom, and comforted him as a woman only can do.

"My own child," he said, as soon as his tears would let him speak, "my own, own child, why should you too be unhappy before it is necessary? It may come to that, that we must leave this place, but till that time comes, why should your young days be clouded?"

"And is that all, papa? If that be all, let us leave it, and have light hearts elsewhere: if that be all, let us go. Oh, papa, you and I could be happy if we had only bread to eat, so long as our hearts were light."

And Eleanor's face was lighted up with enthusiasm as she told her father how he might banish all his care; and a gleam of joy shot across his brow as this idea of escape again presented itself, and he again fancied for a moment that he could spurn away from him the income which the world envied him; that he could give the lie to that wielder of the tomahawk who had dared to write such things of him in the *Jupiter;* that he could leave Sir Abraham, and the archdeacon, and Bold, and the rest of them with their lawsuit among them, and wipe his hands altogether of so sorrow-stirring a concern. Ah, what happiness might there be in the distance, with Eleanor and him in some small cottage, and nothing left of their former grandeur but their music! Yes, they would walk forth with their music books, and their instruments, and shaking the dust from off their feet as they went, leave the ungrateful place. Never did a poor clergyman sigh for a warm benefice more anxiously than our warden did now to be rid of his.

"Give it up, papa," she said again, jumping from his knees and standing on her feet before him, looking boldly into his face; "give it up, papa."

Oh, it was sad to see how that momentary gleam of joy passed away; how the look of hope was dispersed from that sorrowful face, as the remembrance of the archdeacon came back upon our poor warden, and he reflected that he could not stir from his now hated post. He was a man bound with iron, fettered with adamant: he was in no respect a free agent; he had no choice. "Give it up!" Oh if he only could: what an easy way that were out of all his troubles!

"Papa, don't doubt about it," she continued, thinking that his hesitation arose from his unwillingness to abandon so comfortable a home; "is it on my account that you would stay here? Do you think that I cannot be happy without a pony-carriage and a fine drawing-room? Papa, I never can be happy here, as long as there is a question as to your honour in staying here; but I could be gay as the day is long in the smallest tiny little cottage, if I could see you come in and go out with a light heart. Oh! papa, your face tells so much; though you won't speak to me with your voice, I know how it is with you every time I look at you."

How he pressed her to his heart again with almost a spasmodic pressure! How he kissed her as the tears fell like rain from his old eyes! How he blessed her, and called her by a hundred soft sweet names which now came new to his lips! How he chid himself for ever having been unhappy with such a treasure in his house, such a jewel on his bosom, with so sweet a flower in the choice garden of his heart! And then the flood-gates of his tongue were loosed, and, at length, with unsparing detail of circumstances, he told her all that he wished, and all that he could not do. He repeated those arguments of the archdeacon, not agreeing in their truth, but explaining his inability to escape from them—how it had been declared to him that he was bound to remain where he was by the interests of his order, by gratitude to the bishop, by the wishes of his friends, by a sense of duty, which, though he could not understand it, he was fain to acknowledge. He told her how he had been accused of cowardice, and though he was not a man to make much of such a charge before the world, now in the full candour of his heart he explained to her that such an accusation was grievous to him; that he did think it would be unmanly to desert his post, merely to escape his present sufferings, and that, therefore, he must bear as best he might the misery which was prepared for him.

And did she find these details tedious? Oh, no; she encouraged him to dilate on every feeling he expressed, till he laid bare the inmost corners of his heart to her. They spoke together of the archdeacon, as two children might of a stern, unpopular, but still respected schoolmaster, and of the bishop as a parent kind as kind could be, but powerless against an omnipotent pedagogue.

And then, when they had discussed all this, when the father had told all to the child, she could not be less confiding than he had been; and as John Bold's name was mentioned between them, she owned how well she had learned to love him—"had loved him once," she said, "but she would not, could not do so now—no, even had her troth been plighted to him, she would have taken it back again—had she sworn to love him as his wife, she would have discarded him, and not felt herself forsworn, when he proved himself the enemy of her father."

But the warden declared that Bold was no enemy of his, and encouraged her love; and gently rebuked, as he kissed her, the stern resolve she had made to cast him off; and then he spoke to her of happier days when their trials would all be over; and declared that her young heart should not be torn asunder to please either priest or prelate, dean or archdeacon. No, not if all Oxford were to convocate together, and agree as to the necessity of the sacrifice.

And so they greatly comforted each other—and in what sorrow will not such mutual confidence give consolation!—and with a last expression of tender love they parted, and went comparatively happy to their rooms.

XI

Iphigenia

When Eleanor laid her head on her pillow that night, her mind was anxiously intent on some plan by which she might extricate her father from his misery; and, in her warmhearted enthusiasm, self-sacrifice was decided on as the means to be adopted. Was not so good an Agamemnon worthy of an Iphigenia? She would herself personally implore John Bold to desist from his undertaking;

she would explain to him her father's sorrows, the cruel misery of his position; she would tell him how her father would die if he were thus dragged before the public and exposed to such unmerited ignominy; she would appeal to his old friendship, to his generosity, to his manliness, to his mercy; if need were, she would kneel to him for the favour she would ask; but before she did this, the idea of love must be banished. There must be no bargain in the matter. To his mercy, to his generosity, she could appeal; but as a pure maiden, hitherto even unsolicited, she could not appeal to his love, nor under such circumstances could she allow him to do so. Of course, when so provoked he would declare his passion; that was to be expected; there had been enough between them to make such a fact sure; but it was equally certain that he must be rejected. She could not be understood as saying, Make my father free and I am the reward. There would be no sacrifice in that—not so had Jephthah's daughter saved her father—not so could she show to that kindest, dearest of parents how much she was able to bear for his good. No; to one resolve must her whole soul be bound; and so resolving, she felt that she could make her great request to Bold with as much self-assured confidence as she could have done to his grandfather.

And now I own I have fears for my heroine; not as to the upshot of her mission—not in the least as to that; as to the full success of her generous scheme, and the ultimate result of such a project, no one conversant with human nature and novels can have a doubt; but as to the amount of sympathy she may receive from those of her own sex. Girls below twenty and old ladies above sixty will do her justice; for in the female heart the soft springs of sweet romance reopen after many years, and again gush out with waters pure as in earlier days, and greatly refresh the path that leads downwards to the grave. But I fear that the majority of those between these two eras will not approve of Eleanor's plan. I fear that unmarried ladies of thirty-five will declare that there can be no probability of so absurd a project being carried through; that young women on their knees before their lovers are sure to get kissed, and that they would not put themselves in such a position did they not expect it; that Eleanor is going to Bold only because circumstances prevent Bold from coming to her; that she is certainly a little fool, or a little schemer, but that in all probability she is thinking a good deal more about herself than her father.

Dear ladies, you are right as to your appreciation of the

circumstances, but very wrong as to Miss Harding's character. Miss Harding was much younger than you are, and could not, therefore, know, as you may do, to what dangers such an encounter might expose her. She may get kissed; I think it very probable that she will; but I give my solemn word and positive assurance, that the remotest idea of such a catastrophe never occurred to her as she made the great resolve now alluded to.

And then she slept; and then she rose refreshed; and met her father with her kindest embrace and most loving smiles; and on the whole their breakfast was by no means so triste as had been their dinner the day before; and then, making some excuse to her father for so soon leaving him, she started on the commencement of her operations.

She knew that John Bold was in London, and that, therefore, the scene itself could not be enacted to-day; but she also knew that he was soon to be home, probably on the next day, and it was necessary that some little plan for meeting him should be concerted with his sister Mary. When she got up to the house, she went, as usual, into the morning sitting-room, and was startled by perceiving, by a stick, a great coat, and sundry parcels which were lying about, that Bold must already have returned.

"John has come back so suddenly," said Mary, coming into the room; "he has been travelling all night."

"Then I'll come up again some other time," said Eleanor, about to beat a retreat in her sudden dismay.

"He's out now, and will be for the next two hours," said the other; "he's with that horrid Finney; he only came to see him, and he returns by the mail train to-night."

Returns by the mail train to-night, thought Eleanor to herself, as she strove to screw up her courage—away again to-night—then it must be now or never; and she again sat down, having risen to go.

She wished the ordeal could have been postponed: she had fully made up her mind to do the deed, but she had not made up her mind to do it this very day; and now she felt ill at ease, astray, and in difficulty.

"Mary," she began, "I must see your brother before he goes back."

"Oh, yes, of course," said the other; "I know he'll be delighted to see you"; and she tried to treat it as a matter of course, but she was not the less surprised; for Mary and Eleanor had daily talked over John Bold and his conduct, and his love, and Mary would insist on calling Eleanor her sister, and would scold her for not calling Bold by his Christian name; and Eleanor would half confess her love, but like a modest maiden would protest against such familiarities even with the name of her lover; and so they talked hour after hour, and Mary Bold, who was much the elder, looked forward with happy confidence to the day when Eleanor would not be ashamed to call her her sister. She was, however, fully sure that just at present Eleanor would be much more likely to avoid her brother than to seek him.

"Mary, I must see your brother, now, to-day, and beg from him a great favour"; and she spoke with a solemn air, not at all usual to her; and then she went on, and opened to her friend all her plan, her well-weighed scheme for saving her father from a sorrow which would, she said, if it lasted, bring him to his grave. "But, Mary," she continued, "you must now, you know, cease any joking about me and Mr. Bold; you must now say no more about that; I am not ashamed to beg this favour from your brother, but when I have done so, there can never be anything further between us"; and this she said with a staid and solemn air, quite worthy of Jephthah's daughter or of Iphigenia either.

It was quite clear that Mary Bold did not follow the argument. That Eleanor Harding should appeal, on behalf of her father, to Bold's better feelings seemed to Mary quite natural; it seemed quite natural that he should relent, overcome by such filial tears, and by so much beauty; but, to her thinking, it was at any rate equally natural, that having relented, John should put his arm round his mistress's waist, and say: "Now having settled that, let us be man and wife, and all will end happily!" Why his good nature should not be rewarded when such reward would operate to the disadvantage of none, Mary, who had more sense than romance, could not understand; and she said as much.

Eleanor, however, was firm, and made quite an eloquent speech to support her own view of the question: she could not condescend, she said, to ask such a favour on any other terms than those proposed. Mary might, perhaps, think her highflown, but she had her own ideas, and she could not submit to sacrifice her self-respect.

"But I am sure you love him—don't you?" pleaded Mary; "and I am sure he loves you better than anything in the world."

Eleanor was going to make another speech, but a tear came to each eye, and she could not; so she pretended to blow her nose, and walked to the window, and made a little inward call on her own courage, and finding herself somewhat sustained, said sententiously: "Mary, this is nonsense."

"But you do love him," said Mary, who had followed her friend to the window, and now spoke with her arms close wound round the other's waist. "You do love him with all your heart—you know you do; I defy you to deny it."

"I—" commenced Eleanor, turning sharply round to refute the charge; but the intended falsehood stuck in her throat, and never came to utterance. She could not deny her love, so she took plentifully to tears, and leant upon her friend's bosom and sobbed there, and protested that, love or no love, it would make no difference in her resolve, and called Mary, a thousand times, the most cruel of girls, and swore her to secrecy by a hundred oaths, and ended by declaring that the girl who could betray her friend's love, even to a brother, would be as black a traitor as a soldier in a garrison who should open the city gates to the enemy. While they were yet discussing the matter, Bold returned, and Eleanor was forced into sudden action: she had either to accomplish or abandon her plan; and having slipped into her friend's bedroom, as the gentleman closed the hall door, she washed the marks of tears from her eyes, and resolved within herself to go through with it. "Tell him I am here," said she, "and coming in; and mind, whatever you do, don't leave us." So Mary informed her brother, with a somewhat sombre air, that Miss Harding was in the next room, and was coming to speak to him.

Eleanor was certainly thinking more of her father than herself, as she arranged her hair before the glass, and removed the traces of sorrow from her face; and yet I should be untrue if I said that she was not anxious to appear well before her lover: why else was she so sedulous with that stubborn curl that would rebel against her hand, and smooth so eagerly her ruffled ribands? why else did she damp her eyes to dispel the redness, and bite her pretty lips to bring back the colour? Of course she was anxious to look her best, for she was but a mortal angel after all. But had she been immortal, had she flitted back to the sitting-room on a cherub's wings, she could not have had a more faithful heart, or a truer wish to save her father at any cost to herself.

John Bold had not met her since the day when she left him in dudgeon in the cathedral close. Since that his whole time had been occupied in promoting the cause against her father, and not unsuccessfully. He had often thought of her, and turned over in his mind a hundred schemes for showing her how disinterested was his love. He would write to her and beseech her not to allow the performance of a public duty to injure him in her estimation; he would write to Mr. Harding, explain all his views, and boldly claim the warden's daughter, urging that the untoward circumstances between them need be no bar to their ancient friendship, or to a closer tie; he would throw himself on his knees before his mistress; he would wait and marry the daughter when the father had lost his home and his income; he would give up the lawsuit and go to Australia, with her of course, leaving the *Jupiter* and Mr. Finney to complete the case between them. Sometimes as he woke in the morning fevered and impatient, he would blow out his brains and have done with all his cares—but this idea was generally consequent on an imprudent supper enjoyed in company with Tom Towers.

How beautiful Eleanor appeared to him as she slowly walked into the room! Not for nothing had all those little cares been taken. Though her sister, the archdeacon's wife, had spoken slightingly of her charms, Eleanor was very beautiful when seen aright. Hers was not of those impassive faces, which have the beauty of a marble bust; finely chiselled features, perfect in every line, true to the rules of symmetry, as lovely to a stranger as to a friend, unvarying unless in sickness, or as age affects them. She had no startling brilliancy of beauty, no pearly whiteness, no radiant carnation. She had not the majestic contour that rivets attention, demands instant wonder and then disappoints by the coldness of its charms. You might pass Eleanor Harding in the street without notice, but you could hardly pass an evening with her and not lose your heart.

She had never appeared more lovely to her lover than she now did. Her face was animated though it was serious, and her full dark lustrous eyes shone with anxious energy; her hand trembled as she took his, and she could hardly pronounce his name, when she addressed him. Bold wished with all his heart that the Australian scheme was in the act of realisation, and that he and Eleanor were away together, never to hear further of the lawsuit.

He began to talk, asked after her health—said something about London being very stupid, and more about Barchester being very pleasant; declared the weather to be very hot, and then inquired after Mr. Harding.

"My father is not very well," said Eleanor.

John Bold was very sorry, so sorry: he hoped it was nothing serious, and put on the unmeaningly solemn face which people usually use on such occasions.

"I especially want to speak to you about my father, Mr. Bold; indeed, I am now here on purpose to do so. Papa is very unhappy, very unhappy indeed, about this affair of the hospital: you would pity him, Mr. Bold, if you could see how wretched it has made him."

"Oh, Miss Harding!"

"Indeed you would—any one would pity him; but a friend, an old friend as you are—indeed you would. He is an altered man; his cheerfulness has all gone, and his sweet temper, and his kind happy tone of voice; you would hardly know him if you saw him, Mr. Bold, he is so much altered; and—and—if this goes on, he will die." Here Eleanor had recourse to her handkerchief, and so also had her auditors; but she plucked up her courage, and went on with her tale. "He will break his heart, and die. I am sure, Mr. Bold, it was not you who wrote those cruel things in the newspaper——"

John Bold eagerly protested that it was not, but his heart smote him as to his intimate alliance with Tom Towers.

"No, I am sure it was not; and papa has not for a moment thought so; you would not be so cruel—but it has nearly killed him. Papa cannot bear to think that people should so speak to him, and that everybody should hear him so spoken of:—they have called him avaricious, and dishonest, and they say he is robbing the old men, and taking the money of the hospital for nothing."

"I have never said so, Miss Harding. I——"

"No," continued Eleanor, interrupting him, for she was now in the full flood tide of her eloquence; "no, I am sure you have not; but others have said so; and if this goes on, if such things are written again, it will kill papa. Oh! Mr. Bold, if you only knew the state he is in! Now papa does not care much about money."

Both her auditors, brother and sister, assented to this, and declared on their own knowledge that no man lived less addicted to filthy lucre than the warden.

"Oh! it's so kind of you to say so, Mary, and of you too, Mr. Bold. I couldn't bear that people should think unjustly of papa. Do you know he would give up the hospital altogether, only he cannot. The archdeacon says it would be cowardly, and that he would be deserting his order, and injuring the church. Whatever may happen, papa will not do that: he would leave the place to-morrow willingly, and give up his house, and the income and all if the archdeacon——" Eleanor was going to say "would let him," but she stopped herself before she had compromised her father's dignity; and giving a long sigh, she added— "Oh, I do so wish he would."

"No one who knows Mr. Harding personally accuses him for a moment," said Bold.

"It is he that has to bear the punishment; it is he that suffers," said Eleanor; "and what for? what has he done wrong? how has he deserved this persecution? he that never had an unkind thought in his life, he that never said an unkind word!" and here she broke down, and the violence of her sobs stopped her utterance.

Bold, for the fifth or sixth time, declared that neither he nor any of his friends imputed any blame personally to Mr. Harding.

"Then why should he be persecuted?" ejaculated Eleanor through her tears, forgetting in her eagerness that her intention had been to humble herself as a suppliant before John Bold— "why should he be singled out for scorn and disgrace? why should he be made so wretched? Oh! Mr. Bold"—and she turned towards him as though the kneeling scene were about to be commenced—"oh! Mr. Bold, why did you begin all this? You, whom we all so—so—valued!"

To speak the truth, the reformer's punishment was certainly come upon him, for his present plight was not enviable; he had nothing for it but to excuse himself by platitudes about public duty, which it is by no means worth while to repeat, and to reiterate his eulogy on Mr. Harding's character. His position was certainly a cruel one: had any gentleman called upon him on behalf of Mr. Harding he could of course have declined to enter upon the subject; but how could he do so with a beautiful girl, with the daughter of the man whom he had injured, with his own love?

In the meantime Eleanor recollected herself, and again summoned up her energies. "Mr. Bold," said she, "I have come here to implore you to abandon this proceeding." He stood up from his seat, and looked beyond measure distressed. "To implore you to abandon it, to implore you to spare my father, to spare either his life or his reason, for one or the other will pay the forfeit if this goes on. I know how much I am asking, and how little right I have to ask anything; but I think you will listen to me, as it is for my father. Oh, Mr. Bold, pray, pray do this for us—pray do not drive to distraction a man who has loved you so well."

She did not absolutely kneel to him, but she followed him

as he moved from his chair, and laid her soft hands imploringly upon his arm. Ah! at any other time how exquisitely valuable would have been that touch! but now he was distraught, dumbfounded, and unmanned. What could he say to that sweet suppliant; how explain to her that the matter now was probably beyond his control; how tell her that he could not quell the storm which he had raised?

"Surely, surely, John, you cannot refuse her," said his sister.

"I would give her my soul," said he, "if it would serve her."

"Oh, Mr. Bold," said Eleanor, "do not speak so; I ask nothing for myself; and what I ask for my father, it cannot harm you to grant."

"I would give her my soul, if it would serve her," said Bold, still addressing his sister; "everything I have is hers, if she will accept it; my house, my heart, my all; every hope of my breast is centred in her; her smiles are sweeter to me than the sun, and when I see her in sorrow as she now is, every nerve in my body suffers. No man can love better than I love her."

"No, no, no," ejaculated Eleanor; "there can be no talk of love between us. Will you protect my father from the evil you have brought upon him?"

"Oh, Eleanor, I will do anything; let me tell you how I love you!"

"No, no, no"; she almost screamed. "This is unmanly of you, Mr. Bold. Will you, will you, will you leave my father to die in peace in his quiet home?" and seizing him by his arm and hand, she followed him across the room towards the door. "I will not leave you till you promise me; I'll cling to you in the street; I'll kneel to you before all the people. You shall promise me this, you shall promise me this, you shall——" And she clung to him with fixed tenacity, and reiterated her resolve with hysterical passion.

"Speak to her, John; answer her," said Mary, bewildered by the unexpected vehemence of Eleanor's manner; "you cannot have the cruelty to refuse her."

"Promise me, promise me," said Eleanor; "say that my father is safe—one word will do. I know how true you are; say one word, and I will let you go."

She still held him, and looked eagerly into his face, with her hair dishevelled and her eyes all bloodshot. She had no thought now of herself, no care now for her appearance; and yet he thought he had never seen her half so lovely; he was amazed at the intensity of her beauty, and could hardly believe that it was she whom he had dared to love. "Promise me," said she; "I will not leave you till you have promised me."

"I will," said he at length; "I do—all I can do, I will do."

"Then may God Almighty bless you for ever and ever!" said Eleanor; and falling on her knees with her face on Mary's lap, she wept and sobbed like a child: her strength had carried her through her allotted task, but now it was well-nigh exhausted.

In a while she was partly recovered, and got up to go, and would have gone, had not Bold made her understand that it was necessary for him to explain to her how far it was in his power to put an end to the proceedings which had been taken against Mr. Harding. Had he spoken on any other subject, she would have vanished, but on that she was bound to hear him; and now the danger of her position commenced. While she had an active part to play, while she clung to him as a suppliant, it was easy enough for her to reject his proffered love, and cast from her his caressing words; but now—now that he had yielded, and was talking to her calmly and kindly as to her father's welfare, it was hard enough for her to do so. Then Mary Bold assisted her; but now she was quite on her brother's side. Mary said but little, but every word she did say gave some direct and deadly blow. The first thing she did was to make room for her brother between herself and Eleanor on the sofa: as the sofa was full large for three, Eleanor could not resent this, nor could she show suspicion by taking another seat; but she felt it to be a most unkind proceeding. And then Mary would talk as though they three were joined in some close peculiar bond together; as though they were in future always to wish together, contrive together, and act together; and Eleanor could not gainsay this; she could not make another speech, and say, "Mr. Bold and I are strangers, Mary, and are always to remain so!"

He explained to her that, though undoubtedly the proceeding against the hospital had commenced solely with himself, many others were now interested in the matter, some of whom were much more influential than himself; that it was to him alone, however, that the lawyers looked for instruction as to their doings, and, more important still, for the payment of their bills; and he promised that he would at once give them notice that it was his intention to abandon the cause. He thought, he said, that it was not probable that any active steps would be taken after he had seceded from the matter, though it was possible that some passing allusion might still be made to the hospital in the daily *Jupiter*. He promised, however, that he would use his best influence to prevent any further personal allusion being made to Mr. Harding. He then suggested that he would on that afternoon ride over himself to Dr. Grantly, and inform him of his altered intentions on the subject, and with this view, he postponed his immediate return to London.

This was all very pleasant, and Eleanor did enjoy a sort of triumph in the feeling that she had attained the object for which she had sought this interview; but still the part of Iphigenia was to be played out. The gods had heard her prayer, granted her request, and were they not to have their promised sacrifice? Eleanor was not a girl to defraud them wilfully; so, as soon as she decently could, she got up for her bonnet.

"Are you going so soon?" said Bold, who half an hour since would have given a hundred pounds that he was in London, and she still at Barchester.

"Oh yes!" said she. "I am so much obliged to you; papa will feel this to be so kind." She did not quite appreciate all her father's feelings. "Of course I must tell him, and I will say that you will see the archdeacon."

"But may I not say one word for myself?" said Bold.

"I'll fetch you your bonnet, Eleanor," said Mary, in the act of leaving the room.

"Mary, Mary," said she, getting up and catching her by her dress; "don't go, I'll get my bonnet myself." But Mary, the traitress, stood fast by the door, and permitted no such retreat. Poor Iphigenia!

And with a volley of impassioned love, John Bold poured forth the feelings of his heart, swearing, as men do, some truths and many falsehoods; and Eleanor repeated with every shade of vehemence the "No, no, no," which had had a short time since so much effect; but now, alas! its strength was gone. Let her be never so vehement, her vehemence was not respected; all her "No, no, no's" were met with counter asseverations, and at last were overpowered. The ground was cut from under her on every side. She was pressed to say whether her father would object; whether she herself had any aversion (aversion! God help her, poor girl! the word nearly made her jump into his arms); any other preference (this she loudly disclaimed); whether it was impossible that she should love him (Eleanor could not say that it was impossible): and so at last, all her defences demolished, all her maiden barriers swept away, she capitulated, or rather marched out with the honours of war, vanquished evidently, palpably vanquished, but still not reduced to the necessity of confessing it.

And so the altar on the shore of the modern Aulis reeked with no sacrifice.

XII

Mr. Bold's Visit to Plumstead

Whether or no the ill-natured prediction made by certain ladies in the beginning of the last chapter was or was not carried out to the letter, I am not in a position to state. Eleanor, however, certainly did feel herself to have been baffled as she returned home with all her news to her father. Certainly she had been victorious, certainly she had achieved her object, certainly she was not unhappy, and yet she did not feel herself triumphant. Everything would run smooth now. Eleanor was not at all addicted to the Lydian school of romance; she by no means objected to her lover because he came in at the door under the name of Absolute, instead of pulling her out of a window under the name of Beverley; and yet she felt that she had been imposed upon, and could hardly think of Mary Bold with sisterly charity. "I did think I could have trusted Mary," she said to herself over and over again. "Oh, that she should have dared to keep me in the room when I tried to get out!" Eleanor, however, felt that the game was up, and that she had now nothing further to do but to add to the budget of news which was prepared for her father, that John Bold was her accepted lover.

We will, however, now leave her on her way, and go with John Bold to Plumstead Episcopi, merely premising that Eleanor on reaching home will not find things so smooth as she fondly expected; two messengers had come, one to her father and the other to the archdeacon, and each of them much opposed to her quiet mode of solving all their difficulties; the one in the shape of a number of the *Jupiter,* and the other in that of a further opinion from Sir Abraham Haphazard.

John Bold got on his horse and rode off to Plumstead Episcopi; not briskly and with eager spur, as men do ride when self-satisfied with their own intentions; but slowly, modestly, thoughtfully, and somewhat in dread of the coming interview. Now and again he would recur to the scene which was just over, support himself by the remembrance of the silence that gives consent, and exult as a happy lover. But even this feeling was not without a shade of remorse. Had he not shown himself childishly weak thus to yield up the resolve of many hours of thought to the tears of a pretty girl? How was he to meet his lawyer? How was he to back out of a matter in which his name was already so publicly concerned? What, oh what! was he to say to Tom Towers? While meditating these painful things he reached the lodge leading up to the archdeacon's glebe, and for the first time in his life found himself within the sacred precincts.

All the doctor's children were together on the slope of the lawn close to the road, as Bold rode up to the hall door. They were there holding high debate on matters evidently of deep interest at Plumstead Episcopi, and the voices of the boys had been heard before the lodge gate was closed.

Florinda and Grizzel, frightened at the sight of so well-known an enemy to the family, fled on the first appearance of the horseman, and ran in terror to their mother's arms; not for them was it, tender branches, to resent injuries, or as members of a church militant to put on armour against its enemies. But the boys stood their ground like heroes, and boldly demanded the business of the intruder.

"Do you want to see anybody here, sir?" said Henry, with a defiant eye and a hostile tone, which plainly said that at any rate no one there wanted to see the person so addressed; and as he spoke he brandished aloft his garden water-pot, holding it by the spout, ready for the braining of any one.

"Henry," said Charles James slowly, and with a certain dignity of diction, "Mr. Bold of course would not have come without wanting to see some one; if Mr. Bold has a proper ground for wanting to see some person here, of course he has a right to come."

But Samuel stepped lightly up to the horse's head, and offered his services. "Oh, Mr. Bold," said he, "papa, I'm sure, will be glad to see you; I suppose you want to see papa. Shall I hold your horse for you? Oh, what a very pretty horse!'' and he turned his head and winked funnily at his brothers. ''Papa has heard such good news about the old hospital to-day. We know you'll be glad to hear it, because you're such a friend of grandpapa Harding, and so much in love with Aunt Nelly!''

''How d'ye do, lads?'' said Bold, dismounting. ''I want to see your father if he's at home.''

''Lads!'' said Henry, turning on his heel and addressing himself to his brother, but loud enough to be heard by Bold; ''lads, indeed! if we're lads, what does he call himself?''

Charles James condescended to say nothing further, but cocked his hat with much precision, and left the visitor to the care of his youngest brother.

Samuel stayed till the servant came, chatting and patting the horse; but as soon as Bold had disappeared through the front door, he stuck a switch under the animal's tail to make him kick if possible.

The church reformer soon found himself tête-à-tête with the archdeacon in that same room, in that sanctum sanctorum of the rectory, to which we have already been introduced. As he entered he heard the click of a certain patent lock, but it struck him with no surprise; the worthy clergyman was no doubt hiding from eyes profane his last much-studied sermon; for the archdeacon, though he preached but seldom, was famous for his sermons. No room, Bold thought, could have been more becoming for a dignitary of the church; each wall was loaded with theology; over each separate bookcase was printed in small gold letters the names of those great divines whose works were ranged beneath: beginning from the early fathers in due chronological order, there were to be found the precious labours of the chosen servants of the church down to the last pamphlet written in opposition to the consecration of Dr. Hampden; and raised above this were to be seen the busts of the greatest among the great: Chrysostom, St. Augustine, Thomas à Becket, Cardinal Wolsey, Archbishop Laud, and Dr. Philpotts.

Every appliance that could make study pleasant and give ease to the overtoiled brain was there; chairs made to relieve each limb and muscle; reading-desks and writing-desks to suit every attitude; lamps and candles mechanically contrived to throw their light on any favoured spot, as the student might desire; a shoal of newspapers to amuse the few leisure moments which might be stolen from the labours of the day; and then from the window a view right through a bosky vista along which ran a broad green path from the rectory to the church—at the end of which the tawny-tinted fine old tower was seen with all its variegated pinnacles and parapets. Few parish churches in England are in better repair, or better worth keeping so, than that at Plumstead Episcopi; and yet it is built in a faulty style: the body of the church is low—so low, that the nearly flat leaden roof would be visible from the churchyard, were it not for the carved parapet with which it is surrounded. It is cruciform, though the transepts are irregular, one being larger than the other; and the tower is much too high in proportion to the church. But the colour of the building is perfect; it is that rich yellow grey which one finds nowhere but in the south and west of England, and which is so strong a characteristic of most of our old houses of Tudor architecture. The stone work also is beautiful; the mullions of the windows and the thick tracery of the Gothic workmanship is as rich as fancy can desire; and though in gazing on such a structure one knows by rule that the old priests who built it, built it wrong, one cannot bring oneself to wish that they should have made it other than it is.

When Bold was ushered into the book-room, he found its owner standing with his back to the empty fire-place ready to receive him, and he could not but perceive that that expansive brow was elated with triumph, and that those full heavy lips bore more prominently than usual an appearance of arrogant success.

"Well, Mr. Bold," said he—"well, what can I do for you? Very happy, I can assure you, to do anything for such a friend of my father-in-law."

"I hope you'll excuse my calling, Dr. Grantly."

"Certainly, certainly," said the archdeacon; "I can assure you, no apology is necessary from Mr. Bold; only let me know what I can do for him."

Dr. Grantly was standing himself, and he did not ask Bold to sit, and therefore he had to tell his tale standing, leaning on the table, with his hat in his hand. He did, however, manage to tell it; and as the archdeacon never once interrupted him, or even encouraged him by a single word, he was not long in coming to the end of it.

"And so, Mr. Bold, I'm to understand, I believe, that you are desirous of abandoning this attack upon Mr. Harding."

"Oh, Dr. Grantly, there has been no attack, I can assure you——"

"Well, well, we won't quarrel about words; I should call it an attack—most men would so call an endeavour to take away from a man every shilling of income that he has to live upon; but it shan't be an attack, if you don't like it; you wish to abandon this—this little game of backgammon you've begun to play."

"I intend to put an end to the legal proceedings which I have commenced."

"I understand," said the archdeacon. "You've already had enough of it; well, I can't say that I am surprised; carrying on a losing lawsuit where one has nothing to gain, but everything to pay, is not pleasant."

Bold turned very red in the face. "You misinterpret my motives," said he; "but, however, that is of little consequence. I did not come to trouble you with my motives, but to tell you a matter of fact. Good-morning, Dr. Grantly."

"One moment—one moment," said the other. "I don't exactly appreciate the taste which induced you to make any personal communication to me on the subject; but I dare say I'm wrong, I dare say your judgment is the better of the two; but as you have done me the honour—as you have, as it were, forced me into a certain amount of conversation on a subject which had better, perhaps, have been left to our lawyers, you will excuse me if I ask you to hear my reply to your communication."

"I am in no hurry, Dr. Grantly."

"Well, I am, Mr. Bold; my time is not exactly leisure time, and, therefore, if you please, we'll go to the point at once— you're going to abandon this lawsuit?"—and he paused for a reply.

"Yes, Dr. Grantly, I am."

"Having exposed a gentleman who was one of your father's warmest friends to all the ignominy and insolence which the press could heap upon his name, having somewhat ostentatiously declared that it was your duty as a man of high public virtue to protect those poor old fools whom you have humbugged there at the hospital, you now find that the game costs more than it's worth, and so you make up your mind to have done with it. A prudent resolution, Mr. Bold; but it is a pity you should have been so long coming to it. Has it struck you that we may not now choose to give over? that we may find it necessary to punish the injury you have done to us? Are you aware, sir, that we have gone to enormous expense to resist this iniquitous attempt of yours?"

Bold's face was now furiously red, and he nearly crushed his hat between his hands; but he said nothing.

"We have found it necessary to employ the best advice that

money could procure. Are you aware, sir, what may be the probable cost of securing the services of the attorney-general?''

"Not in the least, Dr. Grantly."

"I dare say not, sir. When you recklessly put this affair into the hands of your friend Mr. Finney, whose six and eightpences and thirteen and fourpences may, probably, not amount to a large sum, you were indifferent as to the cost and suffering which such a proceeding might entail on others; but are you aware, sir, that these crushing costs must now come out of your own pocket?''

''Any demand of such a nature which Mr. Harding's lawyer may have to make will doubtless be made to my lawyer.''

"Mr. Harding's lawyer and my lawyer! Did you come here merely to refer me to the lawyers? Upon my word I think the honour of your visit might have been spared! And now, sir, I'll tell you what my opinion is—my opinion is, that we shall not allow you to withdraw this matter from the courts.''

"You can do as you please, Dr. Grantly; good-morning.''

"Hear me out, sir,'' said the archdeacon; ''I have here in my hands the last opinion given in this matter by Sir Abraham Haphazard. I dare say you have already heard of this—I dare say it has had something to do with your visit here to-day.''

"I know nothing whatever of Sir Abraham Haphazard or his opinion.''

"Be that as it may, here it is; he declares most explicitly that under no phasis of the affair whatever have you a leg to stand upon; that Mr. Harding is as safe in his hospital as I am here in my rectory; that a more futile attempt to destroy a man was never made, than this which you have made to ruin Mr. Harding. Here,'' and he slapped the paper on the table, ''I have this opinion from the very first lawyer in the land; and under these circumstances you expect me to make you a low bow for your kind offer to release Mr. Harding from the toils of your net! Sir, your net is not strong enough to hold him; sir, your net has fallen to pieces, and you knew that well enough before I told you—and now, sir, I'll wish you good-morning, for I'm busy.''

Bold was now choking with passion. He had let the arch-deacon run on because he knew not with what words to interrupt him; but now that he had been so defied and insulted, he could not leave the room without some reply.

"Dr. Grantly,'' he commenced.

"I have nothing further to say or to hear,'' said the archdeacon. "I'll do myself the honour to order your horse." And he rang the bell.

"I came here, Dr. Grantly, with the warmest, kindest feelings——"

"Oh, of course you did; nobody doubts it."

"With the kindest feelings—and they have been most grossly outraged by your treatment."

"Of course they have—I have not chosen to see my father-in-law ruined; what an outrage that has been to your feelings!"

"The time will come, Dr. Grantly, when you will understand why I called upon you to-day."

"No doubt, no doubt. Is Mr. Bold's horse there? That's right; open the front door. Good-morning, Mr. Bold"; and the doctor stalked into his own drawing-room, closing the door behind him, and making it quite impossible that John Bold should speak another word.

As he got on his horse, which he was fain to do feeling like a dog turned out of a kitchen, he was again greeted by little Sammy.

"Good-bye, Mr. Bold; I hope we may have the pleasure of seeing you again before long; I am sure papa will always be glad to see you."

That was certainly the bitterest moment in John Bold's life. Not even the remembrance of his successful love could comfort him; nay, when he thought of Eleanor he felt that it was that very love which had brought him to such a pass. That he should have been so insulted, and be unable to reply! That he should have given up so much to the request of a girl, and then have had his motives so misunderstood! That he should have made so gross a mistake as this visit of his to the archdeacon's! He bit the top of his whip, till he penetrated the horn of which it was made: he struck the poor animal in his anger, and then was doubly angry with himself at his futile passion. He had been so completely checkmated, so palpably overcome! and what was he to do? He could not continue his action after pledging himself to abandon it; nor was there any revenge in that—it was the very step to which his enemy had endeavoured to goad him!

He threw the reins to the servant who came to take his horse, and rushed upstairs into his drawing-room, where his sister Mary was sitting.

"If there be a devil," said he, "a real devil here on earth, it is Dr. Grantly." He vouchsafed her no further intelligence, but again seizing his hat, he rushed out, and took his departure for London without another word to any one.

XIII

The Warden's Decision

The meeting between Eleanor and her father was not so stormy as that described in the last chapter, but it was hardly more successful. On her return from Bold's house she found her father in a strange state. He was not sorrowful and silent as he had been on that memorable day when his son-in-law lectured him as to all that he owed to his order; nor was he in his usual quiet mood. When Eleanor reached the hospital, he was walking to and fro upon the lawn, and she soon saw that he was much excited.

"I am going to London, my dear," he said as soon as he saw her.

"London, papa!"

"Yes, my dear, to London; I will have this matter settled some way; there are some things, Eleanor, which I cannot bear."

"Oh, papa, what is it?" said she, leading him by the arm into the house. "I had such good news for you, and now you make me fear I am too late." And then, before he could let her know what had caused this sudden resolve, or could point to the fatal paper which lay on the table, she told him that the lawsuit was over, that Bold had commissioned her to assure her father in his name that it would be abandoned, that there was no further cause for misery, that the whole matter might be looked on as though it had never been discussed. She did not tell him with what determined vehemence she had obtained this concession in his favour, nor did she mention the price she was to pay for it.

The warden did not express himself peculiarly gratified at this intelligence, and Eleanor, though she had not worked for thanks, and was by no means disposed to magnify her own good offices, felt hurt at the manner in which her news was received.

"Mr. Bold can act as he thinks proper, my love," said he; "if Mr. Bold thinks he has been wrong, of course he will discontinue what he is doing; but that cannot change my purpose."

"Oh, papa!" she exclaimed, all but crying with vexation; "I thought you would have been so happy—I thought all would have been right now."

"Mr. Bold," continued he, "has set great people to work—so great that I doubt they are now beyond his control. Read that, my dear." The warden, doubling up a number of the *Jupiter*, pointed to the peculiar article which she was to read. It was to the last of the three leaders, which are generally furnished daily for the support of the nation, that Mr. Harding directed her attention. It dealt some heavy blows on various clerical delinquents; on families who received their tens of thousands yearly for doing nothing; on men who, as the article stated, rolled in wealth which they had neither earned nor inherited, and which was in fact stolen from the poorer clergy. It named some sons of bishops, and grandsons of archbishops; men great in their way, who had redeemed their disgrace in the eyes of many by the enormity of their plunder; and then, having disposed of these leviathans, it descended to Mr. Harding.

"We alluded some weeks since to an instance of similar injustice, though in a more humble scale, in which the warden of an almshouse at Barchester has become possessed of the income of the greater part of the whole institution. Why an almshouse should have a warden we cannot pretend to explain, nor can we say what special need twelve old men can have for the services of a separate clergyman, seeing that they have twelve reserved seats for themselves in Barchester Cathedral. But be this as it may, let the gentleman call himself warden or precentor, or what he will, let him be never so scrupulous in exacting religious duties from his twelve dependants, or never so negligent as regards the services of the cathedral, it appears palpably clear that he can be entitled to no portion of the revenue of the hospital, excepting that which the founder set apart for him; and it is equally clear that the founder did not intend that three-fifths of his charity should be so consumed.

"The case is certainly a paltry one after the tens of thousands with which we have been dealing, for the warden's income is after all but a poor eight hundred a year: eight hundred a year is not magnificent preferment of itself, and the warden may, for anything we know, be worth much more to the church; but if so, let the church pay him out of funds justly at its own disposal.

"We allude to the question of the Barchester almshouse at the present moment, because we understand that a plea has been set up which will be peculiarly revolting to the minds of English churchmen. An action has been taken against Mr. Warden Harding, on behalf of the almsmen, by a gentleman acting solely on public grounds, and it is to be argued that Mr. Harding takes nothing but what he receives as a servant of the hospital, and that he is not himself responsible for the amount of stipend given to him for his work. Such a plea would doubtless be fair, if any one questioned the daily wages of a bricklayer employed on the building, or the fee of the charwoman who cleans it; but we cannot envy the feeling of a clergyman of the Church of England who could allow such an argument to be put in his mouth.

"If this plea be put forward we trust Mr. Harding will be forced as a witness to state the nature of his employment; the amount of work that he does; the income which he receives; and the source from whence he obtained his appointment. We do not think he will receive much public sympathy to atone for the annoyance of such an examination."

As Eleanor read the article her face flushed with indignation, and when she had finished it, she almost feared to look up at her father.

"Well, my dear," said he, "what do you think of that—is it worth while to be a warden at that price?"

"Oh, papa;—dear papa!"

"Mr. Bold can't unwrite that, my dear—Mr. Bold can't say that that shan't be read by every clergyman at Oxford; nay, by every gentleman in the land": and then he walked up and down the room, while Eleanor in mute despair followed him with her eyes. "And I'll tell you what, my dear," he continued, speaking now very calmly, and in a forced manner very unlike himself; "Mr. Bold can't dispute the truth of every word in that article you have just read—nor can I." Eleanor stared at him, as though she scarcely understood the words he was speaking. "Nor can I, Eleanor: that's the worst of all, or would be so if there were no remedy. I have thought much of all this since we were together last night"; and he came and sat beside her, and put his arm round her waist as he had done then. "I have thought much of what the archdeacon has said, and of what this paper says; and I do believe I have no right to be here."

"No right to be warden of the hospital, papa?"

"No right to be warden with eight hundred a year; no right to be warden with such a house as this; no right to spend in luxury money that was intended for charity. Mr. Bold may do as he pleases about his suit, but I hope he will not abandon it for my sake.''

Poor Eleanor! this was hard upon her. Was it for this she had made her great resolve! For this that she had laid aside her quiet demeanour, and taken upon her the rants of a tragedy heroine! One may work and not for thanks, but yet feel hurt at not receiving them; and so it was with Eleanor: one may be disinterested in one's good actions, and yet feel discontented that they are not recognised. Charity may be given with the left hand so privily that the right hand does not know it, and yet the left hand may regret to feel that it has no immediate reward. Eleanor had had no wish to burden her father with a weight of obligation, and yet she had looked forward to much delight from the knowledge that she had freed him from his sorrows: now such hopes were entirely over: all that she had done was of no avail; she had humbled herself to Bold in vain; the evil was utterly beyond her power to cure!

She had thought also how gently she would whisper to her father all that her lover had said to her about herself, and how impossible she had found it to reject him: and then she had anticipated her father's kindly kiss and close embrace as he gave his sanction to her love. Alas! she could say nothing of this now. In speaking of Mr. Bold, her father put him aside as one whose thoughts and sayings and acts could be of no moment. Gentle reader, did you ever feel yourself snubbed? Did you ever, when thinking much of your own importance, find yourself suddenly reduced to a nonentity? Such was Eleanor's feeling now.

"They shall not put forward this plea on my behalf," continued the warden. "Whatever may be the truth of the matter, that at any rate is not true; and the man who wrote that article is right in saying that such a plea is revolting to an honest mind. I will go up to London, my dear, and see these lawyers myself, and if no better excuse can be made for me than that, I and the hospital will part."

"But the archdeacon, papa?"

"I can't help it, my dear; there are some things which a man cannot bear,—I cannot bear that''—and he put his hand upon the newspaper.

"But will the archdeacon go with you?"

To tell the truth, Mr. Harding had made up his mind to steal a march upon the archdeacon. He was aware that he could take no steps without informing his dread son-in-law, but he had resolved that he would send out a note to Plumstead Episcopi detailing his plans, but that the messenger should not leave Barchester till he himself had started for London; so that he might be a day before the doctor, who, he had no doubt, would follow him. In that day, if he had luck, he might arrange it all; he might explain to Sir Abraham that he, as warden, would have nothing further to do with the defence about to be set up; he might send in his official resignation to his friend the bishop, and so make public the whole transaction, that even the doctor would not be able to undo what he had done. He knew too well the doctor's strength and his own weakness to suppose he could do this, if they both reached London together; indeed, he would never be able to get to London, if the doctor knew of his intended journey in time to prevent it.

"No, I think not," said he. "I think I shall start before the archdeacon could be ready—I shall go early to-morrow morning."

"That will be best, papa," said Eleanor, showing that her father's ruse was appreciated.

"Why yes, my love. The fact is, I wish to do all this before the archdeacon can—can interfere. There is a great deal of truth in all he says—he argues very well, and I can't always answer him; but there is an old saying, Nelly: 'Every one knows where his own shoe pinches!' He'll say that I want moral courage, and strength of character, and power of endurance, and it's all true; but I'm sure I ought not to remain here, if I have nothing better to put forward than a quibble: so, Nelly, we shall have to leave this pretty place."

Eleanor's face brightened up, as she assured her father how cordially she agreed with him.

"True, my love," said he, now again quite happy and at ease in his manner. "What good to us is this place or all the money, if we are to be ill-spoken of?"

"Oh, papa, I am so glad!"

"My darling child! It did cost me a pang at first, Nelly, to think that you could lose your pretty drawing-room, and your ponies, and your garden: the garden will be the worst of all—but there is a garden at Crabtree, a very pretty garden."

Crabtree Parva was the name of the small living which Mr. Harding had held as a minor canon, and which still belonged to him. It was only worth some eighty pounds a year, and a small house and glebe, all of which were now handed over to Mr. Harding's curate; but it was to Crabtree glebe that Mr. Harding thought of retiring. This parish must not be mistaken for that other living, Crabtree Canonicorum, as it is called. Crabtree Canonicorum is a very nice thing; there are only two hundred parishioners; there are four hundred acres of glebe; and the great and small tithes, which both go to the rector, are worth four hundred pounds a year more. Crabtree Canonicorum is in the gift of the dean and chapter, and is at this time possessed by the Honourable and Reverend Dr. Vesey Stanhope, who also fills the prebendal stall of Goosegorge in Barchester Chapter, and holds the united rectory of Eiderdown and Stogpingum, or Stoke Pinquium, as it should be written. This is the same Dr. Vesey Stanhope whose hospitable villa on the Lake of Como is so well known to the élite of English travellers, and whose collection of Lombard butterflies is supposed to be unique.

"Yes," said the warden, musing, "there is a very pretty garden at Crabtree; but I shall be sorry to disturb poor Smith." Smith was the curate of Crabtree, a gentleman who was maintaining a wife and half a dozen children on the income arising from his profession.

Eleanor assured her father that, as far as she was concerned, she could leave her house and her ponies without a single regret. She was only so happy that he was going—going where he would escape all this dreadful turmoil.

"But we will take the music, my dear."

And so they went on planning their future happiness, and plotting how they would arrange it all without the interposition of the archdeacon, and at last they again became confidential, and then the warden did thank her for what she had done, and Eleanor, lying on her father's shoulder, did find an opportunity to tell her secret: and the father gave his blessing to his child, and said that the man whom she loved was honest, good, and kind-hearted, and right-thinking in the main—one who wanted only a good wife to put him quite upright—"a man, my love," he ended by saying, "to whom I firmly believe that I can trust my treasure with safety."

"But what will Dr. Grantly say?"

"Well, my dear, it can't be helped—we shall be out at Crabtree then."

And Eleanor ran upstairs to prepare her father's clothes for his journey; and the warden returned to his garden to make his last adieus to every tree, and shrub, and shady nook that he knew so well.

XIV

Mount Olympus

Wretched in spirit, groaning under the feeling of insult, self-condemning, and ill-satisfied in every way, Bold returned to his London lodgings. Ill as he had fared in his interview with the archdeacon, he was not the less under the necessity of carrying out his pledge to Eleanor; and he went about his ungracious task with a heavy heart.

The attorneys whom he had employed in London received his instructions with surprise and evident misgiving; however, they could only obey, and mutter something of their sorrow that such heavy costs should only fall upon their own employer, —especially as nothing was wanting but perseverance to throw them on the opposite party. Bold left the office which he had latterly so much frequented, shaking the dust from off his feet; and before he was down the stairs, an edict had already gone forth for the preparation of the bill.

He next thought of the newspapers. The case had been taken up by more than one; and he was well aware that the keynote had been sounded by the *Jupiter*. He had been very intimate with Tom Towers, and had often discussed with him the affairs of the hospital. Bold could not say that the articles in that paper had been written at his own instigation. He did not even know, as a fact, that they had been written by his friend. Tom Towers had never said that such a view of the case, or such a side in the dispute, would be taken by the paper with which he was connected. Very discreet in such matters was Tom Towers, and altogether indisposed to talk loosely of the concerns of that mighty engine of which it was his high privilege to move in secret some portion. Nonetheless Bold believed that to him were owing those dreadful words which had caused such panic at

Barchester,—and he conceived himself bound to prevent their repetition. With this view he betook himself from the attorneys' to that laboratory where, with amazing chemistry, Tom Towers compounded thunderbolts for the destruction of all that is evil and for the furtherance of all that is good, in this and other hemispheres.

Who has not heard of Mount Olympus,—that high abode of all the powers of type, that favoured seat of the great goddess Pica, that wondrous habitation of gods and devils, from whence, with ceaseless hum of steam and never-ending flow of Castalian ink, issue forth fifty thousand nightly edicts for the governance of a subject nation?

Velvet and gilding do not make a throne, nor gold and jewels a sceptre. It is a throne because the most exalted one sits there;—and a sceptre because the most mighty one wields it. So it is with Mount Olympus. Should a stranger make his way thither at dull noonday, or during the sleepy hours of the silent afternoon, he would find no acknowledged temple of power and beauty, no fitting fane for the great Thunderer, no proud façades and pillared roofs to support the dignity of this greatest of earthly potentates. To the outward and uninitiated eye, Mount Olympus is a somewhat humble spot, undistinguished, unadorned—nay, almost mean. It stands alone, as it were, in a mighty city, close to the densest throng of men, but partaking neither of the noise nor the crowd; a small secluded, dreary spot, tenanted, one would say, by quite unambitious people at the easiest rents. "Is this Mount Olympus?" asks the unbelieving stranger. "Is it from these small, dark, dingy buildings that those infallible laws proceed which cabinets are called upon to obey; by which bishops are to be guided, lords and commons controlled, judges instructed in law, generals in strategy, admirals in naval tactics, and orange-women in the management of their barrows?" "Yes, my friend—from these walls. From here issue the only known infallible bulls for the guidance of British souls and bodies. This little court is the Vatican of England. Here reigns a pope, self-nominated, self-consecrated—ay, and much stranger too—self-believing!—a pope whom, if you cannot obey him, I would advise you to disobey as silently as possible; a pope hitherto afraid of no Luther; a pope who manages his own inquisition, who punishes unbelievers as no most skilful inquisitor of Spain ever dreamt of doing—one who can excommunicate thoroughly, fearfully, radically; put you beyond the pale of men's charity;

make you odious to your dearest friends, and turn you into a monster to be pointed at by the finger!''

Oh heavens! and this is Mount Olympus!

It is a fact amazing to ordinary mortals that the *Jupiter* is never wrong. With what endless care, with what unsparing labour, do we not strive to get together for our great national council the men most fitting to compose it. And how we fail! Parliament is always wrong: look at the *Jupiter,* and see how futile are their meetings, how vain their council, how needless all their trouble! With what pride do we regard our chief ministers, the great servants of state, the oligarchs of the nation on whose wisdom we lean, to whom we look for guidance in our difficulties! But what are they to the writers of the *Jupiter*? They hold council together and with anxious thought painfully elaborate their country's good; but when all is done, the *Jupiter* declares that all is nought. Why should we look to Lord John Russell—why should we regard Palmerston and Gladstone, when Tom Towers without a struggle can put us right? Look at our generals, what faults they make; at our admirals, how inactive they are. What money, honesty, and science can do, is done; and yet how badly are our troops brought together, fed, conveyed, clothed, armed, and managed. The most excellent of our good men do their best to man our ships, with the assistance of all possible external appliances; but in vain. All, all is wrong—alas! alas! Tom Towers, and he alone, knows all about it. Why, oh why, ye earthly ministers, why have ye not followed more closely this heaven-sent messenger that is among us?

Were it not well for us in our ignorance that we confided all things to the *Jupiter*? Would it not be wise in us to abandon useless talking, idle thinking, and profitless labour? Away with majorities in the House of Commons, with verdicts from judicial bench given after much delay, with doubtful laws, and the fallible attempts of humanity! Does not the *Jupiter,* coming forth daily with fifty thousand impressions full of unerring decision on every mortal subject, set all matters sufficiently at rest? Is not Tom Towers here, able to guide us and willing?

Yes indeed, able and willing to guide all men in all things, so long as he is obeyed as autocrat should be obeyed—with undoubting submission: only let not ungrateful ministers seek other colleagues than those whom Tom Towers may approve; let church and state, law and physic, commerce and agriculture, the arts of war, and the arts of peace, all listen and obey, and all will be made perfect. Has not Tom Towers an all-seeing eye? From the diggings of Australia to those of California, right round the habitable globe, does he not know, watch, and chronicle the doings of every one? From a bishopric in New Zealand to an unfortunate director of a North-west passage, is he not the only fit judge of capability? From the sewers of London to the Central Railway of India,—from the palaces of St. Petersburg to the cabins of Connaught, nothing can escape him. Britons have but to read, to obey, and be blessed. None but the fools doubt the wisdom of the *Jupiter;* none but the mad dispute its facts.

No established religion has ever been without its unbelievers, even in the country where it is the most firmly fixed; no creed has been without scoffers; no church has so prospered as to free itself entirely from dissent. There are those who doubt the *Jupiter*! They live and breathe the upper air, walking here unscathed, though scorned—men, born of British mothers and nursed on English milk, who scruple not to say that Mount Olympus has its price, that Tom Towers can be bought for gold!

Such is Mount Olympus, the mouthpiece of all the wisdom of this great country. It may probably be said that no place in this 19th century is more worthy of notice. No treasury mandate armed with the signatures of all the government has half the power of one of those broad sheets, which fly forth from hence so abundantly, armed with no signature at all.

Some great man, some mighty peer—we'll say a noble duke—retires to rest feared and honoured by all his countrymen—fearless himself; if not a good man, at any rate a mighty man—too mighty to care much what men may say about his want of virtue. He rises in the morning degraded, mean, and miserable; an object of men's scorn, anxious only to retire as quickly as may be to some German obscurity, some unseen Italian privacy, or, indeed, anywhere out of sight. What has made this awful change? what has so afflicted him? An article has appeared in the *Jupiter;* some fifty lines of a narrow column have destroyed all his grace's equanimity, and banished him for ever from the world. No man knows who wrote the bitter words; the clubs talk confusedly of the matter, whispering to each other this and that name; while Tom Towers walks quietly along Pall Mall, with his coat buttoned close against the east wind, as though he were a mortal man, and not a god dispensing thunderbolts from Mount Olympus.

It was not to Mount Olympus that our friend Bold betook himself. He had before now wandered round that lonely spot, thinking how grand a thing it was to write articles for the

Jupiter; considering within himself whether by any stretch of the powers within him he could ever come to such distinction; wondering how Tom Towers would take any little humble offering of his talents; calculating that Tom Towers himself must have once had a beginning, have once doubted as to his own success. Towers could not have been born a writer in the *Jupiter*. With such ideas, half ambitious and half awe-struck, had Bold regarded the silent-looking workshop of the gods; but he had never yet by word or sign attempted to influence the slightest word of his unerring friend. On such a course was he now intent; and not without much inward palpitation did he betake himself to the quiet abode of wisdom, where Tom Towers was to be found o' mornings inhaling ambrosia and sipping nectar in the shape of toast and tea.

Not far removed from Mount Olympus, but somewhat nearer to the blessed regions of the West, is the most favoured abode of Themis. Washed by the rich tide which now passes from the towers of Cæsar to Barry's halls of eloquence; and again back, with new offerings of a city's tribute, from the palaces of peers to the mart of merchants, stand those quiet walls which Law has delighted to honour by its presence. What a world within a world is the Temple! how quiet are its "entangled walks," as some one lately has called them, and yet how close to the densest concourse of humanity! how gravely respectable its sober alleys, though removed but by a single step from the profanity of the Strand and the low iniquity of Fleet Street! Old St. Dunstan, with its bell-smiting bludgeoners, has been removed; the ancient shops with their faces full of pleasant history are passing away one by one; the bar itself is to go—its doom has been pronounced by the *Jupiter;* rumour tells us of some huge building that is to appear in these latitudes dedicated to law, subversive of the courts of Westminster, and antagonistic to the Rolls and Lincoln's Inn; but nothing yet threatens the silent beauty of the Temple: it is the mediæval court of the metropolis.

Here, on the choicest spot of this choice ground, stands a lofty row of chambers, looking obliquely upon the sullied Thames; before the windows, the lawn of the Temple Gardens stretches with that dim yet delicious verdure so refreshing to the eyes of Londoners. If doomed to live within the thickest of London smoke you would surely say that that would be your chosen spot. Yes, you, you whom I now address, my dear, middle-aged bachelor friend, can nowhere be so well domiciled as here. No one here will ask whether you are out or at home; alone or with friends; here no Sabbatarian will investigate your Sundays, no censorious landlady will scrutinize your empty bottle, no valetudinarian neighbour will complain of late hours. If you love books, to what place are books so suitable? The whole spot is redolent of typography. Would you worship the Paphian goddess, the groves of Cyprus are not more taciturn than those of the Temple. Wit and wine are always here, and always together; the revels of the Temple are as those of polished Greece, where the wildest worshipper of Bacchus never forgot the dignity of the god whom he adored. Where can retirement be so complete as here? where can you be so sure of all the pleasures of society?

It was here that Tom Towers lived, and cultivated with eminent success the tenth Muse who now governs the periodical press. But let it not be supposed that his chambers were such, or so comfortless, as are frequently the gaunt abodes of legal aspirants. Four chairs, a half-filled deal book-case with hangings of dingy green baize, an old office table covered with dusty papers, which are not moved once in six months, and an older Pembroke brother with rickety legs, for all daily uses; a despatcher for the preparation of lobsters and coffee, and an apparatus for the cooking of toast and mutton chops; such utensils and luxuries as these did not suffice for the well-being of Tom Towers. He indulged in four rooms on the first floor, each of which was furnished, if not with the splendour, with probably more than the comfort of Stafford House. Every addition that science and art have lately made to the luxuries of modern life was to be found there. The room in which he usually sat was surrounded by book-shelves carefully filled; nor was there a volume there which was not entitled to its place in such a collection, both by its intrinsic worth and exterior splendour: a pretty portable set of steps in one corner of the room showed that those even on the higher shelves were intended for use. The chamber contained but two works of art—the one, an admirable bust of Sir Robert Peel, by Power, declared the individual politics of our friend; and the other, a singularly long figure of a female devotee, by Millais, told equally plainly the school of art to which he was addicted. This picture was not hung, as pictures usually are, against the wall; there was no inch of wall vacant for such a purpose: it had a stand or desk erected for its own accommodation; and there on her pedestal, framed and glazed, stood the devotional lady looking intently at a lily as no lady ever looked before.

Our modern artists, whom we style Pre-Raphaelites, have delighted to go back, not only to the finish and peculiar manner, but also to the subjects of the early painters. It is impossible to give them too much praise for the elaborate perseverance with which they have equalled the minute perfections of the masters from whom they take their inspiration: nothing probably can exceed the painting of some of these latter-day pictures. It is, however, singular into what faults they fall as regards their subjects: they are not quite content to take the old stock groups—a Sebastian with his arrows, a Lucia with her eyes in a dish, a Lorenzo with a gridiron, or the Virgin with two children. But they are anything but happy in their change. As a rule, no figure should be drawn in a position which it is impossible to suppose any figure should maintain. The patient endurance of St. Sebastian, the wild ecstasy of St. John in the Wilderness, the maternal love of the Virgin, are feelings naturally portrayed by a fixed posture; but the lady with the stiff back and bent neck, who looks at her flower, and is still looking from hour to hour, gives us an idea of pain without grace, and abstraction without a cause.

It was easy, from his rooms, to see that Tom Towers was a Sybarite, though by no means an idle one. He was lingering over his last cup of tea, surrounded by an ocean of newspapers, through which he had been swimming, when John Bold's card was brought in by his tiger. This tiger never knew that his master was at home, though he often knew that he was not, and thus Tom Towers was never invaded but by his own consent. On this occasion, after twisting the card twice in his fingers, he signified to his attendant imp that he was visible; and the inner door was unbolted, and our friend announced.

I have before said that he of the *Jupiter* and John Bold were intimate. There was no very great difference in their ages, for Towers was still considerably under forty; and when Bold had been attending the London hospitals, Towers, who was not then the great man that he had since become, had been much with him. Then they had often discussed together the objects of their ambition and future prospects; then Tom Towers was struggling hard to maintain himself, as a briefless barrister, by short-hand reporting for any of the papers that would engage him; then he had not dared to dream of writing leaders for the *Jupiter*, or canvassing the conduct of Cabinet ministers. Things had altered since that time: the briefless barrister was still briefless, but he now despised briefs: could he have been sure of a judge's seat, he would hardly have left his present career. It is true he wore no ermine, bore no outward marks of a world's respect; but with what a load of inward importance was he charged! It is true his name appeared in no large capitals; on no wall was chalked up "Tom Towers for ever"—"Freedom of the Press and Tom Towers"; but what member of Parliament had half his power? It is true that in far-off provinces men did not talk daily of Tom Towers but they read the *Jupiter,* and acknowledged that without the *Jupiter* life was not worth having. This kind of hidden but still conscious glory suited the nature of the man. He loved to sit silent in a corner of his club and listen to the loud chattering of politicians, and to think how they all were in his power—how he could smite the loudest of them, were it worth his while to raise his pen for such a purpose. He loved to watch the great men of whom he daily wrote, and flatter himself that he was greater than any of them. Each of them was responsible to his country, each of them must answer if inquired into, each of them must endure abuse with good humour, and insolence without anger. But to whom was he, Tom Towers, responsible? No one could insult him; no one could inquire into him. He could speak out withering words, and no one could answer him: ministers courted him, though perhaps they knew not his name; bishops feared him; judges doubted their own verdicts unless he confirmed them; and generals, in their councils of war, did not consider more deeply what the enemy would do, than what the *Jupiter* would say. Tom Towers never boasted of the *Jupiter;* he scarcely ever named the paper even to the most intimate of his friends; he did not even wish to be spoken of as connected with it; but he did not the less value his privileges, or think the less of his own importance. It is probable that Tom Towers considered himself the most powerful man in Europe; and so he walked on from day to day, studiously striving to look a man, but knowing within his breast that he was a god.

XV

Tom Towers, Dr. Anticant, and Mr. Sentiment

"Ah, Bold! how are you? You haven't breakfasted?"

"Oh yes, hours ago. And how are you?"

When one Esquimau meets another, do the two, as an invariable rule, ask after each other's health? is it inherent in all human nature to make this obliging inquiry? Did any reader of this tale ever meet any friend or acquaintance without asking some such question, and did any one ever listen to the reply? Sometimes a studiously courteous questioner will show so much thought in the matter as to answer it himself, by declaring that had he looked at you he needn't have asked; meaning thereby to signify that you are an absolute personification of health: but such persons are only those who premeditate small effects.

"I suppose you're busy?" inquired Bold.

"Why, yes, rather; or I should say rather not. I have a leisure hour in the day, this is it."

"I want to ask you if you can oblige me in a certain matter."

Towers understood in a moment, from the tone of his friend's voice, that the certain matter referred to the newspaper. He smiled, and nodded his head, but made no promise.

"You know this lawsuit that I've been engaged in," said Bold.

Tom Towers intimated that he was aware of the action which was pending about the hospital.

"Well, I've abandoned it."

Tom Towers merely raised his eyebrows, thrust his hands into his trousers' pockets, and waited for his friend to proceed.

"Yes, I've given it up. I needn't trouble you with all the

115

history; but the fact is that the conduct of Mr. Harding—— Mr. Harding is the——''

"Oh, yes, the master of the place; the man who takes all the money and does nothing," said Tom Towers, interrupting him.

"Well, I don't know about that; but his conduct in the matter has been so excellent, so little selfish, so open, that I cannot proceed in the matter to his detriment." Bold's heart misgave him as to Eleanor as he said this; and yet he felt that what he said was not untrue. "I think nothing should now be done till the wardenship be vacant."

"And be again filled," said Towers, "as it certainly would, before any one heard of the vacancy; and the same objection would again exist. It's an old story that of the vested rights of the incumbent; but suppose the incumbent has only a vested wrong, and that the poor of the town have a vested right, if they only knew how to get at it: is not that something the case here?"

Bold couldn't deny it, but thought it was one of those cases which required a good deal of management before any real good could be done. It was a pity that he had not considered this before he crept into the lion's mouth, in the shape of an attorney's office.

"It will cost you a good deal, I fear," said Towers.

"A few hundreds," said Bold—"perhaps three hundred; I can't help that, and am prepared for it."

"That's philosophical. It's quite refreshing to hear a man talking of his hundreds in so purely indifferent a manner. But I'm sorry you are giving the matter up. It injures a man to commence a thing of this kind, and not carry it through. Have you seen that?" and he threw a small pamphlet across the table, which was all but damp from the press.

Bold had not seen it nor heard of it; but he was well acquainted with the author of it—a gentleman whose pamphlets, condemnatory of all things in these modern days, had been a good deal talked about of late.

Dr. Pessimist Anticant was a Scotchman, who had passed a great portion of his early days in Germany; he had studied there with much effect, and had learnt to look with German subtilty into the root of things, and to examine for himself their intrinsic worth and worthlessness. No man ever resolved more bravely than he to accept as good nothing that was evil; to banish from him as evil nothing that was good. 'Tis a pity that he should not have recognised the fact, that in this world no good is unalloyed, and that there is but little evil that has not in it some seed of what is goodly.

Returning from Germany, he had astonished the reading public by the vigour of his thoughts, put forth in the quaintest language. He cannot write English, said the critics. No matter, said the public; we can read what he does write, and that without yawning. And so Dr. Pessimist Anticant became popular. Popularity spoilt him for all further real use, as it has done many another. While, with some diffidence, he confined his objurgations to the occasional follies or shortcomings of mankind; while he ridiculed the energy of the squire devoted to the slaughter of partridges, or the mistake of some noble patron who turned a poet into a gauger of beer-barrels, it was all well; we were glad to be told our faults and to look forward to the coming millennium, when all men, having sufficiently studied the works of Dr. Anticant, would become truthful and energetic. But the doctor mistook the signs of the times and the minds of men, instituted himself censor of things in general, and began the great task of reprobating everything and everybody, without further promise of any millennium at all. This was not so well; and, to tell the truth, our author did not succeed in his undertaking. His theories were all beautiful, and the code of morals that he taught us certainly an improvement on the practices of the age. We all of us could, and many of us did, learn much from the doctor while he chose to remain vague, mysterious, and cloudy: but when he became practical, the charm was gone.

His allusion to the poet and the partridges was received very well. "Oh, my poor brother," said he, "slaughtered partridges a score of brace to each gun, and poets gauging ale-barrels, with sixty pounds a year, at Dumfries, are not the signs of a great era!—perhaps of the smallest possible era yet written of. Whatever economies we pursue, political or other, let us see at once that this is the maddest of the uneconomic: partridges killed by our land magnates at, shall we say, a guinea a head, to be retailed in Leadenhall at one shilling and ninepence, with one poacher in limbo for every fifty birds! our poet, maker, creator, gauging ale, and that badly, with no leisure for making or creating, only a little leisure for drinking, and such like beer-barrel avocations! Truly, a cutting of blocks with fine razors while we scrape our chins so uncomfortably with rusty knives! Oh, my political economist, master of supply and demand, division of labour and high pressure—oh, my loud-speaking friend, tell me, if so much be in you, what is the demand for poets in these kingdoms of Queen Victoria, and what the vouch-safed supply?''

This was all very well: this gave us some hope. We might do better with our next poet, when we got one; and though the partridges might not be abandoned, something could perhaps be done as to the poachers. We were unwilling, however, to take lessons in politics from so misty a professor; and when he came to tell us that the heroes of Westminster were naught we began to think that he had written enough. His attack upon despatch boxes was not thought to have much in it; but as it is short, the doctor shall again be allowed to speak his sentiments.

"Could utmost ingenuity in the management of red tape avail anything to men lying gasping—we may say, all but dead; could despatch boxes with never-so-much velvet lining and Chubb's patent, be of comfort to a people *in extremis,* I also, with so many others, would, with parched tongue, call on the name of Lord John Russell; or, my brother, at your advice, on Lord Aberdeen; or, my cousin, on Lord Derby, at yours; being, with my parched tongue, indifferent to such matters. 'Tis all one. Oh, Derby! Oh, Gladstone! Oh, Palmerston! Oh, Lord John! Each comes running with serene face and despatch box. Vain physicians! though there were hosts of such, no despatch box will cure this disorder! What! are there other doctors' new names, disciples who have not burdened their souls with tape? Well, let us call again. Oh, Disraeli, great oppositionist, man of the bitter brow! or, Oh, Molesworth, great reformer, thou who promisest Utopia. They come; each with that serene face, and each—alas, me! alas, my country!—each with a despatch box!

"Oh, the serenity of Downing Street!

"My brothers, when hope was over on the battlefield, when no dimmest chance of victory remained, the ancient Roman could hide his face within his toga, and die gracefully. Can you and I do so now? If so, 'twere best for us; if not, oh my brothers, we must die disgracefully, for hope of life and victory I see none left to us in this world below. I for one cannot trust much to serene face and despatch box!''

There might be truth in this, there might be depth of reasoning; but Englishmen did not see enough in the argument to induce them to withdraw their confidence from the present arrangements of the government, and Dr. Anticant's monthly pamphlet on the decay of the world did not receive so much attention as his earlier works. He did not confine himself to politics in these publications, but roamed at large over all matters of public interest, and found everything bad. According to him nobody was true, and not only nobody, but nothing; a man could not take off his hat to a lady without telling a lie—the lady would lie again in smiling. The ruffles of the gentleman's shirt would be fraught with deceit, and the lady's flounces full of falsehood. Was ever anything more severe than that attack of his on chip bonnets, or the anathemas with which he endeavoured to dust the powder out of the bishops' wigs?

The pamphlet which Tom Towers now pushed across the table was entitled *Modern Charity*, and was written with the view of proving how much in the way of charity was done by our predecessors—how little by the present age; and it ended by a comparison between ancient and modern times, very little to the credit of the latter.

"Look at this," said Towers, getting up and turning over the pages of the pamphlet, and pointing to a passage near the end. "Your friend the warden, who is so little selfish, won't like that, I fear." Bold read as follows—

"Heavens, what a sight! Let us with eyes wide open see the godly man of four centuries since, the man of the dark ages; let us see how he does his godlike work, and again, how the godly man of these latter days does his.

"Shall we say that the former is one walking painfully through the world, regarding, as a prudent man, his worldly work, prospering in it as a diligent man will prosper, but always with an eye to that better treasure to which thieves do not creep in? Is there not much nobility in that old man, as, leaning on his oaken staff, he walks down the high street of his native town, and receives from all courteous salutation and acknowledgment of his worth? A noble old man, by august inhabitants of Belgrave Square and such like vicinity—a very noble old man, though employed no better than in the wholesale carding of wool.

"This carding of wool, however, did in those days bring with it much profit, so that our ancient friend, when dying, was declared, in whatever slang then prevailed, to cut up exceeding well. For sons and daughters there was ample sustenance with assistance of due industry; for friends and relatives some relief for grief at this great loss; for aged dependants comfort in declining years. This was much for one old man to get done in that dark fifteenth century. But this was not all: coming generations of poor woolcarders would bless the name of this rich one; and a hospital should be founded and endowed with his wealth for the feeding of such of the trade as could not, by diligent carding, any longer duly feed themselves.

" 'Twas thus that an old man in the fifteenth century did his godlike work to the best of his power, and not ignobly, as appears to me.

"We will now take our godly man of later days. He shall no longer be a woolcarder, for such are not now men of mark. We will suppose him to be one of the best of the good, one who has lacked no opportunities. Our old friend was, after all, but illiterate; our modern friend shall be a man educated in all seemly knowledge; he shall, in short, be that blessed thing—a clergyman of the Church of England!

"And now, in what perfectest manner does he in this lower world get his godlike work done and put out of hand? Heavens! in the strangest of manners. Oh, my brother! in a manner not at all to be believed but by the most minute testimony of eyesight. He does it by the magnitude of his appetite—by the power of his gorge; his only occupation is to swallow the bread prepared with so much anxious care for these impoverished carders of wool—that, and to sing indifferently through his nose once in the week some psalm more or less long—the shorter the better, we should be inclined to say.

"Oh, my civilised friends!—great Britons that never will be slaves, men advanced to infinite state of freedom and knowledge of good and evil—tell me, will you, what becoming monument you will erect to an highly-educated clergyman of the Church of England?"

Bold certainly thought that his friend would not like that: he could not conceive anything that he would like less than this. To what a world of toil and trouble had he, Bold, given rise by his indiscreet attack upon the hospital!

"You see," said Towers, "that this affair has been much talked of, and the public are with you. I am sorry you should give the matter up. Have you seen the first number of the *Almshouse*?"

No; Bold had not seen the *Almshouse*. He had seen advertisements of Mr. Popular Sentiment's new novel of that name, but had in no way connected it with Barchester Hospital, and had never thought a moment on the subject.

"It's a direct attack on the whole system," said Towers. "It'll go a long way to put down Rochester, and Barchester, and Dulwich, and St. Cross, and all such hotbeds of peculation. It's very clear that Sentiment has been down to Barchester, and got up the whole story there; indeed, I thought he must have had it all from you. It's very well done, as you'll see: his first numbers always are.''

Bold declared that Mr. Sentiment had got nothing from him, and that he was deeply grieved to find that the case had become so notorious.

''The fire has gone too far to be quenched,'' said Towers; ''the building must go now; and as the timbers are all rotten, why, I should be inclined to say, the sooner the better. I expected to see you get some éclat in the matter.''

This was all wormwood to Bold. He had done enough to make his friend the warden miserable for life, and had then backed out just when the success of his project was sufficient to make the question one of real interest. How weakly he had managed his business! he had already done the harm, and then stayed his hand when the good which he had in view was to be commenced. How delightful would it have been to have employed all his energy in such a cause—to have been backed by the *Jupiter,* and written up to by two of the most popular authors of the day! The idea opened a view into the very world in which he wished to live. To what might it not have given rise? what delightful intimacies—what public praise—to what Athenian banquets and rich flavour of Attic salt?

This, however, was now past hope. He had pledged himself to abandon the cause; and could he have forgotten the pledge, he had gone too far to retreat. He was now, this moment, sitting in Tom Towers' room with the object of deprecating any further articles in the *Jupiter,* and, greatly as he disliked the job, his petition to that effect must be made.

''I couldn't continue it,'' said he, ''because I found I was in the wrong.''

Tom Towers shrugged his shoulders. How could a successful man be in the wrong! ''In that case,'' said he, ''of course you must abandon it.''

''And I called this morning to ask you also to abandon it,'' said Bold.

''To ask me,'' said Tom Towers, with the most placid of smiles, and a consummate look of gentle surprise, as though Tom Towers was well aware that he of all men was the last to meddle in such matters.

''Yes,'' said Bold, almost trembling with hesitation. ''The *Jupiter,* you know, has taken the matter up very strongly. Mr. Harding has felt what it has said deeply; and I thought that if I could explain to you that he personally has not been to blame, these articles might be discontinued.''

How calmly impassive was Tom Towers' face, as this innocent little proposition was made! Had Bold addressed himself to the doorposts in Mount Olympus, they would have shown as much outward sign of assent or dissent. His quiescence was quite admirable; his discretion certainly more than human.

"My dear fellow,'' said he, when Bold had quite done speaking, "I really cannot answer for the *Jupiter*.''

"But if you saw that these articles were unjust, I think that you would endeavour to put a stop to them. Of course nobody doubts that you could, if you chose.''

"Nobody and everybody are always very kind, but unfortunately are generally very wrong.''

"Come, come, Towers,'' said Bold, plucking up his courage, and remembering that for Eleanor's sake he was bound to make his best exertion; "I have no doubt in my own mind but that you wrote the articles yourself, and very well written they were: it will be a great favour if you will in future abstain from any personal allusions to poor Harding.''

"My dear Bold,'' said Tom Towers, "I have a sincere regard for you. I have known you for many years, and value your friendship; I hope you will let me explain to you, without offence, that none who are connected with the public press can with propriety listen to interference.''

"Interference!'' said Bold, "I don't want to interfere.''

"Ah, but, my dear fellow, you do; what else is it? You think that I am able to keep certain remarks out of a newspaper. Your information is probably incorrect, as most public gossip on such subjects is; but, at any rate, you think I have such power, and you ask me to use it: now that is interference.''

"Well, if you choose to call it so.''

"And now suppose for a moment that I had this power, and used it as you wish: isn't it clear that it would be a great abuse? Certain men are employed in writing for the public press; and if they are induced either to write or to abstain from writing by private motives, surely the public press would soon be of little value. Look at the recognised worth of different newspapers, and see if it does not mainly depend on the assurance which the public feel that such a paper is, or is not, independent. You alluded to the *Jupiter:* surely you cannot but see that the weight of the *Jupiter* is too great to be moved by any private request, even though it should be made to a much more influential person than myself: you've only to think of this, and you'll see that I am right.''

The discretion of Tom Towers was boundless: there was no contradicting what he said, no arguing against such propositions. He took such high ground that there was no getting on it. ''The public is defrauded,'' said he, ''whenever private considerations are allowed to have weight.'' Quite true, thou greatest oracle of the middle of the nineteenth century, thou sententious proclaimer of the purity of the press—the public is defrauded when it is purposely misled. Poor public! how often it is misled! against what a world of fraud has it to contend!

Bold took his leave, and got out of the room as quickly as he could, inwardly denouncing his friend Tom Towers as a prig and a humbug. ''I know he wrote those articles,'' said Bold to himself. ''I know he got his information from me. He was ready enough to take my word for gospel when it suited his own views, and to set Mr. Harding up before the public as an impostor on no other testimony than my chance conversation; but when I offer him real evidence opposed to his own views, he tells me that private motives are detrimental to public justice! Confound his arrogance! What is any public question but a conglomeration of private interests? What is any newspaper article but an expression of the views taken by one side? Truth! it takes an age to ascertain the truth of any question! The idea of Tom Towers talking of public motives and purity of purpose! Why, it wouldn't give him a moment's uneasiness to change his politics to-morrow, if the paper required it.''

Such were John Bold's inward exclamations as he made his way out of the quiet labyrinth of the Temple; and yet there was no position of worldly power so coveted in Bold's ambition as that held by the man of whom he was thinking. It was the impregnability of the place which made Bold so angry with the possessor of it, and it was the same quality which made it appear so desirable.

Passing into the Strand, he saw in a bookseller's window an announcement of the first number of the *Almshouse;* so he purchased a copy, and hurrying back to his lodgings, proceeded to ascertain what Mr. Popular Sentiment had to say to the public on the subject which had lately occupied so much of his own attention.

In former times great objects were attained by great work. When evils were to be reformed, reformers set about their heavy task with grave decorum and laborious argument. An age was occupied in proving a grievance, and philosophical researches were printed in folio pages, which it took a life to write, and an eternity to read. We get on now with a lighter step, and quicker: ridicule is found to be more convincing than argument, imaginary agonies touch more than true sorrows, and monthly novels convince, when learned quartos fail to do so. If the world is to be set right, the work will be done by shilling numbers.

Of all such reformers Mr. Sentiment is the most powerful. It is incredible the number of evil practices he has put down: it is to be feared he will soon lack subjects, and that when he has made the working classes comfortable, and got bitter beer put into proper-sized pint bottles, there will be nothing further for him left to do. Mr. Sentiment is certainly a very powerful man, and perhaps not the less so that his good poor people are so very good; his hard rich people so very hard; and the genuinely honest so very honest. Namby-pamby in these days is not thrown away if it be introduced in the proper quarters. Divine peeresses are no longer interesting, though possessed of every virtue; but a pattern peasant or an immaculate manufacturing hero may talk as much twaddle as one of Mrs. Ratcliffe's heroines, and still be listened to. Perhaps, however, Mr. Sentiment's great attraction is in his second-rate characters. If his heroes and heroines walk upon stilts, as heroes and heroines, I fear, ever must, their attendant satellites are as natural as though one met them in the street: they walk and talk like men and women, and live among our friends a rattling, lively life; yes, live, and will live till the names of their calling shall be forgotten in their own, and Buckett and Mrs. Gamp will be the only words left to us to signify a detective police officer or a monthly nurse.

The Almshouse opened with a scene in a clergyman's house. Every luxury to be purchased by wealth was described as being there: all the appearances of household indulgence generally found amongst the most self-indulgent of the rich were crowded into this abode. Here the reader was introduced to the demon of the book, the Mephistopheles of the drama. What story was ever written without a demon? What novel, what history, what work of any sort, what world, would be perfect without existing principles both of good and evil? The demon of the *Almshouse* was the clerical owner of this comfortable abode. He was a man well stricken in years, but still strong to do evil: he was one who looked cruelly out of a hot, passionate, bloodshot eye; who had a huge red nose with a carbuncle, thick lips, and a great double, flabby chin, which swelled out into solid substance, like a turkey cock's comb, when sudden anger inspired him: he had a hot, furrowed, low brow, from which a few grizzled hairs were not yet rubbed off by the friction of his handkerchief: he wore a loose unstarched white handkerchief, black loose ill-made clothes, and huge loose shoes, adapted to many corns and various bunions: his husky voice told tales of much daily port wine, and his language was not so decorous as became a clergyman. Such was the master of Mr. Sentiment's *Almshouse*. He was a widower, but at present accompanied by two daughters, and a thin and somewhat insipid curate. One of the young ladies was devoted to her father and the fashionable world, and she of course was the favourite; the other was equally addicted to Puseyism and the curate.

The second chapter of course introduced the reader to the more especial inmates of the hospital. Here were discovered eight old men; and it was given to be understood that four vacancies remained unfilled, through the perverse ill-nature of the clerical gentleman with the double chin. The state of these eight paupers was touchingly dreadful: sixpence-farthing a day had been sufficient for their diet when the almshouse was founded; and on sixpence-farthing a day were they still doomed to starve, though food was four times as dear, and money four times as plentiful. It was shocking to find how the conversation of these eight starved old men in their dormitory shamed that of the clergyman's family in his rich drawing-room. The absolute words they uttered were not perhaps spoken in the purest English, and it might be difficult to distinguish from their dialect to what part of the country they belonged; the beauty of the sentiment, however, amply atoned for the imperfection of the language; and it was really a pity that these eight old men could not be sent through the country as moral missionaries, instead of being immured and starved in that wretched almshouse.

Bold finished the number; and as he threw it aside, he thought that that at least had no direct appliance to Mr. Harding, and that the absurdly strong colouring of the picture would disenable the work from doing either good or harm. He was wrong. The artist who paints for the million must use glaring colours, as no one knew better than Mr. Sentiment when he described the inhabitants of his almshouse; and the radical reform which has now swept over such establishments has owed more to the twenty numbers of Mr. Sentiment's novel, than to all the true complaints which have escaped from the public for the last half century.

XVI

A Long Day in London

The warden had to make use of all his very moderate power of intrigue to give his son-in-law the slip, and get out of Barchester without being stopped on his road. No schoolboy ever ran away from school with more precaution and more dread of detection; no convict, slipping down from a prison wall, ever feared to see the gaoler more entirely than Mr. Harding did to see his son-in-law as he drove up in the pony carriage to the railway station, on the morning of his escape to London.

The evening before he went he wrote a note to the archdeacon, explaining that he should start on the morrow on his journey; that it was his intention to see the attorney-general if possible, and to decide on his future plans in accordance with what he heard from that gentleman; he excused himself for giving Dr. Grantly no earlier notice, by stating that his resolve was very sudden; and having entrusted this note to Eleanor, with the perfect, though not expressed, understanding that it was to be sent over to Plumstead Episcopi without haste, he took his departure.

He also prepared and carried with him a note for Sir Abraham Haphazard, in which he stated his name, explaining that he was the defendant in the case of "The Queen on behalf of the Woolcarders of Barchester *v.* Trustees under the will of the late John Hiram," for so was the suit denominated, and begged the illustrious and learned gentleman to vouchsafe to him ten minutes' audience at any hour on the next day. Mr. Harding calculated that for that one day he was safe; his son-in-law, he had no doubt, would arrive in town by an early train, but not early enough to reach the truant till he should have escaped from his hotel after breakfast; and could he thus manage to see the lawyer on that very day, the deed might be done before the archdeacon could interfere.

On his arrival in town the warden drove, as was his wont, to the Chapter Hotel and Coffee House, near St. Paul's. His visits to London of late had not been frequent; but in those happy days when Harding's *Church Music* was going through the press, he had been often there; and as the publisher's house was in Paternoster Row, and the printer's press in Fleet Street, the Chapter Hotel and Coffee House had been convenient. It was a quiet, sombre, clerical house, beseeming such a man as the warden, and thus he afterwards frequented it. Had he dared, he would on this occasion have gone elsewhere to throw the archdeacon further off the scent; but he did not know what violent steps his son-in-law might take for his recovery if he were not found at his usual haunt, and he deemed it not prudent to make himself the object of a hunt through London.

Arrived at his inn, he ordered dinner, and went forth to the attorney-general's chambers. There he learnt that Sir Abraham was in Court, and would not probably return that day. He would go direct from Court to the House; all appointments were, as a rule, made at the chambers; the clerk could by no means promise an interview for the next day; was able, on the other hand, to say that such interview was, he thought, impossible; but that Sir Abraham would certainly be at the House in the course of the night, where an answer from himself might possibly be elicited.

To the House Mr. Harding went, and left his note, not finding Sir Abraham there. He added a most piteous entreaty that he might be favoured with an answer that evening, for which he would return. He then journeyed back sadly to the Chapter Coffee House, digesting his great thoughts, as best he might, in a clattering omnibus, wedged in between a wet old lady and a journeyman glazier returning from his work with his tools in his lap. In melancholy solitude he discussed his mutton chop and pint of port. What is there in this world more melancholy than such a dinner? A dinner, though eaten alone, in a country hotel may be worthy of some energy; the waiter, if you are known, will make much of you; the landlord will make you a bow and perhaps put the fish on the table; if you ring you are attended to, and there is some life about it. A dinner at a London eating-house is also lively enough, if it have no other attraction. There is plenty of noise and stir about it, and the rapid whirl of voices and rattle of dishes disperses sadness. But a solitary dinner in an old, respectable, sombre, solid London inn, where nothing makes any noise but the old waiter's creaking shoes; where one plate slowly goes and another slowly comes without a sound; where the two or three guests would as soon think of knocking each other down as of speaking; where the servants whisper, and the whole household is disturbed if an order be given above the voice—what can be more melancholy than a mutton chop and a pint of port in such a place?

Having gone through this Mr. Harding got into another omnibus, and again returned to the House. Yes, Sir Abraham was there, and was that moment on his legs, fighting eagerly for the hundred and seventh clause of the Convent Custody Bill. Mr. Harding's note had been delivered to him; and if Mr. Harding would wait some two or three hours, Sir Abraham could be asked whether there was any answer. The House was not full, and perhaps Mr. Harding might get admittance into the Strangers' Gallery, which admission, with the help of five shillings, Mr. Harding was able to effect.

This bill of Sir Abraham's had been read a second time and passed into committee. A hundred and six clauses had already been discussed and had occupied only four mornings and five evening sittings: nine of the hundred and six clauses were passed, fifty-five were withdrawn by consent, fourteen had been altered so as to mean the reverse of the original proposition, eleven had been postponed for further consideration, and seventeen had been directly negatived. The hundred and seventh ordered the bodily searching of nuns for Jesuitical symbols by aged clergymen, and was considered to be the real mainstay of the whole bill. No intention had ever existed to pass such a law as that proposed, but the government did not intend to abandon it till their object was fully attained by the discussion of this clause. It was known that it would be insisted on with terrible vehemence by Protestant Irish members, and as vehemently denounced by the Roman Catholic; and it was justly considered that no further union between the parties would be possible after such a battle. The innocent Irish fell into the trap as they always do, and whisky and poplins became a drug in the market.

A florid-faced gentleman with a nice head of hair, from the south of Ireland, had succeeded in catching the speaker's eye by the time that Mr. Harding had got into the gallery, and was denouncing the proposed sacrilege, his whole face glowing with a fine theatrical frenzy.

"And this is a Christian country?" said he. (Loud cheers; counter cheers from the ministerial benches. "Some doubt as to that," from a voice below the gangway.) "No, it can be no Christian country, in which the head of the bar, the lagal adviser (loud laughter and cheers)—yes, I say the lagal adviser of the crown (great cheers and laughter)—can stand up in his seat in this house (prolonged cheers and laughter), and attempt to lagalise indacent assaults on the bodies of religious ladies." (Deafening cheers and laughter, which were prolonged till the honourable member resumed his seat.)

When Mr. Harding had listened to this and much more of the same kind for about three hours, he returned to the door of the House, and received back from the messenger his own note, with the following words scrawled in pencil on the back of it: "To-morrow, 10 P.M.—my chambers.—A.H."

He was so far successful,—but 10 P.M.: what an hour Sir Abraham had named for a legal interview! Mr. Harding felt perfectly sure that long before that Dr. Grantly would be in London. Dr. Grantly could not, however, know that this interview had been arranged, nor could he learn it unless he managed to get hold of Sir Abraham before that hour; and as this was very improbable, Mr. Harding determined to start from his hotel early, merely leaving word that he should dine out, and unless luck were much against him, he might still escape the archdeacon till his return from the attorney-general's chambers.

He was at breakfast at nine, and for the twentieth time consulted his Bradshaw, to see at what earliest hour Dr. Grantly could arrive from Barchester. As he examined the columns, he was nearly petrified by the reflection that perhaps the archdeacon might come up by the night mail-train! His heart sank within him at the horrid idea, and for a moment he felt himself dragged back to Barchester without accomplishing any portion of his object. Then he remembered that had Dr. Grantly done so, he would have been in the hotel, looking for him long since.

"Waiter," said he, timidly.

The waiter approached, creaking in his shoes, but voiceless.

"Did any gentleman—a clergyman, arrive here by the night mail-train?"

"No, sir, not one," whispered the waiter, putting his mouth nearly close to the warden's ear.

Mr. Harding was reassured.

"Waiter," said he again, and the waiter again creaked up.

"If any one calls for me, I am going to dine out, and shall return about eleven o'clock."

The waiter nodded, but did not this time vouchsafe any reply; and Mr. Harding, taking up his hat, proceeded out to pass a long day in the best way he could, somewhere out of sight of the archdeacon.

Bradshaw had told him twenty times that Dr. Grantly could not be at Paddington station till 2 P.M., and our poor friend might therefore have trusted to the shelter of the hotel for some hours longer with perfect safety; but he was nervous. There was no knowing what steps the archdeacon might take for his apprehension: a message by electric telegraph might desire the landlord of the hotel to set a watch upon him; some letter might come which he might find himself unable to disobey; at any rate, he could not feel himself secure in any place at which the archdeacon could expect to find him; and at 10 A.M. he started forth to spend twelve hours in London.

Mr. Harding had friends in town had he chosen to seek them; but he felt that he was in no humour for ordinary calls, and he did not now wish to consult with any one as to the great step which he had determined to take. As he had said to his daughter, no one knows where the shoe pinches but the wearer. There are some points on which no man can be contented to follow the advice of another—some subjects on which a man can consult his own conscience only. Our warden had made up his mind that it was good for him at any cost to get rid of this grievance; his daughter was the only person whose concurrence appeared necessary to him, and she did concur with him most heartily. Under such circumstances he would not, if he could help it, consult any one further, till advice would be useless. Should the archdeacon catch him, indeed, there would be much advice, and much consultation of a kind not to be avoided; but he hoped better things; and as he felt that he could not now converse on indifferent subjects, he resolved to see no one till after his interview with the attorney-general.

He determined to take sanctuary in Westminster Abbey, so he again went thither in an omnibus, and finding that the doors were not open for morning service, he paid his twopence, and went in as a sightseer. It occurred to him that he had no definite place of rest for the day, and that he should be absolutely worn out before his interview if he attempted to walk about from 10 A.M. to 10 P.M., so he sat himself down on a stone step, and gazed

up at the figure of William Pitt, who looks as though he had just
entered the church for the first time in his life and was anything
but pleased at finding himself there.

He had been sitting unmolested about twenty minutes when
the verger asked him whether he wouldn't like to walk around.
Mr. Harding didn't want to walk anywhere, and declined, merely
observing that he was waiting for the morning service. The
verger seeing that he was a clergyman, told him that the doors of
the choir were now open, and showed him into a seat. This was
a great point gained; the archdeacon would certainly not come to
morning service at Westminster Abbey, even though he were in
London; and here the warden could rest quietly, and, when the
time came, duly say his prayers.

He longed to get up from his seat, and examine the music-
books of the choristers, and the copy of the litany from which the
service was chanted, to see how far the little details at Westminster corresponded with those at Barchester, and whether he
thought his own voice would fill the church well from the
Westminster precentor's seat. There would, however, be impropriety in such meddling, and he sat perfectly still, looking up at
the noble roof, and guarding against the coming fatigues of the
day.

By degrees two or three people entered; the very same damp
old woman who had nearly obliterated him in the omnibus, or
some other just like her; a couple of young ladies with their veils
down, and gilt crosses conspicuous on their prayer-books; an old
man on crutches; a party who were seeing the abbey, and
thought they might as well hear the service for their twopence, as
opportunity served; and a young woman with her prayer-book
done up in her handkerchief, who rushed in late, and, in her
hurried entry, tumbled over one of the forms, and made such a
noise that every one, even the officiating minor canon, was
startled, and she herself was so frightened by the echo of her
own catastrophe that she was nearly thrown into fits by the
panic.

Mr. Harding was not much edified by the manner of the
service. The minor canon in question hurried in, somewhat late,
in a surplice not in the neatest order, and was followed by a
dozen choristers, who were also not as trim as they might have
been: they all jostled into their places with a quick hurried step,
and the service was soon commenced. Soon commenced and
soon over—for there was no music, and time was not unnecessar-

ily lost in the chanting. On the whole Mr. Harding was of opinion that things were managed better at Barchester, though even there he knew that there was room for improvement.

It appears to us a question whether any clergyman can go through our church service with decorum, morning after morning, in an immense building, surrounded by not more than a dozen listeners. The best actors cannot act well before empty benches, and though there is, of course, a higher motive in one case than the other, still even the best of clergymen cannot but be influenced by their audience; and to expect that a duty should be well done under such circumstances, would be to require from human nature more than human power.

When the two ladies with the gilt crosses, the old man with his crutch, and the still palpitating housemaid were going, Mr. Harding found himself obliged to go too. The verger stood in his way, and looked at him and looked at the door, and so he went. But he returned again in a few minutes, and re-entered with another twopence. There was no other sanctuary so good for him.

As he walked slowly down the nave, and then up one aisle, and then again down the nave and up the other aisle, he tried to think gravely of the step he was about to take. He was going to give up eight hundred a year voluntarily; and doom himself to live for the rest of his life on about a hundred and fifty. He knew that he had hitherto failed to realise this fact as he ought to do. Could he maintain his own independence and support his daughter on a hundred and fifty pounds a year without being a burden on any one? His son-in-law was rich, but nothing could induce him to lean on his son-in-law after acting, as he intended to do, in direct opposition to his son-in-law's counsel. The bishop was rich, but he was about to throw away the bishop's best gift, and that in a manner to injure materially the patronage of the giver: he could neither expect nor accept anything further from the bishop. There would be not only no merit, but positive disgrace, in giving up his wardenship, if he were not prepared to meet the world without it. Yes, he must from this time forward bound all his human wishes for himself and his daughter to the poor extent of so limited an income. He knew he had not thought sufficiently of this, that he had been carried away by enthusiasm, and had hitherto not brought home to himself the full reality of his position.

He thought most about his daughter, naturally. It was true

that she was engaged, and he knew enough of his proposed son-in-law to be sure that his own altered circumstances would make no obstacle to such a marriage; nay, he was sure that the very fact of his poverty would induce Bold more anxiously to press the matter; but he disliked counting on Bold in this emergency, brought on, as it had been, by his doing. He did not like saying to himself—Bold has turned me out of my house and income, and, therefore, he must relieve me of my daughter; he preferred reckoning on Eleanor as the companion of his poverty and exile—as the sharer of his small income.

Some modest provision for his daughter had been long since made. His life was insured for three thousand pounds, and this sum was to go to Eleanor. The archdeacon, for some years past, had paid the premium, and had secured himself by the immediate possession of a small property which was to have gone to Mrs. Grantly after her father's death. This matter, therefore, had been taken out of the warden's hands long since, as, indeed, had all the business transactions of his family, and his anxiety was, therefore, confined to his own life income.

Yes. A hundred and fifty per annum was very small, but still it might suffice; but how was he to chant the litany at the cathedral on Sunday mornings, and get the service done at Crabtree Parva? True, Crabtree Church was not quite a mile and a half from the cathedral; but he could not be in two places at once? Crabtree was a small village, and afternoon service might suffice, but still this went against his conscience; it was not right that his parishioners should be robbed of any of their privileges on account of his poverty. He might, to be sure, make some arrangements for doing weekday service at the cathedral; but he had chanted the litany at Barchester so long, and had a conscious feeling that he did it so well, that he was unwilling to give up the duty.

Thinking of such things, turning over in his own mind together small desires and grave duties, but never hesitating for a moment as to the necessity of leaving the hospital, Mr. Harding walked up and down the abbey, or sat still meditating on the same stone step, hour after hour. One verger went and another came, but they did not disturb him; every now and then they crept up and looked at him, but they did so with a reverential stare, and, on the whole, Mr. Harding found his retreat well chosen. About four o'clock his comfort was disturbed by an enemy in the shape of hunger. It was necessary that he should dine, and it was clear that he could not dine in the abbey: so he left his sanctuary not willingly, and betook himself to the neighborhood of the Strand to look for food.

His eyes had become so accustomed to the gloom of the church, that they were dazed when he got out into the full light of day, and he felt confused and ashamed of himself, as though people were staring at him. He hurried along, still in dread of the archdeacon, till he came to Charing Cross, and then remembered that in one of his passages through the Strand he had seen the words "Chops and Steaks" on a placard in a shop window. He remembered the shop distinctly; it was next door to a trunk-seller's, and there was a cigar shop on the other side. He couldn't go to his hotel for dinner, which to him hitherto was the only known mode of dining in London at his own expense; and, therefore, he would get a steak at the shop in the Strand. Archdeacon Grantly would certainly not come to such a place for his dinner.

He found the house easily—just as he had observed it, between the trunks and the cigars. He was rather daunted by the huge quantity of fish which he saw in the window. There were barrels of oysters, hecatombs of lobsters, a few tremendous-looking crabs, and a tub full of pickled salmon; not, however, being aware of any connection between shell-fish and iniquity, he entered, and modestly asked a slatternly woman, who was picking oysters out of a great watery reservoir, whether he could have a mutton chop and a potato.

The woman looked somewhat surprised, but answered in the affirmative, and a slipshod girl ushered him into a long back room, filled with boxes for the accommodation of parties, in one of which he took his seat. In a more miserably forlorn place he could not have found himself: the room smelt of fish, and sawdust, and stale tobacco smoke, with a slight taint of escaped gas; everything was rough, and dirty, and disreputable; the cloth which they put before him was abominable; the knives and forks were bruised, and hacked, and filthy; and everything was impregnated with fish. He had one comfort, however: he was quite alone; there was no one there to look on his dismay; nor was it probable that any one would come to do so. It was a London supper-house. About one o'clock at night the place would be lively enough, but at the present time his seclusion was as deep as it had been in the abbey.

In about half an hour the untidy girl, not yet dressed for her evening labours, brought him his chop and potatoes, and Mr. Harding begged for a pint of sherry. He was impressed with an idea, which was generally prevalent a few years since, and is not yet wholly removed from the minds of men, that to order a dinner at any kind of inn, without also ordering a pint of wine for the benefit of the landlord, was a kind of fraud—not punishable, indeed, by law, but not the less abominable on that account. Mr. Harding remembered his coming poverty, and would willingly have saved his half-crown, but he thought he had no alternative; and he was soon put in possession of some horrid mixture procured from the neighbouring public-house.

His chop and potatoes, however, were eatable, and having got over as best he might the disgust created by the knives and forks, he contrived to swallow his dinner. He was not much disturbed: one young man, with pale face and watery fish-like eyes, wearing his hat ominously on one side, did come in and stare at him, and ask the girl, audibly enough, "Who that old cock was"; but the annoyance went no further, and the warden was left seated on his wooden bench in peace, endeavouring to distinguish the different scents arising from lobsters, oysters, and salmon.

Unknowing as Mr. Harding was in the ways of London, he felt that he had somehow selected an ineligible dining-house, and that he had better leave it. It was hardly five o'clock—how was he to pass the time till ten? Five miserable hours! He was already tired, and it was impossible that he should continue walking so long. He thought of getting into an omnibus, and going out to Fulham for the sake of coming back in another: this, however, would be weary work, and as he paid his bill to the woman in the shop, he asked her if there was any place near where he could get a cup of coffee. Though she did keep a shell-fish supper-house, she was very civil, and directed him to the cigar divan on the other side of the street.

Mr. Harding had not a much correcter notion of a cigar divan than he had of a London dinner-house, but he was desperately in want of rest, and went as he was directed. He thought he must have made some mistake when he found himself in a cigar shop, but the man behind the counter saw immediately that he was a stranger, and understood what he wanted. "One shilling, sir—thank ye, sir—cigar, sir?—ticket for coffee, sir—you'll only have to call the waiter. Up those stairs, if you please, sir. Better take the cigar, sir—you can always give it to a friend you know. Well, sir, thank ye, sir—as you are so good, I'll smoke it myself." And so Mr. Harding ascended to the divan, with his ticket for coffee, but minus the cigar.

The place seemed much more suitable to his requirements than the room in which he had dined: there was, to be sure, a strong smell of tobacco, to which he was not accustomed; but after the shell-fish, the tobacco did not seem disagreeable. There were quantities of books, and long rows of sofas. What on earth could be more luxurious than a sofa, a book, and a cup of coffee? An old waiter came up to him, with a couple of magazines and an evening paper. Was ever anything so civil? Would he have a cup of coffee, or would he prefer sherbet? Sherbet! Was he absolutely in an Eastern divan, with the slight addition of all the London periodicals? He had, however, an idea that sherbet should be drunk sitting cross-legged, and as he was not quite up to this, he ordered the coffee.

The coffee came, and was unexceptionable. Why, this divan was a paradise! The civil old waiter suggested to him a game of chess: though a chess player he was not equal to this, so he declined, and, putting up his weary legs on the sofa, leisurely sipped his coffee, and turned over the pages of his Blackwood. He might have been so engaged for about an hour, for the old waiter enticed him to a second cup of coffee, when a musical clock began to play. Mr. Harding then closed his magazine, keeping his place with his finger, and lay, listening with closed eyes to the clock. Soon the clock seemed to turn into a violoncello, with piano accompaniments, and Mr. Harding began to fancy the old waiter was the Bishop of Barchester; he was inexpressibly shocked that the bishop should have brought him his coffee with his own hands; then Dr. Grantly came in, with a basket full of lobsters, which he would not be induced to leave downstairs in the kitchen; and then the warden couldn't quite understand why so many people would smoke in the bishop's drawing-room; and so he fell asleep, and his dreams wandered away to his accustomed stall in Barchester Cathedral, and the twelve old men he was so soon about to leave for ever.

He was fatigued, and slept soundly for some time. Some sudden stop in the musical clock woke him at length, and he jumped up with a start, surprised to find the room quite full: it had been nearly empty when his nap began. With nervous anxiety he pulled out his watch, and found that it was half-past nine. He seized his hat, and, hurrying downstairs, started at a rapid pace for Lincoln's Inn.

It still wanted twenty minutes to ten when the warden found himself at the bottom of Sir Abraham's stairs, so he walked leisurely up and down the quiet inn to cool himself. It was a beautiful evening at the end of August. He had recovered from his fatigue; his sleep and the coffee had refreshed him, and he was surprised to find that he was absolutely enjoying himself, when the inn clock struck ten. The sound was hardly over before he knocked at Sir Abraham's door, and was informed by the clerk who received him that the great man would be with him immediately.

XVII

Sir Abraham Haphazard

Mr. Harding was shown into a comfortable inner sitting-room, looking more like a gentleman's book-room than a lawyer's chambers, and there waited for Sir Abraham. Nor was he kept waiting long: in ten or fifteen minutes he heard a clatter of voices speaking quickly in the passage, and then the attorney-general entered.

"Very sorry to keep you waiting, Mr. Warden," said Sir Abraham, shaking hands with him; "and sorry, too, to name so disagreeable an hour; but your notice was short, and as you said to-day, I named the very earliest hour that was not disposed of."

Mr. Harding assured him that he was aware that it was he that should apologise.

Sir Abraham was a tall thin man, with hair prematurely grey, but bearing no other sign of age; he had a slight stoop, in his neck rather than his back, acquired by his constant habit of leaning forward as he addressed his various audiences. He might be fifty years old, and would have looked young for his age, had not constant work hardened his features, and given him the appearance of a machine with a mind. His face was full of intellect, but devoid of natural expression. You would say he was a man to use, and then have done with; a man to be sought for on great emergencies, but ill adapted for ordinary services; a man whom you would ask to defend your property, but to whom you would be sorry to confide your love. He was bright as a diamond, and as cutting, and also as unimpressionable. He knew every one whom to know was an honour, but he was without a friend; he wanted none, however, and knew not the meaning of the word in other than its parliamentary sense. A friend! Had he not always been sufficient to himself, and now, at fifty, was it likely that he should trust another? He was married, indeed, and had children, but what time had he for the soft idleness of conjugal felicity? His working days or term times were occupied from his time of rising to the late hour at which he went to rest, and even his vacations were more full of labour than the busiest days of other men. He never quarrelled with his wife, but he never talked to her,—he never had time to talk, he was so taken up with speaking. She, poor lady, was not unhappy; she had all that money could give her, she would probably live to be a peeress, and she really thought Sir Abraham the best of husbands.

Sir Abraham was a man of wit, and sparkled among the brightest at the dinner-tables of political grandees: indeed, he always sparkled; whether in society, in the House of Commons, or the courts of law, coruscations flew from him; glittering sparkles, as from hot steel, but no heat; no cold heart was ever cheered by warmth from him, no unhappy soul ever dropped a portion of its burden at his door.

With him success alone was praiseworthy, and he knew none so successful as himself. No one had thrust him forward; no powerful friends had pushed him along on his road to power. No; he was attorney-general, and would, in all human probability, be lord chancellor by sheer dint of his own industry and his own talent. Who else in all the world rose so high with so little help? A premier, indeed! Who had ever been premier without mighty friends? An archbishop! Yes, the son or grandson of a great noble, or else, probably, his tutor. But he, Sir Abraham, had had no mighty lord at his back; his father had been a country apothecary, his mother a farmer's daughter. Why should he respect any but himself? And so he glitters along through the world, the brightest among the bright; and when his glitter is gone, and he is gathered to his fathers, no eye will be dim with a tear, no heart will mourn for its lost friend.

"And so, Mr. Warden," said Sir Abraham, "all our trouble about this lawsuit is at an end."

Mr. Harding said he hoped so, but he didn't at all understand what Sir Abraham meant. Sir Abraham, with all his sharpness, could not have looked into his heart and read his intentions.

"All over. You need trouble yourself no further about it; of course they must pay the costs, and the absolute expense to you and Dr. Grantly will be trifling—that is, compared with what it might have been if it had been continued."

"I fear I don't quite understand you, Sir Abraham."

"Don't you know that their attorneys have noticed us that they have withdrawn the suit?"

Mr. Harding explained to the lawyer that he knew nothing of this, although he had heard in a round-about way that such an intention had been talked of; and he also at length succeeded in making Sir Abraham understand that even this did not satisfy him. The attorney-general stood up, put his hands into his breeches' pockets, and raised his eye-brows, as Mr. Harding proceeded to detail the grievance from which he now wished to rid himself.

"I know I have no right to trouble you personally with this matter, but as it is of most vital importance to me, as all my happiness is concerned in it, I thought I might venture to seek your advice."

Sir Abraham bowed, and declared his clients were entitled to the best advice he could give them; particularly a client so respectable in every way as the Warden of Barchester Hospital.

"A spoken word, Sir Abraham, is often of more value than volumes of written advice. The truth is, I am ill-satisfied with this matter as it stands at present. I do see—I cannot help seeing, that the affairs of the hospital are not arranged according to the will of the founder."

"None of such institutions are, Mr. Harding, nor can they be; the altered circumstances in which we live do not admit of it."

"Quite true—that is quite true; but I can't see that those altered circumstances give me a right to eight hundred a year. I don't know whether I ever read John Hiram's will, but were I to read it now I could not understand it. What I want you, Sir Abraham, to tell me, is this—am I, as warden, legally and distinctly entitled to the proceeds of the property, after the due maintenance of the twelve bedesmen?"

Sir Abraham declared that he couldn't exactly say in so many words that Mr. Harding was legally entitled to, etc., etc.,

etc., and ended in expressing a strong opinion that it would be madness to raise any further question on the matter, as the suit was to be—nay, was, abandoned.

Mr. Harding, seated in his chair, began to play a slow tune on an imaginary violoncello.

"Nay, my dear sir," continued the attorney-general, "there is no further ground for any question; I don't see that you have the power of raising it."

"I can resign," said Mr. Harding, slowly playing away with his right hand, as though the bow were beneath the chair in which he was sitting.

"What! throw it up altogether?" said the attorney-general, gazing with utter astonishment at his client.

"Did you see those articles in the *Jupiter*?" said Mr. Harding, piteously, appealing to the sympathy of the lawyer.

Sir Abraham said he had seen them. This poor little clergyman, cowed into such an act of extreme weakness by a newspaper article, was to Sir Abraham so contemptible an object, that he hardly knew how to talk to him as to a rational being.

"Hadn't you better wait," said he, "till Dr. Grantly is in town with you? Wouldn't it be better to postpone any serious step till you can consult with him?"

Mr. Harding declared vehemently that he could not wait and Sir Abraham began seriously to doubt his sanity.

"Of course," said the latter, "if you have private means sufficient for your wants, and if this——"

"I haven't a sixpence, Sir Abraham," said the warden.

"God bless me! Why, Mr. Harding, how do you mean to live?"

Mr. Harding proceeded to explain to the man of law that he meant to keep his precentorship—that was eighty pounds a year; and, also, that he meant to fall back upon his own little living of Crabtree, which was another eighty pounds. That, to be sure, the duties of the two were hardly compatible; but perhaps he might effect an exchange. And then, recollecting that the attorney-general would hardly care to hear how the service of a cathedral church is divided among the minor canons, stopped short in his explanations.

Sir Abraham listened in pitying wonder. "I really think, Mr. Harding, you had better wait for the archdeacon. This is a most serious step—one for which, in my opinion, there is not the slightest necessity; and, as you have done me the honour of asking my advice, I must implore you to do nothing without the approval of your friends. A man is never the best judge of his own position.''

"A man is the best judge of what he feels himself. I'd sooner beg my bread till my death than read such another article as those two that have appeared, and feel, as I do, that the writer has truth on his side."

"Have you not a daughter, Mr. Harding—an unmarried daughter?"

"I have," said he, now standing also, but still playing away on his fiddle with his hand behind his back. "I have, Sir Abraham; and she and I are completely agreed on this subject."

"Pray excuse me, Mr. Harding, if what I say seems impertinent; but surely it is you that should be prudent on her behalf. She is young, and does not know the meaning of living on an income of a hundred and fifty pounds a year. On her account give up this idea. Believe me, it is sheer Quixotism."

The warden walked away to the window, and then back to his chair; and then, irresolute what to say, took another turn to the window. The attorney-general was really extremely patient, but he was beginning to think that the interview had been long enough.

"But if this income be not justly mine, what if she and I have both to beg?" said the warden at last, sharply, and in a voice so different from that he had hitherto used, that Sir Abraham was startled. "If so, it would be better to beg."

"My dear sir, nobody now questions its justness."

"Yes, Sir Abraham, one does question it—the most important of all witnesses against me—I question it myself. My God knows whether or no I love my daughter; but I would sooner that she and I should both beg, than that she should live in comfort on money which is truly the property of the poor. It may seem strange to you, Sir Abraham, it is strange to myself, that I should have been ten years in that happy home, and not have thought of these things till they were so roughly dinned into my ears. I cannot boast of my conscience, when it required the violence of a public newspaper to awaken it; but, now that it is awake, I must obey it. When I came here I did not know that the suit was withdrawn by Mr. Bold, and my object was to beg you to abandon my defence. As there is no action, there can be no defence; but it is, at any rate, as well that you should know that from to-morrow I shall cease to be the warden of the hospital. My friends and I differ on this subject, Sir Abraham, and that adds much to my sorrow; but it cannot be helped." And, as he finished what he had to say, he played up such a tune as never before had graced the chambers of any attorney-general. He was standing up, gallantly fronting Sir Abraham, and his right arm passed with bold and rapid sweeps before him, as though he were embracing some huge instrument, which allowed him to stand thus erect; and with the fingers of his left hand he stopped, with preternatural velocity, a multitude of strings, which ranged from the top of his collar to the bottom of the lappet of his coat. Sir Abraham listened and looked in wonder. As he had never before seen Mr. Harding, the meaning of these wild gesticulations was lost upon him; but he perceived that the gentleman who had a few minutes since been so subdued as to be unable to speak without hesitation, was now impassioned—nay, almost violent.

"You'll sleep on this, Mr. Harding, and to-morrow——"

"I have done more than sleep upon it," said the warden; "I have laid awake upon it, and that night after night. I found I could not sleep upon it: now I hope to do so."

The attorney-general had no answer to make to this; so he expressed a quiet hope that whatever settlement was finally made would be satisfactory; and Mr. Harding withdrew, thanking the great man for his kind attention.

Mr. Harding was sufficiently satisfied with the interview to feel a glow of comfort as he descended into the small old square of Lincoln's Inn. It was a calm, bright, beautiful night, and by the light of the moon, even the chapel of Lincoln's Inn, and the sombre row of chambers, which surround the quadrangle, looked well. He stood still a moment to collect his thoughts, and reflect on what he had done, and was about to do. He knew that the attorney-general regarded him as little better than a fool, but that he did not mind; he and the attorney-general had not much in common between them; he knew also that others, whom he did care about, would think so too; but Eleanor, he was sure, would exult in what he had done, and the bishop, he trusted, would sympathise with him.

In the meantime he had to meet the archdeacon, and so he walked slowly down Chancery Lane and along Fleet Street, feeling sure that his work for the night was not yet over. When he reached the hotel he rang the bell quietly, and with a palpitating heart; he almost longed to escape round the corner, and delay the coming storm by a further walk round St. Paul's Churchyard, but he heard the slow creaking shoes of the old waiter approaching, and he stood his ground manfully.

XVIII

The Warden Is Very Obstinate

"Dr. Grantly is here, sir," greeted his ears before the door was well open, "and Mrs. Grantly. They have a sitting-room above, and are waiting up for you."

There was something in the tone of the man's voice which seemed to indicate that even he looked upon the warden as a runaway school-boy, just recaptured by his guardian, and that he pitied the culprit, though he could not but be horrified at the crime.

The warden endeavoured to appear unconcerned, as he said, "Oh, indeed! I'll go upstairs at once"; but he failed signally. There was, perhaps, a ray of comfort in the presence of his married daughter; that is to say, of comparative comfort, seeing that his son-in-law was there; but how much would he have preferred that they should both have been safe at Plumstead Episcopi! However, upstairs he went, the waiter slowly preceding him; and on the door being opened the archdeacon was discovered standing in the middle of the room, erect, indeed, as usual, but oh! how sorrowful! and on the dingy sofa behind him reclined his patient wife.

"Papa, I thought you were never coming back," said the lady; "it's twelve o'clock."

"Yes, my dear," said the warden. "The attorney-general named ten for my meeting; to be sure ten is late, but what could I do, you know? Great men will have their own way."

And he gave his daughter a kiss, and shook hands with the doctor, and again tried to look unconcerned.

"And you have absolutely been with the attorney-general?" asked the archdeacon.

Mr. Harding signified that he had.

"Good heavens, how unfortunate!" And the archdeacon raised his huge hands in the manner in which his friends are so accustomed to see him express disapprobation and astonishment. "What will Sir Abraham think of it? Did you not know that it is not customary for clients to go direct to their counsel?"

"Isn't it?" asked the warden, innocently. "Well, at any rate, I've done it now. Sir Abraham didn't seem to think it so very strange."

The archdeacon gave a sigh that would have moved a man-of-war.

"But, papa, what did you say to Sir Abraham?" asked the lady.

"I asked him, my dear, to explain John Hiram's will to me. He couldn't explain it in the only way which would have satisfied me, and so I resigned the wardenship."

"Resigned it!" said the archdeacon, in a solemn voice, sad and low, but yet sufficiently audible—a sort of whisper that Macready would have envied, and the galleries have applauded with a couple of rounds. "Resigned it! Good heavens!" And the dignitary of the church sank back horrified into a horsehair armchair.

"At least I told Sir Abraham that I would resign; and of course I must now do so."

"Not at all," said the archdeacon, catching a ray of hope. "Nothing that you say in such a way to your own counsel can be in any way binding on you; of course you were there to ask his advice. I'm sure Sir Abraham did not advise any such step."

Mr. Harding could not say that he had.

"I am sure he disadvised you from it," continued the reverend cross-examiner.

Mr. Harding could not deny this.

"I'm sure Sir Abraham must have advised you to consult your friends."

To this proposition also Mr. Harding was obliged to assent.

"Then your threat of resignation amounts to nothing, and we are just where we were before."

Mr. Harding was now standing on the rug, moving uneasily from one foot to the other. He made no distinct answer to the archdeacon's last proposition, for his mind was chiefly engaged on thinking how he could escape to bed. That his resignation was a thing finally fixed on, a fact all but completed, was not in his mind a matter of any doubt; he knew his own weakness; he knew how prone he was to be led; but he was not weak enough to give

way now, to go back from the position to which his conscience
had driven him, after having purposely come to London to
declare his determination: he did not in the least doubt his
resolution, but he greatly doubted his power of defending it
against his son-in-law.

"You must be very tired, Susan," said he: "wouldn't you
like to go to bed?"

But Susan didn't want to go till her husband went.—She
had an idea that her papa might be bullied if she were away: she
wasn't tired at all, or at least she said so.

The archdeacon was pacing the room, expressing, by certain noddles of his head, his opinion of the utter fatuity of his
father-in-law.

"Why," at last he said—and angels might have blushed at
the rebuke expressed in his tone and emphasis—"Why did you
go off from Barchester so suddenly? Why did you take such a
step without giving us notice, after what had passed at the
palace?"

The warden hung his head, and made no reply: he could not
condescend to say that he had not intended to give his son-in-law
the slip; and as he had not the courage to avow it, he said
nothing.

"Papa has been too much for you," said the lady.

The archdeacon took another turn, and again ejaculated,
"Good heavens!" this time in a very low whisper, but still
audible.

"I think I'll go to bed," said the warden, taking up a side
candle.

"At any rate, you'll promise me to take no further step
without consultation," said the archdeacon. Mr. Harding made
no answer, but slowly proceeded to light his candle. "Of course,"
continued the other, "such a declaration as that you made to Sir
Abraham means nothing. Come, warden, promise me this. The
whole affair, you see, is already settled, and that with very little
trouble or expense. Bold has been compelled to abandon his
action, and all you have to do is to remain quiet at the hospital."
Mr. Harding still made no reply, but looked meekly into his
son-in-law's face. The archdeacon thought he knew his father-in-
law, but he was mistaken; he thought that he had already talked
over a vacillating man to resign his promise. "Come," said he,
"promise Susan to give up this idea of resigning the wardenship."

The warden looked at his daughter, thinking probably at the
moment that if Eleanor were contented with him, he need not so

much regard his other child, and said, "I am sure Susan will not ask me to break my word, or to do what I know to be wrong."

"Papa," said she, "it would be madness in you to throw up your preferment. What are you to live on?"

"God, that feeds the young ravens, will take care of me also," said Mr. Harding, with a smile, as though afraid of giving offence by making his reference to scripture too solemn.

"Pish!" said the archdeacon, turning away rapidly. "If the ravens persisted in refusing the food prepared for them, they wouldn't be fed." A clergyman generally dislikes to be met in argument by any scriptural quotation; he feels as affronted as a doctor does, when recommended by an old woman to take some favourite dose, or as a lawyer when an unprofessional man attempts to put him down by a quibble.

"I shall have the living of Crabtree," modestly suggested the warden.

"Eighty pounds a year!" sneered the archdeacon.

"And the precentorship," said the father-in-law.

"It goes with the wardenship," said the son-in-law. Mr. Harding was prepared to argue this point, and began to do so, but Dr. Grantly stopped him. "My dear warden," said he, "this is all nonsense. Eighty pounds or a hundred and sixty makes very little difference. You can't live on it—you can't ruin Eleanor's prospects for ever. In point of fact, you can't resign; the bishop wouldn't accept it; the whole thing is settled. What I now want to do is to prevent any inconvenient tittle-tattle—any more newspaper articles."

"That's what I want, too," said the warden.

"And to prevent that," continued the other, "we mustn't let any talk of resignation get abroad."

"But I shall resign," said the warden, very, very meekly.

"Good heavens! Susan, my dear, what can I say to him?"

"But, papa," said Mrs. Grantly, getting up, and putting her arm through that of her father, "what is Eleanor to do if you throw away your income?"

A hot tear stood in each of the warden's eyes as he looked round upon his married daughter. Why should one sister who was so rich predict poverty for another? Some such idea as this was on his mind, but he gave no utterance to it. Then he thought of the pelican feeding its young with blood from its own breast, but he gave no utterance to that either; and then of Eleanor waiting for him at home, waiting to congratulate him on the end of all his trouble.

"Think of Eleanor, papa," said Mrs. Grantly.

"I do think of her," said her father.

"And you will not do this rash thing?" The lady was really moved beyond her usual calm composure.

"It can never be rash to do right," said he. "I shall certainly resign this wardenship."

"Then, Mr. Harding, there is nothing before you but ruin," said the archdeacon, now moved beyond all endurance. "Ruin both for you and Eleanor. How do you mean to pay the monstrous expenses of this action?"

Mrs. Grantly suggested that, as the action was abandoned, the costs would not be heavy.

"Indeed they will, my dear," continued he. "One cannot have the attorney-general up at twelve o'clock at night for nothing; —but of course your father has not thought of this."

"I will sell my furniture," said the warden.

"Furniture!" ejaculated the other, with a most powerful sneer.

"Come, archdeacon," said the lady, "we needn't mind that at present. You know you never expected papa to pay the costs."

"Such absurdity is enough to provoke Job," said the archdeacon, marching quickly up and down the room. "Your father is like a child. Eight hundred pounds a year!—eight hundred and eighty with the house—with nothing to do. The very place for him. And to throw that up because some scoundrel writes an article in a newspaper! Well—I have done my duty. If he chooses to ruin his child I cannot help it"; and he stood still at the fire-place, and looked at himself in a dingy mirror which stood on the chimney-piece.

There was a pause for about a minute, and then the warden, finding that nothing else was coming, lighted his candle, and quietly said, "Good-night."

"Good-night, papa," said the lady.

And so the warden retired; but, as he closed the door behind him, he heard the well-known ejaculation,—slower, lower, and more solemn, more ponderous than ever—"Good heavens!"

XIX

The Warden Resigns

The party met the next morning at breakfast; and a very sombre affair it was—very unlike the breakfasts at Plumstead Episcopi.

There were three thin, small, dry bits of bacon, each an inch long, served up under a huge old plated cover; there were four three-cornered bits of dry toast, and four square bits of buttered toast; there was a loaf of bread, and some oily-looking butter; and on the sideboard there were the remains of a cold shoulder of mutton. The archdeacon, however, had not come up from his rectory to St. Paul's Churchyard to enjoy himself and therefore nothing was said of the scanty fare.

The guests were as sorry as the viands—hardly anything was said over the breakfast-table. The archdeacon munched his toast in ominous silence, turning over bitter thoughts in his deep mind. The warden tried to talk to his daughter, and she tried to answer him; but they both failed. There were no feelings at present in common between them. The warden was thinking only of getting back to Barchester, and calculating whether the archdeacon would expect him to wait for him; and Mrs. Grantly was preparing herself for a grand attack which she was to make on her father, as agreed upon between herself and her husband during their curtain confabulation of that morning.

When the waiter had creaked out of the room with the last of the teacups, the archdeacon got up and went to the window, as though to admire the view. The room looked out on a narrow passage which runs from St. Paul's Churchyard to Paternoster Row; and Dr. Grantly patiently perused the names of the three shopkeepers whose doors were in view. The warden still kept his seat at the table, and examined the pattern of the table-cloth; and Mrs. Grantly, seating herself on the sofa, began to knit.

After awhile the warden pulled his Bradshaw out of his pocket, and began laboriously to consult it. There was a train for Barchester at 10 A.M. That was out of the question, for it was nearly ten already. Another at 3 P.M.; another, the night mail-train, at 9 P.M. The three o'clock train would take him home to tea, and would suit very well.

"My dear," said he, "I think I shall go back home at three o'clock to-day. I shall get home at half-past eight. I don't think there's anything to keep me in London."

"The archdeacon and I return by the early train to-morrow, papa; won't you wait and go back with us?"

"Why, Eleanor will expect me to-night; and I've so much to do; and——"

"Much to do!" said the archdeacon *sotto voce:* but the warden heard him.

"You'd better wait for us, papa."

"Thank ye, my dear! I think I'll go this afternoon." The tamest animal will turn when driven too hard, and even Mr. Harding was beginning to fight for his own way.

"I suppose you won't be back before three?" said the lady, addressing her husband.

"I must leave this at two," said the warden.

"Quite out of the question," said the archdeacon, answering his wife, and still reading the shop-keepers' names; "I don't suppose I shall be back till five."

There was another long pause, during which Mr. Harding continued to study his Bradshaw.

"I must go to Cox and Cumming," said the archdeacon at last.

"Oh, to Cox and Cumming," said the warden. It was quite a matter of indifference to him where his son-in-law went. The names of Cox and Cumming had now no interest in his ears. What had he to do with Cox and Cumming further, having already had his suit finally adjudicated upon in a court of conscience, a judgment without power of appeal fully registered, and the matter settled so that all the lawyers in London could not disturb it. The archdeacon could go to Cox and Cumming, could remain there all day in anxious discussion; but what might be said there was no longer matter of interest to him, who was so soon to lay aside the name of warden of Barchester Hospital.

The archdeacon took up his shining new clerical hat, and put on his black new clerical gloves, and looked heavy, respectable, decorous, and opulent, a decided clergyman of the Church of England, every inch of him. "I suppose I shall see you at Barchester the day after to-morrow," said he.

The warden supposed he would.

"I must once more beseech you to take no further steps till you see my father; if you owe me nothing," and the archdeacon looked as though he thought a great deal were due to him, "at least you owe so much to my father"; and, without waiting for a reply, Dr. Grantly wended his way to Cox and Cumming.

Mrs. Grantly waited till the last fall of her husband's foot was heard, as he turned out of the court into St. Paul's Churchyard, and then commenced her task of talking her father over.

"Papa," she began, "this is a most serious business."

"Indeed it is," said the warden, ringing the bell.

"I greatly feel the distress of mind you must have endured."

"I am sure you do, my dear"; and he ordered the waiter to bring him pen, ink, and paper.

"Are you going to write, papa?"

"Yes, my dear—I am going to write my resignation to the bishop."

"Pray, pray, papa, put it off till our return,—pray put it off till you have seen the bishop,—dear papa! for my sake, for Eleanor's!——"

"It is for your sake and Eleanor's that I do this. I hope, at least, that my children may never have to be ashamed of their father."

"How can you talk about shame, papa?" and she stopped while the waiter creaked in with the paper, and then slowly creaked out again; "how can you talk about shame? you know what all your friends think about this question."

The warden spread his paper on the table, placing it on the meagre blotting-book which the hotel afforded, and sat himself down to write.

"You won't refuse me one request, papa?" continued his daughter; "you won't refuse to delay your letter for two short days? Two days can make no possible difference."

"My dear," said he naïvely, "if I waited till I got to Barchester, I might, perhaps, be prevented."

"But surely you would not wish to offend the bishop?" said she.

"God forbid! The bishop is not apt to take offence, and knows me too well to take in bad part anything that I may be called on to do."

"But, papa——"

"Susan," said he, "my mind on this subject is made up; it is not without much repugnance that I act in opposition to the advice of such men as Sir Abraham Haphazard and the archdeacon; but in this matter I can take no advice, I cannot alter the resolution to which I have come."

"But two days, papa——"

"No—nor can I delay it. You may add to my present unhappiness by pressing me, but you cannot change my purpose; it will be a comfort to me if you will let the matter rest": and, dipping his pen into the inkstand, he fixed his eyes intently on the paper.

There was something in his manner which taught his daughter to perceive that he was in earnest: she had at one time ruled supreme in her father's house, but she knew that there were moments when, mild and meek as he was, he would have his way, and the present was an occasion of the sort. She returned, therefore, to her knitting, and very shortly after left the room.

The warden was now at liberty to compose his letter, and, as it was characteristic of the man, it shall be given at full length. The official letter, which, when written, seemed to him to be too formally cold to be sent alone to so dear a friend, was accompanied by a private note; and both are here inserted.

The letter of resignation ran as follows:

> CHAPTER HOTEL, ST. PAUL'S,
> LONDON,
> *August,* 18—

MY LORD BISHOP,

It is with the greatest pain that I feel myself constrained to resign into your Lordship's hands the wardenship of the hospital at Barchester, which you so kindly conferred upon me, now nearly twelve years since.

I need not explain the circumstances which have made this step appear necessary to me. You are aware that a question has arisen as to the right of the warden to the income which has been allotted to the wardenship; it has seemed to me that this right is not well made out, and I hesitate to incur the risk of taking an income to which my legal claim appears doubtful.

The office of precentor of the cathedral is, as your Lordship is aware, joined to that of the warden; that is to say, the precentor has for many years been the warden of the hospital; there is, however, nothing to make the junction of the two offices necessary, and, unless you or the dean and chapter object to such an arrangement, I would wish to keep the precentorship. The income of this office will now be necessary to me; indeed, I do not know why I should be ashamed to say that I should have difficulty in supporting myself without it.

Your Lordship, and such others as you may please to consult on the matter, will at once see that my resignation of the wardenship need offer not the slightest bar to its occupation by another person. I am thought in the wrong by all those whom I have consulted in the matter; I have very little but an inward and an unguided conviction of my own to bring me to this step, and I shall, indeed, be hurt to find that any slur is thrown on the preferment which your kindness bestowed on me, by my resignation of it. I, at any rate for one, shall look on any successor whom you may appoint as enjoying a clerical situation of the highest respectability, and one to which your Lordship's nomination gives an indefeasible right.

I cannot finish this official letter without again thanking your Lordship for all your great kindness, and I beg to subscribe myself.

Your Lordship's most obedient servant,

SEPTIMUS HARDING,
Warden of Barchester Hospital and
Precentor of the Cathedral.

He then wrote the following private note:

MY DEAR BISHOP,

I cannot send you the accompanying official letter without a warmer expression of thanks for all your kindness than would befit a document which may to a certain degree be made public. You, I know, will understand the feeling, and, perhaps, pity the weakness which makes me resign the hospital. I am not made of calibre strong enough to withstand public attack. Were I convinced that I stood on ground perfectly firm, that I was certainly justified in taking eight hundred a year under Hiram's will, I should feel bound by duty to retain the position, however unendurable might be the nature of the assault; but, as I do not feel this conviction, I cannot believe that you will think me wrong in what I am doing.

I had at one time an idea of keeping only some moderate portion of the income; perhaps three hundred a year, and of remitting the remainder to the trustees; but it occurred to me, and I think with reason, that by so doing I should place my successors in an invidious position, and greatly damage your patronage.

My dear friend, let me have a line from you to say that you do not blame me for what I am doing, and that the officiating vicar of Crabtree Parva will be the same to you as the warden of the hospital.

I am very anxious about the precentorship: the archdeacon thinks it must go with the wardenship; I think not, and, that, having it, I cannot be ousted. I will, however, be guided by you and the dean. No other duty will suit me so well, or come so much within my power of adequate performance.

I thank you from my heart for the preferment which I am now giving up, and for all your kindness, and am, dear bishop, now as always,

> Yours most sincerely,
> SEPTIMUS HARDING.

LONDON,
—*August*, 18—.

Having written these letters and made a copy of the former one for the benefit of the archdeacon, Mr. Harding, whom we must now cease to call the warden, he having designated himself so for the last time, found that it was nearly two o'clock, and that he must prepare for his journey. Yes, from this time he never again admitted the name by which he had been so familiarly known, and in which, to tell the truth, he had rejoiced. The love of titles is common to all men, and a vicar or fellow is as pleased at becoming Mr. Archdeacon or Mr. Provost, as a lieutenant, at getting his captaincy, or a city tallow-chandler in becoming Sir John on the occasion of a Queen's visit to a new bridge. But warden he was no longer, and the name of precentor, though the office was to him so dear, confers in itself no sufficient distinction; our friend, therefore, again became Mi. Harding.

Mrs. Grantly had gone out; he had, therefore, no one to delay him by further entreaties to postpone his journey; he had soon arranged his bag, and paid his bill, and, leaving a note for his daughter, in which he put the copy of his official letter, he got into a cab and drove away to the station with something of triumph in his heart.

Had he not cause for triumph? Had he not been supremely successful? Had he not for the first time in his life held his own purpose against tnat of his son-in-law, and manfully combated against great odds—against the archdeacon's wife as well as the archdeacon? Had he not gained a great victory, and was it not fit that he should step into his cab with triumph?

He had not told Eleanor when he would return, but she was on the look out for him by every train by which he could arrive, and the pony-carriage was at the Barchester station when the train drew up at the platform.

"My dear," said he, sitting beside her, as she steered her little vessel to one side of the road to make room for the clattering omnibus as they passed from the station into the town; "I hope you'll be able to feel a proper degree of respect for the vicar of Crabtree."

"Dear papa," said she, "I am so glad."

There was great comfort in returning home to that pleasant house, though he was to leave it so soon, and in discussing with his daughter all that he had done, and all that he had to do. It must take some time to get out of one house into another; the curate at Crabtree could not be abolished under six months, that is, unless other provision could be made for him; and then the furniture—the most of that must be sold to pay Sir Abraham Haphazard for sitting up till twelve at night. Mr. Harding was strangely ignorant as to lawyers' bills; he had no idea, from twenty pounds to two thousand, as to the sum in which he was indebted for legal assistance. True, he had called in no lawyer himself; true, he had been no consenting party to the employment of either Cox and Cumming, or Sir Abraham; he had never been consulted on such matters;—the archdeacon had managed all this himself, never for a moment suspecting that Mr. Harding would take upon him to end the matter in a way of his own. Had the lawyers' bills been ten thousand pounds, Mr. Harding could not have helped it; but he was not on that account disposed to dispute his own liability. The question never occurred to him; but it did occur to him that he had very little money at his banker's, that he could receive nothing further from the hospital, and that the sale of the furniture was his only resource.

"Not all, papa," said Eleanor pleadingly.

"Not quite all, my dear," said he; "that is, if we can help it. We must have a little at Crabtree—but it can only be a little; we must put a bold front on it, Nelly; it isn't easy to come down from affluence to poverty."

And so they planned their future mode of life; the father taking comfort from the reflection that his daughter would soon be freed from it, and she resolving that her father would soon have in her own house a ready means of escape from the solitude of the Crabtree vicarage.

When the archdeacon left his wife and father-in-law at the Chapter Coffee House to go to Messrs. Cox and Cumming, he had no very defined idea of what he had to do when he got there. Gentlemen when at law, or in any way engaged in matters requiring legal assistance, are very apt to go to their lawyers without much absolute necessity;—gentlemen when doing so, are apt to describe such attendance as quite compulsory, and very disagreeable. The lawyers, on the other hand, do not at all see the necessity, though they quite agree as to the disagreeable nature of the visit;—gentlemen when so engaged are usually somewhat gravelled at finding nothing to say to their learned friends; they generally talk a little politics, a little weather, ask some few foolish questions about their suit, and then withdraw, having passed half an hour in a small dingy waiting-room, in company with some junior assistant-clerk, and ten minutes with the members of the firm; the business is then over for which the gentleman has come up to London, probably a distance of a hundred and fifty miles. To be sure he goes to the play, and dines at his friend's club, and has a bachelor's liberty and bachelor's recreation for three or four days; and he could not probably plead the desire of such gratifications as a reason to his wife for a trip to London.

Married ladies, when your husbands find they are positively obliged to attend their legal advisers, the nature of the duty to be performed is generally of this description.

The archdeacon would not have dreamt of leaving London without going to Cox and Cumming; and yet he had nothing to say to them. The game was up; he plainly saw that Mr. Harding in this matter was not to be moved; his only remaining business on this head was to pay the bill and have done with it: and I think it may be taken for granted, that whatever the cause may be that takes a gentleman to a lawyer's chambers, he never goes there to pay his bill.

Dr. Grantly, however, in the eyes of Messrs. Cox and Cumming, represented the spiritualities of the diocese of Barchester, as Mr. Chadwick did the temporalities, and was, therefore, too great a man to undergo the half-hour in the clerk's room. It will not be necessary that we should listen to the notes of sorrow in which the archdeacon bewailed to Mr. Cox the weakness of his father-in-law, and the end of all their hopes of triumph; nor need we repeat the various exclamations of surprise with which the mournful intelligence was received. No tragedy occurred, though Mr. Cox, a short and somewhat bull-necked man, was very near a fit of apoplexy when he first attempted to ejaculate that fatal word—resign!

Over and over again did Mr. Cox attempt to enforce on the archdeacon the propriety of urging on Mr. Warden the madness of the deed he was about to do.

"Eight hundred a year!" said Mr. Cox.

"And nothing whatever to do!" said Mr. Cumming, who had joined the conference.

"No private fortune, I believe," said Mr. Cox.

"Not a shilling," said Mr. Cumming, in a very low voice, shaking his head.

"I never heard of such a case in all my experience," said Mr. Cox.

"Eight hundred a year, and as nice a house as any gentleman could wish to hang up his hat in," said Mr. Cumming.

"And an unmarried daughter, I believe," said Mr. Cox, with much moral seriousness in his tone. The archdeacon only sighed as each separate wail was uttered, and shook his head, signifying that the fatuity of some people was past belief.

"I'll tell you what he might do," said Mr. Cumming, brightening up. "I'll tell you how you might save it—let him exchange."

"Exchange where?" said the archdeacon.

"Exchange for a living. There's Quiverful, of Puddingdale—he has twelve children, and would be delighted to get the hospital. To be sure Puddingdale is only four hundred, but that would be saving something out of the fire: Mr. Harding would have a curate, and still keep three hundred or three hundred and fifty."

The archdeacon opened his ears and listened; he really thought the scheme might do.

"The newspapers," continued Mr. Cumming, "might hammer away at Quiverful every day for the next six months without his minding them."

The archdeacon took up his hat, and returned to his hotel, thinking the matter over deeply. At any rate he would sound Quiverful. A man with twelve children would do much to double his income.

XX

Farewell

On the morning after Mr. Harding's return home he received a note from the bishop full of affection, condolence, and praise. "Pray come to me at once," wrote the bishop, "that we may see what had better be done; as to the hospital, I will not say a word to dissuade you; but I don't like your going to Crabtree: at any rate, come to me at once."

Mr. Harding did go to him at once; and long and confidential was the consultation between the two old friends. There they sat together the whole long day, plotting to get the better of the archdeacon, and to carry out schemes of their own, which they knew would be opposed by the whole weight of his authority.

The bishop's first idea was, that Mr. Harding, if left to himself, would certainly starve—not in the figurative sense in which so many of our ladies and gentlemen do starve on incomes from one to five hundred a year; not that he would be starved as regarded dress coats, port wine, and pocket-money; but that he would positively perish of inanition for want of bread.

"How is a man to live, when he gives up all his income?" said the bishop to himself. And then the good-natured little man began to consider how his friend might be best rescued from a death so horrid and painful.

His first proposition to Mr. Harding was, that they should

live together at the palace. He, the bishop, positively assured Mr. Harding that he wanted another resident chaplain—not a young, working chaplain, but a steady, middle-aged chaplain; one who would dine and drink a glass of wine with him, talk about the archdeacon, and poke the fire. The bishop did not positively name all these duties, but he gave Mr. Harding to understand that such would be the nature of the service required.

It was not without much difficulty that Mr. Harding made his friend see that this would not suit him; that he could not throw up the bishop's preferment, and then come and hang on at the bishop's table; that he could not allow people to say of him that it was an easy matter to abandon his own income, as he was able to sponge on that of another person. He succeeded, however, in explaining that the plan would not do, and then the bishop brought forward another which he had in his sleeve. He, the bishop, had in his will left certain moneys to Mr. Harding's two daughters, imagining that Mr. Harding would himself want no such assistance during his own lifetime. This legacy amounted to three thousand pounds each, duty free; and he now pressed it as a gift on his friend.

"The girls, you know," said he, "will have it just the same when you're gone—and they won't want it sooner—and as for the interest during my lifetime, it isn't worth talking about. I have more than enough."

With much difficulty and heartfelt sorrow, Mr. Harding refused also this offer. No; his wish was to support himself, however poorly—not to be supported on the charity of anyone. It was hard to make the bishop understand this; it was hard to make him comprehend that the only real favour he could confer was the continuation of his independent friendship; but at last even this was done. At any rate, thought the bishop, he will come and dine with me from time to time, and if he be absolutely starving I shall see it.

Touching the precentorship, the bishop was clearly of opinion that it could be held without the other situation—an opinion from which no one differed; and it was therefore soon settled among all the parties concerned, that Mr. Harding should still be the precentor of the cathedral.

On the day following Mr. Harding's return, the archdeacon reached Plumstead full of Mr. Cumming's scheme regarding Puddingdale and Mr. Quiverful. On the very next morning he drove over to Puddingdale, and obtained the full consent of the wretched clerical Priam, who was endeavouring to feed his poor

Hecuba and a dozen of Hectors on the small proceeds of his ecclesiastical kingdom. Mr. Quiverful had no doubts as to the legal rights of the warden; his conscience would be quite clear as to accepting the income; and as to the *Jupiter*, he begged to assure the archdeacon that he was quite indifferent to any emanations from the profane portion of the periodical press.

Having so far succeeded, he next sounded the bishop; but here he was astonished by most unexpected resistance. The bishop did not think it would do. "Not do, why not?" and seeing that his father was not shaken, he repeated the question in a severer form: "Why not do, my lord?"

His lordship looked very unhappy, and shuffled about in his chair, but still didn't give way; he thought Puddingdale wouldn't do for Mr. Harding; it was too far from Barchester.

"Oh! of course he'll have a curate."

The bishop also thought that Mr. Quiverful wouldn't do for the hospital; such an exchange wouldn't look well at such a time; and, when pressed harder, he declared he didn't think Mr. Harding would accept Puddingdale under any circumstances.

"How is he to live?" demanded the archdeacon.

The bishop, with tears in his eyes, declared that he had not the slightest conception how life was to be sustained within him at all.

The archdeacon then left his father, and went down to the hospital; but Mr. Harding wouldn't listen at all to the Puddingdale scheme. To his eyes it had no attraction; it savoured of simony, and was likely to bring down upon him harder and more deserved strictures than any he had yet received: he positively declined to become vicar of Puddingdale under any circumstances.

The archdeacon waxed wroth, talked big, and looked bigger; he said something about dependence and beggary, spoke of the duty every man was under to earn his bread, made passing allusions to the follies of youth and waywardness of age, as though Mr. Harding were afflicted by both, and ended by declaring that he had done. He felt that he had left no stone unturned to arrange matters on the best and easiest footing; that he had, in fact, so arranged them, that he had so managed that there was no further need of any anxiety in the matter. And how had he been paid? His advice had been systematically rejected; he had been not only slighted, but distrusted and avoided; he and his measures had been utterly thrown over, as had been Sir Abraham, who, he had reason to know, was much pained at what had occurred. He now found it was useless to interfere any further, and he should retire. If any further assistance were required from him, he would probably be called on, and should be again happy to come forward. And so he left the hospital, and has not since entered it from that day to this.

And here we must take leave of Archdeacon Grantly. We fear that he is represented in these pages as being worse than he is; but we have had to do with his foibles, and not with his virtues. We have seen only the weak side of the man, and have lacked the opportunity of bringing him forward on his strong ground. That he is a man somewhat too fond of his own way, and not sufficiently scrupulous in his manner of achieving it, his best friends cannot deny. That he is bigoted in favour, not so much of his doctrines as of his cloth, is also true: and it is true that the possession of a large income is a desire that sits near his heart. Nevertheless, the archdeacon is a gentleman and a man of conscience; he spends his money liberally, and does the work he has to do with the best of his ability; he improves the tone of society of those among whom he lives. His aspirations are of a healthy, if not of the highest, kind. Though never an austere man, he upholds propriety of conduct both by example and precept. He is generous to the poor, and hospitable to the rich; in matters of religion he is sincere, and yet no Pharisee; he is in earnest, and yet no fanatic. On the whole, the Archdeacon of Barchester is a man doing more good than harm—a man to be furthered and supported, though perhaps also to be controlled; and it is matter of regret to us that the course of our narrative has required that we should see more of his weakness than his strength.

Mr. Harding allowed himself no rest till everything was prepared for his departure from the hospital. It may be as well to mention that he was not driven to the stern necessity of selling all his furniture: he had been quite in earnest in his intention to do so, but it was soon made known to him that the claims of Messrs. Cox and Cumming made no such step obligatory. The archdeacon had thought it wise to make use of the threat of the lawyer's bill, to frighten his father-in-law into compliance; but he had no intention to saddle Mr. Harding with costs, which had been incurred by no means exclusively for his benefit. The amount of the bill was added to the diocesan account, and was, in fact, paid out of the bishop's pocket, without any consciousness on the part of his lordship. A great part of his furniture he did resolve to sell, having no other means to dispose of it; and the ponies and carriage were transferred, by private contract, to the use of an old maiden lady in the city.

For his present use Mr. Harding took a lodging in Barchester, and thither were conveyed such articles as he wanted for daily use—his music, books, and instruments, his own arm-chair, and Eleanor's pet sofa; her teapoy and his cellaret, and also the slender but still sufficient contents of his winecellar. Mrs. Grantly had much wished that her sister would reside at Plumstead, till her father's house at Crabtree should be ready for her; but Eleanor herself strongly resisted this proposal. It was in vain urged upon her, that a lady in lodging cost more than a gentleman; and that, under her father's present circumstances, such an expense should be avoided. Eleanor had not pressed her father to give up the hospital in order that she might live at Plumstead Rectory and he alone in his Barchester lodgings; nor did Eleanor think that she would be treating a certain gentleman very fairly, if she betook herself to the house which he would be the least desirous of entering of any in the country. So she got a little bedroom for herself behind the sitting-room, and just over the little back-parlour of the chemist, with whom they were to lodge. There was somewhat of a savour of senna softened by peppermint about the place; but, on the whole, the lodgings were clean and comfortable.

The day had been fixed for the migration of the ex-warden, and all Barchester were in a state of excitement on the subject. Opinion was much divided as to the propriety of Mr. Harding's conduct. The mercantile part of the community, the mayor and corporation, and council, also most of the ladies, were loud in his praise. Nothing could be more noble, nothing more generous, nothing more upright. But the gentry were of a different way of thinking—especially the lawyers and the clergymen. They said such conduct was very weak and undignified; that Mr. Harding evinced a lamentable want of esprit de corps, as well as courage; and that such an abdication must do much harm, and could do but little good.

On the evening before he left, he summoned all the bedesmen into his parlour to wish them good-bye. With Bunce he had been in frequent communication since his return from London, and had been at much pains to explain to the old man the cause of his resignation, without in any way prejudicing the position of his successor. The others, also, he had seen more or less frequently; and had heard from most of them separately some expression of regret at his departure; but he had postponed his farewell till the last evening.

He now bade the maid put wine and glasses on the table; and had the chairs arranged around the room; and sent Bunce to each of the men to request they would come and say farewell to their late warden. Soon the noise of aged scuffling feet was heard upon the gravel and in the little hall, and the eleven men who were enabled to leave their rooms were assembled.

"Come in, my friends, come in," said the warden—he was still warden then. "Come in, and sit down"; and he took the hand of Abel Handy, who was the nearest to him, and led the limping grumbler to a chair. The others followed slowly and bashfully; the infirm, the lame, and the blind: poor wretches! who had been so happy, had they but known it! Now their aged faces were covered with shame, and every kind word from their master was a coal of fire burning on their heads.

When first the news had reached them that Mr. Harding was going to leave the hospital, it had been received with a kind of triumph—his departure was, as it were, a prelude to success. He had admitted his want of right to the money about which they were disputing; and as it did not belong to him, of course it did to them. The one hundred a year to each of them was actually becoming a reality; and Abel Handy was a hero, and Bunce a faint-hearted sycophant, worthy of neither honour nor fellowship. But other tidings soon made their way into the old men's rooms. It was first notified to them that the income abandoned by Mr. Harding would not come to them; and these accounts were confirmed by attorney Finney. They were then informed that Mr. Harding's place would be at once filled by another. That the new warden could not be a kinder man they all knew; that he would be a less friendly one most suspected; and then came the bitter information that, from the moment of Mr. Harding's departure, the twopence a day, his own peculiar gift, must of necessity be withdrawn.

And this was to be the end of all their mighty struggle—of their fight for their rights—of their petition, and their debates, and their hopes! They were to change the best of masters for a possible bad one, and to lose twopence a day each man! No; unfortunate as this was, it was not the worst, or nearly the worst, as will just now be seen.

"Sit down, sit down, my friends," said the warden; "I want to say a word to you and to drink your healths, before I leave you. Come up here, Moody, here is a chair for you; come,

Jonathan Crumple''—and by degrees `he got the men to be seated. It was not surprising that they should hang back with faint hearts, having returned so much kindness with such deep ingratitude. Last of all of them came Bunce, and with sorrowful mien and slow step got into his accustomed seat near the fire-place.

When they were all in their places, Mr. Harding rose to address them; and then finding himself not quite at home on his legs, he sat down again. ''My dear old friends,'' said he, ''you all know that I am going to leave you.''

There was a sort of murmur ran round the room, intended, perhaps, to express regret at his departure; but it was but a murmur, and might have meant that or anything else.

''There has been lately some misunderstanding between us. You have thought, I believe, that you did not get all that you were entitled to, and that the funds of the hospital have not been properly disposed of. As for me, I cannot say what should be the disposition of these moneys, or how they should be managed, and I have therefore thought it best to go.''

''We never wanted to drive your reverence out of it,'' said Handy.

''No, indeed, your reverence,'' said Skulpit. ''We never thought it would come to this. When I signed the petition—that is I didn't sign it, because——''

''Let his reverence speak, can't you?'' said Moody.

''No,'' continued Mr. Harding; ''I am sure you did not wish to turn me out; but I thought it best to leave you. I am not a very good hand at a lawsuit, as you may all guess; and when it seemed necessary that our ordinary quiet mode of living should be disturbed, I thought it better to go. I am neither angry nor offended with any man in the hospital.''

Here Bunce uttered a kind of groan, very clearly expressive of disagreement.

''I am neither angry nor displeased with any man in the hospital,'' repeated Mr. Harding, emphatically. ''If any man has been wrong—and I don't say any man has—he has erred through wrong advice. In this country all are entitled to look for their own rights, and you have done no more. As long as your interests and my interests were at variance, I could give you no counsel on this subject; but the connection between us has ceased; my income can no longer depend on your doings, and therefore, as I leave you, I venture to offer to you my advice.''

The men all declared that they would from henceforth be entirely guided by Mr. Harding's opinion in their affairs.

"Some gentleman will probably take my place here very soon, and I strongly advise you to be prepared to receive him in a kindly spirit and to raise no further question among yourselves as to the amount of his income. Were you to succeed in lessening what he has to receive, you would not increase your own allowance. The surplus would not go to you; your wants are adequately provided for, and your position could hardly be improved."

"God bless your reverence, we knows it," said Spriggs.

"It's all true, your reverence," said Skulpit. "We sees it all now."

"Yes, Mr. Harding," said Bunce, opening his mouth for the first time; "I believe they do understand it now, now that they've driven from under the same roof with them such a master as not one of them will ever know again—now that they're like to be in sore want of a friend."

"Come, come, Bunce," said Mr. Harding, blowing his nose and manœuvring to wipe his eyes at the same time.

"Oh, as to that," said Handy, "we none of us never wanted to do Mr. Harding no harm; if he's going now, it's not along of us; and I don't see for what Mr. Bunce speaks up agen us that way."

"You've ruined yourselves, and you've ruined me too, and that's why," said Bunce.

"Nonsense, Bunce," said Mr. Harding; "there's nobody ruined at all. I hope you'll let me leave you all friends, I hope you'll all drink a glass of wine in friendly feeling with me and with one another. You'll have a good friend, I don't doubt, in your new warden; and if ever you want any other, why after all I'm not going so far off but that I shall sometimes see you"; and then, having finished his speech, Mr. Harding filled all the glasses, and himself handed each a glass to the men round him, and raising his own said—

"God bless you all! you have my heartfelt wishes for your welfare. I hope you may live contented, and die trusting in the Lord Jesus Christ, and thankful to Almighty God for the good things he has given you. God bless you, my friends!" and Mr. Harding drank his wine.

Another murmur, somewhat more articulate than the first, passed round the circle, and this time it was intended to imply a blessing on Mr. Harding. It had, however, but little cordiality in it. Poor old men! how could they be cordial with their sore consciences and shamed faces? how could they bid God bless him with hearty voices and a true benison, knowing, as they did, that their vile cabal had driven him from his happy home, and sent him in his old age to seek shelter under a strange roof-tree? They did their best, however; they drank their wine, and withdrew.

As they left the hall-door, Mr. Harding shook hands with each of the men, and spoke a kind word to them about their individual cases and ailments; and so they departed, answering his questions in the fewest words, and retreated to their dens, a sorrowful repentant crew.

All but Bunce, who still remained to make his own farewell. "There's poor old Bell," said Mr. Harding; "I mustn't go without saying a word to him; come through with me, Bunce, and bring the wine with you"; and so they went through to the men's cottages, and found the old man propped up as usual in his bed.

"I've come to say good-bye to you, Bell," said Mr. Harding, speaking loud, for the old man was deaf.

"And are you going away, then, really?" asked Bell.

"Indeed I am, and I've brought you a glass of wine; so that we may part friends, as we lived, you know."

The old man took the proffered glass in his shaking hands, and drank it eagerly. "God bless you, Bell!" said Mr. Harding; "good-bye, my old friend."

"And so you're really going?" the man again asked.

"Indeed I am, Bell."

The poor old bed-ridden creature still kept Mr. Harding's hand in his own, and the warden thought that he had met with something like warmth of feeling in the one of all his subjects from whom it was the least likely to be expected; for poor old Bell had nearly outlived all human feelings. "And your reverence," said he, and then he paused, while his old palsied head shook horribly, and his shrivelled cheeks sank lower within his jaws, and his glazy eye gleamed with a momentary light; "and your reverence, shall we get the hundred a year, then?"

How gently did Mr. Harding try to extinguish the false hope of money which had been so wretchedly raised to disturb the quiet of the dying man! One other week and his mortal coil would be shuffled off; in one short week would God resume his soul, and set it apart for its irrevocable doom; seven more tedious days and nights of senseless inactivity, and all would be over for poor Bell in this world; and yet, with his last audible words, he was demanding his moneyed rights, and asserting himself to be the proper heir of John Hiram's bounty! Not on him, poor sinner as he was, be the load of such sin!

Mr. Harding returned to his parlour, meditating with a sick heart on what he had seen, and Bunce with him. We will not describe the parting of these two good men, for good men they were. It was in vain that the late warden endeavoured to comfort the heart of the old bedesman; poor old Bunce felt that his days of comfort were gone. The hospital had to him been a happy home, but it could be so no longer. He had had honour there, and friendship; he had recognised his master, and had been recognised; all his wants, both of soul and body, had been supplied, and he had been a happy man. He wept grievously as he parted from his friend, and the tears of an old man are bitter. "It is all over for me in this world," said he, as he gave the last squeeze to Mr. Harding's hand; "I have now to forgive those who have injured me—and to die."

And so the old man went out, and then Mr. Harding gave way to his grief and he too wept aloud.

XXI

Conclusion

Our tale is now done, and it only remains to us to collect the scattered threads of our little story, and to tie them into a seemly knot. This will not be a work of labour, either to the author or to his readers; we have not to deal with many personages, or with stirring events, and were it not for the custom of the thing, we might leave it to the imagination of all concerned to conceive how affairs at Barchester arranged themselves.

On the morning after the day last alluded to, Mr. Harding, at an early hour, walked out of the hospital, with his daughter under his arm, and sat down quietly to breakfast at his lodgings over the chemist's shop. There was no parade about his departure;

no one, not even Bunce, was there to witness it; had he walked to the apothecary's thus early to get a piece of court plaster, or a box of lozenges, he could not have done it with less appearance of an important movement. There was a tear in Eleanor's eye as she passed through the big gateway and over the bridge; but Mr. Harding walked with an elastic step, and entered his new abode with a pleasant face.

"Now, my dear," said he, "you have everything ready, and you can make tea here just as nicely as in the parlour at the hospital." So Eleanor took off her bonnet and made the tea. After this manner did the late Warden of Barchester Hospital accomplish his flitting, and change his residence.

It was not long before the archdeacon brought his father to discuss the subject of a new warden. Of course he looked upon the nomination as his own, and he had in his eye three or four fitting candidates, seeing that Mr. Cumming's plan as to the living of Puddingdale could not be brought to bear. How can I describe the astonishment which confounded him, when his father declared that he would appoint no successor to Mr. Harding? "If we can get the matter set to rights, Mr. Harding will return," said the bishop; "and if we cannot, it will be wrong to put any other gentleman into so cruel a position."

It was in vain that the archdeacon argued and lectured, and even threatened; in vain he my-lorded his poor father in his sternest manner; in vain his "good heavens!" were ejaculated in a tone that might have moved a whole synod, let alone one weak and aged bishop. Nothing could induce his father to fill up the vacancy caused by Mr. Harding's retirement.

Even John Bold would have pitied the feelings with which the archdeacon returned to Plumstead: the church was falling, nay, already in ruins; its dignitaries were yielding without a struggle before the blows of its antagonists; and one of its most respected bishops, his own father—the man considered by all the world as being in such matters under his, Dr. Grantly's, control—had positively resolved to capitulate, and own himself vanquished!

And how fared the hospital under this resolve of its visitor? Badly indeed. It is now some years since Mr. Harding left it, and the warden's house is still tenantless. Old Bell has died, and Billy Gazy; the one-eyed Spriggs has drunk himself to death, and three others of the twelve have been gathered into the churchyard mould. Six have gone, and the six vacancies remain unfilled! Yes, six have died, with no kind friend to solace their last moments, with no wealthy neighbour to administer comforts and ease the stings of death. Mr. Harding, indeed, did not desert them; from him they had such consolation as a dying man may receive from his Christian pastor; but it was the occasional kindness of a stranger which ministered to them, and not the constant presence of a master, a neighbour, and a friend.

Nor were those who remained better off than those who died. Dissensions rose among them, and contests for pre-eminence; and then they began to understand that soon one among them would be the last—some one wretched being would be alone there in that now comfortless hospital—the miserable relic of what had once been so good and so comfortable.

The building of the hospital itself has not been allowed to go to ruins. Mr. Chadwick, who still holds his stewardship, and pays the accruing rents into an account opened at a bank for the purpose, sees to that; but the whole place has become disordered and ugly. The warden's garden is a wretched wilderness, the drive and paths are covered with weeds, the flower-beds are bare, and the unshorn lawn is now a mass of long damp grass and unwholesome moss. The beauty of the place is gone; its attractions have withered. Alas! a very few years since it was the prettiest spot in Barchester, and now it is a disgrace to the city.

Mr. Harding did not go out to Crabtree Parva. An arrangement was made which respected the homestead of Mr. Smith and his happy family, and put Mr. Harding into possession of a small living within the walls of the city. It is the smallest possible parish, containing a part of the Cathedral Close and a few old houses adjoining. The church is a singular little Gothic building, perched over a gateway, through which the Close is entered, and is approached by a flight of stone steps which leads down under the archway of the gate. It is no bigger than an ordinary room— perhaps twenty-seven feet long by eighteen wide—but still it is a perfect church. It contains an old carved pulpit and reading-desk, a tiny altar under a window filled with dark old-coloured glass, a font, some half-dozen pews, and perhaps a dozen seats for the poor; and also a vestry. The roof is high pitched, and of black old oak, and the three large beams which support it run down to the side walls, and terminate in grotesquely carved faces—two devils and an angel on one side, two angels and a devil on the other. Such is the church of St. Cuthbert at Barchester, of which Mr. Harding became rector, with a clear income of seventy-five pounds a year.

Here he performs afternoon service every Sunday, and ad-ministers the Sacrament once in every three months. His audience is not large; and, had they been so, he could not have accommodated them; but enough come to fill his six pews, and on the front seat of those devoted to the poor is always to be seen our old friend Mr. Bunce, decently arrayed in his bedesman's gown.

Mr. Harding is still precentor of Barchester; and it is very rarely the case that those who attend the Sunday morning service miss the gratification of hearing him chant the Litany, as no other man in England can do it. He is neither a discontented nor an unhappy man; he still inhabits the lodgings to which he went on leaving the hospital, but he now has them to himself. Three months after that time Eleanor became Mrs. Bold, and of course removed to her husband's house.

There were some difficulties to be got over on the occasion of the marriage. The archdeacon, who could not so soon overcome his grief, would not be persuaded to grace the ceremony with his presence, but he allowed his wife and children to be there. The marriage took place in the cathedral, and the bishop himself officiated. It was the last occasion on which he ever did so; and, though he still lives, it is not probable that he will ever do so again.

Not long after the marriage, perhaps six months, when Eleanor's bridal-honours were fading, and persons were beginning to call her Mrs. Bold without twittering, the archdeacon consented to meet John Bold at a dinner-party, and since that time they have become almost friends. The archdeacon firmly believes that his brother-in-law was, as a bachelor, an infidel, and unbeliever in the great truths of our religion; but that matrimony has opened his eyes, as it has those of others. And Bold is equally inclined to think that time has softened the asperities of the archdeacon's character. Friends though they are, they do not often revert to the feud of the hospital.

Mr. Harding, we say, is not an unhappy man: he keeps his lodgings, but they are of little use to him, except as being the one spot on earth which he calls his own. His time is spent chiefly at his daughter's or at the palace; he is never left alone, even should he wish to be so; and within a twelve-month of Eleanor's marriage his determination to live at his own lodging had been so far broken through and abandoned, that he consented to have his violoncello permanently removed to his daughter's house.

Every other day a message is brought to him from the bishop. ''The bishop's compliments, and his lordship is not very

well to-day, and he hopes Mr. Harding will dine with him.''
This bulletin as to the old man's health is a myth; for though he
is over eighty he is never ill, and will probably die some day, as
a spark goes out, gradually and without a struggle. Mr. Harding
does dine with him very often, which means going to the palace
at three and remaining till ten; and whenever he does not the
bishop whines, and says that the port wine is corked, and
complains that nobody attends to him, and frets himself off to
bed an hour before his time.

It was long before the people of Barchester forgot to call
Mr. Harding by his long well-known name of Warden. It had
become so customary to say Mr. Warden, that it was not easily
dropped. ''No, no,'' he always says when so addressed, ''not
warden now, only precentor.''

BARCHESTER TOWERS

VOLUME ONE

I

Who Will Be the New Bishop?

In the latter days of July in the year 185—, a most important question was for ten days hourly asked in the cathedral city of Barchester, and answered every hour in various ways—Who was to be the new Bishop?

The death of old Dr. Grantly, who had for many years filled that chair with meek authority, took place exactly as the ministry of Lord —— was going to give place to that of Lord ——. The illness of the good old man was long and lingering, and it became at last a matter of intense interest to those concerned whether the new appointment should be made by a conservative or liberal government.

It was pretty well understood that the out-going premier had made his selection, and that if the question rested with him, the mitre would descend on the head of Archdeacon Grantly, the old bishop's son. The archdeacon had long managed the affairs of the diocese; and for some months previous to the demise of his father, rumour had confidently assigned to him the reversion of his father's honours.

Bishop Grantly died as he had lived, peaceably, slowly, without pain and without excitement. The breath ebbed from him almost imperceptibly, and for a month before his death, it was a question whether he were alive or dead.

A trying time was this for the archdeacon, for whom was designed the reversion of his father's see by those who then had the giving away of episcopal thrones. I would not be understood to say that the prime minister had in so many words promised the bishopric to Dr. Grantly. He was too discreet a man for that. There is a proverb with reference to the killing of cats, and those who know anything either of high or low government places, will be well aware that a promise may be made without positive words, and that an expectant may be put into the highest state of encouragement, though the great man on whose breath he hangs may have done no more than whisper that "Mr. So-and-so is certainly a rising man."

Such a whisper had been made, and was known by those who heard it to signify that the cures of the diocese of Barchester should not be taken out of the hands of the archdeacon. The then prime minister was all in all at Oxford, and had lately passed a night at the house of the master of Lazarus. Now the master of Lazarus—which is, by the bye, in many respects the most comfortable, as well as the richest college at Oxford,—was the archdeacon's most intimate friend and most trusted counsellor. On the occasion of the prime minister's visit, Dr. Grantly was of course present, and the meeting was very gracious. On the following morning Dr. Gwynne, the master, told the archdeacon that in his opinion the thing was settled.

At this time the bishop was quite on his last legs; but the ministry also were tottering. Dr. Grantly returned from Oxford happy and elated, to resume his place in the palace, and to continue to perform for the father the last duties of a son; which, to give him his due, he performed with more tender care than was to be expected from his usual somewhat worldly manners.

A month since the physicians had named four weeks as the outside period during which breath could be supported within the body of the dying man. At the end of the month the physicians wondered, and named another fortnight. The old man lived on wine alone, but at the end of the fortnight he still lived; and the tidings of the fall of the ministry became more frequent. Sir Lamda Mewnew and Sir Omicron Pie, the two great London doctors, now came down for the fifth time, and declared, shaking their learned heads, that another week of life was impossible; and as they sat down to lunch in the episcopal dining-room, whispered to the archdeacon their own private knowledge that the ministry must fall within five days. The son returned to his father's room, and after administering with his own hands the sustaining modicum of madeira, sat down by the bedside to calculate his chances.

The ministry were to be out within five days: his father was to be dead within—No, he rejected that view of the subject. The ministry were to be out, and the diocese might probably be vacant at the same period. There was much doubt as to the names of the men who were to succeed to power, and a week must elapse before a Cabinet was formed. Would not vacancies be filled by the out-going men during this week? Dr. Grantly had a kind of idea that such would be the case, but did not know; and then he wondered at his own ignorance on such a question.

He tried to keep his mind away from the subject, but he could not. The race was so very close, and the stakes were so very high. He then looked at the dying man's impassive, placid face. There was no sign there of death or disease; it was something thinner than of yore, somewhat greyer, and the deep lines of age more marked; but, as far as he could judge, life might yet hang there for weeks to come. Sir Lamda Mewnew and Sir Omicron Pie had thrice been wrong, and might yet be wrong thrice again. The old bishop slept during twenty of the twenty-four hours, but during the short periods of his waking moments, he knew both his son and his dear old friend, Mr. Harding, the archdeacon's father-in-law, and would thank them tenderly for their care and love. Now he lay sleeping like a baby, resting easily on his back, his mouth just open, and his few grey hairs straggling from beneath his cap; his breath was perfectly noiseless, and his thin, wan hand, which lay above the coverlid, never moved. Nothing could be easier than the old man's passage from this world to the next.

But by no means easy were the emotions of him who sat there watching. He knew it must be now or never. He was already over fifty, and there was little chance that his friends who were now leaving office would soon return to it. No probable British prime minister but he who was now in, he who was so soon to be out, would think of making a bishop of Dr. Grantly. Thus he thought long and sadly, in deep silence, and then gazed at that still living face, and then at last dared to ask himself whether he really longed for his father's death.

The effort was a salutary one, and the question was answered in a moment. The proud, wishful, worldly man, sank on his knees by the bedside, and taking the bishop's hand within his own, prayed eagerly that his sins might be forgiven him.

His face was still buried in the clothes when the door of the bed-room opened noiselessly, and Mr. Harding entered with a velvet step. Mr. Harding's attendance at that bedside had been nearly as constant as that of the archdeacon, and his ingress and egress were as much a matter of course as that of his son-in-law. He was standing close beside the archdeacon before he was perceived, and would also have knelt in prayer had he not feared that his doing so might have caused some sudden start, and have disturbed the dying man. Dr. Grantly, however, instantly perceived him, and rose from his knees. As he did so Mr. Harding took both his hands, and pressed them warmly. There was more fellowship between them at that moment than there had ever been before, and it so happened that after circumstances greatly preserved the feeling. As they stood there pressing each other's hands, the tears rolled freely down their cheeks.

"God bless you, my dears,"—said the bishop with feeble voice as he woke—"God bless you—may God bless you both, my dear children": and so he died.

There was no loud rattle in the throat, no dreadful struggle, no palpable sign of death; but the lower jaw fell a little from its place, and the eyes, which had been so constantly closed in sleep, now remained fixed and open. Neither Mr. Harding nor Dr. Grantly knew that life was gone, though both suspected it.

"I believe it's all over," said Mr. Harding, still pressing the other's hands. "I think—nay, I hope it is."

"I will ring the bell," said the other, speaking all but in a whisper. "Mrs. Phillips should be here."

Mrs. Phillips, the nurse, was soon in the room, and immediately, with practised hand, closed those staring eyes.

"It's all over, Mrs. Phillips?" asked Mr. Harding.

"My lord's no more," said Mrs. Phillips, turning round and curtseying low with solemn face; "his lordship's gone more like a sleeping babby than any that I ever saw."

"It's a great relief, archdeacon," said Mr. Harding, "a great relief—dear, good, excellent old man. Oh, that our last moments may be as innocent and as peaceful as his!"

"Surely," said Mrs. Phillips. "The Lord be praised for all his mercies; but, for a meek, mild, gentle-spoken Christian, his lordship was——" and Mrs. Phillips, with unaffected but easy grief, put up her white apron to her flowing eyes.

"You cannot but rejoice that it is over," said Mr. Harding, still consoling his friend. The archdeacon's mind, however, had already travelled from the death chamber to the closet of the prime minister. He had brought himself to pray for his father's life, but now that that life was done, minutes were too precious to be lost. It was now useless to dally with the fact of the bishop's death—useless to lose perhaps everything for the pretence of a foolish sentiment.

But how was he to act while his father-in-law stood there holding his hand? how, without appearing unfeeling, was he to forget his father in the bishop—to overlook what he had lost, and think only of what he might possibly gain?

"No; I suppose not," said he, at last, in answer to Mr. Harding. "We have all expected it so long."

Mr. Harding took him by the arm and led him from the room. "We will see him again to-morrow morning," said he; "we had better leave the room now to the women." And so they went down stairs.

It was already evening and nearly dark. It was most important that the prime minister should know that night that the diocese was vacant. Everything might depend on it; and so, in answer to Mr. Harding's further consolation, the archdeacon suggested that a telegraph message should be immediately sent off to London. Mr. Harding, who had really been somewhat surprised to find Dr. Grantly, as he thought, so much affected, was rather taken aback; but he made no objection. He knew that the archdeacon had some hope of succeeding to his father's place, though he by no means knew how highly raised that hope had been.

"Yes," said Dr. Grantly, collecting himself and shaking off his weakness, "we must send a message at once; we don't know what might be the consequence of delay. Will you do it?"

"I! oh, yes; certainly: I'll do anything, only I don't know exactly what it is you want."

Dr. Grantly sat down before a writing table, and taking pen and ink, wrote a slip of paper as follows:—

By Electric Telegraph.
For the Earl of——, Downing Street, or elsewhere.
"The Bishop of Barchester is dead."
Message sent by the Rev. Septimus Harding.

"There," said he, "just take that to the telegraph office at the railway station, and give it in as it is; they'll probably make you copy it on to one of their own slips; that's all you'll have to do: then you'll have to pay them half-a-crown"; and the archdeacon put his hand in his pocket and pulled out the necessary sum.

Mr. Harding felt very much like an errand-boy, and also felt that he was called on to perform his duties as such at rather an unseemly time; but he said nothing, and took the slip of paper and the proffered coin.

"But you've put my name into it, archdeacon."

"Yes," said the other, "there should be the name of some

clergyman you know, and what name so proper as that of so old a friend as yourself? The earl won't look at the name, you may be sure of that; but my dear Mr. Harding, pray don't lose any time."

Mr. Harding got as far as the library door on his way to the station when he suddenly remembered the news with which he was fraught when he entered the poor bishop's bed-room. He had found the moment so inopportune for any mundane tidings that he had repressed the words which were on his tongue, and immediately afterwards all recollection of the circumstance was for the time banished by the scene which had occurred.

"But, archdeacon," said he, turning back, "I forgot to tell you—The ministry are out."

"Out!" ejaculated the archdeacon, in a tone which too plainly showed his anxiety and dismay, although under the circumstances of the moment he endeavoured to control himself: "Out! who told you so?"

Mr. Harding explained that news to this effect had come down by electric telegraph, and that the tidings had been left at the palace door by Mr. Chadwick.

The archdeacon sat silent for awhile meditating, and Mr. Harding stood looking at him. "Never mind," said the archdeacon at last; "send the message all the same. The news must be sent to some one, and there is at present no one else in a position to receive it. Do it at once, my dear friend; you know I would not trouble you, were I in a state to do it myself. A few minutes' time is of the greatest importance."

Mr. Harding went out and sent the message, and it may be as well that we should follow it to its destination. Within thirty minutes of its leaving Barchester it reached the Earl of —— in his inner library. What elaborate letters, what eloquent appeals, what indignant remonstrances, he might there have to frame, at such a moment, may be conceived, but not described! How he was preparing his thunder for successful rivals, standing like a British peer with his back to the sea-coal fire, and his hands in his breeches pockets—how his fine eye was lit up with anger, and his forehead gleamed with patriotism.—how he stamped his foot as he thought of his heavy associates,—how he all but swore as he remembered how much too clever one of them had been,—my creative readers may imagine. But was he so engaged? No: history and truth compel me to deny it. He was sitting easily in a lounging chair, conning over a Newmarket list, and by his elbow on the table was lying open an uncut French novel on which he was engaged.

He opened the cover in which the message was enclosed, and having read it, he took his pen and wrote on the back of it—

> For the Earl of——,
> With the Earl of——'s compliments,

and sent it off again on its journey.

Thus terminated our unfortunate friend's chance of possessing the glories of a bishopric.

The names of many divines were given in the papers as that of the bishop elect. The *British Grandmother* declared that Dr. Gwynne was to be the man, in compliment to the late ministry. This was a heavy blow to Dr. Grantly, but he was not doomed to see himself superseded by his friend. The *Anglican Devotee* put forward confidently the claims of a great London preacher of austere doctrines; and the *Eastern Hemisphere*, an evening paper supposed to possess much official knowledge, declared in favour of an eminent naturalist, a gentleman most completely versed in the knowledge of rocks and minerals, but supposed by many to hold on religious subjects no special doctrines whatever. The *Jupiter*, that daily paper, which, as we all know, is the only true source of infallibly correct information on all subjects, for a while was silent, but at last spoke out. The merits of all these candidates were discussed and somewhat irreverently disposed of, and then the *Jupiter* declared that Dr. Proudie was to be the man.

Dr. Proudie was the man. Just a month after the demise of the late bishop, Dr. Proudie kissed the Queen's hand as his successor elect.

We must beg to be allowed to draw a curtain over the sorrows of the archdeacon as he sat, sombre and sad at heart, in the study of his parsonage at Plumstead Episcopi. On the day subsequent to the despatch of the message he heard that the Earl of —— had consented to undertake the formation of a ministry, and from that moment he knew that his chance was over. Many will think that he was wicked to grieve for the loss of episcopal power, wicked to have coveted it, nay, wicked even to have thought about it, in the way and at the moments he had done so.

With such censures I cannot profess that I completely agree. The *nolo episcopari*, though still in use, is so directly at variance with the tendency of all human wishes, that it cannot be thought to express the true aspirations of rising priests in the Church of England. A lawyer does not sin in seeking to be a judge, or in compassing his wishes by all honest means. A young diplomat entertains a fair ambition when he looks forward to be the lord of a first-rate embassy; and a poor novelist when he attempts to rival Dickens or rise above Fitzjeames, commits no fault, though he may be foolish. Sydney Smith truly said that in these recreant days we cannot expect to find the majesty of St. Paul beneath the cassock of a curate. If we look to our clergymen to be more than men, we shall probably teach ourselves to think that they are less, and can hardly hope to raise the character of the pastor by denying to him the right to entertain the aspirations of a man.

Our archdeacon was worldly—who among us is not so? He was ambitious—who among us is ashamed to own that "last infirmity of noble minds"! He was avaricious, my readers will say. No—it was for no love of lucre that he wished to be bishop of Barchester. He was his father's only child, and his father had left him great wealth. His preferment brought him in nearly three thousand a year. The bishopric, as cut down by the Ecclesiastical Commission, was only five. He would be a richer man as archdeacon than he could be as bishop. But he certainly did desire to play first fiddle; he did desire to sit in full lawn sleeves among the peers of the realm; and he did desire, if truth must out, to be called "My Lord" by his reverend brethren.

His hopes, however, were they innocent or sinful, were not fated to be realised; and Dr. Proudie was consecrated Bishop of Barchester.

II

Hiram's Hospital According to Act of Parliament

It is hardly necessary that I should here give to the public any lengthened biography of Mr. Harding, up to the period of the commencement of this tale. The public cannot have forgotten how ill that sensitive gentleman bore the attack that was made on him in the columns of the *Jupiter,* with reference to the income which he received as warden of Hiram's hospital, in the city of Barchester. Nor can it yet be forgotten that a law-suit was instituted against him on the matter of that charity by Mr. John Bold, who afterwards married his, Mr. Harding's, younger and then only unmarried daughter. Under pressure of these attacks, Mr. Harding has resigned his wardenship, though strongly recommended to abstain from doing so, both by his friends and by his lawyers. He did, however, resign it, and betook himself manfully to the duties of the small parish of St. Cuthbert's, in the city, of which he was vicar, continuing also to perform those of precentor of the cathedral, a situation of small emolument which had hitherto been supposed to be joined, as a matter of course, to the wardenship of the hospital above spoken of.

When he left the hospital from which he had been so ruthlessly driven, and settled himself down in his own modest manner in the High Street of Barchester, he had not expected that others would make more fuss about it than he was inclined to do himself; and the extent of his hope was, that the movement might have been made in time to prevent any further paragraphs in the *Jupiter*. His affairs, however, were not allowed to subside thus quietly, and people were quite as much inclined to talk about the disinterested sacrifice he had made, as they had before been to upbraid him for his cupidity.

The most remarkable thing that occurred, was the receipt of an autograph letter from the Archbishop of Canterbury, in which the primate very warmly praised his conduct, and begged to know what his intentions were for the future. Mr. Harding replied that he intended to be rector of St. Cuthbert's, in Barchester: and so that matter dropped. Then the newspapers took up his case, the *Jupiter* among the rest, and wafted his name in eulogistic strains through every reading-room in the nation. It was discovered also, that he was the author of that great musical work, Harding's *Church Music,*—and a new edition was spoken of, though, I believe, never printed. It is, however, certain that the work was introduced into the Royal Chapel at St. James's, and that a long criticism appeared in the *Musical Scrutator,* declaring that in no previous work of the kind had so much research been joined with such exalted musical ability, and asserting that the name of Harding would henceforward be known wherever the Arts were cultivated, or Religion valued.

This was high praise, and I will not deny that Mr. Harding was gratified by such flattery; for if Mr. Harding was vain on any subject, it was on that of music. But here the matter rested. The second edition, if printed, was never purchased; the copies which had been introduced into the Royal Chapel disappeared again, and were laid by in peace, with a load of similar literature. Mr. Towers, of the *Jupiter,* and his brethren, occupied themselves with other names, and the undying fame promised to our friend was clearly intended to be posthumous.

Mr. Harding had spent much of his time with his friend the bishop, much with his daughter Mrs. Bold, now, alas, a widow; and had almost daily visited the wretched remnant of his former subjects, the few surviving bedesmen now left at Hiram's hospital. Six of them were still living. The number, according to old Hiram's will, should always have been twelve. But after the abdication of their warden, the bishop had appointed no successor to him, no new occupants of the charity had been nominated, and it appeared as though the hospital at Barchester would fall into abeyance, unless the powers that be should take some steps toward putting it once more into working order.

During the past five years, the powers that be had not overlooked Barchester Hospital, and sundry political doctors had taken the matter in hand. Shortly after Mr. Harding's resignation, the *Jupiter* had very clearly shown what ought to be done. In about half a column it had distributed the income, rebuilt the building, put an end to all bickerings, regenerated kindly feeling, provided for Mr. Harding, and placed the whole thing on a footing which could not but be satisfactory to the city and Bishop of Barchester, and to the nation at large. The wisdom of this scheme was testified by the number of letters which "Common Sense," "Veritas," and "One that loves fair play" sent to the *Jupiter,* all expressing admiration, and amplifying on the details given. It is singular enough that no adverse letter appeared at all, and, therefore, none of course was written.

But Cassandra was not believed, and even the wisdom of the *Jupiter* sometimes falls on deaf ears. Though other plans did not put themselves forward in the columns of the *Jupiter,* reformers of church charities were not slack to make known in various places their different nostrums for setting Hiram's hospital on its feet again. A learned bishop took occasion, in the Upper House, to allude to the matter, intimating that he had communicated on the subject with his right reverend brother of Barchester. The radical member for Staleybridge had suggested that the funds should be alienated for the education of the agricultural poor of the country, and he amused the House by some anecdotes touching the superstition and habits of the agriculturists in question. A political pamphleteer had produced a few dozen pages, which he called *Who Are John Hiram's Heirs?* intending to give an infallible rule for the governance of all such establishments; and, at last, a member of the government promised that in the next session a short bill should be introduced for regulating the affairs of Barchester, and other kindred concerns.

The next session came, and, contrary to custom, the bill came also. Men's minds were then intent on other things. The first threatenings of a huge war hung heavily over the nation, and the question as to Hiram's heirs did not appear to interest very many people either in or out of the house. The bill, however, was read and re-read, and in some undistinguished manner passed through its eleven stages without appeal or dissent. What would John Hiram have said in the matter, could he have predicted that some forty-five gentlemen would take on themselves to make a law altering the whole purport of his will, without in the least knowing at the moment of their making it, what it was that they were doing? It is however to be hoped that the under-secretary for the Home Office knew, for to him had the matter been confided.

The bill, however, did pass, and at the time at which this history is supposed to commence, it had been ordained that there should be, as heretofore, twelve old men in Barchester Hospital, each with 1*s.* 4*d.* a day; that there should also be twelve old women to be located in a house to be built, each with 1*s.* 2*d.* a day; that there should be a matron, with a house and £70 a year; a steward with £150 a year; and latterly, a warden with £450 a year, who should have the spiritual guidance of both establishments, and the temporal guidance of that appertaining to the male sex. The bishop, dean, and warden were, as formerly, to appoint in turn the recipients of the charity, and the bishop was to appoint the officers. There was nothing said as to the wardenship being held by the precentor of the cathedral, nor a word as to Mr. Harding's right to the situation.

It was not, however, till some months after the death of the old bishop, and almost immediately consequent on the installation of his successor, that notice was given that the reform was about to be carried out. The new law and the new bishop were among the earliest works of a new ministry, or rather of a ministry who, having for a while given place to their opponents,

had then returned to power; and the death of Dr. Grantly occurred,
as we have seen, exactly at the period of the change.

Poor Eleanor Bold! How well does that widow's cap become her, and the solemn gravity with which she devotes herself
to her new duties. Poor Eleanor!

Poor Eleanor! I cannot say that with me John Bold was ever
a favourite. I never thought him worthy of the wife he had won.
But in her estimation he was most worthy. Hers was one of those
feminine hearts which cling to a husband, not with idolatry, for
worship can admit of no defect in its idol, but with the perfect
tenacity of ivy. As the parasite plant will follow even the defects
of the trunk which it embraces, so did Eleanor cling to and love
the very faults of her husband. She had once declared that
whatever her father did should in her eyes be right. She then
transferred her allegiance, and became ever ready to defend the
worst failings of her lord and master.

And John Bold was a man to be loved by a woman; he was
himself affectionate, he was confiding and manly; and that arrogance of thought, unsustained by first-rate abilities, that attempt
at being better than his neighbours which jarred so painfully on
the feelings of his acquaintance, did not injure him in the estimation of his wife.

Could she even have admitted that he had a fault, his early
death would have blotted out the memory of it. She wept as for
the loss of the most perfect treasure with which mortal woman
had ever been endowed; for weeks after he was gone the idea of
future happiness in this world was hateful to her; consolation, as
it is called, was insupportable, and tears and sleep were her only
relief.

But God tempers the wind to the shorn lamb. She knew that
she had within her the living source of other cares. She knew
that there was to be created for her another subject of weal or
woe, of unutterable joy or despairing sorrow, as God in his
mercy might vouchsafe to her. At first this did but augment her
grief! To be the mother of a poor infant, orphaned before it was
born, brought forth to the sorrows of an ever desolate hearth,
nurtured amidst tears and wailing, and then turned adrift into the
world without the aid of a father's care! There was at first no joy
in this.

By degrees, however, her heart became anxious for another
object, and, before its birth, the stranger was expected with all
the eagerness of a longing mother. Just eight months after the
father's death a second John Bold was born, and if the worship

of one creature can be innocent in another, let us hope that the adoration offered over the cradle of the fatherless infant may not be imputed as a sin.

It will not be worth our while to define the character of the child, or to point out in how far the faults of the father were redeemed within that little breast by the virtues of the mother. The baby, as a baby, was all that was delightful, and I cannot foresee that it will be necessary for us to inquire into the facts of his after life. Our present business at Barchester will not occupy us above a year or two at the furthest, and I will leave it to some other pen to produce, if necessary, the biography of John Bold the Younger.

But, as a baby, this baby was all that could be desired. This fact no one attempted to deny. "Is he not delightful?" she would say to her father, looking up into his face from her knees, her lustrous eyes overflowing with soft tears, her young face encircled by her close widow's cap and her hands on each side of the cradle in which her treasure was sleeping. The grandfather would gladly admit that the treasure was delightful, and the uncle archdeacon himself would agree, and Mrs. Grantly, Eleanor's sister, would re-echo the word with true sisterly energy; and Mary Bold—but Mary Bold was a second worshipper at the same shrine.

The baby was really delightful; he took his food with a will, struck out his toes merrily whenever his legs were uncovered, and did not have fits. These are supposed to be the strongest points of baby perfection, and in all these our baby excelled.

And thus the widow's deep grief was softened, and a sweet balm was poured into the wound which she had thought nothing but death could heal. How much kinder is God to us than we are willing to be to ourselves! At the loss of every dear face, at the last going of every well beloved one, we all doom ourselves to an eternity of sorrow, and look to waste ourselves away in an ever-running fountain of tears. How seldom does such grief endure! how blessed is the goodness which forbids it to do so! "Let me ever remember my living friends, but forget them as soon as dead," was the prayer of a wise man who understood the mercy of God. Few perhaps would have the courage to express such a wish, and yet to do so would only be to ask for that release from sorrow, which a kind Creator almost always extends to us.

I would not, however, have it imagined that Mrs. Bold forgot her husband. She daily thought of him with all conjugal love, and enshrined his memory in the innermost centre of her heart. But yet she was happy in her baby. It was so sweet to press the living toy to her breast, and feel that a human being existed who did owe, and was to owe everything to her; whose daily food was drawn from herself; whose little wants could all be satisfied by her; whose little heart would first love her and her only; whose infant tongue would make its first effort in calling her by the sweetest name a woman can hear. And so Eleanor's bosom became tranquil, and she set about her new duties eagerly and gratefully.

As regards the concerns of the world, John Bold had left his widow in prosperous circumstances. He had bequeathed to her all that he possessed, and that comprised an income much exceeding what she or her friends thought necessary for her. It amounted to nearly a thousand a year; and when she reflected on its extent, her dearest hope was to hand it over, not only unimpaired but increased, to her husband's son, to her own darling, to the little man who now lay sleeping on her knee, happily ignorant of the cares which were to be accumulated in his behalf.

When John Bold died she earnestly implored her father to come and live with her, but this Mr. Harding declined, though for some weeks he remained with her as a visitor. He could not be prevailed upon to forego the possession of some small home of his own, and so remained in the lodgings he had first selected over a chemist's shop in the High Street of Barchester.

III

Dr. and Mrs. Proudie

This narrative is supposed to commence immediately after the installation of Dr. Proudie. I will not describe the ceremony, as I do not precisely understand its nature. I am ignorant whether a bishop be chaired like a member of Parliament, or carried in a gilt coach like a lord mayor, or sworn in like a justice of peace, or introduced like a peer to the Upper House, or led between two brethren like a knight of the garter; but I do know that every thing was properly done, and that nothing fit or becoming to a young bishop was omitted on the occasion.

Dr. Proudie was not the man to allow anything to be omitted that might be becoming to his new dignity. He understood well the value of forms, and knew that the due observance of rank could not be maintained unless the exterior trappings belonging to it were held in proper esteem. He was a man born to move in high circles; at least so he thought himself, and circumstances had certainly sustained him in this view. He was the nephew of an Irish baron by his mother's side, and his wife was the niece of a Scotch earl. He had for years held some clerical office appertaining to courtly matters, which had enabled him to live in London, and to entrust his parish to his curate. He had been preacher to the royal beef-eaters, curator of theological manuscripts in the Ecclesiastical Courts, chaplain to the Queen's yeomanry guard, and almoner to his Royal Highness the Prince of Rappe-Blankenburg.

His residence in the metropolis, rendered necessary by the duties thus entrusted to him, his high connections, and the peculiar talents and nature of the man, recommended him to persons in power; and Dr. Proudie became known as a useful and rising clergyman.

Some few years since, even within the memory of many who are not yet willing to call themselves old, a liberal clergyman was a person not frequently to be met. Sydney Smith was such, and was looked on as little better than an infidel; a few others also might be named, but they were "raræ aves," and were regarded with doubt and distrust by their brethren. No man was so surely a tory as a country rector—nowhere were the powers that be so cherished as at Oxford.

When, however, Dr. Whately was made an archbishop, and Dr. Hampden some years afterwards regius professor, many wise divines saw that a change was taking place in men's minds, and that more liberal ideas would henceforward be suitable to the priests as well as to the laity. Clergymen began to be heard of who had ceased to anathematise papists on the one hand, or vilify dissenters on the other. It appeared clear that high church principles, as they are called, were no longer to be surest claims to promotion with at any rate one section of statesmen, and Dr. Proudie was one among those who early in life adapted himself to the views held by the whigs on most theological and religious subjects. He bore with the idolatry of Rome, tolerated even the infidelity of Socinianism, and was hand and glove with the Presbyterian Synods of Scotland and Ulster.

Such a man at such a time was found to be useful, and Dr. Proudie's name began to appear in the newspapers. He was made one of a commission who went over to Ireland to arrange matters preparative to the working of the national board; he became honorary secretary to another commission nominated to inquire into the revenues of cathedral chapters; and had had something to do with both the regium donum and the Maynooth grant.

It must not on this account be taken as proved that Dr. Proudie was a man of great mental powers, or even of much capacity for business, for such qualities had not been required in him. In the arrangement of those church reforms with which he was connected, the ideas and original conception of the work to be done were generally furnished by the liberal statesmen of the day, and the labour of the details was borne by officials of a lower rank. It was, however, thought expedient that the name of some clergyman should appear in such matters, and as Dr. Proudie had become known as a tolerating divine, great use of this sort was made of his name. If he did not do much active good, he never did any harm; he was amenable to those who were really in authority, and at the sittings of the various boards to which he belonged maintained a kind of dignity which had its value.

He was certainly possessed of sufficient tact to answer the purpose for which he was required without making himself troublesome; but it must not therefore be surmised that he doubted his own power, or failed to believe that he could himself take a high part in high affairs when his own turn came. He was biding his time, and patiently looking forward to the days when he himself would sit authoritative at some board, and talk and direct, and rule the roast, while lesser stars sat round and obeyed, as he had so well accustomed himself to do.

His reward and his time had now come. He was selected for the vacant bishopric, and on the next vacancy which might occur in any diocese would take his place in the House of Lords, prepared to give not a silent vote in all matters concerning the weal of the church establishment. Toleration was to be the basis on which he was to fight his battles, and in the honest courage of his heart he thought no evil would come to him in encountering even such foes as his brethren of Exeter and Oxford.

Dr. Proudie was an ambitious man, and before he was well consecrated Bishop of Barchester, he had begun to look up to archiepiscopal splendour, and the glories of Lambeth, or at any rate of Bishopsthorpe. He was comparatively young, and had, as he fondly flattered himself, been selected as possessing such gifts, natural and acquired, as must be sure to recommend him to a yet higher notice, now that a higher sphere was opened to him. Dr. Proudie was therefore, quite prepared to take a conspicuous part in all theological affairs appertaining to these realms; and having such views, by no means intended to bury himself at Barchester as his predecessor had done. No: London should still be his ground: a comfortable mansion in a provincial city might be well enough for the dead months of the year. Indeed Dr. Proudie had always felt it necessary to his position to retire from London when other great and fashionable people did so; but London should still be his fixed residence, and it was in London that he resolved to exercise that hospitality so peculiarly recommended to all bishops by St. Paul. How otherwise could he keep himself before the world? how else give to the government, in matters theological, the full benefit of his weight and talents?

This resolution was no doubt a salutary one as regarded the world at large, but was not likely to make him popular either with the clergy or people of Barchester. Dr. Grantly had always lived there; and in truth it was hard for a bishop to be popular after Dr. Grantly. His income had averaged £9000 a year; his successor was to be rigidly limited to £5000. He had but one child on whom to spend his money; Dr. Proudie had seven or eight. He had been a man of few personal expenses, and they had been confined to the tastes of a moderate gentleman; but Dr. Proudie had to maintain a position in fashionable society, and had that to do with comparatively small means. Dr. Grantly had certainly kept his carriage, as became a bishop; but his carriage, horses, and coachman, though they did very well for Barchester, would have been almost ridiculous at Westminster. Mrs. Proudie determined that her husband's equipage should not shame her, and things on which Mrs. Proudie resolved, were generally accomplished.

From all this it was likely to result that Dr. Proudie would not spend much money at Barchester; whereas his predecessor had dealt with the tradesmen of the city in a manner very much to their satisfaction. The Grantlys, father and son, had spent their money like gentlemen; but it soon became whispered in Barchester that Dr. Proudie was not unacquainted with those prudent devices by which the utmost show of wealth is produced from limited means.

In person Dr. Proudie is a good-looking man; spruce and dapper, and very tidy. He is somewhat below middle height, being about five feet four; but he makes up for the inches which he wants by the dignity with which he carries those which he has. It is no fault of his own if he has not a commanding eye, for he studies hard to assume it. His features are well formed, though perhaps the sharpness of his nose may give to his face in the eyes of some people an air of insignificance. If so, it is greatly redeemed by his mouth and chin, of which he is justly proud.

Dr. Proudie may well be said to have been a fortunate man, for he was not born to wealth, and he is now bishop of Barchester; but nevertheless he has his cares. He has a large family, of whom the three eldest are daughters, now all grown up and fit for fashionable life; and he has a wife. It is not my intention to breathe a word against the character of Mrs. Proudie, but still I cannot think that with all her virtues she adds much to her husband's happiness. The truth is that in matters domestic she rules supreme over her titular lord, and rules with a rod of iron. Nor is this all. Things domestic Dr. Proudie might have abandoned to her, if not voluntarily, yet willingly. But Mrs. Proudie is not satisfied with such home dominion, and stretches her power over all his movements, and will not even abstain from things spiritual. In fact, the bishop is henpecked.

The archdeacon's wife, in her happy home at Plumstead, knows how to assume the full privileges of her rank, and express her own mind in becoming tone and place. But Mrs. Grantly's sway, if sway she has, is easy and beneficent. She never shames her husband; before the world she is a pattern of obedience; her voice is never loud, nor her looks sharp: doubtless she values power, and has not unsuccessfully striven to acquire it; but she knows what should be the limits of a woman's rule.

Not so Mrs. Proudie. This lady is habitually authoritative to all, but to her poor husband she is despotic. Successful as has been his career in the eyes of the world, it would seem that in the eyes of his wife he is never right. All hope of defending himself has long passed from him; indeed he rarely even attempts self-justification; and is aware that submission produces the nearest approach to peace which his own house can ever attain.

Mrs. Proudie has not been able to sit at the boards and committees to which her husband has been called by the state;

nor, as he often reflects, can she make her voice heard in the House of Lords. It may be that she will refuse to him permission to attend to this branch of a bishop's duties; it may be that she will insist on his close attendance to his own closet. He has never whispered a word on the subject to living ears, but he has already made his fixed resolve. Should such an attempt be made he will rebel. Dogs have turned against their masters, and even Neapolitans against their rulers, when oppression has been too severe. And Dr. Proudie feels within himself that if the cord be drawn too tight, he also can muster courage and resist.

The state of vassalage in which our bishop has been kept by his wife has not tended to exalt his character in the eyes of his daughters, who assume in addressing their father too much of that authority which is not properly belonging, at any rate, to them. They are, on the whole, fine engaging young ladies. They are tall and robust like their mother, whose high cheek-bones, and——, we may say auburn hair, they all inherit. They think somewhat too much of their grand uncles, who have not hitherto returned the compliment by thinking much of them. But now that their father is a bishop, it is probable that family ties will be drawn closer. Considering their connection with the church, they entertain but few prejudices against the pleasures of the world; and have certainly not distressed their parents, as too many English girls have lately done, by any enthusiastic wish to devote themselves to the seclusion of a protestant nunnery. Dr. Proudie's sons are still at school.

One other marked peculiarity in the character of the bishop's wife must be mentioned. Though not averse to the society and manners of the world, she is in her own way a religious woman; and the form in which this tendency shows itself in her is by a strict observance of Sabbatarian rule. Dissipation and low dresses during the week are, under her control, atoned for by three services, an evening sermon read by herself, and a perfect abstinence from any cheering employment on the Sunday. Unfortunately for those under her roof to whom the dissipation and low dresses are not extended, her servants namely and her husband, the compensating strictness of the Sabbath includes all. Woe betide the recreant housemaid who is found to have been listening to the honey of a sweetheart in the Regent's park, instead of the soul-stirring evening discourse of Mr. Slope. Not only is she sent adrift, but she is so sent with a character which leaves her little hope of a decent place. Woe betide the six-foot hero who escorts Mrs. Proudie to her pew in red plush breeches,

if he slips away to the neighbouring beer-shop, instead of falling
into the back seat appropriated to his use. Mrs. Proudie has the
eyes of Argus for such offenders. Occasional drunkenness in the
week may be overlooked, for six feet on low wages are hardly to
be procured if the morals are always kept at a high pitch; but not
even for grandeur or economy will Mrs. Proudie forgive a
desecration of the Sabbath.

In such matters Mrs. Proudie allows herself to be often
guided by that eloquent preacher, the Rev. Mr. Slope, and as Dr.
Proudie is guided by his wife, it necessarily follows that the
eminent man we have named has obtained a good deal of control
over Dr. Proudie in matters concerning religion. Mr. Slope's
only preferment has hitherto been that of reader and preacher in a
London district church: and on the consecration of his friend the
new bishop, he readily gave this up to undertake the onerous but
congenial duties of domestic chaplain to his lordship.

Mr. Slope, however, on his first introduction must not be
brought before the public at the tail of a chapter.

IV

The Bishop's Chaplain

Of the Rev. Mr. Slope's parentage I am not able to say much. I
have heard it asserted that he is lineally descended from that
eminent physician who assisted at the birth of Mr. T. Shandy,
and that in early years he added an ''e'' to his name, for the sake
of euphony, as other great men have done before him. If this be
so, I presume he was christened Obadiah, for that is his name, in
commemoration of the conflict in which his ancestor so distinguished himself. All my researches on the subject have, however,
failed in enabling me to fix the date on which the family changed
its religion.

He had been a sizar at Cambridge, and had there conducted

himself at any rate successfully, for in due process of time he was an M.A., having university pupils under his care. From thence he was transferred to London, and became preacher at a new district church built on the confines of Baker Street. He was in this position when congenial ideas on religious subjects recommended him to Mrs. Proudie, and the intercourse had become close and confidential.

Having been thus familiarly thrown among the Misses Proudie, it was no more than natural that some softer feeling than friendship should be engendered. There have been some passages of love between him and the eldest hope, Olivia; but they have hitherto resulted in no favourable arrangement. In truth, Mr. Slope having made a declaration of affection, afterwards withdrew it on finding that the doctor had no immediate worldly funds with which to endow his child; and it may easily be conceived that Miss Proudie, after such an announcement on his part, was not readily disposed to receive any further show of affection. On the appointment of Dr. Proudie to the bishopric of Barchester, Mr. Slope's views were in truth somewhat altered. Bishops, even though they be poor, can provide for clerical children, and Mr. Slope began to regret that he had not been more disinterested. He no sooner heard the tidings of the doctor's elevation, than he recommenced his siege, not violently, indeed, but respectfully, and at a distance. Olivia Proudie, however, was a girl of spirit: she had the blood of two peers in her veins, and, better still, she had another lover on her books; so Mr. Slope sighed in vain; and the pair soon found it convenient to establish a mutual bond of inveterate hatred.

It may be thought singular that Mrs. Proudie's friendship for the young clergyman should remain firm after such an affair; but, to tell the truth, she had known nothing of it. Though very fond of Mr. Slope herself, she had never conceived the idea that either of her daughters would become so, and remembering their high birth and social advantages, expected for them matches of a different sort. Neither the gentleman nor the lady found it necessary to enlighten her. Olivia's two sisters had each known of the affair, so had all the servants, so had all the people living in the adjoining houses on either side; but Mrs. Proudie had been kept in the dark.

Mr. Slope soon comforted himself with the reflection, that as he had been selected as chaplain to the bishop, it would probably be in his power to get the good things in the bishop's gift, without troubling himself with the bishop's daughter; and he found himself able to endure the pangs of rejected love. As he sat himself down in the railway carriage, confronting the bishop and Mrs. Proudie, as they started on their first journey to Barchester, he began to form in his own mind a plan for his future life. He knew well his patron's strong points, but he knew the weak ones as well. He understood correctly enough to what attempts the new bishop's high spirit would soar, and he rightly guessed that public life would better suit the great man's taste, than the small details of diocesan duty.

He, therefore, he, Mr. Slope, would in effect be bishop of Barchester. Such was his resolve; and to give Mr. Slope his due, he had both courage and spirit to bear him out in his resolution. He knew that he should have a hard battle to fight, for the power and patronage of the see would be equally coveted by another great mind—Mrs. Proudie would also choose to be bishop of Barchester. Mr. Slope, however, flattered himself that he could out-manœuvre the lady. She must live much in London, while he would always be on the spot. She would necessarily remain ignorant of much, while he would know everything belonging to the diocese. At first, doubtless, he must flatter and cajole, perhaps yield, in some things; but he did not doubt of ultimate triumph. If all other means failed, he could join the bishop against his wife, inspire courage into the unhappy man, lay an axe to the root of the woman's power, and emancipate the husband.

Such were his thoughts as he sat looking at the sleeping pair in the railway carriage, and Mr. Slope is not the man to trouble himself with such thoughts for nothing. He is possessed of more than average abilities, and is of good courage. Though he can stoop to fawn, and stoop low indeed, if need be, he has still within him the power to assume the tyrant; and with the power he has certainly the wish. His acquirements are not of the highest order, but such as they are they are completely under control, and he knows the use of them. He is gifted with a certain kind of pulpit eloquence, not likely indeed to be persuasive with men, but powerful with the softer sex. In his sermons he deals greatly in denunciations, excites the minds of his weaker hearers with a not unpleasant terror, and leaves an impression on their minds that all mankind are in a perilous state, and all womankind too, except those who attend regularly to the evening lectures in Baker Street. His looks and tones are extremely severe, so much so that one cannot but fancy that he regards the greater part of the world as being infinitely too bad for his care. As he walks through the streets, his very face denotes his horror of the world's wickedness; and there is always an anathema lurking in the corner of his eye.

In doctrine, he, like his patron, is tolerant of dissent, if so strict a mind can be called tolerant of anything. With Wesleyan-Methodists he has something in common, but his soul trembles in agony at the iniquities of the Puseyites. His aversion is carried to things outward as well as inward. His gall rises at a new church with a high pitched roof; a full-breasted black silk waistcoat is with him a symbol of Satan; and a profane jest-book would not, in his view, more foully desecrate the church seat of a Christian, than a book of prayer printed with red letters, and ornamented with a cross on the back. Most active clergymen have their hobby, and Sunday observances are his. Sunday, however, is a word which never pollutes his mouth—it is always "the Sabbath." The "desecration of the Sabbath," as he delights to call it, is to him meat and drink:—he thrives upon that as policemen do on the general evil habits of the community. It is the loved subject of all his evening discourses, the source of all his eloquence, the secret of all his power over the female heart. To him the revelation of God appears only in that one law given for Jewish observance. To him the mercies of our Saviour speak in vain, to him in vain has been preached that sermon which fell from divine lips on the mountain—"Blessed are the meek, for they shall inherit the earth"—"Blessed are the merciful, for they shall obtain mercy." To him the New Testament is comparatively of little moment, for from it can he draw no fresh authority for that dominion which he loves to exercise over at least a seventh part of man's allotted time here below.

Mr. Slope is tall, and not ill made. His feet and hands are large, as has ever been the case with all his family, but he has a broad chest and wide shoulders to carry off these excrescences, and on the whole his figure is good. His countenance, however, is not specially prepossessing. His hair is lank, and of a dull pale reddish hue. It is always formed into three straight lumpy masses, each brushed with admirable precision, and cemented with much grease; two of them adhere closely to the sides of his face, and the other lies at right angles above them. He wears no whiskers, and is always punctiliously shaven. His face is nearly of the same colour as his hair, though perhaps a little redder; it is not unlike beef,—beef, however, one would say, of a bad quality. His forehead is capacious and high, but square and heavy, and unpleasantly shining. His mouth is large, though his lips are thin and bloodless; and his big, prominent, pale brown eyes inspire anything but confidence. His nose, however, is his redeeming feature: it is pronounced straight and well-formed; though I myself should have liked it better did it not possess a somewhat spongy, porous appearance, as though it had been cleverly formed out of a red coloured cork.

I never could endure to shake hands with Mr. Slope. A cold, clammy perspiration always exudes from him, the small drops are ever to be seen standing on his brow, and his friendly grasp is unpleasant.

Such is Mr. Slope—such is the man who has suddenly fallen into the midst of Barchester Close, and is destined there to assume the station which has heretofore been filled by the son of the late bishop. Think, oh, my meditative reader, what an associate we have here for those comfortable prebendaries, those gentlemanlike clerical doctors, those happy well-used well-fed minor canons, who have grown into existence at Barchester under the kindly wings of Bishop Grantly!

But not as a mere associate for these does Mr. Slope travel down to Barchester with the bishop and his wife. He intends to be, if not their master, at least the chief among them. He intends to lead, and to have followers; he intends to hold the purse strings of the diocese, and draw round him an obedient herd of his poor and hungry brethren.

And here we can hardly fail to draw a comparison between the archdeacon and our new private chaplain; and despite the manifold faults of the former, one can hardly fail to make it much to his advantage.

Both men are eager, much too eager, to support and increase the power of their order. Both are anxious that the world should be priest-governed, though they have probably never confessed so much, even to themselves. Both begrudge any other kind of dominion held by man over man. Dr. Grantly, if he admits the Queen's supremacy in things spiritual, only admits it as being due to the *quasi* priesthood conveyed in the consecrating qualities of her coronation; and he regards things temporal as being by their nature subject to those which are spiritual. Mr. Slope's ideas of sacerdotal rule are of quite a different class. He cares nothing, one way or the other, for the Queen's supremacy; these to his ears are empty words, meaning nothing. Forms he regards but little, and such titular expressions as supremacy, consecration, ordination, and the like, convey of themselves no significance to him. Let him be supreme who can. The temporal king, judge, or gaoler, can work but on the body. The spiritual master, if he have the necessary gifts, and can duly use them, has a wider field of empire. He works upon the soul. If he can make himself be believed, he can be all powerful over those who listen. If he be careful to meddle with none who are too strong in intellect, or too weak in flesh, he may indeed be supreme. And such was the ambition of Mr. Slope.

Dr. Grantly interfered very little with the worldly doings of those who were in any way subject to him. I do not mean to say that he omitted to notice misconduct among his clergy, immorality in his parish, or omissions in his family; but he was not anxious to do so where the necessity could be avoided. He was not troubled with a propensity to be curious, and as long as those around him were tainted with no heretical leaning towards dissent, as long as they fully and freely admitted the efficacy of Mother Church, he was willing that that mother should be merciful and affectionate, prone to indulgence, and unwilling to chastise. He himself enjoyed the good things of this world, and liked to let it be known that he did so. He cordially despised any brother rector who thought harm of dinner-parties, or dreaded the dangers of a moderate claret-jug; consequently dinner-parties and claret-jugs were common in the diocese. He liked to give laws and to be obeyed in them implicitly, but he endeavoured that his ordinances should be within the compass of the man, and not unpalatable to the gentleman. He had ruled among his clerical neighbours now for sundry years, and as he had maintained his power without becoming unpopular, it may be presumed that he had exercised some wisdom.

Of Mr. Slope's conduct much cannot be said, as his grand career is yet to commence; but it may be premised that his tastes will be very different from those of the archdeacon. He conceives it to be his duty to know all the private doings and desires of the flock entrusted to his care. From the poorer classes he exacts an unconditional obedience to set rules of conduct, and if disobeyed he has recourse, like his great ancestor, to the fulminations of an Ernulfus: "Thou shalt be damned in thy going in and in thy coming out—in thy eating and thy drinking," &c. &c. &c. With the rich, experience has already taught him that a different line of action is necessary. Men in the upper walks of life do not mind being cursed, and the women, presuming that it be done in delicate phrase, rather like it. But he has not, therefore, given up so important a portion of believing Christians. With the men, indeed, he is generally at variance; they are hardened

sinners, on whom the voice of the priestly charmer too often falls
in vain; but with the ladies, old and young, firm and frail, devout
and dissipated, he is, as he conceives, all powerful. He can
reprove faults with so much flattery, and utter censure in so
caressing a manner, that the female heart, if it glow with a spark
of low church susceptibility, cannot withstand him. In many
houses he is thus an admired guest; the husbands, for their
wives' sake, are fain to admit him; and when once admitted it is
not easy to shake him off. He has, however, a pawing, greasy
way with him, which does not endear him to those who do not
value him for their souls' sake, and he is not a man to make
himself at once popular in a large circle such as is now likely to
surround him at Barchester.

V

A Morning Visit

It was known that Dr. Proudie would immediately have to
reappoint to the wardenship of the hospital under the act of
Parliament to which allusion has been made; but no one imagined that any choice was left to him—no one for a moment
thought that he could appoint any other than Mr. Harding. Mr.
Harding himself, when he heard how the matter had been settled,
without troubling himself much on the subject, considered it as
certain that he would go back to his pleasant house and garden.
And though there would be much that was melancholy, nay,
almost heartrending, in such a return, he still was glad that it was
to be so. His daughter might probably be persuaded to return
there with him. She had, indeed, all but promised to do so,
though she still entertained an idea that that greatest of mortals,
that important atom of humanity, that little god upon earth,
Johnny Bold her baby, ought to have a house of his own over his
head.

Such being the state of Mr. Harding's mind in the matter, he did not feel any peculiar personal interest in the appointment of Dr. Proudie to the bishopric. He, as well as others at Barchester, regretted that a man should be sent among them who, they were aware, was not of their way of thinking; but Mr. Harding himself was not a bigoted man on points of church doctrine, and he was quite prepared to welcome Dr. Proudie to Barchester in a graceful and becoming manner. He had nothing to seek and nothing to fear; he felt that it behoved him to be on good terms with his bishop, and he did not anticipate any obstacle that would prevent it.

In such a frame of mind he proceeded to pay his respects at the palace the second day after the arrival of the bishop and his chaplain. But he did not go alone. Dr. Grantly proposed to accompany him, and Mr. Harding was not sorry to have a companion, who would remove from his shoulders the burden of the conversation in such an interview. In the affair of the consecration Dr. Grantly had been introduced to the bishop, and Mr. Harding had also been there. He had, however, kept himself in the background, and he was now to be presented to the great man for the first time.

The archdeacon's feelings were of a much stronger nature. He was not exactly the man to overlook his own slighted claims, or to forgive the preference shown to another. Dr. Proudie was playing Venus to his Juno, and he was prepared to wage an internecine war against the owner of the wished-for apple, and all his satellites, private chaplains, and others.

Nevertheless, it behoved him also to conduct himself towards the intruder as an old archdeacon should conduct himself to an incoming bishop; and though he was well aware of all Dr. Proudie's abominable opinions as regarded dissenters, church reform, the hebdomadal council, and such like; though he disliked the man, and hated the doctrines, still he was prepared to show respect to the station of the bishop. So he and Mr. Harding called together at the palace.

His lordship was at home, and the two visitors were shown through the accustomed hall into the well-known room, where the good old bishop used to sit. The furniture had been bought at a valuation, and every chair and table, every book-shelf against the wall, and every square in the carpet, was as well known to each of them as their own bedrooms. Nevertheless they at once felt that they were strangers there. The furniture was for the most part the same, yet the place had been metamorphosed. A new

sofa had been introduced, a horrid chintz affair, most unprelatical
and almost irreligious: such a sofa as never yet stood in the study
of any decent high church clergyman of the Church of England.
The old curtains had also given way. They had, to be sure,
become dingy, and that which had been originally a rich and
goodly ruby had degenerated into a reddish brown. Mr. Harding,
however, thought the old reddish brown much preferable to the
gaudy buff-coloured trumpery moreen which Mrs. Proudie had
deemed good enough for her husband's own room in the provincial city of Barchester.

Our friends found Dr. Proudie sitting on the old bishop's
chair, looking very nice in his new apron; they found, too, Mr.
Slope standing on the hearthrug, persuasive and eager, just as the
archdeacon used to stand; but on the sofa they also found Mrs.
Proudie, an innovation for which a precedent might in vain be
sought in all the annals of the Barchester bishopric!

There she was, however, and they could only make the best
of her. The introductions were gone through in much form. The
archdeacon shook hands with the bishop, and named Mr. Harding,
who received such an amount of greeting as was due from a
bishop to a precentor. His lordship then presented them to his
lady wife; the archdeacon first, with archidiaconal honours, and
then the precentor with diminished parade. After this Mr. Slope
presented himself. The bishop, it is true, did mention his name,
and so did Mrs. Proudie too, in a louder tone; but Mr. Slope
took upon himself the chief burden of his own introduction. He
had great pleasure in making himself acquainted with Dr. Grantly;
he had heard much of the archdeacon's good works in that part
of the diocese in which his duties as archdeacon had been
exercised (thus purposely ignoring the archdeacon's hitherto un-
limited dominion over the diocese at large). He was aware that
his lordship depended greatly on the assistance which Dr. Grantly
would be able to give him in that portion of his diocese. He then
thrust out his hand, and grasping that of his new foe, bedewed it
unmercifully. Dr. Grantly in return bowed, looked stiff, con-
tracted his eyebrows, and wiped his hand with his pocket-
handkerchief. Nothing abashed, Mr. Slope then noticed the
precentor, and descended to the grade of the lower clergy. He
gave him a squeeze of the hand, damp indeed, but affectionate,
and was very glad to make the acquaintance of Mr.——; oh,
yes, Mr. Harding; he had not exactly caught the name—"Precentor
in the cathedral," surmised Mr. Slope. Mr. Harding confessed
that such was the humble sphere of his work. "Some parish duty

as well," suggested Mr. Slope. Mr. Harding acknowledged the diminutive incumbency of St. Cuthbert's. Mr. Slope then left him alone, having condescended sufficiently, and joined the conversation among the higher powers.

There were four persons there, each of whom considered himself the most important personage in the diocese; himself, indeed, or herself, as Mrs. Proudie was one of them; and with such a difference of opinion it was not probable that they would get on pleasantly together. The bishop himself actually wore the visible apron, and trusted mainly to that—to that and his title, both being facts which could not be overlooked. The archdeacon knew his subject, and really understood the business of bishoping, which the others did not; and this was his strong ground. Mrs. Proudie had her sex to back her, and her habit of command, and was nothing daunted by the high tone of Dr. Grantly's face and figure. Mr. Slope had only himself and his own courage and tact to depend on, but he nevertheless was perfectly self-assured, and did not doubt but that he should soon get the better of weak men who trusted so much to externals, as both bishop and archdeacon appeared to do.

"Do you reside in Barchester, Dr. Grantly?" asked the lady with her sweetest smile.

Dr. Grantly explained that he lived in his own parish of Plumstead Episcopi, a few miles out of the city. Whereupon the lady hoped that the distance was not too great for country visiting, as she would be so glad to make the acquaintance of Mrs. Grantly. She would take the earliest opportunity, after the arrival of her horses at Barchester; their horses were at present in London; their horses were not immediately coming down, as the bishop would be obliged in a few days, to return to town. Dr. Grantly was no doubt aware that the bishop was at present much called upon by the "University Improvement Committee": indeed, the Committee could not well proceed without him, as their final report had now to be drawn up. The bishop had also to prepare a scheme for the "Manufacturing Towns Morning and Evening Sunday School Society," of which he was a patron, or president, or director, and therefore the horses would not come down to Barchester at present; but whenever the horses did come down, she would take the earliest opportunity of calling at Plumstead Episcopi, providing the distance was not too great for country visiting.

The archdeacon made his fifth bow: he had made one at each mention of the horses; and promised that Mrs. Grantly would do herself the honour of calling at the palace on an early day. Mrs. Proudie declared that she would be delighted: she hadn't liked to ask, not being quite sure whether Mrs. Grantly had horses; besides, the distance might have been, &c. &c.

Dr. Grantly again bowed, but said nothing. He could have bought every individual possession of the whole family of the Proudies, and have restored them as a gift, without much feeling the loss; and had kept a separate pair of horses for the exclusive use of his wife since the day of his marriage; whereas Mrs. Proudie had been hitherto jobbed about the streets of London at so much a month during the season; and at other times had managed to walk, or hire a smart fly from the livery stables.

"Are the arrangements with reference to the Sabbath-day schools generally pretty good in your archdeaconry?" asked Mr. Slope.

"Sabbath-day schools!" repeated the archdeacon with an affectation of surprise. "Upon my word, I can't tell; it depends mainly on the parson's wife and daughters. There is none at Plumstead."

This was almost a fib on the part of the archdeacon, for Mrs. Grantly has a very nice school. To be sure it is not a Sunday school exclusively, and is not so designated; but that exemplary lady always attends there an hour before church, and hears the children say their catechism, and sees that they are clean and tidy for church, with their hands washed, and their shoes tied; and Grisel and Florinda, her daughters carry thither a basket of large buns, baked on the Saturday afternoon, and distribute them to all the children not especially under disgrace, which buns are carried home after church with considerable content, and eaten hot at tea, being then split and toasted. The children of Plumstead would indeed open their eyes if they heard their venerated pastor declare that there was no Sunday school in his parish.

Mr. Slope merely opened his eyes wider, and slightly shrugged his shoulders. He was not, however, prepared to give up his darling project.

"I fear there is a great deal of Sabbath travelling here," said he. "On looking at the 'Bradshaw,' I see that there are three trains in and three out every Sabbath. Could nothing be done to induce the company to withdraw them? Don't you think, Dr. Grantly, that a little energy might diminish the evil?"

"Not being a director, I really can't say. But if you can withdraw the passengers, the company, I dare say, will withdraw the trains,'' said the doctor. ''It's merely a question of dividends.''

''But surely, Dr. Grantly,'' said the lady, ''surely we should look at it differently. You and I, for instance, in our position: surely we should do all that we can to control so grievous a sin. Don't you think so, Mr. Harding?'' and she turned to the precentor, who was sitting mute and unhappy.

Mr. Harding thought that all porters and stokers, guards, breaksmen, and pointsmen ought to have an opportunity of going to church, and he hoped that they all had.

''But surely, surely,'' continued Mrs. Proudie, ''surely that is not enough. Surely that will not secure such an observance of the Sabbath as we are taught to conceive is not only expedient but indispensable; surely——''

Come what come might, Dr. Grantly was not to be forced into a dissertation on a point of doctrine with Mrs. Proudie, nor yet with Mr. Slope; so without much ceremony he turned his back upon the sofa, and began to hope that Dr. Proudie had found that the palace repairs had been such as to meet his wishes.

''Yes, yes,'' said his lordship; upon the whole he thought so—upon the whole, he didn't know that there was much ground for complaint; the architect, perhaps, might have—but his double, Mr. Slope, who had sidled over to the bishop's chair, would not allow his lordship to finish his ambiguous speech.

''There is one point I would like to mention, Mr. Archdeacon. His lordship asked me to step through the premises, and I see that the stalls in the second stable are not perfect.''

''Why—there's standing there for a dozen horses,'' said the archdeacon.

''Perhaps so,'' said the other; ''indeed, I've no doubt of it; but visitors, you know, often require so much accommodation. There are so many of the bishop's relatives who always bring their own horses.''

Dr. Grantly promised that due próvision for the relatives' horses should be made, as far at least as the extent of the original stable building would allow. He would himself communicate with the architect.

''And the coach-house, Dr. Grantly,'' continued Mr. Slope; ''there is really hardly room for a second carriage in the large coach-house, and the smaller one, of course, holds only one.''

''And the gas,'' chimed in the lady; ''there is no gas through the house, none whatever, but in the kitchen and passages.

Surely the palace should have been fitted through with pipes for gas, and hot water too. There is no hot water laid on anywhere above the ground-floor; surely there should be the means of getting hot water in the bed-rooms without having it brought in jugs from the kitchen.''

The bishop had a decided opinion that there should be pipes for hot water. Hot water was very essential for the comfort of the palace. It was, indeed, a requisite in any decent gentleman's house.

Mr. Slope had remarked that the coping on the garden wall was in many places imperfect.

Mrs. Proudie had discovered a large hole, evidently the work of rats, in the servants' hall.

The bishop expressed an utter detestation of rats. There was nothing, he believed, in this world, that he so much hated as a rat.

Mr. Slope had, moreover, observed that the locks of the out-houses were very imperfect: he might specify the coal-cellar, and the wood-house.

Mrs. Proudie had also seen that those on the doors of the servants' bed-rooms were in an equally bad condition; indeed the locks all through the house were old-fashioned and unserviceable.

The bishop thought that a great deal depended on a good lock, and quite as much on the key. He had observed that the fault very often lay with the key, especially if the wards were in any way twisted.

Mr. Slope was going on with his catalogue of grievances, when he was somewhat loudly interrupted by the archdeacon, who succeeded in explaining that the diocesan architect, or rather his foreman, was the person to be addressed on such subjects; and that he, Dr. Grantly, had inquired as to the comfort of the palace, merely as a point of compliment. He was sorry, however, that so many things had been found amiss: and then he rose from his chair to escape.

Mrs. Proudie, though she had contrived to lend her assistance in recapitulating the palatial dilapidations, had not on that account given up her hold of Mr. Harding, nor ceased from her cross-examinations as to the iniquity of Sabbatical amusements. Over and over again had she thrown out her ''Surely, surely,'' at Mr. Harding's devoted head, and ill had that gentleman been able to parry the attack.

He had never before found himself subjected to such a nuisance. Ladies hitherto, when they had consulted him on religious subjects, had listened to what he might choose to say with some deference, and had differed, if they differed, in silence. But Mrs. Proudie interrogated him, and then lectured. "Neither thou, nor thy son, nor thy daughter, nor thy man servant, nor thy maid servant," said she, impressively, and more than once, as though Mr. Harding had forgotten the words. She shook her finger at him as she quoted the favourite law, as though menacing him with punishment; and then called upon him categorically to state whether he did not think that travelling on the Sabbath was an abomination and a desecration.

Mr. Harding had never been so hard pressed in his life. He felt that he ought to rebuke the lady for presuming so to talk to a gentleman and a clergyman many years her senior; but he recoiled from the idea of scolding the bishop's wife, in the bishop's presence, on his first visit to the palace; moreover, to tell the truth, he was somewhat afraid of her. She, seeing him sit silent and absorbed, by no means refrained from the attack.

"I hope, Mr. Harding," said she, shaking her head slowly and solemnly, "I hope you will not leave me to think that you approve of Sabbath travelling," and she looked a look of unutterable meaning into his eyes.

There was no standing this, for Mr. Slope was now looking at him, and so was the bishop, and so was the archdeacon, who had completed his adieux on that side of the room. Mr. Harding therefore got up also, and putting out his hand to Mrs. Proudie said: "If you will come to St. Cuthbert's some Sunday, I will preach you a sermon on that subject."

And so the archdeacon and the precentor took their departure, bowing low to the lady, shaking hands with the lord, and escaping from Mr. Slope in the best manner each could. Mr. Harding was again maltreated; but Dr. Grantly swore deeply in the bottom of his heart, that no earthly consideration should ever again induce him to touch the paw of that impure and filthy animal.

And now, had I the pen of a mighty poet, would I sing in epic verse the noble wrath of the archdeacon. The palace steps descend to a broad gravel sweep, from whence a small gate opens out into the street, very near the covered gateway leading into the close. The road from the palace door turns to the left, through the spacious gardens, and terminates on the London-road, half a mile from the cathedral.

Till they had both passed this small gate and entered the close, neither of them spoke a word; but the precentor clearly saw from his companion's face that a tornado was to be expected, nor was he himself inclined to stop it. Though by nature far less irritable than the archdeacon, even he was angry: he even—that mild and courteous man—was inclined to express himself in anything but courteous terms.

VI

War

"Good heavens!" exclaimed the archdeacon, as he placed his foot on the gravel walk of the close, and raising his hat with one hand, passed the other somewhat violently over his now grizzled locks; smoke issued forth from the uplifted beaver as it were a cloud of wrath, and the safety-valve of his anger opened, and emitted a visible steam, preventing positive explosion and probable apoplexy. "Good heavens!"—and the archdeacon looked up to the gray pinnacles of the cathedral tower, making a mute appeal to that still living witness which had looked down on the doings of so many bishops of Barchester.

"I don't think I shall ever like that Mr. Slope," said Mr. Harding.

"Like him!" roared the archdeacon, standing still for a moment to give more force to his voice; "like him!" All the ravens of the close cawed their assent. The old bells of the tower, in chiming the hour, echoed the words; and the swallows flying out from their nests mutely expressed a similar opinion. Like Mr. Slope! Why no, it was not very probable that any Barchester-bred living thing should like Mr. Slope!

"Nor Mrs. Proudie either," said Mr. Harding.

The archdeacon hereupon forgot himself. I will not follow his example, nor shock my readers by transcribing the term in which he expressed his feeling as to the lady who had been named. The ravens and the last lingering notes of the clock bells were less scrupulous, and repeated in corresponding echoes the very improper exclamation. The archdeacon again raised his hat, and another salutary escape of steam was effected.

There was a pause, during which the precentor tried to realise the fact that the wife of a bishop of Barchester had been thus designated, in the close of the cathedral, by the lips of its own archdeacon: but he could not do it.

"The bishop seems to be a quiet man enough," suggested Mr. Harding, having acknowledged to himself his own failure.

"Idiot!" exclaimed the doctor, who for the nonce was not capable of more than such spasmodic attempts at utterance.

"Well, he did not seem very bright," said Mr. Harding, "and yet he has always had the reputation of a clever man. I suppose he's cautious and not inclined to express himself very freely."

The new bishop of Barchester was already so contemptible a creature in Dr. Grantly's eyes, that he could not condescend to discuss his character. He was a puppet to be played by others; a mere wax doll, done up in an apron and a shovel hat, to be stuck on a throne or elsewhere, and pulled about by wires as others chose. Dr. Grantly did not choose to let himself down low enough to talk about Dr. Proudie; but he saw that he would have to talk about the other members of his household, the coadjutor bishops, who had brought his lordship down, as it were, in a box, and were about to handle the wires as they willed. This in itself was a terrible vexation to the archdeacon. Could he have ignored the chaplain, and have fought the bishop, there would have been, at any rate, nothing degrading in such a contest. Let the Queen make whom she would bishop of Barchester; a man, or even an ape, when once a bishop, would be a respectable adversary, if he would but fight, himself. But what was such a person as Dr. Grantly to do, when such another person as Mr. Slope was put forward as his antagonist?

If he, our archdeacon, refused to combat, Mr. Slope would walk triumphant over the field, and have the diocese of Barchester under his heel.

If, on the other hand, the archdeacon accepted as his enemy the man whom the new puppet bishop put before him as such, he would have to talk about Mr. Slope, and write about Mr. Slope, and in all matters treat with Mr. Slope, as a being standing, in some degree, on ground similar to his own. He would have to meet Mr. Slope; to——Bah! the idea was sickening. He could not bring himself to have to do with Mr. Slope.

"He is the most thoroughly bestial creature that ever I set my eyes upon," said the archdeacon.

"Who—the bishop?" asked the other, innocently.

"Bishop! no—I'm not talking about the bishop. How on earth such a creature got ordained!—they'll ordain anybody now, I know; but he's been in the church these ten years; and they used to be a little careful ten years ago."

"Oh! you mean Mr. Slope."

"Did you ever see any animal less like a gentleman?" asked Dr. Grantly.

"I can't say I felt myself much disposed to like him."

"Like him!" again shouted the doctor, and the assenting ravens again cawed an echo; "of course, you don't like him: it's not a question of liking. But what are we to do with him?"

"Do with him?" asked Mr. Harding.

"Yes—what are we to do with him? How are we to treat him? There he is, and there he'll stay. He has put his foot in that palace, and he will never take it out again till he's driven. How are we to get rid of him?"

"I don't suppose he can do us much harm."

"Not do harm!—Well, I think you'll find yourself of a different opinion before a month is gone. What would you say now, if he got himself put into the hospital? Would that be harm?"

Mr. Harding mused awhile, and then said he didn't think the new bishop would put Mr. Slope into the hospital.

"If he doesn't put him there, he'll put him somewhere else where he'll be as bad. I tell you that that man, to all intents and purposes, will be Bishop of Barchester"; and again Dr. Grantly raised his hat, and rubbed his hand thoughtfully and sadly over his head.

"Impudent scoundrel!" he continued after a while. "To dare to cross-examine me about the Sunday schools in the diocese, and Sunday travelling too: I never in my life met his equal for sheer impudence. Why, he must have thought we were two candidates for ordination!"

"I declare I thought Mrs. Proudie was the worst of the two," said Mr. Harding.

"When a woman is impertinent, one must only put up with it, and keep out of her way in future; but I am not inclined to put up with Mr. Slope. 'Sabbath travelling!' " and the doctor attempted to imitate the peculiar drawl of the man he so much disliked. " 'Sabbath travelling!' Those are the sort of men who will ruin the Church of England, and make the profession of a clergyman disreputable. It is not the dissenters or the papists that we should fear, but the set of canting, low-bred hypocrites who are wriggling their way in among us; men who have no fixed principle, no standard ideas of religion or doctrine, but who take up some popular cry, as this fellow has done about 'Sabbath travelling.' ''

Dr. Grantly did not again repeat the question aloud, but he did so constantly to himself, "What were they to do with Mr. Slope?" How was he openly, before the world, to show that he utterly disapproved of and abhorred such a man?

Hitherto Barchester had escaped the taint of any extreme rigour of church doctrine. The clergymen of the city and neighbourhood, though very well inclined to promote high-church principles, privileges, and prerogatives, had never committed themselves to tendencies, which are somewhat too loosely called Puseyite practices. They all preached in their black gowns, as their fathers had done before them; they wore ordinary black cloth waistcoats; they had no candles on their altars, either lighted or unlighted; they made no private genuflexions, and were contented to confine themselves to such ceremonial observances as had been in vogue for the last hundred years. The services were decently and demurely read in their parish churches, chanting was confined to the cathedral, and the science of intoning was unknown. One young man who had come direct from Oxford as a curate to Plumstead had, after the lapse of two or three Sundays, made a faint attempt, much to the bewilderment of the poorer part of the congregation. Dr. Grantly had not been present on the occasion; but Mrs. Grantly, who had her own opinion on the subject, immediately after the service expressed a hope that the young gentleman had not been taken ill, and offered to send him all kinds of condiments supposed to be good for a sore throat. After that there had been no more intoning at Plumstead Episcopi.

But now the archdeacon began to meditate on some strong measures of absolute opposition. Dr. Proudie and his crew were of the lowest possible order of Church of England clergymen, and therefore it behoved him, Dr. Grantly, to be of the very highest. Dr. Proudie would abolish all forms and ceremonies, and therefore Dr. Grantly felt the sudden necessity of multiplying them. Dr. Proudie would consent to deprive the church of all collective authority and rule, and therefore Dr. Grantly would stand up for the full power of convocation, and the renewal of all its ancient privileges.

It was true that he could not himself intone the service, but he could procure the co-operation of any number of gentleman-like curates well trained in the mystery of doing so. He would not willingly alter his own fashion of dress, but he could people Barchester with young clergymen dressed in the longest frocks, and in the highest-breasted silk waistcoats. He certainly was not prepared to cross himself, or to advocate the real presence; but, without going this length, there were various observances, by adopting which he could plainly show his antipathy to such men as Dr. Proudie and Mr. Slope.

All these things passed through his mind as he paced up and down the close with Mr. Harding. War, war, internecine war was in his heart. He felt that, as regarded himself and Mr. Slope, one of the two must be annihilated as far as the city of Barchester was concerned; and he did not intend to give way until there was not left to him an inch of ground on which he could stand. He still flattered himself that he could make Barchester too hot to hold Mr. Slope, and he had no weakness of spirit to prevent his bringing about such a consummation if it were in his power.

"I suppose Susan must call at the palace," said Mr. Harding.

"Yes, she shall call there; but it shall be once and once only. I dare say 'the horses' won't find it convenient to come out to Plumstead very soon, and when that once is done the matter may drop."

"I don't suppose Eleanor need call. I don't think Eleanor would get on at all well with Mrs. Proudie."

"Not the least necessity in life," replied the archdeacon, not without the reflection that a ceremony which was necessary for his wife, might not be at all binding on the widow of John Bold. "Not the slightest reason on earth why she should do so, if she doesn't like it. For myself, I don't think that any decent young woman should be subjected to the nuisance of being in the same room with that man."

And so the two clergymen parted, Mr. Harding going to his daughter's house, and the archdeacon seeking the seclusion of his brougham.

The new inhabitants of the palace did not express any higher opinion of their visitors than their visitors had expressed of them. Though they did not use quite such strong language as Dr. Grantly had done, they felt as much personal aversion, and were quite as well aware as he was that there would be a battle to be fought, and that there was hardly room for Proudieism in Barchester as long as Grantlyism was predominant.

Indeed, it may be doubted whether Mr. Slope had not already within his breast a better prepared system of strategy, a more accurately defined line of hostile conduct than the archdeacon. Dr. Grantly was going to fight because he found that he hated the man. Mr. Slope had predetermined to hate the man, because he foresaw the necessity of fighting him. When he had first reviewed the *carte du pays,* previous to his entry into Barchester, the idea had occurred to him of conciliating the archdeacon, of cajoling and flattering him into submission, and of obtaining the upper hand by cunning instead of courage. A little inquiry, however, sufficed to convince him that all his cunning would fail to win over such a man as Dr. Grantly to such a mode of action as that to be adopted by Mr. Slope; and then he determined to fall back upon his courage. He at once saw that open battle against Dr. Grantly and all Dr. Grantly's adherents was a necessity of his position, and he deliberately planned the most expedient methods of giving offence.

Soon after his arrival the bishop had intimated to the dean that, with the permission of the canon then in residence, his chaplain would preach in the cathedral on the next Sunday. The canon in residence happened to be the Hon. and Rev. Dr. Vesey Stanhope, who at this time was very busy on the shores of the Lake of Como, adding to that unique collection of butterflies for which he is so famous. Or, rather, he would have been in residence but for the butterflies and other such summer-day considerations; and the vicar-choral, who was to take his place in the pulpit, by no means objected to having his work done for him by Mr. Slope.

Mr. Slope accordingly preached, and if a preacher can have satisfaction in being listened to, Mr. Slope ought to have been gratified. I have reason to think that he was gratified, and that he left the pulpit with the conviction that he had done what he intended to do when he entered it.

On this occasion the new bishop took his seat for the first time in the throne allotted to him. New scarlet cushions and drapery had been prepared, with new gilt binding and new fringe. The old carved oak-wood of the throne, ascending with its numerous grotesque pinnacles half-way up to the roof of the choir, had been washed, and dusted, and rubbed, and it all looked very smart. Ah! how often sitting there, in happy early days, on those lowly benches in front of the altar, have I whiled away the tedium of a sermon in considering how best I might thread my way up amidst those wooden towers, and climb safely to the topmost pinnacle!

All Barchester went to hear Mr. Slope; either for that or to gaze at the new bishop. All the best bonnets of the city were there, and moreover all the best glossy clerical hats. Not a stall but had its fitting occupant; for though some of the prebendaries might be away in Italy or elsewhere, their places were filled by brethren, who flocked into Barchester on the occasion. The dean was there, a heavy old man, now too old, indeed, to attend frequently in his place; and so was the archdeacon. So also were the chancellor, the treasurer, the precentor, sundry canons and minor canons, and every lay member of the choir, prepared to sing the new bishop in with due melody and harmonious expression of sacred welcome.

The service was certainly very well performed. Such was always the case at Barchester, as the musical education of the choir had been good, and the voices had been carefully selected. The psalms were beautifully chanted; the Te Deum was magnificently sung; and the litany was given in a manner, which is still to be found at Barchester, but, if my taste be correct, is to be found nowhere else. The litany in Barchester cathedral has long been the special task to which Mr. Harding's skill and voice have been devoted. Crowded audiences generally make good performers, and though Mr. Harding was not aware of any extraordinary exertion on his part, yet probably he rather exceeded his usual mark. Others were doing their best, and it was natural that he should emulate his brethren. So the service went on, and at last Mr. Slope got into the pulpit.

He chose for his text a verse from the precepts addressed by St. Paul to Timothy, as to the conduct necessary in a spiritual pastor and guide, and it was immediately evident that the good clergy of Barchester were to have a lesson.

"Study to show thyself approved unto God, a workman that needeth not to be ashamed, rightly dividing the word of truth." These were the words of his text, and with such a subject in such a place, it may be supposed that such a preacher would be listened to by such an audience. He was listened to with breathless attention, and not without considerable surprise. Whatever opinion of Mr. Slope might have been held in Barchester before he commenced his discourse, none of his hearers, when it was over, could mistake him either for a fool or a coward.

It would not be becoming were I to travesty a sermon, or even to repeat the language of it in the pages of a novel. In endeavouring to depict the characters of the persons of whom I write, I am to a certain extent forced to speak of sacred things. I trust, however, that I shall not be thought to scoff at the pulpit, though some may imagine that I do not feel all the reverence that is due to the cloth. I may question the infallibility of the teachers, but I hope that I shall not therefore be accused of doubt as to the thing to be taught.

Mr. Slope, in commencing his sermon, showed no slight tact in his ambiguous manner of hinting that, humble as he was himself, he stood there as the mouthpiece of the illustrious divine who sat opposite to him; and having premised so much, he gave forth a very accurate definition of the conduct which that prelate would rejoice to see in the clergymen now brought under his jurisdiction. It is only necessary to say, that the peculiar points insisted upon were exactly those which were most distasteful to the clergy of the diocese, and most averse to their practice and opinions; and that all those peculiar habits and privileges which have always been dear to high-church priests, to that party which is now scandalously called the high-and-dry church, were ridiculed, abused, and anathematised. Now, the clergymen of the diocese of Barchester are all of the high-and-dry church.

Having thus, according to his own opinion, explained how a clergyman should show himself approved unto God, as a workman that needeth not to be ashamed, he went on to explain how the word of truth should be divided; and here he took a rather narrow view of the question, and fetched his arguments from afar. His object was to express his abomination of all ceremonious modes of utterance, to cry down any religious feeling which might be excited, not by the sense, but by the sound of words, and in fact to insult cathedral practices. Had St. Paul spoken of rightly pronouncing instead of rightly dividing the word of truth, this part of his sermon would have been more to the purpose; but the preacher's immediate object was to preach Mr. Slope's doctrine, and not St. Paul's, and he contrived to give the necessary twist to the text with some skill.

He could not exactly say, preaching from a cathedral pulpit, that chanting should be abandoned in cathedral services. By such an assertion, he would have overshot his mark and rendered himself absurd, to the delight of his hearers. He could, however, and did, allude with heavy denunciations to the practice of intoning in parish churches, although the practice was all but unknown in the diocese; and from thence he came round to the undue preponderance, which he asserted, music had over meaning in the beautiful service which they had just heard. He was aware, he said, that the practices of our ancestors could not be abandoned at a moment's notice; the feelings of the aged would be outraged, and the minds of respectable men would be shocked. There were many, he was aware, of not sufficient calibre of thought to perceive, of not sufficient education to know, that a mode of service, which was effective when outward ceremonies were of more moment than inward feelings, had become all but barbarous at a time when inward conviction was everything, when each word of the minister's lips should fall intelligibly into the listener's heart. Formerly the religion of the multitude had been an affair of the imagination: now, in these latter days, it had become necessary that a Christian should have a reason for his faith—should not only believe, but digest—not only hear, but understand. The words of our morning service, how beautiful, how apposite, how intelligible they were, when read with simple and distinct decorum! but how much of the meaning of the words was lost when they were produced with all the meretricious charms of melody! &c. &c.

Here was a sermon to be preached before Mr. Archdeacon Grantly, Mr. Precentor Harding, and the rest of them! before a whole dean and chapter assembled in their own cathedral! before men who had grown old in the exercise of their peculiar services, with a full conviction of their excellence for all intended purposes! This too from such a man, a clerical *parvenu*, a man without a cure, a mere chaplain, an intruder among them; a fellow raked up, so said Dr. Grantly, from the gutters of Marylebone! They had to sit through it! None of them, not even Dr. Grantly, could close his ears, nor leave the house of God during the hours of service. They were under an obligation of listening, and that too, without any immediate power of reply.

There is, perhaps, no greater hardship at present inflicted on mankind in civilised and free countries, than the necessity of listening to sermons. No one but a preaching clergyman has, in these realms, the power of compelling an audience to sit silent, and be tormented. No one but a preaching clergyman can revel in platitudes, truisms, and untruisms, and yet receive, as his undisputed privilege, the same respectful demeanour as though words of impassioned eloquence, or persuasive logic, fell from his lips. Let a professor of law or physic find his place in a lecture-room and there pour forth jejune words and useless empty phrases and he will pour them forth to empty benches. Let a barrister attempt to talk without talking well, and he will talk but

seldom. A judge's charge need be listened to per force by none
but the jury, prisoner, and gaoler. A member of Parliament can
be coughed down or counted out. Town-councillors can be tabooed.
But no one can rid himself of the preaching clergyman. He is the
bore of the age, the old man whom we Sindbads cannot shake
off, the nightmare that disturbs our Sunday's rest, the incubus
that overloads our religion and makes God's service distasteful.
We are not forced into church! No: but we desire more than that.
We desire not to be forced to stay away. We desire, nay, we are
resolute, to enjoy the comfort of public worship; but we desire
also that we may do so without an amount of tedium which
ordinary human nature cannot endure with patience; that we may
be able to leave the house of God, without that anxious longing
for escape, which is the common consequence of common sermons.

With what complacency will a young parson deduce false
conclusions from misunderstood texts, and then threaten us with
all the penalties of Hades if we neglect to comply with the
injunctions he has given us! Yes, my too self-confident juvenile
friend, I do believe in those mysteries, which are so common in
your mouth; I do believe in the unadulterated word which you
hold there in your hand; but you must pardon me if, in some
things, I doubt your interpretation. The Bible is good, the prayer-
book is good, nay, you yourself would be acceptable, if you
would read to me some portion of those time-honoured discourses which our great divines have elaborated in the full
maturity of their powers. But you must excuse me, my insufficient young lecturer, if I yawn over your imperfect sentences,
your repeated phrases, your false pathos, your drawlings and
denouncings, your humming and hawing, your oh-ing and ah-
ing, your black gloves and your white handkerchief. To me, it
all means nothing; and hours are too precious to be so wasted——if
one could only avoid it.

And here I must make a protest against the pretence, so
often put forward by the working clergy, that they are overburdened by the multitude of sermons to be preached. We are all too
fond of our own voices, and a preacher is encouraged in the
vanity of making his heard by the privilege of a compelled
audience. His sermon is the pleasant morsel of his life, his
delicious moment of self-exaltation. "I have preached nine sermons this week," said a young friend to me the other day, with
hand languidly raised to his brow, the picture of an overburdened
martyr. "Nine this week, seven last week, four the week before.
I have preached twenty-three sermons this month. It is really

too much." "Too much, indeed," said I, shuddering; "too much for the strength of any one." "Yes," he answered meekly, "indeed it is; I am beginning to feel it painfully." "Would," said I, "you could feel it—would that you could be made to feel it." But he never guessed that my heart was wrung for the poor listeners.

There was, at any rate, no tedium felt in listening to Mr. Slope on the occasion in question. His subject came too home to his audience to be dull; and, to tell the truth, Mr. Slope had the gift of using words forcibly. He was heard through his thirty minutes of eloquence with mute attention and open ears; but with angry eyes, which glared round from one enraged person to another, with wide-spread nostrils from which already burst forth fumes of indignation, and with many shufflings of the feet and uneasy motions of the body, which betokened minds disturbed, and hearts not at peace with all the world.

At last the bishop, who, of all the congregation, had been most surprised, and whose hair almost stood on end with terror, gave the blessing in a manner not at all equal to that in which he had long been practising it in his own study, and the congregation was free to go their way.

VII

The Dean and Chapter Take Counsel

All Barchester was in a tumult. Dr. Grantly could hardly get himself out of the cathedral porch before he exploded in his wrath. The old dean betook himself silently to his deanery, afraid to speak; and there sat, half stupefied, pondering many things in vain. Mr. Harding crept forth solitary and unhappy; and, slowly passing beneath the elms of the close, could scarcely bring himself to believe that the words which he had heard had proceeded from the pulpit of Barchester Cathedral. Was he again to be disturbed? was his whole life to be shown up as a useless sham a second time? would he have to abdicate his precentorship, as he had his wardenship, and to give up chanting, as he had given up his twelve old bedesmen? And what if he did! Some other *Jupiter,* some other Mr. Slope, would come and turn him out of St. Cuthbert's. Surely he could not have been wrong all his life in chanting the litany as he had done! He began, however, to have his doubts. Doubting himself was Mr. Harding's weakness. It is not, however, the usual fault of his order.

Yes! all Barchester was in a tumult. It was not only the clergy who were affected. The laity also had listened to Mr. Slope's new doctrine, all with surprise, some with indignation, and some with a mixed feeling, in which dislike of the preacher was not so strongly blended. The old bishop and his chaplains, the dean and his canons and minor canons, the old choir, and especially Mr. Harding who was at the head of it, had all been popular in Barchester. They had spent their money and done good; the poor had not been ground down; the clergy in society had neither been overbearing nor austere; and the whole repute of the city was due to its ecclesiastical importance. Yet there were those who had heard Mr. Slope with satisfaction.

It is so pleasant to receive a fillip of excitement when suffering from the dull routine of every-day life! The anthems and Te Deums were in themselves delightful, but they had been heard so often! Mr. Slope was certainly not delightful, but he was new, and, moreover, clever. They had long thought it slow, so said now many of the Barchesterians, to go on as they had done in their old humdrum way, giving ear to none of the religious changes which were moving the world without. People in advance of the age now had new ideas, and it was quite time that Barchester should go in advance. Mr. Slope might be right. Sunday certainly had not been strictly kept in Barchester, except as regarded the cathedral services. Indeed the two hours between services had long been appropriated to morning calls and hot luncheons. Then Sunday schools! really more ought to have been done as to Sunday schools; Sabbath-day schools Mr. Slope had called them. The late bishop had really not thought of Sunday schools as he should have done. (These people probably did not reflect that catechisms and collects are quite as hard work to the young mind as book-keeping is to the elderly; and that quite as little feeling of worship enters into the one task as the other.) And then, as regarded that great question of musical services, there might be much to be said on Mr. Slope's side of the question. It certainly was the fact, that people went to the cathedral to hear the music, &c. &c.

And so a party absolutely formed itself in Barchester on Mr. Slope's side of the question! This consisted, among the upper classes, chiefly of ladies. No man—that is, no gentleman—could possibly be attracted by Mr. Slope, or consent to sit at the feet of so abhorrent a Gamaliel. Ladies are sometimes less nice in their appreciation of physical disqualification; and, provided that a man speak to them well, they will listen, though he speak from a mouth never so deformed and hideous. Wilkes was most fortunate as a lover; and the damp, sandy-haired, saucer-eyed, red-fisted Mr. Slope was powerful only over the female breast.

There were, however, one or two of the neighbouring clergy who thought it not quite safe to neglect the baskets in which for the nonce were stored the loaves and fishes of the diocese of Barchester. They, and they only, came to call on Mr. Slope after his performance in the cathedral pulpit. Among these Mr. Quiverful, the rector of Puddingdale, whose wife still continued to present him from year to year with fresh pledges of her love, and so to increase his cares and, it is to be hoped, his happiness equally. Who can wonder that a gentleman, with fourteen living children and a bare income of £400 a year, should look after the loaves and fishes, even when they are under the thumb of Mr. Slope?

Very soon after the Sunday on which the sermon was preached, the leading clergy of the neighbourhood held high debate together as to how Mr. Slope should be put down. In the first place he should never again preach from the pulpit of Barchester Cathedral. This was Dr. Grantly's earliest dictum; and they all agreed, providing only that they had the power to exclude him. Dr. Grantly declared that the power rested with the dean and chapter, observing that no clergyman out of the chapter had a claim to preach there, saving only the bishop himself. To this the dean assented, but alleged that contests on such a subject would be unseemly; to which rejoined a meagre little doctor, one of the cathedral prebendaries, that the contest must be all on the side of Mr. Slope if every prebendary were always there ready to take his own place in the pulpit. Cunning little meagre doctor, whom it suits well to live in his own cosy house within Barchester close, and who is well content to have his little fling at Dr. Vesey Stanhope and other absentees, whose Italian villas, or enticing London homes, are more tempting than cathedral stalls and residences!

To this answered the burly chancellor, a man rather silent indeed, but very sensible, that absent prebendaries had their vicars, and that in such case the vicar's right to the pulpit was the same as that of the higher order. To which the dean assented, groaning deeply at these truths. Thereupon, however, the meagre doctor remarked that they would be in the hands of their minor canons, one of whom might at any hour betray his trust. Whereon was heard from the burly chancellor an ejaculation sounding somewhat like "Pooh, pooh, pooh!" but it might be that the worthy man was but blowing out the heavy breath from his windpipe. Why silence him at all? suggested Mr. Harding. Let them not be ashamed to hear what any man might have to preach to them, unless he preached false doctrine; in which case, let the bishop silence him. So spoke our friend; vainly; for human ends must be attained by human means. But the dean saw a ray of hope out of those purblind old eyes of his. Yes, let them tell the bishop how distasteful to them was this Mr. Slope: a new bishop just come to his seat could not wish to insult his clergy while the gloss was yet fresh on his first apron.

Then up rose Dr. Grantly; and, having thus collected the scattered wisdom of his association, spoke forth with words of deep authority. When I say up rose the archdeacon, I speak of the inner man, which then sprang up to more immediate action, for the doctor had, bodily, been standing all along with his back to the dean's empty fire-grate, and the tails of his frock coat supported over his two arms. His hands were in his breeches pockets.

"It is quite clear that this man must not be allowed to preach again in this cathedral. We all see that, except our dear friend here, the milk of whose nature runs so softly, that he would not have the heart to refuse the Pope the loan of his pulpit, if the Pope would come and ask it. We must not, however, allow the man to preach again here. It is not because his opinion on church matters may be different from ours—with that one would not quarrel. It is because he has purposely insulted us. When he went up into the pulpit last Sunday, his studied object was to give offence to men who had grown old in reverence of those things of which he dared to speak so slightingly. What! to come here a stranger, a young, unknown, and unfriended stranger, and tell us, in the name of the bishop his master, that we are ignorant of our duties, old-fashioned, and useless! I don't know whether most to admire his courage or his impudence! And one thing I will tell you: that sermon originated solely with the man himself. The bishop was no more a party to it than was the dean here. You all know how grieved I am to see a bishop in this diocese holding the latitudinarian ideas by which Dr. Proudie has made himself conspicuous. You all know how greatly I should distrust the opinion of such a man. But in this matter I hold him to be blameless. I believe Dr. Proudie has lived too long among gentlemen to be guilty, or to instigate another to be guilty, of so gross an outrage. No! that man uttered what was untrue when he hinted that he was speaking as the mouthpiece of the bishop. It suited his ambitious views at once to throw down the gauntlet to us—at once to defy us here in the quiet of our own religious duties—here within the walls of our own loved cathedral—here where we have for so many years exercised our ministry without schism and with good repute. Such an attack upon us, coming from such a quarter, is abominable."

"Abominable," groaned the dean. "Abominable," muttered the meagre doctor. "Abominable," re-echoed the chancellor, uttering the sound from the bottom of his deep chest. "I really think it was," said Mr. Harding.

"Most abominable and most unjustifiable," continued the archdeacon. "But, Mr. Dean, thank God, that pulpit is still our own: your own, I should say. That pulpit belongs solely to the dean and chapter of Barchester Cathedral, and, as yet, Mr. Slope is no part of that chapter. You, Mr. Dean, have suggested that we should appeal to the bishop to abstain from forcing this man on us; but what if the bishop allow himself to be ruled by his chaplain? In my opinion, the matter is in our own hands. Mr. Slope cannot preach there without permission asked and obtained, and let that permission be invariably refused. Let all participation in the ministry of the cathedral service be refused to him. Then, if the bishop choose to interfere, we shall know what answer to make to the bishop. My friend here has suggested that this man may again find his way into the pulpit by undertaking the duty of some of your minor canons; but I am sure that we may fully trust to these gentlemen to support us, when it is known that the dean objects to any such transfer."

"Of course you may," said the chancellor.

There was much more discussion among the learned conclave, all of which, of course, ended in obedience to the archdeacon's commands. They had too long been accustomed to his rule to shake it off so soon; and in this particular case they had none of them a wish to abet the man whom he was so anxious to put down.

Such a meeting as that we have just recorded is not held in such a city as Barchester unknown and untold of. Not only was the fact of the meeting talked of in every respectable house, including the palace, but the very speeches of the dean, the archdeacon, and chancellor were repeated; not without many additions and imaginary circumstances, according to the tastes and opinions of the relaters.

All, however, agreed in saying that Mr. Slope was to be debarred from opening his mouth in the cathedral of Barchester; many believed that the vergers were to be ordered to refuse him even the accommodation of a seat; and some of the most far-going advocates for strong measures, declared that his sermon was looked upon as an indictable offence, and that proceedings were to be taken against him for brawling.

The party who were inclined to defend him—the enthusiastically religious young ladies, and the middle-aged spinsters desirous of a move—of course took up his defence the more warmly on account of this attack. If they could not hear Mr. Slope in the cathedral, they would hear him elsewhere; they would leave the dull dean, the dull old prebendaries, and the scarcely less dull young minor canons, to preach to each other; they would work slippers and cushions, and hem bands for Mr. Slope, make him a happy martyr, and stick him up in some new Sion or Bethesda, and put the cathedral quite out of fashion.

Dr. and Mrs. Proudie at once returned to London. They thought it expedient not to have to encounter any personal application from the dean and chapter respecting the sermon, till the violence of the storm had expended itself; but they left Mr. Slope behind them nothing daunted, and he went about his work zealously, flattering such as would listen to his flattery, whispering religious twaddle into the ears of foolish women, ingratiating himself with the few clergy who would receive him, visiting the houses of the poor, inquiring into all people, prying into everything, and searching with his minutest eye into all palatial dilapidations. He did not, however, make any immediate attempt to preach again in the cathedral.

An so all Barchester was by the ears.

VIII

The Ex-Warden Rejoices in His Probable Return to the Hospital

Among the ladies in Barchester who have hitherto acknowledged Mr. Slope as their spiritual director, must not be reckoned either the widow Bold, or her sister-in-law. On the first outbreak of the wrath of the denizens of the close, none had been more animated against the intruder than these two ladies. And this was natural. Who could be so proud of the musical distinction of their own cathedral as the favourite daughter of the precentor? Who would be so likely to resent an insult offered to the old choir? And in such matters Miss Bold and her sister-in-law had but one opinion.

This wrath, however, has in some degree been mitigated, and I regret to say that these ladies allowed Mr. Slope to be his own apologist. About a fortnight after the sermon had been preached, they were both of them not a little surprised by hearing Mr. Slope announced, as the page in buttons opened Mrs. Bold's drawing-room door. Indeed, what living man could, by a mere morning visit, have surprised them more? Here was the great enemy of all that was good in Barchester coming into their own drawing-room, and they had no strong man, no ready tongue, near at hand for their protection. The widow snatched her baby out of its cradle into her lap, and Mary Bold stood up ready to die manfully in that baby's behalf, should, under any circumstances, such a sacrifice become necessary.

In this manner was Mr. Slope received. But when he left, he was allowed by each lady to take her hand, and to make his adieux as gentlemen do who have been graciously entertained! Yes; he shook hands with them, and was curtseyed out courteously, the buttoned page opening the door, as he would have done for the best canon of them all. He had touched the baby's little hand

and blessed him with a fervid blessing; he had spoken to the widow of her early sorrows, and Eleanor's silent tears had not rebuked him; he had told Mary Bold that her devotion would be rewarded, and Mary Bold had heard the praise without disgust. And how had he done all this? how had he so quickly turned aversion into, at any rate, acquaintance? how had he overcome the enmity with which these ladies had been ready to receive him, and made his peace with them so easily?

My readers will guess from what I have written that I myself do not like Mr. Slope; but I am constrained to admit that he is a man of parts. He knows how to say a soft word in the proper place; he knows how to adapt his flattery to the ears of his hearers; he knows the wiles of the serpent, and he uses them. Could Mr. Slope have adapted his manners to men as well as to women, could he ever have learnt the ways of a gentleman, he might have risen to great things.

He commenced his acquaintance with Eleanor by praising her father. He had, he said, become aware that he had unfortunately offended the feelings of a man of whom he could not speak too highly; he would not now allude to a subject which was probably too serious for drawing-room conversation, but he would say, that it had been very far from him to utter a word in disparagement of a man, of whom all the world, at least the clerical world, spoke so highly as it did of Mr. Harding. And so he went on, unsaying a great deal of his sermon, expressing his highest admiration for the precentor's musical talents, eulogising the father and the daughter and the sister-in-law, speaking in that low silky whisper which he always had specially prepared for feminine ears, and, ultimately, gaining his object. When he left, he expressed a hope that he might again be allowed to call; and though Eleanor gave no verbal assent to this, she did not express dissent: and so Mr. Slope's right to visit at the widow's house was established.

The day after this visit Eleanor told her father of it, and expressed an opinion that Mr. Slope was not quite so black as he had been painted. Mr. Harding opened his eyes rather wider than usual when he heard what had occurred, but he said little; he could not agree in any praise of Mr. Slope, and it was not his practice to say much evil of any one. He did not, however, like the visit, and simple-minded as he was, he felt sure that Mr. Slope had some deeper motive than the mere pleasure of making soft speeches to two ladies.

Mr. Harding, however, had come to see his daughter with other purpose than that of speaking either good or evil of Mr. Slope. He had come to tell her that the place of warden in Hiram's hospital was again to be filled up, and that in all probability he would once more return to his old home and his twelve bedesmen.

"But," said he, laughing, "I shall be greatly shorn of my ancient glory."

"Why so, papa?"

"This new act of parliament, that is to put us all on our feet again," continued he, "settles my income at four hundred and fifty pounds per annum."

"Four hundred and fifty," said she, "instead of eight hundred! Well: that is rather shabby. But still, papa, you'll have the dear old house and the garden?"

"My dear," said he, "it's worth twice the money"; and as he spoke he showed a jaunty kind of satisfaction in his tone and manner, and in the quick, pleasant way in which he paced Eleanor's drawing-room. "It's worth twice the money. I shall have the house and the garden, and a larger income than I can possibly want."

"At any rate, you'll have no extravagant daughter to provide for"; and as she spoke, the young widow put her arm within his, and made him sit on the sofa beside her; "at any rate you'll not have that expense."

"No, my dear; and I shall be rather lonely without her; but we won't think of that now. As regards income I shall have plenty for all I want. I shall have my old house; and I don't mind owning now that I have felt sometimes the inconvenience of living in a lodging. Lodgings are very nice for young men, but at my time of life there is a want of——I hardly know what to call it, perhaps not respectability——"

"Oh, papa! I'm sure there's been nothing like that. Nobody has thought it; nobody in all Barchester has been more respected than you have been since you took those rooms in High Street. Nobody! Not the dean in his deanery, or the archdeacon out at Plumstead."

"The archdeacon would not be much obliged to you if he heard you," said he, smiling somewhat at the exclusive manner in which his daughter confined her illustration to the church dignitaries of the chapter of Barchester; "but at any rate I shall be glad to get back to the old house. Since I heard that it was all settled, I have begun to fancy that I can't be comfortable without my two sitting-rooms.''

"Come and stay with me, papa, till it is settled—there's a dear papa.''

"Thank ye, Nelly. But no; I won't do that. It would make two movings. I shall be very glad to get back to my old men again. Alas! alas! There have six of them gone in these few last years. Six out of twelve! And the others I fear have had but a sorry life of it there. Poor Bunce, poor old Bunce!''

Bunce was one of the surviving recipients of Hiram's charity; an old man, now over ninety, who had long been a favourite of Mr. Harding's.

"How happy old Bunce will be,'' said Mrs. Bold, clapping her soft hands softly. "How happy they all will be to have you back again. You may be sure there will soon be friendship among them again when you are there.''

"But,'' said he, half laughing, "I am to have new troubles, which will be terrible to me. There are to be twelve old women, and a matron. How shall I manage twelve women and a matron!''

"The matron will manage the women of course.''

"And who'll manage the matron?'' said he.

"She won't want to be managed. She'll be a great lady herself, I suppose. But, papa, where will the matron live? She is not to live in the warden's house with you, is she?''

"Well, I hope not, my dear.''

"Oh, papa, I tell you fairly, I won't have a matron for a new step-mother.''

"You shan't, my dear; that is, if I can help it. But they are going to build another house for the matron and the women; and I believe they haven't even fixed yet on the site of the building.''

"And have they appointed the matron?'' said Eleanor.

"They haven't appointed the warden yet,'' replied he.

"But there's no doubt about that, I suppose,'' said his daughter.

Mr. Harding explained that he thought there was no doubt; that the archdeacon had declared as much, saying that the bishop and his chaplain between them had not the power to appoint any one else, even if they had the will to do so, and sufficient impudence to carry out such a will. The archdeacon was of opinion, that though Mr. Harding had resigned his wardenship, and had done so unconditionally, he had done so under circumstances which left the bishop no choice as to his re-appointment, now that the affairs of the hospital had been settled on a new basis by act of Parliament. Such was the archdeacon's opinion, and his father-in-law received it without a shadow of doubt.

Dr. Grantly had always been strongly opposed to Mr. Harding's resignation of the place. He had done all in his power to dissuade him from it. He had considered that Mr. Harding was bound to withstand the popular clamour with which he was attacked for receiving so large an income as eight hundred a year from such a charity, and was not even yet satisfied that his father-in-law's conduct had not been pusillanimous and undignified. He looked also on this reduction of the warden's income as a shabby, paltry scheme on the part of government for escaping from a difficulty into which it had been brought by the public press. Dr. Grantly observed that the government had no more right to dispose of a sum of four hundred and fifty pounds a year out of the income of Hiram's legacy, than of nine hundred; whereas, as he said, the bishop, dean, and chapter clearly had a right to settle what sum should be paid. He also declared that the government had no more right to saddle the charity with twelve old women than with twelve hundred; and he was, therefore, very indignant on the matter. He probably forgot when so talking that government had done nothing of the kind, and had never assumed any such might or any such right. He made the common mistake of attributing to the government, which in such matters is powerless, the doings of Parliament, which in such matters is omnipotent.

But though he felt that the glory and honour of the situation of warden of Barchester Hospital were indeed curtailed by the new arrangement; that the whole establishment had to a certain degree been made vile by the touch of Whig commissioners; that the place with its lessened income, its old women, and other innovations, was very different from the hospital of former days; still the archdeacon was too practical a man of the world to wish that his father-in-law, who had at present little more than £200 per annum for all his wants, should refuse the situation, defiled, undignified, and commission-ridden as it was.

Mr. Harding had, accordingly, made up his mind that he would return to his old home at the hospital, and to tell the truth, had experienced almost a childish pleasure in the idea of doing so. The diminished income was to him not even the source of momentary regret. The matron and the old women did rather go against the grain; but he was able to console himself with the reflection, that, after all, such an arrangement might be of real service to the poor of the city. The thought that he must receive his re-appointment as the gift of the new bishop, and probably through the hands of Mr. Slope, annoyed him a little; but his mind was set at rest by the assurance of the archdeacon that there would be no favour in such a presentation. The re-appointment of the old warden would be regarded by all the world as a matter of course. Mr. Harding, therefore, felt no hesitation in telling his daughter that they might look upon his return to his old quarters as a settled matter.

"And you won't have to ask for it, papa."

"Certainly not, my dear. There is no ground on which I could ask for any favour from the bishop, whom, indeed, I hardly know. Nor would I ask a favour, the granting of which might possibly be made a question to be settled by Mr. Slope. No," said he, moved for a moment by a spirit very unlike his own, "I certainly shall be very glad to go back to the hospital; but I should never go there, if it were necessary that my doing so should be the subject of a request to Mr. Slope."

This little outbreak of her father's anger jarred on the present tone of Eleanor's mind. She had not learnt to like Mr. Slope, but she had learnt to think that he had much respect for her father; and she would, therefore, willingly use her efforts to induce something like good feeling between them.

"Papa," said she, "I think you somewhat mistake Mr. Slope's character."

"Do I?" said he, placidly.

"I think you do, papa. I think he intended no personal disrespect to you when he preached the sermon which made the archdeacon and the dean so angry!"

"I never supposed he did, my dear. I hope I never inquired within myself whether he did or no. Such a matter would be unworthy of any inquiry, and very unworthy of the consideration of the chapter. But I fear he intended disrespect to the ministration of God's services, as conducted in conformity with the rules of the Church of England."

"But might it not be that he thought it his duty to express his dissent from that which you, and the dean, and all of us here so much approve?"

"It can hardly be the duty of a young man rudely to assail the religious convictions of his elders in the church. Courtesy should have kept him silent, even if neither charity nor modesty could do so."

"But Mr. Slope would say that on such a subject the commands of his heavenly Master do not admit of his being silent."

"Nor of his being courteous, Eleanor?"

"He did not say that, papa."

"Believe me, my child, that Christian ministers are never called on by God's word to insult the convictions, or even the prejudices of their brethren; and that religion is at any rate not less susceptible of urbane and courteous conduct among men, than any other study which men may take up. I am sorry to say that I cannot defend Mr. Slope's sermon in the cathedral. But come, my dear, put on your bonnet, and let us walk round the dear old gardens at the hospital. I have never yet had the heart to go beyond the court-yard since we left the place. Now I think I can venture to enter."

Eleanor rang the bell, and gave a variety of imperative charges as to the welfare of the precious baby, whom, all but unwillingly, she was about to leave for an hour or so, and then sauntered forth with her father to revisit the old hospital. It had been forbidden ground to her as well as to him since the day on which they had walked forth together from its walls.

IX

The Stanhope Family

It is now three months since Dr. Proudie began his reign, and changes have already been effected in the diocese which show at least the energy of an active mind. Among other things absentee clergymen have been favoured with hints much too strong to be overlooked. Poor dear old Bishop Grantly had on this matter been too lenient, and the archdeacon had never been inclined to be severe with those who were absent on reputable pretences, and who provided for their duties in a liberal way.

Among the greatest of the diocesan sinners in this respect was Dr. Vesey Stanhope. Years had now passed since he had done a day's duty; and yet there was no reason against his doing duty except a want of inclination on his own part. He held a prebendal stall in the diocese; one of the best residences in the close; and the two large rectories of Crabtree Canonicorum, and Stogpingum. Indeed, he had the cure of three parishes, for that of Eiderdown was joined to Stogpingum. He had resided in Italy for twelve years. His first going there had been attributed to a sore throat; and that sore throat, though never repeated in any violent manner, had stood him in such stead, that it had enabled him to live in easy idleness ever since.

He had now been summoned home—not, indeed, with rough violence, or by any peremptory command, but by a mandate which he found himself unable to disregard. Mr. Slope had written to him by the bishop's desire. In the first place, the bishop much wanted the valuable co-operation of Dr. Vesey Stanhope in the diocese; in the next, the bishop thought it his imperative duty to become personally acquainted with the most conspicuous of his diocesan clergy; then the bishop thought it essentially necessary for Dr. Stanhope's own interests, that Dr. Stanhope should, at any rate for a time, return to Barchester; and last, it was said that so strong a feeling was at the present moment evinced by the hierarchs of the church with reference to the absence of its clerical members, that it behoved Dr. Vesey Stanhope not to allow his name to stand among those which would probably in a few months be submitted to the councils of the nation.

There was something so ambiguously frightful in this last threat that Dr. Stanhope determined to spend two or three summer months at his residence in Barchester. His rectories were inhabited by his curates, and he felt himself from disuse to be unfit for parochial duty; but his prebendal home was kept empty for him, and he thought it probable that he might be able now and again to preach a prebendal sermon. He arrived, therefore, with all his family at Barchester, and he and they must be introduced to my readers.

The great family characteristic of the Stanhopes might probably be said to be heartlessness: but this want of feeling was, in most of them, accompanied by so great an amount of good nature as to make itself but little noticeable to the world. They were so prone to oblige their neighbours that their neighbours failed to perceive how indifferent to them was the happiness and well-being of those around them. The Stanhopes would visit you in your sickness (provided it were not contagious), would bring you oranges, French novels, and the last new bit of scandal, and then hear of your death or your recovery with an equally indifferent composure. Their conduct to each other was the same as to the world; they bore and forbore: and there was sometimes, as will be seen, much necessity for forbearing; but their love among themselves rarely reached above this. It is astonishing how much each of the family was able to do, and how much each did, to prevent the well-being of the other four.

For there were five in all; the doctor, namely, and Mrs. Stanhope, two daughters, and one son. The doctor, perhaps, was the least singular and most estimable of them all, and yet such good qualities as he possessed were all negative. He was a good-looking rather plethoric gentleman of about sixty years of age. His hair was snow white, very plentiful, and somewhat like wool of the finest description. His whiskers were very large and very white, and gave to his face the appearance of a benevolent sleepy old lion. His dress was always unexceptionable. Although he had lived so many years in Italy it was invariably of a decent clerical hue, but it never was hyperclerical. He was a man not given to much talking, but what little he did say was generally well said. His reading seldom went beyond romances and poetry of the lightest and not always most moral description. He was thoroughly a *bon vivant;* an accomplished judge of wine, though he never drank to excess; and a most inexorable critic in all affairs touching the kitchen. He had had much to forgive in his own family, since a family had grown up around him, and had forgiven everything—except inattention to his dinner. His weakness in that respect was now fully understood, and his temper but seldom tried. As Dr. Stanhope was a clergyman, it may be supposed that his religious convictions made up a considerable part of his character; but this was not so. That he had religious convictions must be believed; but he rarely obtruded them, even on his children. This abstinence on his part was not systematic, but very characteristic of the man. It was not that he had predetermined never to influence their thoughts; but he was so habitually idle that his time for doing so had never come till the opportunity for doing so was gone for ever. Whatever conviction the father may have had, the children were at any rate but indifferent members of the church from which he drew his income.

Such was Dr. Stanhope. The features of Mrs. Stanhope's character were even less plainly marked than those of her lord. The *far niente* of her Italian life had entered into her very soul, and brought her to regard a state of inactivity as the only earthly good. In manner and appearance she was exceedingly prepossessing. She had been a beauty, and even now, at fifty-five, she was a handsome woman. Her dress was always perfect; she never dressed but once in the day, and never appeared till between three and four; but when she did appear, she appeared at her best. Whether the toil rested partly with her, or wholly with her handmaid, it is not for such a one as the author even to imagine. The structure of her attire was always elaborate, and yet never over laboured. She was rich in apparel, but not bedizened with finery; her ornaments were costly, rare, and such as could not fail to attract notice, but they did not look as though worn with that purpose. She well knew the great architectural secret of decorating her constructions, and never descended to construct a decoration. But when we have said that Mrs. Stanhope knew how to dress, and used her knowledge daily, we have said all. Other purpose in life she had none. It was something, indeed, that she did not interfere with the purposes of others. In early life she had undergone great trials with reference to the doctor's dinners; but for the last ten or twelve years her eldest daughter Charlotte had taken that labour off her hands, and she had had little to trouble her;—little, that is, till the edict for this terrible English journey had gone forth; since then, indeed, her life had been laborious enough. For such a one, the toil of being carried from the shores of Como to the city of Barchester is more than labour enough, let the care of the carriers be ever so vigilant. Mrs. Stanhope had been obliged to have every one of her dresses taken in from the effects of the journey.

Charlotte Stanhope was at this time about thirty-five years old; and, whatever may have been her faults, she had none of those which belong particularly to old young ladies. She neither dressed young, nor talked young, nor indeed looked young. She appeared to be perfectly content with her time of life, and in no way affected the graces of youth. She was a fine young woman; and had she been a man, would have been a very fine young man. All that was done in the house, and that was not done by servants, was done by her. She gave the orders, paid the bills, hired and dismissed the domestics, made the tea, carved the meat, and managed everything in the Stanhope household. She, and she alone, could ever induce her father to look into the state of his worldly concerns. She, and she alone, could in any degree control the absurdities of her sister. She, and she alone, prevented the whole family from falling into utter disrepute and beggary. It was by her advice that they now found themselves very unpleasantly situated in Barchester.

So far, the character of Charlotte Stanhope is not unprepossessing. But it remains to be said, that the influence which she had in her family, though it had been used to a certain extent for their worldly well-being, had not been used to their real benefit, as it might have been. She had aided her father in his indifference to his professional duties, counselling him that his livings were as much his individual property as the estates of his elder brother were the property of that worthy peer. She had for years past stifled every little rising wish for a return to England which the doctor had from time to time expressed. She had encouraged her mother in her idleness in order that she herself might be mistress and manager of the Stanhope household. She had encouraged and fostered the follies of her sister, though she was always willing, and often able, to protect her from their probable result. She had done her best, and had thoroughly succeeded in spoiling her brother, and turning him loose upon the world an idle man without a profession, and without a shilling that he could call his own.

Miss Stanhope was a clever woman, able to talk on most subjects, and quite indifferent as to what the subject was. She prided herself on her freedom from English prejudice, and she might have added, from feminine delicacy. On religion she was a pure freethinker, and with much want of true affection, delighted to throw out her own views before the troubled mind of her father. To have shaken what remained of his Church of England faith would have gratified her much; but the idea of his abandoning his preferment in the church had never once presented itself to her mind. How could he indeed, when he had no income from any other source?

But the two most prominent members of the family still remain to be described. The second child had been christened Madeline, and had been a great beauty. We need not say had been, for she was never more beautiful than at the time of which we write, though her person for many years had been disfigured by an accident. It is unnecessary that we should give in detail the early history of Madeline Stanhope. She had gone to Italy when about seventeen years of age, and had been allowed to make the most of her surpassing beauty in the saloons of Milan, and among the crowded villas along the shores of the Lake of Como. She had become famous for adventures in which her character was just not lost, and had destroyed the hearts of a dozen cavaliers without once being touched in her own. Blood had flowed in quarrels about her charms, and she heard of these encounters with pleasurable excitement. It had been told of her that on one occasion she had stood by in the disguise of a page, and had seen her lover fall.

As is so often the case, she had married the very worst of those who sought her hand. Why she had chosen Paulo Neroni, a man of no birth and no property, a mere captain in the Pope's guard, one who had come up to Milan either simply as an adventurer or else as a spy, a man of harsh temper and oily manners, mean in figure, swarthy in face, and so false in words as to be hourly detected, need not now be told. When the moment for doing so came, she had probably no alternative. He, at any rate, had become her husband; and after a prolonged honeymoon among the lakes, they had gone together to Rome, the papal captain having vainly endeavoured to induce his wife to remain behind him.

Six months afterwards she arrived at her father's house a cripple, and a mother. She had arrived without even notice, with hardly clothes to cover her, and without one of those many ornaments which had graced her bridal *trousseau*. Her baby was in the arms of a poor girl from Milan, whom she had taken in exchange for the Roman maid who had accompanied her thus far, and who had then, as her mistress said, become homesick and had returned. It was clear that the lady had determined that there should be no witness to tell stories of her life in Rome.

She had fallen, she said, in ascending a ruin, and had fatally injured the sinews of her knee; so fatally, that when she stood she lost eight inches of her accustomed height; so fatally, that when she essayed to move, she could only drag herself painfully along, with protruded hip and extended foot in a manner less graceful than that of a hunchback. She had consequently made up her mind, once and for ever, that she would never stand, and never attempt to move herself.

Stories were not slow to follow her, averring that she had been cruelly ill-used by Neroni, and that to his violence had she owed her accident. Be that as it may, little had been said about her husband, but that little had made it clearly intelligible to the family that Signor Neroni was to be seen and heard of no more. There was no question as to re-admitting the poor ill-used beauty to her old family rights, no question as to adopting her infant daughter beneath the Stanhope roof-tree. Though heartless, the Stanhopes were not selfish. The two were taken in, petted, made much of, for a time all but adored, and then felt by the two parents to be great nuisances in the house. But in the house the lady was, and there she remained, having her own way, though that way was not very conformable with the customary usages of an English clergyman.

Madame Neroni, though forced to give up all motion in the world, had no intention whatever of giving up the world itself. The beauty of her face was uninjured, and that beauty was of a peculiar kind. Her copious rich brown hair was worn in Grecian *bandeaux* round her head, displaying as much as possible of her forehead and cheeks. Her forehead, though rather low, was very beautiful from its perfect contour and pearly whiteness. Her eyes were long and large, and marvellously bright; might I venture to say, bright as Lucifer's, I should perhaps best express the depth of their brilliancy. They were dreadful eyes to look at, such as would absolutely deter any man of quiet mind and easy spirit from attempting a passage of arms with such foes. There was talent in them, and the fire of passion and the play of wit, but there was no love. Cruelty was there instead, and courage, a desire of masterhood, cunning, and a wish for mischief. And yet, as eyes, they were very beautiful. The eyelashes were long and perfect, and the long steady unabashed gaze, with which she would look into the face of her admirer, fascinated while it frightened him. She was a basilisk from whom an ardent lover of beauty could make no escape. Her nose and mouth and teeth and chin and neck and bust were perfect, much more so at twenty-eight than they had been at eighteen. What wonder that with such charms still glowing in her face, and with such deformity destroying her figure, she should resolve to be seen, but only to be seen reclining on a sofa.

Her resolve had not been carried out without difficulty. She had still frequented the opera at Milan; she had still been seen occasionally in the saloons of the *noblesse;* she had caused herself to be carried in and out from her carriage, and that in such a manner as in no wise to disturb her charms, disarrange her dress, or expose her deformities. Her sister always accompanied her and a maid, a man-servant also, and on state occasions, two. It was impossible that her purpose could have been achieved with less: and yet, poor as she was, she had achieved her purpose. And then again the more dissolute Italian youths of Milan frequented the Stanhope villa and surrounded her couch, not greatly to her father's satisfaction. Sometimes his spirit would rise, a dark spot would show itself on his cheek, and he would

rebel; but Charlotte would assuage him with some peculiar triumph
of her culinary art, and all again would be smooth for a while.

Madeline affected all manner of rich and quaint devices in the
garniture of her room, her person, and her feminine belongings.
In nothing was this more apparent than in the visiting card which
she had prepared for her use. For such an article one would say
that she, in her present state, could have but small need, seeing
how improbable it was that she should make a morning call: but
not such was her own opinion. Her card was surrounded by a
deep border of gilding; on this she had imprinted, in three
lines,—

La Signora Madeline
Vesey Neroni
—Nata Stanhope.

And over the name she had a bright gilt coronet, which certainly
looked very magnificent. How she had come to concoct such a
name for herself it would be difficult to explain. Her father had
been christened Vesey, as another man is christened Thomas;
and she had no more right to assume it than would have the
daughter of a Mr. Josiah Jones to call herself Mrs. Josiah Smith,
on marrying a man of the latter name. The gold coronet was
equally out of place, and perhaps inserted with even less excuse.
Paulo Neroni had had not the faintest title to call himself a scion
of even Italian nobility. Had the pair met in England Neroni
would probably have been a count; but they had met in Italy, and
any such pretence on his part would have been simply ridiculous.
A coronet, however, was a pretty ornament, and if it could
solace a poor cripple to have such on her card, who would
begrudge it to her?

Of her husband, or of his individual family, she never
spoke; but with her admirers she would often allude in a mysterious way to her married life and isolated state, and, pointing to
her daughter, would call her the last of the blood of the emperors,
thus referring Neroni's extraction to the old Roman family from
which the worst of the Cæsars sprang.

The "Signora" was not without talent, and not without a
certain sort of industry; she was an indomitable letter writer, and
her letters were worth the postage: they were full of wit, mischief,
satire, love, latitudinarian philosophy, free religion, and,
sometimes, alas! loose ribaldry. The subject, however, depended
entirely on the recipient, and she was prepared to correspond

with any one but moral young ladies or stiff old women. She wrote also a kind of poetry, generally in Italian, and short romances, generally in French. She read much of a desultory sort of literature, and as a modern linguist had really made great proficiency. Such was the lady who had now come to wound the hearts of the men of Barchester.

Ethelbert Stanhope was in some respects like his younger sister, but he was less inestimable as a man than she as a woman. His great fault was an entire absence of that principle which should have induced him, as the son of a man without fortune, to earn his own bread. Many attempts had been made to get him to do so, but these had all been frustrated, not so much by idleness on his part, as by a disinclination to exert himself in any way not to his taste. He had been educated at Eton, and had been intended for the Church, but had left Cambridge in disgust after a single term, and notified to his father his intention to study for the bar. Preparatory to that, he thought it well that he should attend a German university, and consequently went to Leipsic. There he remained two years, and brought away a knowledge of German and a taste for the fine arts. He still, however, intended himself for the bar, took chambers, engaged himself to sit at the feet of a learned pundit, and spent a season in London. He there found that all his aptitudes inclined him to the life of an artist, and he determined to live by painting. With this object he returned to Milan, and had himself rigged out for Rome. As a painter he might have earned his bread, for he wanted only diligence to excel; but when at Rome his mind was carried away by other things: he soon wrote home for money, saying that he had been converted to the Mother Church, that he was already an acolyte of the Jesuits, and that he was about to start with others to Palestine on a mission for converting Jews. He did go to Judea, but being unable to convert the Jews, was converted by them. He again wrote home, to say that Moses was the only giver of perfect laws to the world, that the coming of the true Messiah was at hand, that great things were doing in Palestine, and that he had met one of the family of Sidonia, a most remarkable man, who was now on his way to Western Europe, and whom he had induced to deviate from his route with the object of calling at the Stanhope villa. Ethelbert then expressed his hope that his mother and sisters would listen to this wonderful prophet. His father he knew could not do so from pecuniary considerations. This Sidonia, however, did not take so strong a fancy to him as another of that family once did to a

young English nobleman. At least he provided him with no
heaps of gold as large as lions; so that the Judaised Ethelbert was
again obliged to draw on the revenues of the Christian Church.

It is needless to tell how the father swore that he would send
no more money and receive no Jew; nor how Charlotte declared
that Ethelbert could not be left penniless in Jerusalem, and how
"La Signora Neroni" resolved to have Sidonia at her feet. The
money was sent, and the Jew did come. The Jew did come, but
he was not at all to the taste of "La Signora." He was a dirty
little old man, and though he had provided no golden lions, he
had, it seems, relieved young Stanhope's necessities. He positively refused to leave the villa till he had got a bill from the
doctor on his London bankers.

Ethelbert did not long remain a Jew. He soon reappeared at
the villa without prejudices on the subject of his religion, and
with a firm resolve to achieve fame and fortune as a sculptor. He
brought with him some models which he had originated at
Rome, and which really gave such fair promise that his father
was induced to go to further expense in furthering these views.
Ethelbert opened an establishment, or rather took lodgings and a
workshop, at Carrara, and there spoilt much marble, and made
some few pretty images. Since that period, now four years ago,
he had alternated between Carrara and the villa, but his sojourns
at the workshop became shorter and shorter, and those at the
villa longer and longer. 'Twas no wonder; for Carrara is not a
spot in which an Englishman would like to dwell.

When the family started for England he had resolved not to
be left behind, and with the assistance of his elder sister had
carried his point against his father's wishes. It was necessary, he
said, that he should come to England for orders. How otherwise
was he to bring his profession to account?

In personal appearance Ethelbert Stanhope was the most
singular of beings. He was certainly very handsome. He had his
sister Madeline's eyes without their stare, and without their hard
cunning cruel firmness. They were also very much lighter, and
of so light and clear a blue as to make his face remarkable, if
nothing else did so. On entering a room with him, Ethelbert's
blue eyes would be the first thing you would see, and on leaving
it almost the last you would forget. His light hair was very long
and silky, coming down over his coat. His beard had been
prepared in the Holy Land, and was patriarchal. He never shaved,
and rarely trimmed it. It was glossy, soft, clean, and altogether not
unprepossessing. It was such, that ladies might desire to reel it

off and work it into their patterns in lieu of floss silk. His complexion was fair and almost pink, he was small in height, and slender in limb, but well-made, and his voice was of peculiar sweetness.

In manner and dress he was equally remarkable. He had none of the *mauvaise honte* of an Englishman. He required no introduction to make himself agreeable to any person. He habitually addressed strangers, ladies as well as men, without any such formality, and in doing so never seemed to meet with rebuke. His costume cannot be described, because it was so various; but it was always totally opposed in every principle of colour and construction to the dress of those with whom he for the time consorted.

He was habitually addicted to making love to ladies, and did so without any scruple of conscience, or any idea that such a practice was amiss. He had no heart to touch himself, and was literally unaware that humanity was subject to such an infliction. He had not thought much about it; but, had he been asked, would have said, that ill-treating a lady's heart meant injuring her promotion in the world. His principles therefore forbade him to pay attention to a girl, if he thought any man was present whom it might suit her to marry. In this manner, his good nature frequently interfered with his amusement; but he had no other motive in abstaining from the fullest declarations of love to every girl that pleased his eye.

Bertie Stanhope, as he was generally called, was, however, popular with both sexes; and with Italians as well as English. His circle of acquaintance was very large, and embraced people of all sorts. He had no respect for rank, and no aversion to those below him. He had lived on familiar terms with English peers, German shopkeepers, and Roman priests. All people were nearly alike to him. He was above, or rather below, all prejudices. No virtue could charm him, no vice shock him. He had about him a natural good manner, which seemed to qualify him for the highest circles, and yet he was never out of place in the lowest. He had no principle, no regard for others, no self-respect, no desire to be other than a drone in the hive, if only he could, as a drone, get what honey was sufficient for him. Of honey, in his latter days, it may probably be presaged, that he will have but short allowance.

Such was the family of the Stanhopes, who, at this period, suddenly joined themselves to the ecclesiastical circle of Barchester close. Any stranger union, it would be impossible perhaps to conceive. And it was not as though they all fell down into the cathedral precincts hitherto unknown and untalked of. In such case no amalgamation would have been at all probable between the newcomers and either the Proudie set or the Grantly set. But such was far from being the case. The Stanhopes were all known by name in Barchester, and Barchester was prepared to receive them with open arms. The doctor was one of her prebendaries, one of her rectors, one of her pillars of strength; and was, moreover, counted on, as a sure ally, both by Proudies and Grantlys.

He himself was the brother of one peer, and his wife was the sister of another—and both these peers were lords of whiggish tendency, with whom the new bishop had some sort of alliance. This was sufficient to give to Mr. Slope high hope that he might enlist Dr. Stanhope on his side, before his enemies could out-manœuvre him. On the other hand, the old dean had many many years ago, in the days of the doctor's clerical energies, been instrumental in assisting him in his views as to preferment; and many many years ago also, the two doctors, Stanhope and Grantly, had, as young parsons, been joyous together in the common rooms of Oxford. Dr. Grantly, consequently, did not doubt but that the newcomer would range himself under his banners.

Little did any of them dream of what ingredients the Stanhope family was now composed.

X

Mrs. Proudie's Reception—Commenced

The bishop and his wife had only spent three or four days in Barchester on the occasion of their first visit. His lordship had, as we have seen, taken his seat on his throne; but his demeanour there, into which it had been his intention to infuse much hierar-

chal dignity, had been a good deal disarranged by the audacity of
his chaplain's sermon. He had hardly dared to look his clergy in
the face, and to declare by the severity of his countenance that in
truth he meant all that his factotum was saying on his behalf; nor
yet did he dare to throw Mr. Slope over, and show to those
around him that he was no party to the sermon, and would resent
it.

He had accordingly blessed his people in a shambling manner,
not at all to his own satisfaction, and had walked back to his
palace with his mind very doubtful as to what he would say to
his chaplain on the subject. He did not remain long in doubt. He
had hardly doffed his lawn when the partner of all his toils
entered his study, and exclaimed even before she had seated
herself—

"Bishop, did you ever hear a more sublime, more spirit-
moving, more appropriate discourse than that?"

"Well, my love; ha—hum—he!" The bishop did not know
what to say.

"I hope, my lord, you don't mean to say you disapprove?"

There was a look about the lady's eye which did not admit of
my lord's disapproving at that moment. He felt that if he intended to disapprove, it must be now or never; but he also felt
that it could not be now. It was not in him to say to the wife of
his bosom that Mr. Slope's sermon was ill-timed, impertinent
and vexatious.

"No, no," replied the bishop. "No, I can't say I disapprove—
a very clever sermon and very well intended, and I dare say will
do a great deal of good." This last praise was added, seeing that
what he had already said by no means satisfied Mrs. Proudie.

"I hope it will," said she. "I am sure it was well deserved.
Did you ever in your life, bishop, hear anything so like play-
acting as the way in which Mr. Harding sings the litany? I shall
beg Mr. Slope to continue a course of sermons on the subject till
all that is altered. We will have at any rate, in our cathedral, a
decent, godly, modest morning service. There must be no more
play-acting here now"; and so the lady rang for lunch.

The bishop knew more about cathedrals and deans, and
precentors and church services than his wife did, and also more
of a bishop's powers. But he thought it better at present to let the
subject drop.

"My dear," said he, "I think we must go back to London
on Tuesday. I find my staying here will be very inconvenient to
the Government."

The bishop knew that to this proposal his wife would not object; and he also felt that by thus retreating from the ground of battle, the heat of the fight might be got over in his absence.

"Mr. Slope will remain here, of course?" said the lady.

"Oh, of course," said the bishop.

Thus, after less than a week's sojourn in his palace, did the bishop fly from Barchester; nor did he return to it for two months, the London season being then over. During that time Mr. Slope was not idle, but he did not again essay to preach in the cathedral. In answer to Mrs. Proudie's letters, advising a course of sermons, he had pleaded that he would at any rate wish to put off such an undertaking till she was there to hear them.

He had employed his time in consolidating a Proudie and Slope party—or rather a Slope and Proudie party, and he had not employed his time in vain. He did not meddle with the dean and chapter, except by giving them little teasing intimations of the bishop's wishes about this and the bishop's feelings about that, in a manner which was to them sufficiently annoying, but which they could not resent. He preached once or twice in a distant church in the suburbs of the city, but made no allusion to the cathedral service. He commenced the establishment of two "Bishop's Barchester Sabbath-day Schools," gave notice of a proposed "Bishop's Barchester Young Men's Sabbath Evening Lecture Room,"—and wrote three or four letters to the manager of the Barchester branch railway, informing him how anxious the bishop was that the Sunday trains should be discontinued.

At the end of two months, however, the bishop and the lady reappeared; and as a happy harbinger of their return, heralded their advent by the promise of an evening party on the largest scale. The tickets of invitation were sent out from London—they were dated from Bruton Street, and were despatched by the odious Sabbath breaking railway, in a huge brown paper parcel to Mr. Slope. Everybody calling himself a gentleman, or herself a lady, within the city of Barchester, and a circle of two miles round it, was included. Tickets were sent to all the diocesan clergy, and also to many other persons of priestly note, of whose absence the bishop, or at least the bishop's wife, felt tolerably confident. It was intended, however, to be a thronged and noticeable affair, and preparations were made for receiving some hundred.

And now there arose considerable agitation among the Grantlyites whether or no they would attend the episcopal bidding. The first feeling with them all was to send the briefest excuses both for themselves and their wives and daughters. But by degrees policy prevailed over passion. The archdeacon perceived that he would be making a false step if he allowed the cathedral clergy to give the bishop just ground of umbrage. They all met in conclave and agreed to go. They would show that they were willing to respect the office, much as they might dislike the man. They agreed to go. The old dean would crawl in, if it were but for half an hour. The chancellor, treasurer, archdeacon, prebendaries, and minor canons would all go, and would all take their wives. Mr. Harding was especially bidden to do so, resolving in his heart to keep himself far removed from Mrs. Proudie. And Mrs. Bold was determined to go, though assured by her father that there was no necessity for such a sacrifice on her part. When all Barchester was to be there, neither Eleanor nor Mary Bold understood why they should stay away. Had they not been invited separately? and had not a separate little note from the chaplain, couched in the most respectful language, been enclosed with the huge episcopal card?

And the Stanhopes would be there, one and all. Even the lethargic mother would so far bestir herself on such an occasion. They had only just arrived. The card was at the residence waiting for them. No one in Barchester had seen them; and what better opportunity could they have of showing themselves to the Barchester world? Some few old friends, such as the archdeacon and his wife, had called, and had found the doctor and his eldest daughter; but the *élite* of the family were not yet known.

The doctor indeed wished in his heart to prevent the signora from accepting the bishop's invitation; but she herself had fully determined that she would accept it. If her father was ashamed of having his daughter carried into a bishop's palace, she had no such feeling.

"Indeed, I shall," she had said to her sister who had gently endeavoured to dissuade her, by saying that the company would consist wholly of parsons and parsons' wives. "Parsons, I suppose, are much the same as other men, if you strip them of their black coats; and as to their wives, I dare say they won't trouble me. You may tell papa I don't at all mean to be left at home."

Papa was told, and felt that he could do nothing but yield. He also felt that it was useless for him now to be ashamed of his children. Such as they were, they had become such under his auspices; as he had made his bed, so he must lie upon it; as he had sown his seed, so must he reap his corn. He did not indeed utter such reflections in such language, but such was the gist of his thoughts. It was not because Madeline was a cripple that he shrank from seeing her make one of the bishop's guests; but because he knew that she would practise her accustomed lures, and behave herself in a way that could not fail of being distasteful to the propriety of Englishwomen. These things had annoyed but not shocked him in Italy. There they had shocked no one; but here in Barchester, here among his fellow parsons, he was ashamed that they should be seen. Such had been his feelings, but he repressed them. What if his brother clergymen were shocked! They could not take from him his preferment because the manners of his married daughter were too free.

La Signora Neroni had, at any rate, no fear that she would shock anybody. Her ambition was to create a sensation, to have parsons at her feet, seeing that the manhood of Barchester consisted mainly of parsons, and to send, if possible, every parson's wife home with a green fit of jealousy. None could be too old for her, and hardly any too young. None too sanctified, and none too worldly. She was quite prepared to entrap the bishop himself, and then to turn up her nose at the bishop's wife. She did not doubt of success, for she had always succeeded; but one thing was absolutely necessary, she must secure the entire use of a sofa.

The card sent to Dr. and Mrs. Stanhope and family, had been so sent in an envelope, having on the cover Mr. Slope's name. The signora soon learnt that Mrs. Proudie was not yet at the palace, and that the chaplain was managing everything. It was much more in her line to apply to him than to the lady, and she accordingly wrote him the prettiest little billet in the world. In five lines she explained everything, declared how impossible it was for her not to be desirous to make the acquaintance of such persons as the Bishop of Barchester and his wife, and she might add also of Mr. Slope, depicted her own grievous state, and concluded by being assured that Mrs. Proudie would forgive her extreme hardihood in petitioning to be allowed to be carried to a sofa. She then enclosed one of her beautiful cards. In return she received as polite an answer from Mr. Slope—a sofa should be kept in the large drawing-room, immediately at the top of the grand stairs, especially for her use.

And now the day of the party had arrived. The bishop and his wife came down from town, only on the morning of the eventful day, as behoved such great people to do; but Mr. Slope had toiled day and night to see that everything should be in right order. There had been much to do. No company had been seen in the palace since heaven knows when. New furniture had been required, new pots and pans, new cups and saucers, new dishes and plates. Mrs. Proudie had at first declared that she would condescend to nothing so vulgar as eating and drinking; but Mr. Slope had talked or rather written her out of economy! Bishops should be given to hospitality, and hospitality meant eating and drinking. So the supper was conceded; the guests, however, were to stand as they consumed it.

There were four rooms opening into each other on the first floor of the house, which were denominated the drawing-rooms, the reception-room, and Mrs. Proudie's boudoir. In olden days one of these had been Bishop Grantly's bed-room, and another his common sitting-room and study. The present bishop, however, had been moved down into a back parlour, and had been given to understand, that he could very well receive his clergy in the dining-room, should they arrive in too large a flock to be admitted into his small sanctum. He had been unwilling to yield, but after a short debate had yielded.

Mrs. Proudie's heart beat high as she inspected her suite of rooms. They were really very magnificent, or at least would be so by candlelight; and they had nevertheless been got up with commendable economy. Large rooms when full of people and full of light look well, because they are large, and are full, and are light. Small rooms are those which require costly fittings and rich furniture. Mrs. Proudie knew this, and made the most of it; she had therefore a huge gas lamp with a dozen burners hanging from each of the ceilings.

People were to arrive at ten, supper was to last from twelve till one, and at half-past one everybody was to be gone. Carriages were to come in at the gate in the town and depart at the gate outside. They were desired to take up at a quarter before one. It was managed excellently, and Mr. Slope was invaluable.

At half-past nine the bishop and his wife and their three daughters entered the great reception-room, and very grand and very solemn they were. Mr. Slope was down-stairs giving the last orders about the wine. He well understood that curates and country vicars with their belongings did not require so generous an article as the dignitaries of the close. There is a useful gradation in such things, and Marsala at 20s. a dozen did very well for the exterior supplementary tables in the corner.

"Bishop," said the lady, as his lordship sat himself down, "don't sit on that sofa, if you please; it is to be kept separate for a lady."

The bishop jumped up and seated himself on a cane-bottomed chair. "A lady?" he inquired meekly; "do you mean one particular lady, my dear?"

"Yes, Bishop, one particular lady," said his wife, disdaining to explain.

"She has got no legs, papa," said the youngest daughter, tittering.

"No legs!" said the bishop, opening his eyes.

"Nonsense, Netta, what stuff you talk," said Olivia. "She has got legs, but she can't use them. She has always to be kept lying down, and three or four men carry her about everywhere."

"Laws, how odd!" said Augusta. "Always carried about by four men! I'm sure I shouldn't like it. Am I right behind, mamma? I feel as if I was open"; and she turned her back to her anxious parent.

"Open! to be sure you are," said she, "and a yard of petticoat strings hanging out. I don't know why I pay such high wages to Mrs. Richards, if she can't take the trouble to see whether or no you are fit to be looked at," and Mrs. Proudie poked the strings here, and twitched the dress there, and gave her daughter a shove and a shake, and then pronounced it all right.

"But," rejoined the bishop, who was dying with curiosity about the mysterious lady and her legs, "who is it that is to have the sofa? What's her name, Netta?"

A thundering rap at the front door interrupted the conversation. Mrs. Proudie stood up and shook herself gently, and touched her cap on each side as she looked in the mirror. Each of the girls stood on tiptoe, and re-arranged the bows on their bosoms; and Mr. Slope rushed upstairs three steps at a time.

"But who is it, Netta?" whispered the bishop to his youngest daughter.

"La Signora Madeline Vesey Neroni," whispered back the daughter; "and mind you don't let any one sit upon the sofa."

"La Signora Madeline Vicinironi!" muttered, to himself, the bewildered prelate. Had he been told that the Begum of Oude was to be there, or Queen Pomara of the Western Isles, he could not have been more astonished. La Signora Madeline Vicinironi, who, having no legs to stand on, had bespoken a sofa in his drawing-room!—who could she be? He however could now make no further inquiry, as Dr. and Mrs. Stanhope were announced. They had been sent on out of the way a little before

the time, in order that the signora might have plenty of time to
get herself conveniently packed into the carriage.

The bishop was all smiles for the prebendary's wife, and the
bishop's wife was all smiles for the prebendary. Mr. Slope was
presented, and was delighted to make the acquaintance of one of
whom he had heard so much. The doctor bowed very low, and
then looked as though he could not return the compliment as
regarded Mr. Slope, of whom, indeed, he had heard nothing.
The doctor, in spite of his long absence, knew an English
gentleman when he saw him.

And then the guests came in shoals: Mr. and Mrs. Quiverful
and their three grown daughters. Mr. and Mrs. Chadwick and
their three daughters. The burly chancellor and his wife and
clerical son from Oxford. The meagre little doctor without
incumbrance. Mr. Harding with Eleanor and Miss Bold. The
dean leaning on a gaunt spinster, his only child now living with
him, a lady very learned in stones, ferns, plants, and vermin,
and who had written a book about petals. A wonderful woman in
her way was Miss Trefoil. Mr. Finney, the attorney, with his
wife, was to be seen, much to the dismay of many who had
never met him in a drawing-room before. The five Barchester
doctors were all there, and old Scalpen, the retired apothecary
and toothdrawer, who was first taught to consider himself as
belonging to the higher orders by the receipt of the bishop's
card. Then came the archdeacon and his wife, with their elder
daughter Griselda, a slim pale retiring girl of seventeen, who kept
close to her mother, and looked out on the world with quiet
watchful eyes, one who gave promise of much beauty when time
should have ripened it.

And so the rooms became full, and knots were formed, and
every newcomer paid his respects to my lord and passed on, not
presuming to occupy too much of the great man's attention. The
archdeacon shook hands very heartily with Dr. Stanhope, and
Mrs. Grantly seated herself by the doctor's wife. And Mrs.
Proudie moved about with well-regulated grace, measuring out
the quantity of her favours to the quality of her guests, just as
Mr. Slope had been doing with the wine. But the sofa was still
empty, and five-and-twenty ladies and five gentlemen had been
courteously warned off it by the mindful chaplain.

"Why doesn't she come?" said the bishop to himself. His
mind was so preoccupied with the signora, that he hardly remembered how to behave himself *en bishop*.

At last a carriage dashed up to the hall steps with a very

different manner of approach from that of any other vehicle that
had been there that evening. A perfect commotion took place.
The doctor, who heard it as he was standing in the drawing-
room, knew that his daughter was coming, and retired into the
furthest corner, where he might not see her entrance. Mrs.
Proudie perked herself up, feeling that some important piece of
business was in hand. The bishop was instinctively aware that La
Signora Vicinironi was come at last, and Mr. Slope hurried into
the hall to give his assistance.

He was, however, nearly knocked down and trampled on by
the cortège that he encountered on the hall steps. He got himself
picked up as well as he could, and followed the cortège up stairs.
The signora was carried head foremost, her head being the care
of her brother and an Italian man-servant who was accustomed to
the work; her feet were in the care of the lady's maid and the
lady's Italian page; and Charlotte Stanhope followed to see that
all was done with due grace and decorum. In this manner they
climbed easily into the drawing-room, and a broad way through
the crowd having been opened, the signora rested safely on her
couch. She had sent a servant beforehand to learn whether it was
a right or a left hand sofa, for it required that she should dress
accordingly, particularly as regarded her bracelets.

And very becoming her dress was. It was white velvet,
without any other garniture than rich white lace worked with
pearls across her bosom, and the same round the armlets of her
dress. Across her brow she wore a band of red velvet, on the
centre of which shone a magnificent Cupid in mosaic, the tints
of whose wings were of the most lovely azure, and the colour of
his chubby cheeks the clearest pink. On the one arm which her
position required her to expose she wore three magnificent
bracelets, each of different stones. Beneath her on the sofa, and
over the cushion and head of it, was spread a crimson silk mantle
or shawl, which went under her whole body and concealed her
feet. Dressed as she was and looking as she did, so beautiful and
yet so motionless, with the pure brilliancy of her white dress
brought out and strengthened by the colour beneath it, with that
lovely head, and those large bold bright staring eyes, it was
impossible that either man or woman should do other than look
at her.

Neither man nor woman for some minutes did do other.

Her bearers too were worthy of note. The three servants
were Italian, and though perhaps not peculiar in their own country,
were very much so in the palace at Barchester. The man espe-

cially attracted notice, and created a doubt in the mind of some whether he were a friend or a domestic. The same doubt was felt as to Ethelbert. The man was attired in a loose-fitting common black cloth morning coat. He had a jaunty fat well-pleased clean face, on which no atom of beard appeared, and he wore round his neck a loose black silk neck-handkerchief. The bishop essayed to make him a bow, but the man, who was well-trained, took no notice of him, and walked out of the room quite at his ease, followed by the woman and the boy.

Ethelbert Stanhope was dressed in light blue from head to foot. He had on the loosest possible blue coat, cut square like a shooting coat, and very short. It was lined with silk of azure blue. He had on a blue satin waistcoat, a blue neck-handkerchief which was fastened beneath his throat with a coral ring, and very loose blue trowsers which almost concealed his feet. His soft glossy beard was softer and more glossy than ever.

The bishop, who had made one mistake, thought that he also was a servant, and therefore tried to make way for him to pass. But Ethelbert soon corrected the error.

XI

Mrs. Proudie's Reception—Concluded

"Bishop of Barchester, I presume?" said Bertie Stanhope, putting out his hand, frankly; "I am delighted to make your acquaintance. We are in rather close quarters here, a'nt we?"

In truth they were. They had been crowded up behind the head of the sofa: the bishop in waiting to receive his guest, and the other in carrying her; and they now had hardly room to move themselves.

The bishop gave his hand quickly, and made his little studied bow, and was delighted to make——. He couldn't go on, for he did not know whether his friend was a signor, or a count, or a prince.

"My sister really puts you all to great trouble," said Bertie.

"Not at all!" The bishop was delighted to have the opportunity of welcoming the Signora Vicinironi—so at least he said—and attempted to force his way round to the front of the sofa. He had, at any rate, learnt that his strange guests were brother and sister. The man, he presumed, must be Signor Vicinironi—or count, or prince, as it might be. It was wonderful what good English he spoke. There was just a twang of foreign accent, and no more.

"Do you like Barchester on the whole?" asked Bertie.

The bishop, looking dignified. said that he did like Barchester.

"You've not been here very long, I believe," said Bertie.

"No—not long," said the bishop, and tried again to make his way between the back of the sofa and a heavy rector, who was staring over it at the grimaces of the signora.

"You weren't a bishop before, were you?"

Dr. Proudie explained that this was the first diocese he had held.

"Ah—I thought so," said Bertie; "but you are changed about sometimes, a'nt you?"

"Translations are occasionally made," said Dr. Proudie; "but not so frequently as in former days."

"They've cut them all down to pretty nearly the same figure, haven't they?" said Bertie.

To this the bishop could not bring himself to make any answer, but again attempted to move the rector.

"But the work, I suppose, is different?" continued Bertie. "Is there much to do here, at Barchester?" This was said exactly in the tone that a young Admiralty clerk might use in asking the same question of a brother acolyte at the Treasury.

"The work of a bishop of the Church of England," said Dr. Proudie, with considerable dignity, "is not easy. The responsibility which he has to bear is very great indeed."

"Is it?" said Bertie, opening wide his wonderful blue eyes. "Well: I never was afraid of responsibility. I once had thoughts of being a bishop, myself."

"Had thoughts of being a bishop!" said Dr. Proudie, much amazed.

"That is, a parson—a parson first, you know, and a bishop afterwards. If I had once begun, I'd have stuck to it. But, on the whole, I like the Church of Rome best."

The bishop could not discuss the point, so he remained silent.

"Now, there's my father," continued Bertie; "he hasn't stuck to it. I fancy he didn't like saying the same thing over so often. By the bye, Bishop, have you seen my father?"

The bishop was more amazed than ever. Had he seen his father? "No," he replied; he had not yet had the pleasure: he hoped he might; and, as he said so, he resolved to bear heavy on that fat, immovable rector, if ever he had the power of doing so.

"He's in the room somewhere," said Bertie, "and he'll turn up soon. By the bye, do you know much about the Jews?"

At last the bishop saw a way out. "I beg your pardon," said he; "but I'm forced to go round the room."

"Well—I believe I'll follow in your wake," said Bertie. "Terribly hot—isn't it?" This he addressed to the fat rector with whom he had brought himself into the closest contact. "They've got this sofa into the worst possible part of the room; suppose we move it. Take care, Madeline."

The sofa had certainly been so placed that those who were behind it found great difficulty in getting out;—there was but a narrow gangway, which one person could stop. This was a bad arrangement, and one which Bertie thought it might be well to improve.

"Take care, Madeline," said he; and turning to the fat rector, added, "Just help me with a slight push."

The rector's weight was resting on the sofa, and unwittingly lent all its impetus to accelerate and increase the motion which Bertie intentionally originated. The sofa rushed from its moorings, and ran half-way into the middle of the room. Mrs. Proudie was standing with Mr. Slope in front of the signora, and had been trying to be condescending and sociable; but she was not in the very best of tempers; for she found that, whenever she spoke to the lady, the lady replied by speaking to Mr. Slope. Mr. Slope was a favourite, no doubt; but Mrs. Proudie had no idea of being less thought of than the chaplain. She was beginning to be stately, stiff, and offended, when unfortunately the castor of the sofa caught itself in her lace train, and carried away there is no saying how much of her garniture. Gathers were heard to go, stitches to crack, plaits to fly open, flounces were seen to fall, and breadths to expose themselves;—a long ruin of rent lace disfigured the carpet, and still clung to the vile wheel on which the sofa moved.

So, when a granite battery is raised, excellent to the eyes of warfaring men, is its strength and symmetry admired. It is the work of years. Its neat embrasures, its finished parapets, its casemated stories, show all the skill of modern science. But, anon, a small spark is applied to the treacherous fusee—a cloud of dust arises to the heavens—and then nothing is to be seen but dirt and dust and ugly fragments.

We know what was the wrath of Juno when her beauty was despised. We know too what storms of passion even celestial minds can yield. As Juno may have looked at Paris on Mount Ida, so did Mrs. Proudie look on Ethelbert Stanhope when he pushed the leg of the sofa into her lace train.

"Oh, you idiot, Bertie!" said the signora, seeing what had been done, and what were to be the consequences.

"Idiot!" re-echoed Mrs. Proudie, as though the word were not half strong enough to express the required meaning; "I'll let him know——"; and then looking round to learn, at a glance, the worst, she saw that at present it behoved her to collect the scattered *débris* of her dress.

Bertie, when he saw what he had done, rushed over the sofa, and threw himself on one knee before the offended lady. His object, doubtless, was to liberate the torn lace from the castor; but he looked as though he were imploring pardon from a goddess.

"Unhand it, sir!" said Mrs. Proudie. From what scrap of dramatic poetry she had extracted the word cannot be said; but it must have rested on her memory, and now seemed opportunely dignified for the occasion.

"I'll fly to the looms of the fairies to repair the damage, if you'll only forgive me," said Ethelbert, still on his knees.

"Unhand it, sir!" said Mrs. Proudie, with redoubled emphasis, and all but furious wrath. This allusion to the fairies was a direct mockery, and intended to turn her into ridicule. So at least it seemed to her. "Unhand it, sir!" she almost screamed.

"It's not me; it's the cursed sofa," said Bertie, looking imploringly in her face, and holding up both his hands to show that he was not touching her belongings, but still remaining on his knees.

Hereupon the signora laughed; not loud, indeed, but yet audibly. And as the tigress bereft of her young will turn with equal anger on any within reach, so did Mrs. Proudie turn upon her female guest.

"Madam!" she said—and it is beyond the power of prose to tell of the fire which flashed from her eyes.

The signora stared her full in the face for a moment, and then turning to her brother said, playfully, "Bertie, you idiot, get up."

By this time the bishop, and Mr. Slope, and her three daughters were around her, and had collected together the wide ruins of her magnificence. The girls fell into circular rank behind their mother, and thus following her and carrying out the fragments, they left the reception-rooms in a manner not altogether devoid of dignity. Mrs. Proudie had to retire and re-array herself.

As soon as the constellation had swept by, Ethelbert rose from his knees, and turning with mock anger to the fat rector, said: "After all it was your doing, sir—not mine. But perhaps you are waiting for preferment, and so I bore it."

Whereupon there was a laugh against the fat rector, in which both the bishop and the chaplain joined; and thus things got themselves again into order.

"Oh! my lord, I am so sorry for this accident," said the signora, putting out her hand so as to force the bishop to take it. "My brother is so thoughtless. Pray sit down, and let me have the pleasure of making your acquaintance. Though I am so poor a creature as to want a sofa, I am not so selfish as to requite it all." Madeline could always dispose herself so as to make room for a gentleman, though, as she declared, the crinoline of her lady friends was much too bulky to be so accommodated.

"It was solely for the pleasure of meeting you that I have had myself dragged here," she continued. "Of course, with your occupation, one cannot even hope that you should have time to come to us, that is, in the way of calling. And at your English dinner-parties all is so dull and so stately. Do you know, my lord, that in coming to England my only consolation has been the thought that I should know you"; and she looked at him with the look of a she-devil.

The bishop, however, thought that she looked very like an angel, and accepting the proffered seat, sat down beside her. He uttered some platitude as to his deep obligation for the trouble she had taken, and wondered more and more who she was.

"Of course you know my sad story?" she continued.

The bishop didn't know a word of it. He knew, however, or thought he knew, that she couldn't walk into a room like other people, and so made the most of that. He put on a look of ineffable distress, and said that he was aware how God had afflicted her.

The signora just touched the corner of her eyes with the

most lovely of pocket-handkerchiefs. Yes, she said—she had been sorely tried—tried, she thought, beyond the common endurance of humanity; but while her child was left to her, everything was left. "Oh! my lord," she exclaimed, "you must see that infant—the last bud of a wondrous tree: you must let a mother hope that you will lay your holy hands on her innocent head, and consecrate her for female virtues. May I hope it?" said she, looking into the bishop's eye, and touching the bishop's arm with her hand.

The bishop was but a man, and said she might. After all, what was it but a request that he would confirm her daughter?—a request, indeed, very unnecessary to make, as he should do so as a matter of course, if the young lady came forward in the usual way.

"The blood of Tiberius," said the signora, in all but a whisper; "the blood of Tiberius flows in her veins. She is the last of the Neros!"

The bishop had heard of the last of the Visigoths, and had floating in his brain some indistinct idea of the last of the Mohicans, but to have the last of the Neros thus brought before him for a blessing was very staggering. Still he liked the lady: she had a proper way of thinking, and talked with more propriety than her brother. But who were they? It was now quite clear that that blue madman with the silky beard was not a Prince Vicinironi. The lady was married, and was of course one of the Vicinironis by right of the husband. So the bishop went on learning.

"When will you see her?" said the signora with a start.

"See whom?" said the bishop.

"My child," said the mother.

"What is the young lady's age?" asked the bishop.

"She is just seven," said the signora.

"Oh," said the bishop, shaking his head; "she is much too young—very much too young."

"But in sunny Italy you know, we do not count by years," and the signora gave the bishop one of her very sweetest smiles.

"But indeed, she is a great deal too young," persisted the bishop; "we never confirm before——"

"But you might speak to her; you might let her hear from your consecrated lips, that she is not a castaway because she is a Roman; that she may be a Nero and yet a Christian; that she may owe her black locks and dark cheeks to the blood of the pagan Cæsars, and yet herself be a child of grace; you will tell her this, won't you, my friend?"

The friend said he would, and asked if the child could say her catechism.

"No," said the signora, "I would not allow her to learn lessons such as those in a land ridden over by priests, and polluted by the idolatry of Rome. It is here, here in Barchester, that she must first be taught to lisp those holy words. Oh, that you could be her instructor!"

Now, Dr. Proudie certainly liked the lady, but, seeing that he was a bishop, it was not probable that he was going to instruct a little girl in the first rudiments of her catechism; so he said he'd send a teacher.

"But you'll see her, yourself, my lord?"

The bishop said he would, but where should he call.

"At papa's house," said the signora, with an air of some little surprise at the question.

The bishop actually wanted the courage to ask her who was her papa; so he was forced at last to leave her without fathoming the mystery. Mrs. Proudie, in her second best, had now returned to the rooms, and her husband thought it as well that he should not remain in too close conversation with the lady whom his wife appeared to hold in such slight esteem. Presently he came across his youngest daughter.

"Netta," said he, "do you know who is the father of that Signora Vicinironi?"

"It isn't Vicinironi, papa," said Netta; "but Vesey Neroni, and she's Dr. Stanhope's daughter. But I must go and do the civil to Griselda Grantly; I declare nobody has spoken a word to the poor girl this evening."

Dr. Stanhope! Dr. Vesey Stanhope! Dr. Vesey Stanhope's daughter, of whose marriage with a dissolute Italian scamp he now remembered to have heard something! And that impertinent blue cub who had examined him as to his episcopal bearings was old Stanhope's son, and the lady who had entreated him to come and teach her child the catechism was old Stanhope's daughter! the daughter of one of his own prebendaries! As these things flashed across his mind, he was nearly as angry as his wife had been. Nevertheless, he could not but own that the mother of the last of the Neros was an agreeable woman.

Dr. Proudie tripped out into the adjoining room, in which were congregated a crowd of Grantlyite clergymen, among whom the archdeacon was standing pre-eminent, while the old dean was sitting nearly buried in a huge arm-chair by the fire-place. The bishop was very anxious to be gracious, and, if possible, to diminish the bitterness which his chaplain had occasioned. Let Mr. Slope do the *fortiter in re*, he himself would pour in the *suaviter in modo*.

"Pray don't stir, Mr. Dean, pray don't stir," he said, as the old man essayed to get up; "I take it as a great kindness, your coming to such an *omnium gatherum* as this. But we have hardly got settled yet, and Mrs. Proudie has not been able to see her friends as she would wish to do. Well, Mr. Archdeacon, after all, we have not been so hard upon you at Oxford."

"No," said the archdeacon; "you've only drawn our teeth and cut out our tongues; you've allowed us still to breathe and swallow."

"Ha, ha, ha!" laughed the bishop; "it's not quite so easy to cut out the tongue of an Oxford magnate,—and as for teeth,—ha, ha, ha! Why, in the way we've left the matter, it's very odd if the heads of colleges don't have their own way quite as fully as when the hebdomadal board was in all its glory; what do you say, Mr. Dean?"

"An old man, my lord, never likes changes," said the dean.

"You must have been sad bunglers if it is so," said the archdeacon; "and indeed, to tell the truth, I think you have bungled it. At any rate, you must own this; you have not done the half what you boasted you would do."

"Now, as regards your system of professors——" began the chancellor slowly. He was never destined to get beyond such beginning.

"Talking of professors," said a soft clear voice, close behind the chancellor's elbow; "how much you Englishmen might learn from Germany; only you are all too proud."

The bishop looking round, perceived that that abominable young Stanhope had pursued him. The dean stared at him, as though he were some unearthly apparition; so also did two or three prebendaries and minor canons. The archdeacon laughed.

"The German professors are men of learning," said Mr. Harding, "but——"

"German professors!" groaned out the chancellor, as though his nervous system had received a shock which nothing but a week of Oxford air could cure.

"Yes," continued Ethelbert; not at all understanding why a German professor should be contemptible in the eyes of an Oxford don. "Not but what the name is best earned at Oxford. In Germany the professors do teach; at Oxford, I believe they only profess to do so, and sometimes not even that. You'll have those universities of yours about your ears soon, if you don't consent to take a lesson from Germany."

There was no answering this. Dignified clergymen of sixty years of age could not condescend to discuss such a matter with a young man with such clothes and such a beard.

"Have you got good water out at Plumstead, Mr. Arch-deacon?" said the bishop by way of changing the conversation.

"Pretty good," said Dr. Grantly.

"But by no means as good as his wine, my lord," said a witty minor canon.

"Nor so generally used," said another; "that is for inward application."

"Ha, ha, ha!" laughed the bishop, "a good cellar of wine is a very comfortable thing in a house."

"Your German professors, sir, prefer beer, I believe," said the sarcastic little meagre prebendary.

"They don't think much of either," said Ethelbert; "and that perhaps accounts for their superiority. Now the Jewish professor——"

The insult was becoming too deep for the spirit of Oxford to endure, so the archdeacon walked off one way and the chancellor another, followed by their disciples, and the bishop and the young reformer were left together on the hearth-rug.

"I was a Jew once myself," began Bertie.

The bishop was determined not to stand another examination, or be led on any terms into Palestine; so he again remembered that he had to do something very particular, and left young Stanhope with the dean. The dean did not get the worst of it, for Ethelbert gave him a true account of his remarkable doings in the Holy Land.

"Oh, Mr. Harding," said the bishop, overtaking the *ci-devant* warden; "I wanted to say one word about the hospital. You know, of course, that it is to be filled up."

Mr. Harding's heart beat a little, and he said that he had heard so.

"Of course," continued the bishop; "there can be only one man whom I could wish to see in that situation. I don't know what your own views may be, Mr. Harding——"

"They are very simply told, my lord," said the other; "to take the place if it be offered me, and to put up with the want of it should another man get it."

The bishop professed himself delighted to hear it; Mr.

Harding might be quite sure that no other man would get it. There were some few circumstances which would in a slight degree change the nature of the duties. Mr. Harding was probably aware of this, and would, perhaps, not object to discuss the matter with Mr. Slope. It was a subject to which Mr. Slope had given a good deal of attention.

Mr. Harding felt, he knew not why, oppressed and annoyed. What could Mr. Slope do to him? He knew that there were to be changes. The nature of them must be communicated to the warden through somebody, and through whom so naturally as the bishop's chaplain. 'Twas thus he tried to argue himself back to an easy mind, but in vain.

Mr. Slope in the mean time had taken the seat which the bishop had vacated on the signora's sofa, and remained with that lady till it was time to marshal the folk to supper. Not with contented eyes had Mrs. Proudie seen this. Had not this woman laughed at her distress, and had not Mr. Slope heard it? Was she not an intriguing Italian woman, half wife and half not, full of affectation, airs, and impudence? Was she not horribly bedizened with velvet and pearls, with velvet and pearls, too, which had not been torn off her back? Above all, did she not pretend to be more beautiful than her neighbours? To say that Mrs. Proudie was jealous would give a wrong idea of her feelings. She had not the slightest desire that Mr. Slope should be in love with herself. But she desired the incense of Mr. Slope's spiritual and temporal services, and did not choose that they should be turned out of their course to such an object as Signora Neroni. She considered also that Mr. Slope ought in duty to hate the signora; and it appeared from his manner that he was very far from hating her.

"Come, Mr. Slope," she said, sweeping by, and looking all that she felt; "can't you make yourself useful? Do pray take Mrs. Grantly down to supper."

Mrs. Grantly heard and escaped. The words were hardly out of Mrs. Proudie's mouth, before the intended victim had stuck her hand through the arm of one of her husband's curates, and saved herself. What would the archdeacon have said had he seen her walking down stairs with Mr. Slope?

Mr. Slope heard also, but was by no means so obedient as was expected. Indeed, the period of Mr. Slope's obedience to Mrs. Proudie was drawing to a close. He did not wish yet to break with her, nor to break with her at all, if it could be avoided. But he intended to be master in that palace, and as she

had made the same resolution it was not improbable that they
might come to blows.

Before leaving the signora he arranged a little table before
her, and begged to know what he should bring her. She was
quite indifferent, she said—nothing—anything. It was now she
felt the misery of her position, now that she must be left alone.
Well, a little chicken, some ham, and a glass of champagne.

Mr. Slope had to explain, not without blushing for his
patron, that there was no champagne.

Sherry would do just as well. And then Mr. Slope descended with the learned Miss Trefoil on his arm. Could she tell
him, he asked, whether the ferns of Barsetshire were equal to
those of Cumberland? His strongest worldly passion was for
ferns—and before she could answer him he left her wedged
between the door and the sideboard. It was fifty minutes before
she escaped, and even then unfed.

"You are not leaving us, Mr. Slope," said the watchful
lady of the house, seeing her slave escaping towards the door,
with stores of provisions held high above the heads of the guests.

Mr. Slope explained that the Signora Neroni was in want of
her supper.

"Pray, Mr. Slope, let her brother take it to her," said Mrs.
Proudie, quite out loud. "It is out of the question that you should
be so employed. Pray, Mr. Slope, oblige me; I am sure Mr.
Stanhope will wait upon his sister."

Ethelbert was most agreeably occupied in the furthest corner
of the room, making himself both useful and agreeable to Mrs.
Proudie's youngest daughter.

"I couldn't get out, madam, if Madeline were starving for
her supper," said he; "I'm physically fixed, unless I could fly."

The lady's anger was increased by seeing that her daughter
also had gone over to the enemy; and when she saw that in spite
of her remonstrances, in the teeth of her positive orders, Mr.
Slope went off to the drawing-room, the cup of her indignation
ran over, and she could not restrain herself. "Such manners I
never saw," she said, muttering. "I cannot, and will not permit
it"; and then, after fussing and fuming for a few minutes, she
pushed her way through the crowd, and followed Mr. Slope.

When she reached the room above, she found it absolutely
deserted, except by the guilty pair. The signora was sitting very
comfortably up to her supper, and Mr. Slope was leaning over
her and administering to her wants. They had been discussing the
merits of Sabbath-day schools, and the lady had suggested that

as she could not possibly go to the children, she might be indulged in the wish of her heart by having the children brought to her.

"And when shall it be, Mr. Slope?" said she.

Mr. Slope was saved the necessity of committing himself to a promise by the entry of Mrs. Proudie. She swept close up to the sofa so as to confront the guilty pair, stared full at them for a moment, and then said as she passed on to the next room, "Mr. Slope, his lordship is especially desirous of your attendance below; you will greatly oblige me if you will join him." And so she stalked on.

Mr. Slope muttered something in reply, and prepared to go down stairs. As for the bishop's wanting him, he knew his lady patroness well enough to take that assertion at what it was worth; but he did not wish to make himself the hero of a scene, or to become conspicuous for more gallantry than the occasion required.

"Is she always like this?" said the signora.

"Yes—always—madam," said Mrs. Proudie, returning; "always the same—always equally adverse to impropriety of conduct of every description"; and she stalked back through the room again, following Mr. Slope out of the door.

The signora couldn't follow her, or she certainly would have done so. But she laughed loud, and sent the sound of it ringing through the lobby and down the stairs after Mrs. Proudie's feet. Had she been as active as Grimaldi, she could probably have taken no better revenge.

"Mr. Slope," said Mrs. Proudie, catching the delinquent at the door, "I am surprised that you should leave my company to attend on such a painted Jezebel as that."

"But she's lame, Mrs. Proudie, and cannot move. Somebody must have waited upon her."

"Lame," said Mrs. Proudie; "I'd lame her if she belonged to me. What business had she here at all?—such impertinence—such affectation."

In the hall and adjacent rooms all manner of cloaking and shawling was going on, and the Barchester folk were getting themselves gone. Mrs. Proudie did her best to smirk at each and every one, as they made their adieux, but she was hardly successful. Her temper had been tried fearfully. By slow degrees, the guests went.

"Send back the carriage quick," said Ethelbert, as Dr. and Mrs. Stanhope took their departure.

The younger Stanhopes were left to the very last, and an

uncomfortable party they made with the bishop's family. They
all went into the dining-room, and then the bishop observing
that "the lady" was alone in the drawing-room, they followed
him up. Mrs. Proudie kept Mr. Slope and her daughters in
close conversation, resolving that he should not be indulged,
nor they polluted. The bishop, in mortal dread of Bertie and
the Jews, tried to converse with Charlotte Stanhope about the
climate of Italy. Bertie and the signora had no resource but in
each other.

"Did you get your supper, at last, Madeline?" said the
impudent or else mischievous young man.

"Oh, yes," said Madeline; "Mr. Slope was so very kind as
to bring it me. I fear, however, he put himself to more inconvenience than I wished."

Mrs. Proudie looked at her, but said nothing. The meaning
of her look might have been thus translated: "If ever you
find yourself within these walls again, I'll give you leave to
be as impudent and affected, and as mischievous as you please."

At last the carriage returned with the three Italian servants,
and La Signora Madeline Vesey Neroni was carried out, as she
had been carried in.

The lady of the palace retired to her chamber by no means
contented with the result of her first grand party at Barchester.

XII

Slope Versus Harding

Two or three days after the party, Mr. Harding received a note,
begging him to call on Mr. Slope, at the palace, at an early hour
the following morning. There was nothing uncivil in the
communication, and yet the tone of it was thoroughly displeasing.
It was as follows:

My dear Mr. Harding,—Will you favour me by calling on me at the palace to-morrow morning at 9:30 A.M. The bishop wishes me to speak to you touching the hospital. I hope you will excuse my naming so early an hour. I do so as my time is greatly occupied. If, however, it is positively inconvenient to you, I will change it to 10. You will, perhaps, be kind enough to let me have a note in reply.

> Believe me to be,
> My dear Mr. Harding,
> Your assured friend,
> OBH. SLOPE.

The Palace, Monday morning,
   20th August, 185—.

Mr. Harding neither could nor would believe anything of the sort; and he thought, moreover, that Mr. Slope was rather impertinent to call himself by such a name. His assured friend, indeed! How many assured friends generally fall to the lot of a man in this world? And by what process are they made? and how much of such process had taken place as yet between Mr. Harding and Mr. Slope? Mr Harding could not help asking himself these questions as he read and re-read the note before him. He answered it, however, as follows:

Dear Sir,—I will call at the palace to-morrow at 9:30 A.M. as you desire.

> Truly yours,
> S. HARDING.

High Street, Barchester, Monday.

And on the following morning, punctually at half-past nine, he knocked at the palace door, and asked for Mr. Slope.

The bishop had one small room allotted to him on the ground-floor, and Mr. Slope had another. Into this latter Mr. Harding was shown, and asked to sit down. Mr. Slope was not yet there. The ex-warden stood up at the window looking into the garden, and could not help thinking how very short a time had passed since the whole of that house had been open to him, as though he had been a child of the family, born and bred in it. He remembered how the old servants used to smile as they opened the door to him; how the familiar butler would say, when he had been absent a few hours longer than usual, "A sight of you, Mr. Harding, is good for sore eyes"; how the fussy house-keeper would swear that he couldn't have dined, or couldn't have breakfasted, or couldn't have lunched. And then, above all, he remembered the pleasant gleam of inward satisfaction which always spread itself over the old bishop's face, whenever his friend entered his room.

A tear came into each eye as he reflected that all this was gone. What use would the hospital be to him now? He was alone in the world, and getting old; he would soon, very soon have to go, and leave it all, as his dear old friend had gone;—go, and leave the hospital, and his accustomed place in the cathedral, and his haunts and pleasures, to younger and perhaps wiser men. That chanting of his!—perhaps, in truth, the time for it had gone by. He felt as though the world were sinking from his feet; as though this, this was the time for him to turn with confidence to those hopes which he had preached with confidence to others. "What," said he to himself, "can a man's religion be worth, if it does not support him against the natural melancholy of declining years?" And, as he looked out through his dimmed eyes into the bright parterres of the bishop's garden, he felt that he had the support which he wanted.

Nevertheless, he did not like to be thus kept waiting. If Mr. Slope did not really wish to see him at half-past nine o'clock, why force him to come away from his lodgings with his breakfast in his throat? To tell the truth, it was policy on the part of Mr. Slope. Mr. Slope had made up his mind that Mr. Harding should either accept the hospital with abject submission, or else refuse it altogether; and had calculated that he would probably be more quick to do the latter, if he could be got to enter upon the subject in an ill-humour. Perhaps Mr. Slope was not altogether wrong in his calculation.

It was nearly ten when Mr. Slope hurried into the room, and, muttering something about the bishop and diocesan duties, shook Mr. Harding's hand ruthlessly, and begged him to be seated.

Now the air of superiority which this man assumed, did go against the grain of Mr. Harding; and yet he did not know how to resent it. The whole tendency of his mind and disposition was opposed to any contra-assumption of grandeur on his own part, and he hadn't the worldly spirit or quickness necessary to put down insolent pretensions by downright and open rebuke, as the archdeacon would have done. There was nothing for Mr. Harding but to submit, and he accordingly did so.

"About the hospital, Mr. Harding?" began Mr. Slope, speaking of it as the head of a college at Cambridge might speak of some sizarship which had to be disposed of.

Mr. Harding crossed one leg over another, and then one hand over the other on the top of them, and looked Mr. Slope in the face; but he said nothing.

"It's to be filled up again," said Mr. Slope. Mr. Harding said that he had understood so.

"Of course, you know, the income will be very much reduced," continued Mr. Slope. "The bishop wished to be liberal, and he therefore told the government that he thought it ought to be put at not less than £450. I think on the whole the bishop was right; for though the services required will not be of a very onerous nature, they will be more so than they were before. And it is, perhaps, well that the clergy immediately attached to the cathedral town should be made as comfortable as the extent of the ecclesiastical means at our disposal will allow. Those are the bishop's ideas, and I must say mine also."

Mr. Harding sat rubbing one hand on the other, but said not a word.

"So much for the income, Mr. Harding. The house will, of course, remain to the warden, as before. It should, however, I think, be stipulated that he should paint inside every seven years, and outside every three years, and be subject to dilapidations, in the event of vacating, either by death or otherwise. But this is a matter on which the bishop must yet be consulted."

Mr. Harding still rubbed his hands, and still sat silent, gazing up into Mr. Slope's unprepossessing face.

"Then, as to the duties," continued he, "I believe, if I am rightly informed, there can hardly be said to have been any duties hitherto," and he gave a sort of half laugh, as though to pass off the accusation in the guise of a pleasantry.

Mr. Harding thought of the happy, easy years he had passed in his old home; of the worn-out, aged men whom he had succoured; of his good intentions; and of his work, which had certainly been of the lightest. He thought of these things, doubting for a moment whether he did or did not deserve the sarcasm. He gave his enemy the benefit of the doubt, and did not rebuke him. He merely observed, very tranquilly, and perhaps with too much humility, that the duties of the situation, such as they were, had, he believed, been done to the satisfaction of the late bishop.

Mr. Slope again smiled, and this time the smile was intended to operate against the memory of the late bishop, rather than against the energy of the ex-warden; and so it was understood by Mr. Harding. The colour rose to his cheeks, and he began to feel very angry.

"You must be aware, Mr. Harding, that things are a good deal changed in Barchester," said Mr. Slope.

Mr. Harding said that he was aware of it. "And not only in Barchester, Mr. Harding, but in the world at large. It is not only in Barchester that a new man is carrying out new measures and casting away the useless rubbish of past centuries. The same thing is going on throughout the country. Work is now required from every man who receives wages; and they who have to superintend the doing of work, and the paying of wages, are bound to see that this rule is carried out. New men, Mr. Harding, are now needed, and are now forthcoming in the church, as well as in other professions."

All this was wormwood to our old friend. He had never rated very high his own abilities or activity; but all the feelings of his heart were with the old clergy, and any antipathies of which his heart was susceptible, were directed against those new, busy, uncharitable, self-lauding men, of whom Mr. Slope was so good an example.

"Perhaps," said he, "the bishop will prefer a new man at the hospital?"

"By no means," said Mr. Slope. "The bishop is very anxious that you should accept the appointment: but he wishes you should understand beforehand what will be the required duties. In the first place, a Sabbath-day school will be attached to the hospital."

"What! for the old men?" asked Mr. Harding.

"No, Mr. Harding, not for the old men, but for the benefit of the children of such of the poor of Barchester as it may suit. The bishop will expect that you shall attend this school, and the teachers shall be under your inspection and care."

Mr. Harding slipped his topmost hand off the other, and began to rub the calf of the leg which was supported.

"As to the old men," continued Mr. Slope, "and the old women who are to form a part of the hospital, the bishop is desirous that you shall have morning and evening service on the premises every Sabbath, and one week-day service; that you shall preach to them once at least on Sundays; and that the whole hospital be always collected for morning and evening prayer. The bishop thinks that this will render it unnecessary that any separate seats in the cathedral should be reserved for the hospital inmates.''

Mr. Slope paused, but Mr. Harding still said nothing.

"Indeed, it would be difficult to find seats for the women; and, on the whole, Mr. Harding, I may as well say at once, that for the people of that class the cathedral service does not appear to me the most useful,—even if it be so for any class of people.''

"We will not discuss that, if you please,'' said Mr. Harding.

"I am not desirous of doing so; at least, not at the present moment. I hope, however, you fully understand the bishop's wishes about the new establishment of the hospital; and if, as I do not doubt, I shall receive from you an assurance that you accord with his lordship's views, it will give me very great pleasure to be the bearer from his lordship to you of the presentation to the appointment.''

"But if I disagree with his lordship's views?'' asked Mr. Harding.

"But I hope you do not,'' said Mr. Slope.

"But if I do?'' again asked the other.

"If such unfortunately should be the case, which I can hardly conceive, I presume your own feelings will dictate to you the propriety of declining the appointment.''

"But if I accept the appointment, and yet disagree with the bishop, what then?''

This question rather bothered Mr. Slope. It was true that he had talked the matter over with the bishop, and had received a sort of authority for suggesting to Mr. Harding the propriety of a Sunday school, and certain hospital services; but he had no authority for saying that these propositions were to be made peremptory conditions attached to the appointment. The bishop's idea had been that Mr. Harding would of course consent, and that the school would become, like the rest of those new establishments in the city, under the control of his wife and his chaplain. Mr. Slope's idea had been more correct. He intended that Mr. Harding should refuse the situation, and that an ally of his own should get it; but he had not conceived the possibility of Mr. Harding openly accepting the appointment, and as openly rejecting the conditions.

"It is not, I presume, probable,'' said he, "that you will accept from the hands of the bishop a piece of preferment, with a fixed predetermination to disacknowledge the duties attached to it.''

"If I become warden,'' said Mr. Harding, "and neglect my

duty, the bishop has means by which he can remedy the grievance.''

"I hardly expected such an argument from you, or I may say the suggestion of such a line of conduct," said Mr. Slope, with a great look of injured virtue.

"Nor did I expect such a proposition."

"I shall be glad at any rate to know what answer I am to make to his lordship," said Mr. Slope.

"I will take an early opportunity of seeing his lordship myself," said Mr. Harding.

"Such an arrangement," said Mr. Slope, "will hardly give his lordship satisfaction. Indeed, it is impossible that the bishop should himself see every clergyman in the diocese on every subject of patronage that may arise. The bishop, I believe, did see you on the matter and I really cannot see why he should be troubled to do so again."

"Do you know, Mr. Slope, how long I have been officiating as a clergyman in this city?" Mr. Slope's wish was now nearly fulfilled. Mr. Harding had become angry, and it was probable that he might commit himself.

"I really do not see what that has to do with the question. You cannot think the bishop would be justified in allowing you to regard as a sinecure a situation that requires an active man, merely because you have been employed for many years in the cathedral."

"But it might induce the bishop to see me, if I asked him to do so. I shall consult my friends in this matter, Mr. Slope; but I mean to be guilty of no subterfuge,—you may tell the bishop that as I altogether disagree with his views about the hospital, I shall decline the situation if I find that any such conditions are attached to it as those you have suggested," and so saying, Mr. Harding took his hat and went his way.

Mr. Slope was contented. He considered himself at liberty to accept Mr. Harding's last speech as an absolute refusal of the appointment. At least, he so represented it to the bishop and to Mrs. Proudie.

"That is very surprising," said the bishop.

"Not at all," said Mrs. Proudie; "you little know how determined the whole set of them are to withstand your authority."

"But Mr. Harding was so anxious for it," said the bishop.

"Yes," said Mr. Slope, "if he can hold it without the slightest acknowledgment of your lordship's jurisdiction."

"That is out of the question," said the bishop.

"I should imagine it to be quite so," said the chaplain.

"Indeed, I should think so," said the lady.

"I really am sorry for it," said the bishop.

"I don't know that there is much cause for sorrow," said the lady. "Mr. Quiverful is a much more deserving man, more in need of it, and one who will make himself much more useful in the close neighbourhood of the palace."

"I suppose I had better see Quiverful?" said the chaplain.

"I suppose you had," said the bishop.

XIII

The Rubbish Cart

Mr. Harding was not a happy man as he walked down the palace pathway, and stepped out into the close. His preferment and pleasant house were a second time gone from him; but that he could endure. He had been schooled and insulted by a man young enough to be his son; but that he could put up with. He could even draw from the very injuries, which had been inflicted on him, some of that consolation, which we may believe martyrs always receive from the injustice of their own sufferings, and which is generally proportioned in its strength to the extent of cruelty with which martyrs are treated. He had admitted to his daughter that he wanted the comfort of his old home, and yet he could have returned to his lodgings in the High Street, if not with exultation, at least with satisfaction, had that been all. But the venom of the chaplain's harangue had worked into his blood, and sapped the life of his sweet contentment.

"New men are carrying out new measures, and are carting away the useless rubbish of past centuries!" What cruel words these had been; and how often are they now used with all the heartless cruelty of a Slope! A man is sufficiently condemned if it can only be shown that either in politics or religion he does not belong to some new school established within the last score of years. He may then regard himself as rubbish and expect to be carted away. A man is nothing now unless he has within him a full appreciation of the new era; an era in which it would seem that neither honesty nor truth is very desirable, but in which success is the only touchstone of merit. We must laugh at every thing that is established. Let the joke be ever so bad, ever so untrue to the real principles of joking; nevertheless we must laugh—or else beware the cart. We must talk, think, and live up to the spirit of the times, and write up to it too, if that cacoethes be upon us, or else we are nought. New men and new measures, long credit and few scruples, great success or wonderful ruin, such are now the tastes of Englishmen who know how to live. Alas, alas! under such circumstances Mr. Harding could not but feel that he was an Englishman who did not know how to live. This new doctrine of Mr. Slope and the rubbish cart, new at least at Barchester, sadly disturbed his equanimity.

"The same thing is going on throughout the whole country!" "Work is now required from every man who receives wages!" And had he been living all his life receiving wages, and doing no work? Had he in truth so lived as to be now in his old age justly reckoned as rubbish fit only to be hidden away in some huge dust hole? The school of men to whom he professes to belong, the Grantlys, the Gwynnes, and the old high set of Oxford divines, are afflicted with no such self-accusations as these which troubled Mr. Harding. They, as a rule, are as satisfied with the wisdom and propriety of their own conduct as can be any Mr. Slope, or any Dr. Proudie, with his own. But unfortunately for himself Mr. Harding had little of this self-reliance. When he heard himself designated as rubbish by the Slopes of the world, he had no other resource than to make inquiry within his own bosom as to the truth of the designation. Alas, alas! the evidence seemed generally to go against him.

He had professed to himself in the bishop's parlour that in these coming sources of the sorrow of age, in these fits of sad regret from which the latter years of few reflecting men can be free, religion would suffice to comfort him. Yes, religion could console him for the loss of any worldly good; but was his religion of that active sort which would enable him so to repent of misspent years as to pass those that were left to him in a spirit of hope for the future? And such repentance itself, is it not a work of agony and of tears? It is very easy to talk of repentance; but a man has to walk over hot ploughshares before he can

complete it; to be skinned alive as was St. Bartholomew; to be
stuck full of arrows as was St. Sebastian; to lie broiling on a
gridiron like St. Lorenzo! How if his past life required such
repentance as this? had he the energy to go through with it?

Mr. Harding after leaving the palace, walked slowly for an
hour or so beneath the shady elms of the close, and then betook
himself to his daughter's house. He had at any rate made up his
mind that he would go out to Plumstead to consult Dr. Grantly,
and that he would in the first instance tell Eleanor what had
occurred.

And now he was doomed to undergo another misery. Mr.
Slope had forestalled him at the widow's house. He had called
there on the preceding afternoon. He could not, he had said,
deny himself the pleasure of telling Mrs. Bold that her father was
about to return to the pretty house at Hiram's hospital. He had
been instructed by the bishop to inform Mr. Harding that the
appointment would now be made at once. The bishop was of
course only too happy to be able to be the means of restoring to
Mr. Harding the preferment which he had so long adorned. And
then by degrees Mr. Slope had introduced the subject of the
pretty school which he hoped before long to see attached to the
hospital. He had quite fascinated Mrs. Bold by his description of
this picturesque, useful, and charitable appendage, and she had
gone so far as to say that she had no doubt her father would
approve, and that she herself would gladly undertake a class.

Any one who had heard the entirely different tone, and seen
the entirely different manner in which Mr. Slope had spoken of
this projected institution to the daughter and to the father, could
not have failed to own that Mr. Slope was a man of genius. He
said nothing to Mrs. Bold about the hospital sermons and services,
nothing about the exclusion of the old men from the cathedral,
nothing about dilapidation and painting, nothing about carting
away the rubbish. Eleanor had said to herself that certainly she
did not like Mr. Slope personally, but that he was a very active,
zealous clergyman, and would no doubt be useful in Barchester.
All this paved the way for much additional misery to Mr.
Harding.

Eleanor put on her happiest face as she heard her father on
the stairs, for she thought she had only to congratulate him; but
directly she saw his face, she knew that there was but little matter
for congratulation. She had seen him with the same weary look
of sorrow on one or two occasions before, and remembered it
well. She had seen him when he first read that attack upon

himself in the *Jupiter* which had ultimately caused him to resign the hospital; and she had seen him also when the archdeacon had persuaded him to remain there against his own sense of propriety and honour. She knew at a glance that his spirit was in deep trouble.

"Oh, papa, what is it?" said she, putting down her boy to crawl upon the floor.

"I came to tell you, my dear," said he, "that I am going out to Plumstead; you won't come with me, I suppose?"

"To Plumstead, papa? Shall you stay there?"

"I suppose I shall, to-night: I must consult the archdeacon about this weary hospital. Ah me! I wish I had never thought of it again."

"Why, papa, what is the matter?"

"I've been with Mr. Slope, my dear, and he isn't the pleasantest companion in the world, at least not to me." Eleanor gave a sort of half blush; but she was wrong if she imagined that her father in any way alluded to her acquaintance with Mr. Slope.

"Well, papa."

"He wants to turn the hospital into a Sunday school and a preaching house; and I suppose he will have his way. I do not feel myself adapted for such an establishment, and therefore, I suppose, I must refuse the appointment."

"What would be the harm of the school, papa?"

"The want of a proper schoolmaster, my dear."

"But that would of course be supplied."

"Mr. Slope wishes to supply it by making me his schoolmaster. But as I am hardly fit for such work, I intend to decline."

"Oh, papa! Mr. Slope doesn't intend that. He was here yesterday, and what he intends——"

"He was here yesterday, was he?" asked Mr. Harding.

"Yes, papa."

"And talking about the hospital?"

"He was saying how glad he would be, and the bishop too, to see you back there again. And then he spoke about the Sunday school; and to tell the truth I agreed with him; and I thought you would have done so too. Mr. Slope spoke of a school, not inside the hospital, but just connected with it, of which you would be the patron and visitor; and I thought you would have liked such a school as that; and I promised to look after it and to take a class—and it all seemed so very——. But, oh, papa! I shall be so miserable if I find I have done wrong."

"Nothing wrong at all, my dear," said he, gently, very gently rejecting his daughter's caress. "There can be nothing wrong in your wishing to make yourself useful; indeed, you ought to do so by all means. Every one must now exert himself who would not choose to go to the wall." Poor Mr. Harding thus attempted in his misery to preach the new doctrine to his child. "Himself or herself, it's all the same," he continued; "you will be quite right, my dear, to do something of this sort; but——"

"Well, papa."

"I am not quite sure that if I were you I would select Mr. Slope for my guide."

"But I never have done so, and never shall."

"It would be very wicked of me to speak evil of him, for to tell the truth I know no evil of him; but I am not quite sure that he is honest. That he is not gentleman-like in his manners, of that I am quite sure."

"I never thought of taking him for my guide, papa."

"As for myself, my dear," continued he, "we know the old proverb—'It's bad teaching an old dog tricks.' I must decline the Sunday school, and shall therefore probably decline the hospital also. But I will first see your brother-in-law." So he took up his hat, kissed the baby, and withdrew, leaving Eleanor in as low spirits as himself.

All this was a great aggravation to his misery. He had so few with whom to sympathise, that he could not afford to be cut off from the one whose sympathy was of the most value to him. And yet it seemed probable that this would be the case. He did not own to himself that he wished his daughter to hate Mr. Slope; yet had she expressed such a feeling there would have been very little bitterness in the rebuke he would have given her for so uncharitable a state of mind. The fact, however, was that she was on friendly terms with Mr. Slope, that she coincided with his views, adhered at once to his plans, and listened with delight to his teaching. Mr. Harding hardly wished his daughter to hate the man, but he would have preferred that to her loving him.

He walked away to the inn to order a fly, went home to put up his carpet bag, and then started for Plumstead. There was, at any rate, no danger that the archdeacon would fraternise with Mr. Slope; but then he would recommend internecine war, public appeals, loud reproaches, and all the paraphernalia of open battle. Now that alternative was hardly more to Mr. Harding's taste than the other.

When Mr. Harding reached the parsonage he found that the

archdeacon was out, and would not be home till dinnertime, so he began his complaint to his elder daughter. Mrs. Grantly entertained quite as strong an antagonism to Mr. Slope as did her husband; she was also quite as alive to the necessity of combating the Proudie faction, of supporting the old church interest of the close, of keeping in her own set such of the loaves and fishes as duly belonged to it; and was quite as well prepared as her lord to carry on the battle without giving or taking quarter. Not that she was a woman prone to quarrelling, or ill inclined to live at peace with her clerical neighbours; but she felt, as did the archdeacon, that the presence of Mr. Slope in Barchester was an insult to every one connected with the late bishop, and that his assumed dominion in the diocese was a spiritual injury to her husband. Hitherto people had little guessed how bitter Mrs. Grantly could be. She lived on the best of terms with all the rectors' wives around her. She had been popular with all the ladies connected with the close. Though much the wealthiest of the ecclesiastical matrons of the county, she had so managed her affairs that her carriage and horses had given umbrage to none. She had never thrown herself among the county grandees so as to excite the envy of other clergymen's wives. She had never talked too loudly of earls and countesses, or boasted that she gave her governess sixty pounds a year, or her cook seventy. Mrs. Grantly had lived the life of a wise, discreet, peace-making woman; and the people of Barchester were surprised at the amount of military vigour she displayed as general of the feminine Grantlyite forces.

Mrs. Grantly soon learnt that her sister Eleanor had promised to assist Mr. Slope in the affairs of the hospital; and it was on this point that her attention soon fixed itself.

"How can Eleanor endure him?" said she.

"He is a very crafty man," said her father, "and his craft has been successful in making Eleanor think that he is a meek, charitable, good clergyman. God forgive me if I wrong him, but such is not his true character in my opinion."

"His true character, indeed!" said she, with something approaching to scorn for her father's moderation. "I only hope he won't have craft enough to make Eleanor forget herself and her position."

"Do you mean marry him?" said he, startled out of his usual demeanour by the abruptness and horror of so dreadful a proposition.

"What is there so improbable in it? Of course that would be

his own object if he thought he had any chance of success. Eleanor has a thousand a year entirely at her own disposal, and what better fortune could fall to Mr. Slope's lot than the transferring of the disposal of such a fortune to himself?''

''But you can't think she likes him, Susan?''

''Why not?'' said Susan. ''Why shouldn't she like him? He's just the sort of man to get on with a woman left as she is, with no one to look after her.''

''Look after her!'' said the unhappy father; ''don't we look after her?''

''Ah, papa, how innocent you are! Of course it was to be expected that Eleanor should marry again. I should be the last to advise her against it, if she would only wait the proper time, and then marry at least a gentleman.''

''But you don't really mean to say that you suppose Eleanor has ever thought of marrying Mr. Slope? Why, Mr. Bold has only been dead a year.''

''Eighteen months,'' said his daughter. ''But I don't suppose Eleanor has ever thought about it. It is very probable, though, that he has, and that he will try and make her do so; and that he will succeed too, if we don't take care what we are about.''

This was quite a new phase of the affair to poor Mr. Harding. To have thrust upon him as his son-in-law, as the husband of his favourite child, the only man in the world whom he really positively disliked, would be a misfortune which he felt he would not know how to endure patiently. But then, could there be any ground for so dreadful a surmise? In all worldly matters he was apt to look upon the opinion of his eldest daughter, as one generally sound and trustworthy. In her appreciation of character, of motives, and the probable conduct both of men and women, she was usually not far wrong. She had early foreseen the marriage of Eleanor and John Bold; she had at a glance deciphered the character of the new bishop and his chaplain; could it possibly be that her present surmise should ever come forth as true?

''But you don't think that she likes him?'' said Mr. Harding again.

''Well, papa, I can't say that I think she dislikes him as she ought to do. Why is he visiting there as a confidential friend, when he never ought to have been admitted inside the house? Why is it that she speaks to him about your welfare and your position, as she clearly has done? At the bishop's party the other night, I saw her talking to him for half an hour at the stretch.''

"I thought Mr. Slope seemed to talk to nobody there but that daughter of Stanhope's," said Mr. Harding, wishing to defend his child.

"Oh, Mr. Slope is a cleverer man than you think of, papa, and keeps more than one iron in the fire."

To give Eleanor her due, any suspicion as to the slightest inclination on her part towards Mr. Slope was a wrong to her. She had no more idea of marrying Mr. Slope than she had of marrying the bishop; and the idea that Mr. Slope would present himself as a suitor had never occurred to her. Indeed, to give her her due again, she had never thought about suitors since her husband's death. But nevertheless it was true that she had overcome all that repugnance to the man which was so strongly felt for him by the rest of the Grantly faction. She had forgiven him his sermon. She had forgiven him his low church tendencies, his Sabbath schools, and puritanical observances. She had forgiven his pharisaical arrogance, and even his greasy face and oily vulgar manners. Having agreed to overlook such offences as these, why should she not in time be taught to regard Mr. Slope as a suitor?

And as to him, it must also be affirmed that he was hitherto equally innocent of the crime imputed to him. How it had come to pass that a man whose eyes were generally so widely open to everything around him had not perceived that this young widow was rich as well as beautiful, cannot probably now be explained. But such was the fact. Mr. Slope had ingratiated himself with Mrs. Bold, merely as he had done with other ladies, in order to strengthen his party in the city. He subsequently amended his error; but it was not till after the interview between him and Mr. Harding.

XIV

The New Champion

The archdeacon did not return to the parsonage till close upon the hour of dinner, and there was therefore no time to discuss matters before that important ceremony. He seemed to be in an especial good humour, and welcomed his father-in-law with a sort of jovial earnestness that was usual with him when things on which he was intent were going on as he would have them.

"It's all settled, my dear," said he to his wife as he washed his hands in his dressing-room, while she, according to her wont, sat listening in the bedroom; "Arabin has agreed to accept the living. He'll be here next week." And the archdeacon scrubbed his hands and rubbed his face with a violent alacrity, which showed that Arabin's coming was a great point gained.

"Will he come here to Plumstead?" said the wife.

"He has promised to stay a month with us," said the archdeacon, "so that he may see what his parish is like. You'll like Arabin very much. He's a gentleman in every respect, and full of humour."

"He's very queer, isn't he?" asked the lady.

"Well—he is a little odd in some of his fancies; but there's nothing about him you won't like. He is as staunch a churchman as there is at Oxford. I really don't know what we should do without Arabin. It's a great thing for me to have him so near me; and if anything can put Slope down, Arabin will do it."

The Reverend Francis Arabin was a fellow of Lazarus, the favoured disciple of the great Dr. Gwynne, a high churchman at all points; so high, indeed, that at one period of his career he had all but toppled over into the cesspool of Rome; a poet and also a polemical writer, a great pet in the common rooms at Oxford, an eloquent clergyman, a droll, odd, humourous, energetic, consci-

275

entious man, and, as the archdeacon had boasted of him, a thorough gentleman. As he will hereafter be brought more closely to our notice, it is now only necessary to add, that he had just been presented to the vicarage of St. Ewold by Dr. Grantly, in whose gift as archdeacon the living lay. St. Ewold is a parish lying just without the city of Barchester. The suburbs of the new town, indeed, are partly within its precincts, and the pretty church and parsonage are not much above a mile distant from the city gate.

St. Ewold is not a rich piece of preferment—it is worth some three or four hundred a year at most, and has generally been held by a clergyman attached to the cathedral choir. The archdeacon, however, felt, when the living on this occasion became vacant, that it imperatively behoved him to aid the force of his party with some tower of strength, if any such tower could be got to occupy St. Ewold's. He had discussed the matter with his brethren in Barchester; not in any weak spirit as the holder of patronage to be used for his own or his family's benefit, but as one to whom was committed a trust, on the due administration of which much of the church's welfare might depend. He had submitted to them the name of Mr. Arabin, as though the choice had rested with them all in conclave, and they had unanimously admitted that, if Mr. Arabin would accept St. Ewold's, no better choice could possibly be made.

If Mr. Arabin would accept St. Ewold's! There lay the difficulty. Mr. Arabin was a man standing somewhat prominently before the world, that is, before the Church of England world. He was not a rich man, it is true, for he held no preferment but his fellowship; but he was a man not over anxious for riches, not married of course, and one whose time was greatly taken up in discussing, both in print and on platforms, the privileges and practices of the church to which he belonged. As the archdeacon had done battle for its temporalities, so did Mr. Arabin do battle for its spiritualities; and both had done so conscientiously; that is, not so much each for his own benefit as for that of others.

Holding such a position as Mr. Arabin did, there was much reason to doubt whether he would consent to become the parson of St. Ewold's, and Dr. Grantly had taken the trouble to go himself to Oxford on the matter. Dr. Gwynne and Dr. Grantly together had succeeded in persuading this eminent divine that duty required him to go to Barchester. There were wheels within wheels in this affair. For some time past Mr. Arabin had been engaged in a tremendous controversy with no less a person than Mr. Slope, respecting the apostolic succession. These two gentlemen had never seen each other, but they had been extremely bitter in print. Mr. Slope had endeavoured to strengthen his cause`by calling Mr. Arabin an owl, and Mr. Arabin had retaliated by hinting that Mr. Slope was an infidel. This battle had been commenced in the columns of the daily *Jupiter,* a powerful newspaper, the manager of which was very friendly to Mr. Slope's view of the case. The matter, however, had become too tedious for the readers of the *Jupiter,* and a little note had therefore been appended to one of Mr. Slope's most telling rejoinders, in which it had been stated that no further letters from the reverend gentlemen could be inserted except as advertisements.

Other methods of publication were, however, found less expensive than advertisements in the *Jupiter;* and the war went on merrily. Mr. Slope declared that the main part of the consecration of a clergyman was the self-devotion of the inner man to the duties of the ministry. Mr. Arabin contended that a man was not consecrated at all, had, indeed, no single attribute of a clergyman, unless he became so through the imposition of some bishop's hands, who had become a bishop through the imposition of other hands, and so on in a direct line to one of the apostles. Each had repeatedly hung the other on the horns of a dilemma; but neither seemed to be a whit the worse for the hanging; and so the war went on merrily.

Whether or no the near neighbourhood of the foe may have acted in any way as an inducement to Mr. Arabin to accept the living of St. Ewold, we will not pretend to say; but it had at any rate been settled in Dr. Gwynne's library, at Lazarus, that he would accept it, and that he would lend his assistance towards driving the enemy out of Barchester, or, at any rate, silencing him while he remained there. Mr. Arabin intended to keep his rooms at Oxford, and to have the assistance of a curate at St. Ewold; but he promised to give as much time as possible to the neighbourhood of Barchester, and from so great a man Dr. Grantly was quite satisfied with such a promise. It was no small part of the satisfaction derivable from such an arrangement that Bishop Proudie would be forced to institute into a living, immediately under his own nose, the enemy of his favourite chaplain.

All through dinner the archdeacon's good humour shone brightly in his face. He ate of the good things heartily, he drank wine with his wife and daughter, he talked pleasantly of his doings at Oxford, told his father-in-law that he ought to visit Dr.

Gwynne at Lazarus, and launched out again in praise of Mr. Arabin.

"Is Mr. Arabin married, papa?" asked Griselda.

"No, my dear; the fellow of a collge is never married."

"Is he a young man, papa?"

"About forty, I believe," said the archdeacon.

"Oh!" said Griselda. Had her father said eighty, Mr. Arabin would not have appeared to her to be very much older.

When the two gentlemen were left alone over their wine, Mr. Harding told his tale of woe. But even this, sad as it was, did not much diminish the archdeacon's good humour, though it greatly added to his pugnacity.

"He can't do it," said Dr. Grantly over and over again, as his father-in-law explained to him the terms on which the new warden of the hospital was to be appointed; "he can't do it. What he says is not worth the trouble of listening to. He can't alter the duties of the place."

"Who can't?" asked the ex-warden.

"Neither the bishop nor the chaplain, nor yet the bishop's wife, who, I take it, has really more to say to such matters than either of the other two. The whole body corporate of the palace together have no power to turn the warden of the hospital into a Sunday schoolmaster."

"But the bishop has the power to appoint whom he pleases, and——"

"I don't know that; I rather think he'll find he has no such power. Let him try it, and see what the press will say. For once we shall have the popular cry on our side. But Proudie, ass as he is, knows the world too well to get such a hornet's nest about his ears."

Mr. Harding winced at the idea of the press. He had had enough of that sort of publicity, and was unwilling to be shown up a second time either as a monster or as a martyr. He gently remarked that he hoped the newspapers would not get hold of his name again, and then suggested that perhaps it would be better that he should abandon his object. "I am getting old," said he; "and after all I doubt whether I am fit to undertake new duties."

"New duties!" said the archdeacon: "don't I tell you there shall be no new duties?"

"Or, perhaps, old duties either," said Mr. Harding; "I think I will remain content as I am." The picture of Mr. Slope carting away the rubbish was still present to his mind.

The archdeacon drank off his glass of claret, and prepared

himself to be energetic. "I do hope," said he, "that you are not going to be so weak as to allow such a man as Mr. Slope to deter you from doing what you know it is your duty to do. You know it is your duty to resume your place at the hospital now that Parliament has so settled the stipend as to remove those difficulties which induced you to resign it. You cannot deny this; and should your timidity now prevent you from doing so, your conscience will hereafter never forgive you"; and as he finished this clause of his speech, he pushed over the bottle to his companion.

"Your conscience will never forgive you," he continued. "You resigned the place from conscientious scruples, scruples which I greatly respected, though I did not share them. All your friends respected them, and you left your old house as rich in reputation as you were ruined in fortune. It is now expected that you will return. Dr. Gwynne was saying only the other day——"

"Dr. Gwynne does not reflect how much older a man I am now than when he last saw me."

"Old—nonsense!" said the archdeacon; "you never thought yourself old till you listened to the impudent trash of that coxcomb at the palace."

"I shall be sixty-five if I live till November," said Mr. Harding.

"And seventy-five, if you live till November ten years," said the archdeacon. "And you bid fair to be as efficient then as you were ten years ago. But for heaven's sake let us have no pretence in this matter. Your plea of old age is only a pretence. But you're not drinking your wine. It is only a pretence. The fact is, you are half afraid of this Slope, and would rather subject yourself to comparative poverty and discomfort, than come to blows with a man who will trample on you, if you let him."

"I certainly don't like coming to blows, if I can help it."

"Nor I neither—but sometimes we can't help it. This man's object is to induce you to refuse the hospital, that he may put some creature of his own into it; that he may show his power, and insult us all by insulting you, whose cause and character are so intimately bound up with that of the chapter. You owe it to us all to resist him in this, even if you have no solicitude for yourself. But surely, for your own sake, you will not be so lily-livered as to fall into this trap which he has baited for you, and let him take the very bread out of your mouth without a struggle."

Mr. Harding did not like being called lily-livered, and was

rather inclined to resent it. "I doubt there is any true courage," said he, "in squabbling for money."

"If honest men did not squabble for money, in this wicked world of ours, the dishonest men would get it all; and I do not see that the cause of virtue would be much improved. No,—we must use the means which we have. If we were to carry your argument home, we might give away every shilling of revenue which the church has; and I presume you are not prepared to say that the church would be strengthened by such a sacrifice." The archdeacon filled his glass and then emptied it, drinking with much reverence a silent toast to the well-being and permanent security of those temporalities which were so dear to his soul.

"I think all quarrels between a clergyman and his bishop should be avoided," said Mr. Harding.

"I think so too; but it is quite as much the duty of the bishop to look to that as of his inferior. I tell you what, my friend; I'll see the bishop in this matter, that is, if you will allow me; and you may be sure I will not compromise you. My opinion is, that all his trash about the Sunday-schools and the sermons has originated wholly with Slope and Mrs. Proudie, and that the bishop knows nothing about it. The bishop can't very well refuse to see me, and I'll come upon him when he has neither his wife nor his chaplain by him. I think you'll find that it will end in his sending you the appointment without any condition whatever. And as to the seats in the cathedral, we may safely leave that to Mr. Dean. I believe the fool positively thinks that the bishop could walk away with the cathedral if he pleased."

And so the matter was arranged between them. Mr. Harding had come expressly for advice, and therefore felt himself bound to take the advice given him. He had known, moreover, beforehand, that the archdeacon would not hear of his giving the matter up, and accordingly though he had in perfect good faith put forward his own views, he was prepared to yield.

They therefore went into the drawing-room in good humour with each other, and the evening passed pleasantly in prophetic discussions on the future wars of Arabin and Slope. The frogs and the mice would be nothing to them, nor the angers of Agamemnon and Achilles. How the archdeacon rubbed his hands, and plumed himself on the success of his last move. He could not himself descend into the arena with Slope, but Arabin would have no such scruples. Arabin was exactly the man for such work, and the only man whom he knew that was fit for it.

The archdeacon's good humour and high buoyancy continued till, when reclining on his pillow, Mrs. Grantly commenced to give him her view of the state of affairs at Barchester. And then certainly he was startled. The last words he said that night were as follows:—

"If she does, by heaven I'll never speak to her again. She dragged me into the mire once, but I'll not pollute myself with such filth as that——" And the archdeacon gave a shudder which shook the whole room, so violently was he convulsed with the thought which then agitated his mind.

Now in this matter, the widow Bold was scandalously ill-treated by her relatives. She had spoken to the man three or four times, and had expressed her willingness to teach in a Sunday-school. Such was the full extent of her sins in the matter of Mr. Slope. Poor Eleanor! But time will show.

The next morning Mr. Harding returned to Barchester, no further word having been spoken in his hearing respecting Mr. Slope's acquaintance with his younger daughter. But he observed that the archdeacon at breakfast was less cordial than he had been on the preceding evening.

XV

The Widow's Suitors

Mr. Slope lost no time in availing himself of the bishop's permission to see Mr. Quiverful, and it was in his interview with this worthy pastor that he first learned that Mrs. Bold was worth the wooing. He rode out to Puddingdale to communicate to the embryo warden the good will of the bishop in his favour, and during the discussion on the matter it was not unnatural that the pecuniary resources of Mr. Harding and his family should become the subject of remark.

Mr. Quiverful, with his fourteen children and his four hundred a year, was a very poor man, and the prospect of this new preferment, which was to be held together with his living, was very grateful to him. To what clergyman so circumstanced would not such a prospect be very grateful? But Mr. Quiverful had long been acquainted with Mr. Harding, and had received kindness at his hands, so that his heart misgave him as he thought of supplanting a friend at the hospital. Nevertheless, he was extremely civil, cringingly civil, to Mr. Slope; treated him quite as the great man; entreated this great man to do him the honour to drink a glass of sherry, at which, as it was very poor Marsala, the now pampered Slope turned up his nose; and ended by declaring his extreme obligation to the bishop and Mr. Slope, and his great desire to accept the hospital, if—if it were certainly the case that Mr. Harding had refused it.

What man, as needy as Mr. Quiverful, would have been more disinterested?

"Mr. Harding did positively refuse it," said Mr. Slope, with a certain air of offended dignity, "when he heard of the conditions to which the appointment is now subjected. Of course, you understand, Mr. Quiverful, that the same conditions will be imposed on yourself."

Mr. Quiverful cared nothing for the conditions. He would have undertaken to preach any number of sermons Mr. Slope might have chosen to dictate, and to pass every remaining hour of his Sundays within the walls of a Sunday-school. What sacrifices, or, at any rate, what promises, would have been too much to make for such an addition to his income, and for such a house! But his mind still recurred to Mr. Harding.

"To be sure," said he; "Mr. Harding's daughter is very rich, and why should he trouble himself with the hospital?"

"You mean Mrs. Grantly," said Slope.

"I meant his widowed daughter," said the other. "Mrs. Bold has twelve hundred a year of her own, and I suppose Mr. Harding means to live with her."

"Twelve hundred a year of her own!" said Slope, and very shortly afterwards took his leave, avoiding, as far as it was possible for him to do, any further allusion to the hospital. Twelve hundred a year, said he to himself, as he rode slowly home. If it were the fact that Mrs. Bold had twelve hundred a year of her own, what a fool would he be to oppose her father's return to his old place. The train of Mr. Slope's ideas will probably be plain to all my readers. Why should he not make the twelve hundred a year his own? and if he did so, would it not be well for him to have a father-in-law comfortably provided with the good things of this world? would it not, moreover, be much more easy for him to gain the daughter, if he did all in his power to forward the father's views?

These questions presented themselves to him in a very forcible way, and yet there were many points of doubt. If he resolved to restore to Mr. Harding his former place, he must take the necessary steps for doing so at once; he must immediately talk over the bishop, quarrel on the matter with Mrs. Proudie whom he knew he could not talk over, and let Mr. Quiverful know that he had been a little too precipitate as to Mr. Harding's positive refusal. That he could effect all this, he did not doubt; but he did not wish to effect it for nothing. He did not wish to give way to Mr. Harding, and then be rejected by the daughter. He did not wish to lose one influential friend before he had gained another.

And thus he rode home, meditating many things in his mind. It occurred to him that Mrs. Bold was sister-in-law to the archdeacon; and that not even for twelve hundred a year would he submit to that imperious man. A rich wife was a great desideratum to him, but success in his profession was still greater; there were, moreover, other rich women who might be willing to become wives; and after all, this twelve hundred a year might, when inquired into, melt away into some small sum utterly beneath his notice. Then also he remembered that Mrs. Bold had a son.

Another circumstance also much influenced him, though it was one which may almost be said to have influenced him against his will. The vision of the Signora Neroni was perpetually before his eyes. It would be too much to say that Mr. Slope was lost in love, but yet he thought, and kept continually thinking, that he had never seen so beautiful a woman. He was a man whose nature was open to such impulses, and the wiles of the Italianised charmer had been thoroughly successful in imposing upon his thoughts. We will not talk about his heart: not that he had no heart, but because his heart had little to do with his present feelings. His taste had been pleased, his eyes charmed, and his vanity gratified. He had been dazzled by a sort of loveliness which he had never before seen, and had been caught by an easy, free, voluptuous manner which was perfectly new to him. He had never been so tempted before, and the temptation was now irresistible. He had not owned to himself that he cared for this woman more than for others around him; but yet he thought often of the time when he might see her next, and made, almost unconsciously, little cunning plans for seeing her frequently.

He had called at Dr. Stanhope's house the day after the bishop's party, and then the warmth of admiration had been fed with fresh fuel. If the signora had been kind in her manner and flattering in her speech when lying upon the bishop's sofa, with the eyes of so many on her, she had been much more so in her mother's drawing-room, with no one present but her sister to repress either her nature or her art. Mr. Slope had thus left her quite bewildered, and could not willingly admit into his brain any scheme, a part of which would be the necessity of his abandoning all further special friendship with this lady.

And so he slowly rode along very meditative.

And here the author must beg it to be remembered that Mr. Slope was not in all things a bad man. His motives, like those of most men, were mixed; and though his conduct was generally very different from that which we would wish to praise, it was actuated perhaps as often as that of the majority of the world by a desire to do his duty. He believed in the religion which he taught, harsh, unpalatable, uncharitable as that religion was. He believed those whom he wished to get under his hoof, the Grantlys and Gwynnes of the church, to be the enemies of that religion. He believed himself to be a pillar of strength, destined to do great things; and with that subtle, selfish, ambiguous sophistry to which the minds of all men are so subject, he had taught himself to think that in doing much for the promotion of his own interests he was doing much also for the promotion of religion. But Mr. Slope had never been an immoral man. Indeed, he had resisted temptations to immorality with a strength of purpose that was creditable to him. He had early in life devoted himself to works which were not compatible with the ordinary pleasures of youth, and he had abandoned such pleasures not without a struggle. It must therefore be conceived that he did not admit to himself that he warmly admired the beauty of a married woman without heartfelt stings of conscience; and to pacify that conscience, he had to teach himself that the nature of his admiration was innocent.

And thus he rode along meditative and ill at ease. His conscience had not a word to say against his choosing the widow and her fortune. That he looked upon as a godly work rather than otherwise; as a deed which, if carried through, would rebound to his credit as a Christian. On that side lay no future remorse, no conduct which he might probably have to forget, no inward stings. If it should turn out to be really the fact that Mrs. Bold had twelve hundred a year at her own disposal, Mr. Slope would rather look upon it as a duty which he owed his religion to make himself the master of the wife and the money; as a duty too, in which some amount of self-sacrifice would be necessary. He would have to give up his friendship with the signora, his resistance to Mr. Harding, his antipathy—no, he found on mature self-examination, that he could not bring himself to give up his antipathy to Dr. Grantly. He would marry the lady as the enemy of her brother-in-law if such an arrangement suited her; if not, she must look elsewhere for a husband.

It was with such resolve as this that he reached Barchester. He would at once ascertain what the truth might be as to the lady's wealth, and having done this, he would be ruled by circumstances in his conduct respecting the hospital. If he found that he could turn round and secure the place for Mr. Harding without much self-sacrifice, he would do so; but if not, he would woo the daughter in opposition to the father. But in no case would he succumb to the archdeacon.

He saw his horse taken round to the stable, and immediately went forth to commence his inquiries. To give Mr. Slope his due, he was not a man who ever let much grass grow under his feet.

Poor Eleanor! She was doomed to be the intended victim of more schemes than one.

About the time that Mr. Slope was visiting the vicar of Puddingdale, a discussion took place respecting her charms and wealth at Dr. Stanhope's house in the close. There had been morning callers there, and people had told some truth and also some falsehood respecting the property which John Bold had left behind him. By degrees the visitors went, and as the doctor went with them, and as the doctor's wife had not made her appearance, Charlotte Stanhope and her brother were left together. He was sitting idly at the table, scrawling caricatures of Barchester notables, then yawning, then turning over a book or two, and evidently at a loss how to kill his time without much labour.

"You haven't done much, Bertie, about getting any orders," said his sister.

"Orders!" said he; "who on earth is there at Barchester to give one orders? Who among the people here could possibly think it worth his while to have his head done into marble?"

"Then you mean to give up your profession," said she.

"No, I don't," said he, going on with some absurd portrait of the bishop. "Look at that, Lotte; isn't it the little man all over, apron and all? I'd go on with my profession at once, as you call it, if the governor would set me up with a studio in London; but as to sculpture at Barchester—I suppose half the people here don't know what a torso means."

"The governor will not give you a shilling to start you in London," said Lotte. "Indeed, he can't give you what would be sufficient, for he has not got it. But you might start yourself very well, if you pleased."

"How the deuce am I to do it?" said he.

"To tell you the truth, Bertie, you'll never make a penny by any profession."

"That's what I often think myself," said he, not in the least offended. "Some men have a great gift of making money, but they can't spend it. Others can't put two shillings together, but they have a great talent for all sorts of outlay. I begin to think that my genius is wholly in the latter line."

"How do you mean to live then?" asked the sister.

"I suppose I must regard myself as a young raven, and look for heavenly manna; besides, we have all got something when the governor goes."

"Yes—you'll have enough to supply yourself with gloves and boots; that is, if the Jews have not got the possession of it all. I believe they have the most of it already. I wonder, Bertie, at your indifference; that you, with your talents and personal advantages, should never try to settle yourself in life. I look forward with dread to the time when the governor must go. Mother, and Madeline, and I,—we shall be poor enough, but you will have absolutely nothing."

"Sufficient for the day is the evil thereof," said Bertie.

"Will you take my advice?" said his sister.

"*Cela dépend*," said the brother.

"Will you marry a wife with money?"

"At any rate," said he, "I won't marry one without: wives with money a'nt so easy to get now-a-days; the parsons pick them all up."

"And a parson will pick up the wife I mean for you, if you do not look quickly about it; the wife I mean is Mrs. Bold."

"Whew-w-w-w!" whistled Bertie, "a widow!"

"She is very beautiful," said Charlotte.

"With a son and heir all ready to my hand," said Bertie.

"A baby that will very likely die," said Charlotte.

"I don't see that," said Bertie. "But however, he may live for me—I don't wish to kill him; only, it must be owned that a ready-made family is a drawback."

"There is only one after all," pleaded Charlotte.

"And that a very little one, as the maid-servant said," rejoined Bertie.

"Beggars mustn't be choosers, Bertie; you can't have everything."

"God knows I am not unreasonable," said he, "nor yet opinionated; and if you'll arrange it all for me, Lotte, I'll marry the lady. Only mark this; the money must be sure, and the income at my own disposal, at any rate for the lady's life."

Charlotte was explaining to her brother that he must make love for himself if he meant to carry on the matter, and was encouraging him to do so, by warm eulogiums on Eleanor's beauty, when the signora was brought into the drawing-room. When at home, and subject to the gaze of none but her own family, she allowed herself to be dragged about by two persons, and her two bearers now deposited her on the sofa. She was not quite so grand in her apparel as she had been at the bishop's party, but yet she was dressed with much care, and though there was a look of care and pain about her eyes, she was, even by daylight, extremely beautiful.

"Well, Madeline; so I'm going to be married," Bertie began, as soon as the servants had withdrawn.

"There's no other foolish thing left, that you haven't done," said Madeline, "and therefore you are quite right to try that."

"Oh, you think it's a foolish thing, do you?" said he. "There's Lotte advising me to marry by all means. But on such a subject your opinion ought to be the best; you have experience to guide you."

"Yes, I have," said Madeline, with a sort of harsh sadness in her tone, which seemed to say—What is it to you if I am sad? I have never asked your sympathy.

Bertie was sorry when he saw that she was hurt by what he said, and he came and squatted on the floor close before her face to make his peace with her.

"Come, Mad, I was only joking; you know that. But in sober earnest, Lotte is advising me to marry. She wants me to marry this Mrs. Bold. She's a widow with lots of tin, a fine baby, a beautiful complexion, and the George and Dragon hotel up in the High Street. By Jove, Lotte, if I marry her, I'll keep the public house myself—it's just the life to suit me."

"What?" said Madeline, "that vapid swarthy creature in the widow's cap, who looked as though her clothes had been stuck on her back with a pitchfork!'' The signora never allowed any woman to be beautiful.

"Instead of being vapid," said Lotte, "I call her a very lovely woman. She was by far the loveliest woman in the rooms the other night; that is, excepting you, Madeline."

Even the compliment did not soften the asperity of the maimed beauty. "Every woman is charming according to Lotte," she said; "I never knew an eye with so little true appreciation. In the first place, what woman on earth could look well in such a thing as that she had on her head?"

"Of course she wears a widow's cap; but she'll put that off when Bertie marries her."

"I don't see any of course in it," said Madeline. "The death of twenty husbands should not make me undergo such a penance. It is as much a relic of paganism as the sacrifice of a Hindoo woman at the burning of her husband's body. If not so bloody, it is quite as barbarous, and quite as useless."

"But you don't blame her for that," said Bertie. "She does it because it's the custom of the country. People would think ill of her if she didn't do it."

"Exactly," said Madeline. "She is just one of those English nonentities who would tie her head up in a bag for three months every summer, if her mother and grandmother had tied up their heads before her. It would never occur to her, to think whether there was any use in submitting to such a nuisance."

"It's very hard, in a country like England, for a young woman to set herself in opposition to prejudices of that sort," said the prudent Charlotte.

"What you mean is, that it's very hard for a fool not to be a fool," said Madeline.

Bertie Stanhope had been so much knocked about the world from his earliest years, that he had not retained much respect for the gravity of English customs; but even to his mind an idea presented itself, that, perhaps in a wife, true British prejudice would not in the long run be less agreeable than Anglo-Italian freedom from restraint. He did not exactly say so, but he expressed the idea in another way.

"I fancy," said he, "that if I were to die, and then walk, I should think that my widow looked better in one of those caps than any other kind of head-dress."

"Yes—and you'd fancy also that she could do nothing better than shut herself up and cry for you, or else burn herself. But she would think differently. She'd probably wear one of those horrid she-helmets, because she'd want the courage not to do so; but she'd wear it with a heart longing for the time when she might be allowed to throw it off. I hate such shallow false pretences. For my part, I would let the world say what it pleased, and show no grief if I felt none;—and perhaps not, if I did.''

"But wearing a widow's cap won't lessen her fortune," said Charlotte.

"Or increase it," said Madeline. "Then why on earth does she do it?"

"But Lotte's object is to make her put it off," said Bertie.

"If it be true that she has got twelve hundred a year quite at her own disposal, and she be not utterly vulgar in her manners, I would advise you to marry her. I dare say she is to be had for the asking: and as you are not going to marry her for love, it doesn't much matter whether she is good-looking or not. As to your really marrying a woman for love, I don't believe *you* are fool enough for that.''

"Oh, Madeline!" exclaimed her sister.

"And oh, Charlotte!" said the other.

"You don't mean to say that no man can love a woman unless he be a fool?"

"I mean very much the same thing,—that any man who is willing to sacrifice his interest to get possession of a pretty face is a fool. Pretty faces are to be had cheaper than that. I hate your mawkish sentimentality, Lotte. You know as well as I do in what way husbands and wives generally live together; you know how far the warmth of conjugal affection can withstand the trial of a bad dinner, of a rainy day, or of the least privation which poverty brings with it; you know what freedom a man claims for himself, what slavery he would exact from his wife if he could! And you know also how wives generally obey. Marriage means tyranny on one side and deceit on the other. I say that a man is a fool to sacrifice his interests for such a bargain. A woman, too generally, has no other way of living.''

"But Bertie has no other way of living," said Charlotte.

"Then, in God's name, let him marry Mrs. Bold," said Madeline. And so it was settled between them.

But let the gentle-hearted reader be under no apprehension whatsoever. It is not destined that Eleanor shall marry Mr. Slope or Bertie Stanhope. And here, perhaps, it may be allowed to the novelist to explain his views on a very important point in the art of telling tales. He ventures to reprobate that system which goes so far to violate all proper confidence between the author and his readers, by maintaining nearly to the end of the third volume a mystery as to the fate of their favourite personage. Nay, more, and worse than this, is too frequently done. Have not often the profoundest efforts of genius been used to baffle the aspirations of the reader, to raise false hopes and false fears, and to give rise to expectations which are never to be realised? Are not promises all but made of delightful horrors, in lieu of which the writer produces nothing but most commonplace realities in his final chapter? And is there not a species of deceit in this to which the honesty of the present age should lend no countenance?

And what can be the worth of that solicitude which a peep into the third volume can utterly dissipate? What the value of those literary charms which are absolutely destroyed by their enjoyment? When we have once learnt what was that picture before which was hung Mrs. Ratcliffe's solemn curtain, we feel no further interest about either the frame or the veil. They are to us, merely a receptacle for old bones, an inappropriate coffin, which we would wish to have decently buried out of our sight.

And then, how grievous a thing it is to have the pleasure of your novel destroyed by the ill-considered triumph of a previous reader. "Oh, you needn't be alarmed for Augusta, of course she accepts Gustavus in the end." "How very ill-natured you are, Susan," says Kitty, with tears in her eyes; "I don't care a bit about it now." Dear Kitty, if you will read my book, you may defy the ill-nature of your sister. There shall be no secret that she can tell you. Nay, take the last chapter if you please—learn from its pages all the results of our troubled story, and the story shall have lost none of its interest, if indeed there be any interest in it to lose.

Our doctrine is, that the author and the reader should move along together in full confidence with each other. Let the personages of the drama undergo ever so complete a comedy of errors among themselves, but let the spectator never mistake the Syracusan for the Ephesian; otherwise he is one of the dupes, and the part of a dupe is never dignified.

I would not for the value of this chapter have it believed by a single reader that my Eleanor could bring herself to marry Mr. Slope, or that she should be sacrificed to a Bertie Stanhope. But among the good folk of Barchester many believed both the one and the other.

XVI

Baby Worship

"Diddle, diddle, diddle, diddle, dum, dum, dum," said or sung Eleanor Bold.

"Diddle, diddle, diddle, diddle, dum, dum, dum," continued Mary Bold, taking up the second part in this concerted piece.

The only audience at the concert was the baby, who however gave such vociferous applause, that the performers presuming it to amount to an encore, commenced again.

"Diddle, diddle, diddle, diddle, dum, dum, dum: hasn't he got lovely legs?" said the rapturous mother.

"H'm 'm 'm 'm 'm," simmered Mary, burying her lips in the little fellow's fat neck, by way of kissing him.

"H'm 'm 'm 'm 'm," simmered the mamma, burying her lips also in his fat round short legs. "He's a dawty little bold darling, so he is; and he has the nicest little pink legs in all the world, so he has"; and the simmering and the kissing went on over again, and as though the ladies were very hungry, and determined to eat him.

"Well, then, he's his own mother's own darling: well, he shall—oh, oh—Mary, Mary—did you ever see? What am I to do? My naughty, naughty, naughty, naughty little Johnny." All these energetic exclamations were elicited by the delight of the mother in finding that her son was strong enough, and mischievous enough, to pull all her hair out from under her cap. "He's been and pulled down all mamma's hair, and he's the naughtiest, naughtiest, naughtiest little man that ever, ever, ever, ever, ever——"

A regular service of baby worship was going on. Mary Bold was sitting on a low easy chair, with the boy in her lap, and

Eleanor was kneeling before the object of her idolatry. As she tried to cover up the little fellow's face with her long, glossy, dark brown locks, and permitted him to pull them hither and thither, as he would, she looked very beautiful in spite of the widow's cap which she still wore. There was a quiet, enduring, grateful sweetness about her face, which grew so strongly upon those who knew her, as to make the great praise of her beauty which came from her old friends, appear marvellously exaggerated to those who were only slightly acquainted with her. Her loveliness was like that of many landscapes, which require to be often seen to be fully enjoyed. There was a depth of dark clear brightness in her eyes which was lost upon a quick observer, a character about her mouth which only showed itself to those with whom she familiarly conversed, a glorious form of head the perfect symmetry of which required the eye of an artist for its appreciation. She had none of that dazzling brilliancy, of that voluptuous Rubens beauty, of that pearly whiteness, and those vermilion tints, which immediately entranced with the power of a basilisk men who came within reach of Madeline Neroni. It was all but impossible to resist the signora, but no one was called upon for any resistance towards Eleanor. You might begin to talk to her as though she were your sister, and it would not be till your head was on your pillow, that the truth and intensity of her beauty would flash upon you; that the sweetness of her voice would come upon your ear. A sudden half-hour with the Neroni, was like falling into a pit; an evening spent with Eleanor like an unexpected ramble in some quiet fields of asphodel.

"We'll cover him up till there sha'n't be a morsel of his little 'ittle 'ittle 'ittle nose to be seen," said the mother, stretching her streaming locks over the infant's face. The child screamed with delight, and kicked till Mary Bold was hardly able to hold him.

At this moment the door opened, and Mr. Slope was announced. Up jumped Eleanor, and with a sudden quick motion of her hands pushed back her hair over her shoulders. It would have been perhaps better for her that she had not, for she thus showed more of her confusion than she would have done had she remained as she was. Mr. Slope, however, immediately recognised her loveliness, and thought to himself, that irrespective of her fortune, she would be an inmate that a man might well desire for his house, a partner for his bosom's care very well qualified to make care lie easy. Eleanor hurried out of the room to re-adjust her cap, muttering some unnecessary apology about her baby. And while she is gone, we will briefly go back and state what had been hitherto the results of Mr. Slope's meditations on his scheme of matrimony.

His inquiries as to the widow's income had at any rate been so far successful as to induce him to determine to go on with the speculation. As regarded Mr. Harding, he had also resolved to do what he could without injury to himself. To Mrs. Proudie he determined not to speak on the matter, at least not at present. His object was to instigate a little rebellion on the part of the bishop. He thought that such a state of things would be advisable not only in respect to Messrs. Harding and Quiverful, but also in the affairs of the diocese generally. Mr. Slope was by no means of opinion that Dr. Proudie was fit to rule, but he conscientiously thought it wrong that his brother clergy should be subjected to petticoat government. He therefore made up his mind to infuse a little of his spirit into the bishop, sufficient to induce him to oppose his wife, though not enough to make him altogether insubordinate.

He had therefore taken an opportunity of again speaking to his lordship about the hospital, and had endeavoured to make it appear that after all it would be unwise to exclude Mr. Harding from the appointment. Mr. Slope, however, had a harder task than he had imagined. Mrs. Proudie, anxious to assume to herself as much as possible of the merit of patronage, had written to Mrs. Quiverful, requesting her to call at the palace; and had then explained to that matron, with much mystery, condescension, and dignity, the good that was in store for her and her progeny. Indeed Mrs. Proudie had been so engaged at the very time that Mr. Slope had been doing the same with the husband at Puddingdale Vicarage, and had thus in a measure committed herself. The thanks, the humility, the gratitude, the surprise of Mrs. Quiverful had been very overpowering; she had all but embraced the knees of her patroness, and had promised that the prayers of fourteen unprovided babes (so Mrs. Quiverful had described her own family, the eldest of which was a stout young woman of three-and-twenty) should be put up to heaven morning and evening for the munificent friend whom God had sent to them. Such incense as this was not unpleasing to Mrs. Proudie, and she made the most of it. She offered her general assistance to the fourteen unprovided babes, if, as she had no doubt, she should find them worthy; expressed a hope that the eldest of them would be fit to undertake tuition in her Sabbath schools, and altogether made herself a very great lady in the estimation of Mrs. Quiverful.

Having done this, she thought it prudent to drop a few words before the bishop, letting him know that she had acquainted the Puddingdale family with their good fortune; so that he might perceive that he stood committed to the appointment. The husband well understood the *ruse* of his wife, but he did not resent it. He knew that she was taking the patronage out of his hands; he was resolved to put an end to her interference, and re-assume his powers. But then he thought this was not the best time to do it. He put off the evil hour, as many a man in similar circumstances has done before him.

Such having been the case, Mr. Slope naturally encountered a difficulty in talking over the bishop, a difficulty indeed which he found could not be overcome except at the cost of a general outbreak at the palace. A general outbreak at the present moment might be good policy, but it also might not. It was at any rate not a step to be lightly taken. He began by whispering to the bishop that he feared that public opinion would be against him if Mr. Harding did not reappear at the hospital. The bishop answered with some warmth that Mr. Quiverful had been promised the appointment on Mr. Slope's advice. "Not promised!" said Mr. Slope. "Yes, promised," replied the bishop, "and Mrs. Proudie has seen Mrs. Quiverful on the subject." This was quite unexpected on the part of Mr. Slope, but his presence of mind did not fail him, and he turned the statement to his own account.

"Ah, my lord," said he, "we shall all be in scrapes if the ladies interfere."

This was too much in unison with my lord's feelings to be altogether unpalatable, and yet such an allusion to interference demanded a rebuke. My lord was somewhat astounded also, though not altogether made miserable, by finding that there was a point of difference between his wife and his chaplain.

"I don't know what you mean by interference," said the bishop mildly. "When Mrs. Proudie heard that Mr. Quiverful was to be appointed, it was not unnatural that she should wish to see Mrs. Quiverful about the schools. I really cannot say that I see any interference."

"I only speak, my lord, for your own comfort," said Slope; "for your own comfort and dignity in the diocese. I can have no other motive. As far as personal feelings go, Mrs. Proudie is the best friend I have. I must always remember that. But still, in my present position, my first duty is to your lordship."

"I'm sure of that, Mr. Slope, I am quite sure of that," said the bishop mollified: "and you really think that Mr. Harding should have the hospital?"

"Upon my word, I'm inclined to think so. I am quite prepared to take upon myself the blame of first suggesting Mr. Quiverful's name. But since doing so, I have found that there is so strong a feeling in the diocese in favour of Mr. Harding, that I think your lordship should give way. I hear also that Mr. Harding has modified the objections he first felt to your lordship's propositions. And as to what has passed between Mrs. Proudie and Mrs. Quiverful, the circumstance may be a little inconvenient, but I really do not think that that should weigh in a matter of so much moment."

And thus the poor bishop was left in a dreadfully undecided state as to what he should do. His mind, however, slightly inclined itself to the appointment of Mr. Harding, seeing that by such a step, he should have the assistance of Mr. Slope in opposing Mrs. Proudie.

Such was the state of affairs at the palace, when Mr. Slope called at Mrs. Bold's house, and found her playing with her baby. When she ran out of the room, Mr. Slope began praising the weather to Mary Bold, then he praised the baby and kissed him, and then he praised the mother, and then he praised Miss Bold herself. Mrs. Bold, however, was not long before she came back.

"I have to apologise for calling at so very early an hour," began Mr. Slope, "but I was really so anxious to speak to you that I hope you and Miss Bold will excuse me."

Eleanor muttered something in which the words "certainly," and "of course," and "not early at all," were just audible, and then apologised for her own appearance, declaring with a smile, that her baby was becoming such a big boy that he was quite unmanageable.

"He's a great big naughty boy," said she to the child; "and we must send him away to a great big rough romping school, where they have great big rods, and do terrible things to naughty boys who don't do what their mammas tell them"; and she then commenced another course of kissing, being actuated thereto by the terrible idea of sending her child away which her own imagination had depicted.

"And where the masters don't have such beautiful long hair to be dishevelled," said Mr. Slope, taking up the joke and paying a compliment at the same time.

Eleanor thought he might as well have left the compliment

alone; she had said nothing and looked nothing, being occupied as she was with the baby.

"Let me take him," said Mary. "His clothes are nearly off his back with his romping," and so saying she left the room with the child. Miss Bold had heard Mr. Slope say he had something pressing to say to Eleanor, and thinking that she might be *de trop*, took this opportunity of getting herself out of the room.

"Don't be long, Mary," said Eleanor, as Miss Bold shut the door.

"I am glad, Mrs. Bold, to have the opportunity of having ten minutes' conversation with you alone," began Mr. Slope. "Will you let me openly ask you a plain question?"

"Certainly," said she.

"And I am sure you will give me a plain and open answer."

"Either that or none at all," said she, laughing.

"My question is this, Mrs. Bold; is your father really anxious to go back to the hospital?"

"Why do you ask me?" said she. "Why don't you ask himself?"

"My dear Mrs. Bold, I'll tell you why. There are wheels within wheels, all of which I would explain to you, only I fear that there is not time. It is essentially necessary that I should have an answer to this question, otherwise I cannot know how to advance your father's wishes; and it is quite impossible that I should ask himself. No one can esteem your father more than I do, but I doubt if this feeling is reciprocal." It certainly was not. "I must be candid with you as the only means of avoiding ultimate consequences, which may be most injurious to Mr. Harding. I fear there is a feeling, I will not even call it a prejudice, with regard to myself in Barchester, which is not in my favour. You remember that sermon——"

"Oh! Mr. Slope, we need not go back to that," said Eleanor.

"For one moment, Mrs. Bold. It is not that I may talk of myself, but because it is so essential that you should understand how matters stand. That sermon may have been ill-judged,—it was certainly misunderstood; but I will say nothing about that now; only this, that it did give rise to a feeling against myself which your father shares with others. It may be that he has proper cause, but the result is that he is not inclined to meet me on friendly terms. I put it to yourself whether you do not know this to be the case."

Eleanor made no answer, and Mr. Slope, in the eagerness

of his address, edged his chair a little nearer to the widow's seat, unperceived by her.

"Such being so," continued Mr. Slope, "I cannot ask him this question as I can ask it of you. In spite of my delinquencies since I came to Barchester you have allowed me to regard you as a friend." Eleanor made a little motion with her head which was hardly confirmatory, but Mr. Slope if he noticed it, did not appear to do so. "To you I can speak openly, and explain the feelings of my heart. This your father would not allow. Unfortunately the bishop has thought it right that this matter of hospital should pass through my hands. There have been some details to get up with which he would not trouble himself, and thus it has come to pass that I was forced to have an interview with your father on the matter."

"I am aware of that," said Eleanor.

"Of course," said he. "In that interview Mr. Harding left the impression on my mind that he did not wish to return to the hospital."

"How could that be?" said Eleanor, at last stirred up to forget the cold propriety of demeanour which she had determined to maintain.

"My dear Mrs. Bold, I give you my word that such was the case," said he, again getting a little nearer to her. "And what is more than that, before my interview with Mr. Harding, certain persons at the palace, I do not mean the bishop, had told me that such was the fact. I own, I hardly believed it; I own, I thought that your father would wish on every account, for conscience' sake, for the sake of those old men, for old association, and the memory of dear days long gone by, on every account I thought that he would wish to resume his duties. But I was told that such was not his wish; and he certainly left me with the impression that I had been told the truth."

"Well!" said Eleanor, now sufficiently roused on the matter.

"I hear Miss Bold's step," said Mr. Slope; "would it be asking too great a favour to beg you to—I know you can manage anything with Miss Bold."

Eleanor did not like the word manage, but still she went out, and asked Mary to leave them alone for another quarter of an hour.

"Thank you, Mrs. Bold,—I am so very grateful for this confidence. Well, I left your father with this impression. Indeed, I may say that he made me understand that he declined the appointment."

"Not the appointment," said Eleanor. "I am sure he did not decline the appointment. But he said that he would not agree,—that is, that he did not like the scheme about the schools and the services, and all that. I am quite sure he never said that he wished to refuse the place."

"Oh, Mrs. Bold!" said Mr. Slope, in a manner almost impassioned. "I would not, for the world, say to so good a daughter a word against so good a father. But you must, for his sake, let me show you exactly how the matter stands at present. Mr. Harding was a little flurried when I told him of the bishop's wishes about the school. I did so, perhaps, with the less caution because you yourself had so perfectly agreed with me on the same subject. He was a little put out and spoke warmly. 'Tell the bishop,' said he, 'that I quite disagree with him,—and shall not return to the hospital as such conditions are attached to it.' What he said was to that effect; indeed, his words were, if anything, stronger than those. I had no alternative but to repeat them to his lordship, who said that he could look on them in no other light than a refusal. He also had heard the report that your father did not wish for the appointment, and putting all these things together, he thought he had no choice but to look for some one else. He has consequently offered the place to Mr. Quiverful."

"Offered the place to Mr. Quiverful!" repeated Eleanor, her eyes suffused with tears. "Then, Mr. Slope, there is an end of it."

"No, my friend—not so," said he. "It is to prevent such being the end of it that I am now here. I may at any rate presume that I have got an answer to my question, and that Mr. Harding is desirous of returning."

"Desirous of returning—of course he is," said Eleanor; "of course he wishes to have back his house and his income, and his place in the world; to have back what he gave up with such self-denying honesty, if he can have them without restraints on his conduct to which at his age it would be impossible that he should submit. How can the bishop ask a man of his age to turn schoolmaster to a pack of children?"

"Out of the question," said Mr. Slope, laughing slightly; "of course no such demand shall be made on your father. I can at any rate promise you that I will not be the medium of any so absurd a requisition. We wished your father to preach in the hospital, as the inmates may naturally be too old to leave it; but even that shall not be insisted on. We wished also to attach a Sabbath-day school to the hospital, thinking that such an establishment could not be useful under the surveillance of so good a clergyman as Mr. Harding, and also under your own. But, dear Mrs. Bold; we won't talk of these things now. One thing is clear; we must do what we can to annul this rash offer the bishop has made to Mr. Quiverful. Your father wouldn't see Quiverful, would he? Quiverful is an honourable man, and would not, for a moment, stand in your father's way."

"What?" said Eleanor; "ask a man with fourteen children to give up his preferment! I am quite sure he will do no such thing."

"I suppose not," said Slope; and he again drew near to Mrs. Bold, so that now they were very close to each other. Eleanor did not think much about it, but instinctively moved away a little. How greatly would she have increased the distance could she have guessed what had been said about her at Plumstead! "I suppose not. But it is out of the question that Quiverful should supersede your father,—quite out of the question. The bishop has been too rash. An idea occurs to me, which may, perhaps, with God's blessing, put us right. My dear Mrs. Bold, would you object to seeing the bishop yourself?"

"Why should not my father see him?" said Eleanor. She had once before in her life interfered in her father's affairs, and then not to much advantage. She was older now, and felt that she should take no step in a matter so vital to him without his consent.

"Why, to tell the truth," said Mr. Slope, with a look of sorrow, as though he greatly bewailed the want of charity in his patron, "the bishop fancies that he has cause of anger against your father. I fear an interview would lead to further ill will."

"Why," said Eleanor, "my father is the mildest, the gentlest man living."

"I only know," said Slope, "that he has the best of daughters. So you would not see the bishop? As to getting an interview, I could manage that for you without the slightest annoyance to yourself."

"I could do nothing, Mr. Slope, without consulting my father."

"Ah!" said he, "that would be useless; you would then only be your father's messenger. Does anything occur to yourself? Something must be done. Your father shall not be ruined by so ridiculous a misunderstanding."

Eleanor said that nothing occurred to her, but that it was very hard; and the tears came to her eyes and rolled down her cheeks. Mr. Slope would have given much to have had the privilege of drying them; but he had tact enough to know that he had still a great deal to do before he could even hope for any privilege with Mrs. Bold.

"It cuts me to the heart to see you so grieved," said he. "But pray let me assure you that your father's interests shall not be sacrificed if it be possible for me to protect them. I will tell the bishop openly what are the facts. I will explain to him that he has hardly the right to appoint any other than your father, and will show him that if he does so he will be guilty of great injustice,—and you, Mrs. Bold, you will have the charity at any rate to believe this of me, that I am truly anxious for your father's welfare,—for his and for your own."

The widow hardly knew what answer to make. She was quite aware that her father would not be at all thankful to Mr. Slope; she had a strong wish to share her father's feelings; and yet she could not but acknowledge that Mr. Slope was very kind. Her father, who was generally so charitable to all men, who seldom spoke ill of any one, had warned her against Mr. Slope, and yet she did not know how to abstain from thanking him. What interest could he have in the matter but that which he professed? Nevertheless there was that in his manner which even she distrusted. She felt, she did not know why, that there was something about him which ought to put her on her guard.

Mr. Slope read all this in her hesitating manner just as plainly as though she had opened her heart to him. It was the talent of the man that he could so read the inward feelings of women with whom he conversed. He knew that Eleanor was doubting him, and that if she thanked him she would only do so because she could not help it; but yet this did not make him angry or even annoy him. Rome was not built in a day.

"I did not come for thanks," continued he, seeing her hesitation; "and do not want them—at any rate before they are merited. But this I do want, Mrs. Bold, that I may make to myself friends in this fold to which it has pleased God to call me as one of the humblest of his shepherds. If I cannot do so, my task here must indeed be a sad one. I will at any rate endeavour to deserve them."

"I'm sure," said she, "you will soon make plenty of friends." She felt herself obliged to say something.

"That will be nothing unless they are such as will sympathise with my feelings; unless they are such as I can reverence and admire—and love. If the best and purest turn away from me,

I cannot bring myself to be satisfied with the friendship of the less estimable. In such case I must live alone.''

"Oh! I'm sure you will not do that, Mr. Slope." Eleanor meant nothing, but it suited him to appear to think some special allusion had been intended.

"Indeed, Mrs. Bold, I shall live alone, quite alone as far as the heart is concerned, if those with whom I yearn to ally myself turn away from me. But enough of this; I have called you my friend, and I hope you will not contradict me. I trust the time may come when I may also call your father so. May God bless you, Mrs. Bold, you and your darling boy. And tell your father from me that what can be done for his interest shall be done.''

And so he took his leave, pressing the widow's hand rather more closely than usual. Circumstances, however, seemed just then to make this intelligible, and the lady did not feel called on to resent it.

"I cannot understand him," said Eleanor to Mary Bold, a few minutes afterwards. "I do not know whether he is a good man or a bad man—whether he is true or false.''

"Then give him the benefit of the doubt," said Mary, "and believe the best.''

"On the whole, I think I do," said Eleanor. "I think I do believe that he means well—and if so, it is a shame that we should revile him, and make him miserable while he is among us. But, oh, Mary, I fear papa will be disappointed in the hospital.''

XVII

Who Shall Be Cock of the Walk?

All this time things were going on somewhat uneasily at the palace. The hint or two which Mr. Slope had given was by no means thrown away upon the bishop. He had a feeling that if he ever meant to oppose the now almost unendurable despotism of his wife, he must lose no further time in doing so; that if he ever meant to be himself master of his own diocese, let alone his own house, he should begin at once. It would have been easier to have done so from the day of his consecration than now, but easier now than when Mrs. Proudie should have succeeded in thoroughly mastering the diocesan details. Then the proffered assistance of Mr. Slope was a great thing for him, a most unexpected and invaluable aid. Hitherto he had looked on the two as allied forces; and had considered that as allies they were impregnable. He had begun to believe that his only chance of escape would be by the advancement of Mr. Slope to some distant and rich preferment. But now it seemed that one of his enemies, certainly the least potent of them, but nevertheless one very important, was willing to desert his own camp. Assisted by Mr. Slope what might he not do? He walked up and down his little study, almost thinking that the time might come when he would be able to appropriate to his own use the big room up stairs, in which his predecessor had always sat.

As he revolved these things in his mind a note was brought to him from Archdeacon Grantly, in which that divine begged his lordship to do him the honour of seeing him on the morrow— would his lordship have the kindness to name an hour? Dr. Grantly's proposed visit would have reference to the reappointment of Mr. Harding to the wardenship of Barchester hospital. The bishop having read his note was informed that the archdeacon's servant was waiting for an answer.

Here at once a great opportunity offered itself to the bishop of acting on his own responsibility. He bethought himself however of his new ally, and rang the bell for Mr. Slope. It turned out that Mr. Slope was not in the house; and then, greatly daring, the bishop with his own unassisted spirit wrote a note to the archdeacon saying that he would see him, and naming an hour for doing so. Having watched from his study-window that the messenger got safely off from the premises with this despatch, he began to turn over in his mind what step he should next take.

To-morrow he would have to declare to the archdeacon either that Mr. Harding should have the appointment, or that he should not have it. The bishop felt that he could not honestly throw over the Quiverfuls without informing Mrs. Proudie, and he resolved at last to brave the lioness in her den and tell her that circumstances were such that it behoved him to reappoint Mr. Harding. He did not feel that he should at all derogate from his new courage by promising Mrs. Proudie that the very first piece

of available preferment at his disposal should be given to Quiverful
to atone for the injury done to him. If he could mollify the
lioness with such a sop, how happy would he think his first
efforts to have been!

Not without many misgivings did he find himself in Mrs.
Proudie's boudoir. He had at first thought of sending for her. But
it was not at all impossible that she might choose to take such a
message amiss, and then also it might be some protection to him
to have his daughters present at the interview. He found her
sitting with her account books before her nibbling the end of her
pencil evidently mersed in pecuniary difficulties, and harassed in
mind by the multiplicity of palatial expenses, and the heavy cost
of episcopal grandeur. Her daughters were around her. Olivia
was reading a novel, Augusta was crossing a note to her bosom
friend in Baker Street, and Netta was working diminutive coach
wheels for the bottom of a petticoat. If the bishop could get the
better of his wife in her present mood, he would be a man
indeed. He might then consider the victory his own for ever.
After all, in such case, the matter between husband and wife
stands much the same as it does between two boys at the same
school, two cocks in the same yard, or two armies on the same
continent. The conqueror once is generally the conqueror for
ever after. The prestige of victory is everything.

"Ahem—my dear," began the bishop, "if you are disen-
gaged, I wish to speak to you." Mrs. Proudie put her pencil
down carefully at the point to which she had dotted her figures,
marked down in her memory the sum she had arrived at, and
then looked up, sourly enough, into her helpmate's face. "If you
are busy, another time will do as well," continued the bishop,
whose courage like Bob Acres' had oozed out, now that he
found himself on the ground of battle.

"What is it about, Bishop?" asked the lady.

"Well—it was about those Quiverfuls—but I see you are
engaged. Another time will do just as well for me."

"What about the Quiverfuls? It is quite understood I believe,
that they are to come to the hospital. There is to be no doubt
about that, is there?" and as she spoke she kept her pencil sternly
and vigorously fixed on the column of figures before her.

"Why, my dear, there is a difficulty," said the bishop.

"A difficulty!" said Mrs. Proudie, "what difficulty? The
place has been promised to Mr. Quiverful, and of course he must
have it. He has made all his arrangements. He has written for a
curate for Puddingdale, he has spoken to the auctioneer about

selling his farm, horses, and cows, and in all respects considers the place as his own. Of course he must have it.''

Now, bishop, look well to thyself, and call up all the manhood that is in thee. Think how much is at stake. If now thou art not true to thy guns, no Slope can hereafter aid thee. How can he who deserts his own colours at the first smell of gunpowder expect faith in any ally. Thou thyself hast sought the battlefield; fight out the battle manfully now thou art there. Courage, bishop, courage! Frowns cannot kill, nor can sharp words break any bones. After all the apron is thine own. She can appoint no wardens, give away no benefices, nominate no chaplains, an' thou art but true to thyself. Up, man, and at her with a constant heart.

Some little monitor within the bishop's breast so addressed him. But then there was another monitor there which advised him differently, and as follows. Remember, bishop, she is a woman, and such a woman too as thou well knowest: a battle of words with such a woman is the very mischief. Were it not better for thee to carry on this war, if it must be waged, from behind thine own table in thine own study? Does not every cock fight best on his own dunghill? Thy daughters also are here, the pledges of thy love, the fruits of thy loins; is it well that they should see thee in the hour of thy victory over their mother? nay, is it well that they should see thee in the possible hour of thy defeat? Besides, hast thou not chosen thy opportunity with wonderful little skill, indeed with no touch of that sagacity for which thou art famous? Will it not turn out that thou art wrong in this matter, and thine enemy right; that thou hast actually pledged thyself in this manner of the hospital, and that now thou wouldest turn upon thy wife because she requires from thee but the fulfilment of thy promise? Art thou not a Christian bishop, and is not thy word to be held sacred whatever be the result? Return, bishop, to thy sanctum on the lower floor, and postpone thy combative propensities for some occasion in which at least thou mayest fight the battle against odds less tremendously against thee.

All this passed within the bishop's bosom while Mrs. Proudie still sat with her fixed pencil, and the figures of her sum still enduring on the tablets of memory. ''£4 17s. 7d.'' she said to herself. ''Of course Mr. Quiverful must have the hospital,'' she said out loud to her lord.

''Well, my dear, I merely wanted to suggest to you that Mr. Slope seems to think that if Mr. Harding be not appointed, public feeling in the matter would be against us, and that the press might perhaps take it up.''

"Mr. Slope seems to think!'' said Mrs. Proudie, in a tone of voice which plainly showed the bishop that he was right in looking for a breach in that quarter. "And what has Mr. Slope to do with it? I hope, my lord, you are not going to allow yourself to be governed by a chaplain.'' And now in her eagerness the lady lost her place in her account.

"Certainly not, my dear. Nothing I can assure you is less probable. But still Mr. Slope may be useful in finding how the wind blows, and I really thought that if we could give something else as good to the Quiverfuls——''

"Nonsense,'' said Mrs. Proudie; "it would be years before you could give them anything else that could suit them half as well, and as for the press and the public, and all that, remember there are two ways of telling a story. If Mr. Harding is fool enough to tell his tale, we can also tell ours. The place was offered to him, and he refused it. It has now been given to some-one else, and there's an end of it. At least, I should think so.''

"Well, my dear, I rather believe you are right''; said the bishop, and sneaking out of the room, he went down stairs, troubled in his mind as to how he should receive the archdeacon on the morrow. He felt himself not very well just at present; and began to consider that he might, not improbably, be detained in his room the next morning by an attack of bile. He was, unfortunately, very subject to bilious annoyances.

"Mr. Slope, indeed! I'll Slope him,'' said the indignant matron to her listening progeny. "I don't know what has come to Mr. Slope. I believe he thinks he is to be Bishop of Barchester himself, because I've taken him by the hand, and got your father to make him his domestic chaplain.''

"He was always full of impudence,'' said Olivia; "I told you so once before, mamma.'' Olivia, however, had not thought him too impudent when once before he had proposed to make her Mrs. Slope.

"Well, Olivia, I always thought you liked him,'' said Augusta, who at that moment had some grudge against her sister. "I always disliked the man, because I think him thoroughly vulgar.''

"There you're wrong,'' said Mrs. Proudie; "he's not vulgar at all; and what is more, he is a soul-stirring, eloquent preacher; but he must be taught to know his place if he is to remain in this house.''

"He has the horridest eyes I ever saw in a man's head," said Netta; "and I tell you what, he's terribly greedy; did you see all the currant pie he ate yesterday?"

When Mr. Slope got home he soon learnt from the bishop, as much from his manner as his words, that Mrs. Proudie's behests in the matter of the hospital were to be obeyed. Dr. Proudie let fall something as to "this occasion only," and "keeping all affairs about patronage exclusively in his own hands." But he was quite decided about Mr. Harding; and as Mr. Slope did not wish to have both the prelate and the prelatess against him, he did not at present see that he could do anything but yield.

He merely remarked that he would of course carry out the bishop's views, and that he was quite sure that if the bishop trusted to his own judgment things in the diocese would certainly be well ordered. Mr. Slope knew that if you hit a nail on the head often enough, it will penetrate at last.

He was sitting alone in his room on the same evening when a light knock was made on his door, and before he could answer it the door was opened, and his patroness appeared. He was all smiles in a moment, but so was not she also. She took, however, the chair that was offered to her, and thus began her expostulation:—

"Mr. Slope, I did not at all approve your conduct the other night with that Italian woman. Any one would have thought that you were her lover."

"Good gracious, my dear madam," said Mr. Slope, with a look of horror. "Why, she is a married woman."

"That's more than I know," said Mrs. Proudie; "however she chooses to pass for such. But married or not married, such attention as you paid to her was improper. I cannot believe that you would wish to give offence in my drawing-room, Mr. Slope; but I owe it to myself and my daughters to tell you that I disapprove your conduct."

Mr. Slope opened wide his huge protruding eyes, and stared out of them with a look of well-feigned surprise. "Why Mrs. Proudie," said he, "I did but fetch her something to eat when she said she was hungry."

"And you have called on her since," continued she, looking at the culprit with the stern look of a detective policeman in the act of declaring himself.

Mr. Slope turned over in his mind whether it would be well for him to tell this termagant at once that he should call on whom he liked, and do what he liked; but he remembered that his footing in Barchester was not yet sufficiently firm, and that it would be better for him to pacify her.

"I certainly called since at Dr. Stanhope's house, and certainly saw Madam Neroni."

"Yes, and you saw her alone," said the episcopal Argus.

"Undoubtedly, I did," said Mr. Slope, "but that was because nobody else happened to be in the room. Surely it was no fault of mine if the rest of the family were out."

"Perhaps not; but I assure you, Mr. Slope, you will fall greatly in my estimation if I find that you allow yourself to be caught by the lures of that woman. I know women better than you do, Mr. Slope, and you may believe me that that signora, as she calls herself, is not a fitting companion for a strict evangelical, unmarried young clergyman."

How Mr. Slope would have liked to laugh at her, had he dared! But he did not dare. So he merely said, "I can assure you, Mrs. Proudie, the lady in question is nothing to me."

"Well, I hope not, Mr. Slope. But I have considered it my duty to give you this caution; and now there is another thing I feel myself called on to speak about; it is your conduct to the bishop, Mr. Slope."

"My conduct to the bishop," said he, now truly surprised and ignorant what the lady alluded to.

"Yes, Mr. Slope; your conduct to the bishop. It is by no means what I would wish to see it."

"Has the bishop said anything, Mrs. Proudie?"

"No, the bishop has said nothing. He probably thinks that any remarks on the matter will come better from me, who first introduced you to his lordship's notice. The fact is, Mr. Slope, you are a little inclined to take too much upon yourself."

An angry spot showed itself on Mr. Slope's cheeks, and it was with difficulty that he controlled himself. But he did do so, and sat quite silent while the lady went on.

"It is the fault of many young men in your position, and therefore the bishop is not inclined at present to resent it. You will, no doubt, soon learn what is required from you, and what is not. If you will take my advice, however, you will be careful not to obtrude advice upon the bishop in any matter touching patronage. If his lordship wants advice, he knows where to look for it." And then having added to her counsel a string of platitudes as to what was desirable and what was not desirable in the conduct of a strictly evangelical, unmarried young clergyman, Mrs. Proudie retreated, leaving the chaplain to his thoughts.

The upshot of his thoughts was this, that there certainly was not room in the diocese for the energies of both himself and Mrs. Proudie, and that it behoved him quickly to ascertain whether his energies or hers were to prevail.

XVIII

The Widow's Persecution

Early on the following morning Mr. Slope was summoned to the bishop's dressing-room, and went there fully expecting that he should find his lordship very indignant, and spirited up by his wife to repeat the rebuke which she had administered on the previous day. Mr. Slope had resolved that at any rate from him he would not stand it, and entered the dressing-room in rather a combative disposition; but he found the bishop in the most placid and gentlest of humours. His lordship complained of being rather unwell, had a slight headache, and was not quite the thing in his stomach; but there was nothing the matter with his temper.

"Oh, Slope," said he, taking the chaplain's proffered hand. "Archdeacon Grantly is to call on me this morning, and I really am not fit to see him. I fear I must trouble you, to see him for me"; and then Dr. Proudie proceeded to explain what it was that must be said to Dr. Grantly. He was to be told in fact in the civilest words in which the tidings could be conveyed, that Mr. Harding having refused the wardenship, the appointment had been offered to Mr. Quiverful and accepted by him.

Mr. Slope again pointed out to his patron that he thought he was perhaps not quite wise in his decision, and this he did *sotto voce*. But even with this precaution it was not safe to say much, and during the little he did say, the bishop made a very slight, but still a very ominous gesture with his thumb towards the door which opened from his dressing-room to some inner sanctuary. Mr. Slope at once took the hint, and said no more; but he perceived that there was to be confidence between him and his patron, that the league desired by him was to be made, and that this appointment of Mr. Quiverful was to be the last sacrifice offered on the altar of conjugal obedience. All this Mr. Slope read in the slight motion of the bishop's thumb, and he read it correctly. There was no need of parchments and seals, of attestations, explanations, and professions. The bargain was understood between them, and Mr. Slope gave the bishop his hand upon it. The bishop understood the little extra squeeze, and an intelligible gleam of assent twinkled in his eye.

"Pray be civil to the archdeacon, Mr. Slope," said he out loud; "but make him quite understand that in this matter Mr. Harding has put it out of my power to oblige him."

It would be a calumny on Mrs. Proudie to suggest that she was sitting in her bed-room with her ear at the keyhole during this interview. She had within her a spirit of decorum which prevented her from descending to such baseness. To put her ear to a key-hole or to listen at a chink, was a trick for a housemaid.

Mrs. Proudie knew this, and therefore she did not do it; but she stationed herself as near to the door as she well could, that she might, if possible, get the advantage which the housemaid would have had, without descending to the housemaid's artifice.

It was little, however, that she heard, and that little was only sufficient to deceive her. She saw nothing of that friendly pressure, perceived nothing of that concluded bargain; she did not even dream of the treacherous resolves which those two false men had made together to upset her in the pride of her station, to dash the cup from her lip before she drank of it, to sweep away all her power before she had tasted its sweets! Traitors that they were; the husband of her bosom, and the outcast whom she had fostered and brought to the warmth of the world's brightest fireside! But neither of them had the magnanimity of this woman. Though two men have thus leagued themselves together against her, even yet the battle is not lost.

Mr. Slope felt pretty sure that Dr. Grantly would decline the honour of seeing him, and such turned out to be the case. The archdeacon, when the palace door was opened to him, was greeted by a note. Mr. Slope presented his compliments, &c. &c. The bishop was ill in his room, and very greatly regretted, &c. &c. Mr. Slope had been charged with the bishop's views, and if agreeable to the archdeacon, would do himself the honour, &c. &c. The archdeacon, however, was not agreeable, and having read his note in the hall, crumpled it up in his hand, and

muttering something about sorrow for his lordship's illness, took
his leave, without sending as much as a verbal message in
answer to Mr. Slope's note.

"Ill!" said the archdeacon to himself as he flung himself
into his brougham. "The man is absolutely a coward. He is
afraid to see me. Ill, indeed!" The archdeacon was never ill
himself, and did not therefore understand that any one else could
in truth be prevented by illness from keeping an appointment. He
regarded all such excuses as subterfuges, and in the present
instance he was not far from wrong.

Dr. Grantly desired to be driven to his father-in-law's lodgings in the High Street, and hearing from the servant that Mr.
Harding was at his daughter's, followed him to Mrs. Bold's
house, and there found him. The archdeacon was fuming with
rage when he got into the drawing-room, and had by this time
nearly forgotten the pusillanimity of the bishop in the villany of
the chaplain.

"Look at that," said he, throwing Mr. Slope's crumpled
note to Mr. Harding. "I am to be told that if I choose I may have
the honour of seeing Mr. Slope, and that too, after a positive
engagement with the bishop."

"But he says the bishop is ill," said Mr. Harding.

"Pshaw! You don't mean to say that you are deceived by
such an excuse as that. He was well enough yesterday. Now I
tell you what, I will see the bishop; and I will tell him also very
plainly what I think of his conduct. I will see him, or else
Barchester will soon be too hot to hold him."

Eleanor was sitting in the room, but Mr. Grantly had hardly
noticed her in his anger. Eleanor now said to him, with the
greatest innocence, "I wish you had seen Mr. Slope, Dr. Grantly,
because I think perhaps it might have done good."

The archdeacon turned on her with almost brutal wrath. Had
she at once owned that she had accepted Mr. Slope for her
second husband, he could hardly have felt more convinced of her
belonging body and soul to the Slope and Proudie party than he
now did on hearing her express such a wish as this. Poor
Eleanor!

"See him!" said the archdeacon glaring at her; "and why
am I to be called on to lower myself in the world's esteem and
my own by coming in contact with such a man as that? I have
hitherto lived among gentlemen, and do not mean to be dragged
into other company by anybody."

Poor Mr. Harding well knew what the archdeacon meant,

but Eleanor was as innocent as her own baby. She could not understand how the archdeacon could consider himself to be dragged into bad company by condescending to speak to Mr. Slope for a few minutes when the interests of her father might be served by his doing so.

"I was talking for a full hour yesterday to Mr. Slope," said she, with some little assumption of dignity, "and I did not find myself lowered by it."

"Perhaps not," said he. "But if you'll be good enough to allow me, I shall judge for myself in such matters. And I tell you what, Eleanor, it will be much better for you if you will allow yourself to be guided also by the advice of those who are your friends. If you do not you will be apt to find that you have no friends left who can advise you."

Eleanor blushed up to the roots of her hair. But even now she had not the slightest idea of what was passing in the archdeacon's mind. No thought of love-making or love-receiving had yet found its way to her heart since the death of poor John Bold; and if it were possible that such a thought should spring there, the man must be far different from Mr. Slope that could give it birth.

Nevertheless Eleanor blushed deeply, for she felt she was charged with improper conduct, and she did so with the more inward pain because her father did not instantly rally to her side; that father for whose sake and love she had submitted to be the receptacle of Mr. Slope's confidence. She had given a detailed account of all that had passed to her father; and though he had not absolutely agreed with her about Mr. Slope's views touching the hospital, yet he had said nothing to make her think that she had been wrong in talking to him.

She was far too angry to humble herself before her brother-in-law. Indeed, she had never accustomed herself to be very abject before him, and they had never been confidential allies. "I do not the least understand what you mean, Dr. Grantly," said she. "I do not know that I can accuse myself of doing anything that my friends should disapprove. Mr. Slope called here expressly to ask what papa's wishes were about the hospital; and as I believe he called with friendly intentions I told him."

"Friendly intentions!" sneered the archdeacon.

"I believe you greatly wrong Mr. Slope," continued Eleanor; "but I have explained this to papa already; and as you do not seem to approve of what I say, Dr. Grantly, I will with your permission leave you and papa together,'' and so saying she walked slowly out of the room.

All this made Mr. Harding very unhappy. It was quite clear that the archdeacon and his wife had made up their minds that Eleanor was going to marry Mr. Slope. Mr. Harding could not really bring himself to think that she would do so, but yet he could not deny that circumstances made it appear that the man's company was not disagreeable to her. She was now constantly seeing him, and yet she received visits from no other unmarried gentleman. She always took his part when his conduct was canvassed, although she was aware how personally objectionable he was to her friends. Then, again, Mr. Harding felt that if she should choose to become Mrs. Slope, he had nothing that he could justly urge against her doing so. She had full right to please herself, and he, as a father, could not say that she would disgrace herself by marrying a clergyman who stood so well before the world as Mr. Slope did. As for quarrelling with his daughter on account of such a marriage, and separating himself from her as the archdeacon had threatened to do, that, with Mr. Harding, would be out of the question. If she should determine to marry this man, he must get over his aversion as best he could. His Eleanor, his own old companion in their old happy home, must still be the friend of his bosom, the child of his heart. Let who would cast her off, he would not. If it were fated that he should have to sit in his old age at the same table with that same man whom of all men he disliked the most, he would meet his fate as best he might. Anything to him would be preferable to the loss of his daughter.

Such being his feelings, he hardly knew how to take part with Eleanor against the archdeacon, or with the archdeacon against Eleanor. It will be said that he should never have suspected her.—Alas! he never should have done so. But Mr. Harding was by no means a perfect character. In his indecision, his weakness, his proneness to be led by others, his want of self-confidence, he was very far from being perfect. And then it must be remembered that such a marriage as that which the archdeacon contemplated with disgust, which we who know Mr. Slope so well would regard with equal disgust, did not appear so monstrous to Mr. Harding, because in his charity he did not hate the chaplain as the archdeacon did, and as we do.

He was, however, very unhappy when his daughter left the room, and he had recourse to an old trick of his that was customary to him in his times of sadness. He began playing some slow tune upon an imaginary violoncello, drawing one hand slowly backwards and forwards, as though he held a bow in it, and modulating the unreal cords with the other.

"She'll marry that man as sure as two and two make four," said the practical archdeacon.

"I hope not, I hope not," said the father. "But if she does, what can I say to her? I have no right to object to him."

"No right!" exclaimed Dr. Grantly.

"No right as her father. He is in my own profession, and for aught we know a good man."

To this the archdeacon would by no means assent. It was not well, however, to argue the case against Eleanor in her own drawing-room, and so they both walked forth and discussed the matter in all its bearings under the elm trees of the close. Mr. Harding also explained to his son-in-law what had been the purport, at any rate the alleged purport, of Mr. Slope's last visit to the widow. He, however, stated that he could not bring himself to believe that Mr. Slope had any real anxiety such as that he had pretended. "I cannot forget his demeanour to myself," said Mr. Harding, "and it is not possible that his ideas should have changed so soon."

"I see it all," said the archdeacon. "The sly *tartufe*! He thinks to buy the daughter by providing for the father. He means to show how powerful he is, how good he is, and how much he is willing to do for her *beaux yeux;* yes, I see it all now. But we'll be too many for him yet, Mr. Harding"; he said, turning to his companion with some gravity, and pressing his hand upon the other's arm. "It would, perhaps, be better for you to lose the hospital than get it on such terms."

"Lose it!" said Mr. Harding; "why I've lost it already. I don't want it. I've made up my mind to do without it. I'll withdraw altogether. I'll just go and write a line to the bishop and tell him that I withdraw my claim altogether."

Nothing would have pleased him better than to be allowed to escape from the trouble and difficulty in such a manner. But he was now going too fast for the archdeacon.

"No—no—no! we'll do no such thing," said Dr. Grantly; "we'll still have the hospital. I hardly doubt but that we'll have it. But not by Mr. Slope's assistance. If that be necessary we'll lose it; but we'll have it, spite of his teeth, if we can. Arabin will be at Plumstead to-morrow; you must come over and talk to him."

The two now turned into the cathedral library, which was used by the clergymen of the close as a sort of ecclesiastical club-room, for writing sermons and sometimes letters; also for reading theological works, and sometimes magazines and newspapers. The theological works were not disturbed, perhaps, quite as often as from the appearance of the building the outside public might have been led to expect. Here the two allies settled on their course of action. The archdeacon wrote a letter to the bishop, strongly worded, but still respectful, in which he put forward his father-in-law's claim to the appointment, and expressed his own regret that he had not been able to see his lordship when he called. Of Mr. Slope he made no mention whatsoever. It was then settled that Mr. Harding should go out to Plumstead on the following day; and after considerable discussion on the matter, the archdeacon proposed to ask Eleanor there also, so as to withdraw her, if possible, from Mr. Slope's attentions. "A week or two," said he, "may teach her what he is, and while she is there she will be out of harm's way. Mr. Slope won't come there after her."

Eleanor was not a little surprised when her brother-in-law came back and very civilly pressed her to go out to Plumstead with her father. She instantly perceived that her father had been fighting her battles for her behind her back. She felt thankful to him, and for his sake she would not show her resentment to the archdeacon by refusing his invitation. But she could not, she said, go on the morrow; she had an invitation to drink tea at the Stanhopes which she had promised to accept. She would, she added, go with her father on the next day, if he would wait; or she would follow him.

"The Stanhopes!" said Dr. Grantly; "I did not know you were so intimate with them."

"I did not know it myself," said she, "till Miss Stanhope called yesterday. However, I like her very much, and I have promised to go and play chess with some of them."

"Have they a party there?" said the archdeacon, still fearful of Mr. Slope.

"Oh, no," said Eleanor; "Miss Stanhope said there was to be nobody at all. But she had heard that Mary had left me for a few weeks, and she had learnt from some one that I play chess, and so she came over on purpose to ask me to go in."

"Well, that's very friendly," said the ex-warden. "They certainly do look more like foreigners than English people, but I dare say they are none the worse for that."

The archdeacon was inclined to look upon the Stanhopes with favourable eyes, and had nothing to object on the matter. It

was therefore arranged that Mr. Harding should postpone his
visit to Plumstead for one day, and then take with him Eleanor,
the baby, and the nurse.

Mr. Slope is certainly becoming of some importance in
Barchester.

XIX

Barchester by Moonlight

There was much cause for grief and occasional perturbation of
spirits in the Stanhope family, but yet they rarely seemed to be
grieved or to be disturbed. It was the peculiar gift of each of
them that each was able to bear his or her own burden without
complaint, and perhaps without sympathy. They habitually looked
on the sunny side of the wall, if there was a gleam on either side
for them to look at; and, if there was none, they endured the
shade with an indifference which, if not stoical, answered the
end at which the Stoics aimed. Old Stanhope could not but feel
that he had ill-performed his duties as a father and a clergyman;
and could hardly look forward to his own death without grief at
the position in which he would leave his family. His income for
many years had been as high as £3000 a year, and yet they had
among them no other provision than their mother's fortune of
£10,000. He had not only spent his income, but was in debt.
Yet with all this, he seldom showed much outward sign of
trouble.

It was the same with the mother. If she added little to the
pleasures of her children she detracted still less: she neither
grumbled at her lot, nor spoke much of her past or future
sufferings; as long as she had a maid to adjust her dress, and had
those dresses well made, nature with her was satisfied. It was the
same with the children. Charlotte never rebuked her father with
the prospect of their future poverty, nor did it seem to grieve her

that she was becoming an old maid so quickly; her temper was rarely ruffled, and, if we might judge by her appearance, she was always happy. The signora was not so sweet-tempered, but she possessed much enduring courage; she seldom complained—never, indeed, to her family. Though she had a cause for affliction which would have utterly broken down the heart of most women as beautiful as she and as devoid of all religious support, yet, she bore her suffering in silence, or alluded to it only to elicit the sympathy and stimulate the admiration of the men with whom she flirted. As to Bertie, one would have imagined from the sound of his voice and the gleam of his eye that he had not a sorrow nor a care in the world. Nor had he. He was incapable of anticipating to-morrow's griefs. The prospect of future want no more disturbed his appetite than does that of the butcher's knife disturb the appetite of the sheep.

Such was the usual tenour of their way; but there were rare exceptions. Occasionally the father would allow an angry glance to fall from his eye, and the lion would send forth a low dangerous roar as though he meditated some deed of blood. Occasionally also Madame Neroni would become bitter against mankind, more than usually antagonistic to the world's decencies, and would seem as though she was about to break from her moorings and allow herself to be carried forth by the tide of her feelings to utter ruin and whipwreck. She, however, like the rest of them, had no real feelings, could feel no true passion. In that was her security. Before she resolved on any contemplated escapade she would make a small calculation, and generally summed up that the Stanhope villa or even Barchester close was better than the world at large.

They were most irregular in their hours. The father was generally the earliest in the breakfast-parlour, and Charlotte would soon follow and give him his coffee; but the others breakfasted anywhere, anyhow, and at any time. On the morning after the archdeacon's futile visit to the palace, Dr. Stanhope came down stairs with an ominously dark look about his eyebrows; his white locks were rougher than usual, and he breathed thickly and loudly as he took his seat in his arm-chair. He had open letters in his hand, and when Charlotte came into the room he was still reading them. She went up and kissed him as was her wont, but he hardly noticed her as she did so, and she knew at once that something was the matter.

"What's the meaning of that?" said he, throwing over the table a letter with a Milan post-mark. Charlotte was a little frightened as she took it up, but her mind was relieved when she saw that it was merely the bill of their Italian milliner. The sum total was certainly large, but not so large as to create an important row.

"It's for our clothes, papa, for six months before we came here. The three of us can't dress for nothing you know."

"Nothing, indeed!" said he, looking at the figures, which in Milanese denominations were certainly monstrous.

"The man should have sent it to me," said Charlotte.

"I wish he had with all my heart—if you would have paid it. I see enough in it, to know that three quarters of it are for Madeline."

"She has little else to amuse her, sir," said Charlotte with true good nature.

"And I suppose he has nothing else to amuse him," said the doctor, throwing over another letter to his daughter. It was from some member of the family of Sidonia, and politely requested the father to pay a small trifle of £700, being the amount of a bill discounted in favour of Mr. Ethelbert Stanhope, and now overdue for a period of nine months.

Charlotte read the letter, slowly folded it up, and put it under the edge of the tea-tray.

"I suppose he has nothing to amuse him but discounting bills with Jews. Does he think I'll pay that?"

"I am sure he thinks no such thing," said she.

"And who does he think will pay it?"

"As far as honesty goes I suppose it won't much matter if it is never paid," said she. "I dare say he got very little of it."

"I suppose it won't much matter either," said the father, "if he goes to prison and rots there. It seems to me that that's the other alternative."

Dr. Stanhope spoke of the custom of his youth. But his daughter, though she had lived so long abroad, was much more completely versed in the ways of the English world. "If the man arrests him," said she, "he must go through the court."

It is thus, thou great family of Sidonia—it is thus that we Gentiles treat thee, when, in our extremest need, thou and thine have aided us with mountains of gold as big as lions,—and occasionally with wine-warrants and orders for dozens of dressing-cases.

"What, and become an insolvent?" said the doctor.

"He's that already," said Charlotte, wishing always to get over a difficulty.

"What a condition," said the doctor, "for the son of a clergyman of the Church of England."

"I don't see why clergymen's sons should pay their debts more than other young men," said Charlotte.

"He's had as much from me since he left school as is held sufficient for the eldest son of many a nobleman," said the angry father.

"Well, sir," said Charlotte, "give him another chance."

"What!" said the doctor, "do you mean that I am to pay that Jew?"

"Oh no! I wouldn't pay him, he must take his chance; and if the worst comes to the worst, Bertie must go abroad. But I want you to be civil to Bertie, and let him remain here as long as we stop. He has a plan in his head, that may put him on his feet after all."

"Has he any plan for following up his profession?"

"Oh, he'll do that too; but that must follow. He's thinking of getting married."

Just at that moment the door opened, and Bertie came in whistling. The doctor immediately devoted himself to his egg, and allowed Bertie to whistle himself round to his sister's side without noticing him.

Charlotte gave a sign to him with her eye, first glancing at her father, and then at the letter, the corner of which peeped out from under the tea-tray. Bertie saw and understood, and with the quiet motion of a cat abstracted the letter, and made himself acquainted with its contents. The doctor, however, had seen him, deep as he appeared to be mersed in his eggshell, and said in his harshest voice, "Well, sir, do you know that gentleman?"

"Yes, sir," said Bertie. "I have a sort of acquaintance with him, but none that can justify him in troubling you. If you will allow me, sir, I will answer this."

"At any rate I sha'n't," said the father, and then he added, after a pause, "Is it true, sir, that you owe the man £700?"

"Well," said Bertie, "I think I should be inclined to dispute the amount, if I were in a condition to pay him such of it as I really do owe him."

"Has he your bill for £700?" said the father, speaking very loudly and very angrily.

"Well, I believe he has," said Bertie; "but all the money I ever got from him was £150."

"And what became of the £550?"

"Why, sir; the commission was £100 or so, and I took the remainder in paving-stones and rocking-horses."

"Paving-stones and rocking-horses!" said the doctor, "where are they?"

"Oh, sir, I suppose they are in London somewhere—but I'll inquire if you wish for them."

"He's an idiot," said the doctor, "and it's sheer folly to waste more money on him. Nothing can save him from ruin," and so saying, the unhappy father walked out of the room.

"Would the governor like to have the paving-stones?" said Bertie to his sister.

"I'll tell you what," said she. "If you don't take care, you will find yourself loose upon the world without even a house over your head: you don't know him as well as I do. He's very angry."

Bertie stroked his big beard, sipped his tea, chatted over his misfortunes in a half comic, half serious tone, and ended by promising his sister that he would do his very best to make himself agreeable to the widow Bold. Then Charlotte followed her father to his own room and softened down his wrath, and persuaded him to say nothing more about the Jew bill discounter, at any rate for a few weeks. He even went so far as to say he would pay the £700, or at any rate settle the bill, if he saw a certainty of his son's securing for himself anything like a decent provision in life. Nothing was said openly between them about poor Eleanor: but the father and the daughter understood each other.

They all met together in the drawing-room at nine o'clock, in perfect good humour with each other; and about that hour Mrs. Bold was announced. She had never been in the house before, though she had of course called; and now she felt it strange to find herself there in her usual evening dress, entering the drawing-room of these strangers in this friendly unceremonious way, as though she had known them all her life. But in three minutes they made her at home. Charlotte tripped down stairs and took her bonnet from her, and Bertie came to relieve her from her shawl, and the signora smiled on her as she could smile when she chose to be gracious, and the old doctor shook hands with her in a kind benedictory manner that went to her heart at once, and made her feel that he must be a good man.

She had not been seated for above five minutes when the door again opened, and Mr. Slope was announced. She felt rather surprised, because she was told that nobody was to be there, and it was very evident from the manner of some of them, that Mr. Slope was unexpected. But still there was not much in it. In such invitations a bachelor or two more or less are always spoken of as nobodies, and there was no reason why Mr. Slope should not drink tea at Dr. Stanhope's as well as Eleanor herself. He, however, was very much surprised and not very much gratified at finding that his own embryo spouse made one of the party. He had come there to gratify himself by gazing on Madame Neroni's beauty, and listening to and returning her flattery: and though he had not owned as much to himself, he still felt that if he spent the evening as he had intended to do, he might probably not thereby advance his suit with Mrs. Bold.

The signora, who had no idea of a rival, received Mr. Slope with her usual marks of distinction. As he took her hand, she made some confidential communication to him in a low voice, declaring that she had a plan to communicate to him after tea, and was evidently prepared to go on with her work of reducing the chaplain to a state of captivity. Poor Mr. Slope was rather beside himself. He thought that Eleanor could not but have learnt from his demeanour that he was an admirer of her own, and he had also flattered himself that the idea was not unacceptable to her. What would she think of him if he now devoted himself to a married woman!

But Eleanor was not inclined to be severe in her criticisms on him in this respect, and felt no annoyance of any kind, when she found herself seated between Bertie and Charlotte Stanhope. She had no suspicion of Mr. Slope's intentions; she had no suspicion even of the suspicion of other people; but still she felt well pleased not to have Mr. Slope too near to her.

And she was not ill-pleased to have Bertie Stanhope near her. It was rarely indeed that he failed to make an agreeable impression on strangers. With a bishop indeed who thought much of his own dignity it was possible that he might fail, but hardly with a young and pretty woman. He possessed the tact of becoming instantly intimate with women without giving rise to any fear of impertinence. He had about him somewhat of the propensities of a tame cat. It seemed quite natural that he should be petted, caressed, and treated with familiar good nature, and that in return he should purr, and be sleek and graceful, and above all never show his claws. Like other tame cats, however, he had his claws, and sometimes made them dangerous.

When tea was over Charlotte went to the open window and declared loudly that the full harvest moon was much too beautiful to be disregarded, and called them all to look at it. To tell the truth, there was but one there who cared much about the moon's beauty, and that one was not Charlotte; but she knew how valuable an aid to her purpose the chaste goddess might become, and could easily create a little enthusiasm for the purpose of the moment. Eleanor and Bertie were soon with her. The doctor was now quiet in his arm-chair, and Mrs. Stanhope in hers, both prepared for slumber.

"Are you a Whewellite or a Brewsterite, or a t'othermanite, Mrs. Bold?" said Charlotte, who knew a little about everything, and had read about a third of each of the books to which she alluded.

"Oh!" said Eleanor; "I have not read any of the books, but I feel sure that there is one man in the moon at least, if not more."

"You don't believe in the pulpy gelatinous matter?" said Bertie.

"I heard about that," said Eleanor; "and I really think it's almost wicked to talk in such a manner. How can we argue about God's power in the other stars from the laws which he has given for our rule in this one?"

"How indeed!" said Bertie. "Why shouldn't there be a race of salamanders in Venus? and even if there be nothing but fish in Jupiter, why shouldn't the fish there be as wide awake as the men and women here?"

"That would be saying very little for them," said Charlotte. "I am for Dr. Whewell myself; for I do not think that men and women are worth being repeated in such countless worlds. There may be souls in other stars, but I doubt their having any bodies attached to them. But come, Mrs. Bold, let us put our bonnets on and walk round the close. If we are to discuss sidereal questions, we shall do so much better under the towers of the cathedral, than stuck in this narrow window."

Mrs. Bold made no objection, and a party was made to walk out. Charlotte Stanhope well knew the rule as to three being no company, and she had therefore to induce her sister to allow Mr. Slope to accompany them.

"Come, Mr. Slope," she said; "I'm sure you'll join us. We shall be in again in a quarter of an hour, Madeline."

Madeline read in her eye all that she had to say, knew her object, and as she had to depend on her sister for so many of her amusements, she felt that she must yield. It was hard to be left alone while others of her own age walked out to feel the soft influence of the bright night, but it would be harder still to be without the sort of sanction which Charlotte gave to all her flirtations and intrigues. Charlotte's eye told her that she must give up just at present for the good of the family, and so Madeline obeyed.

But Charlotte's eyes said nothing of the sort to Mr. Slope. He had no objection at all to the *tête-à-tête* with the signora, which the departure of the other three would allow him, and gently whispered to her, "I shall not leave you alone."

"Oh, yes," said she; "go—pray go, pray go, for my sake. Do not think that I am so selfish. It is understood that nobody is kept within for me. You will understand this too when you know me better. Pray join them, Mr. Slope, but when you come in speak to me for five minutes before you leave us."

Mr. Slope understood that he was to go, and he therefore joined the party in the hall. He would have had no objection at all to this arrangement, if he could have secured Mrs. Bold's arm; but this of course was out of the question. Indeed, his fate was very soon settled, for no sooner had he reached the hall-door than Miss Stanhope put her hand within his arm, and Bertie walked off with Eleanor just as naturally as though she were already his own property.

And so they sauntered forth; first they walked round the close, according to their avowed intent; then they went under the old arched gateway below St. Cuthbert's little church, and then they turned behind the grounds of the bishop's palace, and so on till they came to the bridge just at the edge of the town, from which passers-by can look down into the gardens of Hiram's hospital; and here Charlotte and Mr. Slope, who were in advance, stopped till the other two came up to them. Mr. Slope knew that the gable-ends and old brick chimneys which stood up so prettily in the moonlight, were those of Mr. Harding's late abode, and would not have stopped on such a spot, in such company, if he could have avoided it; but Miss Stanhope would not take the hint which he tried to give.

"This is a very pretty place, Mrs. Bold," said Charlotte; "by far the prettiest place near Barchester. I wonder your father gave it up."

It was a very pretty place, and now by the deceitful light of the moon looked twice larger, twice prettier, twice more antiquely picturesque than it would have done in truth-telling daylight. Who does not know the air of complex multiplicity and the mysterious interesting grace which the moon always lends to old gable buildings half surrounded, as was the hospital, by fine trees! As seen from the bridge on the night of which we are speaking, Mr. Harding's late abode did look very lovely; and though Eleanor did not grieve at her father's having left it, she felt at the moment an intense wish that he might be allowed to return.

"He is going to return to it almost immediately, is he not?" asked Bertie.

Eleanor made no immediate reply. Many such a question passes unanswered, without the notice of the questioner; but such was not now the case. They all remained silent as though expecting her to reply, and after a moment or two, Charlotte said, "I believe it is settled that Mr. Harding returns to the hospital, is it not?"

"I don't think anything about it is settled yet," said Eleanor.

"But it must be a matter of course," said Bertie; "that is, if your father wishes it; who else on earth could hold it after what has occurred?"

Eleanor quietly made her companion understand that the matter was one which she could not discuss in the present company; and then they passed on; Charlotte said she would go a short way up the hill out of the town so as to look back upon the towers of the cathedral, and as Eleanor leant upon Bertie's arm for assistance in the walk, she told him how the matter stood between her father and the bishop.

"And he," said Bertie, pointing on to Mr. Slope, "what part does he take in it?"

Eleanor explained how Mr. Slope had at first endeavoured to tyrannise over her father, but how he had latterly come round, and done all he could to talk the bishop over in Mr. Harding's favour. "But my father," said she, "is hardly inclined to trust him; they all say he is so arrogant to the old clergymen of the city."

"Take my word for it," said Bertie, "your father is right. If I am not very much mistaken, that man is both arrogant and false."

They strolled up to the top of the hill, and then returned through the fields by a footpath which leads by a small wooden bridge, or rather a plank with a rustic rail to it, over the river to the other side of the cathedral from that at which they had started. They had thus walked round the bishop's grounds, through which the river runs, and round the cathedral and adjacent fields, and it was past eleven before they reached the doctor's door.

"It is very late," said Eleanor, "it will be a shame to disturb your mother again at such an hour."

"Oh," said Charlotte, laughing, "you won't disturb mamma;

I dare say she is in bed by this time, and Madeline would be furious if you did not come in and see her. Come, Bertie, take Mrs. Bold's bonnet from her.''

They went up stairs, and found the signora alone, reading. She looked somewhat sad and melancholy, but not more so perhaps than was sufficient to excite additional interest in the bosom of Mr. Slope; and she was soon deep in whispered intercourse with that happy gentleman, who was allowed to find a resting-place on her sofa. The signora had a way of whispering that was peculiarly her own, and was exactly the reverse of that which prevails among great tragedians. The great tragedian hisses out a positive whisper, made with bated breath, and produced by inarticulated tongue-formed sounds, but yet he is audible through the whole house. The signora however used no hisses, and produced all her words in a clear silver tone, but they could only be heard by the ear into which they were poured.

Charlotte hurried and skurried about the room hither and thither, doing, or pretending to do many things; and then saying something about seeing her mother, ran up stairs. Eleanor was thus left alone with Bertie, and she hardly felt an hour fly by her. To give Bertie his due credit, he could not have played his cards better. He did not make love to her, nor sigh, nor look languishing; but he was amusing and familiar, yet respectful; and when he left Eleanor at her own door at one o'clock, which he did by the bye with the assistance of the now jealous Slope, she thought that he was one of the most agreeable men, and the Stanhopes decidedly the most agreeable family, that she had ever met.

VOLUME TWO

XX

Mr. Arabin

The Rev. Francis Arabin, fellow of Lazarus, late professor of poetry at Oxford, and present vicar of St. Ewold, in the diocese of Barchester, must now be introduced personally to the reader. And as he will fill a conspicuous place in the volume, it is desirable that he should be made to stand before the reader's eye by the aid of such portraiture as the author is able to produce.

It is to be regretted that no mental method of daguerreotype or photography has yet been discovered, by which the characters of men can be reduced to writing and put into grammatical language with an unerring precision of truthful description. How often does the novelist feel, ay, and the historian also and the biographer, that he has conceived within his mind and accurately depicted on the tablet of his brain the full character and personage of a man, and that nevertheless, when he flies to pen and ink to perpetuate the portrait, his words forsake, elude, disappoint, and play the deuce with him, till at the end of a dozen pages the man described has no more resemblance to the man conceived than the sign board at the corner of the street has to the Duke of Cambridge?

And yet such mechanical descriptive skill would hardly give more satisfaction to the reader than the skill of the photographer does to the anxious mother desirous to possess an absolute duplicate of her beloved child. The likeness is indeed true; but it is a dull, dead, unfeeling, inauspicious likeness. The face is indeed there, and those looking at it will know at once whose image it is; but the owner of the face will not be proud of the resemblance.

There is no royal road to learning; no short cut to the acquirement of any valuable art. Let photographers and daguerreotypers do what they will, and improve as they may with further skill on that which skill has already done, they will never achieve a portrait of the human face divine. Let biographers, novelists, and the rest of us groan as we may under the burdens which we so often feel too heavy for our shoulders; we must either bear them up like men, or own ourselves too weak for the work we have undertaken. There is no way of writing well and also of writing easily.

Labor omnia vincit improbus. Such should be the chosen motto of every labourer, and it may be that labour, if adequately enduring, may suffice at last to produce even some not untrue resemblance of the Rev. Francis Arabin.

Of his doings in the world, and of the sort of fame which he has achieved, enough has been already said. It has also been said that he is forty years of age, and still unmarried. He was the younger son of a country gentleman of small fortune in the north of England. At an early age he went to Winchester, and was intended by his father for New College; but though studious as a boy, he was not studious within the prescribed limits; and at the age of eighteen he left school with a character for talent, but without a scholarship. All that he had obtained, over and above the advantage of his character, was a gold medal for English verse, and hence was derived a strong presumption on the part of his friends that he was destined to add another name to the imperishable list of English poets.

From Winchester he went to Oxford, and was entered as a commoner at Balliol. Here his special career very soon commenced. He utterly eschewed the society of fast men, gave no wine parties, kept no horses, rowed no boats, joined no rows, and was the pride of his college tutor. Such at least was his career till he had taken his little go; and then he commenced a course of action which, though not less creditable to himself as a man, was hardly so much to the taste of the tutor. He became a member of a vigorous debating society, and rendered himself remarkable there for humorous energy. Though always in earnest, yet his earnestness was always droll. To be true in his ideas, unanswerable in his syllogisms, and just in his aspirations was not enough for him. He had failed, failed in his own opinion as well as that of others when others came to know him, if he could not reduce the arguments of his opponents to an absurdity, and conquer both by wit and reason. To say that his object was ever to raise a laugh, would be most untrue. He hated such common and unnecessary evidence of satisfaction on the party of his hearers. A joke that required to be laughed at was, with him, not worth uttering. He could appreciate by a keener sense than that of his ears the success of his wit, and would see in the eyes of his auditory whether or no he was understood and appreciated.

He had been a religious lad before he left school. That is, he had addicted himself to a party in religion, and having done so had received that benefit which most men do who become partisans in such a cause. We are much too apt to look at schism in our church as an unmitigated evil. Moderate schism, if there may be such a thing, at any rate calls attention to the subject, draws in supporters who would otherwise have been inattentive to the matter, and teaches men to think upon religion. How great an amount of good of this description has followed that movement in the Church of England which commenced with the publication of Froude's Remains!

As a boy young Arabin took up the cudgels on the side of the Tractarians, and at Oxford he sat for a while at the feet of the great Newman. To this cause he lent all his faculties. For it he concocted verses, for it he made speeches, for it he scintillated the brightest sparks of his quiet wit. For it he ate and drank and dressed, and had his being. In due process of time he took his degree, and wrote himself B.A., but he did not do so with any remarkable amount of academical éclat. He had occupied himself too much with high church matters, and the polemics, politics, and outward demonstrations usually concurrent with high churchmanship, to devote himself with sufficient vigour to the acquisition of a double first. He was not a double first, nor even a first class man; but he revenged himself on the university by putting firsts and double firsts out of fashion for the year, and laughing down a species of pedantry which at the age of twenty-three leaves no room in a man's mind for graver subjects than conic sections or Greek accents.

Greek accents, however, and conic sections were esteemed necessaries at Balliol, and there was no admittance there for Mr. Arabin within the list of its fellows. Lazarus, however, the richest and the most comfortable abode of Oxford dons, opened its bosom to the young champion of a church militant. Mr. Arabin was ordained, and became a fellow soon after taking his degree, and shortly after that was chosen professor of poetry.

And now came the moment of his great danger. After many mental struggles, and an agony of doubt which may be well surmised, the great prophet of the Tractarians confessed himself a Roman Catholic. Mr. Newman left the Church of England, and with him carried many a waverer. He did not carry off Mr. Arabin, but the escape which that gentlaman had was a very narrow one. He left Oxford for a while that he might meditate in complete peace on the step which appeared to him to be all but unavoidable, and shut himself up in a little village on the sea-shore of one of our remotest counties, that he might learn by communing with his own soul whether or no he could with a safe conscience remain within the pale of his mother church.

Things would have gone badly with him there had he been left entirely to himself. Every thing was against him: all his worldly interests required him to remain a Protestant; and he looked on his worldly interests as a legion of foes, to get the better of whom was a point of extremest honour. In his then state of ecstatic agony such a conquest would have cost him little; he could easily have thrown away all his livelihood; but it cost him much to get over the idea that by choosing the Church of England he should be open in his own mind to the charge that he had been led to such a choice by unworthy motives. Then his heart was against him: he loved with a strong and eager love the man who had hitherto been his guide, and yearned to follow his footsteps. His tastes were against him; the ceremonies and pomps of the Church of Rome, their august feasts and solemn fasts, invited his imagination and pleased his eye. His flesh was against him: how great an aid would it be to a poor, weak, wavering man to be constrained to high moral duties, self-denial, obedience, and chastity by laws which were certain in their enactments, and not to be broken without loud, palpable, unmistakable sin! Then his faith was against him: he required to believe so much; panted so eagerly to give signs of his belief; deemed it so insufficient to wash himself simply in the waters of Jordan; that some great deed, such as that of forsaking everything for a true church, had for him allurements almost past withstanding.

Mr. Arabin was at this time a very young man, and when he left Oxford for his far retreat was much too confident in his powers of fence, and too apt to look down on the ordinary sense of ordinary people, to expect aid in the battle that he had to fight from any chance inhabitants of the spot which he had selected. But Providence was good to him; and there, in that all but desolate place, on the storm-beat shore of that distant sea, he met one who gradually calmed his mind, quieted his imagination, and taught him something of a Christian's duty. When Mr. Arabin left Oxford, he was inclined to look upon the rural clergymen of most English parishes almost with contempt. It was his ambition, should he remain within the fold of their church, to do somewhat towards redeeming and rectifying their inferiority, and to assist in infusing energy and faith into the hearts of Christian ministers, who were, as he thought, too often satisfied to go through life without much show of either.

And yet it was from such a one that Mr. Arabin in his extremest need received that aid which he so much required. It was from the poor curate of a small Cornish parish that he first learnt to know that the highest laws for the governance of a Christian's duty must act from within and not from without; that no man can become a serviceable servant solely by obedience to written edicts; and that the safety which he was about to seek within the gates of Rome was no other than the selfish freedom from personal danger which the bad soldier attempts to gain who counterfeits illness on the eve of battle.

Mr. Arabin returned to Oxford a humbler but a better and a happier man; and from that time forth he put his shoulder to the wheel as a clergyman of the Church for which he had been educated. The intercourse of those among whom he familiarly lived kept him staunch to the principles of that system of the Church to which he had always belonged. Since his severance from Mr. Newman, no one had had so strong an influence over him as the head of his college. During the time of his expected apostacy, Dr. Gwynne had not felt much predisposition in favour of the young fellow. Though a High Churchman himself within moderate limits, Dr. Gwynne felt no sympathy with men who could not satisfy their faiths with the Thirty-nine Articles. He regarded the enthusiasm of such as Newman as a state of mind more nearly allied to madness than to religion; and when he saw it evinced by very young men, was inclined to attribute a good deal of it to vanity. Dr. Gwynne himself, though a religious man, was also a thoroughly practical man of the world, and he regarded with no favourable eye the tenets of any one who looked on the two things as incompatible. When he found that Mr. Arabin was a half Roman, he began to regret all he had done towards bestowing a fellowship on so unworthy a recipient; and when again he learnt that Mr. Arabin would probably complete his journey to Rome, he regarded with some satisfaction the fact that in such case the fellowship would be again vacant.

When, however, Mr. Arabin returned and professed himself a confirmed Protestant, the master of Lazarus again opened his arms to him, and gradually he became the pet of the college. For some little time he was saturnine, silent, and unwilling to take

any prominent part in university broils; but gradually his mind
recovered, or rather made its tone, and he became known as a
man always ready at a moment's notice to take up the cudgels in
opposition to anything that savoured of an evangelical bearing.
He was great in sermons, great on platforms, great at after dinner
conversations, and always pleasant as well as great. He took
delight in elections, served on committees, opposed tooth and
nail all projects of university reform, and talked jovially over his
glass of port of the ruin to be anticipated by the Church, and of
the sacrilege daily committed by the Whigs. The ordeal through
which he had gone, in resisting the blandishments of the lady of
Rome, had certainly done much towards the strengthening of his
character. Although in small and outward matters he was self-
confident enough, nevertheless in things affecting the inner man
he aimed at a humility of spirit which would never have been
attractive to him but for that visit to the coast of Cornwall. This
visit he now repeated every year.

Such is an interior view of Mr. Arabin at the time when he
accepted the living of St. Ewold. Exteriorly, he was not a
remarkable person. He was above the middle height, well made,
and very active. His hair which had been jet black, was now
tinged with grey, but his face bore no sign of years. It would
perhaps be wrong to say that he was handsome, but his face was,
nevertheless, pleasant to look upon. The cheek bones were rather
too high for beauty, and the formation of the forehead too
massive and heavy: but the eyes, nose, and mouth were perfect.
There was a continual play of lambent fire about his eyes, which
gave promise of either pathos or humour whenever he essayed to
speak, and that promise was rarely broken. There was a gentle
play about his mouth which declared that his wit never descended to sarcasm, and that there was no ill-nature in his
repartee.

Mr. Arabin was a popular man among women, but more so
as a general than a special favourite. Living as a fellow at
Oxford, marriage with him had been out of the question, and it
may be doubted whether he had ever allowed his heart to be
touched. Though belonging to a Church in which celibacy is not
the required lot of its ministers, he had come to regard himself as
one of those clergymen to whom to be a bachelor is almost a
necessity. He had never looked for parochial duty, and his career
at Oxford was utterly incompatible with such domestic joys as a
wife and nursery. He looked on women, therefore, in the same
light that one sees them regarded by many Romish priests. He

liked to have near him that which was pretty and amusing, but women generally were little more to him than children. He talked to them without putting out all his powers, and listened to them without any idea that what he should hear from them could either actuate his conduct or influence his opinion.

Such was Mr. Arabin, the new vicar of St. Ewold, who is going to stay with the Grantlys, at Plumstead Episcopi.

Mr. Arabin reached Plumstead the day before Mr. Harding and Eleanor, and the Grantly family were thus enabled to make his acquaintance and discuss his qualifications before the arrival of the other guests. Griselda was surprised to find that he looked so young; but she told Florinda her younger sister, when they had retired for the night, that he did not talk at all like a young man: and she decided with the authority that seventeen has over sixteen, that he was not at all nice, although his eyes were lovely. As usual, sixteen implicitly acceded to the dictum of seventeen in such a matter, and said that he certainly was not nice. They then branched off on the relative merits of other clerical bachelors in the vicinity, and both determined without any feeling of jealousy between them that a certain Rev. Augustus Green was by many·degrees the most estimable of the lot. The gentleman in question had certainly much in his favour, as, having a comfortable allowance from his father, he could devote the whole proceeds of his curacy to violet gloves and unexceptionable neck ties. Having thus fixedly resolved that the new comer had nothing about him to shake the pre-eminence of the exalted Green, the two girls went to sleep in each other's arms, contented with themselves and the world.

Mrs. Grantly at first sight came to much the same conclusion about her husband's favourite as her daughers had done, though, in seeking to measure his relative value, she did not compare him to Mr. Green; indeed, she made no comparison by name between him and any one else; but she remarked to her husband that one person's swans were very often another person's geese, thereby clearly showing that Mr. Arabin had not yet proved his qualifications in swanhood to her satisfaction.

"Well, Susan," said he, rather offended at hearing his friend spoken of so disrespectfully, "if you take Mr. Arabin for a goose, I cannot say that I think very highly of your discrimination."

"A goose! No of course, he's not a goose. I've no doubt he's a very clever man. But you're so matter-of-fact, archdeacon, when it suits your purpose, that one can't trust oneself to any *façon de parler.* I've no doubt Mr. Arabin is a very valuable man—at Oxford, and that he'll be a good vicar at St. Ewold. All I mean is, that having passed one evening with him, I don't find him to be absolutely a paragon. In the first place, if I am not mistaken, he is a little inclined to be conceited."

"Of all the men that I know intimately," said the archdeacon, "Arabin is, in my opinion, the most free from any taint of self-conceit. His fault is that he's too diffident."

"Perhaps so," said the lady; "only I must own I did not find it out this evening."

Nothing further was said about him. Dr. Grantly thought that his wife was abusing Mr. Arabin merely because he had praised him; and Mrs. Grantly knew that it was useless arguing for or against any person in favour of or in opposition to whom the archdeacon had already pronounced a strong opinion.

In truth they were both right. Mr. Arabin was a diffident man in social intercourse with those whom he did not intimately know; when placed in situations which it was his business to fill, and discussing matters with which it was his duty to be conversant, Mr. Arabin was from habit brazen-faced enough. When standing on a platform in Exeter Hall, no man would be less mazed than he by the eyes of the crowd before him; for such was the work which his profession had called on him to perform; but he shrank from a strong expression of opinion in general society, and his doing so not uncommonly made it appear that he considered the company not worth the trouble of his energy. He was averse to dictate when the place did not seem to him to justify dictation; and as those subjects on which people wished to hear him speak were such as he was accustomed to treat with decision, he generally shunned the traps there were laid to allure him into discussion, and, by doing so, not unfrequently subjected himself to such charges as those brought against him by Mrs. Grantly.

Mr. Arabin, as he sat at his open window, enjoying the delicious moonlight and gazing at the grey towers of the church, which stood almost within the rectory grounds, little dreamed that he was the subject of so many friendly or unfriendly criticisms. Considering how much we are all given to discuss the characters of others, and discuss them often not in the strictest spirit of charity, it is singular how little we are inclined to think that others can speak ill-naturedly of us, and how angry and hurt we are when proof reaches us that they have done so. It is hardly too much to say that we all of us occasionally speak of our dearest friends in a manner in which those dearest friends would very little like to hear themselves mentioned; and that we nevertheless expect that our dearest friends shall invariably speak of us as though they were blind to all our faults, but keenly alive to every shade of our virtues.

It did not occur to Mr. Arabin that he was spoken of at all. It seemed to him, when he compared himself with his host, that he was a person of so little consequence to any, that he was worth no one's words or thoughts. He was utterly alone in the world as regarded domestic ties and those inner familiar relations which are hardly possible between others than husbands and wives, parents and children, or brothers and sisters. He had often discussed with himself the necessity of such bonds for a man's happiness in this world, and had generally satisfied himself with the answer that happiness in this world is not a necessity. Herein he deceived himself, or rather tried to do so. He, like others, yearned for the enjoyment of whatever he saw enjoyable; and though he attempted, with the modern stoicism of so many Christians, to make himself believe that joy and sorrow were matters which here should be held as perfectly indifferent, these things were not indifferent to him. He was tired of his Oxford rooms and his college life. He regarded the wife and children of his friend with something like envy; he all but coveted the pleasant drawing-room, with its pretty windows opening on to lawns and flowerbeds, the apparel of the comfortable house, and—above all—the air of home which encompassed it all.

It will be said that no time can have been so fitted for such desires on his part as this, when he had just possessed himself of a country parish, of a living among fields and gardens, of a house which a wife would grace. It is true there was a difference between the opulence of Plumstead and the modest economy of St. Ewold; but surely Mr. Arabin was not a man to sigh after wealth! Of all men, his friends would have unanimously declared he was the last to do so. But how little our friends know us! In his period of stoical rejection of this world's happiness, he had cast from him as utter dross all anxiety as to fortune. He had, as it were, proclaimed himself to be indifferent to promotion, and those who chiefly admired his talents, and would mainly have exerted themselves to secure to them their deserved reward, had taken him at his word. And now, if the truth must out, he felt himself disappointed—disappointed not by them but by himself. The daydream of his youth was over, and at the age of forty he felt that he was not fit to work in the spirit of an apostle. He had mistaken himself, and learned his mistake when it was past remedy. He had professed himself indifferent to mitres and diaconal residences, to rich livings and pleasant glebes, and now he had to own to himself that he was sighing for the good things of other men, on whom in his pride he had ventured to look down.

Not for wealth, in its vulgar sense, had he ever sighed; not for the enjoyment of rich things had he ever longed; but for the allotted share of worldly bliss, which a wife, and children, and happy home could give him, for that usual amount of comfort which he had ventured to reject as unnecessary for him, he did now feel that he would have been wiser to have searched.

He knew that his talents, his position, and his friends would have won for him promotion, had he put himself in the way of winning it. Instead of doing so, he had allowed himself to be persuaded to accept a living which would give him an income of some £300 a year, should he, by marrying, throw up his fellowship. Such, at the age of forty, was the worldly result of labour, which the world had chosen to regard as successful. The world also thought that Mr. Arabin was, in his own estimation, sufficiently paid. Alas! alas! the world was mistaken; and Mr. Arabin was beginning to ascertain that such was the case.

And here, may I beg the reader not to be hard in his judgment upon this man. Is not the state at which he has arrived, the natural result of efforts to reach that which is not the condition of humanity? Is not modern stoicism, built though it be on Christianity, as great an outrage on human nature as was the stoicism of the ancients? The philosophy of Zeno was built on true laws, but on true laws misunderstood, and therefore misapplied. It is the same with our Stoics here, who would teach us that wealth and worldly comfort and happiness on earth are not worth the search. Alas, for a doctrine which can find no believing pupils and no true teachers!

The case of Mr. Arabin was the more singular, as he belonged to a branch of the Church of England well inclined to regard its temporalities with avowed favour, and had habitually lived with men who were accustomed to much worldly comfort. But such was his idiosyncrasy, that these very facts had produced within him, in early life, a state of mind that was not natural to him. He was content to be a High Churchman, if he could be so on principles of his own, and could strike out a course showing a marked difference from those with whom he consorted. He was ready to be a partisan as long as he was allowed to have a course of action and of thought unlike that of his party. His party had indulged him, and he began to feel that his party was right and himself wrong, just when such a conviction was too late to be of service to him. He discovered, when such discovery was no longer serviceable, that it *would* have been worth his while to have worked for the usual pay assigned to work in this world, and have earned a wife and children, with a carriage for them to sit in; to have earned a pleasant dining-room, in which his friends could drink his wine, and the power of walking up the High Street of his country town, with the knowledge that all its tradesmen would have gladly welcomed him within their doors. Other men arrived at those convictions in their start in life, and so worked up to them. To him they had come when they were too late to be of use.

It has been said that Mr. Arabin was a man of pleasantry; and it may be thought that such a state of mind as that described, would be antagonistic to humour. But surely such is not the case. Wit is the outward mental casing of the man, and has no more to do with the inner mind of thoughts and feelings than have the rich brocaded garments of the priest at the altar with the asceticism of the anchorite below them, whose skin is tormented with sackcloth, and whose body is half flayed with rods. Nay, will not such a one often rejoice more than any other in the rich show of his outer apparel? Will it not be food for his pride to feel that he groans inwardly, while he shines outwardly? So it is with the mental efforts which men make. Those which they show forth daily to the world are often the opposites of the inner workings of the spirit.

In the archdeacon's drawing-room. Mr. Arabin had sparkled with his usual unaffected brilliancy, but when he retired to his bed-room, he sat there sad, at his open window, repining within himself that he also had no wife, no bairns, no soft sward of lawn duly mown for him to lie on, no herd of attendant curates, no bowings from the banker's clerks, no rich rectory. That apostleship that he had thought of had evaded his grasp, and he was now only vicar of St. Ewold's, with a taste for a mitre. Truly he had fallen between two stools.

XXI

St. Ewold's Parsonage

When Mr. Harding and Mrs. Bold reached the rectory on the
following morning, the archdeacon and his friend were at St.
Ewold's. They had gone over that the new vicar might inspect
his church, and be introduced to the squire, and were not expected back before dinner. Mr. Harding rambled out by himself,
and strolled, as was his wont at Plumstead, about the lawn and
round the church; and as he did so, the two sisters naturally fell
into conversation about Barchester.

There was not much sisterly confidence between them. Mrs.
Grantly was ten years older than Eleanor, and had been married
while Eleanor was yet a child. They had never, therefore, poured
into each other's ears their hopes and loves; and now that one
was a wife and the other a widow, it was not probable that they
would begin to do so. They lived too much asunder to be able to
fall into that kind of intercourse which makes confidence between sisters almost a necessity; and, moreover, that which is
so easy at eighteen is often very difficult at twenty-eight. Mrs.
Grantly knew this, and did not, therefore, expect confidence
from her sister; and yet she longed to ask her whether in real
truth Mr. Slope was agreeable to her.

It was by no means difficult to turn the conversation to Mr.
Slope. That gentleman had become so famous at Barchester, had
so much to do with all clergymen connected with the city, and
was so specially concerned in the affairs of Mr. Harding, that it
would have been odd if Mr. Harding's daughters had not talked
about him. Mrs. Grantly was soon abusing him, which she did
with her whole heart; and Mrs. Bold was nearly as eager to
defend him. She positively disliked the man, would have been
delighted to learn that he had taken himself off so that she should

never see him again, had indeed almost a fear of him, and yet she constantly found herself taking his part. The abuse of other people, and abuse of a nature that she felt to be unjust, imposed this necessity on her, and at last made Mr. Slope's defence an habitual course of argument with her.

From Mr. Slope the conversation turned to the Stanhopes, and Mrs. Grantly was listening with some interest to Eleanor's account of the family, when it dropped out that Mr. Slope made one of the party.

"What!" said the lady of the rectory, "was Mr. Slope there too?"

Eleanor merely replied that such had been the case.

"Why, Eleanor, he must be very fond of you, I think; he seems to follow you everywhere."

Even this did not open Eleanor's eyes. She merely laughed, and said that she imagined Mr. Slope found other attraction at Dr. Stanhope's. And so they parted. Mrs. Grantly felt quite convinced that the odious match would take place; and Mrs. Bold as convinced that that unfortunate chaplain, disagreeable as he must be allowed to be, was more sinned against than sinning.

The archdeacon of course heard before dinner that Eleanor had remained the day before in Barchester with the view of meeting Mr. Slope, and that she had so met him. He remembered how she had positively stated that there were to be no guests at the Stanhopes, and he did not hesitate to accuse her of deceit. Moreover, the fact, or rather presumed fact, of her being deceitful on such a matter, spoke but too plainly in evidence against her as to her imputed crime of receiving Mr. Slope as a lover.

"I am afraid that anything we can do will be too late," said the archdeacon. "I own I am fairly surprised. I never liked your sister's taste with regard to men; but still I did not give her credit for—ugh!"

"And so soon, too," said Mrs. Grantly, who thought more, perhaps, of her sister's indecorum in having a lover before she had put off her weeds, than her bad taste in having such a lover as Mr. Slope.

"Well, my dear, I shall be sorry to be harsh, or to do anything that can hurt your father; but, positively, neither that man nor his wife shall come within my doors."

Mrs. Grantly sighed, and then attempted to console herself and her lord by remarking that, after all, the thing was not accomplished yet. Now that Eleanor was at Plumstead, much might be done to wean her from her fatal passion. Poor Eleanor!

The evening passed off without anything to make it remarkable. Mr. Arabin discussed the parish of St. Ewold with the archdeacon, and Mrs. Grantly and Mr. Harding, who knew the personages of the parish, joined in. Eleanor also knew them, but she said little. Mr. Arabin did not apparently take much notice of her, and she was not in a humour to receive at that time with any special grace any special favourite of her brother-in-law. Her first idea on reaching her bedroom was that a much pleasanter family party might be met at Dr. Stanhope's than at the rectory. She began to think that she was getting tired of clergymen and their respectable humdrum wearisome mode of living, and that after all, people in the outer world, who had lived in Italy, London, or elsewhere, need not necessarily be regarded as atrocious and abominable. The Stanhopes, she had thought, were a giddy, thoughtless, extravagant set of people; but she had seen nothing wrong about them, and had, on the other hand, found that they thoroughly knew how to make their house agreeable. It was a thousand pities, she thought, that the archdeacon should not have a little of the same *savoir vivre*. Mr. Arabin, as we have said, did not apparently take much notice of her; but yet he did not go to bed without feeling that he had been in company with a very pretty woman; and as is the case with most bachelors, and some married men, regarded the prospect of his month's visit at Plumstead in a pleasanter light, when he learnt that a very pretty woman was to share it with him.

Before they all retired it was settled that the whole party should drive over on the following day to inspect the parsonage at St. Ewold. The three clergymen were to discuss dilapidations, and the two ladies were to lend their assistance in suggesting such changes as might be necessary for a bachelor's abode. Accordingly, soon after breakfast, the carriage was at the door. There was only room for four inside, and the archdeacon got upon the box. Eleanor found herself opposite to Mr. Arabin, and was, therefore, in a manner forced into conversation with him. They were soon on comfortable terms together; and had she thought about it, she would have thought that, in spite of his black cloth, Mr. Arabin would not have been a bad addition to the Stanhope family party.

Now that the archdeacon was away, they could all trifle. Mr. Harding began by telling them in the most innocent manner

imaginable an old legend about Mr. Arabin's new parish. There
was, he said, in days of yore, an illustrious priestess of St.
Ewold, famed through the whole country for curing all manner
of diseases. She had a well, as all priestesses have ever had,
which well was extant to this day, and shared in the minds of
many of the people the sanctity which belonged to the consecrated ground of the parish church. Mr. Arabin declared that he
should look on such tenets on the part of his parishioners as
anything but orthodox. And Mrs. Grantly replied that she so
entirely disagreed with him as to think that no parish was in a
proper state that had not its priestess as well as its priest. "The
duties are never well done," said she, "unless they are so
divided."

"I suppose, papa," said Eleanor, "that in the olden times
the priestess bore all the sway herself. Mr. Arabin, perhaps,
thinks that such might be too much the case now if a sacred lady
were admitted within the parish."

"I think, at any rate," said he, "that it is safer to run no
such risk. No priestly pride has ever exceeded that of sacerdotal
females. A very lowly curate I might, perhaps, essay to rule; but
a curatess would be sure to get the better of me."

"There are certainly examples of such accidents happening,"
said Mrs. Grantly. "They do say that there is a priestess at
Barchester who is very imperious in all things touching the altar.
Perhaps the fear of such a fate as that is before your eyes."

When they were joined by the archdeacon on the gravel
before the vicarage, they descended again to grave dulness. Not
that Archdeacon Grantly was a dull man; but his frolic humours
were of a cumbrous kind; and his wit, when he was witty, did
not generally extend itself to his auditory. On the present occasion he was soon making speeches about wounded roofs and
walls, which he declared to be in want of some surgeon's art.
There was not a partition that he did not tap, nor a block of
chimneys that he did not narrowly examine; all water-pipes,
flues, cisterns, and sewers underwent an investigation; and he
even descended, in the care of his friend, so far as to bore sundry
boards in the floors with a bradawl.

Mr. Arabin accompanied him through the rooms, trying to
look wise in such domestic matters, and the other three also
followed. Mrs. Grantly showed that she had not herself been
priestess of a parish twenty years for nothing, and examined the
bells and window panes in a very knowing way.

"You will, at any rate, have a beautiful prospect out of

your own window, if this is to be your private sanctum," said Eleanor. She was standing at the lattice of a little room up stairs, from which the view certainly was very lovely. It was from the back of the vicarage, and there was nothing to interrupt the eye between the house and the glorious grey pile of the cathedral. The intermediate ground, however, was beautifully studded with timber. In the immediate foreground ran the little river which afterwards skirted the city; and, just to the right of the cathedral, the pointed gables and chimneys of Hiram's hospital peeped out of the elms which encompass it.

"Yes," said he, joining her. "I shall have a beautifully complete view of my adversaries. I shall sit down before the hostile town, and fire away at them at a very pleasant distance. I shall just be able to lodge a shot in the hospital, should the enemy ever get possession of it; and as for the palace, I have it within full range."

"I never saw anything like you clergymen," said Eleanor; "you are always thinking of fighting each other."

"Either that," said he, "or else supporting each other. The pity is that we cannot do the one without the other. But are we not here to fight? Is not ours a church militant? What is all our work but fighting, and hard fighting, if it be well done?"

"But not with each other."

"That's as it may be. The same complaint which you make of me for battling with another clergyman of our own church, the Mohammedan would make against me for battling with the error of a priest of Rome. Yet, surely, you would not be inclined to say that I should be wrong to do battle with such as him. A pagan, too, with his multiplicity of gods, would think it equally odd that the Christian and the Mohammedan should disagree."

"Ah! but you wage your wars about trifles so bitterly."

"Wars about trifles," said he, "are always bitter, especially among neighbours. When the differences are great, and the parties comparative strangers, men quarrel with courtesy. What combatants are ever so eager as two brothers?"

"But do not such contentions bring scandal on the church?"

"More scandal would fall on the church if there were no such contentions. We have but one way to avoid them—that of acknowledging a common head of our church, whose word on all points of doctrine shall be authoritative. Such a termination of our difficulties is alluring enough. It has charms which are irresistible to many, and all but irresistible, I own, to me."

"You speak now of the Church of Rome?" said Eleanor.

"No," said he, "not necessarily of the Church of Rome; but of *a* church with *a* head. Had it pleased God to vouchsafe to us such a church our path would have been easy. But easy paths have not been thought good for us." He paused and stood silent for a while, thinking of the time when he had so nearly sacrificed all he had, his powers of mind, his free agency, the fresh running waters of his mind's fountain, his very inner self, for an easy path in which no fighting would be needed; and then he continued:—"What you say is partly true; our contentions do bring on us some scandal. The outer world, though it constantly reviles us for our human infirmities, and throws in our teeth the fact that being clergymen we are still no more than men, demands of us that we should do our work with godlike perfection. There is nothing godlike about us: we differ from each other with the acerbity common to man—we triumph over each other with human frailty—we allow differences on subjects of divine origin to produce among us antipathies and enmities which are anything but divine. This is all true. But what would you have in place of it? There is no infallible head for a church on earth. This dream of believing man has been tried, and we see in Italy and in Spain what has come of it. Grant that there are and have been no bickerings within the pale of the Pope's Church. Such an assumption would be utterly untrue; but let us grant it, and then let us say which church has incurred the heavier scandals."

There was a quiet earnestness about Mr. Arabin, as he half acknowledged and half defended himself from the charge brought against him, which surprised Eleanor. She had been used all her life to listen to clerical discussion; but the points at issue between the disputants had so seldom been of more than temporal significance as to have left on her mind no feeling of reverence for such subjects. There had always been a hard worldly leaven of the love either of income or of power in the strains she had heard; there had been no panting for the truth; no aspirations after religious purity. It had always been taken for granted by those around her that they were indubitably right, that there was no ground for doubt, that the hard uphill work of ascertaining what the duty of a clergyman should be had been already accomplished in full; and that what remained for an active militant parson to do, was to hold his own against all comers. Her father, it is true, was an exception to this; but then he was so essentially anti-militant in all things, that she classed him in her own mind apart from all others. She had never argued the matter within herself, or considered whether this common tone was or was not faulty; but she was sick of it without knowing that she was so. And now she found to her surprise and not without a certain pleasurable excitement, that this newcomer among them spoke in a manner very different from that to which she was accustomed.

"It is so easy to condemn," said he, continuing the thread of his thoughts. "I know no life that must be so delicious as that of a writer for newspapers, or a leading member of the opposition—to thunder forth accusations against men in power; show up the worst side of everything that is produced; to pick holes in every coat; to be indignant, sarcastic, jocose, moral, or supercilious; to damn with faint praise, or crush with open calumny! What can be so easy as this when the critic has to be responsible for nothing? You condemn what I do; but put yourself in my position and do the reverse, and then see if I cannot condemn you."

"Oh! Mr. Arabin, I do not condemn you."

"Pardon me, you do, Mrs. Bold—you as one of the world; you are now composing your leading article, and well and bitterly you do it. 'Let dogs delight to bark and bite'; you fitly begin with an elegant quotation; 'but if we are to have a church at all, in heaven's name let the pastors who preside over it keep their hands from each other's throats. Lawyers can live without befouling each other's names; doctors do not fight duels. Why is it that clergymen alone should indulge themselves in such unrestrained liberty of abuse against each other?' and so you go on reviling us for our ungodly quarrels, our sectarian propensities, and scandalous differences. It will, however, give you no trouble to write another article next week in which we, or some of us, shall be twitted with an unseemly apathy in matters of our vocation. It will not fall on you to reconcile the discrepancy; your readers will never ask you how the poor parson is to be urgent in season and out of season, and yet never come in contact with men who think widely differently from him. You, when you condemn this foreign treaty, or that official arrangement, will have to incur no blame for the graver faults of any different measure. It is so easy to condemn; and so pleasant too; for eulogy charms no listeners as detraction does."

Eleanor only half followed him in his raillery, but she caught his meaning. "I know I ought to apologise for presuming to criticise you," she said; "but I was thinking with sorrow of the ill-will that has lately come among us at Barchester, and I spoke more freely than I should have done."

"Peace on earth and good-will among men, are, like heaven, promises for the future"; said he, following rather his own thoughts than hers. "When prophecy is accomplished there will no longer be any need for clergymen."

Here they were interrupted by the archdeacon, whose voice was heard from the cellar shouting to the vicar.

"Arabin, Arabin,"—and then turning to his wife, who was apparently at his elbow—"where has he gone to? This cellar is perfectly abominable. It would be murder to put a bottle of wine into it till it has been roofed, walled, and floored. How on earth old Goodenough ever got on with it, I cannot guess. But then Goodenough never had a glass of wine that any man could drink."

"What is it, archdeacon?" said the vicar, running down stairs, and leaving Eleanor above to her meditations.

"This cellar must be roofed, walled, and floored," repeated the archdeacon. "Now mind what I say, and don't let the architect persuade you that it will do; half of these fellows know nothing about wine. This place as it is now would be damp and cold in winter, and hot and muggy in summer. I wouldn't give a straw for the best wine that ever was vinted, after it had lain here a couple of years."

Mr. Arabin assented, and promised that the cellar should be reconstructed according to the archdeacon's receipt.

"And, Arabin, look here; was such an attempt at a kitchen grate ever seen?"

"The grate is really very bad," said Mrs. Grantly; "I am sure the priestess won't approve of it, when she is brought home to the scene of her future duties. Really, Mr. Arabin, no priestess accustomed to such an excellent well as that above could put up with such a grate as this."

"If there must be a priestess at St. Ewold's at all, Mrs. Grantly, I think we will leave her to her well, and not call down her divine wrath on any of the imperfections rising from our human poverty. However, I own I am amenable to the attractions of a well-cooked dinner, and the grate shall certainly be changed."

By this time the archdeacon had again ascended, and was now in the dining-room. "Arabin," said he, speaking in his usual loud clear voice, and with that tone of dictation which was so common to him; "you must positively alter this dining-room, that is, remodel it altogether; look here, it is just sixteen feet by fifteen; did anybody ever hear of a dining-room of such proportions!" and the archdeacon stepped the room long-ways and cross-ways with ponderous steps, as though a certain amount of ecclesiatical dignity could be imparted even to such an occupation as that by the manner of doing it. "Barely sixteen; you may call it a square."

"It would do very well for a round table," suggested the ex-warden.

Now there was something peculiarly unorthodox in the archdeacon's estimation in the idea of a round table. He had always been accustomed to a goodly board of decent length, comfortably elongating itself according to the number of the guests, nearly black with perpetual rubbing, and as bright as a mirror. Now round dinner tables are generally of oak, or else of such new construction as not to have acquired the peculiar hue which was so pleasing to him. He connected them with what he called the nasty new-fangled method of leaving a cloth on the table, as though to warn people that they were not to sit long. In his eyes there was something democratic and parvenue in a round table. He imagined that dissenters and calico-printers chiefly used them, and perhaps a few literary lions more conspicuous for their wit than their gentility. He was a little flurried at the idea of such an article being introduced into the diocese by a protégé of his own, and at the instigation of his father-in-law.

"A round dinner-table," said he, with some heat, "is the most abominable article of furniture that ever was invented. I hope that Arabin has more taste than to allow such a thing in his house."

Poor Mr. Harding felt himself completely snubbed, and of course said nothing further; but Mr. Arabin, who had yielded submissively in the small matters of the cellar and kitchen grate, found himself obliged to oppose reforms which might be of a nature too expensive for his pocket.

"But it seems to me, archdeacon, that I can't very well lengthen the room without pulling down the wall, and if I pull down the wall, I must build it up again; then if I throw out a bow on this side, I must do the same on the other, then if I do it for the ground floor, I must carry it up to the floor above. That will be putting a new front to the house, and will cost, I suppose, a couple of hundred pounds. The ecclesiastical commissioners will hardly assist me when they hear that my grievance consists in having a dining-room only sixteen feet long."

The archdeacon proceeded to explain that nothing would be easier than adding six feet to the front of the dining-room, without touching any other in the house. Such irregularities of construction in small country houses were, he said, rather graceful than otherwise, and he offered to pay for the whole thing out of his own pocket if it cost more than forty pounds. Mr. Arabin, however, was firm, and, although the archdeacon fussed and fumed about it, would not give way.

Forty pounds, he said, was a matter of serious moment to him, and his friends, if under such circumstances they would be good-natured enough to come to him at all, must put up with the misery of a square room. He was willing to compromise matters by disclaiming any intention of having a round table.

"But," said Mrs. Grantly, "what if the priestess insists on having both the rooms enlarged?"

"The priestess in that case must do it for herself, Mrs. Grantly."

"I have no doubt she will be well able to do so," replied the lady; "to do that and many more wonderful things. I am quite sure that the priestess of St. Ewold, when she does come, won't come empty-handed."

Mr. Arabin, however, did not appear well inclined to enter into speculative expenses on such a chance as this, and therefore, any material alterations in the house, the cost of which could not fairly be made to lie at the door either of the ecclesiastical commissioners or of the estate of the late incumbent, were tabooed. With this essential exception, the archdeacon ordered, suggested, and carried all points before him in a manner very much to his own satisfaction. A close observer, had there been one there, might have seen that his wife had been quite as useful in the matter as himself. No one knew better than Mrs. Grantly the appurtenances necessary to a comfortable house. She did not, however, think it necessary to lay claim to any of the glory which her lord and master was so ready to appropriate as his own.

Having gone through their work effectually and systematically, the party returned to Plumstead well satisfied with their expedition.

XXII

The Thornes of Ullathorne

On the following Sunday Mr. Arabin was to read himself in at his new church. It was agreed at the rectory that the archdeacon should go over with him and assist at the reading-desk, and that Mr. Harding should take the archdeacon's duty at Plumstead Church. Mrs. Grantly had her school and her buns to attend to, and professed that she could not be spared; but Mrs. Bold was to accompany them. It was further agreed also, that they would lunch at the squire's house, and return home after the afternoon service.

Wilfred Thorne, Esq., of Ullathorne, was the squire of St. Ewold's; or rather the squire of Ullathorne; for the domain of the modern landlord was of wider notoriety than the fame of the ancient saint. He was a fair specimen of what that race has come to in our days, which a century ago was, as we are told, fairly represented by Squire Western. If that representation be a true one, few classes of men can have made faster strides in improvement. Mr. Thorne, however, was a man possessed of quite a sufficient number of foibles to lay him open to much ridicule. He was still a bachelor, being about fifty, and was not a little proud of his person. When living at home at Ullathorne there was not much room for such pride, and there therefore he always looked like a gentleman, and like that which he certainly was, the first man in his parish. But during the month or six weeks which he annually spent in London, he tried so hard to look like a great man there also, which he certainly was not, that he was put down as a fool by many at his club. He was a man of considerable literary attainment in a certain way and on certain subjects. His favourite authors were Montaigne and Burton, and he knew more perhaps than any other man in his own county,

346

and the next to it, of the English essayists of the two last centuries. He possessed complete sets of the *Idler,* the *Spectator,* the *Tatler,* the *Guardian,* and the *Rambler;* and would discourse by hours together on the superiority of such publications to anything which has since been produced in our Edinburghs and Quarterlies. He was a great proficient in all questions of genealogy, and knew enough of almost every gentleman's family in England to say of what blood and lineage were descended all those who had any claim to be considered as possessors of any such luxuries. For blood and lineage he himself had a most profound respect. He counted back his own ancestors to some period long anteced- ent to the Conquest; and could tell you, if you would listen to him, how it had come to pass that they, like Cedric the Saxon, had been permitted to hold their own among the Norman barons. It was not, according to his showing, on account of any weak complaisance on the part of his family towards their Norman neighbours. Some Ealfried of Ullathorne once fortified his own castle, and held out, not only that, but the then existing cathedral of Barchester also, against one Geoffrey De Burgh, in the time of King John; and Mr. Thorne possessed the whole history of the siege written on vellum, and illuminated in a most costly manner. It little signified that no one could read the writing, as, had that been possible, no one could have understood the language. Mr. Thorne could, however, give you all the particulars in good English, and had no objection to do so.

It would be unjust to say that he looked down on men whose families were of recent date. He did not do so. He frequently consorted with such, and had chosen many of his friends from among them. But he looked on them as great millionaires are apt to look on those who have small incomes; as men who have Sophocles at their fingers' ends regard those who know nothing of Greek. They might doubtless be good sort of people, entitled to much praise for virtue, very admirable for talent, highly respectable in every way; but they were without the one great good gift. Such was Mr. Thorne's way of thinking on this matter; nothing could atone for the loss of good blood; nothing could neutralise its good effects. Few indeed were now possessed of it, but the possession was on that account the more precious. It was very pleasant to hear Mr. Thorne descant on this matter. Were you in your ignorance to surmise that such a one was of a good family because the head of his family was a baronet of an old date, he would open his eyes with a delightful look of affected surprise, and modestly remind you that baronetcies only dated from James I. He would gently sigh if you spoke of the blood of the Fitzgeralds and De Burghs; would hardly allow the claims of the Howards and Lowthers; and has before now alluded to the Talbots as a family who had hardly yet achieved the full honours of a pedigree.

In speaking once of a wide spread race whose name had received the honours of three coronets, scions from which sat for various constituencies, some one of whose members had been in almost every cabinet formed during the present century, a brilliant race such as there are few in England, Mr. Thorne had called them all "dirt." He had not intended any disrespect to these men. He admired them in many senses, and allowed them their privileges without envy. He had merely meant to express his feeling that the streams which ran through their veins were not yet purified by time to that perfection, had not become so genuine an ichor, as to be worthy of being called blood in the genealogical sense.

When Mr. Arabin was first introduced to him, Mr. Thorne had immediately suggested that he was one of the Arabins of Uphill Stanton. Mr. Arabin replied that he was a very distant relative of the family alluded to. To this Mr. Thorne surmised that the relationship could not be very distant. Mr. Arabin assured him that it was so distant that the families knew nothing of each other. Mr. Thorne laughed his gentle laugh at this, and told Mr. Arabin that there was now existing no branch of his family separated from the parent stock at an earlier date than the reign of Elizabeth; and that therefore Mr. Arabin could not call himself distant. Mr. Arabin himself was quite clearly an Arabin of Uphill Stanton.

"But," said the vicar, "Uphill Stanton has been sold to the De Greys, and has been in their hands for the last fifty years."

"And when it has been there one hundred and fifty, if it unluckily remain there so long," said Mr. Thorne, "your descendants will not be a whit the less entitled to describe themselves as being of the family of Uphill Stanton. Thank God, no De Grey can buy that—and, thank God—no Arabin, and no Thorne, can sell it."

In politics, Mr. Thorne was an unflinching conservative. He looked on those fifty-three Trojans, who, as Mr. Dod tells us, censured free trade in November, 1852, as the only patriots left among the public men of England. When that terrible crisis of free trade had arrived, when the repeal of the Corn Laws was carried by those very men whom Mr. Thorne had hitherto regarded as the only possible saviours of his country, he was for a time paralysed. His country was lost; but that was comparatively a small thing. Other countries had flourished and fallen, and the human race still went on improving under God's Providence. But now all trust in human faith must for ever be at an end. Not only must ruin come, but it must come through the apostasy of those who had been regarded as the truest of true believers. Politics in England, as a pursuit for gentlemen, must be at an end. Had Mr. Thorne been trodden under foot by a Whig, he could have borne it as a Tory and a martyr; but to be so utterly thrown over and deceived by those he had so earnestly supported, so thoroughly trusted, was more than he could endure and live. He therefore ceased to live as a politician, and refused to hold any converse with the world at large on the state of the country.

Such were Mr. Thorne's impressions for the first two or three years after Sir Robert Peel's apostasy; but by degrees his temper, as did that of others, cooled down. He began once more to move about, to frequent the bench and the market, and to be seen at dinners, shoulder to shoulder with some of those who had so cruelly betrayed him. It was a necessity for him to live, and that plan of his for avoiding the world did not answer. He, however, and others around him who still maintained the same staunch principles of protection—men like himself, who were too true to flinch at the cry of a mob—had their own way of consoling themselves. They were, and felt themselves to be, the only true depositaries left of certain Eleusinian mysteries, of certain deep and wondrous services of worship by which alone the gods could be rightly approached. To them and them only was it now given to know these things, and to perpetuate them, if that might still be done, by the careful and secret education of their children.

We have read how private and peculiar forms of worship have been carried on from age to age in families, which to the outer world have apparently adhered to the services of some ordinary church. And so by degrees it was with Mr. Thorne. He learnt at length to listen calmly while protection was talked of as a thing dead, although he knew within himself that it was still quick with a mystic life. Nor was he without a certain pleasure that such knowledge though given to him should be debarred from the multitude. He became accustomed to hear, even among country gentlemen, that free trade was after all not so bad, and to hear this without dispute, although conscious within himself that everything good in England had gone with his old palladium. He had within him something of the feeling of Cato, who gloried that he could kill himself because Romans were no longer worthy of their name. Mr. Thorne had no thought of killing himself, being a Christian, and still possessing his £4000 a year; but the feeling was not on that account the less comfortable.

Mr. Thorne was a sportsman, and had been active though not outrageous in his sports. Previous to the great downfall of politics in his country, he had supported the hunt by every means in his power. He had preserved game till no goose or turkey could show a tail in the parish of St. Ewold's. He had planted gorse covers with more care than oaks and larches. He had been more anxious for the comfort of his foxes than of his ewes and lambs. No meet had been more popular than Ullathorne; no man's stables had been more liberally open to the horses of distant men than Mr. Thorne's; no man had said more, written more, or done more to keep the club up. The theory of protection could expand itself so thoroughly in the practices of a country hunt! But when the great ruin came; when the noble master of the Barsetshire hounds supported the recreant minister in the House of Lords, and basely surrendered his truth, his manhood, his friends, and his honour for the hope of a garter, then Mr. Thorne gave up the hunt. He did not cut his covers, for that would not have been the act of a gentleman. He did not kill his foxes, for that according to his light would have been murder. He did not say that his covers should not be drawn, or his earths stopped, for that would have been illegal according to the by-laws prevailing among country gentlemen. But he absented himself from home on the occasion of every meet at Ullathorne, left the covers to their fate, and could not be persuaded to take his pink coat out of the press, or his hunters out of his stable. This lasted for two years, and then by degrees he came round. He first appeared at a neighbouring meet on a pony, dressed in his shooting coat, as though he had trotted in by accident; then he walked up one morning on foot to see his favourite gorse drawn, and when his groom brought his mare out by chance, he did not refuse to mount her. He was next persuaded, by one of the immortal fifty-three, to bring his hunting materials over to the other side of the county, and take a fortnight with the hounds there; and so gradually he returned to his old life. But in hunting as in other things he was only supported by an inward feeling of mystic superiority to those with whom he shared the common breath of outer life.

Mr. Thorne did not live in solitude at Ullathorne. He had a sister, who was ten years older than himself, and who participated in his prejudices and feelings so strongly, that she was a living caricature of all his foibles. She would not open a modern quarterly, did not choose to see a magazine in her drawing-room, and would not have polluted her fingers with a shred of the *Times* for any consideration. She spoke of Addison, Swift, and Steele, as though they were still living, regarded De Foe as the best known novelist of his country, and thought of Fielding as a young but meritorious novice in the fields of romance. In poetry, she was familiar with names as late as Dryden, and had once been seduced into reading the *Rape of the Lock*; but she regarded Spenser as the purest type of her country's literature in this line. Genealogy was her favourite insanity. Those things which are the pride of most genealogists were to her contemptible. Arms and mottoes set her beside herself. Ealfried of Ullathorne had wanted no motto to assist him in cleaving to the brisket Geoffrey De Burgh; and Ealfried's great grandfather, the gigantic Ullafrid, had required no other arms than those which nature gave him to hurl from the top of his own castle a cousin of the base invading Norman. To her all modern English names were equally insignificant: Hengist, Horsa, and such like, had for her ears the only true savour of nobility. She was not contented unless she could go beyond the Saxons; and would certainly have christened her children, had she had children, by the names of the ancient Britons. In some respects she was not unlike Scott's Ulrica, and had she been given to cursing, she would certainly have done so in the names of Mista, Skogula, and Zernebock. Not having submitted to the embraces of any polluting Norman, as poor Ulrica had done, and having assisted no parricide, the milk of human kindness was not curdled in her bosom. She never cursed, therefore, but blessed rather. This, however, she did in a strange uncouth Saxon manner that would have been unintelligible to any peasants but her own.

As a politician, Miss Thorne had been so thoroughly disgusted with public life by base deeds long antecedent to the Corn Law question, that that had but little moved her. In her estimation her brother had been a fast young man, hurried away by a too ardent temperament into democratic tendencies. Now happily he was brought to sounder views by seeing the iniquity of the world. She had not yet reconciled herself to the Reform Bill, and still groaned in spirit over the defalcations of the Duke as touching the Catholic Emancipation. If asked whom she thought

the Queen should take as her counsellor, she would probably
have named Lord Eldon; and when reminded that that venerable
man was no longer present in the flesh to assist us, she would
probably have answered with a sigh that none now could help us
but the dead.

In religion, Miss Thorne was a pure Druidess. We would
not have it understood by that, that she did actually in these latter
days assist at any human sacrifices, or that she was in fact hostile
to the Church of Christ. She had adopted the Christian religion
as a milder form of the worship of her ancestors, and always
appealed to her doing so as evidence that she had no prejudices
against reform, when it could be shown that reform was salutary.
This reform was the most modern of any to which she had as yet
acceded, it being presumed that British ladies had given up their
paint and taken to some sort of petticoats before the days of St.
Augustine. That further feminine step in advance which com-
bines paint and petticoats together, had not found a votary in
Miss Thorne.

But she was a Druidess in this, that she regretted she knew
not what in the usages and practices of her Church. She sometimes talked and constantly thought of good things gone by,
though she had but the faintest idea of what those good things
had been. She imagined that a purity had existed which was now
gone; that a piety had adorned our pastors and a simple docility
our people, for which it may be feared history gave her but little
true warrant. She was accustomed to speak of Cranmer as though
he had been the firmest and most simple-minded of martyrs, and
of Elizabeth as though the pure Protestant faith of her people had
been the one anxiety of her life. It would have been cruel to
undeceive her, had it been possible; but it would have been
impossible to make her believe that the one was a time-serving
priest, willing to go any length to keep his place, and that the
other was in heart a papist, with this sole proviso, that she
should be her own pope.

And so Miss Thorne went on sighing and regretting, looking back to the divine right of kings as the ruling axiom of a
golden age, and cherishing, low down in the bottom of her heart
of hearts, a dear unmentioned wish for the restoration of some
exiled Stuart. Who would deny her the luxury of her sighs, or
the sweetness of her soft regrets!

In her person and her dress she was perfect, and well she
knew her own perfection. She was a small elegantly made old
woman, with a face from which the glow of her youth had not

departed without leaving some streaks of a roseate hue. She was proud of her colour, proud of her grey hair which she wore in short crisp curls peering out all around her face from the dainty white lace cap. To think of all the money that she spent in lace used to break the heart of poor Mrs. Quiverful with her seven daughters. She was proud of her teeth, which were still white and numerous, proud of her bright cheery eye, proud of her short jaunty step, and very proud of the neat, precise, small feet with which those steps were taken. She was proud also, ay, very proud, of the rich brocaded silk in which it was her custom to ruffle through her drawing-room.

We know what was the custom of the lady of Branksome—

> Nine-and-twenty knights of fame
> Hung their shields in Branksome Hall.

The lady of Ullathorne was not so martial in her habits, but hardly less costly. She might have boasted that nine-and-twenty silken skirts might have been produced in her chamber, each fit to stand alone. The nine-and-twenty shields of the Scottish heroes were less independent, and hardly more potent to withstand any attack that might be made on them. Miss Thorne when fully dressed might be said to have been armed cap-a-pie, and she was always fully dressed, as far as was ever known to mortal man.

For all this rich attire Miss Thorne was not indebted to the generosity of her brother. She had a very comfortable independence of her own, which she divided among juvenile relatives, the milliners, and the poor, giving much the largest share to the latter. It may be imagined, therefore, that with all her little follies she was not unpopular. All her follies have, we believe, been told. Her virtues were too numerous to describe, and not sufficiently interesting to deserve description.

While we are on the subject of the Thornes, one word must be said of the house they lived in. It was not a large house, nor a fine house, nor perhaps to modern ideas a very commodious house; but by those who love the peculiar colour and peculiar ornaments of genuine Tudor architecture it was considered a perfect gem. We beg to own ourselves among the number, and therefore take this opportunity to express our surprise that so little is known by English men and women of the beauties of English architecture. The ruins of the Colosseum, the Campanile at Florence, St. Mark's, Cologne, the Bourse and Notre Dame, are with our tourists as familiar as household words; but they know nothing of the glories of Wiltshire, Dorsetshire, and Somersetshire. Nay, we much question whether many noted travellers, men who have pitched their tents perhaps under Mount Sinai, are not still ignorant that there are glories in Wiltshire, Dorsetshire, and Somersetshire. We beg that they will go and see.

Mr. Thorne's house was called Ullathorne Court, and was properly so called; for the house itself formed two sides of a quadrangle, which was completed on the other two sides by a wall about twenty feet high. This wall was built of cut stone, rudely cut indeed, and now much worn, but of a beautiful rich tawny yellow colour, the effect of that stonecrop of minute growth, which it had taken three centuries to produce. The top of this wall was ornamented by huge round stone balls of the same colour as the wall itself. Entrance into the court was had through a pair of iron gates, so massive that no one could comfortably open or close them, consequently they were rarely disturbed. From the gateway two paths led obliquely across the court; that to the left reaching the hall-door, which was in the corner made by the angle of the house, and that to the right leading to the back entrance, which was at the further end of the longer portion of the building.

With those who are now adepts in contriving house accommodation, it will militate much against Ullathorne Court, that no carriage could be brought to the hall-door. If you enter Ullathorne at all, you must do so, fair reader, on foot, or at least in a bath-chair. No vehicle drawn by horses ever comes within that iron gate. But this is nothing to the next horror that will encounter you. On entering the front door, which you do by no very grand portal, you find yourself immediately in the dining-room. What,—no hall? exclaims my luxurious friend, accustomed to all the comfortable appurtenances of modern life. Yes, kind sir; a noble hall, if you will but observe it; a true old Ensligh hall of excellent dimensions for a country gentleman's family; but, if you please, no dining-parlour.

Both Mr. and Miss Thorne were proud of this peculiarity of their dwelling, though the brother was once all but tempted by his friends to alter it. They delighted in the knowledge that they, like Cedric, positively dined in their true hall, even though they so dined tête-à-tête. But though they had never owned, they had felt and endeavoured to remedy the discomfort of such an arrangement. A huge screen partitioned off the front door and a portion of the hall, and from the angle so screened off a second door led into a passage, which ran along the larger side of the house next to the courtyard. Either my reader or I must be a bad hand at topography, if it be not clear that the great hall forms the ground-floor of the smaller portion of the mansion, that which was to your left as you entered the iron gate, and that it occupies the whole of this wing of the building. It must be equally clear that it looks out on a trim mown lawn, through three quadrangular windows with stone mullions, each window divided into a larger portion at the bottom, and a smaller portion at the top, and each portion again divided into five by perpendicular stone supporters. There may be windows which give a better light than such as these, and it may be, as my utilitarian friend observes, that the giving of light is the desired object of a window. I will not argue the point with him. Indeed I cannot. But I shall not the less die in the assured conviction that no sort of description of window is capable of imparting half so much happiness to mankind as that which had been adopted at Ullathorne Court. What—not an oriel? says Miss Diana de Midellage. No, Miss Diana; not even an oriel, beautiful as is an oriel window. It has not about it so perfect a feeling of quiet English homely comfort. Let oriel windows grace a college, or the half public mansion of a potent peer; but for the sitting room of quiet country ladies, of ordinary homely folk, nothing can equal the square mullioned windows of the Tudor architects.

The hall was hung round with family female insipidities by Lely, and unprepossessing male Thornes in red coats by Kneller; each Thorne having been let into a panel in the wainscoting, in the proper manner. At the further end of the room was a huge fire-place, which afforded much ground of difference between the brother and sister. An antiquated grate that would hold about a hundred weight of coal, had been stuck on to the hearth, by Mr. Thorne's father. This hearth had of course been intended for the consumption of wood fagots, and the iron dogs for the purpose were still standing, though half buried in the masonry of the grate. Miss Thorne was very anxious to revert to the dogs. The dear good old creature was always glad to revert to anything, and had she been systematically indulged, would doubtless in time have reflected that fingers were made before forks, and have reverted accordingly. But in the affairs of the fire-place, Mr. Thorne would not revert. Country gentlemen around him, all had comfortable grates in their dining-rooms. He not exactly the man to have suggested a modern usage; but he was not so far prejudiced as to banish those which his father had prepared for his use. Mr. Thorne had, indeed, once suggested that with very little contrivance the front door might have been so altered, as to open at least into the passage; but on hearing this, his sister Monica, such was Miss Thorne's name, had been taken ill, and had remained so for a week. Before she came down stairs she received a pledge from her brother that the entrance should never be changed in her lifetime.

At the end of the hall opposite to the fire-place a door led into the drawing-room, which was of equal size, and lighted with precisely similar windows. But yet the aspect of the room was very different. It was papered, and the ceiling, which in the hall showed the old rafters, was whitened and finished with a modern cornice. Miss Thorne's drawing-room, or, as she always called it, withdrawing-room, was a beautiful apartment. The windows opened on to the full extent of the lovely trim garden; immediately before the windows were plots of flowers in stiff, stately, stubborn little beds, each bed surrounded by a stone coping of its own; beyond, there was a low parapet wall, on which stood urns and images, fawns, nymphs, satyrs, and a whole tribe of Pan's followers; and then again, beyond that, a beautiful lawn sloped away to a sunk fence which divided the garden from the park. Mr. Thorne's study was at the end of the drawing-room, and beyond that were the kitchen and the offices. Doors opened into both Miss Thorne's withdrawing-room and Mr. Thorne's sanctum from the passage above alluded to; which, as it came to the latter room, widened itself so as to make space for the huge black oak stairs, which led to the upper regions.

Such was the interior of Ullathorne Court. But having thus described it, perhaps somewhat too tediously, we beg to say that it is not the interior to which we wish to call the English tourist's attention, though we advise him to lose no legitimate opportunity of becoming acquainted with it in a friendly manner. It is the outside of Ullathorne that is so lovely. Let the tourist get admission at least into the garden, and fling himself on that soft sward just opposite to the exterior angle of the house. He will there get the double frontage, and enjoy that which is so lovely— the expanse of architectural beauty without the formal dulness of one long line.

It is the colour of Ullathorne that is so remarkable. It is all of that delicious tawny hue which no stone can give, unless it has on it the vegetable richness of centuries. Strike the wall with your hand, and you will think that the stone has on it no covering, but rub it carefully, and you will find that the colour comes off upon your finger. No colourist that ever yet worked from a palette has been able to come up to this rich colouring of years crowding themselves on years.

Ullathorne is a high building for a country house, for it possesses three stories; and in each story, the windows are of the same sort as that described, though varying in size, and varying also in their lines athwart the house. Those of the ground floor are all uniform in size and position. But those above are irregular both in size and place, and this irregularity gives a bizarre and not unpicturesque appearance to the building. Along the top, on every side, runs a low parapet, which nearly hides the roof, and at the corners are more figures of fawns and satyrs.

Such is Ullathorne House. But we must say one word of the approach to it, which shall include all the description which we mean to give of the church also. The picturesque old church of St. Ewold's stands immediately opposite to the iron gates which open into the court, and is all but surrounded by the branches of the lime trees, which form the avenue leading up to the house from both sides. This avenue is magnificent, but it would lose much of its value in the eyes of many proprietors, by the fact that the road through it is not private property. It is a public lane between hedge rows, with a broad grass margin on each side of the road, from which the lime trees spring. Ullathorne Court, therefore, does not stand absolutely surrounded by its own grounds, though Mr. Thorne is owner of all the adjacent land. This, however, is the source of very little annoyance to him. Men, when they are acquiring property, think much of such things, but they who live where their ancestors have lived for years, do not feel the misfortune. It never occurred either to Mr. or Miss Thorne that they were not sufficiently private, because the world at large might, if it so wished, walk or drive by their iron gates. That part of the world which availed itself of the privilege was however very small.

Such a year or two since were the Thornes of Ullathorne. Such, we believe, are the inhabitants of many an English country home. May it be long before their number diminishes.

XXIII

Mr. Arabin Reads Himself in at St. Ewold's

On the Sunday morning the archdeacon with his sister-in-law and Mr. Arabin drove over to Ullathorne, as had been arranged. On their way thither the new vicar declared himself to be considerably disturbed in his mind at the idea of thus facing his parishioners for the first time. He had, he said, been always subject to *mauvaise honte* and an annoying degree of bashfulness, which often unfitted him for any work of a novel description; and now he felt this so strongly that he feared he should acquit himself badly in St. Ewold's reading-desk. He knew, he said, that those sharp little eyes of Miss Thorne would be on him, and that they would not approve. All this the archdeacon greatly ridiculed. He himself knew not, and had never known, what it was to be shy. He could not conceive that Miss Thorne, surrounded as she would be by the peasants of Ullathorne, and a few of the poorer inhabitants of the suburbs of Barchester, could in any way affect the composure of a man well accustomed to address the learned congregation of St. Mary's at Oxford, and he laughed accordingly at the idea of Mr. Arabin's modesty.

Thereupon Mr. Arabin commenced to subtilise. The change, he said, from St. Mary's to St. Ewold's was quite as powerful on the spirits as would be that from St. Ewold's to St. Mary's. Would not a peer who, by chance of fortune, might suddenly be driven to herd among navvies be as afraid of the jeers of his companions, as would any navvy suddenly exalted to a seat among the peers? Whereupon the archdeacon declared with a loud laugh that he would tell Miss Thorne that her new minister had likened her to a navvy. Eleanor, however, pronounced such a conclusion to be unfair; a comparison might be very just in its proportions which did not at all assimilate the things compared.

But Mr. Arabin went on subtilising, regarding neither the archdeacon's raillery nor Eleanor's defence. A young lady, he said, would execute with most perfect self-possession a difficult piece of music in a room crowded with strangers, who would not be able to express herself in intelligible language, even on any ordinary subject and among her most intimate friends, if she were required to do so standing on a box somewhat elevated among them. It was all an affair of education, and he at forty found it difficult to educate himself anew.

Eleanor dissented on the matter of the box; and averred she could speak very well about dresses, or babies, or legs of mutton from any box, provided it were big enough for her to stand upon without fear, even though all her friends were listening to her. The archdeacon was sure she would not be able to say a word; but this proved nothing in favour of Mr. Arabin. Mr. Arabin said that he would try the question out with Mrs. Bold, and get her on a box some day when the rectory might be full of visitors. To this Eleanor assented, making condition that the visitors should be of their own set, and the archdeacon cogitated in his mind, whether by such a condition it was intended that Mr. Slope should be included, resolving also that, if so, the trial would certainly never take place in the rectory drawing-room at Plumstead.

And so arguing, they drove up to the iron gates of Ullathorne Court.

Mr. and Miss Thorne were standing ready dressed for church in the hall, and greeted their clerical visitors with cordiality. The archdeacon was an old favourite. He was a clergyman of the old school, and this recommended him to the lady. He had always been an opponent of free trade as long as free trade was an open question; and now that it was no longer so, he, being a clergyman, had not been obliged, like most of his lay Tory companions, to read his recantation. He could therefore be regarded as a supporter of the immaculate fifty-three, and was on this account a favourite with Mr. Thorne. The little bell was tinkling, and the rural population of the parish were standing about the lane, leaning on the church stile, and against the walls of the old court, anxious to get a look at their new minister as he passed from the house to the rectory. The archdeacon's servant had already preceded them thither with the vestments.

They all went forth together; and when the ladies passed into the church the three gentlemen tarried a moment in the lane, that Mr. Thorne might name to the vicar with some kind of one-sided introduction, the most leading among his parishioners.

"Here are our churchwardens, Mr. Arabin; Farmer Greenacre and Mr. Stiles. Mr. Stiles has the mill as you go into Barchester; and very good churchwardens they are."

"Not very severe, I hope," said Mr. Arabin: the two ecclesiastical officers touched their hats, and each made a leg in the approved rural fashion, assuring the vicar that they were very glad to have the honour of seeing him, and adding that the weather was very good for the harvest. Mr. Stiles being a man somewhat versed in town life, had an impression of his own dignity, and did not quite like leaving his pastor under the erroneous idea that he being a churchwarden kept the children in order during church time. 'Twas thus he understood Mr. Arabin's allusion to his severity, and hastened to put matters right by observing that "Sexton Clodheve looked to the younguns, and perhaps sometimes there may be a thought too much stick going on during sermon." Mr. Arabin's bright eye twinkled as he caught that of the archdeacon's; and he smiled to himself as he observed how ignorant his officers were of the nature of their authority, and of the surveillance which it was their duty to keep even over himself.

Mr. Arabin read the lessons and preached. It was enough to put a man a little out, let him have been ever so used to pulpit reading, to see the knowing way in which the farmers cocked their ears, and set about a mental criticism as to whether their new minister did or did not fall short of the excellence of him who had lately departed from them. A mental and silent criticism it was for the existing moment, but soon to be made public among the elders of St. Ewold's over the green graves of their children and forefathers. The excellence, however, of poor old Mr. Goodenough had not been wonderful, and there were few there who did not deem that Mr. Arabin did his work sufficiently well, in spite of the slightly nervous affection which at first impeded him, and which nearly drove the archdeacon beside himself.

But the sermon was the thing to try the man. It often surprises us that very young men can muster courage to preach for the first time to a strange congregation. Men who are as yet but little more than boys, who have but just left, what indeed we may not call a school, but a seminary intended for their tuition as scholars, whose thoughts have been mostly of boating, cricketing, and wine parties, ascend a rostrum high above the heads of the submissive crowd, not that they may read God's word to those below, but that they may preach their own word for the edification of their hearers. It seems strange to us that they are not stricken dumb by the new and awful solemnity of their position. How am I, just turned twenty-three, who have never yet passed ten thoughtful days since the power of thought first came to me, how am I to instruct these greybeards, who with the weary thinking of so many years have approached so near the grave? Can I teach them their duty? Can I explain to them that which I so imperfectly understand, that which years of study may have made so plain to them? Has my newly acquired privilege, as one of God's ministers, imparted to me as yet any fitness for the wonderful work of a preacher?

It must be supposed that such ideas do occur to young clergymen, and yet they overcome, apparently with ease, this difficulty which to us appears to be all but insurmountable. We have never been subjected in the way of ordination to the power of a bishop's hands. It may be that there is in them something that sustains the spirit and banishes the natural modesty of youth. But for ourselves we must own that the deep affection which Dominie Sampson felt for his young pupils has not more endeared him to us than the bashful spirit which sent him mute and inglorious from the pulpit when he rose there with the futile attempt to preach God's gospel.

There is a rule in our church which forbids the younger order of our clergymen to perform a certain portion of the service. The absolution must be read by a minister in priest's orders. If there be no such minister present, the congregation can have the benefit of no absolution but that which each may succeed in administering to himself. The rule may be a good one, though the necessity for it hardly comes home to the general understanding. But this forbearance on the part of youth would be much more appreciated if it were extended likewise to sermons. The only danger would be that congregations would be too anxious to prevent their young clergymen from advancing themselves in the ranks of the ministry. Clergymen who could not preach would be such blessings that they would be bribed to adhere to their incompetence.

Mr. Arabin, however, had not the modesty of youth to impede him, and he succeeded with his sermon even better than with the lessons. He took for his text two verses out of the second epistle of St. John. "Whosoever transgresseth, and abideth not in the doctrine of Christ, hath not God. He that abideth in the doctrine of Christ he hath both the Father and Son. If there come any unto you and bring not this doctrine, receive him not into your house, neither bid him God speed.'' He told them that the house of theirs to which he alluded was this their church in which he now addressed them for the first time; that their most welcome and proper manner of bidding him God speed would be their patient obedience to his teaching of the gospel; but that he could put forward no claim to such conduct on their part unless he taught them the great Christian doctrine of works and faith combined. On this he enlarged, but not very amply, and after twenty minutes succeeded in sending his new friends home to their baked mutton and pudding well pleased with their new minister.

Then came the lunch at Ullathorne. As soon as they were in the hall Miss Thorne took Mr. Arabin's hand, and assured him that she received him into her house, into the temple, she said, in which she worshipped, and bade him God speed with all her heart. Mr. Arabin was touched, and squeezed the spinster's hand without uttering a word in reply. Then Mr. Thorne expressed a hope that Mr. Arabin found the church easy to fill, and Mr. Arabin having replied that he had no doubt he should do so as soon as he had learnt to pitch his voice to the building, they all sat down to the good things before them.

Miss Thorne took special care of Mrs. Bold. Eleanor still wore her widow's weeds, and therefore had about her that air of grave and sad maternity which is the lot of recent widows. This opened the soft heart of Miss Thorne, and made her look on her young guest as though too much could not be done for her. She heaped chicken and ham upon her plate, and poured out for her a full bumper of port wine. When Eleanor, who was not sorry to get it, had drunk a little of it, Miss Thorne at once essayed to fill it again. To this Eleanor objected, but in vain. Miss Thorne winked and nodded and whispered, saying that it was the proper thing and must be done, and that she knew all about it; and so she desired Mrs. Bold to drink it up, and not mind any body.

"It is your duty, you know, to support yourself," she said into the ear of the young mother; "there's more than yourself depending on it"; and thus she coshered up Eleanor with cold fowl and port wine. How it is that poor men's wives, who have no cold fowl and port wine on which to be coshered up, nurse their children without difficulty, whereas the wives of rich men, who eat and drink everything that is good, cannot do so, we will for the present leave to the doctors and the mothers to settle between them.

And then Miss Thorne was great about teeth. Little Johnny Bold had been troubled for the last few days with his first incipient masticator, and with that freemasonry which exists among ladies, Miss Thorne became aware of the fact before Eleanor had half finished her wing. The old lady prescribed at once a receipt which had been much in vogue in the young days of her grandmother, and warned Eleanor with solemn voice against the fallacies of modern medicine.

"Take his coral, my dear," said she, "and rub it well with carrot-juice; rub it till the juice dries on it, and then give it to him to play with——"

"But he hasn't got a coral," said Eleanor.

"Not got a coral!" said Miss Thorne, with almost angry vehemence. "Not got a coral—how can you expect that he should cut his teeth? Have you got Daffy's Elixir?"

Eleanor explained that she had not. It had not been ordered by Mr. Rerechild, the Barchester doctor whom she employed; and then the young mother mentioned some shockingly modern succedaneum, which Mr. Rerechild's new lights had taught him to recommend.

Miss Thorne looked awfully severe. "Take care, my dear, she said, "that the man knows what he's about; take care he doesn't destroy your little boy. But"—and she softened into sorrow as she said it, and spoke more in pity than in anger— "but I don't know who there is in Barchester now that you can trust. Poor dear old Dr. Bumpwell, indeed——"

"Why, Miss Thorne, he died when I was a little girl."

"Yes, my dear, he did, and an unfortunate day it was for Barchester. As to those young men that have come up since" (Mr. Rerechild, by the bye, was quite as old as Miss Thorne herself), "one doesn't know where they came from or who they are, or whether they know anything about their business or not."

"I think there are very clever men in Barchester," said Eleanor.

"Perhaps there may be; only I don't know them; and it's admitted on all sides that medical men aren't now what they used to be. They used to be talented, observing, educated men. But now any whipper-snapper out of an apothecary's shop can call himself a doctor. I believe no kind of education is now thought necessary."

Eleanor was herself the widow of a medical man, and felt a

little inclined to resent all these hard sayings. But Miss Thorne
was so essentially good-natured that it was impossible to resent
anything she said. She therefore sipped her wine and finished her
chicken.

"At any rate, my dear, don't forget the carrot-juice, and by
all means get him a coral at once. My grandmother Thorne had
the best teeth in the county, and carried them to the grave with
her at eighty. I have heard her say it was all the carrot-juice. She
couldn't bear the Barchester doctors. Even poor old Dr. Bumpwell
didn't please her." It clearly never occurred to Miss Thorne that
some fifty years ago Dr. Bumpwell was only a rising man, and
therefore as much in need of character in the eyes of the then
ladies of Ullathorne, as the present doctors were in her own.

The archdeacon made a very good lunch, and talked to his
host about turnip-drillers and new machines for reaping; while
the host, thinking it only polite to attend to a stranger, and
fearing that perhaps he might not care about turnip crops on a
Sunday, mooted all manner of ecclesiastical subjects.

"I never saw a heavier lot of wheat, Thorne, than you've
got there in that field beyond the copse. I suppose that's guano,"
said the archdeacon.

"Yes, guano. I get it from Bristol myself. You'll find you
often have a tolerable congregation of Barchester people out
here, Mr. Arabin. They are very fond of St. Ewold's, particularly of an afternoon, when the weather is not too hot for the
walk."

"I am under an obligation to them for staying away to-day,
at any rate," said the vicar. "The congregation can never be too
small for a maiden sermon."

"I got a ton and a half at Bradley's in High Street," said
the archdeacon, "and it was a complete take in. I don't believe
there was five hundred-weight of guano in it."

"That Bradley never has anything good," said Miss Thorne,
who had just caught the name during her whisperings with
Eleanor. "And such a nice shop as there used to be in that very
house before he came. Wilfred, don't you remember what good
things old Ambleoff used to have?"

"There have been three men since Ambleoff's time," said
the archdeacon, "and each as bad as the other. But who gets it
for you at Bristol, Thorne?"

"I ran up myself this year and bought it out of the ship. I
am afraid as the evenings get shorter, Mr. Arabin, you'll find the

reading-desk too dark. I must send a fellow with an axe and make him lop off some of those branches.''

Mr. Arabin declared that the morning light at any rate was perfect, and deprecated any interference with the lime trees. And then they took a stroll out among the trim parterres, and Mr. Arabin explained to Mrs. Bold the difference between a naiad and a dryad, and dilated on vases and the shapes of urns. Miss Thorne busied herself among her pansies; and her brother, finding it quite impracticable to give anything of a peculiarly Sunday tone to the conversation, abandoned the attempt, and had it out with the archdeacon about the Bristol guano.

At three o'clock they again went into church; and now Mr. Arabin read the service and the archdeacon preached. Nearly the same congregation was present, with some adventurous pedestrians from the city, who had not thought the heat of the mid-day August sun too great to deter them. The archdeacon took his text from the Epistle of Philemon. ''I beseech thee for my son Onesimus, whom I have begotten in my bonds.'' From such a text it may be imagined the kind of sermon which Dr. Grantly preached, and on the whole it was neither dull, nor bad, nor out of place.

He told them that it had become his duty to look about for a pastor for them, to supply the place of one who had been long among them; and that in this manner he regarded as a son him whom he had selected, as St. Paul had regarded the young disciple whom he sent forth. Then he took a little merit to himself for having studiously provided the best man he could without reference to patronage or favour; but he did not say that the best man according to his views was he who was best able to subdue Mr. Slope, and make that gentleman's situation in Barchester too hot to be comfortable. As to the bonds, they had consisted in the exceeding struggle which he had made to get a good clergyman for them. He deprecated any comparison between himself and St. Paul, but said that he was entitled to beseech them for their good-will towards Mr. Arabin, in the same manner that the apostle had besought Philemon and his household with regard to Onesimus.

The archdeacon's sermon, text, blessing and all, was concluded within the half hour. Then they shook hands with their Ullathorne friends, and returned to Plumstead. 'Twas thus that Mr. Arabin read himself in at St. Ewold's.

XXIV

Mr. Slope Manages Matters Very Cleverly at Puddingdale

The next two weeks passed pleasantly enough at Plumstead. The whole party there assembled seemed to get on well together. Eleanor made the house agreeable, and the archdeacon and Mrs. Grantly seemed to have forgotten her iniquity as regarded Mr. Slope. Mr. Harding had his violoncello, and played to them while his daughters accompanied him. Johnny Bold, by the help either of Mr. Rerechild or else by that of his coral and carrot-juice, got through his teething troubles. There had been gaieties too of all sorts. They had dined at Ullathorne, and the Thornes had dined at the rectory. Eleanor had been duly put to stand on her box, and in that position had found herself quite unable to express her opinion on the merits of flounces, such having been the subject given to try her elocution. Mr. Arabin had of course been much in his own parish, looking to the doings at his vicarage, calling on his parishioners, and taking on himself the duties of his new calling. But still he had been every evening at Plumstead, and Mrs. Grantly was partly willing to agree with her husband that he was a pleasant inmate in a house.

They had also been at a dinner party at Dr. Stanhope's, of which Mr. Arabin had made one. He also, moth-like, burnt his wings in the flames of the signora's candle. Mrs. Bold, too, had been there, and had felt somewhat displeased with the taste, want of taste she called it, shown by Mr. Arabin in paying so much attention to Madame Neroni. It was as infallible that Madeline should displease and irritate the women, as that she should charm and captivate the men. The one result followed naturally on the other. It was quite true that Mr. Arabin had been charmed. He thought her a very clever and a very handsome woman; he thought also that her peculiar affliction entitled her to the sympathy of all. He had never, he said, met so much suffering joined to such perfect beauty and so clear a mind. 'Twas thus he spoke of the signora coming home in the archdeacon's carriage; and Eleanor by no means liked to hear the praise. It was, however, exceedingly unjust of her to be angry with Mr. Arabin, as she had herself spent a very pleasant evening with Bertie Stanhope, who had taken her down to dinner, and had not left her side for one moment after the gentlemen came out of the dining-room. It was unfair that she should amuse herself with Bertie and yet begrudge her new friend his license of amusement himself with Bertie's sister. And yet she did so. She was half angry with him in the carriage, and said something about meretricious manners. Mr. Arabin did not understand the ways of women very well, or else he might have flattered himself that Eleanor was in love with him.

But Eleanor was not in love with him. How many shades there are between love and indifference, and how little the graduated scale is understood! She had now been nearly three weeks in the same house with Mr. Arabin, and had received much of his attention, and listened daily to his conversation. He had usually devoted at least some portion of his evening to her exclusively. At Dr. Stanhope's he had devoted himself exclusively to another. It does not require that a woman should be in love to be irritated at this; it does not require that she should even acknowledge to herself that it is unpleasant to her. Eleanor had no such self-knowledge. She thought in her own heart that it was only on Mr. Arabin's account that she regretted that he could condescend to be amused by the signora. "I thought he had more mind," she said to herself, as she sat watching her baby's cradle on her return from the party. "After all, I believe Mr. Stanhope is the pleasanter man of the two." Alas for the memory of poor John Bold! Eleanor was not in love with Bertie Stanhope, nor was she in love with Mr. Arabin. But her devotion to her late husband was fast fading, when she could revolve in her mind, over the cradle of his infant, the faults and failings of other aspirants to her favour.

Will any one blame my heroine for this? Let him or her rather thank God for all His goodness,—for His mercy endureth for ever.

Eleanor, in truth, was not in love; neither was Mr. Arabin. Neither indeed was Bertie Stanhope, though he had already found occasion to say nearly as much as that he was. The widow's cap had prevented him from making a positive declaration, when otherwise he would have considered himself entitled to do so on a third or fourth interview. It was, after all, but a small cap now, and had but little of the weeping-willow left in its construction. It is singular how these emblems of grief fade away by unseen gradations. Each pretends to be the counterpart of the forerunner, and yet the last little bit of crimped white crape that sits so jauntily on the back of the head, is as dissimilar to the first huge mountain of woe which disfigured the face of the weeper, as the state of the Hindoo is to the jointure of the English dowager.

But let it be clearly understood that Eleanor was in love with no one, and that no one was in love with Eleanor. Under these circumstances her anger against Mr. Arabin did not last long, and before two days were over they were both as good friends as ever. She could not but like him, for every hour spent in his company was spent pleasantly. And yet she could not quite like him, for there was always apparent in his conversation a certain feeling on his part that he hardly thought it worth his while to be in earnest. It was almost as though he were playing with a child. She knew well enough that he was in truth a sober thoughtful man, who in some matters and on some occasions could endure an agony of earnestness. And yet to her he was always gently playful. Could she have seen his brow once clouded she might have learnt to love him.

So things went on at Plumstead, and on the whole not unpleasantly, till a huge storm darkened the horizon, and came down upon the inhabitants of the rectory with all the fury of a water-spout. It was astonishing how in a few minutes the whole face of the heavens was changed. The party broke up from breakfast in perfect harmony; but fierce passions had arisen before the evening, which did not admit of their sitting at the same board for dinner. To explain this, it will be necessary to go back a little.

It will be remembered that the bishop expressed to Mr. Slope in his dressing-room, his determination that Mr. Quiverful should be confirmed in his appointment to the hospital, and that his lordship requested Mr. Slope to communicate this decision to the archdeacon. It will also be remembered that the archdeacon had indignantly declined seeing Mr. Slope, and had, instead, written a strong letter to the bishop, in which he all but demanded the situation of warden for Mr. Harding. To this letter the archdeacon received an immediate formal reply from Mr. Slope, in which it was stated, that the bishop had received and would give his best consideration to the archdeacon's letter.

The archdeacon felt himself somewhat checkmated by this reply. What could he do with a man who would neither see him, nor argue with him by letter, and who had undoubtedly the power of appointing any clergyman he pleased? He had consulted with Mr. Arabin, who had suggested the propriety of calling in the aid of the master of Lazarus. "If," said he, "you and Dr. Gwynne formally declare your intention of waiting upon the bishop, the bishop will not dare to refuse to see you; and if two such men as you are see him together, you will probably not leave him without carrying your point."

The archdeacon did not quite like admitting the necessity of his being backed by the master of Lazarus before he could obtain admission into the episcopal palace of Barchester; but still he felt that the advice was good, and he resolved to take it. He wrote again to the bishop, expressing a hope that nothing further would be done in the matter of the hospital, till the consideration promised by his lordship had been given, and then sent off a warm appeal to his friend the master, imploring him to come to Plumstead and assist in driving the bishop into compliance. The master had rejoined, raising some difficulty, but not declining; and the archdeacon had again pressed his point, insisting on the necessity for immediate action. Dr. Gwynne unfortunately had the gout, and could therefore name no immediate day, but still agreed to come, if it should be finally found necessary. So the matter stood, as regarded the party at Plumstead.

But Mr. Harding had another friend fighting his battle for him, quite as powerful as the master of Lazarus, and this was Mr. Slope. Though the bishop had so pertinaciously insisted on giving way to his wife in the matter of the hospital, Mr. Slope did not think it necessary to abandon his object. He had, he thought, daily more and more reason to imagine that the widow would receive his overtures favourably, and he could not but feel that Mr. Harding at the hospital, and placed there by his means, would be more likely to receive him as a son-in-law, than Mr. Harding growling in opposition and disappointment under the archdeacon's wing at Plumstead. Moreover, to give Mr. Slope due credit, he was actuated by greater motives even than these. He wanted a wife, and he wanted money, but he wanted power more than either. He had fully realised the fact that he must come to blows with Mrs. Proudie. He had no desire to remain in Barchester as her chaplain. Sooner than do so, he would risk the loss of his whole connection with the diocese. What! was he to feel within him the possession of no ordinary talents; was he to know himself to be courageous, firm, and, in matters where his conscience did not interfere, unscrupulous; and yet be contented to be the working factotum of a woman-prelate? Mr. Slope had higher ideas of his own destiny. Either he or Mrs. Proudie must go to the wall; and now had come the time when he would try which it should be.

The bishop had declared that Mr. Quiverful should be the new warden. As Mr. Slope went down stairs prepared to see the archdeacon if necessary, but fully satisfied that no such necessity would arise, he declared to himself that Mr. Harding should be warden. With the object of carrying this point, he rode over to Puddingdale, and had a further interview with the worthy expectant of clerical good things. Mr. Quiverful was on the whole a worthy man. The impossible task of bringing up as ladies and gentlemen fourteen children on an income which was insufficient to give them with decency the common necessaries of life, had had an effect upon him not beneficial either to his spirit, or his keen sense of honour. Who can boast that he would have supported such a burden with a different result? Mr. Quiverful was an honest, painstaking, drudging man; anxious, indeed, for bread and meat, anxious for means to quiet his butcher and cover with returning smiles the now sour countenance of the baker's wife, but anxious also to be right with his own conscience. He was not careful, as another might be who sat on an easier worldly seat, to stand well with those around him, to shun a breath which might sully his name, or a rumour which might affect his honour. He could not afford such niceties of conduct, such moral luxuries. It must suffice for him to be ordinarily honest according to the ordinary honesty of the world's ways, and to let men's tongues wag as they would.

He had felt that his brother clergymen, men whom he had known for the last twenty years, looked coldly on him from the first moment that he had shown himself willing to sit at the feet of Mr. Slope; he had seen that their looks grew colder still, when it became bruited about that he was to be the bishop's new warden at Hiram's hospital. This was painful enough; but it was the cross which he was doomed to bear. He thought of his wife, whose last new silk dress was six years in wear. He thought of all his young flock, whom he could hardly take to church with him on Sundays, for there were not decent shoes and stockings for them all to wear. He thought of the well-worn sleeves of his own black coat, and of the stern face of the draper from whom he would fain ask for cloth to make another, did he not know that the credit would be refused him. Then he thought of the comfortable house in Barchester, of the comfortable income, of his boys sent to school, of his girls with books in their hands instead of darning needles, of his wife's face again covered with smiles, and of his daily board again covered with plenty. He thought of these things; and do thou also, reader, think of them, and then wonder, if thou canst, that Mr. Slope had appeared to him to possess all those good gifts which could grace a bishop's chaplain. "How beautiful upon the mountains are the feet of him that bringeth good tidings."

Why, moreover, should the Barchester clergy have looked coldly on Mr. Quiverful? Had they not all shown that they regarded with complacency the loaves and fishes of their mother church? Had they not all, by some hook or crook, done better for themselves than he had done? They were not burdened as he was burdened. Dr. Grantly had five children, and nearly as many thousands a year on which to feed them. It was very well for him to turn up his nose at a new bishop who could do nothing for him, and a chaplain who was beneath his notice; but it was cruel in a man so circumstanced to set the world against the father of fourteen children because he was anxious to obtain for them an honourable support! He, Mr. Quiverful, had not asked for the wardenship; he had not even accepted it till he had been assured that Mr. Harding had refused it. How hard then that he should be blamed for doing that which not to have done would have argued a most insane imprudence?

Thus in this matter of the hospital poor Mr. Quiverful had his trials; and he had also his consolations. On the whole the consolations were the more vivid of the two. The stern draper heard of the coming promotion, and the wealth of his warehouse was at Mr. Quiverful's disposal. Coming events cast their shadows before, and the coming event of Mr. Quiverful's transference to Barchester produced a delicious shadow in the shape of a new outfit for Mrs. Quiverful and her three elder daughters. Such consolations come home to the heart of a man, and quite home to the heart of a woman. Whatever the husband might feel, the wife cared nothing for frowns of dean, archdeacon, or prebendary. To her the outsides and insides of her husband and fourteen children were everything. In her bosom every other ambition had been swallowed up in that maternal ambition of seeing them and him and herself duly clad and properly fed. It had come to that with her that life had now no other purpose. She recked nothing of the imaginary rights of others. She had no

patience with her husband when he declared to her that he could
not accept the hospital unless he knew that Mr. Harding had
refused it. Her husband had no right to be Quixotic at the
expense of fourteen children. The narrow escape of throwing
away his good fortune which her lord had had, almost paralysed
her. Now, indeed, they had received the full promise not only
from Mr. Slope, but also from Mrs. Proudie. Now, indeed, they
might reckon with safety on their good fortune. But what if all
had been lost? What if her fourteen bairns had been resteeped to
the hips in poverty by the morbid sentimentality of their father?
Mrs. Quiverful was just at present a happy woman, but yet it
nearly took her breath away when she thought of the risk they
had run.

"I don't know what your father means when he talks so
much of what is due to Mr. Harding," she said to her eldest
daughter. "Does he think that Mr. Harding would give him
£450 a year out of fine feeling? And what signifies it whom he
offends, as long as he gets the place? He does not expect
anything better. It passes me to think how your father can be so
soft, while everybody around him is so griping."

Thus, while the outer world was accusing Mr. Quiverful of
rapacity for promotion and of disregard to his honour, the inner
world of his own household was falling foul of him, with equal
vehemence, for his willingness to sacrifice their interest to a
false feeling of sentimental pride. It is astonishing how much
difference the point of view makes in the aspect of all that we
look at!

Such were the feelings of the different members of the
family at Puddingdale on the occasion of Mr. Slope's second
visit. Mrs. Quiverful, as soon as she saw his horse coming up
the avenue from the vicarage gate, hastily packed up her huge
basket of needlework, and hurried herself and her daughter out
of the room in which she was sitting with her husband. 'It's Mr.
Slope," she said. "He's come to settle with you about the
hospital. I do hope we shall now be able to move at once." And
she hastened to bid the maid of all work go to the door, so that
the welcome great man might not be kept waiting.

Mr. Slope thus found Mr. Quiverful alone. Mrs. Quiverful
went off to her kitchen and back settlements with anxious beating heart, almost dreading that there might be some slip between
the cup of her happiness and the lip of her fruition, but yet
comforting herself with the reflection that after what had taken
place, any such slip could hardly be possible.

Mr. Slope was all smiles as he shook his brother clergyman's hand, and said that he had ridden over because he thought it right at once to put Mr. Quiverful in possession of the facts of the matter regarding the wardenship of the hospital. As he spoke, the poor expectant husband and father saw at a glance that his brilliant hopes were to be dashed to the ground, and that his visitor was now there for the purpose of unsaying what on his former visit he had said. There was something in the tone of the voice, something in the glance of the eye, which told the tale. Mr. Quiverful knew it all at once. He maintained his self-possession, however, smiled with a slight unmeaning smile, and merely said that he was obliged to Mr. Slope for the trouble he was taking.

"It has been a troublesome matter from first to last," said Mr. Slope; "and the bishop has hardly known how to act. Between ourselves—but mind this of course must go no further, Mr. Quiverful."

Mr. Quiverful said that of course it should not. "The truth is, that poor Mr. Harding has hardly known his own mind. You remember our last conversation, no doubt."

Mr. Quiverful assured him that he remembered it very well indeed.

"You will remember that I told you that Mr. Harding had refused to return to the hospital."

Mr. Quiverful declared that nothing could be more distinct on his memory.

"And acting on this refusal, I suggested that you should take the hospital," continued Mr. Slope.

"I understood you to say that the bishop had authorised you to offer it to me."

"Did I? did I go as far as that? Well, perhaps it may be, that in my anxiety in your behalf I did commit myself further than I should have done. So far as my own memory serves me, I don't think I did go quite so far as that. But I own I was very anxious that you should get it; and I may have said more than was quite prudent."

"But," said Quiverful, in his deep anxiety to prove his case, "my wife received as distinct a promise from Mrs. Proudie as one human being could give to another."

Mr. Slope smiled, and gently shook his head. He meant that smile for a pleasant smile, but it was diabolical in the eyes of the man he was speaking to. "Mrs. Proudie!" he said. "If we are to go to what passes between the ladies in these matters, we shall really be in a nest of troubles from which we shall never extricate ourselves. Mrs. Proudie is a most excellent lady, kindhearted, charitable, pious, and in every way estimable. But, my dear Mr. Quiverful, the patronage of the diocese is not in her hands."

Mr. Quiverful for a moment sat panic-stricken and silent. "Am I to understand, then, that I have received no promise?" he said, as soon as he had sufficiently collected his thoughts.

"If you will allow me, I will tell you exactly how the matter rests. You certainly did receive a promise conditional on Mr. Harding's refusal. I am sure you will do me the justice to remember that you yourself declared that you could accept the appointment on no other condition than the knowledge that Mr. Harding had declined it."

"Yes," said Mr. Quiverful; "I did say that, certainly."

"Well; it now appears that he did not refuse it."

"But surely you told me, and repeated it more than once, that he had done so in your own hearing."

"So I understood him. But it seems I was in error. But don't for a moment, Mr. Quiverful, suppose that I mean to throw you over. No. Having held out my hand to a man in your position, with your large family and pressing claims, I am not now going to draw it back again. I only want you to act with me fairly and honestly."

"Whatever I do, I shall endeavour at any rate to act fairly," said the poor man, feeling that he had to fall back for support on the spirit of martyrdom within him.

"I am sure you will," said the other. "I am sure you have no wish to obtain possession of an income which belongs by all right to another. No man knows better than you do Mr. Harding's history, or can better appreciate his character. Mr. Harding is very desirous of returning to his old position, and the bishop feels that he is at the present moment somewhat hampered, though of course he is not bound, by the conversation which took place on the matter between you and me."

"Well," said Mr. Quiverful, dreadfully doubtful as to what his conduct under such circumstances should be, and fruitlessly striving to harden his nerves with some of that instinct of self-preservation which made his wife so bold.

"The wardenship of this little hospital is not the only thing in the bishop's gift, Mr. Quiverful, nor is it by many degrees the best. And his lordship is not the man to forget any one whom he has once marked with approval. If you would allow me to advise you as a friend——"

"Indeed I shall be most grateful to you," said the poor vicar of Puddingdale——

"I should advise you to withdraw from any opposition to Mr. Harding's claims. If you persist in your demand, I do not think you will ultimately succeed. Mr. Harding has all but a positive right to the place. But if you will allow me to inform the bishop that you decline to stand in Mr. Harding's way, I think I may promise you—though, by the bye, it must not be taken as a formal promise—that the bishop will not allow you to be a poorer man than you would have been had you become warden."

Mr. Quiverful sat in his arm-chair silent, gazing at vacancy. What was he to say? All this that came from Mr. Slope was so true. Mr. Harding had a right to the hospital. The bishop had a great many good things to give away. Both the bishop and Mr. Slope would be excellent friends and terrible enemies to a man in his position. And then he had no proof of any promise; he could not force the bishop to appoint him.

"Well, Mr. Quiverful, what do you say about it?"

"Oh, of course, whatever you think fit, Mr. Slope. It's a great disappointment, a very great disappointment. I won't deny that I am a very poor man, Mr. Slope."

"In the end, Mr. Quiverful, you will find that it will have been better for you."

The interview ended in Mr. Slope receiving a full renunciation from Mr. Quiverful of any claim he might have to the appointment in question. It was only given verbally and without witnesses; but then the original promise was made in the same way.

Mr. Slope again assured him that he should not be forgotten, and then rode back to Barchester, satisfied that he would now be able to mould the bishop to his wishes.

XXV

Fourteen Arguments in Favour of Mr. Quiverful's Claims

We have most of us heard of the terrible anger of a lioness when, surrounded by her cubs, she guards her prey. Few of us wish to disturb the mother of a litter of puppies when mouthing a bone in the midst of her young family. Medea and her children are familiar to us, and so is the grief of Constance. Mrs. Quiverful, when she first heard from her husband the news which he had to impart, felt within her bosom all the rage of a lioness, the rapacity of the hound, the fury of the tragic queen, and the deep despair of the bereaved mother.

Doubting, but yet hardly fearing, what might have been the tenour of Mr. Slope's discourse, she rushed back to her husband as soon as the front door was closed behind the visitor. It was well for Mr. Slope that he so escaped,—the anger of such a woman, at such a moment, would have cowed even him. As a general rule, it is highly desirable that ladies should keep their temper; a woman when she storms always makes herself ugly, and usually ridiculous also. There is nothing so odious to man as a virago. Though Theseus loved an Amazon, he showed his love but roughly; and from the time of Theseus downward, no man ever wished to have his wife remarkable rather for forward prowess than retiring gentleness. A low voice "is an excellent thing in woman."

Such may be laid down as a very general rule; and few women should allow themselves to deviate from it, and then only on rare occasions. But if there be a time when a woman may let her hair to the winds, when she may loose her arms, and scream out trumpet-tongued to the ears of men, it is when nature calls out within her not for her own wants, but for the wants of those whom her womb has borne, whom her breasts have suckled, for those who look to her for their daily bread as naturally as man looks to his Creator.

There was nothing poetic in the nature of Mrs. Quiverful. She was neither a Medea nor a Constance. When angry, she spoke out her anger in plain words, and in a tone which might have been modulated with advantage; but she did so, at any rate, without affectation. Now, without knowing it, she rose to a tragic vein.

"Well, my dear; we are not to have it." Such were the words with which her ears were greeted when she entered the parlour, still hot from the kitchen fire. And the face of her husband spoke even more plainly than his words:—

> E'en such a man, so faint, so spiritless,
> So dull, so dead in look, so woe-begone,
> Drew Priam's curtain in the dead of night.

"What!" said she,—and Mrs. Siddons could not have put more passion into a single syllable.—"What! not have it? who says so?" And she sat opposite to her husband, with her elbows on the table, her hands clasped together, and her coarse, solid, but once handsome face stretched over it towards him.

She sat as silent as death while he told his story, and very dreadful to him her silence was. He told it very lamely and badly, but still in such a manner that she soon understood the whole of it.

"And so you have resigned it?" said she.

"I have had no opportunity of accepting it," he replied. "I had no witnesses to Mr. Slope's offer, even if that offer would bind the bishop. It was better for me, on the whole, to keep on good terms with such men than to fight for what I should never get!"

"Witnesses!" she screamed, rising quickly to her feet, and walking up and down the room. "Do clergymen require witnesses to their words? He made the promise in the bishop's name, and if it is to be broken I'll know the reason why. Did he not positively say that the bishop had sent him to offer you the place?"

"He did, my dear. But that is now nothing to the purpose."

"It is everything to the purpose, Mr. Quiverful. Witnesses indeed! and then to talk of *your* honour being questioned, because you wish to provide for fourteen children. It is everything to the purpose; and so they shall know, if I scream it into their ears from the town cross of Barchester.''

"You forget, Letitia, that the bishop has so many things in his gift. We must wait a little longer. That is all.''

"Wait! Shall we feed the children by waiting? Will waiting put George, and Tom, and Sam, out into the world? Will it enable my poor girls to give up some of their drudgery? Will waiting make Bessy and Jane fit even to be governesses? Will waiting pay for the things we got in Barchester last week?''

"It is all we can do, my dear. The disappointment is as much to me as to you; and yet, God knows, I feel it more for your sake than my own.''

Mrs. Quiverful was looking full into her husband's face, and saw a small hot tear appear on each of those furrowed cheeks. This was too much for her woman's heart. He also had risen, and was standing with his back to the empty grate. She rushed towards him, and, seizing him in her arms, sobbed aloud upon his bosom.

"You are too good, too soft, too yielding,'' she said at last. "These men, when they want you, they use you like a cat's-paw; and when they want you no longer, they throw you aside like an old shoe. This is twice they have treated you so.''

"In one way this will be all for the better,'' argued he. "It will make the bishop feel that he is bound to do something for me.''

"At any rate, he shall hear of it,'' said the lady, again reverting to her more angry mood. "At any rate he shall hear of it, and that loudly; and so shall she. She little knows Letitia Quiverful, if she thinks I will sit down quietly with the loss after all that passed between us at the palace. If there's any feeling within her, I'll make her ashamed of herself,''—and she paced the room again, stamping the floor as she went with her fat heavy foot. "Good heavens! what a heart she must have within her to treat in such a way as this the father of fourteen unprovided children!''

Mr. Quiverful proceeded to explain that he didn't think that Mrs. Proudie had had anything to do with it.

"Don't tell me,'' said Mrs. Quiverful; "I know more about it than that. Doesn't all the world know that Mrs. Proudie is bishop of Barchester, and that Mr. Slope is merely her creature? Wasn't it she that made me the promise, just as though the thing was in her own particular gift? I tell you, it was that woman who sent him over here to-day, because, for some reason of her own, she wants to go back from her word.''

''My dear, you're wrong——''

''Now, Q., don't be so soft,'' she continued. ''Take my word for it, the bishop knows no more about it than Jemima does.'' Jemima was the two-year-old. ''And if you'll take my advice, you'll lose no time in going over and seeing him yourself.''

Soft, however, as Mr. Quiverful might be, he would not allow himself to be talked out of his opinion on this occasion; and proceeded with much minuteness to explain to his wife the tone in which Mr. Slope had spoken of Mrs. Proudie's interference in diocesan matters. As he did so, a new idea gradually instilled itself into the matron's head, and a new course of conduct presented itself to her judgment. What if, after all, Mrs. Proudie knew nothing of this visit of Mr. Slope's? In that case, might it not be possible that that lady would still be staunch to her in this matter, still stand her friend, and, perhaps, possibly carry her through in opposition to Mr. Slope? Mrs. Quiverful said nothing as this vague hope occurred to her, but listened with more than ordinary patience to what her husband had to say. While he was still explaining that in all probability the world was wrong in its estimation of Mrs. Proudie's power and authority, she had fully made up her mind as to her course of action. She did not, however, proclaim her intention. She shook her head ominously as he continued his narration; and when he had completed she rose to go, merely observing that it was cruel, cruel treatment. She then asked him if he would mind waiting for a late dinner instead of dining at their usual hour of three, and, having received from him a concession on this point, she proceeded to carry her purpose into execution.

She determined that she would at once go to the palace; that she would do so, if possible, before Mrs. Proudie could have had an interview with Mr. Slope; and that she would be either submissive piteous and pathetic, or else indignant violent and exacting, according to the manner in which she was received.

She was quite confident in her own power. Strengthened as she was by the pressing wants of fourteen children, she felt that she could make her way through legions of episcopal servants, and force herself, if need be, into the presence of the lady who had so wronged her. She had no shame about it, no *mauvaise honte*, no dread of archdeacons. She would, as she declared to her husband, make her wail heard in the marketplace if she did not get redress and justice. It might be very well for an unmarried young curate to be shamefaced in such matters; it might be all right that a snug rector, really in want of nothing, but still looking for better preferment, should carry on his affairs decently under the rose. But Mrs. Quiverful, with fourteen children, had given over being shamefaced, and, in some things, had given over being decent. If it were intended that she should be ill used in the manner proposed by Mr. Slope, it should not be done under the rose. All the world should know of it.

In her present mood, Mrs. Quiverful was not over careful about her attire. She tied her bonnet under her chin, threw her shawl over her shoulders, armed herself with the old family cotton umbrella, and started for Barchester. A journey to the palace was not quite so easy a thing for Mrs. Quiverful as for our friend at Plumstead. Plumstead is nine miles from Barchester, and Puddingdale is but four. But the archdeacon could order round his brougham, and his high-trotting fast bay gelding would take him into the city within the hour. There was no brougham in the coach-house of Puddingdale vicarage, no bay horse in the stables. There was no method of locomotion for its inhabitants but that which nature has assigned to man.

Mrs. Quiverful was a broad heavy woman, not young, nor given to walking. In her kitchen, and in the family dormitories, she was active enough; but her pace and gait were not adapted for the road. A walk into Barchester and back in the middle of an August day would be to her a terrible task, if not altogether impracticable. There was living in the parish, about half a mile from the vicarage on the road to the city, a decent, kindly farmer, well to do as regards this world, and so far mindful of the next that he attended his parish church with decent regularity. To him Mrs. Quiverful had before now appealed in some of her more pressing family troubles, and had not appealed in vain. At his door she now presented herself, and, having explained to his wife that most urgent business required her to go at once to Barchester, begged that Farmer Subsoil would take her thither in his tax-cart. The farmer did not reject her plan; and, as soon as Prince could be got into his collar, they started on their journey.

Mrs. Quiverful did not mention the purpose of her business, nor did the farmer alloy his kindness by any unseemly questions. She merely begged to be put down at the bridge going into the city, and to be taken up again at the same place in the course of two hours. The farmer promised to be punctual to his appointment, and the lady, supported by her umbrella, took the short cut to the close, and in a few minutes was at the bishop's door.

Hitherto she had felt no dread with regard to the coming interview. She had felt nothing but an indignant longing to pour forth her claims, and declare her wrongs, if those claims were not fully admitted. But now the difficulty of her situation touched her a little. She had been at the palace once before, but then she went to give grateful thanks. Those who have thanks to return for favours received find easy admittance to the halls of the great. Such is not always the case with men, or even with women, who have favours to beg. Still less easy is access for those who demand the fulfilment of promises already made.

Mrs. Quiverful had not been slow to learn the ways of the world. She knew all this, and she knew also that her cotton umbrella and all but ragged shawl would not command respect in the eyes of the palatial servants. If she were too humble, she knew well that she would never succeed. To overcome by imperious overbearing with such a shawl as hers upon her shoulders, and such a bonnet on her head, would have required a personal bearing very superior to that with which nature had endowed her. Of this also Mrs. Quiverful was aware. She must make it known that she was the wife of a gentleman and a clergyman, and must yet condescend to conciliate.

The poor lady knew but one way to overcome these difficulties at the very threshold of her enterprise, and to this she resorted. Low as were the domestic funds at Puddingdale, she still retained possession of half-a-crown, and this she sacrificed to the avarice of Mrs. Proudie's metropolitan sesquipedalian serving-man. She was, she said, Mrs. Quiverful of Puddingdale, the wife of the Rev. Mr. Quiverful. She wished to see Mrs. Proudie. It was indeed quite indispensable that she should see Mrs. Proudie. James Fitzplush looked worse than dubious, did not know whether his lady were out, or engaged, or in her bed-room; thought it most probable she was subject to one of these or to some other cause that would make her invisible; but Mrs. Quiverful could sit down in the waiting-room while inquiry was being made of Mrs. Proudie's maid.

"Look here, my man," said Mrs. Quiverful; "I must see her"; and she put her card and half-a-crown—think of it, my reader, think of it; her last half-crown—into the man's hand, and sat herself down on a chair in the waiting-room.

Whether the bribe carried the day, or whether the bishop's wife really chose to see the vicar's wife, it boots not now to inquire. The man returned, and begging Mrs. Quiverful to follow him, ushered her into the presence of the mistress of the diocese.

Mrs. Quiverful at once saw that her patroness was in a
smiling humour. Triumph sat throned upon her brow, and all the
joys of dominion hovered about her curls. Her lord had that
morning contested with her a great point. He had received an
invitation to spend a couple of days with the archbishop. His
soul longed for the gratification. Not a word, however, in his
grace's note alluded to the fact of his being a married man; and,
if he went at all, he must go alone. This necessity would have
presented no insurmountable bar to the visit, or have militated
much against the pleasure, had he been able to go without any
reference to Mrs. Proudie. But this he could not do. He could
not order his portmanteau to be packed, and start with his own
man, merely telling the lady of his heart that he would probably
be back on Saturday. There are men—may we not rather say
monsters?—who do such things; and there are wives—may we
not rather say slaves?—who put up with such usage. But Dr.
and Mrs. Proudie were not among the number.

The bishop, with some beating about the bush, made the
lady understand that he very much wished to go. The lady,
without any beating about the bush, made the bishop understand
that she wouldn't hear of it. It would be useless here to repeat
the arguments that were used on each side, and needless to
record the result. Those who are married will understand very
well how the battle was lost and won; and those who are single
will never understand it till they learn the lesson which experience alone can give. When Mrs. Quiverful was shown into Mrs.
Proudie's room, that lady had only returned a few minutes from
her lord. But before she left him she had seen the answer to the
archbishop's note written and sealed. No wonder that her face
was wreathed with smiles as she received Mrs. Quiverful.

She instantly spoke of the subject which was so near the
heart of her visitor. "Well, Mrs. Quiverful," said she, "is it
decided yet when you are to move into Barchester?"

"That woman," as she had an hour or two since been
called, became instantly re-endowed with all the graces that can
adorn a bishop's wife. Mrs. Quiverful immediately saw that her
business was to be piteous, and that nothing was to be gained by
indignation; nothing, indeed, unless she could be indignant in
company with her patroness.

"Oh, Mrs. Proudie," she began, "I fear we are not to
move to Barchester at all."

"Why not?" said that lady sharply, dropping at a moment's

notice her smiles and condescension, and turning with her sharp
quick way to business which she saw at a glance was important.

And then Mrs. Quiverful told her tale. As she progressed in
the history of her wrongs she perceived that the heavier she leant
upon Mr. Slope the blacker became Mrs. Proudie's brow, but
that such blackness was not injurious to her own cause. When
Mr. Slope was at Puddingdale vicarage that morning she had
regarded him as the creature of the lady-bishop; now she perceived that they were enemies. She admitted her mistake to
herself without any pain or humiliation. She had but one feeling,
and that was confined to her family. She cared little how she
twisted and turned among these new comers at the bishop's
palace so long as she could twist her husband into the warden's
house. She cared not which was her friend or which was her
enemy, if only she could get this preferment which she so sorely
wanted.

She told her tale, and Mrs. Proudie listened to it almost in
silence. She told how Mr. Slope had cozened her husband into
resigning his claim, and had declared that it was the bishop's
will that none but Mr. Harding should be warden. Mrs. Proudie's
brow became blacker and blacker. At last she started from her
chair, and begging Mrs. Quiverful to sit and wait for her return,
marched out of the room.

"Oh, Mrs. Proudie, it's for fourteen children—for fourteen
children." Such was the burden that fell on her ear as she closed
the door behind her.

XXVI

Mrs. Proudie Wrestles and Gets a Fall

It was hardly an hour since Mrs. Proudie had left her husband's
apartment victorious, and yet so indomitable was her courage
that she now returned thither panting for another combat. She was

greatly angry with what she thought was his duplicity. He had so
clearly given her a promise on this matter of the hospital. He had
been already so absolutely vanquished on that point. Mrs. Proudie
began to feel that if every affair was to be thus discussed and
battled about twice and even thrice, the work of the diocese
would be too much even for her.

Without knocking at the door she walked quickly into her
husband's room, and found him seated at his office table, with
Mr. Slope opposite to him. Between his fingers was the very
note which he had written to the archbishop in her presence——
and it was open! Yes, he had absolutely violated the seal which
had been made sacred by her approval. They were sitting in deep
conclave, and it was too clear that the purport of the archbishop's
invitation had been absolutely canvassed again, after it had been
already debated and decided on in obedience to her behests! Mr.
Slope rose from his chair, and bowed slightly. The two opposing
spirits looked each other fully in the face, and they knew that
they were looking each at an enemy.

"What is this, bishop, about Mr. Quiverful?" said she,
coming to the end of the table and standing there.

Mr. Slope did not allow the bishop to answer, but replied
himself. "I have been out to Puddingdale this morning, ma'am,
and have seen Mr. Quiverful. Mr. Quiverful has abandoned his
claim to the hospital, because he is now aware that Mr. Harding
is desirous to fill his old place. Under these circumstances I have
strongly advised his lordship to nominate Mr. Harding."

"Mr. Quiverful has not abandoned anything," said the
lady, with a very imperious voice. "His lordship's word has
been pledged to him, and it must be respected."

The bishop still remained silent. He was anxiously desirous
of making his old enemy bite the dust beneath his feet. His new
ally had told him that nothing was more easy for him than to do
so. The ally was there now at his elbow to help him, and yet his
courage failed him. It is so hard to conquer when the prestige of
former victories is all against one. It is so hard for the cock who
has once been beaten out of his yard to resume his courage and
again take a proud place upon a dunghill.

"Perhaps I ought not to interfere," said Mr. Slope, "but
yet——"

"Certainly you ought not," said the infuriated dame.

"But yet," continued Mr. Slope, not regarding the interruption, "I have thought it my imperative duty to recommend the
bishop not to slight Mr. Harding's claims."

"Mr. Harding should have known his own mind," said the lady.

"If Mr. Harding be not replaced at the hospital, his lordship will have to encounter much ill will, not only in the diocese, but in the world at large. Besides, taking a higher ground, his lordship, as I understood, feels it to be his duty to gratify, in this matter, so very worthy a man and so good a clergyman as Mr. Harding."

"And what is to become of the Sabbath-day school, and of the Sunday services in the hospital?" said Mrs. Proudie, with something very nearly approaching to a sneer on her face.

"I understand that Mr. Harding makes no objection to the Sabbath-day school," said Mr. Slope. "And as to the hospital services, that matter will be best discussed after his appointment. If he has any permanent objection, then, I fear, the matter must rest."

"You have a very easy conscience in such matters, Mr. Slope," said she.

"I should not have an easy conscience," he rejoined, "but a conscience very far from being easy, if anything said or done by me should lead the bishop to act unadvisedly in this matter. It is clear that in the interview I had with Mr. Harding, I misunderstood him——"

"And it is equally clear that you have misunderstood Mr. Quiverful," said she, now at the top of her wrath. "What business have you at all with these interviews? Who desired you to go to Mr. Quiverful this morning? Who commissioned you to manage this affair? Will you answer me, sir?—who sent you to Mr. Quiverful this morning?"

There was a dead pause in the room. Mr. Slope had risen from his chair, and was standing with his hand on the back of it, looking at first very solemn and now very black. Mrs. Proudie was standing as she had at first placed herself, at the end of the table, and as she interrogated her foe she struck her hand upon it with almost more than feminine vigour. The bishop was sitting in his easy chair twiddling his thumbs, turning his eyes now to his wife, and now to his chaplain, as each took up the cudgels. How comfortable it would be if they could fight it out between them without the necessity of any interference on his part; fight it out so that one should kill the other utterly, as far as diocesan life was concerned, so that he, the bishop, might know clearly by whom it behoved him to be led. There would be the comfort of quiet in either case; but if the bishop had a wish as to which might prove the victor, that wish was certainly not antagonistic to Mr. Slope.

"Better the d—— you know than the d—— you don't know," is an old saying, and perhaps a true one; but the bishop had not yet realised the truth of it.

"Will you answer me, sir?" she repeated. "Who instructed you to call on Mr. Quiverful this morning?" There was another pause. "Do you intend to answer me, sir?"

"I think, Mrs. Proudie, that under all the circumstances it will be better for me not to answer such a question," said Mr. Slope. Mr. Slope had many tones in his voice, all duly under his command; among them was a sanctified low tone, and a sanctified loud tone; and he now used the former.

"Did any one send you, sir?"

"Mrs. Proudie," said Mr. Slope, "I am quite aware how much I owe to your kindness. I am aware also what is due by courtesy from a gentleman to a lady. But there are higher considerations than either of those, and I hope I shall be forgiven if I now allow myself to be actuated solely by them. My duty in this matter is to his lordship, and I can admit of no questioning but from him. He has approved of what I have done, and you must excuse me if I say, that having that approval and my own, I want none other."

What horrid words were these which greeted the ear of Mrs. Proudie? The matter was indeed too clear. There was premeditated mutiny in the camp. Not only had ill-conditioned minds become insubordinate by the fruition of a little power, but sedition had been overtly taught and preached. The bishop had not yet been twelve months in his chair, and rebellion had already reared her hideous head within the palace. Anarchy and misrule would quickly follow, unless she took immediate and strong measures to put down the conspiracy which she had detected.

"Mr. Slope," she said, with slow and dignified voice, differing much from that which she had hitherto used, "Mr. Slope, I will trouble you, if you please, to leave the apartment. I wish to speak to my lord alone."

Mr. Slope also felt that everything depended on the present interview. Should the bishop now be repetticoated, his thraldom would be complete and for ever. The present moment was peculiarly propitious for rebellion. The bishop had clearly committed himself by breaking the seal of the answer to the archbishop; he had therefore fear to influence him. Mr. Slope had told him that no consideration ought to induce him to refuse the archbishop's invitation; he had therefore hope to influence him. He had accepted Mr. Quiverful's resignation, and therefore dreaded having to renew that matter with his wife. He had been screwed up to the pitch of asserting a will of his own, and might possibly be carried on till by an absolute success he should have been taught how possible it was to succeed. Now was the moment for victory or rout. It was now that Mr. Slope must make himself master of the diocese, or else resign his place and begin his search for fortune again. He saw all this plainly. After what had taken place any compromise between him and the lady was impossible. Let him once leave the room at her bidding, and leave the bishop in her hands, and he might at once pack up his portmanteau and bid adieu to episcopal honours, Mrs. Bold, and the Signora Neroni.

And yet it was not so easy to keep his ground when he was bidden by a lady to go; or to continue to make a third in a party between a husband and wife when the wife expressed a wish for a *tête-à-tête* with her husband.

"Mr. Slope," she repeated, "I wish to be alone with my lord."

"His lordship has summoned me on most important diocesan business," said Mr. Slope, glancing with uneasy eye at Dr. Proudie. He felt that he must trust something to the bishop, and yet that trust was so woefully ill-placed. "My leaving him at the present moment is, I fear, impossible."

"Do you bandy words with me, you ungrateful man?" said she. "My lord, will you do me the favour to beg Mr. Slope to leave the room?"

My lord scratched his head, but for the moment said nothing. This was as much as Mr. Slope expected from him, and was on the whole, for him, an active exercise of marital rights.

"My lord," said the lady, "is Mr. Slope to leave this room, or am I?"

Here Mrs. Proudie made a false step. She should not have alluded to the possibility of retreat on her part. She should not have expressed the idea that her order for Mr. Slope's expulsion could be treated otherwise than by immediate obedience. In answer to such a question the bishop naturally said in his own mind, that as it was necessary that one should leave the room, perhaps it might be as well that Mrs. Proudie did so. He did say so in his own mind, but externally he again scratched his head and again twiddled his thumbs.

Mrs. Proudie was boiling over with wrath. Alas, alas! could she but have kept her temper as her enemy did, she would have conquered as she had ever conquered. But divine anger got the better of her, as it has done of other heroines, and she fell.

"My lord," said she, "am I to be vouchsafed an answer or am I not?"

At last he broke his deep silence and proclaimed himself a Slopeite. "Why, my dear," said he, "Mr. Slope and I are very busy."

That was all. There was nothing more necessary. He had gone to the battle-field, stood the dust and heat of the day, encountered the fury of the foe, and won the victory. How easy is success to those who will only be true to themselves!

Mr. Slope saw at once the full amount of his gain, and turned on the vanquished lady a look of triumph which she never forgot and never forgave. Here he was wrong. He should have looked humbly at her, and with meek entreating eye have deprecated her anger. He should have said by his glance that he asked pardon for his success, and that he hoped forgiveness for the stand which he had been forced to make in the cause of duty. So might he perchance have somewhat mollified that imperious bosom, and prepared the way for future terms. But Mr. Slope meant to rule without terms. Ah, forgetful, inexperienced man! Can you cause that little trembling victim to be divorced from the woman that possesses him? Can you provide that they shall be separated at bed and board? Is he not flesh of her flesh and bone of her bone, and must he not so continue? It is very well now for you to stand your ground, and triumph as she is driven ignominiously from the room; but can you be present when those curtains are drawn, when that awful helmet of proof has been tied beneath the chin, when the small remnants of the bishop's prowess shall be cowed by the tassel above his head? Can you then intrude yourself when the wife wishes "to speak to my lord alone?"

But for the moment Mr. Slope's triumph was complete; for Mrs. Proudie without further parley left the room, and did not forget to shut the door after her. Then followed a close conference between the new allies, in which was said much which it astonished Mr. Slope to say and the bishop to hear. And yet the one said it and the other heard it without ill will. There was no mincing of matters now. The chaplain plainly told the bishop that the world gave him credit for being under the governance of his wife; that his credit and character in the diocese were suffering; that he would surely get himself into hot water if he allowed Mrs. Proudie to interfere in matters which were not suitable for a

woman's powers; and in fact that he would become contemptible
if he did not throw off the yoke under which he groaned. The
bishop at first hummed and hawed, and affected to deny the truth
of what was said. But his denial was not stout and quickly broke
down. He soon admitted by silence his state of vassalage, and
pledged himself, with Mr. Slope's assistance, to change his
courses. Mr. Slope also did not make out a bad case for himself.
He explained how it grieved him to run counter to a lady who
had always been his patroness, who had befriended him in so
many ways, who had, in fact, recommended him to the bishop's
notice; but, as he stated, his duty was now imperative: he held a
situation of peculiar confidence, and was immediately and especially attached to the bishop's person. In such a situation his
conscience required that he should regard solely the bishop's
interests, and therefore he had ventured to speak out.

The bishop took this for what it was worth, and Mr. Slope
only intended that he should do so. It gilded the pill which Mr.
Slope had to administer, and which the bishop thought would be
less bitter than that other pill which he had so long been taking.

"My lord" had his immediate reward, like a good child.
He was instructed to write and at once did write another note to
the archbishop accepting his grace's invitation. This note Mr.
Slope, more prudent than the lady, himself took away and posted
with his own hands. Thus he made sure that this act of self-
jurisdiction should be as nearly as possible a *fait accompli*. He
begged, and coaxed, and threatened the bishop with a view of
making him also write at once to Mr. Harding; but the bishop,
though temporarily emancipated from his wife, was not yet
enthralled to Mr. Slope. He said, and probably said truly, that
such an offer must be made in some official form; that he was
not yet prepared to sign the form; and that he should prefer
seeing Mr. Harding before he did so. Mr. Slope might, however,
beg Mr. Harding to call upon him. Not disappointed with his
achievement Mr. Slope went his way. He first posted the precious note which he had in his pocket, and then pursued other
enterprises in which we must follow him in other chapters.

Mrs. Proudie, having received such satisfaction as was to be
derived from slamming her husband's door, did not at once
betake herself to Mrs. Quiverful. Indeed for the first few moments after her repulse she felt that she could not again see that
lady. She would have to own that she had been beaten, to
confess that the diadem had passed from her brow, and the
sceptre from her hand! No, she would send a message to her

with the promise of a letter on the next day or the day after. Thus resolving, she betook herself to her bed-room; but here she again changed her mind. The air of that sacred enclosure somewhat restored her courage, and gave her more heart. As Achilles warmed at the sight of his armour, as Don Quixote's heart grew strong when he grasped his lance, so did Mrs. Proudie look forward to fresh laurels, as her eye fell on her husband's pillow. She would not despair. Having so resolved, she descended with dignified mien and refreshed countenance to Mrs. Quiverful.

This scene in the bishop's study took longer in the acting than in the telling. We have not, perhaps, had the whole of the conversation. At any rate Mrs. Quiverful was beginning to be very impatient, and was thinking that farmer Subsoil would be tired of waiting for her, when Mrs. Proudie returned. Oh! who can tell the palpitations of that maternal heart, as the suppliant looked into the face of the great lady to see written there either a promise of house, income, comfort and future competence, or else the doom of continued and ever increasing poverty. Poor mother! poor wife! there was little there to comfort you!

"Mrs. Quiverful," thus spoke the lady with considerable austerity, and without sitting down herself, "I find that your husband has behaved in this matter in a very weak and foolish manner."

Mrs. Quiverful immediately rose upon her feet, thinking it disrespectful to remain sitting while the wife of the bishop stood. But she was desired to sit down again, and made to do so, so that Mrs. Proudie might stand and preach over her. It is generally considered an offensive thing for a gentleman to keep his seat while another is kept standing before him, and we presume the same law holds with regard to ladies. It often is so felt; but we are inclined to say that it never produces half the discomfort or half the feeling of implied inferiority that is shown by a great man who desires his visitor to be seated while he himself speaks from his legs. Such a solecism in good breeding, when construed into English, means this: "The accepted rules of courtesy in the world require that I should offer you a seat; if I did not do so, you would bring a charge against me in the world of being arrogant and ill-mannered; I will obey the world; but, nevertheless, I will not put myself on an equality with you. You may sit down, but I won't sit with you. Sit, therefore, at my bidding, and I'll stand and talk at you!"

This was just what Mrs. Proudie meant to say; and Mrs. Quiverful, though she was too anxious and too flurried thus to translate the full meaning of the manœuvre, did not fail to feel its effect. She was cowed and uncomfortable, and a second time essayed to rise from her chair.

"Pray be seated, Mrs. Quiverful, pray keep your seat. Your husband, I say, has been most weak and most foolish. It is impossible, Mrs. Quiverful, to help people who will not help themselves. I much fear that I can now do nothing for you in this matter."

"Oh! Mrs. Proudie—don't say so," said the poor woman again jumping up.

"*Pray* be seated Mrs. Quiverful. I much fear that I can do nothing further for you in this matter. Your husband has, in a most unaccountable manner, taken upon himself to resign that which I was empowered to offer him. As a matter of course, the bishop expects that his clergy shall know their own minds. What he may ultimately do—what we may finally decide on doing—I cannot now say. Knowing the extent of your family—"

"Fourteen children, Mrs. Proudie, fourteen of them! and barely bread,—barely, bread! It's hard for the children of a clergyman, it's hard for one who has always done his duty respectably!" Not a word fell from her about herself; but the tears came streaming down her big coarse cheeks, on which the dust of the August road had left its traces.

Mrs. Proudie has not been portrayed in these pages as an agreeable or an amiable lady. There has been no intention to impress the reader much in her favour. It is ordained that all novels should have a male and a female angel, and a male and a female devil. If it be considered that this rule is obeyed in these pages, the latter character must be supposed to have fallen to the lot of Mrs. Proudie. But she was not all devil. There was a heart inside that stiff-ribbed bodice, though not, perhaps, of large dimensions, and certainly not easily accessible. Mrs. Quiverful, however, did gain access, and Mrs. Proudie proved herself a woman. Whether it was the fourteen children with their probable bare bread and their possible bare backs, or the respectability of the father's work, or the mingled dust and tears on the mother's face, we will not pretend to say. But Mrs. Proudie was touched.

She did not show it as other women might have done. She did not give Mrs. Quiverful eau-de-Cologne, or order her a glass of wine. She did not take her to her toilet table, and offer her the use of brushes and combs, towels and water. She did not say soft little speeches and coax her kindly back to equanimity. Mrs. Quiverful, despite her rough appearance, would have been as amenable to such little tender cares as any lady in the land. But none such were forthcoming. Instead of this, Mrs. Proudie slapped one hand upon the other, and declared—not with an oath; for as a lady and a Sabbatarian and a she-bishop, she could not swear, —but with an adjuration, that "she wouldn't have it done."

The meaning of this was that she wouldn't have Mr. Quiverful's promised appointment cozened away by the treachery of Mr. Slope and the weakness of her husband. This meaning she very soon explained to Mrs. Quiverful.

"Why was your husband such a fool," said she, now dismounted from her high horse and sitting confidentially down close to her visitor, "as to take the bait which that man threw to him? If he had not been so utterly foolish, nothing could have prevented your going to the hospital."

Poor Mrs. Quiverful was ready enough with her own tongue in accusing her husband to his face of being soft, and perhaps did not always speak of him to her children quite so respectfully as she might have done. But she did not at all like to hear him abused by others, and began to vindicate him, and to explain that of course he had taken Mr. Slope to be an emissary from Mrs. Proudie herself; that Mr. Slope was thought to be peculiarly her friend; and that, therefore, Mr. Quiverful would have been failing in respect to her had he assumed to doubt what Mr. Slope had said.

Thus mollified Mrs. Proudie again declared that "she would not have it done," and at last sent Mrs. Quiverful home with an assurance that, to the furthest stretch of her power and influence in the palace, the appointment of Mr. Quiverful should be insisted on. As she repeated the word "insisted," she thought of the bishop in his night-cap, and with compressed lips slightly shook her head. Oh! my aspiring pastors, divines to whose ears *nolo episcopari* are the sweetest of words, which of you would be a bishop on such terms as these?

Mrs. Quiverful got home in the farmer's cart, not indeed with a light heart, but satisfied that she had done right in making her visit.

XXVII

A Love Scene

Mr. Slope, as we have said, left the palace with a feeling of considerable triumph. Not that he thought that his difficulties were all over; he did not so deceive himself; but he felt that he had played his first move well, as well as the pieces on the board would allow; and that he had nothing with which to reproach himself. He first of all posted the letter to the archbishop, and having made that sure he proceeded to push the advantage which he had gained. Had Mrs. Bold been at home, he would have called on her; but he knew that she was at Plumstead, so he wrote the following note. It was the beginning of what, he trusted, might be a long and tender series of epistles.

> My dear Mrs. Bold,—You will understand perfectly that I cannot at present correspond with your father. I heartily wish that I could, and hope the day may be not long distant when mists shall have cleared away, and we may know each other. But I cannot preclude myself from the pleasure of sending you these few lines to say that Mr. Q. has to-day, in my presence, resigned any title that he ever had to the wardenship of the hospital, and that the bishop has assured me that it is his intention to offer it to your esteemed father.
>
> Will you, with my respectful compliments, ask him, who I believe is now a fellow-visitor with you, to call on the bishop either on Wednesday or Thursday, between ten and one. *This is by the bishop's desire*. If you will so far oblige me as to let me have a line naming either day, and the hour which will suit Mr. Harding, I will take care that the servants shall have

orders to show him in without delay. Perhaps I should say
no more,—but still I wish you could make your father
understand that no subject will be mooted between his
lordship and him, which will refer at all to the method
in which he may choose to perform his duty. I for one,
am persuaded that no clergyman could perform it more
satisfactorily than he did, or than he will do again.

On a former occasion I was indiscreet and much
too impatient, considering your father's age and my
own. I hope he will not now refuse my apology. I still
hope also that with your aid and sweet pious labours,
we may live to attach such a Sabbath school to the old
endowment, as may, by God's grace and furtherance,
be a blessing to the poor of this city.

You will see at once that this letter is confidential.
The subject, of course, makes it so. But, equally of
course, it is for your parent's eye as well as for your
own, should you think proper to show it to him.

I hope my darling little friend Johnny is as strong
as ever,—dear little fellow. Does he still continue his
rude assaults on those beautiful silken tresses?

I can assure you your friends miss you from
Barchester sorely; but it would be cruel to begrudge
you your sojourn among flowers and fields during this
truly sultry weather.

> Pray believe me, my dear Mrs. Bold,
> Yours most sincerely,
> OBADIAH SLOPE.

Barchester, Friday.

Now this letter, taken as a whole, and with the consideration that Mr. Slope wished to assume a great degree of intimacy
with Eleanor, would not have been bad, but for the allusion to
the tresses. Gentlemen do not write to ladies about their tresses,
unless they are on very intimate terms indeed. But Mr. Slope
could not be expected to be aware of this. He longed to put a
little affection into his epistle, and yet he thought it injudicious,
as the letter would, he knew, be shown to Mr. Harding. He
would have insisted that the letter should be strictly private and
seen by no eyes but Eleanor's own, had he not felt that such an
injunction would have been disobeyed. He therefore restrained

his passion, did not sign himself "yours affectionately," and contented himself instead with the compliment to the tresses.

Having finished his letter, he took it to Mrs. Bold's house, and learning there, from the servant, that things were to be sent out to Plumstead that afternoon, left it, with many injunctions, in her hands.

We will now follow Mr. Slope so as to complete the day with him, and then return to his letter and its momentous fate in the next chapter.

There is an old song which gives us some very good advice about courting:—

> It's gude to be off with the auld luve
> Before ye be on wi' the new.

Of the wisdom of this maxim Mr. Slope was ignorant, and accordingly, having written his letter to Mrs. Bold, he proceeded to call upon the Signora Neroni. Indeed it was hard to say which was the old love and which the new, Mr. Slope having been smitten with both so nearly at the same time. Perhaps he thought it not amiss to have two strings to his bow. But two strings to Cupid's bow are always dangerous to him on whose behalf they are to be used. A man should remember that between two stools he may fall to the ground.

But in sooth Mr. Slope was pursuing Mrs. Bold in obedience to his better instincts, and the signora in obedience to his worser. Had he won the widow and worn her, no one could have blamed him. You, O reader, and I, and Eleanor's other friends would have received the story of such a winning with much disgust and disappointment; but we should have been angry with Eleanor, not with Mr. Slope. Bishop, male and female, dean and chapter and diocesan clergy in full congress, could have found nothing to disapprove of in such an alliance. Convocation itself, that mysterious and mighty synod, could in no wise have fallen foul of it. The possession of £1000 a year and a beautiful wife would not at all have hurt the voice of the pulpit charmer, or lessened the grace and piety of the exemplary clergyman.

But not of such a nature were likely to be his dealings with the Signora Neroni. In the first place he knew that her husband was living, and therefore he could not woo her honestly. Then again she had nothing to recommend her to his honest wooing had such been possible. She was not only portionless, but also from misfortune unfitted to be chosen as the wife of any man who wanted a useful mate. Mr. Slope was aware that she was a helpless hopeless cripple.

But Mr. Slope could not help himself. He knew that he was wrong in devoting his time to the back drawing-room in Dr. Stanhope's house. He knew that what took place there would if divulged utterly ruin him with Mrs. Bold. He knew that scandal would soon come upon his heels and spread abroad among the black coats of Barchester some tidings, exaggerated tidings, of the sighs which he poured into the lady's ears. He knew that he was acting against the recognised principles of his life, against those laws of conduct by which he hoped to achieve much higher success. But as we have said, he could not help himself. Passion, for the first time in his life, passion was too strong for him.

As for the signora, no such plea can be put forward for her, for in truth she cared no more for Mr. Slope than she did for twenty others who had been at her feet before him. She willingly, nay greedily, accepted his homage. He was the finest fly that Barchester had hitherto afforded to her web; and the signora was a powerful spider that made wondrous webs, and could in no way live without catching flies. Her taste in this respect was abominable, for she had no use for the victims when caught. She could not eat them matrimonially, as young lady-flies do whose webs are most frequently of their mothers' weaving. Nor could she devour them by any escapade of a less legitimate description. Her unfortunate affliction precluded her from all hope of levanting with a lover. It would be impossible to run away with a lady who required three servants to move her from a sofa.

The signora was subdued by no passion. Her time for love was gone. She had lived out her heart, such heart as she had ever had, in her early years, at an age when Mr. Slope was thinking of the second book of Euclid and his unpaid bill at the buttery hatch. In age the lady was younger than the gentleman; but in feelings, in knowledge of the affairs of love, in intrigue, he was immeasurably her junior. It was necessary to her to have some man at her feet. It was the one customary excitement of her life. She delighted in the exercise of power which this gave her; it was now nearly the only food for her ambition; she would boast to her sister that she could make a fool of any man, and the sister, as little imbued with feminine delicacy as herself, good naturedly thought it but fair that such amusement should be afforded to a poor invalid who was debarred from the ordinary pleasures of life.

Mr. Slope was madly in love, but hardly knew it. The

signora spitted him, as a boy does a cockchafer on a cork, that she might enjoy the energetic agony of his gyrations. And she knew very well what she was doing.

Mr. Slope having added to his person all such adornments as are possible to a clergyman making a morning visit, such as a clean neck tie, clean handkerchief, new gloves, and a *soupçon* of not unnecessary scent, called about three o'clock at the doctor's door. At about this hour the signora was almost always alone in the back drawing-room. The mother had not come down. The doctor was out or in his own room. Bertie was out, and Charlotte at any rate left the room if any one called whose object was specially with her sister. Such was her idea of being charitable and sisterly.

Mr. Slope, as was his custom, asked for Mr. Stanhope, and was told, as was the servant's custom, that the signora was in the drawing-room. Upstairs he accordingly went. He found her, as he always did, lying on her sofa with a French volume before her, and a beautiful little inlaid writing case open on her table. At the moment of his entrance she was in the act of writing.

"Ah, my friend," said she, putting out her left hand to him across her desk, "I did not expect you to-day and was this very instant writing to you——"

Mr. Slope, taking the soft fair delicate hand in his, and very soft and fair and delicate it was, bowed over it his huge red head and kissed it. It was a sight to see, a deed to record if the author could fitly do it, a picture to put on canvass. Mr. Slope was big, awkward, cumbrous, and having his heart in his pursuit was ill at ease. The lady was fair, as we have said, and delicate; every thing about her was fine and refined; her hand in his looked like a rose lying among carrots, and when he kissed it he looked as a cow might do on finding such a flower among her food. She was graceful as a couchant goddess, and, moreover, as self-possessed as Venus must have been when courting Adonis.

Oh, that such grace and such beauty should have condescended to waste itself on such a pursuit!

"I was in the act of writing to you," said she, "but now my scrawl may go into the basket"; and she raised the sheet of gilded note paper from off her desk as though to tear it.

"Indeed it shall not," said he, laying the embargo of half a stone weight of human flesh and blood upon the devoted paper. "Nothing that you write for my eyes, signora, shall be so desecrated," and he took up the letter, put that also among the carrots and fed on it, and then proceeded to read it.

"Gracious me! Mr. Slope," said she, "I hope you don't mean to say that you keep all the trash I write to you. Half my time I don't know what I write, and when I do, I know it is only fit for the back of the fire. I hope you have not that ugly trick of keeping letters."

"At any rate, I don't throw them into a waste-paper basket. If destruction is their doomed lot, they perish worthily, and are burnt on a pyre, as Dido was of old."

"With a steel pen stuck through them, of course," said she, "to make the simile more complete. Of all the ladies of my acquaintance I think Lady Dido was the most absurd. Why did she not do as Cleopatra did? Why did she not take out her ships and insist on going with him? She could not bear to lose the land she had got by a swindle; and then she could not bear the loss of her lover. So she fell between two stools. Mr. Slope, whatever you do, never mingle love and business."

Mr. Slope blushed up to his eyes, and over his mottled forehead to the very roots of his hair. He felt sure that the signora knew all about his intentions with reference to Mrs. Bold. His conscience told him that he was detected. His doom was to be spoken; he was to be punished for his duplicity, and rejected by the beautiful creature before him. Poor man. He little dreamt that had all his intentions with reference to Mrs. Bold been known to the signora, it would only have added zest to that lady's amusement. It was all very well to have Mr. Slope at her feet, to show her power by making an utter fool of a clergyman, to gratify her own infidelity by thus proving the little strength which religion had in controlling the passions even of a religious man; but it would be an increased gratification if she could be made to understand that she was at the same time alluring her victim away from another, whose love if secured would be in every way beneficent and salutary.

The signora had indeed discovered with the keen instinct of such a woman, that Mr. Slope was bent on matrimony with Mrs. Bold, but in alluding to Dido she had not thought of it. She instantly perceived, however, from her lover's blushes, what was on his mind, and was not slow in taking advantage of it.

She looked him full in the face, not angrily, nor yet with a smile, but with an intense and overpowering gaze; and then holding up her forefinger, and slightly shaking her head she said:—

"Whatever you do, my friend, do not mingle love and business. Either stick to your treasure and your city of wealth, or else follow your love like a true man. But never attempt both. If you do, you'll have to die with a broken heart as did poor Dido. Which is it to be with you, Mr. Slope, love or money?''

Mr. Slope was not so ready with a pathetic answer as he usually was with touching episodes in his extempore sermons. He felt that he ought to say something pretty, something also that should remove the impression on the mind of his lady love. But he was rather put about how to do it.

"Love," said he, "true overpowering love, must be the strongest passion a man can feel; it must control every other wish, and put aside every other pursuit. But with me love will never act in that way unless it be returned''; and he threw upon the signora a look of tenderness which was intended to make up for all the deficiences of his speech.

"Take my advice," said she. "Never mind love. After all, what is it? The dream of a few weeks. That is all its joy. The disappointment of a life is its Nemesis. Who was ever successful in true love? Success in love argues that the love is false. True love is always despondent or tragical. Juliet loved, Haidee loved, Dido loved, and what came of it? Troilus loved and ceased to be a man.''

"Troilus loved and was fooled," said the more manly chaplain. "A man may love and yet not be a Troilus. All women are not Cressids.''

"No; all women are not Cressids. The falsehood is not always on the woman's side. Imogen was true, but how was she rewarded? Her lord believed her to be the paramour of the first he who came near her in his absence. Desdemona was true and was smothered. Ophelia was true and went mad. There is no happiness in love, except at the end of an English novel. But in wealth, money, houses, lands, goods and chattels, in the good things of this world, yes, in them there is something tangible, something that can be retained and enjoyed.''

"Oh, no," said Mr. Slope, feeling himself bound to enter some protest against so very unorthodox a doctrine, "this world's wealth will make no one happy.''

"And what will make you happy—you—you?" said she, raising herself up, and speaking to him with energy across the table. "From what source do you look for happiness? Do not say that you look for none? I shall not believe you. It is a search in which every human being spends an existence.''

"And the search is always in vain," said Mr. Slope. "We

look for happiness on earth, while we ought to be content to hope for it in heaven.''

"Pshaw! you preach a doctrine which you know you don't believe. It is the way with you all. If you know that there is no earthly happiness, why do you long to be a bishop or a dean? Why do you want lands and income?''

"I have the natural ambition of a man," said he.

"Of course you have, and the natural passions; and therefore I say that you don't believe the doctrine you preach. St. Paul was an enthusiast. He believed so that his ambition and passions did not war against his creed. So does the Eastern fanatic who passes half his life erect upon a pillar. As for me, I will believe in no belief that does not make itself manifest by outward signs. I will think no preaching sincere that is not recommended by the practice of the preacher.''

Mr. Slope was startled and horrified, but he felt that he could not answer. How could he stand up and preach the lessons of his Master, being there as he was, on the devil's business? He was a true believer, otherwise this would have been nothing to him. He had audacity for most things, but he had not audacity to make a plaything of the Lord's word. All this the signora understood and felt much interest as she saw her cockchafer whirl round upon her pin.

"Your wit delights in such arguments," said he, "but your heart and your reason do not go along with them.''

"My heart!" said she; "you quite mistake the principles of my composition if you imagine that there is such a thing about me.'' After all, there was very little that was false in anything that the signora said. If Mr. Slope allowed himself to be deceived it was his own fault. Nothing could have been more open than her declarations about herself.

The little writing table with her desk was still standing before her, a barrier, as it were, against the enemy. She was sitting as nearly upright as she ever did, and he had brought a chair close to the sofa, so that there was only the corner of the table between him and her. It so happened that as she spoke her hand lay upon the table, and as Mr. Slope answered her he put his hand upon hers.

"No heart!" said he. "That is a heavy charge which you bring against yourself, and one of which I cannot find you guilty——''

She withdrew her hand, not quickly and angrily, as though insulted by his touch, but gently and slowly.

"You are in no condition to give a verdict on the matter," said she, "as you have not tried me. No; don't say that you intend doing so, for you know you have no intention of the kind; nor indeed have I either. As for you, you will take your vows where they will result in something more substantial than the pursuit of such a ghostlike, ghastly love as mine——"

"Your love should be sufficient to satisfy the dream of a monarch," said Mr. Slope, not quite clear as to the meaning of his words.

"Say an archbishop, Mr. Slope," said she. Poor fellow! she was very cruel to him. He went round again upon his cork on this allusion to his profession. He tried, however, to smile, and gently accused her of joking on a matter, which was, he said, to him of such vital moment.

"Why—what gulls do you men make of us," she replied. "How you fool us to the top of our bent; and of all men you clergymen are the most fluent of your honeyed caressing words. Now look me in the face, Mr. Slope, boldly and openly."

Mr. Slope did look at her with a languishing loving eye, and as he did so, he again put forth his hand to get hold of hers.

"I told you to look at me boldly, Mr. Slope; but confine your boldness to your eyes."

"Oh, Madeline!" he sighed.

"Well, my name is Madeline," said she; "but none except my own family usually call me so. Now look me in the face, Mr. Slope. Am I to understand that you say you love me?"

Mr. Slope never had said so. If he had come there with any formed plan at all, his intention was to make love to the lady without uttering any such declaration. It was, however, quite impossible that he should now deny his love. He had, therefore, nothing for it, but to go down on his knees distractedly against the sofa, and swear that he did love her with a love passing the love of man.

The signora received the assurance with very little palpitation or appearance of surprise. "And now answer me another question," said she; "when are you to be married to my dear friend Eleanor Bold?"

Poor Mr. Slope went round and round in mortal agony. In such a condition as his it was really very hard for him to know what answer to give. And yet no answer would be his surest condemnation. He might as well at once plead guilty to the charge brought against him.

"And why do you accuse me of such dissimulation?" said he.

"Dissimulation! I said nothing of dissimulation. I made no charge against you, and make none. Pray don't defend yourself to me. You swear that you are devoted to my beauty, and yet you are on the eve of matrimony with another. I feel this to be rather a compliment. It is to Mrs. Bold that you must defend yourself. That you may find difficult; unless, indeed, you can keep her in the dark. You clergymen are cleverer than other men."

"Signora, I have told you that I loved you, and now you rail at me?"

"Rail at you. God bless the man; what would he have? Come, answer me this at your leisure,—not without thinking now, but leisurely and with consideration,—Are you not going to be married to Mrs. Bold?"

"I am not," said he. And as he said it, he almost hated, with an exquisite hatred, the woman whom he could not help loving with an exquisite love.

"But surely you are a worshipper of hers?"

"I am not," said Mr. Slope, to whom the word worshipper was peculiarly distasteful. The signora had conceived that it would be so.

"I wonder at that," said she. "Do you not admire her? To my eye she is the perfection of English beauty. And then she is rich too. I should have thought she was just the person to attract you. Come, Mr. Slope, let me give you advice on this matter. Marry the charming widow! she will be a good mother to your children, and an excellent mistress of a clergyman's household."

"Oh, signora, how can you be so cruel?"

"Cruel," said she, changing the voice of banter which she had been using for one which was expressively earnest in its tone; "is that cruelty?"

"How can I love another, while my heart is entirely your own?"

"If that were cruelty, Mr. Slope, what might you say of me if I were to declare that I returned your passion? What would you think if I bound you even by a lover's oath to do daily penance at this couch of mine? What can I give in return for a man's love? Ah, dear friend, you have not realised the conditions of my fate."

Mr. Slope was not on his knees all this time. After his declaration of love he had risen from them as quickly as he thought consistent with the new position which he now filled, and as he stood was leaning on the back of his chair. This outburst of tenderness on the signora's part quite overcame him, and made him feel for the moment that he could sacrifice everything to be assured of the love of the beautiful creature before him, maimed, lame, and already married as she was.

"And can I not sympathise with your lot?" said he, now seating himself on her sofa, and pushing away the table with his foot.

"Sympathy is so near to pity!" said she. "If you pity me, cripple as I am, I shall spurn you from me."

"Oh, Madeline, I will only love you," and again he caught her hand and devoured it with kisses. Now she did not draw it from him, but sat there as he kissed it, looking at him with her great eyes, just as a great spider would look at a great fly that was quite securely caught.

"Suppose Signor Neroni were to come to Barchester," said she, "would you make his acquaintance?"

"Signor Neroni!" said he.

"Would you introduce him to the bishop, and Mrs. Proudie, and the young ladies?" said she, again having recourse to that horrid quizzing voice which Mr. Slope so particularly hated.

"Why do you ask such a question?" said he.

"Because it is necessary that you should know that there is a Signor Neroni. I think you had forgotten it."

"If I thought that you retained for that wretch one particle of the love of which he was never worthy, I would die before I would distract you by telling you what I feel. No! were your husband the master of your heart, I might perhaps love you; but you should never know it."

"My heart again! how you talk. And you consider then, that if a husband be not master of his wife's heart, he has no right to her fealty; if a wife ceases to love, she may cease to be true. Is that your doctrine on this matter, as a minister of the Church of England?"

Mr. Slope tried hard within himself to cast off the pollution with which he felt that he was defiling his soul. He strove to tear himself away from the noxious siren that had bewitched him. But he could not do it. He could not be again heart free. He had looked for rapturous joy in loving this lovely creature, and he already found that he met with little but disappointment and self-rebuke. He had come across the fruit of the Dead Sea, so sweet and delicious to the eye, so bitter and nauseous to the taste. He had put the apple to his mouth, and it had turned to ashes between his teeth. Yet he could not tear himself away. He knew, he could not but know, that she jeered at him, ridiculed his love, and insulted the weakness of his religion. But she half permitted his adoration, and that half permission added such fuel to his fire that all the fountain of his piety could not quench it. He began to feel savage, irritated, and revengeful. He meditated some severity of speech, some taunt that should cut her, as her taunts cut him. He reflected as he stood there for a moment, silent before her, that if he desired to quell her proud spirit, he should do so by being prouder even than herself; that if he wished to have her at his feet suppliant for his love it behoved him to conquer her by indifference. All this passed through his mind. As far as dead knowledge went, he knew, or thought he knew, how a woman should be tamed. But when he essayed to bring his tactics to bear, he failed like a child. What chance has dead knowledge with experience in any of the transactions between man and man? What possible chance between man and woman? Mr. Slope loved furiously, insanely, and truly; but he had never played the game of love. The signora did not love at all, but she was up to every move of the board. It was Philidor pitted against a school-boy.

And so she continued to insult him, and he continued to bear it.

"Sacrifice the world for love!" said she, in answer to some renewed vapid declaration of his passion, "how often has the same thing been said, and how invariably with the same falsehood!"

"Falsehood," said he. "Do you say that I am false to you? do you say that my love is not real?"

"False? of course it is false, false as the father of falsehood—if indeed falsehoods need a sire and are not self-begotten since the world began. You are ready to sacrifice the world for love? Come let us see what you will sacrifice. I care nothing for nuptial vows. The wretch, I think you were kind enough to call him so, whom I swore to love and obey, is so base that he can only be thought of with repulsive disgust. In the council chamber of my heart I have divorced him. To me that is as good as though aged lords had gloated for months over the details of his licentious life. I care nothing for what the world can say. Will you be as frank? Will you take me to your home as your wife? Will you call me Mrs. Slope before bishop, dean, and prebendaries?" The poor tortured wretch stood silent, not knowing what to say. "What! you won't do that. Tell me, then, what part of the world is it that you will sacrifice for my charms?"

"Were you free to marry, I would take you to my house tomorrow and wish no higher privilege."

"I am free"; said she, almost starting up in her energy. For though there was no truth in her pretended regard for her clerical admirer, there was a mixture of real feeling in the scorn and satire with which she spoke of love and marriage generally. "I am free; free as the winds. Come; will you take me as I am? Have your wish; sacrifice the world, and prove yourself a true man."

Mr. Slope should have taken her at her word. She would have drawn back, and he would have had the full advantage of the offer. But he did not. Instead of doing so, he stood wrapt in astonishment, passing his fingers through his lank red hair, and thinking as he stared upon her animated countenance that her wondrous beauty grew more and more wonderful as he gazed on it. "Ha! ha! ha!" she laughed out loud. "Come Mr. Slope; don't talk of sacrificing the world again. People beyond one-and-twenty should never dream of such a thing. You and I, if we have the dregs of any love left in us, if we have the remnants of a passion remaining in our hearts, should husband our resources better. We are not in our *première jeunesse*. The world is a very nice place. Your world, at any rate, is so. You have all manner of fat rectories to get, and possible bishoprics to enjoy. Come, confess; on second thoughts you would not sacrifice such things for the smiles of a lame lady?"

It was impossible for him to answer this. In order to be in any way dignified, he felt that he must be silent.

"Come," said she—"don't boody with me: don't be angry because I speak out some home truths. Alas, the world, as I have found it, has taught me bitter truths. Come, tell me that I am forgiven. Are we not to be friends?" and she again put out her hand to him.

He sat himself down in the chair beside her, and took her proffered hand and leant over her.

"There," said she, with her sweetest softest smile—a smile to withstand which a man should be cased in triple steel, "there; seal your forgiveness on it," and she raised it towards his face. He kissed it again and again, and stretched over her as though desirous of extending the charity of his pardon beyond the hand that was offered to him. She managed, however, to check his ardour. For one so easily allured as this poor chaplain, her hand was surely enough.

"Oh, Madeline!" said he, "tell me that you love me—do you—do you love me?"

"Hush," said she. "There is my mother's step. Our *tête-à-tête* has been of monstrous length. Now you had better go. But we shall see you soon again, shall we not?"

Mr. Slope promised that he would call again on the following day.

"And, Mr. Slope," she continued, "pray answer my note. You have it in your hand, though I declare during these two hours you have not been gracious enough to read it. It is about the Sabbath school and the children. You know how anxious I am to have them here. I have been learning the catechism myself, on purpose. You must manage it for me next week. I will teach them, at any rate, to submit themselves to their spiritual pastors and masters."

Mr. Slope said but little on the subject of Sabbath schools, but he made his adieu, and betook himself home with a sad heart, troubled mind, and uneasy conscience.

XXVIII

Mrs. Bold Is Entertained by Dr. and Mrs. Grantly at Plumstead

It will be remembered that Mr. Slope, when leaving his *billet doux* at the house of Mrs. Bold, had been informed that it would be sent out to her at Plumstead that afternoon. The archdeacon and Mr. Harding had in fact come into town together in the brougham, and it had been arranged that they should call for Eleanor's parcels as they left on their way home. Accordingly they did so call, and the maid, as she handed to the coachman a small basket and large bundle carefully and neatly packed, gave in at the carriage window Mr. Slope's epistle. The archdeacon, who was sitting next to the window, took it, and immediately recognised the hand-writing of his enemy.

"Who left this?" said he.

"Mr. Slope called with it himself, your reverence," said the girl; "and was very anxious that missus should have it to-day."

So the brougham drove off, and the letter was left in the archdeacon's hand. He looked at it as though he held a basket of adders. He could not have thought worse of the document had he read it and discovered it to be licentious and atheistical. He did, moreover, what so many wise people are accustomed to do in similar circumstances; he immediately condemned the person to whom the letter was written, as though she were necessarily a *particeps criminis*.

Poor Mr. Harding, though by no means inclined to forward Mr. Slope's intimacy with his daughter, would have given anything to have kept the letter from his son-in-law. But that was now impossible. There it was in his hand; and he looked as thoroughly disgusted as though he were quite sure that it contained all the rhapsodies of a favoured lover.

"It's very hard on me," said he, after awhile, "that this should go on under my roof."

Now here the archdeacon was certainly most unreasonable. Having invited his sister-in-law to his house, it was a natural consequence that she should receive her letters there. And if Mr. Slope chose to write to her, his letter would, as a matter of course, be sent after her. Moreover, the very fact of an invitation to one's house implies confidence on the part of the inviter. He had shown that he thought Mrs. Bold to be a fit person to stay with him by his asking her to do so, and it was most cruel to her that he should complain of her violating the sanctity of his roof-tree, when the laches committed were none of her committing.

Mr. Harding felt this; and felt also that when the archdeacon talked thus about his roof, what he said was most offensive to himself as Eleanor's father. If Eleanor did receive a letter from Mr. Slope, what was there in that to pollute the purity of Dr. Grantly's household? He was indignant that his daughter should be so judged and so spoken of; and he made up his mind that even as Mrs. Slope she must be dearer to him than any other creature on God's earth. He almost broke out, and said as much; but for the moment he restrained himself.

"Here," said the archdeacon, handing the offensive missile

to his father-in-law; "I am not going to be the bearer of his love letters. You are her father, and may do as you think fit with it."

By doing as he thought fit with it, the archdeacon certainly meant that Mr. Harding would be justified in opening and reading the letter, and taking any steps which might in consequence be necessary. To tell the truth, Dr. Grantly did feel rather a stronger curiosity than was justified by his outraged virtue, to see the contents of the letter. Of course he could not open it himself, but he wished to make Mr. Harding understand that he, as Eleanor's father, would be fully justified in doing so. The idea of such a proceeding never occurred to Mr. Harding. His authority over Eleanor ceased when she became the wife of John Bold. He had not the slightest wish to pry into her correspondence. He consequently put the letter into his pocket, and only wished that he had been able to do so without the archdeacon's knowledge. They both sat silent during half the journey home, and then Dr. Grantly said, "Perhaps Susan had better give it to her. She can explain to her sister, better than either you or I can do, how deep is the disgrace of such an acquaintance."

"I think you are very hard upon Eleanor," replied Mr. Harding. "I will not allow that she has disgraced herself, nor do I think it likely that she will do so. She has a right to correspond with whom she pleases, and I shall not take upon myself to blame her because she gets a letter from Slope."

"I suppose," said Dr. Grantly, "you don't wish her to marry the man. I suppose you'll admit that she would disgrace herself if she did so."

"I do not wish her to marry him," said the perplexed father; "I do not like him, and do not think he would make a good husband. But if Eleanor chooses to do so, I shall certainly not think that she disgraces herself."

"Good heavens!" exclaimed Dr. Grantly, and threw himself back into the corner of his brougham. Mr. Harding said nothing more, but commenced playing a dirge, with an imaginary fiddle bow upon an imaginary violoncello, for which there did not appear to be quite room enough in the carriage; and he continued the tune, with sundry variations, till he arrived at the rectory door.

The archdeacon had been meditating sad things in his mind. Hitherto he had always looked on his father-in-law as a true partisan, though he knew him to be a man devoid of all the combative qualifications for that character. He had felt no fear that Mr. Harding would go over to the enemy, though he had never counted much on the ex-warden's prowess in breaking the hostile ranks. Now, however, it seemed that Eleanor, with her wiles, had completely trepanned and bewildered her father, cheated him out of his judgment, robbed him of the predilections and tastes of his life, and caused him to be tolerant of a man whose arrogance and vulgarity would, a few years since, have been unendurable to him. That the whole thing was as good as arranged between Eleanor and Mr. Slope there was no longer any room to doubt. That Mr. Harding knew that such was the case, even this could hardly be doubted. It was too manifest that he at any rate suspected it, and was prepared to sanction it.

And to tell the truth, such was the case. Mr. Harding disliked Mr. Slope as much as it was in his nature to dislike any man. Had his daughter wished to do her worst to displease him by a second marriage, she could hardly have succeeded better than by marrying Mr. Slope. But, as he said to himself now very often, what right had he to condemn her if she did nothing that was really wrong? If she liked Mr. Slope it was her affair. It was indeed miraculous to him that a woman with such a mind, so educated, so refined, so nice in her tastes, should like such a man. Then he asked himself whether it was possible that she did so?

Ah, thou weak man; most charitable, most Christian, but weakest of men! Why couldst thou not have asked herself? Was she not the daughter of thy loins, the child of thy heart, the best beloved to thee of all humanity? Had she not proved to thee, by years of closest affection, her truth and goodness and filial obedience? And yet, knowing and feeling all this, thou couldst endure to go groping in darkness, hearing her named in strains which wounded thy loving heart, and being unable to defend her as thou shouldst have done!

Mr. Harding had not believed, did not believe, that his daughter meant to marry this man; but he feared to commit himself to such an opinion. If she did do it there would be then no means of retreat. The wishes of his heart were—First, that there should be no truth in the archdeacon's surmises; and in this wish he would have fain trusted entirely, had he dared so to do; Secondly, that the match might be prevented, if unfortunately, it had been contemplated by Eleanor; Thirdly, that should she be so infatuated as to marry this man, he might justify his conduct, and declare that no cause existed for his separating himself from her.

He wanted to believe her incapable of such a marriage; he

wanted to show that he so believed of her; but he wanted also to be able to say hereafter, that she had done nothing amiss, if she should unfortunately prove herself to be different from what he thought her to be.

Nothing but affection could justify such fickleness; but affection did justify it. There was but little of the Roman about Mr. Harding. He could not sacrifice his Lucretia even though she should be polluted by the accepted addresses of the clerical Tarquin at the palace. If Tarquin could be prevented, well and good; but if not, the father would still open his heart to his daughter, and accept her as she presented herself, Tarquin and all.

Dr. Grantly's mind was of a stronger calibre, and he was by no means deficient in heart. He loved with an honest genuine love his wife and children and friends. He loved his father-in-law; and was quite prepared to love Eleanor too, if she would be one of his party, if she would be on his side, if she would regard the Slopes and the Proudies as the enemies of mankind, and acknowledge and feel the comfortable merits of the Gwynnes and Arabins. He wished to be what he called "safe" with all those whom he had admitted to the penetralia of his house and heart. He could luxuriate in no society that was deficient in a certain feeling of faithful staunch high-churchism, which to him was tantamount to freemasonry. He was not strict in his lines of definition. He endured without impatience many different shades of Anglo-church conservatism; but with the Slopes and Proudies he could not go on all fours.

He was wanting in, moreover, or perhaps it would be more correct to say, he was not troubled by that womanly tenderness which was so peculiar to Mr. Harding. His feelings towards his friends were, that while they stuck to him he would stick to them; that he would work with them shoulder and shoulder; that he would be faithful to the faithful. He knew nothing of that beautiful love which can be true to a false friend.

And thus these two men, each miserable enough in his own way, returned to Plumstead.

It was getting late when they arrived there, and the ladies had already gone up to dress. Nothing more was said as the two parted in the hall. As Mr. Harding passed to his own room he knocked at Eleanor's door and handed in the letter. The archdeacon hurried to his own territory, there to unburden his heart to his faithful partner.

What colloquy took place between the marital chamber and the adjoining dressing-room shall not be detailed. The reader, now intimate with the persons concerned, can well imagine it. The whole tenour of it also might be read in Mrs. Grantly's brow as she came down to dinner.

Eleanor, when she received the letter from her father's hand, had no idea from whom it came. She had never seen Mr. Slope's hand-writing, or if so had forgotten it; and did not think of him as she twisted the letter as people do twist letters when they do not immediately recognise their correspondents either by the writing or the seal. She was sitting at her glass brushing her hair, and rising every other minute to play with her boy who was sprawling on the bed, and who engaged pretty nearly the whole attention of the maid as well as of his mother.

At last, sitting before her toilet table, she broke the seal, and turning over the leaf saw Mr. Slope's name. She first felt surprised, and then annoyed, and then anxious. As she read it she became interested. She was so delighted to find that all obstacles to her father's return to the hospital were apparently removed that she did not observe the fulsome language in which the tidings were conveyed. She merely perceived that she was commissioned to tell her father that such was the case, and she did not realise the fact that such a communication should not have been made, in the first instance, to her by an unmarried young clergyman. She felt, on the whole, grateful to Mr. Slope, and anxious to get on her dress that she might run with the news to her father. Then she came to the allusion to her own pious labours, and she said in her heart that Mr. Slope was an affected ass. Then she went on again and was offended by her boy being called Mr. Slope's darling—he was nobody's darling but her own; or at any rate not the darling of a disagreeable stranger like Mr. Slope. Lastly she arrived at the tresses and felt a qualm of disgust. She looked up in the glass, and there they were before her, long and silken, certainly, and very beautiful. I will not say but that she knew them to be so, but she felt angry with them and brushed them roughly and carelessly. She crumpled the letter up with angry violence, and resolved, almost without thinking of it, that she would not show it to her father. She would merely tell him the contents of it. She then comforted herself again with her boy, had her dress fastened, and went down to dinner.

As she tripped down the stairs she began to ascertain that there was some difficulty in her situation. She could not keep from her father the news about the hospital, nor could she comfortably confess the letter from Mr. Slope before the Grantlys. Her father had already gone down. She had heard his step upon the lobby. She resolved therefore to take him aside, and tell him her little bit of news. Poor girl! she had no idea how severely the unfortunate letter had already been discussed.

When she entered the drawing-room the whole party were there, including Mr. Arabin, and the whole party looked glum and sour. The two girls sat silent and apart as though they were aware that something was wrong. Even Mr. Arabin was solemn and silent. Eleanor had not seen him since breakfast. He had been the whole day at St. Ewold's, and such having been the case it was natural that he should tell how matters were going on there. He did nothing of the kind, however, but remained solemn and silent. They were all solemn and silent. Eleanor knew in her heart that they had been talking about her, and her heart misgave her as she thought of Mr. Slope and his letter. At any rate she felt it to be quite impossible to speak to her father alone while matters were in this state.

Dinner was soon announced, and Dr. Grantly, as was his wont, gave Eleanor his arm. But he did so as though the doing it were an outrage on his feelings rendered necessary by sternest necessity. With quick sympathy Eleanor felt this, and hardly put her fingers on his coat sleeve. It may be guessed in what way the dinner-hour was passed. Dr. Grantly said a few words to Mr. Arabin, Mr. Arabin said a few words to Mrs. Grantly, she said a few words to her father, and he tried to say a few words to Eleanor. She felt that she had been tried and found guilty of something, though she knew not what. She longed to say out to them all, "Well, what is it that I have done; out with it, and let me know my crime; for heaven's sake let me hear the worst of it"; but she could not. She could say nothing, but sat there silent, half feeling that she was guilty, and trying in vain to pretend even to eat her dinner.

At last the cloth was drawn, and the ladies were not long following it. When they were gone the gentlemen were somewhat more sociable but not much so. They could not of course talk over Eleanor's sins. The archdeacon had indeed so far betrayed his sister-in-law as to whisper into Mr. Arabin's ear in the study, as they met there before dinner, a hint of what he feared. He did so with the gravest and saddest of fears, and Mr. Arabin became grave and apparently sad enough as he heard it. He opened his eyes and his mouth and said in a sort of whisper, "Mr. Slope!" in the same way as he might have said "The

Cholera,'' had his friend told him that that horrid disease was in his nursery. "I fear so, I fear so," said the archdeacon, and then together they left the room.

We will not accurately analyse Mr. Arabin's feelings on receipt of such astounding tidings. It will suffice to say that he was surprised, vexed, sorrowful, and ill at ease. He had not perhaps thought very much about Eleanor, but he had appreciated her influence, and had felt that close intimacy with her in a country house was pleasant to him, and also beneficial. He had spoken highly of her intelligence to the archdeacon, and had walked about the shrubberies with her, carrying her boy on his back. When Mr. Arabin had called Johnny his darling, Eleanor was not angry.

Thus the three men sat over their wine, all thinking of the same subject, but unable to speak of it to each other. So we will leave them, and follow the ladies into the drawing-room.

Mrs. Grantly had received a commission from her husband, and had undertaken it with some unwillingness. He had desired her to speak gravely to Eleanor, and to tell her that, if she persisted in her adherence to Mr. Slope, she could no longer look for the countenance of her present friends. Mrs. Grantly probably knew her sister better than the doctor did, and assured him that it would be in vain to talk to her. The only course likely to be of any service in her opinion was to keep Eleanor away from Barchester. Perhaps she might have added, for she had a very keen eye in such things, that there might also be ground for hope in keeping Eleanor near Mr. Arabin. Of this, however, she said nothing. But the archdeacon would not be talked over; he spoke much of his conscience, and declared that if Mrs. Grantly would not do it he would. So instigated, the lady undertook the task, stating, however, her full conviction that her interference would be worse than useless. And so it proved.

As soon as they were in the drawing-room Mrs. Grantly found some excuse for sending her girls away, and then began her task. She knew well that she could exercise but very slight authority over her sister. Their various modes of life, and the distance between their residences, had prevented any very close confidence. They had hardly lived together since Eleanor was a child. Eleanor had moreover, especially in latter years, resented in a quiet sort of way the dictatorial authority which the archdeacon seemed to exercise over her father, and on this account had been unwilling to allow the archdeacon's wife to exercise authority over herself.

"You got a note just before dinner, I believe," began the eldest sister.

Eleanor acknowledged that she had done so, and felt that she turned red as she acknowledged it. She would have given anything to have kept her colour, but the more she tried to do so the more signally she failed.

"Was it not from Mr. Slope?"

Eleanor said that the letter was from Mr. Slope.

"Is he a regular correspondent of yours, Eleanor?"

"Not exactly," said she, already beginning to feel angry at the cross-examination. She determined, and why it would be difficult to say, that nothing should induce her to tell her sister Susan what was the subject of the letter. Mrs. Grantly, she knew, was instigated by the archdeacon, and she would not plead to any arraignment made against her by him.

"But, Eleanor dear, why do you get letters from Mr. Slope at all, knowing, as you do, he is a person so distasteful to papa, and to the archdeacon, and indeed to all your friends?"

"In the first place, Susan, I don't get letters from him; and in the next place, as Mr. Slope wrote the one letter which I have got, and as I only received it, which I could not very well help doing, as papa handed it to me, I think you had better ask Mr. Slope instead of me."

"What was his letter about, Eleanor?"

"I cannot tell you," said she, "because it was confidential. It was on business respecting a third person."

"It was in no way personal to yourself, then?"

"I won't exactly say that, Susan," said she, getting more and more angry at her sister's questions.

"Well, I must say it's rather singular," said Mrs. Grantly, affecting to laugh, "that a young lady in your position should receive a letter from an unmarried gentleman of which she will not tell the contents, and which she is ashamed to show to her sister."

"I am not ashamed," said Eleanor blazing up; "I am not ashamed of anything in the matter; only I do not choose to be cross-examined as to my letters by any one."

"Well, dear," said the other, "I cannot but tell you that I do not think Mr. Slope a proper correspondent for you."

"If he be ever so improper, how can I help his having written to me? But you are all prejudiced against him to such an extent, that that which would be kind and generous in another man is odious and impudent in him. I hate a religion that teaches one to be so onesided in one's charity."

"I am sorry, Eleanor, that you hate the religion you find here; but surely you should remember that in such matters the archdeacon must know more of the world than you do. I don't ask you to respect or comply with me, although I am, unfortunately, so many years your senior; but surely, in such a matter as this, you might consent to be guided by the archdeacon. He is most anxious to be your friend if you will let him."

"In such a matter as what?" said Eleanor very testily. "Upon my word I don't know what this is all about."

"We all want you to drop Mr. Slope."

"You all want me to be as illiberal as yourselves. That I shall never be. I see no harm in Mr. Slope's acquaintance, and I shall not insult the man by telling him that I do. He has thought it necessary to write to me, and I do not want the archdeacon's advice about the letter. If I did I would not ask it."

"Then, Eleanor, it is my duty to tell you," and now she spoke with a tremendous gravity, "that the archdeacon thinks that such a correspondence is disgraceful, and that he cannot allow it to go on in his house."

Eleanor's eyes flashed fire as she answered her sister, jumping up from her seat as she did so. "You may tell the archdeacon that wherever I am I shall receive what letters I please and from whom I please. And as for the word disgraceful, if Dr. Grantly has used it of me he has been unmanly and inhospitable," and she walked off to the door. "When papa comes from the dining-room I will thank you to ask him to step up to my bed-room. I will show him Mr. Slope's letter, but I will show it to no one else." And so saying she retreated to her baby.

She had no conception of the crime with which she was charged. The idea that she could be thought by her friends to regard Mr. Slope as a lover, had never flashed upon her. She conceived that they were all prejudiced and illiberal in their persecution of him, and therefore she would not join in the persecution, even though she greatly disliked the man.

Eleanor was very angry as she seated herself in a low chair by her open window at the foot of her child's bed. "To dare to say I have disgraced myself," she repeated to herself more than once. "How papa can put up with that man's arrogance! I will certainly not sit down to dinner in his house again unless he begs my pardon for that word." And then a thought struck her that Mr. Arabin might perchance hear of her "disgraceful" correspondence with Mr. Slope, and she turned crimson with pure vexation. Oh, if she had known the truth? If she could have conceived that Mr. Arabin had been informed as a fact that she was going to marry Mr. Slope!

She had not been long in her room before her father joined her. As he left the drawing-room Mrs. Grantly took her husband into the recess of the window, and told him how signally she had failed.

"I will speak to her myself before I go to bed," said the archdeacon.

"Pray do no such thing," said she; "you can do no good and will only make an unseemly quarrel in the house. You have no idea how headstrong she can be."

The archdeacon declared that as to that he was quite indifferent. He knew his duty and would do it. Mr. Harding was weak in the extreme in such matters. He would not have it hereafter on his conscience that he had not done all that in him lay to prevent so disgraceful an alliance. It was in vain that Mrs. Grantly assured him that speaking to Eleanor angrily would only hasten such a crisis, and render it certain if at present there were any doubt. He was angry, self-willed, and sore. The fact that a lady of his household had received a letter from Mr. Slope had wounded his pride in the sorest place, and nothing could control him.

Mr. Harding looked worn and woebegone as he entered his daughter's room. These sorrows worried him sadly. He felt that if they were continued he must go to the wall in the manner so kindly prophesied to him by the chaplain. He knocked gently at his daughter's door, waited till he was distinctly bade to enter, and then appeared as though he and not she were the suspected criminal.

Eleanor's arm was soon within his, and she had soon kissed his forehead and caressed him, not with joyous but with eager love. "Oh, papa," she said, "I do so want to speak to you. They have been talking about me down stairs to-night; don't you know they have, papa?"

Mr. Harding confessed with a sort of murmur that the archdeacon had been speaking of her.

"I shall hate Dr. Grantly soon—"

"Oh, my dear!"

"Well; I shall. I cannot help it. He is so uncharitable, so unkind, so suspicious of every one that does not worship himself:

and then he is so monstrously arrogant to other people who have a right to their opinions as well as he has to his own.''

"He is an earnest eager man, my dear: but he never means to be unkind.''

"He is unkind, papa, most unkind. There, I got that letter from Mr. Slope before dinner. It was you yourself who gave it to me. There; pray read it. It is all for you. It should have been addressed to you. You know how they have been talking about it down stairs. You know how they behaved to me at dinner. And since dinner Susan has been preaching to me, till I could not remain in the room with her. Read it, papa; and then say whether that is a letter that need make Dr. Grantly so outrageous.''

Mr. Harding took his arm from his daughter's waist, and slowly read the letter. She expected to see his countenance lit with joy as he learnt that his path back to the hospital was made so smooth; but she was doomed to disappointment, as had once been the case before on a somewhat similar occasion. His first feeling was one of unmitigated disgust that Mr. Slope should have chosen to interfere in his behalf. He had been anxious to get back to the hospital, but he would have infinitely sooner resigned all pretensions to the place, than have owed it in any manner to Mr. Slope's influence in his favour. Then he thoroughly disliked the tone of Mr. Slope's letter; it was unctuous, false, and unwholesome, like the man. He saw, which Eleanor had failed to see, that much more had been intended than was expressed. The appeal to Eleanor's pious labours as separate from his own grated sadly against his feelings as a father. And then when he came to the "darling boy" and the "silken tresses," he slowly closed and folded the letter in despair. It was impossible that Mr. Slope should so write unless he had been encouraged. It was impossible Eleanor should have received such a letter, and have received it without annoyance, unless she were willing to encourage him. So at least Mr. Harding argued to himself.

How hard it is to judge accurately of the feelings of others. Mr. Harding, as he came to the close of the letter, in his heart condemned his daughter for indelicacy, and it made him miserable to do so. She was not responsible for what Mr. Slope might write. True. But then she expressed no disgust at it. She had rather expressed approval of the letter as a whole. She had given it to him to read, as a vindication for herself and also for him. The father's spirits sank within him as he felt that he could not acquit her.

And yet it was the true feminine delicacy of Eleanor's mind

which brought on her this condemnation. Listen to me, ladies, and I beseech *you* to acquit her. She thought of this man, this lover of whom she was so unconscious, exactly as her father did, exactly as the Grantlys did. At least she esteemed him personally as they did. But she believed him to be in the main an honest man, and one truly inclined to assist her father. She felt herself bound, after what had passed, to show this letter to Mr. Harding. She thought it necessary that he should know what Mr. Slope had to say. But she did not think it necessary to apologise for, or condemn, or even allude to the vulgarity of the man's tone, which arose, as does all vulgarity, from ignorance. It was nauseous to her to have a man like Mr. Slope commenting on her personal attractions; and she did not think it necessary to dilate with her father upon what was nauseous. She never supposed they could disagree on such a subject. It would have been painful for her to point it out, painful for her to speak strongly against a man of whom, on the whole, she was anxious to think and speak well. In encountering such a man she had encountered what was disagreeable, as she might do in walking the streets. But in such encounters she never thought it necessary to dwell on what disgusted her.

And he, foolish weak loving man, would not say one word, though one word would have cleared up everything. There would have been a deluge of tears, and in ten minutes every one in the house would have understood how matters really were. The father would have been delighted. The sister would have kissed her sister and begged a thousand pardons. The archdeacon would have apologised and wondered, and raised his eyebrows, and gone to bed a happy man. And Mr. Arabin—Mr. Arabin would have dreamt of Eleanor, have awoke in the morning with ideas of love, and retired to rest the next evening with schemes of marriage. But, alas! all this was not to be.

Mr. Harding slowly folded the letter, handed it back to her, kissed her forehead and bade God bless her. He then crept slowly away to his own room.

As soon as he had left the passage another knock was given at Eleanor's door, and Mrs. Grantly's very demure own maid, entering on tiptoe, wanted to know would Mrs. Bold be so kind as to speak to the archdeacon for two minutes, in the archdeacon's study, if not disagreeable. The archdeacon's compliments, and he wouldn't detain her two minutes.

Eleanor thought it was very disagreeable; she was tired and fagged and sick at heart; her present feelings towards Dr. Grantly were anything but those of affection. She was, however, no coward, and therefore promised to be in the study in five minutes. So she arranged her hair, tied on her cap, and went down with a palpitating heart.

XXIX

A Serious Interview

There are people who delight in serious interviews, especially when to them appertains the part of offering advice or administering rebuke, and perhaps the archdeacon was one of these. Yet on this occasion he did not prepare himself for the coming conversation with much anticipation of pleasure. Whatever might be his faults he was not an inhospitable man, and he almost felt that he was sinning against hospitality in upbraiding Eleanor in his own house. Then, also he was not quite sure that he would get the best of it. His wife had told him that he decidedly would not, and he usually gave credit to what his wife said. He was, however, so convinced of what he considered to be the impropriety of Eleanor's conduct, and so assured also of his own duty in trying to check it, that his conscience would not allow him to take his wife's advice and go to bed quietly.

Eleanor's face as she entered the room was not such as to reassure him. As a rule she was always mild in manner and gentle in conduct; but there was that in her eyes which made it not an easy task to scold her. In truth she had been little used to scolding. No one since her childhood had tried it but the archdeacon, and he had generally failed when he did try it. He had never done so since her marriage; and now, when he saw her quiet easy step, as she entered his room, he almost wished that he had taken his wife's advice.

He began by apologising for the trouble he was giving her. She begged him not to mention it, assured him that walking down stairs was no trouble to her at all, and then took a seat and waited patiently for him to begin his attack.

"My dear Eleanor," he said, "I hope you believe me when I assure you that you have no sincerer friend than I am." To this Eleanor answered nothing, and therefore he proceeded. "If you had a brother of your own I should not probably trouble you with what I am going to say. But as it is I cannot but think that it must be a comfort to you to know that you have near you one who is as anxious for your welfare as any brother of your own could be."

"I never had a brother," said she.

"I know you never had, and it is therefore that I speak to you."

"I never had a brother," she repeated; "but I have hardly felt the want. Papa has been to me both father and brother."

"Your father is the fondest and most affectionate of men. But—"

"He is—the fondest and most affectionate of men, and the best of counsellors. While he lives I can never want advice."

This rather put the archdeacon out. He could not exactly contradict what his sister-in-law said about her father; and yet he did not at all agree with her. He wanted her to understand that he tendered his assistance because her father was a soft good-natured gentleman, not sufficiently knowing in the ways of the world; but he could not say this to her. So he had to rush into the subject-matter of his proffered counsel without any acknowledgment on her part that she could need it, or would be grateful for it.

"Susan tells me that you received a letter this evening from Mr. Slope."

"Yes; papa brought it in the brougham. Did he not tell you?"

"And Susan says that you objected to let her know what it was about."

"I don't think she asked me. But had she done so I should not have told her. I don't think it nice to be asked about one's letters. If one wishes to show them one does so without being asked."

"True. Quite so. What you say is quite true. But is not the fact of your receiving letters from Mr. Slope, which you do not wish to show to your friends, a circumstance which must excite some—some surprise—some suspicion—"

"Suspicion!" said she, not speaking above her usual voice,

speaking still in a soft womanly tone, but yet with indignation; "suspicion! and who suspects me, and of what?" And then there was a pause, for the archdeacon was not quite ready to explain the ground of his suspicion. "No, Dr. Grantly. I did not choose to show Mr. Slope's letter to Susan. I could not show it to any one till papa had seen it. If you have any wish to read it now, you can do so," and she handed the letter to him over the table.

This was an amount of compliance which he had not at all expected, and which rather upset him in his tactics. However, he took the letter, perused it carefully, and then refolding it, kept it on the table under his hand. To him it appeared to be in almost every respect the letter of a declared lover; it seemed to corroborate his worst suspicions; and the fact of Eleanor's showing it to him was all but tantamount to a declaration on her part, that it was her pleasure to receive love-letters from Mr. Slope. He almost entirely overlooked the real subject-matter of the epistle; so intent was he on the forthcoming courtship and marriage.

"I'll thank you to give it me back, if you please, Dr. Grantly."

He took it in his hand and held it up, but made no immediate overture to return it. "And Mr. Harding has seen this?" said he.

"Of course he has," said she; "it was written that he might see it. It refers solely to his business—of course I showed it to him."

"And, Eleanor, do you think that that is a proper letter for you—for a person in your condition—to receive from Mr. Slope?"

"Quite a proper letter," said she, speaking, perhaps, a little out of obstinacy; probably forgetting at the moment the objectionable mention of her silken curls.

"Then, Eleanor, it is my duty to tell you that I wholly differ from you."

"So I suppose," said she, instigated now by sheer opposition and determination not to succumb. "You think Mr. Slope is a messenger direct from Satan. I think he is an industrious, well-meaning clergyman. It's a pity that we differ as we do. But, as we do differ, we had probably better not talk about it."

Here Eleanor undoubtedly put herself in the wrong. She might probably have refused to talk to Dr. Grantly on the matter in dispute without any impropriety; but having consented to listen to him, she had no business to tell him that he regarded Mr. Slope as an emissary from the evil one; nor was she justified in praising Mr. Slope, seeing that in her heart of hearts she did not think well of him. She was, however, wounded in spirit, and angry and bitter. She had been subjected to contumely and cross-questioning and ill-usage through the whole evening. No one, not even Mr. Arabin, not even her father, had been kind to her. All this she attributed to the prejudice and conceit of the archdeacon, and therefore she resolved to set no bounds to her antagonism to him. She would neither give nor take quarter. He had greatly presumed in daring to question her about her correspondence, and she was determined to show that she thought so.

"Eleanor, you are forgetting yourself," said he, looking very sternly at her. "Otherwise you could never tell me that I conceive any man to be a messenger from Satan."

"But you do," said she. "Nothing is too bad for him. Give me that letter, if you please"; and she stretched out her hand and took it from him. "He had been doing his best to serve papa, doing more than any of papa's friends could do; and yet, because he is the chaplain of a bishop whom you don't like, you speak of him as though he had no right to the usage of a gentleman."

"He has done nothing for your father."

"I believe that he has done a great deal; and, as far as I am concerned, I am grateful to him. Nothing that you can say can prevent my being so. I judge people by their acts, and his, as far as I can see them, are good." She then paused for a moment. "If you have nothing further to say, I shall be obliged by being permitted to say good-night—I am very tired."

Dr. Grantly had, as he thought, done his best to be gracious to his sister-in-law. He had endeavoured not to be harsh to her, and had striven to pluck the sting from his rebuke. But he did not intend that she should leave him without hearing him.

"I have something to say, Eleanor; and I fear I must trouble you to hear it. You profess that it is quite proper that you should receive from Mr. Slope such letters as that you have in your hand. Susan and I think very differently. You are, of course, your own mistress, and much as we both must grieve should anything separate you from us, we have no power to prevent you from taking steps which may lead to such a separation. If you are so wilful as to reject the counsel of your friends, you must be allowed to cater for yourself. But Eleanor, I may at any rate ask you this. Is it worth your while to break away from all those you have loved—from all who love you—for the sake of Mr. Slope?"

"I don't know what you mean, Dr. Grantly; I don't know

what you're talking about. I don't want to break away from anybody."

"But you will do so if you connect yourself with Mr. Slope. Eleanor, I must speak out to you. You must choose between your sister and myself and our friends, and Mr. Slope and his friends. I say nothing of your father, as you may probably understand his feelings better than I do."

"What do you mean, Dr. Grantly? What am I to understand? I never heard such wicked prejudice in my life."

"It is no prejudice, Eleanor. I have known the world longer than you have done. Mr. Slope is altogether beneath you. You ought to know and feel that he is so. Pray—pray think of this before it is too late."

"Too late!"

"Or if you will not believe me, ask Susan; you cannot think she is prejudiced against you. Or even consult your father, he is not prejudiced against you. Ask Mr. Arabin——"

"You haven't spoken to Mr. Arabin about this!" said she, jumping up and standing before him.

"Eleanor, all the world in and about Barchester will be speaking of it soon."

"But have you spoken to Mr. Arabin about me and Mr. Slope?"

"Certainly I have, and he quite agrees with me."

"Agrees with what?" said she. "I think you are trying to drive me mad."

"He agrees with me and Susan that it is quite impossible you should be received at Plumstead as Mrs. Slope."

Not being favourites with the tragic muse we do not dare to attempt any description of Eleanor's face when she first heard the name of Mrs. Slope pronounced as that which would or should or might at some time appertain to herself. The look, such as it was, Dr. Grantly did not soon forget. For a moment or two she could find no words to express her deep anger and deep disgust; and, indeed, at this conjuncture, words did not come to her very freely.

"How dare you be so impertinent?" at last she said; and then hurried out of the room, without giving the archdeacon the opportunity of uttering another word. It was with difficulty she contained herself till she reached her own room; and then locking the door, she threw herself on her bed and sobbed as though her heart would break.

But even yet she had no conception of the truth. She had no

idea that her father and her sister had for days past conceived in sober earnest the idea that she was going to marry this man. She did not even then believe that the archdeacon thought that she would do so. By some manœuvre of her brain, she attributed the origin of the accusation to Mr. Arabin, and as she did so her anger against him was excessive, and the vexation of her spirit almost unendurable. She could not bring herself to think that the charge was made seriously. It appeared to her most probably that the archdeacon and Mr. Arabin had talked over her objectionable acquaintance with Mr. Slope; that Mr. Arabin, in his jeering, sarcastic way, had suggested the odious match as being the severest way of treating with contumely her acquaintance with his enemy; and that the archdeacon, taking the idea from him, thought proper to punish her by the allusion. The whole night she lay awake thinking of what had been said, and this appeared to be the most probable solution.

But the reflection that Mr. Arabin should have in any way mentioned her name in connection with that of Mr. Slope was overpowering; and the spiteful ill-nature of the archdeacon, in repeating the charge to her, made her wish to leave his house almost before the day had broken. One thing was certain: nothing should make her stay there beyond the following morning, and nothing should make her sit down to breakfast in company with Dr. Grantly. When she thought of the man whose name had been linked with her own, she cried from sheer disgust. It was only because she would be thus disgusted, thus pained and shocked and cut to the quick, that the archdeacon had spoken the horrid word. He wanted to make her quarrel with Mr. Slope, and therefore he had outraged her by his abominable vulgarity. She determined that at any rate he should know that she appreciated it.

Nor was the archdeacon a bit better satisfied with the result of his serious interview than was Eleanor. He gathered from it, as indeed he could hardly fail to do, that she was very angry with him; but he thought that she was thus angry, not because she was suspected of an intention to marry Mr. Slope, but because such an intention was imputed to her as a crime. Dr. Grantly regarded this supposed union with disgust; but it never occurred to him that Eleanor was outraged, because she looked at it exactly in the same light.

He returned to his wife vexed and somewhat disconsolate, but, nevertheless, confirmed in his wrath against his sister-in-law. "Her whole behaviour," said he, "has been most objectionable. She handed me his love letter to read as though she were proud of it. And she is proud of it. She is proud of having this slavering, greedy man at her feet. She will throw herself and John Bold's money into his lap; she will ruin her boy, disgrace her father and you, and be a wretched miserable woman.''

His spouse, who was sitting at her toilet table, continued her avocations, making no answer to all this. She had known that the archdeacon would gain nothing by interfering; but she was too charitable to provoke him by saying so while he was in such deep sorrow.

"This comes of a man making such a will as that of Bold's,'' he continued. "Eleanor is no more fitted to be trusted with such an amount of money in her own hands than is a charity-school girl.'' Still Mrs. Grantly made no reply. "But I have done my duty; I can do nothing further. I have told her plainly that she cannot be allowed to form a link of connection between me and that man. From henceforth it will not be in my power to make her welcome at Plumstead. I cannot have Mr. Slope's love letters coming here. Susan, I think you had better let her understand that as her mind on this subject seems to be irrevocably fixed, it will be better for all parties that she should return to Barchester.''

Now Mrs. Grantly was angry with Eleanor, nearly as angry as her husband; but she had no idea of turning her sister out of the house. She, therefore, at length spoke out, and explained to the archdeacon in her own mild seducing way, that he was fuming and fussing and fretting himself very unnecessarily. She declared that things, if left alone, would arrange themselves much better than he could arrange them; and at last succeeded in inducing him to go to bed in a somewhat less inhospitable state of mind.

On the following morning Eleanor's maid was commissioned to send word into the dining-room that her mistress was not well enough to attend prayers, and that she would breakfast in her own room. Here she was visited by her father and declared to him her intention of returning immediately to Barchester. He was hardly surprised by the announcement. All the household seemed to be aware that something had gone wrong. Every one walked about with subdued feet, and people's shoes seemed to creak more than usual. There was a look of conscious intelligence on the faces of the women; and the men attempted, but in vain, to converse as though nothing were the matter. All this had weighed heavily on the heart of Mr. Harding; and when Eleanor told him that her immediate return to Barchester was a necessity, he merely sighed piteously, and said that he would be ready to accompany her.

But here she objected strenuously. She had a great wish, she said, to go alone; a great desire that it might be seen that her father was not implicated in her quarrel with Dr. Grantly. To this at last he gave way; but not a word passed between them about Mr. Slope—not a word was said, not a question asked as to the serious interview on the preceding evening. There was, indeed, very little confidence between them, though neither of them knew why it should be so. Eleanor once asked him whether he would not call upon the bishop; but he answered rather tartly that he did not know—he did not think he should, but he could not say just at present. And so they parted. Each was miserably anxious for some show of affection, for some return of confidence, for some sign of the feeling that usually bound them together. But none was given. The father could not bring himself to question his daughter about her supposed lover; and the daughter would not sully her mouth by repeating the odious word with which Dr. Grantly had roused her wrath. And so they parted.

There was some trouble in arranging the method of Eleanor's return. She begged her father to send for a post-chaise; but when Mrs. Grantly heard of this, she objected strongly. If Eleanor would go away in dudgeon with the archdeacon, why should she let all the servants and all the neighbourhood know that she had done so? So at last Eleanor consented to make use of the Plumstead carriage; and as the archdeacon had gone out immediately after breakfast and was not to return till dinner-time, she also consented to postpone her journey till after lunch, and to join the family at that time. As to the subject of the quarrel not a word was said by any one. The affair of the carriage was arranged by Mr. Harding, who acted as Mercury between the two ladies; they, when they met, kissed each other very lovingly, and then sat down each to her crochet work as though nothing was amiss in all the world.

XXX

Another Love Scene

But there was another visitor at the rectory whose feelings in this unfortunate matter must be somewhat strictly analysed. Mr. Arabin had heard from his friend of the probability of Eleanor's marriage with Mr. Slope with amazement, but not with incredulity. It has been said that he was not in love with Eleanor, and up to this period this certainly had been true. But as soon as he heard that she loved some one else, he began to be very fond of her himself. He did not make up his mind that he wished to have her for his wife; he had never thought of her, and did not now think of her, in connection with himself; but he experienced an inward indefinable feeling of deep regret, a gnawing sorrow, an unconquerable depression of spirits, and also a species of self-abasement that he—he, Mr. Arabin—had not done something to prevent that other he, that vile he, whom he so thoroughly despised, from carrying off this sweet prize.

Whatever man may have reached the age of forty unmarried without knowing something of such feelings must have been very successful or else very cold-hearted.

Mr. Arabin had never thought of trimming the sails of his bark so that he might sail as convoy to this rich argosy. He had seen that Mrs. Bold was beautiful, but he had not dreamt of making her beauty his own. He knew that Mrs. Bold was rich, but he had had no more idea of appropriating her wealth than that of Dr. Grantly. He had discovered that Mrs. Bold was intelligent, warm-hearted, agreeable, sensible, all, in fact, that a man could wish his wife to be; but the higher were her attractions, the greater her claims to consideration, the less had he imagined that he might possibly become the possessor of them. Such had been his instinct rather than his thoughts, so humble and so diffident. Now his diffidence was to be rewarded by his seeing this woman, whose beauty was to his eyes perfect, whose wealth was such as to have deterred him from thinking of her, whose widowhood would have silenced him had he not been so deterred, by his seeing her become the prey of——Obadiah Slope!

On the morning of Mrs. Bold's departure he got on his horse to ride over to St. Ewold's. As he rode he kept muttering to himself a line from Van Artevelde,

> How little flattering is woman's love.

And he strove to recall his mind and to think of other affairs, his parish, his college, his creed—but his thoughts would revert to Mr. Slope and the Flemish chieftain.—

> When we think upon it,
> How little flattering is woman's love,
> Given commonly to whosoe'er is nearest
> And propped with most advantage.

It was not that Mrs. Bold should marry any one but him; he had not put himself forward as a suitor; but that she should marry Mr. Slope—and so he repeated over again—

> Outward grace
> Nor inward light is needful—day by day
> Men wanting both are mated with the best
> And loftiest of God's feminine creation,
> Whose love takes no distinction but of gender,
> And ridicules the very name of choice.

And so he went on, troubled much in his mind.

He had but an uneasy ride of it that morning, and little good did he do at St. Ewold's.

The necessary alterations in his house were being fast completed, and he walked through the rooms, and went up and down the stairs and rambled through the garden; but he could not wake himself to much interest about them. He stood still at every window to look out and think upon Mr. Slope. At almost every window he had before stood and chatted with Eleanor. She and Mrs. Grantly had been there continually, and while Mrs. Grantly had been giving orders, and seeing that orders had been complied with, he and Eleanor had conversed on all things appertaining to a clergyman's profession. He thought how often he had laid down the law to her, and how sweetly she had borne with his somewhat dictatorial decrees. He remembered her listening intelligence, her gentle but quick replies, her interest in all that concerned the church, in all that concerned him; and then he struck his riding whip against the window sill, and declared to himself that it was impossible that Eleanor Bold should marry Mr. Slope.

And yet he did not really believe, as he should have done, that it was impossible. He should have known her well enough to feel that it was truly impossible. He should have been aware that Eleanor had that within her which would surely protect her from such degradation. But he, like so many others, was deficient in confidence in woman. He said to himself over and over again that it was impossible that Eleanor Bold should become Mrs. Slope, and yet he believed that she would do so. And so he rambled about, and could do and think of nothing. He was thoroughly uncomfortable, thoroughly ill at ease, cross with himself and everybody else, and feeding in his heart on animosity towards Mr. Slope. This was not as it should be, as he knew and felt; but he could not help himself. In truth Mr. Arabin was now in love with Mrs. Bold, though ignorant of the fact himself. He was in love, and, though forty years old, was in love without being aware of it. He fumed and fretted, and did not know what was the matter, as a youth might do at one-and-twenty. And so having done no good at St. Ewold's, he rode back much earlier than was usual with him, instigated by some inward unacknowledged hope that he might see Mrs. Bold before she left.

Eleanor had not passed a pleasant morning. She was irritated with every one, and not least with herself. She felt that she had been hardly used, but she felt also that she had not played her own cards well. She should have held herself so far above suspicion as to have received her sister's innuendoes and the archdeacon's lecture with indifference. She had not done this, but had shown herself angry and sore, and was now ashamed of her own petulance, and yet unable to discontinue it.

The greater part of the morning she had spent alone; but after a while her father joined her. He had fully made up his mind that, come what come might, nothing should separate him from his younger daughter. It was a hard task for him to reconcile himself to the idea of seeing her at the head of Mr. Slope's table; but he got through it. Mr. Slope, as he argued to himself, was a respectable man and a clergyman; and he, as Eleanor's father, had no right even to endeavour to prevent her from marrying such a one. He longed to tell her how he had determined to prefer her to all the world, how he was prepared to admit that she was not wrong, how thoroughly he differed from Dr. Grantly; but he could not bring himself to mention Mr. Slope's name. There was yet a chance that they were all wrong in their surmise! and being thus in doubt, he could not bring himself to speak openly to her on the subject.

He was sitting with her in the drawing-room, with his arm round her waist, saying every now and then some little soft words of affection, and working hard with his imaginary fiddle-bow, when Mr. Arabin entered the room. He immediately got up, and the two made some trite remarks to each other, neither thinking of what he was saying, while Eleanor kept her seat on the sofa mute and moody. Mr. Arabin was included in the list of those against whom her anger was excited. He, too, had dared to talk about her acquaintance with Mr. Slope; he, too, had dared to blame her for not making an enemy of his enemy. She had not intended to see him before her departure, and was now but little inclined to be gracious.

There was a feeling through the whole house that something was wrong. Mr. Arabin, when he saw Eleanor, could not succeed in looking or in speaking as though he knew nothing of all this. He could not be cheerful and positive and contradictory with her, as was his wont. He had not been two minutes in the room before he felt that he had done wrong to return; and the moment he heard her voice, he thoroughly wished himself back at St. Ewold's. Why, indeed, should he have wished to have aught further to say to the future wife of Mr. Slope?

"I am sorry to hear that you are to leave us so soon," said he, striving in vain to use his ordinary voice. In answer to this she muttered something about the necessity of her being in Barchester, and betook herself most industriously to her crochet work.

Then there was a little more trite conversation between Mr. Arabin and Mr. Harding; trite, and hard, and vapid, and senseless. Neither of them had anything to say to the other, and yet neither at such a moment liked to remain silent. At last Mr. Harding, taking advantage of a pause, escaped out of the room, and Eleanor and Mr. Arabin were left together.

"Your going will be a great break-up to our party," said he.

She again muttered something which was all but inaudible; but kept her eyes fixed upon her work.

"We have had a very pleasant month here," said he; "at least I have; and I am sorry it should be so soon over."

"I have already been from home longer than I intended," said she; "and it is time that I should return."

"Well, pleasant hours and pleasant days must come to an end. It is a pity that so few of them are pleasant; or perhaps, rather"——

"It is a pity, certainly, that men and women do so much to destroy the pleasantness of their days," said she, interrupting him. "It is a pity that there should be so little charity abroad."

"Charity should begin at home," said he; and he was proceeding to explain that he as a clergyman could not be what she would call charitable at the expense of those principles which he considered it his duty to teach, when he remembered that it would be worse than vain to argue on such a matter with the future wife of Mr. Slope. "But you are just leaving us," he continued, "and I will not weary your last hour with another lecture. As it is, I fear I have given you too many."

"You should practice as well as preach, Mr. Arabin."

"Undoubtedly I should. So should we all. All of us who presume to teach are bound to do our utmost towards fulfilling our own lessons. I thoroughly allow my deficiency in doing so: but I do not quite know now to what you allude. Have you any special reason for telling me now that I should practice as well as preach?"

Eleanor made no answer. She longed to let him know the cause of her anger, to upbraid him for speaking of her disrespectfully, and then at last to forgive him, and so part friends. She felt that she would be unhappy to leave him in her present frame of mind; but yet she could hardly bring herself to speak to him of Mr. Slope. And how could she allude to the innuendo thrown out by the archdeacon, and thrown out, as she believed, at the instigation of Mr. Arabin? She wanted to make him know that he was wrong, to make him aware that he had ill-treated her, in order that the sweetness of her forgiveness might be enhanced. She felt that she liked him too well to be contented to part with him in displeasure; and yet she could not get over her deep displeasure without some explanation, some acknowledgment on his part, some assurance that he would never again so sin against her.

"Why do you tell me that I should practise what I preach?" continued he.

"All men should do so."

"Certainly. That is as it were understood and acknowledged. But you do not say so to all men, or to all clergymen. The advice, good as it is, is not given except in allusion to some special deficiency. If you will tell me my special deficiency, I will endeavour to profit by the advice."

She paused for a while, and then looking full in his face, she said, "You are not bold enough, Mr. Arabin, to speak out to me openly and plainly, and yet you expect me, a woman, to speak openly to you. Why did you speak calumny of me to Dr. Grantly behind my back?"

"Calumny!" said he, and his whole face became suffused with blood; "what calumny? If I have spoken calumny of you, I will beg your pardon, and his to whom I spoke it, and God's pardon also. But what calumny have I spoken of you to Dr. Grantly?"

She also blushed deeply. She could not bring herself to ask him whether he had not spoken of her as another man's wife. "You know that best yourself," said she; "but I ask you as a man of honour, if you have not spoken of me as you would not have spoken of your own sister; or rather I will not ask you," she continued, finding that he did not immediately answer her. "I will not put you to the necessity of answering such a question. Dr. Grantly has told me what you said."

"Dr. Grantly certainly asked me for my advice, and I gave it. He asked me"——

"I know he did, Mr. Arabin. He asked you whether he would be doing right to receive me at Plumstead, if I continued my acquaintance with a gentleman who happens to be personally disagreeable to yourself and to him?"

"You are mistaken, Mrs. Bold. I have no personal knowledge of Mr. Slope; I never met him in my life."

"You are not the less individually hostile to him. It is not for me to question the propriety of your enmity; but I had a right to expect that my name should not have been mixed up in your hostilities. This has been done, and been done by you in a manner the most injurious and the most distressing to me as a woman. I must confess, Mr. Arabin, that from you I expected a different sort of usage."

As she spoke she with difficulty restrained her tears; but she did restrain them. Had she given way and sobbed aloud, as in such cases a woman should do, he would have melted at once, implored her pardon, perhaps knelt at her feet and declared his love. Everything would have been explained, and Eleanor would have gone back to Barchester with a contented mind. How easily would she have forgiven and forgotten the archdeacon's suspicions had she but heard the whole truth from Mr. Arabin. But then where would have been my novel? She did not cry, and Mr. Arabin did not melt.

"You do me an injustice," said he. "My advice was asked by Dr. Grantly, and I was obliged to give it."

"Dr. Grantly has been most officious, most impertinent. I have as complete a right to form my acquaintance as he has to form his. What would you have said, had I consulted you as to the propriety of my banishing Dr. Grantly from my house because he knows Lord Tattenham Corner? I am sure Lord Tattenham is quite as objectionable an acquaintance for a clergyman as Mr. Slope is for a clergyman's daughter."

"I do not know Lord Tattenham Corner."

"No; but Dr. Grantly does. It is nothing to me if he knows all the young lords on every racecourse in England. I shall not interfere with him; nor shall he with me."

"I am sorry to differ with you, Mrs. Bold; but as you have spoken to me on this matter, and especially as you blame me for what little I said on the subject, I must tell you that I do differ from you. Dr. Grantly's position as a man in the world gives him a right to choose his own acquaintances, subject to certain influences. If he chooses them badly, those influences will be used. If he consorts with persons unsuitable to him, his bishop will interfere. What the bishop is to Dr. Grantly, Dr. Grantly is to you."

"I deny it. I utterly deny it," said Eleanor, jumping from her seat, and literally flashing before Mr. Arabin, as she stood on the drawing-room floor. He had never seen her so excited, he had never seen her look half so beautiful.

"I utterly deny it," said she. "Dr. Grantly has no sort of jurisdiction over me whatsoever. Do you and he forget that I am not altogether alone in the world? Do you forget that I have a father? Dr. Grantly, I believe, always has forgotten it.

"From you, Mr. Arabin," she continued, "I would have listened to advice because I should have expected it to have been given as one friend may advise another; not as a schoolmaster gives an order to a pupil. I might have differed from you; on this matter I should have done so; but had you spoken to me in your usual manner and with your usual freedom I should not have been angry. But now——was it manly of you, Mr. Arabin, to speak of me in this way——, so disrespectful— so——? I cannot bring myself to repeat what you said. You must understand what I feel. Was it just of you to speak of me in such a way, and to advise my sister's husband to turn me out of my sister's house, because I chose to know a man of whose doctrine you disapprove?''

"I have no alternative left to me, Mrs. Bold," said he, standing with his back to the fire-place, looking down intently at the carpet pattern, and speaking with a slow measured voice, "but to tell you plainly what did take place between me and Dr. Grantly."

"Well," said she, finding that he paused for a moment.

"I am afraid that what I may say may pain you."

"It cannot well do so more than what you have already done," said she.

"Dr. Grantly asked me whether I thought it would be prudent for him to receive you in his house as the wife of Mr. Slope, and I told him that I thought it would be imprudent. Believing it to be utterly impossible that Mr. Slope and——"

"Thank you, Mr. Arabin, that is sufficient. I do not want to know your reasons," said she, speaking with a terribly calm voice. "I have shown to this gentleman the common-place civility of a neighbour; and because I have done so, because I have not indulged against him in all the rancour and hatred which you and Dr. Grantly consider due to all clergymen who do not agree with yourselves, you conclude that I am to marry him;—or rather you do not conclude so—no rational man could really come to such an outrageous conclusion without better ground;—you have not thought so—but, as I am in a position in which such an accusation must be peculiarly painful, it is made in order that I may be terrified into hostility against this enemy of yours.''

As she finished speaking, she walked to the drawing-room window and stepped out into the garden. Mr. Arabin was left in the room, still occupied in counting the pattern on the carpet. He had, however, distinctly heard and accurately marked every word that she had spoken. Was it not clear from what she had said, that the archdeacon had been wrong in imputing to her any attachment to Mr. Slope? Was it not clear that Eleanor was still free to make another choice? It may seem strange that he should for a moment have had a doubt; and yet he did doubt. She had not absolutely denied the charge; she had not expressly said that it was untrue. Mr. Arabin understood little of the nature of a woman's feelings, or he would have known how improbable it was that she should make any clearer declaration than she had done. Few men do understand the nature of a woman's heart, till years have robbed such understanding of its value. And it is well that it should be so, or men would triumph too easily.

Mr. Arabin stood counting the carpet, unhappy, wretchedly unhappy, at the hard words that had been spoken to him; and yet happy, exquisitely happy, as he thought that after all the woman whom he so regarded was not to become the wife of the man whom he so much disliked. As he stood there he began to be aware that he was himself in love. Forty years had passed over his head, and as yet woman's beauty had never given him an uneasy hour. His present hour was very uneasy.

Not that he remained there for half or a quarter of that time. In spite of what Eleanor had said, Mr. Arabin was, in truth, a manly man. Having ascertained that he loved this woman, and having now reason to believe that she was free to receive his love, at least if she pleased to do so, he followed her into the garden to make such wooing as he could.

He was not long in finding her. She was walking to and fro beneath the avenue of elms that stood in the archdeacon's grounds, skirting the churchyard. What had passed between her and Mr. Arabin, had not, alas, tended to lessen the acerbity of her spirit. She was very angry; more angry with him than with any one. How could he have so misunderstood her? She had been so intimate with him, had allowed him such latitude in what he had chosen to say to her, had complied with his ideas, cherished his views, fostered his precepts, cared for his comforts, made much of him in every way in which a pretty woman can make much of an unmarried man without committing herself or her feelings! She had been doing this, and while she had been doing it he had regarded her as the affianced wife of another man.

As she passed along the avenue, every now and then an unbidden tear would force itself on her cheek, and as she raised her hand to brush it away she stamped with her little foot upon the sward with very spite to think that she had been so treated.

Mr. Arabin was very near to her when she first saw him, and she turned short round and retraced her steps down the avenue, trying to rid her cheeks of all trace of the tell-tale tears. It was a needless endeavour, for Mr. Arabin was in a state of mind that hardly allowed him to observe such trifles. He followed her down the walk, and overtook her just as she reached the end of it.

He had not considered how he would address her; he had not thought what he would say. He had only felt that it was wretchedness to him to quarrel with her, and that it would be happiness to be allowed to love her. And yet he could not lower himself by asking her pardon. He had done her no wrong. He had not calumniated her, not injured her, as she had accused him of doing. He could not confess sins of which he had not been guilty. He could only let the past be past, and ask her as to her and his hopes for the future.

"I hope we are not to part as enemies?" said he.

"There shall be no enmity on my part," said Eleanor; "I endeavour to avoid all enmities. It would be a hollow pretence were I to say that there can be true friendship between us after what has just passed. People cannot make their friends of those whom they despise."

"And am I despised?"

"*I* must have been so before you could have spoken of me as you did. And I was deceived, cruelly deceived. I believed that you thought well of me; I believed that you esteemed me."

"Thought well of you and esteemed you!" said he. "In justifying myself before you, I must use stronger words than those." He paused for a moment, and Eleanor's heart beat with painful violence within her bosom as she waited for him to go on. "I have esteemed, do esteem you, as I never yet esteemed any woman. Think well of you! I never thought to think so well, so much of any human creature. Speak calumny of you! Insult you! Wilfully injure you! I wish it were my privilege to shield you from calumny, insult, and injury. Calumny! ah, me. 'Twere almost better that it were so. Better than to worship with a sinful worship; sinful and vain also." And then he walked along beside her, with his hands clasped behind his back, looking down on the grass beneath his feet, and utterly at a loss how to express his meaning. And Eleanor walked beside him determined at least to give him no assistance.

"Ah me!" he uttered at last, speaking rather to himself than to her. "Ah me! these Plumstead walks were pleasant enough, if one could have but heart's ease; but without that the dull dead stones of Oxford were far preferable; and St. Ewold's too; Mrs. Bold, I am beginning to think that I mistook myself when I came hither. A Romish priest now would have escaped all this. Oh, Father of heaven! how good for us would it be, if thou couldest vouchsafe to us a certain rule."

"And have we not a certain rule, Mr. Arabin?"

"Yes—yes, surely; 'Lead us not into temptation but deliver us from evil.' But what is temptation? what is evil? Is this evil,—is this temptation?"

Poor Mr. Arabin! It would not come out of him, that deep true love of his. He could not bring himself to utter it in plain language that would require and demand an answer. He knew not how to say to the woman by his side, "Since the fact is that you do not love that other man, that you are not to be his wife, can you love me, will you be my wife?" These were the words which were in his heart, but with all his sighs he could not draw them to his lips. He would have given anything, everything for power to ask this simple question; but glib as was his tongue in pulpits and on platforms, now he could not find a word wherewith to express the plain wish of his heart.

And yet Eleanor understood him as thoroughly as though he had declared his passion with all the elegant fluency of a practised Lothario. With a woman's instinct she followed every bend of his mind, as he spoke of the pleasantness of Plumstead and the stones of Oxford, as he alluded to the safety of the Romish priest and the hidden perils of temptation. She knew that it all meant love. She knew that this man at her side, this accomplished scholar, this practised orator, this great polemical combatant, was striving and striving in vain to tell her that his heart was no longer his own.

She knew this, and felt a sort of joy in knowing it; and yet she would not come to his aid. He had offended her deeply, had treated her unworthily, the more unworthily seeing that he had learnt to love her, and Eleanor could not bring herself to abandon her revenge. She did not ask herself whether or no she would ultimately accept his love. She did not even acknowledge to herself that she now perceived it with pleasure. At the present moment it did not touch her heart; it merely appeased her pride and flattered her vanity. Mr. Arabin had dared to associate her name with that of Mr. Slope, and now her spirit was soothed by finding that he would fain associate it with his own. And so she walked on beside him inhaling incense, but giving out no sweetness in return.

"Answer me this," said Mr. Arabin, stopping suddenly in his walk, and stepping forward so that he faced his companion. "Answer me this one question. You do not love Mr. Slope? you do not intend to be his wife?"

Mr. Arabin certainly did not go the right way to win such a woman as Eleanor Bold. Just as her wrath was evaporating, as it

was disappearing before the true warmth of his untold love, he
re-kindled it by a most useless repetition of his original sin. Had
he known what he was about he should never have mentioned
Mr. Slope's name before Eleanor Bold, till he had made her all
his own. Then, and not till then, he might have talked of Mr.
Slope with as much triumph as he chose.

"I shall answer no such question," said she; "and what is
more, I must tell you that nothing can justify your asking it.
Good-morning!"

And so saying she stepped proudly across the lawn, and
passing through the drawing-room window joined her father
and sister at lunch in the dining-room. Half an hour afterwards
she was in the carriage, and so she left Plumstead without again
seeing Mr. Arabin.

His walk was long and sad among the sombre trees that
overshadowed the churchyard. He left the archdeacon's grounds
that he might escape attention, and sauntered among the green hill-
ocks under which lay at rest so many of the once loving swains
and forgotten beauties of Plumstead. To his ears Eleanor's last
words sounded like a knell never to be reversed. He could not
comprehend that she might be angry with him, indignant with
him, remorseless with him, and yet love him. He could not make
up his mind whether or no Mr. Slope was in truth a favoured
rival. If not, why should she not have answered his question?

Poor Mr. Arabin—untaught, illiterate, boorish, ignorant man!
That at forty years of age you should know so little of the
workings of a woman's heart!

XXXI

The Bishop's Library

And thus the pleasant party at Plumstead was broken up. It had
been a very pleasant party as long as they had all remained in

good humour with one another. Mrs. Grantly had felt her house to be gayer and brighter than it had been for many a long day, and the archdeacon had been aware that the month had passed pleasantly without attributing the pleasure to any other special merits than those of his own hospitality. Within three or four days of Eleanor's departure Mr. Harding had also returned, and Mr. Arabin had gone to Oxford to spend one week there previous to his settling at the vicarage of St. Ewold's. He had gone laden with many messages to Dr. Gwynne touching the iniquity of the doings in Barchester palace, and the peril in which it was believed the hospital still stood in spite of the assurances contained in Mr. Slope's inauspicious letter.

During Eleanor's drive into Barchester she had not much opportunity of reflecting on Mr. Arabin. She had been constrained to divert her mind both from his sins and his love by the necessity of conversing with her sister, and maintaining the appearance of parting with her on good terms. When the carriage reached her own door, and while she was in the act of giving her last kiss to her sister and nieces, Mary Bold ran out and exclaimed,

"Oh! Eleanor,—have you heard?—oh! Mrs. Grantly, have you heard what has happened? The poor dean!"

"Good heavens!" said Mrs. Grantly; "what—what has happened?"

"This morning at nine he had a fit of apoplexy, and he has not spoken since. I very much fear that by this time he is no more."

Mrs. Grantly had been very intimate with the dean, and was therefore much shocked. Eleanor had not known him so well; nevertheless she was sufficiently acquainted with his person and manners to feel startled and grieved also at the tidings she now received. "I will go at once to the deanery," said Mrs. Grantly; "the archdeacon, I am sure, will be there. If there is any news to send you I will let Thomas call before he leaves town." And so the carriage drove off, leaving Eleanor and her baby with Mary Bold.

Mrs. Grantly had been quite right. The archdeacon was at the deanery. He had come into Barchester that morning by himself, not caring to intrude himself upon Eleanor, and he also immediately on his arrival had heard of the dean's fit. There was, as we have before said, a library or reading room connecting the cathedral with the dean's house. This was generally called the bishop's library, because a certain bishop of Barchester was supposed to have added it to the cathedral. It was built immediately over a portion of the cloisters, and a flight of stairs descended from it into the room in which the cathedral clergymen put their surplices on and off. As it also opened directly into the dean's house, it was the passage through which that dignitary usually went to his public devotions. Who had or had not the right of entry into it, it might be difficult to say; but the people of Barchester believed that it belonged to the dean, and the clergymen of Barchester believed that it belonged to the chapter.

On the morning in question most of the resident clergymen who constituted the chapter, and some few others, were here assembled, and among them as usual the archdeacon towered with high authority. He had heard of the dean's fit before he was over the bridge which led into the town, and had at once come to the well-known clerical trysting place. He had been there by eleven o'clock, and had remained ever since. From time to time the medical men who had been called in came through from the deanery into the library, uttered little bulletins, and then returned. There was it appears very little hope of the old man's rallying, indeed no hope of any thing like a final recovery. The only question was whether he must die at once speechless, unconscious, stricken to death by his first heavy fit; or whether by due aid of medical skill he might not be so far brought back to this world as to become conscious of his state, and enabled to address one prayer to his Maker before he was called to meet Him face to face at the judgment seat.

Sir Omicron Pie had been sent for from London. That great man had shown himself a wonderful adept at keeping life still moving within an old man's heart in the case of good old Bishop Grantly, and it might be reasonably expected that he would be equally successful with a dean. In the meantime Dr. Fillgrave and Mr. Rerechild were doing their best; and poor Miss Trefoil sat at the head of her father's bed, longing, as in such cases daughters do long, to be allowed to do something to show her love; if it were only to chafe his feet with her hands, or wait in menial offices on those autocratic doctors; anything so that now in the time of need she might be of use.

The archdeacon alone of the attendant clergy had been admitted for a moment into the sick man's chamber. He had crept in with creaking shoes, had said with smothered voice a word of consolation to the sorrowing daughter, and looked on the distorted face of his old friend with solemn but yet eager scrutinising eye, as though he said in his heart "and so some day it will probably be with me"; and then having whispered an unmeaning word or two to the doctors, had creaked his way back again into the library.

"He'll never speak again, I fear," said the archdeacon as he noiselessly closed the door, as though the unconscious dying man, from whom all sense had fled, would have heard in his distant chamber the spring of the lock which was now so carefully handled.

"Indeed! indeed! is he so bad?" said the meagre little prebendary, turning over in his own mind all the probable candidates for the deanery, and wondering whether the archdeacon would think it worth his while to accept it. "The fit must have been very violent."

"When a man over seventy has a stroke of apoplexy, it seldom comes very lightly," said the burly chancellor.

"He was an excellent, sweet-tempered man," said one of the vicars choral. "Heaven knows how we shall repair his loss."

"He was indeed," said a minor canon; "and a great blessing to all those privileged to take a share of the services of our cathedral. I suppose the government will appoint, Mr. Archdeacon. I trust we may have no stranger."

"We will not talk about his successor," said the archdeacon, "while there is yet hope."

"Oh no, of course not," said the minor canon. "It would be exceedingly indecorous? but——"

"I know of no man," said the meagre little prebendary, "who has better interest with the present government than Mr. Slope."

"Mr. Slope," said two or three at once almost sotto voce. "Mr. Slope dean of Barchester!"

"Pooh!" exclaimed the burly chancellor.

"The bishop would do anything for him," said the little prebendary.

"And so would Mrs. Proudie," said the vicar choral.

"Pooh!" said the chancellor.

The archdeacon had almost turned pale at the idea. What if Mr. Slope should become dean of Barchester? To be sure there was no adequate ground, indeed no ground at all, for presuming that such a desecration could even be contemplated. But nevertheless it was on the cards. Dr. Proudie had interest with the government, and the man carried as it were Dr. Proudie in his pocket. How should they all conduct themselves if Mr. Slope were to become dean of Barchester? The bare idea for a moment struck even Dr. Grantly dumb.

"It would certainly not be very pleasant for us to have Mr. Slope at the deanery," said the little prebendary, chuckling inwardly at the evident consternation which his surmise had created.

"About as pleasant and as probable as having you in the palace," said the chancellor.

"I should think such an appointment highly improbable," said the minor canon, "and, moreover, extremely injudicious. Should not you, Mr. Archdeacon?"

"I should presume such a thing to be quite out of the question," said the archdeacon; "but at the present moment I am thinking rather of our poor friend who is lying so near us than of Mr. Slope."

"Of course, of course," said the vicar choral with a very solemn air; "of couse you are. So are we all. Poor Dr. Trefoil; the best of men, but——"

"It's the most comfortable dean's residence in England," said a second prebendary. "Fifteen acres in the grounds. It is better than many of the bishops' palaces."

"And full two thousand a year," said the meagre doctor.

"It is cut down to £1200," said the chancellor.

"No," said the second prebendary. "It is to be fifteen. A special case was made."

"No such thing," said the chancellor.

"You'll find I'm right," said the prebendary.

"I'm sure I read it in the report," said the minor canon.

"Nonsense," said the chancellor. "They couldn't do it. There were to be no exceptions but London and Durham."

"And Canterbury and York," said the vicar choral, modestly.

"What do you say, Grantly?" said the meagre little doctor.

"Say about what?" said the archdeacon, who had been looking as though he were thinking about his friend the dean, but who had in reality been thinking about Mr. Slope.

"What is the next dean to have, twelve or fifteen?"

"Twelve," said the archdeacon authoritatively, thereby putting an end at once to all doubt and dispute among his subordinates as far as that subject was concerned.

"Well, I certainly thought it was fifteen," said the minor canon.

"Pooh!" said the burly chancellor. At this moment the door opened, and in came Dr. Fillgrave.

"How is he?" "Is he conscious?" "Can he speak?" "I hope not dead?" "No worse news, doctor, I trust?" "I hope, I trust, something better, doctor?'' said half a dozen voices all at once each in a tone of extremest anxiety. It was pleasant to see how popular the good old dean was among his clergy.

"No change, gentlemen; not the slightest change—but a telegraphic message has arrived—Sir Omicron Pie will be here by the 9:15 P.M. train. If any man can do anything Sir Omicron Pie will do it. But all that skill can do has been done.''

"We are sure of that Dr. Fillgrave,'' said the archdeacon; "we are quite sure of that. But yet you know——''

"Oh! quite right,'' said the doctor, "quite right—I should have done just the same—I advised it at once. I said to Rerechild at once that with such a life and such a man, Sir Omicron should be summoned—of course I knew the expense was nothing—so distinguished, you know, and so popular. Nevertheless, all that human skill can do has been done.''

Just at this period Mrs. Grantly's carriage drove into the close, and the archdeacon went down to confirm the news which she had heard before.

By the 9:15 P.M. train Sir Omicron Pie did arrive. And in the course of the night a sort of consciousness returned to the poor dean. Whether this was due to Sir Omicron Pie is a question on which it may be well not to offer an opinion. Dr. Fillgrave was very clear in his own mind, but Sir Omicron himself is thought to have differed from that learned doctor. At any rate Sir Omicron expressed an opinion that the dean had yet some days to live.

For the eight or ten next days, accordingly, the poor dean remained in the same state, half conscious and half comatose, and the attendant clergy began to think that no new appointment would be necessary for some few months to come.

XXXII

A New Candidate for Ecclesiastical Honours

The dean's illness occasioned much mental turmoil in other places besides the deanery and adjoining library; and the idea which occurred to the meagre little prebendary about Mr. Slope did not occur to him alone.

The bishop was sitting listlessly in his study when the news reached him of the dean's illness. It was brought to him by Mr. Slope, who of course was not the last person in Barchester to hear it. It was also not slow in finding its way to Mrs. Proudie's ears. It may be presumed that there was not just then much friendly intercourse between these two rival claimants for his lordship's obedience. Indeed, though living in the same house, they had not met since the stormy interview between them in the bishop's study on the preceding day.

On that occasion Mrs. Proudie had been defeated. That the prestige of continual victory should have been torn from her standards was a subject of great sorrow to that militant lady; but though defeated, she was not overcome. She felt that she might yet recover her lost ground, that she might yet hurl Mr. Slope down to the dust from which she had picked him, and force her sinning lord to sue for pardon in sackcloth and ashes.

On that memorable day, memorable for his mutiny and rebellion against her high behests, he had carried his way with a high hand, and had really begun to think it possible that the days of his slavery were counted. He had begun to hope that he was now about to enter into a free land, a land delicious with milk which he himself might quaff, and honey which would not tantalise him by being only honey to the eye. When Mrs. Proudie banged the door, as she left his room, he felt himself every inch a bishop. To be sure his spirit had been a little cowed by his chaplain's subsequent lecture; but on the whole he was highly pleased with himself, and flattered himself that the worst was over. *"Ce n'est que le premier pas qui coûte,"* he reflected; and now that the first step had been so magnanimously taken, all the rest would follow easily.

He met his wife as a matter of course at dinner, where little or nothing was said that could ruffle the bishop's happiness. His daughters and the servants were present and protected him.

He made one or two trifling remarks on the subject of his projected visit to the archbishop, in order to show to all concerned that he intended to have his own way; and the very servants perceiving the change transferred a little of their reverence from their mistress to their master. All which the master perceived; and so also did the mistress. But Mrs. Proudie bided her time.

After dinner he returned to his study where Mr. Slope soon found him, and there they had tea together and planned many things. For some few minutes the bishop was really happy; but as the clock on the chimney piece warned him that the stilly hours of night were drawing on, as he looked at his chamber candlestick and knew that he must use it, his heart sank within him again. He was as a ghost, all whose power of wandering free through these upper regions ceases at cockcrow; or rather he was the opposite of the ghost, for till cockcrow he must again be a serf. And would that be all? Could he trust himself to come down to breakfast a free man in the morning.

He was nearly an hour later than usual, when he betook himself to his rest. Rest! what rest? However, he took a couple of glasses of sherry, and mounted the stairs. Far be it from us to follow him thither. There are some things which no novelist, no historian, should attempt; some few scenes in life's drama which even no poet should dare to paint. Let that which passed between Dr. Proudie and his wife on this night be understood to be among them.

He came down the following morning a sad and thoughtful man. He was attenuated in appearance; one might almost say emaciated. I doubt whether his now grizzled locks had not palpably become more grey than on the preceding evening. At any rate he had aged materially. Years do not make a man old gradually and at an even pace. Look through the world and see if this is not so always, except in those rare cases in which the human being lives and dies without joys and without sorrows, like a vegetable. A man shall be possessed of florid youthful

blooming health till, it matters not what age. Thirty—forty—
fifty, then comes some nipping frost, some period of agony, that
robs the fibres of the body of their succulence, and the hale and
hearty man is counted among the old.

He came down and breakfasted alone; Mrs. Proudie being
indisposed took her coffee in her bed-room, and her daughters
waited upon her there. He ate his breakfast alone, and then,
hardly knowing what he did, he betook himself to his usual seat
in his study. He tried to solace himself with his coming visit to
the archbishop. That effort of his own free will at any rate
remained to him as an enduring triumph. But somehow, now that
he had achieved it, he did not seem to care so much about it. It
was his ambition that had prompted him to take his place at the
archiepiscopal table, and his ambition was now quite dead within
him.

He was thus seated when Mr. Slope made his appearance
with breathless impatience.

"My lord, the dean is dead."

"Good heavens!" exclaimed the bishop, startled out of his
apathy by an announcement so sad and so sudden.

"He is either dead or now dying. He has had an apoplectic
fit, and I am told that there is not the slightest hope; indeed, I do
not doubt that by this time he is no more."

Bells were rung, and servants were immediately sent to
inquire. In the course of the morning, the bishop, leaning on his
chaplain's arm, himself called at the deanery door. Mrs. Proudie
sent to Miss Trefoil all manner of offers of assistance. The Miss
Proudies sent also, and there was immense sympathy between
the palace and the deanery. The answer to all inquiries was
unvaried. The dean was just the same; and Sir Omicron Pie was
expected down by the 9:15 P.M. train.

And then Mr. Slope began to meditate, as others also had
done, as to who might possibly be the new dean; and it occurred
to him, as it had also occurred to others, that it might be possible
that he should be the new dean himself. And then the question as
to the twelve hundred, or fifteen hundred, or two thousand, ran
in his mind, as it had run through those of the other clergymen in
the cathedral library.

Whether it might be two thousand, or fifteen or twelve
hundred, it would in any case undoubtedly be a great thing for
him, if he could get it. The gratification to his ambition would be
greater even than that of his covetousness. How glorious to
out-top the archdeacon in his own cathedral city; to sit above

prebendaries and canons, and have the cathedral pulpit and all the cathedral services altogether at his own disposal!

But it might be easier to wish for this than to obtain it. Mr. Slope, however, was not without some means of forwarding his views, and he at any rate did not let the grass grow under his feet. In the first place he thought—and not vainly—that he could count upon what assistance the bishop could give him. He immediately changed his views with regard to his patron; he made up his mind that if he became dean, he would hand his lordship back again to his wife's vassalage; and he thought it possible that his lordship might not be sorry to rid himself of one of his mentors. Mr. Slope had also taken some steps towards making his name known to other men in power. There was a certain chief-commissioner of national schools who at the present moment was presumed to stand especially high in the good graces of the government big wigs, and with him Mr. Slope had contrived to establish a sort of epistolary intimacy. He thought that he might safely apply to Sir Nicholas Fitzwhiggin; and he felt sure that if Sir Nicholas chose to exert himself, the promise of such a piece of preferment would be had for the asking for.

Then he also had the press at his bidding, or flattered himself that he had so. The daily *Jupiter* had taken his part in a very thorough manner in those polemical contests of his with Mr. Arabin; he had on more than one occasion absolutely had an interview with a gentleman on the staff of that paper, who, if not the editor, was as good as the editor; and had long been in the habit of writing telling letters on all manner of ecclesiastical abuses, which he signed with his initials, and sent to his editorial friend with private notes signed in his own name. Indeed, he and Mr. Towers—such was the name of the powerful gentleman of the press with whom he was connected—were generally very amiable with each other. Mr. Slope's little productions were always printed and occasionally commented upon; and thus, in a small sort of way, he had become a literary celebrity. This public life had great charms for him, though it certainly also had its drawbacks. On one occasion, when speaking in the presence of reporters, he had failed to uphold and praise and swear by that special line of conduct which had been upheld and praised and sworn by in the *Jupiter*, and then he had been much surprised and at the moment not a little irritated to find himself lacerated most unmercifully by his old ally. He was quizzed and bespattered and made a fool of, just as though, or rather worse than if, he had been a constant enemy instead of a constant friend. He had hitherto not learnt that a man who aspires to be on the staff of the *Jupiter* must surrender all individuality. But ultimately this little castigation had broken no bones between him and his friend Mr. Towers. Mr. Slope was one of those who understood the world too well to show himself angry with such a potentate as the *Jupiter*. He had kissed the rod that scourged him, and now thought that he might fairly look for his reward. He determined that he would at once let Mr. Towers know that he was a candidate for the place which was about to become vacant. More than one piece of preferment had lately been given away much in accordance with advice tendered to the government in the columns of the *Jupiter*.

But it was incumbent on Mr. Slope first to secure the bishop. He specially felt that it behoved him to do this before the visit to the archbishop was made. It was really quite providential that the dean should have fallen ill just at the very nick of time. If Dr. Proudie could be instigated to take the matter up warmly, he might manage a good deal while staying at the archbishop's palace. Feeling this very strongly Mr. Slope determined to sound the bishop that very afternoon. He was to start on the following morning to London and therefore not a moment could be lost with safety.

He went into the bishop's study about five o'clock, and found him still sitting alone. It might have been supposed that he had hardly moved since the little excitement occasioned by his walk to the dean's door. He still wore on his face that dull dead look of half unconscious suffering. He was doing nothing, reading nothing, thinking of nothing, but simply gazing on vacancy when Mr. Slope for the second time that day entered his room.

"Well, Slope," said he, somewhat impatiently; for, to tell the truth, he was not anxious just at present to have much conversation with Mr. Slope.

"Your lordship will be sorry to hear that as yet the poor dean has shown no sign of amendment."

"Oh—ah—hasn't he? Poor man! I'm sure I'm very sorry. I suppose Sir Omicron has not arrived yet?"

"No; not till the 9:15 P.M. train."

"I wonder they didn't have a special. They say Dr. Trefoil is very rich."

"Very rich, I believe," said Mr. Slope. "But the truth is, all the doctors in London can do no good; no other good than to show that every possible care has been taken. Poor Dr. Trefoil is not long for this world, my lord."

"I suppose not—I suppose not."

"Oh no; indeed, his best friends could not wish that he should outlive such a shock, for his intellects cannot possibly survive it."

"Poor man! poor man!" said the bishop.

"It will naturally be a matter of much moment to your lordship who is to succeed him," said Mr. Slope. "It would be a great thing if you could secure the appointment for some person of your own way of thinking on important points. The party hostile to us are very strong here in Barchester—much too strong."

"Yes, yes. If poor Dr. Trefoil is to go, it will be a great thing to get a good man in his place."

"It will be everything to your lordship to get a man on whose co-operation you can reckon. Only think what trouble we might have if Dr. Grantly, or Dr. Hyandry, or any of that way of thinking, were to get it."

"It is not very probable that Lord —— will give it to any of that school; why should he?"

"No. Not probable; certainly not; but it's possible. Great interest will probably be made. If I might venture to advise your lordship, I would suggest that you should discuss the matter with his grace next week. I have no doubt that your wishes, if made known and backed by his grace, would be paramount with Lord ——."

"Well, I don't know that; Lord —— has always been very kind to me, very kind. But I am unwilling to interfere in such matters unless asked. And indeed if asked, I don't know whom, at this moment, I should recommend."

Mr. Slope, even Mr. Slope, felt at the present rather abashed. He hardly knew how to frame his little request in language sufficiently modest. He had recognised and acknowledged to himself the necessity of shocking the bishop in the first instance by the temerity of his application, and his difficulty was how best to remedy that by his adroitness and eloquence. "I doubted myself," said he, "whether your lordship would have any one immediately in your eye, and it is on this account that I venture to submit to you an idea that I have been turning over in my own mind. If poor Dr. Trefoil must go, I really do not see why, with your lordship's assistance, I should not hold the preferment myself."

"You!" exclaimed the bishop, in a manner that Mr. Slope could hardly have considered complimentary.

The ice was now broken, and Mr. Slope became fluent enough. "I have been thinking of looking for it. If your lordship will press the matter on the archbishop, I do not doubt but I shall succeed. You see I shall be the first to move, which is a great matter. Then I can count upon assistance from the public press: my name is known, I may say, somewhat favourably known to that portion of the press which is now most influential with the government, and I have friends also in the government. But, nevertheless, it is to you, my lord, that I look for assistance. It is from your hands that I would most willingly receive the benefit. And, which should ever be the chief consideration in such matters, you must know better than any other person whatsoever what qualifications I possess."

The bishop sat for a while dumbfounded. Mr. Slope dean of Barchester! The idea of such a transformation of character would never have occurred to his own unaided intellect. At first he went on thinking why, for what reasons, on what account, Mr. Slope should be dean of Barchester. But by degrees the direction of his thoughts changed, and he began to think why, for what reasons, on what account, Mr. Slope should not be dean of Barchester. As far as he himself, the bishop, was concerned, he could well spare the services of his chaplain. That little idea of using Mr. Slope as a counterpoise to his wife had well nigh evaporated. He had all but acknowledged the futility of the scheme. If indeed he could have slept in his chaplain's bedroom instead of his wife's there might have been something in it. But―― ――. And thus as Mr. Slope was speaking, the bishop began to recognise the idea that that gentleman might become dean of Barchester without impropriety; not moved, indeed, by Mr. Slope's eloquence, for he did not follow the tenour of his speech; but led thereto by his own cogitations.

"I need not say," continued Mr. Slope, "that it would be my chief desire to act in all matters connected with the cathedral as far as possible in accordance with your views. I know your lordship so well (and I hope you know me well enough to have the same feelings), that I am satisfied that my being in that position would add materially to your own comfort, and enable you to extend the sphere of your useful influence. As I said before, it is most desirable that there should be but one opinion among the dignitaries of the same diocese. I doubt much whether I would accept such an appointment in any diocese in which I should be constrained to differ much from the bishop. In this case there would be a delightful uniformity of opinion."

Mr. Slope perfectly well perceived that the bishop did not follow a word that he said, but nevertheless he went on talking. He knew it was necessary that Dr. Proudie should recover from his surprise, and he knew also that he must give him the opportunity of appearing to have been persuaded by argument. So he went on, and produced a multitude of fitting reasons all tending to show that no one on earth could make so good a dean of Barchester as himself, that the government and the public would assuredly coincide in desiring that he, Mr. Slope, should be dean of Barchester; but that for high considerations of ecclesiastical polity it would be especially desirable that this piece of preferment should be so bestowed through the instrumentality of the bishop of the diocese.

"But I really don't know what I could do in the matter," said the bishop.

"If you would mention it to the archbishop; if you could tell his grace that you consider such an appointment very desirable, that you have it much at heart with a view to putting an end to schism in the diocese; if you did this with your usual energy, you would probably find no difficulty in inducing his grace to promise that he would mention it to Lord ——. Of course you would let the archbishop know that I am not looking for the preferment solely through his intervention; that you do not exactly require him to ask it as a favour; that you expect that I shall get it through other sources, as is indeed the case; but that you are very anxious that his grace should express his approval of such an arrangement to Lord ——."

It ended in the bishop promising to do as he was bid. Not that he so promised without a stipulation. "About that hospital," he said, in the middle of the conference. "I was never so troubled in my life"; which was about the truth. "You haven't spoken to Mr. Harding since I saw you?"

Mr. Slope assured his patron that he had not.

"Ah well, then—I think upon the whole it will be better to let Quiverful have it. It has been half promised to him, and he has a large family and is very poor. I think on the whole it will be better to make out the nomination for Mr. Quiverful."

"But, my lord," said Mr. Slope, still thinking that he was bound to make a fight for his own view on this matter, and remembering that it still behoved him to maintain his lately acquired supremacy over Mrs. Proudie, lest he should fail in his views regarding the deanery,—"but my lord, I am really much afraid——"

"Remember, Mr. Slope," said the bishop, "I can hold out no sort of hope to you in this matter of succeeding poor Dr. Trefoil. I will certainly speak to the archbishop, as you wish it, but I cannot think——"

"Well, my lord," said Mr. Slope, fully understanding the bishop, and in his turn interrupting him, "perhaps your lordship is right about Mr. Quiverful. I have no doubt I can easily arrange matters with Mr. Harding, and I will make out the nomination for your signature as you direct."

"Yes, Slope, I think that will be best; and you may be sure that any little that I can do to forward your views shall be done."

And so they parted.

Mr. Slope had now much business on his hands. He had to make his daily visit to the signora. This common prudence should have now induced him to omit, but he was infatuated; and could not bring himself to be commonly prudent. He determined therefore that he would drink tea at the Stanhopes'; and he determined also, or thought that he determined, that having done so he would go thither no more. He had also to arrange his matters with Mrs. Bold. He was of opinion that Eleanor would grace the deanery as perfectly as she would the chaplain's cottage; and he thought, moreover, that Eleanor's fortune would excellently repair any dilapidations and curtailments in the dean's stipend which might have been made by that ruthless ecclesiastical commission.

Touching Mrs. Bold his hopes now soared high. Mr. Slope was one of that numerous multitude of swains who think that all is fair in love, and he had accordingly not refrained from using the services of Mrs. Bold's own maid. From her he had learnt much of what had taken place at Plumstead; not exactly with truth, for "the old maid" had not been able to divine the exact truth, but with some sort of similitude to it. He had been told that the archdeacon and Mrs. Grantly and Mr. Harding and Mr. Arabin had all quarrelled with "missus" for having received a letter from Mr. Slope; that "missus" had positively refused to give the letter up; that she had received from the archdeacon the option of giving up either Mr. Slope and his letter, or else the society of Plumstead rectory; and that "missus" had declared with much indignation, that "she didn't care a straw for the society of Plumstead rectory," and that she wouldn't give up Mr. Slope for any of them.

Considering the source from whence this came, it was not quite so untrue as might have been expected. It showed pretty plainly what had been the nature of the conversation in the servants' hall; and coupled as it was with the certainty of Eleanor's sudden return, it appeared to Mr. Slope to be so far worthy of credit as to justify him in thinking that the fair widow would in all human probability accept his offer.

All this work was therefore to be done. It was desirable he thought that he should make his offer before it was known that Mr. Quiverful was finally appointed to the hospital. In his letter to Eleanor he had plainly declared that Mr. Harding was to have the appointment. It would be very difficult to explain this away; and were he to write another letter to Eleanor, telling the truth and throwing the blame on the bishop, it would naturally injure him in her estimation. He determined therefore to let that matter disclose itself as it would, and to lose no time in throwing himself at her feet.

Then he had to solicit the assistance of Sir Nicholas Fitzwhiggin and Mr. Towers, and he went directly from the bishop's presence to compose his letters to those gentlemen. As Mr. Slope was esteemed an adept at letter writing, they shall be given in full.

(Private.)   Palace, Barchester, Sept. 185—.

My dear Sir Nicholas,—I hope that the intercourse which has been between us will preclude you from regarding my present application as an intrusion. You cannot I imagine have yet heard that poor dear old Dr. Trefoil has been seized with apoplexy. It is a subject of profound grief to every one in Barchester, for he has always been an excellent man—excellent as a man and as a clergyman. He is, however, full of years, and his life could not under any circumstances have been much longer spared. You may probably have known him.

There is, it appears, no probable chance of his recovery. Sir Omicron Pie is, I believe, at present with him. At any rate the medical men here have declared that one to two days more must limit the tether of his mortal coil. I sincerely trust that his soul may wing its flight to that haven where it may for ever be at rest and for ever be happy.

The bishop has been speaking to me about the preferment, and he is anxious that it should be conferred on me. I confess that I can hardly venture, at my age, to look for such advancement; but I am so far encouraged by his lordship, that I believe I shall be induced to do so. His lordship goes to —— to-morrow, and is intent on mentioning the subject to the archbishop.

I know well how deservedly great is your weight with the present government. In any matter touching church preferment you would of course be listened to. Now that the matter has been put into my head, I am of course anxious to be successful. If you can assist me by your good word, you will confer on me one additional favour.

I had better add, that Lord —— cannot as yet know of this piece of preferment having fallen in, or rather of its certainty of falling (for poor dear Dr. Trefoil is past hope). Should Lord —— first hear it from you, that might probably be thought to give you a fair claim to express your opinion.

Of course our grand object is, that we should all be of one opinion in church matters. This is most desirable at Barchester; it is this that makes our good bishop so anxious about it. You may probably think it expedient to point this out to Lord —— if it shall be in your power to oblige me by mentioning the subject to his lordship.

Believe me, my dear Sir Nicholas,
Your most faithful servant,
OBADIAH SLOPE.

His letter to Mr. Towers was written in quite a different strain. Mr. Slope conceived that he completely understood the difference in character and position of the two men whom he addressed. He knew that for such a man as Sir Nicholas Fitzwhiggin a little flummery was necessary, and that it might be of the easy every-day description. Accordingly his letter to Sir Nicholas was written *currente calamo,* with very little trouble. But to such a man as Mr. Towers it was not so easy to write a letter that should be effective and yet not offensive, that should carry its point without undue interference. It was not difficult to flatter Dr. Proudie or Sir Nicholas Fitzwhiggin, but very difficult to flatter Mr. Towers without letting the flattery declare itself. This, however, had to be done. Moreover, this letter must, in appearance at least, be written without effort, and be fluent, unconstrained, and demonstrative of no doubt or fear on the part of the writer. Therefore the epistle to Mr. Towers was studied,

and recopied, and elaborated at the cost of so many minutes, that
Mr. Slope had hardly time to dress himself and reach Dr.
Stanhope's that evening.

When despatched it ran as follows:—

(Private.)   Barchester. Sept. 185—.

(He purposely omitted any allusion to the "palace," thinking
that Mr. Towers might not like it. A great man, he remembered,
had been once much condemned for dating a letter from Winsdor
Castle.)

My dear Sir,—We were all a good deal shocked here
this morning by hearing that poor old Dean Trefoil had
been stricken with apoplexy. The fit took him about 9
A.M. I am writing now to save the post, and he is still
alive, but past all hope, or possibility I believe, of
living. Sir Omicron Pie is here, or will be very shortly;
but all that even Sir Omicron can do, is to ratify the
sentence of his less distinguished brethren that nothing
can be done. Poor Dr. Trefoil's race on this side the
grave is run. I do not know whether you knew him. He
was a good, quiet, charitable man, of the old school of
course, as any clergyman over seventy years of age
must necessarily be.

But I do not write merely with the object of sending
you such news as this: doubtless some one of your
Mercuries will have seen and heard and reported so
much; I write, as you usually do yourself, rather with a
view to the future than to the past.

Rumour is already rife here as to Dr. Trefoil's
successor, and among those named as possible future
deans your humble servant is, I believe, not the least
frequently spoken of; in short I am looking for the
preferment. You may probably know that since Bishop
Proudie came to this diocese I have exerted myself here
a good deal; and I may certainly say not without some
success. He and I are nearly always of the same opinion
on points of doctrine as well as church discipline, and
therefore I have had, as his confidential chaplain, very
much in my own hands; but I confess to you that I have
a higher ambition than to remain the chaplain of any
bishop.

There are no positions in which more energy is now needed than those of our deans. The whole of our enormous cathedral establishments have been allowed to go to sleep—nay, they are all but dead and ready for the sepulchre! And yet of what prodigious moment they might be made, if, as was intended, they were so managed as to lead the way and show an example for all our parochial clergy!

The bishop here is most anxious for my success; indeed, he goes to-morrow to press the matter on the archbishop. I believe also I may count on the support of at least one most effective member of the government. But I confess that the support of the *Jupiter,* if I be thought worthy of it, would be more gratifying to me than any other; more gratifying if by it I should be successful; and more gratifying also, if, although so supported, I should be unsuccessful.

The time has, in fact, come in which no government can venture to fill up the high places of the Church in defiance of the public press. The age of honourable bishops and noble deans has gone by; and any clergy-man however humbly born can now hope for success, if his industry, talent, and character be sufficient to call forth the manifest opinion of the public in his favour.

At the present moment we all feel that any counsel given in such matters by the *Jupiter* has the greatest weight—is, indeed, generally followed; and we feel also—I am speaking of clergymen of my own age and standing—that it should be so. There can be no patron less interested than the *Jupiter,* and none that more thoroughly understands the wants of the people.

I am sure you will not suspect me of asking from you any support which the paper with which you are connected cannot conscientiously give me. My object in writing is to let you know that I am a candidate for the appointment. It is for you to judge whether or no you can assist my views. I should not, of course, have written to you on such a matter had I not believed (and I have had good reason so to believe) that the *Jupiter* approves of my views on ecclesiastical polity.

The bishop expresses a fear that I may be considered too young for such a station, my age being thirty-six. I cannot think that at the present day any hesitation need be felt on such a point. The public has lost its love for antiquated servants. If a man will ever be fit to do good work he will be fit at thirty-six years of age.

Believe me very faithfully yours,

OBADIAH SLOPE.

T. TOWERS, ESQ.
——Court,
Middle Temple.

Having thus exerted himself, Mr. Slope posted his letters, and passed the remainder of the evening at the feet of his mistress.

Mr. Slope will be accused of deceit in his mode of canvassing. It will be said that he lied in the application he made to each of his three patrons. I believe it must be owned that he did so. He could not hesitate on account of his youth, and yet be quite assured that he was not too young. He could not count chiefly on the bishop's support, and chiefly also on that of the newspaper. He did not think that the bishop was going to —— to press the matter on the archbishop. It must be owned that in his canvassing Mr. Slope was as fake as he well could be.

Let it, however, be asked of those who are conversant with such matters, whether he was more false than men usually are on such occasions. We English gentlemen hate the name of a lie; but how often do we find public men who believe each other's words?

XXXIII

Mrs. Proudie Victrix

The next week passed over at Barchester with much apparent tranquillity. The hearts, however, of some of the inhabitants were not so tranquil as the streets of the city. The poor old dean still continued to live, just as Sir Omicron Pie had prophesied that he would do, much to the amazement, and some thought disgust, of Dr. Fillgrave. The bishop still remained away. He had stayed a day or two in town, and had also remained longer at the archbishop's than he had intended. Mr. Slope had as yet received no line in answer to either of his letters; but he had learnt the cause of this. Sir Nicholas was stalking a deer, or attending the Queen, in the Highlands; and even the indefatigable Mr. Towers had stolen an autumn holiday, and had made one of the yearly tribe who now ascend Mont Blanc. Mr. Slope learnt that he was not expected back till the last day of September.

Mrs. Bold was thrown much with the Stanhopes, of whom she became fonder and fonder. If asked, she would have said that Charlotte Stanhope was her especial friend, and so she would have thought. But, to tell the truth, she liked Bertie nearly as well; she had no more idea of regarding him as a lover than she would have had of looking at a big tame dog in such a light. Bertie had become very intimate with her, and made little speeches to her, and said little things of a sort very different from the speeches and sayings of other men. But then this was almost always done before his sisters; and he, with his long silken beard, his light blue eyes and strange dress, was so unlike other men. She admitted him to a kind of familiarity which she had never known with any one else, and of which she by no means understood the danger. She blushed once at finding that she had called him Bertie, and on the same day only barely remembered her position in time to check herself from playing upon him some personal practical joke to which she was instigated by Charlotte.

In all this Eleanor was perfectly innocent, and Bertie Stanhope could hardly be called guilty. But every familarity into which Eleanor was entrapped was deliberately planned by his sister. She knew well how to play her game, and played it without mercy; she knew, none so well, what was her brother's character, and she would have handed over to him the young widow, and the young widow's money, and the money of the widow's child, without remorse. With her pretended friendship and warm cordiality, she strove to connect Eleanor so closely with her brother as to make it impossible that she should go back even if she wished it. But Charlotte Stanhope knew really nothing of Eleanor's character; did not even understand that there were such characters. She did not comprehend that a young and pretty woman could be playful and familiar with a man such as

Bertie Stanhope, and yet have no idea in her head, no feeling in her heart that she would have been ashamed to own to all the world. Charlotte Stanhope did not in the least conceive that her new friend was a woman whom nothing could entrap into an inconsiderate marriage, whose mind would have revolted from the slightest impropriety had she been aware that any impropriety existed.

Miss Stanhope, however, had tact enough to make herself and her father's house very agreeable to Mrs. Bold. There was with them all an absence of stiffness and formality which was peculiarly agreeable to Eleanor after the great dose of clerical arrogance which she had lately been constrained to take. She played chess with them, walked with them, and drank tea with them; studied or pretended to study astronomy; assisted them in writing stories in rhyme, in turning prose tragedy into comic verse, or comic stories into would-be tragic poetry. She had no idea before that she had any such talents. She had not conceived the possibility of her doing such things as she now did. She found with the Stanhopes new amusements and employments, new pursuits, which in themselves could not be wrong, and which were exceedingly alluring.

Is it not a pity that people who are bright and clever should so often be exceedingly improper? and that those who are never improper should so often be dull and heavy? Now Charlotte Stanhope was always bright, and never heavy: but her propriety was doubtful.

But during all this time Eleanor by no means forgot Mr. Arabin, nor did she forget Mr. Slope. She had parted from Mr. Arabin in her anger. She was still angry at what she regarded as his impertinent interference; but nevertheless she looked forward to meeting him again, and also looked forward to forgiving him. The words that Mr. Arabin had uttered still sounded in her ears. She knew that if not intended for a declaration of love, they did signify that he loved her; and she felt also that if he ever did make such a declaration, it might be that she should not receive it unkindly. She was still angry with him, very angry with him; so angry that she would bite her lip and stamp her foot as she thought of what he had said and done. But nevertheless she yearned to let him know that he was forgiven; all that she required was that he should own that he had sinned.

She was to meet him at Ullathorne on the last day of the present month. Miss Thorne had invited all the country round to a breakfast on the lawn. There were to be tents, and archery, and dancing for the ladies on the lawn, and for the swains and girls in the paddock. There were to be fiddlers and fifers, races for the boys, poles to be climbed, ditches full of water to be jumped over, horse-collars to be grinned through (this latter amusement was an addition of the stewards, and not arranged by Miss Thorne in the original programme), and every game to be played which, in a long course of reading, Miss Thorne could ascertain to have been played in the good days of Queen Elizabeth. Everything of more modern growth was to be tabooed, if possible. On one subject Miss Thorne was very unhappy. She had been turning in her mind the matter of a bull-ring, but could not succeed in making anything of it. She would not for the world have done, or allowed to be done, anything that was cruel; as to the promoting the torture of a bull for the amusement of her young neighbours, it need hardly be said that Miss Thorne would be the last to think of it. And yet there was something so charming in the name. A bull-ring, however, without a bull would only be a memento of the decadence of the times, and she felt herself constrained to abandon the idea. Quintains, however, she was determined to have, and had poles and swivels and bags of flour prepared accordingly. She would no doubt have been anxious for something small in the way of a tournament; but, as she said to her brother, that had been tried, and the age had proved itself too decidedly inferior to its fore-runners to admit of such a pastime. Mr. Thorne did not seem to participate much in her regret, feeling perhaps that a full suit of chain-armour would have added but little to his own personal comfort.

This party at Ullathorne had been planned in the first place as a sort of welcoming to Mr. Arabin on his entrance into St. Ewold's parsonage; an intended harvest-home gala for the labourers and their wives and children had subsequently been amalgamated with it, and thus it had grown to its present dimensions. All the Plumstead party had of course been asked, and at the time of the invitation Eleanor had intended to have gone with her sister. Now her plans were altered, and she was going with the Stanhopes. The Proudies were also to be there; and as Mr. Slope had not been included in the invitation to the palace, the signora, whose impudence never deserted her, asked permission of Miss Thorne to bring him.

This permission Miss Thorne gave, having no other alternative; but she did so with a trembling heart, fearing Mr. Arabin would be offended. Immediately on his return she apologised, almost with tears, so dire an enmity was presumed to rage between the two gentlemen. But Mr. Arabin comforted her by an assurance that he should meet Mr. Slope with the greatest pleasure imaginable and made her promise that she would introduce them to each other.

But this triumph of Mr. Slope's was not so agreeable to Eleanor, who since her return to Barchester had done her best to avoid him. She would not give way to the Plumstead folk when they so ungenerously accused her of being in love with this odious man; but, nevertheless, knowing that she was so accused, she was fully alive to the expediency of keeping out of his way and dropping him by degrees. She had seen very little of him since her return. Her servant had been instructed to say to all visitors that she was out. She could not bring herself to specify Mr. Slope particularly, and in order to avoid him she had thus debarred herself from all her friends. She had excepted Charlotte Stanhope, and by degrees a few others also. Once she had met him at the Stanhopes'; but, as a rule, Mr. Slope's visits there were made in the morning, and hers in the evening. On that one occasion Charlotte had managed to preserve her from any annoyance. This was very good-natured on the part of Charlotte, as Eleanor thought, and also very sharp-witted, as Eleanor had told her friend nothing of her reasons for wishing to avoid that gentleman. The fact, however, was, that Charlotte had learnt from her sister that Mr. Slope would probably put himself forward as a suitor for the widow's hand, and she was consequently sufficiently alive to the expediency of guarding Bertie's future wife from any danger in that quarter.

Nevertheless the Stanhopes were pledged to take Mr. Slope with them to Ullathorne. An arrangement was therefore necessarily made, which was very disagreeable to Eleanor. Dr. Stanhope, with herself, Charlotte, and Mr. Slope, were to go together, and Bertie was to follow with his sister Madeline. It was clearly visible by Eleanor's face that this assortment was very disagreeable to her; and Charlotte, who was much encouraged thereby in her own little plan, made a thousand apologies.

"I see you don't like it, my dear," said she, "but we could not manage otherwise. Bertie would give his eyes to go with you, but Madeline cannot possibly go without him. Nor could we possibly put Mr. Slope and Madeline in the same carriage without any one else. They'd both be ruined for ever, you know, and not admitted inside Ullathorne gates, I should imagine, after such an impropriety."

"Of course that wouldn't do," said Eleanor; "but couldn't I go in the carriage with the signora and your brother?"

"Impossible!" said Charlotte. "When she is there, there is only room for two." The signora, in truth, did not care to do her travelling in the presence of strangers.

"Well, then," said Eleanor, "you are all so kind, Charlotte, and so good to me, that I am sure you won't be offended; but I think I'll not go at all."

"Not go at all!—what nonsense!—indeed you shall." It had been absolutely determined in family council that Bertie should propose on that very occasion.

"Or I can take a fly," said Eleanor. "You know I am not embarrassed by so many difficulties as you young ladies; I can go alone."

"Nonsense! my dear. Don't think of such a thing; after all it is only for an hour or so; and, to tell the truth, I don't know what it is you dislike so. I thought you and Mr. Slope were great friends. What is it you dislike?"

"Oh! nothing particular," said Eleanor; "only I thought it would be a family party."

"Of course it would be much nicer, much more snug, if Bertie could go with us. It is he that is badly treated. I can assure you he is much more afraid of Mr. Slope than you are. But you see Madeline cannot go out without him,—and she, poor creature, goes out so seldom! I am sure you don't begrudge her this, though her vagary does knock about our own party a little."

Of course Eleanor made a thousand protestations, and uttered a thousand hopes that Madeline would enjoy herself. And of course she had to give way, and undertake to go in the carriage with Mr. Slope. In fact, she was driven either to do this, or to explain why she would not do so. Now she could not bring herself to explain to Charlotte Stanhope all that had passed at Plumstead.

But it was to her a sore necessity. She thought of a thousand little schemes for avoiding it; she would plead illness, and not go at all; she would persuade Mary Bold to go although not asked, and then make a necessity of having a carriage of her own to take her sister-in-law; anything, in fact, she could do, rather than be seen by Mr. Arabin getting out of the same carriage with Mr. Slope. However, when the momentous morning came she had no scheme matured, and then Mr. Slope handed her into Dr. Stanhope's carriage, and following her steps, sat opposite to her.

The bishop returned on the eve of the Ullathorne party, and

was received at home with radiant smiles by the partner of all his cares. On his arrival he crept up to his dressing-room with somewhat of a palpitating heart; he had overstayed his allotted time by three days, and was not without much fear of penalties. Nothing, however, could be more affectionately cordial than the greeting he received: the girls came out and kissed him in a manner that was quite soothing to his spirit; and Mrs. Proudie, "albeit, unused to the melting mood," squeezed him in her arms, and almost in words called him her dear, darling, good, pet, little bishop. All this was a very pleasant surprise.

Mrs. Proudie had somewhat changed her tactics; not that she had seen any cause to disapprove of her former line of conduct, but she had now brought matters to such a point that she calculated that she might safely do so. She had got the better of Mr. Slope, and she now thought well to show her husband that when allowed to get the better of everybody, when obeyed by him and permitted to rule over others, she would take care that he should have his reward. Mr. Slope had not a chance against her; not only could she stun the poor bishop by her midnight anger, but she could assuage and soothe him, if she so willed, by daily indulgences. She could furnish his room for him, turn him out as smart a bishop as any on the bench, give him good dinners, warm fires, and an easy life; all this she would do if he would but be quietly obedient. But if not ——! To speak sooth, however, his sufferings on that dreadful night had been so poignant, as to leave him little spirit for further rebellion.

As soon as he had dressed himself she returned to his room. "I hope you enjoyed yourself at ——" said she, seating herself on one side of the fire while he remained in his arm-chair on the other, stroking the calves of his legs. It was the first time he had had a fire in his room since the summer, and it pleased him; for the good bishop loved to be warm and cozy. Yes, he said, he had enjoyed himself very much. Nothing could be more polite than the archbishop; and Mrs. Archbishop had been equally charming.

Mrs. Proudie was delighted to hear it; nothing, she declared, pleased her so much as to think

Her bairn respectit like the lave.

She did not put it precisely in these words, but what she said came to the same thing; and then, having petted and fondled her little man sufficiently, she proceeded to business.

"The poor dean is still alive," said she.

"So I hear, so I hear," said the bishop. "I'll go to the deanery directly after breakfast to-morrow."

"We are going to this party at Ullathorne to-morrow morning, my dear; we must be there early, you know,—by twelve o'clock I suppose."

"Oh,—ah!" said the bishop; "then I'll certainly call the next day."

"Was much said about it at ——?" asked Mrs. Proudie.

"About what?" said the bishop.

"Filling up the dean's place," said Mrs. Proudie. As she spoke a spark of the wonted fire returned to her eye, and the bishop felt himself to be a little less comfortable than before.

"Filling up the dean's place; that is, if the dean dies?—very little, my dear. It was mentioned, just mentioned."

"And what did you say about it, bishop?"

"Why, I said that I thought that if, that is, should—should the dean die, that is, I said I thought——" As he went on stammering and floundering, he saw that his wife's eye was fixed sternly on him. Why should he encounter such evil for a man whom he loved so slightly as Mr. Slope? Why should he give up his enjoyments and his ease, and such dignity as might be allowed to him, to fight a losing battle for a chaplain? The chaplain after all, if successful, would be as great a tyrant as his wife. Why fight at all? why contend? why be uneasy? From that moment he determined to fling Mr. Slope to the winds and take the goods the gods provided.

"I am told," said Mrs. Proudie, speaking very slowly, "that Mr. Slope is looking to be the new dean."

"Yes,—certainly, I believe he is," said the bishop.

"And what does the archbishop say about that?" asked Mrs. Proudie.

"Well, my dear, to tell the truth, I promised Mr. Slope to speak to the archbishop. Mr. Slope spoke to me about it. It is very arrogant of him, I must say,—but that is nothing to me."

"Arrogant!" said Mrs. Proudie; "it is the most impudent piece of pretension I ever heard of in my life. Mr. Slope dean of Barchester, indeed! And what did you do in the matter, Bishop?"

"Why, my dear, I did speak to the archbishop."

"You don't mean to tell me," said Mrs. Proudie, "that you are going to make yourself ridiculous by lending your name to such a preposterous attempt as this? Mr. Slope dean of Barchester, indeed!" And she tossed her head, and put her arms a-kimbo, with an air of confident defiance that made her husband quite sure that Mr. Slope never would be dean of Barchester. In truth, Mrs. Proudie was all but invincible; had she married Petruchio, it may be doubted whether that arch wife-tamer would have been able to keep her legs out of those garments which are presumed by men to be peculiarly unfitted for feminine use.

"It is preposterous, my dear."

"Then why have you endeavoured to assist him?"

"Why,—my dear, I haven't assisted him—much."

"But why have you done it at all? why have you mixed your name up in any thing so ridiculous? What was it you did say to the archbishop?"

"Why, I just did mention it; I just did say that—that in the event of the poor dean's death, Mr. Slope would—would——"

"Would what?"

"I forget how I put it,—would take it if he could get it; something of that sort. I didn't say much more than that."

"You shouldn't have said anything at all. And what did the archbishop say?"

"He didn't say anything; he just bowed and rubbed his hands. Somebody else came up at the moment, and as we were discussing the new parochial universal school committee, the matter of the new dean dropped; after that I didn't think it wise to renew it."

"Renew it! I am very sorry you ever mentioned it. What will the archbishop think of you?"

"You may be sure, my dear, the archbishop thought very little about it."

"But why did you think about it, bishop? how could you think of making such a creature as that Dean of Barchester? —Dean of Barchester! I suppose he'll be looking for a bishopric some of these days—a man that hardly knows who his own father was; a man that I found without bread to his mouth, or a coat to his back. Dean of Barchester, indeed! I'll dean him."

Mrs. Proudie considered herself to be in politics a pure Whig; all her family belonged to the Whig party. Now among all ranks of Englishmen and Englishwomen (Mrs. Proudie should, I think, be ranked among the former, on the score of her great strength of mind), no one is so hostile to lowly born pretenders to high station as the pure Whig.

The bishop thought it necessary to exculpate himself. "Why, my dear," said he, "it appeared to me that you and Mr. Slope did not get on quite so well as you used to do."

"Get on!" said Mrs. Proudie, moving her foot uneasily on the hearth-rug, and compressing her lips in a manner that betokened much danger to the subject of their discourse.

"I began to find that he was objectionable to you,"—Mrs. Proudie's foot worked on the hearth-rug with great rapidity, —"and that you would be more comfortable if he was out of the palace,"—Mrs. Proudie smiled, as a hyena may probably smile before he begins his laugh,—"and therefore I thought that if he got this place, and so ceased to be my chaplain, you might be pleased at such an arrangement."

And then the hyena laughed out. Pleased at such an arrangement! pleased at having her enemy converted into a dean with twelve hundred a year! Medea, when she describes the customs of her native country (I am quoting from Robson's edition), assures her astonished auditor that in her land captives, when taken, are eaten. "You pardon them?" says Medea. "We do indeed," says the mild Grecian. "We eat them!" says she of Colchis, with terrific energy. Mrs. Proudie was the Medea of Barchester; she had no idea of not eating Mr. Slope. Pardon him! merely get rid of him! make a dean of him! It was not so they did with their captives in her country, among people of her sort! Mr. Slope had no such mercy to expect; she would pick him to the very last bone.

"Oh, yes, my dear, of course he'll cease to be your chaplain," said she. "After what has passed, that must be a matter of course. I couldn't for a moment think of living in the same house with such a man. Besides, he has shown himself quite unfit for such a situation; making broils and quarrels among the clergy, getting you, my dear, into scrapes, and taking upon himself as though he were as good as bishop himself. Of course he'll go. But because he leaves the palace, that is no reason why he should get into the deanery."

"Oh, of course not!" said the bishop; "but to save appearances you know, my dear——"

"I don't want to save appearances; I want Mr. Slope to appear just what he is—a false, designing, mean, intriguing man. I have my eye on him; he little knows what I see. He is misconducting himself in the most disgraceful way with that lame Italian woman. That family is a disgrace to Barchester, and Mr. Slope is a disgrace to Barchester! If he doesn't look well to it, he'll have his gown stripped off his back instead of having a dean's hat on his head. Dean, indeed! The man has gone mad with arrogance."

The bishop said nothing further to excuse either himself or his chaplain, and having shown himself passive and docile was again taken into favour. They soon went to dinner, and he spent the pleasantest evening he had had in his own house for a long time. His daughter played and sang to him as he sipped his coffee and read his newspaper, and Mrs. Proudie asked good-natured little questions about the archbishop; and then he went happily to bed, and slept as quietly as though Mrs. Proudie had been Griselda herself. While shaving himself in the morning and preparing for the festivities of Ullathorne, he fully resolved to run no more tilts against a warrior so fully armed at all points as was Mrs. Proudie.

XXXIV

Oxford—The Master and Tutor of Lazarus

Mr. Arabin, as we have said, had but a sad walk of it under the trees of Plumstead churchyard. He did not appear to any of the family till dinner time, and then he seemed, as far as their judgment went, to be quite himself. He had, as was his wont, asked himself a great many questions, and given himself a great many answers; and the upshot of this was that he had set himself down for an ass. He had determined that he was much too old and much too rusty to commence the manœuvres of love-making; that he had let the time slip through his hands which should have been used for such purposes; and that now he must lie on his bed as he had made it. Then he asked himself whether in truth he did love this woman; and he answered himself, not without a long struggle, but at last honestly, that he certainly did love her. He then asked himself whether he did not also love her money; and he again answered himself that he did so. But here he did not answer honestly. It was and ever had been his weakness to look for impure motives for his own conduct. No doubt, circumstanced as he was, with a small living and a fellowship, accustomed as he had been to collegiate luxuries and expensive comforts, he might have hesitated to marry a penniless woman had he felt ever so strong a predilection for the woman herself; no doubt Eleanor's fortune put all such difficulties out of the question: but it was equally without doubt that his love for her had crept upon him without the slightest idea on his part that he could ever benefit his own condition by sharing her wealth.

When he had stood on the hearth-rug, counting the pattern, and counting also the future chances of his own life, the remembrance of Mrs. Bold's comfortable income had not certainly damped his first assured feeling of love for her. And why should it have done so? Need it have done so with the purest of men? Be that as it may, Mr. Arabin decided against himself; he decided that it had done so in his case, and that he was not the purest of men.

He also decided, which was more to his purpose, that Eleanor did not care a straw for him, and that very probably she did care a straw for his rival. Then he made up his mind not to think of her any more, and went on thinking of her till he was almost in a state to drown himself in the little brook which ran at the bottom of the archdeacon's grounds.

And ever and again his mind would revert to the Signora Neroni, and he would make comparisons between her and Eleanor Bold, not always in favour of the latter. The signora had listened to him, and flattered him, and believed in him; at least she had told him so. Mrs. Bold had also listened to him, but had never flattered him; and had not always believed in him: and now had broken from him in violent rage. The signora, too, was the more lovely woman of the two, and had also the additional attraction of her affliction; for to him it was an attraction.

But he never could have loved the Signora Neroni as he felt that he now loved Eleanor! and so he flung stones into the brook, instead of flinging in himself, and sat down on its margin as sad a gentleman as you shall meet in á summer's day.

He heard the dinner-bell ring from the churchyard, and he knew that it was time to recover his self-possession. He felt that he was disgracing himself in his own eyes, that he had been idling his time and neglecting the high duties which he had taken upon himself to perform. He should have spent this afternoon among the poor at St. Ewold's, instead of wandering about at Plumstead, an ancient love-lorn swain, dejected and sighing, full of imaginary sorrows and Wertherian grief. He was thoroughly ashamed of himself, and determined to lose no time in retrieving his character, so damaged in his own eyes. Thus when he appeared at dinner he was as animated as ever, and was the author of most of the conversation which graced the archdeacon's board on that evening. Mr. Harding was ill at ease and sick at heart, and did not care to appear more comfortable than he really was; what little he did say was said to his daughter. He thought that the archdeacon and Mr. Arabin had leagued together against Eleanor's comfort; and his wish now was to break away from the pair, and undergo in his Barchester lodgings whatever Fate had in store for him. He hated the name of the hospital; his attempt to regain his lost inheritance there had brought upon him so much suffering. As far as he was concerned, Mr. Quiverful was now welcome to the place.

And the archdeacon was not very lively. The poor dean's illness was of course discussed in the first place. Dr. Grantly did not mention Mr. Slope's name in connexion with the expected event of Dr. Trefoil's death; he did not wish to say anything about Mr. Slope just at present, nor did he wish to make known his sad surmises; but the idea that his enemy might possibly become Dean of Barchester made him very gloomy. Should such an event take place, such a dire catastrophe come about, there would be an end to his life as far as his life was connected with the city of Barchester. He must give up all his old haunts, all his old habits, and live quietly as a retired rector at Plumstead. It had been a severe trial for him to have Dr. Proudie in the palace; but with Mr. Slope also in the deanery, he felt that he should be unable to draw his breath in Barchester close.

Thus it came to pass that in spite of the sorrow at his heart, Mr. Arabin was apparently the gayest of the party. Both Mr. Harding and Mrs. Grantly were in a slight degree angry with him on account of his want of gloom. To the one it appeared as though he were triumphing at Eleanor's banishment, and to the other that he was not affected as he should have been by all the sad circumstances of the day, Eleanor's obstinacy, Mr. Slope's success, and the poor dean's apoplexy. And so they were all at cross purposes.

Mr. Harding left the room almost together with the ladies, and then the archdeacon opened his heart to Mr. Arabin. He still harped upon the hospital. "What did that fellow mean," said he, "by saying in his letter to Mrs. Bold, that if Mr. Harding would call on the bishop it would be all right? Of course I would not be guided by anything he might say; but still it may be well that Mr.

Harding should see the bishop. It would be foolish to let the thing slip through our fingers because Mrs. Bold is determined to make a fool of herself.''

Mr. Arabin hinted that he was not quite so sure that Mrs. Bold would make a fool of herself. He said that he was not convinced that she did regard Mr. Slope so warmly as she was supposed to do. The archdeacon questioned and cross-questioned him about this, but elicited nothing; and at last remained firm in his own conviction that he was destined, *malgré lui*, to be the brother-in-law of Mr. Slope. Mr. Arabin strongly advised that Mr. Harding should take no step regarding the hospital in connexion with, or in consequence of, Mr. Slope's letter. "If the bishop really means to confer the appointment on Mr. Harding," argued Mr. Arabin, "he will take care to let him have some other intimation than a message conveyed through a letter to a lady. Were Mr. Harding to present himself at the palace he might merely be playing Mr. Slope's game''; and thus it was settled that nothing should be done till the great Dr. Gwynne's arrival, or at any rate without that potentate's sanction.

It was droll to observe how these men talked of Mr. Harding as though he were a puppet, and planned their intrigues and small ecclesiastical manœuvres in reference to Mr. Harding's future position, without dreaming of taking him into their confidence. There was a comfortable house and income in question, and it was very desirable, and certainly very just, that Mr. Harding should have them; but that, at present, was not the main point; it was expedient to beat the bishop, and if possible to smash Mr. Slope. Mr. Slope had set up, or was supposed to have set up, a rival candidate. Of all things the most desirable would have been to have had Mr. Quiverful's appointment published to the public, and then annulled by the clamour of an indignant world, loud in the defence of Mr. Harding's rights. But of such an event the chance was small; a slight fraction only of the world would be indignant, and that fraction would be one not accustomed to loud speaking. And then the preferment had in a sort of way been offered to Mr. Harding, and had in a sort of way been refused by him.

Mr. Slope's wicked, cunning hand had been peculiarly conspicuous in the way in which this had been brought to pass, and it was the success of Mr. Slope's cunning which was so painfully grating to the feelings of the archdeacon. That which of all things he most dreaded was that he should be out-generalled by Mr. Slope: and just at present it appeared probable that Mr.

Slope would turn his flank, steal a march on him, cut off his provisions, carry his strong town by a *coup de main*, and at last beat him thoroughly in a regular pitched battle. The archdeacon felt that his flank had been turned when desired to wait on Mr. Slope instead of the bishop, that a march had been stolen when Mr. Harding was induced to refuse the bishop's offer, that his provisions would be cut off when Mr. Quiverful got the hospital, that Eleanor was the strong town doomed to be taken, and that Mr. Slope, as Dean of Barchester, would be regarded by all the world as the conqueror in the final conflict.

Dr. Gwynne was the *Deus ex machina* who was to come down upon the Barchester stage, and bring about deliverance from these terrible evils. But how can melodramatic *dénouements* be properly brought about, how can vice and Mr. Slope be punished, and virtue and the archdeacon be rewarded, while the avenging god is laid up with the gout? In the mean time evil may be triumphant, and poor innocence, transfixed to the earth by an arrow from Dr. Proudie's quiver, may lie dead upon the ground, not to be resuscitated even by Dr. Gwynne.

Two or three days after Eleanor's departure, Mr. Arabin went to Oxford, and soon found himself closeted with the august head of his college. It was quite clear that Dr. Gwynne was not very sanguine as to the effects of his journey to Barchester, and not over anxious to interfere with the bishop. He had had the gout but was very nearly convalescent, and Mr. Arabin at once saw that had the mission been one of which the master thoroughly approved, he would before this have been at Plumstead.

As it was, Dr. Gwynne was resolved on visiting his friend, and willingly promised to return to Barchester with Mr. Arabin. He could not bring himself to believe that there was any probability that Mr. Slope would be made Dean of Barchester. Rumour, he said, had reached even his ears, not at all favourable to that gentleman's character, and he expressed himself strongly of opinion that any such appointment was quite out of the question. At this stage of the proceedings, the master's right-hand man, Tom Staple, was called in to assist at the conference. Tom Staple was the Tutor of Lazarus, and moreover a great man at Oxford. Though universally known by a species of nomenclature so very undignified, Tom Staple was one who maintained a high dignity in the University. He was, as it were, the leader of the Oxford tutors, a body of men who consider themselves collectively as being by very little, if at all, second in importance to the heads themselves. It is not always the case that the master, or warden, or provost, or principal can hit it off exactly with his tutor. A tutor is by no means indisposed to have a will of his own. But at Lazarus they were great friends and firm allies at the time of which we are writing.

Tom Staple was a hale strong man of about forty-five; short in stature, swarthy in face, with strong sturdy black hair, and crisp black beard, of which very little was allowed to show itself in shape of whiskers. He always wore a white neckcloth, clean indeed, but not tied with that scrupulous care which now distinguishes some of our younger clergy. He was, of course, always clothed in a seemly suit of solemn black. Mr. Staple was a decent cleanly liver, not over addicted to any sensuality; but nevertheless a somewhat warmish hue was beginning to adorn his nose, the peculiar effect, as his friends averred, of a certain pipe of port introduced into the cellars of Lazarus the very same year in which the tutor entered it as a freshman. There was also, perhaps, a little redolence of port wine, as it were the slightest possible twang, in Mr. Staple's voice.

In these latter days Tom Staple was not a happy man; University reform had long been his bugbear, and now was his bane. It was not with him as with most others, an affair of politics, respecting which, when the need existed, he could for parties' sake or on behalf of principle, maintain a certain amount of necessary zeal; it was not with him a subject for dilettante warfare, and courteous common-place opposition. To him it was life and death. The *statu quo* of the University was his only idea of life, and any reformation was as bad to him as death. He would willingly have been a martyr in the cause, had the cause admitted of martyrdom.

At the present day, unfortunately, public affairs will allow of no martyrs, and therefore it is that there is such a deficiency of zeal. Could gentlemen of £10,000 a year have died on their own door-steps in defence of protection, no doubt some half-dozen glorious old baronets would have so fallen, and the school of protection would at this day have been crowded with scholars. Who can fight strenuously in any combat in which there is no danger? Tom Staple would have willingly been impaled before a Committee of the House, could he by such self-sacrifice have infused his own spirit into the component members of the hebdomadal board.

Tom Staple was one of those who in his heart approved of the credit system which had of old been in vogue between the students and tradesmen of the University. He knew and acknowledged to himself that it was useless in these degenerate days publicly to contend with the *Jupiter* on such a subject. The *Jupiter* had undertaken to rule the University, and Tom Staple was well aware that the *Jupiter* was too powerful for him. But in secret, and among his safe companions, he would argue that the system of credit was an ordeal good for young men to undergo.

The bad men, said he, the weak and worthless, blunder into danger and burn their feet; but the good men, they who have any character, they who have that within them which can reflect credit on their Alma Mater, they come through scatheless. What merit will there be to a young man to get through safely, if he be guarded and protected and restrained like a school-boy? By so doing, the period of the ordeal is only postponed, and the manhood of the man will be deferred from the age of twenty to that of twenty-four. If you bind him with leading-strings at college, he will break loose while reading for the bar in London; bind him there, and he will break loose afterwards, when he is a married man. The wild oats must be sown somewhere. 'Twas thus that Tom Staple would argue of young men; not, indeed, with much consistency, but still with some practical knowledge of the subject gathered from long experience.

And now Tom Staple proffered such wisdom as he had for the assistance of Dr. Gwynne and Mr. Arabin.

"Quite out of the question," said he, arguing that Mr. Slope could not possibly be made the new Dean of Barchester.

"So I think," said the master. "He has no standing, and, if all I hear be true, very little character."

"As to character," said Tom Staple, "I don't think much of that. They rather like loose parsons for deans; a little fast living, or a dash of infidelity, is no bad recommendation to a cathedral close. But they couldn't make Mr. Slope; the last two deans have been Cambridge men; you'll not show me an instance of their making three men running from the same University. We don't get our share, and never shall, I suppose; but we must at least have one out of three."

"Those sort of rules are all gone by now," said Mr. Arabin.

"Everything has gone by, I believe," said Tom Staple. "The cigar has been smoked out, and we are the ashes."

"Speak for yourself, Staple," said the master.

"I speak for all," said the tutor, stoutly. "It is coming to that, that there will be no life left anywhere in the country. No one is any longer fit to rule himself, or those belonging to him.

The Government is to find us all in everything, and the press is to find the Government. Nevertheless, Mr. Slope won't be Dean of Barchester.''

"And who will be warden of the hospital?" said Mr. Arabin.

"I hear that Mr. Quiverful is already appointed," said Tom Staple.

"I think not," said the master. "And I think, moreover, that Dr. Proudie will not be so short-sighted as to run against such a rock: Mr. Slope should himself have sense enough to prevent it.''

"But perhaps Mr. Slope may have no objection to see his patron on a rock," said the suspicious tutor.

"What could he get by that?" asked Mr. Arabin.

"It is impossible to see the doubles of such a man," said Mr. Staple. "It seems quite clear that Bishop Proudie is altogether in his hands, and it is equally clear that he has been moving heaven and earth to get this Mr. Quiverful into the hospital, although he must know that such an appointment would be most damaging to the bishop. It is impossible to understand such a man, and dreadful to think," added Tom Staple, sighing deeply, "that the welfare and fortunes of good men may depend on his intrigues.''

Dr. Gwynne or Mr. Staple were not in the least aware, nor even was Mr. Arabin, that this Mr. Slope, of whom they were talking, had been using his utmost efforts to put their own candidate into the hospital; and that in lieu of being permanent in the palace, his own expulsion therefrom had been already decided on by the high powers of the diocese.

"I'll tell you what," said the tutor, "if this Quiverful is thrust into the hospital and Dr. Trefoil does die, I should not wonder if the Government were to make Mr. Harding Dean of Barchester. They would feel bound to do something for him after all that was said when he resigned.''

Dr. Gwynne at the moment made no reply to this suggestion; but it did not the less impress itself on his mind. If Mr. Harding could not be warden of the hospital, why should he not be Dean of Barchester?

And so the conference ended without any very fixed resolution, and Dr. Gwynne and Mr. Arabin prepared for their journey to Plumstead on the morrow.

VOLUME THREE

XXXV

Miss Thorne's Fête Champêtre

The day of the Ullathorne party arrived, and all the world were there; or at least so much of the world as had been included in Miss Thorne's invitation. As we have said, the bishop returned home on the previous evening, and on the same evening, and by the same train, came Dr. Gwynne and Mr. Arabin from Oxford. The archdeacon with his brougham was in waiting for the Master of Lazarus, so that there was a goodly show of church dignitaries on the platform of the railway.

The Stanhope party was finally arranged in the odious manner already described, and Eleanor got into the doctor's carriage full of apprehension and presentiment of further misfortune, whereas Mr. Slope entered the vehicle elate with triumph.

He had received that morning a very civil note from Sir Nicholas Fitzwhiggin; not promising much indeed; but then Mr. Slope knew, or fancied that he knew, that it was not etiquette for government officers to make promises. Though Sir Nicholas promised nothing he implied a good deal; declared his conviction that Mr. Slope would make an excellent dean, and wished him every kind of success. To be sure he added that, not being in the cabinet, he was never consulted on such matters, and that even if he spoke on the subject his voice would go for nothing. But all this Mr. Slope took for the prudent reserve of official life. To complete his anticipated triumphs, another letter was brought to him just as he was about to start to Ullathorne.

Mr. Slope also enjoyed the idea of handing Mrs. Bold out of Mr. Stanhope's carriage before the multitude at Ullathorne gate, as much as Eleanor dreaded the same ceremony. He had fully made up his mind to throw himself and his fortune at the widow's feet, and had almost determined to select the present

475

propitious morning for doing so. The signora had of late been less than civil to him. She had indeed admitted his visits, and listened, at any rate without anger, to his love; but she had tortured him and reviled him, jeered at him and ridiculed him, while she allowed him to call her the most beautiful of living women, to kiss her hand, and to proclaim himself with reiterated oaths her adorer, her slave, and worshipper.

Miss Thorne was in great perturbation, yet in great glory, on the morning of the gala day. Mr. Thorne also, though the party was none of his giving, had much heavy work on his hands. But perhaps the most overtasked, the most anxious and the most effective of all the Ullathorne household was Mr. Plomacy, the steward. This last personage had, in the time of Mr. Thorne's father, when the Directory held dominion in France, gone over to Paris with letters in his boot heel for some of the royal party; and such had been his good luck that he had returned safe. He had then been very young and was now very old, but the exploit gave him a character for political enterprise and secret discretion which still availed him as thoroughly as it had done in its freshest gloss. Mr. Plomacy had been steward of Ullathorne for more than fifty years, and a very easy life he had had of it. Who could require much absolute work from a man who had carried safely at his heel that which if discovered would have cost him his head? Consequently Mr. Plomacy had never worked hard, and of latter years had never worked at all. He had a taste for timber, and therefore he marked the trees that were to be cut down; he had a taste for gardening, and would therefore allow no shrub to be planted or bed to be made without his express sanction. In these matters he was sometimes driven to run counter to his mistress, but he rarely allowed his mistress to carry the point against him.

But on occasions such as the present Mr. Plomacy came out strong. He had the honour of the family at heart; he thoroughly appreciated the duties of hospitality; and therefore, when gala doings were going on, always took the management into his own hands and reigned supreme over master and mistress.

To give Mr. Plomacy his due, old as he was, he thoroughly understood such work as he had in hand, and did it well.

The order of the day was to be as follows. The quality, as the upper classes in rural districts are designated by the lower with so much true discrimination, were to eat a breakfast, and the non-quality were to eat a dinner. Two marquees had been erected for these two banquets, that for the quality on the esoteric or garden side of a certain deep ha-ha; and that for the non-quality on the exoteric or paddock side of the same. Both were of huge dimensions; that on the outer side was, one may say, on an egregious scale; but Mr. Plomacy declared that neither would be sufficient. To remedy this, an auxiliary banquet was prepared in the dining-room, and a subsidiary board was to be spread *sub dio* for the accommodation of the lower class of yokels on the Ullathorne property.

No one who has not had a hand in the preparation of such an affair can understand the manifold difficulties which Miss Thorne encountered in her project. Had she not been made throughout of the very finest whalebone, riveted with the best Yorkshire steel, she must have sunk under them. Had not Mr. Plomacy felt how much was justly expected from a man who at one time carried the destinies of Europe in his boot, he would have given way; and his mistress, so deserted, must have perished among her poles and canvas.

In the first place there was a dreadful line to be drawn. Who were to dispose themselves within the ha-ha, and who without? To this the unthinking will give an off-hand answer, as they will to every ponderous question. Oh, the bishop and such like within the ha-ha; and Farmer Greenacre and such like without. True, my unthinking friend; but who shall define these such-likes? It is in such definitions that the whole difficulty of society consists. To seat the bishop on an arm-chair on the lawn and place Farmer Greenacre at the end of a long table in the paddock is easy enough; but where will you put Mrs. Lookaloft, whose husband, though a tenant on the estate, hunts in a red coat, whose daughters go to a fashionable seminary in Barchester, who calls her farm house Rosebank, and who has a pianoforte in her drawing-room? The Misses Lookaloft, as they call themselves, won't sit contented among the bumpkins. Mrs. Lookaloft won't squeeze her fine clothes on a bench and talk familiarly about cream and ducklings to good Mrs. Greenacre. And yet Mrs. Lookaloft is no fit companion and never has been the associate of the Thornes and the Grantlys. And if Mrs. Lookaloft be admitted within the sanctum of fashionable life, if she be allowed with her three daughters to leap the ha-ha, why not the wives and daughters of the other families also? Mrs. Greenacre is at present well contented with the paddock, but she might cease to be so if she saw Mrs. Lookaloft on the lawn. And thus poor Miss Thorne had a hard time of it.

And how was she to divide her guests between the marquee

and the parlour? She had a countess coming, an Honourable John
and an Honourable George, and a whole bevy of Ladies Amelia,
Rosina, Margaretta, &c.; she had a leash of baronets with their
baronnettes; and, as we all know, she had a bishop. If she put
them on the lawn, no one would go into the parlour; if she put
them into the parlour, no one would go into the tent. She thought
of keeping the old people in the house, and leaving the lawn to
the lovers. She might as well have seated herself at once in a
hornet's nest. Mr. Plomacy knew better than this. "Bless your
soul, Ma'am," said he, "there won't be no old ladies; not one,
barring yourself and old Mrs. Clantantram."

Personally Miss Thorne accepted this distinction in her
favour as a compliment to her good sense; but nevertheless she
had no desire to be closeted on the coming occasion with Mrs.
Clantantram. She gave up all idea of any arbitrary division of her
guests, and determined if possible to put the bishop on the lawn
and the countess in the house, to sprinkle the baronets, and thus
divide the attractions. What to do with the Lookalofts even Mr.
Plomacy could not decide. They must take their chance. They
had been specially told in the invitation that all the tenants had
been invited; and they might probably have the good sense to
stay away if they objected to mix with the rest of the tenantry.

Then Mr. Plomacy declared his apprehension that the Honourable Johns and Honourable Georges would come in a sort of
amphibious costume, half morning, half evening, satin neck-
handkerchiefs, frock coats, primrose gloves, and polished boots;
and that, being so dressed, they would decline riding at the
quintain, or taking part in any of the athletic games which Miss
Thorne had prepared with so much fond care. If the Lord Johns
and Lord Georges didn't ride at the quintain, Miss Thorne might
be sure that nobody else would.

"But," said she in dolorous voice, all but overcome by her
cares; "it was specially signified that there were to be sports."

"And so there will be, of course," said Mr. Plomacy.
"They'll all be sporting with the young ladies in the laurel walks.
Them's the sports they care most about now-a-days. If you gets
the young men at the quintain, you'll have all the young women
in the pouts."

"Can't they look on, as their great grandmothers did before
them?" said Miss Thorne.

"It seems to me that the ladies ain't contented with looking
now-a-days. Whatever the men do they'll do. If you'll have side

saddles on the nags, and let them go at the quintain too, it'll answer capital, no doubt."

Miss Thorne made no reply. She felt that she had no good ground on which to defend her sex of the present generation from the sarcasm of Mr. Plomacy. She had once declared, in one of her warmer moments, "that now-a-days the gentlemen were all women, and the ladies all men." She could not alter the debased character of the age. But, such being the case, why should she take on herself to cater for the amusement of people of such degraded tastes? This question she asked herself more than once, and she could only answer herself with a sigh. There was her own brother Wilfred, on whose shoulders rested all the ancient honours of Ullathorne house; it was very doubtful whether even he would consent to "go at the quintain," as Mr. Plomacy not injudiciously expressed it.

And now the morning arrived. The Ullathorne household was early on the move. Cooks were cooking in the kitchen long before daylight, and men were dragging out tables and hammering red baize on to benches at the earliest dawn. With what dread eagerness did Miss Thorne look out at the weather as soon as the parting veil of night permitted her to look at all! In this respect at any rate there was nothing to grieve her. The glass had been rising for the last three days, and the morning broke with that dull chill steady grey haze which in autumn generally presages a clear and dry day. By seven she was dressed and down. Miss Thorne knew nothing of the modern luxury of *déshabilles*. She would as soon have thought of appearing before her brother without her stockings as without her stays; and Miss Thorne's stays were no trifle.

And yet there was nothing for her to do when down. She fidgeted out to the lawn, and then back into the kitchen. She put on her high-heeled clogs, and fidgeted out into the paddock. Then she went into the small home park where the quintain was erected. The pole and cross bar and the swivel, and the target and the bag of flour were all complete. She got up on a carpenter's bench and touched the target with her hand; it went round with beautiful ease; the swivel had been oiled to perfection. She almost wished to take old Plomacy at his word, to get on a side saddle and have a tilt at it herself. What must a young man be, thought she, who could prefer maundering among laurel trees with a wishy-washy school-girl to such fun as this? "Well," said she aloud to herself, "one man can take a horse to water, but a thousand can't make him drink. There it is. If they haven't the spirit to enjoy it, the fault shan't be mine''; and so she returned to the house.

At a little after eight her brother came down, and they had a sort of scrap breakfast in his study. The tea was made without the customary urn, and they dispensed with the usual rolls and toast. Eggs also were missing, for every egg in the parish had been whipped into custards, baked into pies, or boiled into lobster salad. The allowance of fresh butter was short, and Mr. Thorne was obliged to eat the leg of a fowl without having it devilled in the manner he loved.

"I have been looking at the quintain, Wilfred," said she, "and it appears to be quite right."

"Oh—ah; yes"; said he. "It seemed to be so yesterday when I saw it." Mr. Thorne was beginning to be rather bored by his sister's love of sports, and had especially no affection for this quintain post.

"I wish you'd just try it after breakfast," said she. "You could have the saddle put on Mark Antony, and the pole is there all handy. You can take the flour bag off, you know, if you think Mark Antony won't be quick enough," added Miss Thorne, seeing that her brother's countenance was not indicative of complete accordance with her little proposition.

Now Mark Antony was a valuable old hunter, excellently suited to Mr. Thorne's usual requirements, steady indeed at his fences, but extremely sure, very good in deep ground, and safe on the roads. But he had never yet been ridden at a quintain, and Mr. Thorne was not inclined to put him to the trial, either with or without the bag of flour. He hummed and hawed, and finally declared that he was afraid Mark Antony would shy.

"Then try the cob," said the indefatigable Miss Thorne.

"He's in physic," said Wilfred.

"There's the Belzebub colt," said his sister; "I know he's in the stable, because I saw Peter exercising him just now."

"My dear Monica, he's so wild, that it's as much as I can do to manage him at all. He'd destroy himself and me too, if I attempted to ride him at such a rattletrap as that."

A rattletrap! The quintain that she had put up with so much anxious care; the game that she had prepared for the amusement of the stalwart yeomen of the country; the sport that had been honoured by the affection of so many of their ancestors! It cut her to the heart to hear it so denominated by her own brother. There were but the two of them left together in the world; and it had ever been one of the rules by which Miss Thorne had regulated her conduct through life, to say nothing that could provoke her brother. She had often had to suffer from his indifference to time-honoured British customs; but she had always suffered in silence. It was part of her creed that the head of the family should never be upbraided in his own house; and Miss Thorne had lived up to her creed. Now, however, she was greatly tried. The colour mounted to her ancient cheek, and the fire blazed in her still bright eye; but yet she said nothing. She resolved that, at any rate, to him nothing more should be said about the quintain that day.

She sipped her tea in silent sorrow, and thought with painful regret of the glorious days when her great ancestor Ealfried had successfully held Ullathorne against a Norman invader. There was no such spirit now left in her family except that small useless spark which burnt in her own bosom. And she herself, was not she at this moment intent on entertaining a descendant of those very Normans, a vain proud countess with a frenchified name, who would only think that she graced Ullathorne too highly by entering its portals? Was it likely that an honourable John, the son of an Earl De Courcy, should ride at a quintain in company with Saxon yeomen? And why should she expect her brother to do that which her brother's guests would decline to do?

Some dim faint idea of the impracticability of her own views flitted across her brain. Perhaps it was necessary that races doomed to live on the same soil should give way to each other, and adopt each other's pursuits. Perhaps it was impossible that after more than five centuries of close intercourse, Normans should remain Normans, and Saxons, Saxons. Perhaps after all her neighbours were wiser than herself. Such ideas did occasionally present themselves to Miss Thorne's mind, and make her sad enough. But it never occurred to her that her favourite quintain was but a modern copy of a Norman knight's amusement, an adaptation of the noble tourney to the tastes and habits of the Saxon yeomen. Of this she was ignorant, and it would have been cruelty to instruct her.

When Mr. Thorne saw the tear in her eye, he repented himself of his contemptuous expression. By him also it was recognised as a binding law that every whim of his sister was to be respected. He was not perhaps so firm in his observances to her, as she was in hers to him. But his intentions were equally good, and whenever he found that he had forgotten them it was matter of grief to him.

"My dear Monica," said he, "I beg your pardon; I don't in the least mean to speak ill of the game. When I called it a rattletrap, I merely meant that it was so for a man of my age. You know you always forget that I an't a young man."

"I am quite sure you are not an old man, Wilfred," said she, accepting the apology in her heart, and smiling at him with the tear still on her cheek.

"If I was five-and-twenty, or thirty," continued he, "I should like nothing better than riding at the quintain all day."

"But you are not too old to hunt or to shoot," said she. "If you can jump over a ditch and hedge I am sure you could turn the quintain round."

"But when I ride over the hedges, my dear—and it isn't very often I do that—but when I do ride over the hedges there isn't any bag of flour coming after me. Think how I'd look taking the countess out to breakfast with the back of my head all covered with meal."

Miss Thorne said nothing further. She didn't like the allusion to the countess. She couldn't be satisfied with the reflection that the sports of Ullathorne should be interfered with by the personal attentions necessary for a Lady De Courcy. But she saw that it was useless for her to push the matter further. It was conceded that Mr. Thorne was to be spared the quintain; and Miss Thorne determined to trust wholly to a youthful knight of hers, an immense favourite, who, as she often declared, was a pattern to the young men of the age, and an excellent sample of an English yeoman.

This was Farmer Greenacre's eldest son; who, to tell the truth, had from his earliest years taken the exact measure of Miss Thorne's foot. In his boyhood he had never failed to obtain from her, apples, pocket money, and forgiveness for his numerous trespasses; and now in his early manhood he got privileges and immunities which were equally valuable. He was allowed a day or two's shooting in September; he schooled the squire's horses; got slips of trees out of the orchard, and roots of flowers out of the garden; and had the fishing of the little river altogether in his own hands. He had undertaken to come mounted on a nag of his father's, and show the way at the quintain post. Whatever young Greenacre did the others would do after him. The juvenile Lookalofts might stand aloof, but the rest of the youth of Ullathorne would be sure to venture if Harry Greenacre showed the way. And so Miss Thorne made up her mind to dispense with the noble Johns and Georges, and trust, as her ancestors had done before her, to the thews and sinews of native Ullathorne growth.

At about nine the lower orders began to congregate in the paddock and park, under the surveillance of Mr. Plomacy and the head gardener and head groom, who were sworn in as his deputies, and were to assist him in keeping the peace and promoting the sports. Many of the younger inhabitants of the neighbourhood, thinking that they could not have too much of a good thing, had come at a very early hour, and the road between the house and the church had been thronged for some time before the gates were thrown open.

And then another difficulty of huge dimensions arose, a difficulty which Mr. Plomacy had indeed foreseen and for which he was in some sort provided. Some of those who wished to share Miss Thorne's hospitality were not so particular as they should have been as to the preliminary ceremony of an invitation. They doubtless conceived that they had been overlooked by accident; and instead of taking this in dudgeon, as their betters would have done, they good-naturedly put up with the slight, and showed that they did so by presenting themselves at the gate in their Sunday best.

Mr. Plomacy, however, well knew who were welcome and who were not. To some, even though uninvited, he allowed ingress. "Don't be too particular, Plomacy," his mistress had said; "especially with the children. If they live anywhere near, let them in."

Acting on this hint, Mr. Plomacy did let in many an eager urchin, and a few tidily dressed girls with their swains, who in no way belonged to the property. But to the denizens of the city he was inexorable. Many a Barchester apprentice made his appearance there that day, and urged with piteous supplication that he had been working all the week in making saddles and boots for the use of Ullathorne, in compounding doses for the horses, or cutting up carcases for the kitchen. No such claim was allowed. Mr. Plomacy knew nothing about the city apprentices; he was to admit the tenants and labourers on the estate; Miss Thorne wasn't going to take in the whole city of Barchester; and so on.

Nevertheless, before the day was half over, all this was found to be useless. Almost anybody who chose to come made his way into the park, and the care of the guardians was transferred to the tables on which the banquet was spread. Even here there was many an unauthorized claimant for a place, of whom it was impossible to get quit without more commotion than the place and food were worth.

XXXVI

Ullathorne Sports—Act I

The trouble in civilised life of entertaining company, as it is called too generally without much regard to strict veracity, is so great that it cannot but be matter of wonder that people are so fond of attempting it. It is difficult to ascertain what is the *quid pro quo*. If they who give such laborious parties, and who endure such toil and turmoil in the vain hope of giving them successfully, really enjoyed the parties given by others, the matter could be understood. A sense of justice would induce men and women to undergo, in behalf of others, those miseries which others had undergone in their behalf. But they all profess that going out is as great a bore as receiving; and to look at them when they are out, one cannot but believe them.

Entertain! Who shall have sufficient self-assurance, who shall feel sufficient confidence in his own powers to dare to boast that he can entertain his company? A clown can sometimes do so, and sometimes a dancer in short petticoats and stuffed pink legs; occasionally, perhaps, a singer. But beyond these, success in this art of entertaining is not often achieved. Young men and girls linking themselves kind with kind, pairing like birds in spring because nature wills it, they, after a simple fashion, do entertain each other. Few others even try.

Ladies, when they open their houses, modestly confessing, it may be presumed, their own incapacity, mainly trust to wax candles and upholstery. Gentlemen seem to rely on their white waistcoats. To these are added, for the delight of the more sensual, champagne and such good things of the table as fashion allows to be still considered as comestible. Even in this respect the world is deteriorating. All the good soups are now tabooed; and at the houses of one's accustomed friends, small barristers, doctors, government clerks, and such like (for we cannot all of us always live as grandees, surrounded by an elysium of livery servants), one gets a cold potato handed to one as a sort of finale to one's slice of mutton. Alas! for those happy days when one could say to one's neighbourhood, "Jones, shall I give you some mashed turnip?—may I trouble you for a little cabbage?" And then the pleasure of drinking wine with Mrs. Jones and Miss Smith; with all the Joneses and all the Smiths! These latter-day habits are certainly more economical.

Miss Thorne, however, boldly attempted to leave the modern beaten track, and made a positive effort to entertain her guests. Alas! she did so with but moderate success. They had all their own way of going, and would not go her way. She piped to them, but they would not dance. She offered to them good honest household cake, made of currants and flour and eggs and sweetmeat; but they would feed themselves on trashy wafers from the shop of the Barchester pastry-cook, on chalk and gum and adulterated sugar. Poor Miss Thorne! yours is not the first honest soul that has vainly striven to recall the glories of happy days gone by! If fashion suggests to a Lady De Courcy that when invited to a *déjeûner* at twelve she ought to come at three, no eloquence of thine will teach her the advantage of a nearer approach to punctuality.

She had fondly thought that when she called on her friends to come at twelve, and specially begged them to believe that she meant it, she would be able to see them comfortably seated in their tents at two. Vain woman—or rather ignorant woman—ignorant of the advances of that civilisation which the world had witnessed while she was growing old. At twelve she found herself alone, dressed in all the glory of the newest of her many suits of raiment; with strong shoes however, and a serviceable bonnet on her head, and a warm rich shawl on her shoulders. Thus clad she peered out into the tent, went to the ha-ha, and satisfied herself that at any rate the youngsters were amusing themselves, spoke a word to Mrs. Greenacre over the ditch, and took one look at the quintain. Three or four young farmers were turning the machine round and round, and poking at the bag of flour in a manner not at all intended by the inventor of the game; but no mounted sportsmen were there. Miss Thorne looked at her watch. It was only fifteen minutes past twelve, and it was understood that Harry Greenacre was not to begin till the half hour.

Miss Thorne returned to her drawing-room rather quicker than was her wont, fearing that the countess might come and find none to welcome her. She need not have hurried, for no one was there. At half-past twelve she peeped into the kitchen; at a quarter to one she was joined by her brother; and just then the first fashionable arrival took place. Mrs. Clantantram was announced.

No announcement was necessary, indeed; for the good lady's voice was heard as she walked across the court-yard to the house scolding the unfortunate postilion who had driven her from Barchester. At the moment, Miss Thorne could not but be thankful that the other guests were more fashionable, and were thus spared the fury of Mrs. Clantantram's indignation.

"Oh Miss Thorne, look here!" said she, as soon as she found herself in the drawing-room; "do look at my roquelaure! It's clean spoilt, and for ever. I wouldn't but wear it because I knew you wished us all to be grand to-day; and yet I had my misgivings. Oh dear, oh dear! It was five-and-twenty shillings a yard."

The Barchester post horses had misbehaved in some unfortunate manner just as Mrs. Clantantram was getting out of the chaise and had nearly thrown her under the wheel.

Mrs. Clantantram belonged to other days, and therefore, though she had but little else to recommend her, Miss Thorne was to a certain extent fond of her. She sent the roquelaure away to be cleaned, and lent her one of her best shawls out of her own wardrobe.

The next comer was Mr. Arabin, who was immediately informed of Mrs. Clantantram's misfortune, and of her determination to pay neither master nor post-boy; although, as she remarked, she intended to get her lift home before she made known her mind upon that matter. Then a good deal of rustling was heard in the sort of lobby that was used for the ladies' outside cloaks; and the door having been thrown wide open, the servant announced, not in the most confident of voices, Mrs. Lookaloft, and the Miss Lookalofts, and Mr. Augustus Lookaloft.

Poor man!—we mean the footman. He knew, none better, that Mrs. Lookaloft had no business there, that she was not wanted there, and would not be welcome. But he had not the courage to tell a stout lady with a low dress, short sleeves, and satin at eight shillings a yard, that she had come to the wrong tent; he had not dared to hint to young ladies with white dancing shoes and long gloves, that there was a place ready for them in the paddock. And thus Mrs. Lookaloft carried her point, broke through the guards, and made her way into the citadel. That she would have to pass an uncomfortable time there, she had surmised before. But nothing now could rob her of the power of boasting that she had consorted on the lawn with the squire and Miss Thorne, with a countess, a bishop, and the country grandees, while Mrs. Greenacre and such like were walking about with the ploughboys in the park. It was a great point gained by Mrs. Lookaloft, and it might be fairly expected that from this time forward the tradesmen of Barchester would, with undoubting pens, address her husband as T. Lookaloft, Esquire.

Mrs. Lookaloft's pluck carried her through everything, and she walked triumphant into the Ullathorne drawing-room; but her children did feel a little abashed at the sort of reception they met with. It was not in Miss Thorne's heart to insult her own guests; but neither was it in her disposition to overlook such effrontery.

"Oh, Mrs. Lookaloft, is this you," said she; "and your daughters and son? Well, we're very glad to see you; but I'm sorry you've come in such low dresses, as we are all going out of doors. Could we lend you anything?"

"Oh dear no! thank ye, Miss Thorne," said the mother; "the girls and myself are quite used to low dresses, when we're out."

"Are you indeed?" said Miss Thorne shuddering; but the shudder was lost on Mrs. Lookaloft.

"And where's Lookaloft?" said the master of the house, coming up to welcome his tenant's wife. Let the faults of the family be what they would, he could not but remember that their rent was well paid; he was therefore not willing to give them a cold shoulder.

"Such a headache, Mr. Thorne!" said Mrs. Lookaloft. "In fact he couldn't stir, or you may be certain on such a day he would not have absented hisself."

"Dear me," said Miss Thorne. "If he is so ill, I'm sure you'd wish to be with him."

"Not at all!" said Mrs. Lookaloft. "Not at all, Miss Thorne. It is only bilious you know, and when he's that way he can bear nobody nigh him."

The fact however was that Mr. Lookaloft, having either more sense or less courage than his wife, had not chosen to intrude on Miss Thorne's drawing-room; and as he could not very well have gone among the plebeians while his wife was with the patricians, he thought it most expedient to remain at Rosebank.

Mrs. Lookaloft soon found herself on a sofa, and the Miss Lookalofts on two chairs, while Mr. Augustus stood near the door; and here they remained till in due time they were seated all four together at the bottom of the dining-room table.

Then the Grantlys came; the archdeacon and Mrs. Grantly and the two girls, and Dr. Gwynne and Mr. Harding; and as ill luck would have it, they were closely followed by Dr. Stanhope's carriage. As Eleanor looked out of the carriage window, she saw her brother-in-law helping the ladies out, and threw herself back into her seat, dreading to be discovered. She had had an odious journey. Mr. Slope's civility had been more than ordinarily greasy; and now, though he had not in fact said anything which she could notice, she had for the first time entertained a suspicion that he was intending to make love to her. Was it after all true that she had been conducting herself in a way that justified the world in thinking that she liked the man? After all, could it be possible that the archdeacon and Mr. Arabin were right, and that she was wrong? Charlotte Stanhope had also been watching Mr. Slope, and had come to the conclusion that it behoved her brother to lose no further time, if he meant to gain the widow. She almost regretted that it had not been contrived that Bertie should be at Ullathorne before them.

Dr. Grantly did not see his sister-in-law in company with Mr. Slope, but Mr. Arabin did. Mr. Arabin came out with Mr. Thorne to the front door to welcome Mrs. Grantly, and he remained in the court-yard till all their party had passed on. Eleanor hung back in the carriage as long as she well could, but she was nearest to the door, and when Mr. Slope, having alighted, offered her his hand, she had no alternative but to take it. Mr. Arabin standing at the open door, while Mrs. Grantly was shaking hands with some one within, saw a clergyman alight from the carriage whom he at once knew to be Mr. Slope, and then he saw this clergyman hand out Mrs. Bold. Having seen so much, Mr. Arabin, rather sick at heart, followed Mrs. Grantly into the house.

Eleanor was, however, spared any further immediate degradation, for Dr. Stanhope gave her his arm across the courtyard, and Mr. Slope was fain to throw away his attention upon Charlotte.

They had hardly passed into the house, and from the house

to the lawn, when, with a loud rattle and such noise as great men and great women are entitled to make in their passage through the world, the Proudies drove up. It was soon apparent that no every-day comer was at the door. One servant whispered to another that it was the bishop, and the word soon ran through all the hangers-on and strange grooms and coachmen about the place. There was quite a little cortége to see the bishop and his "lady" walk across the court-yard, and the good man was pleased to see that the church was held in such respect in the parish of St. Ewold's.

And now the guests came fast and thick, and the lawn began to be crowded, and the room to be full. Voices buzzed, silk rustled against silk, and muslin crumpled against muslin. Miss Thorne became more happy than she had been, and again bethought her of her sports. There were targets and bows and arrows prepared at the further end of the lawn. Here the gardens of the place encroached with a somewhat wide sweep upon the paddock, and gave ample room for the doings of the toxophilites. Miss Thorne got together such daughters of Diana as could bend a bow, and marshalled them to the targets. There were the Grantly girls and the Proudie girls and the Chadwick girls, and the two daughters of the burly chancellor, and Miss Knowle; and with them went Frederick and Augustus Chadwick, and young Knowle of Knowle park, and Frank Foster of the Elms, and Mr. Vellem Deeds the dashing attorney of the High Street, and the Rev. Mr. Green, and the Rev. Mr. Brown, and the Rev. Mr. White, all of whom, as in duty bound, attended the steps of the three Miss Proudies.

"Did you ever ride at the quintain, Mr. Foster?" said Miss Thorne, as she walked with her party, across the lawn.

"The quintain?" said young Foster, who considered him-self a dab at horsemanship. "Is it a sort of gate, Miss Thorne?"

Miss Thorne had to explain the noble game she spoke of, and Frank Foster had to own that he never had ridden at the quintain.

"Would you like to come and see?" said Miss Thorne. "There'll be plenty here without you, if you like it."

"Well, I don't mind," said Frank; "I suppose the ladies can come too."

"Oh yes," said Miss Thorne; "those who like it; I have no doubt they'll go to see your prowess, if you'll ride, Mr. Foster."

Mr. Foster looked down at a most unexceptionable pair of pantaloons, which had arrived from London only the day before.

They were the very things, at least he thought so, for a picnic or fête champêtre; but he was not prepared to ride in them. Nor was he more encouraged than had been Mr. Thorne, by the idea of being attacked from behind by the bag of flour which Miss Thorne had graphically described to him.

"Well, I don't know about riding, Miss Thorne," said he; "I fear I'm not quite prepared."

Miss Thorne sighed, but said nothing further. She left the toxophilites to their bows and arrows, and returned towards the house. But as she passed by the entrance to the small park, she thought that she might at any rate encourage the yeomen by her presence, as she could not induce her more fashionable guests to mix with them in their manly amusements. Accordingly she once more betook herself to the quintain post.

Here to her great delight she found Harry Greenacre ready mounted, with his pole in his hand, and a lot of comrades standing round him, encouraging him to the assault. She stood at a little distance and nodded to him in token of her good pleasure.

"Shall I begin, ma'am?" said Harry fingering his long staff in a rather awkward way, while his horse moved uneasily beneath him, not accustomed to a rider armed with such a weapon.

"Yes, yes," said Miss Thorne, standing triumphant as the queen of beauty, on an inverted tub which some chance had brought thither from the farm-yard.

"Here goes then," said Harry as he wheeled his horse round to get the necessary momentum of a sharp gallop. The quintain post stood right before him, and the square board at which he was to tilt was fairly in his way. If he hit that duly in the middle, and maintained his pace as he did so, it was calculated that he would be carried out of reach of the flour bag, which, suspended at the other end of the cross-bar on the post, would swing round when the board was struck. It was also calculated that if the rider did not maintain his pace, he would get a blow from the flour bag just at the back of his head, and bear about him the signs of his awkwardness to the great amusement of the lookers-on.

Harry Greenacre did not object to being powdered with flour in the service of his mistress, and therefore gallantly touched his steed with his spur, having laid his lance in rest to the best of his ability. But his ability in this respect was not great, and his appurtenances probably not very good; consequently, he struck his horse with his pole unintentionally on the side of the head as he started. The animal swerved and shied, and galloped off wide

of the quintain. Harry well accustomed to manage a horse, but
not to do so with a twelve-foot rod on his arm, lowered his right
hand to the bridle and thus the end of the lance came to the
ground, and got between the legs of the steed. Down came rider
and steed and staff. Young Greenacre was thrown some six feet
over the horse's head, and poor Miss Thorne almost fell off her
tub in a swoon.

"Oh gracious, he's killed," shrieked a woman who was
near him when he fell.

"The Lord be good to him! his poor mother, his poor
mother!" said another.

"Well, drat them dangerous plays all the world over," said
an old crone.

"He has broke his neck sure enough, if ever man did," said
a fourth.

Poor Miss Thorne. She heard all this and yet did not quite
swoon. She made her way through the crowd as best she could,
sick herself almost to death. Oh, his mother—his poor mother!
how could she ever forgive herself. The agony of that moment
was terrific. She could hardly get to the place where the poor lad
was lying, as three or four men in front were about the horse
which had risen with some difficulty; but at last she found
herself close to the young farmer.

"Has he marked himself? for heaven's sake tell me that; has
he marked his knees?" said Harry, slowly rising and rubbing his
left shoulder with his right hand, and thinking only of his horse's
legs. Miss Thorne soon found that he had not broken his neck,
nor any of his bones, nor been injured in any essential way. But
from that time forth she never instigated any one to ride at a
quintain.

Eleanor left Dr. Stanhope as soon as she could do so civilly,
and went in quest of her father whom she found on the lawn in
company with Mr. Arabin. She was not sorry to find them
together. She was anxious to disabuse at any rate her father's
mind as to this report which had got abroad respecting her, and
would have been well pleased to have been able to do the same
with regard to Mr. Arabin. She put her own through her father's
arm, coming up behind his back, and then tendered her hand also
to the vicar of St. Ewold's.

"And how did you come?" said Mr. Harding, when the
first greeting was over.

"The Stanhopes brought me," said she; "their carriage was
obliged to come twice, and has now gone back for the signora."

As she spoke she caught Mr. Arabin's eye, and saw that he was looking pointedly at her with a severe expression. She understood at once the accusation contained in his glance. It said as plainly as an eye could speak, "Yes, you came with the Stanhopes, but you did so in order that you might be in company with Mr. Slope."

"Our party," said she, still addressing her father, "consisted of the doctor and Charlotte Stanhope, myself, and Mr. Slope." As she mentioned the last name she felt her father's arm quiver slightly beneath her touch. At the same moment Mr. Arabin turned away from them, and joining his hands behind his back strolled slowly away by one of the paths.

"Papa," said she, "it was impossible to help coming in the same carriage with Mr. Slope; it was quite impossible. I had promised to come with them before I dreamt of his coming, and afterwards I could not get out of it without explaining and giving rise to talk. You weren't at home, you know, I couldn't possibly help it." She said all this so quickly that by the time her apology was spoken she was quite out of breath.

"I don't know why you should have wished to help it, my dear," said her father.

"Yes, papa, you do; you must know, you do know all the things they said at Plumstead. I am sure you do. You know all the archdeacon said. How unjust he was; and Mr. Arabin too. He's a horrid man, a horrid odious man, but——"

"Who is an odious man, my dear? Mr. Arabin?"

"No; but Mr. Slope. You know I mean Mr. Slope. He's the most odious man I ever met in my life, and it was most unfortunate my having to come here in the same carriage with him. But how could I help it?"

A great weight began to move itself off Mr. Harding's mind. So, after all, the archdeacon with all his wisdom, and Mrs. Grantly with all her tact, and Mr. Arabin with all his talents, were in the wrong. His own child, his Eleanor, the daughter of whom he was so proud was not to become the wife of a Mr. Slope. He had been about to give his sanction to the marriage, so certified had he been of the fact; and now he learnt that this imputed lover of Eleanor's was at any rate as much disliked by her as by any one of the family. Mr. Harding, however, was by no means sufficiently a man of the world to conceal the blunder he had made. He could not pretend that he had entertained no suspicion; he could not make believe that he had never joined the archdeacon in his surmises. He was greatly surprised, and gratified beyond measure, and he could not help showing that such was the case.

"My darling girl," said he, "I am so delighted, so overjoyed. My own child; you have taken such a weight off my mind."

"But surely, papa, *you* didn't think——"

"I didn't know what to think, my dear. The archdeacon told me that——"

"The archdeacon!" said Eleanor, her face lighting up with passion. "A man like the archdeacon might, one would think, be better employed than in traducing his sister-in-law, and creating bitterness between a father and his daughter!"

"He didn't mean to do that, Eleanor."

"What did he mean then? Why did he interfere with me, and fill your mind with such falsehood?"

"Never mind it now, my child; never mind it now. We shall all know you better now."

"Oh, papa, that you should have thought it! that you should have suspected me!"

"I don't know what you mean by suspicion, Eleanor. There would be nothing disgraceful, you know; nothing wrong in such a marriage. Nothing that could have justified my interfering as your father." And Mr. Harding would have proceeded in his own defence to make out that Mr. Slope after all was a very good sort of man, and a very fitting second husband for a young widow, had he not been interrupted by Eleanor's greater energy.

"It would be disgraceful," said she; "it would be wrong; it would be abominable. Could I do such a horrid thing, I should expect no one to speak to me. Ugh——" and she shuddered as she thought of the matrimonial torch which her friends had been so ready to light on her behalf. "I don't wonder at Dr. Grantly; I don't wonder at Susan; but, oh, papa, I do wonder at you. How could you, how could you believe it?" Poor Eleanor, as she thought of her father's defalcation, could resist her tears no longer, and was forced to cover her face with her handkerchief.

The place was not very opportune for her grief. They were walking through the shrubberies, and there were many people near them. Poor Mr. Harding stammered out his excuse as best he could, and Eleanor with an effort controlled her tears, and returned her handkerchief to her pocket. She did not find it difficult to forgive her father, nor could she altogether refuse to join him in the returning gaiety of spirit to which her present avowal gave rise. It was such a load off his heart to think that he should not be called on to welcome Mr. Slope as his son-in-law.

It was such a relief to him to find that his daughter's feelings and his own were now, as they ever had been, in unison. He had been so unhappy for the last six weeks about this wretched Mr. Slope! He was so indifferent as to the loss of the hospital, so thankful for the recovery of his daughter, that, strong as was the ground for Eleanor's anger, she could not find it in her heart to be long angry with him.

"Dear papa," she said, hanging closely to his arm, "never suspect me again: promise me that you never will. Whatever I do, you may be sure I shall tell you first; you may be sure I shall consult you."

And Mr. Harding did promise, and owned his sin, and promised again. And so, while he promised amendment and she uttered forgiveness, they returned together to the drawing-room windows.

And what had Eleanor meant when she declared that *whatever she did*, she would tell her father first? What was she thinking of doing?

So ended the first act of the melodrama which Eleanor was called on to perform this day at Ullathorne.

XXXVII

The Signora Neroni, the Countess De Courcy, and Mrs. Proudie Meet Each Other at Ullathorne

And now there were new arrivals. Just as Eleanor reached the drawing-room the signora was being wheeled into it. She had been brought out of the carriage into the dining-room and there placed on a sofa, and was now in the act of entering the other room, by the joint aid of her brother and sister, Mr. Arabin, and two servants in livery. She was all in her glory and looked so pathetically happy, so full of affliction and grace, was so beautiful, so pitiable, and so charming, that it was almost impossible not to be glad she was there.

Miss Thorne was unaffectedly glad to welcome her. In fact, the signora was a sort of lion; and though there was no drop of the Leohunter blood in Miss Thorne's veins, she nevertheless did like to see attractive people at her house. The signora was attractive, and on her first settlement in the dining-room she had whispered two or three soft feminine words into Miss Thorne's ear, which, at the moment, had quite touched that lady's heart.

"Oh, Miss Thorne; where is Miss Thorne?" she said, as soon as her attendants had placed her in her position just before one of the windows, from whence she could see all that was going on upon the lawn; "How am I to thank you for permitting a creature like me to be here? But if you knew the pleasure you give me, I am sure you would excuse the trouble I bring with me." And as she spoke she squeezed the spinster's little hand between her own.

"We are delighted to see you here," said Miss Thorne; "you give us no trouble at all, and we think it a great favour conferred by you to come and see us; don't we, Wilfred?"

"A very great favour indeed," said Mr. Thorne, with a gallant bow, but of a somewhat less cordial welcome than that conceded by his sister. Mr. Thorne had heard perhaps more of the antecedents of his guest than his sister had done, and had not as yet undergone the power of the signora's charms.

But while the mother of the last of the Neros was thus in her full splendour, with crowds of people gazing at her and the *élite* of the company standing round her couch, her glory was paled by the arrival of the Countess De Courcy. Miss Thorne had now been waiting three hours for the countess, and could not therefore but show very evident gratification when the arrival at last took place. She and her brother of course went off to welcome the titled grandees, and with them, alas, went many of the signora's admirers.

"Oh, Mr. Thorne," said the countess, while in the act of being disrobed of her fur cloaks, and re-robed in her gauze shawls, "what dreadful roads you have; perfectly frightful."

It happened that Mr. Thorne was way-warden for the district, and not liking the attack, began to excuse his roads.

"Oh yes, indeed they are," said the countess, not minding him in the least, "perfectly dreadful; are they not, Margaretta? Why, my dear Miss Thorne, we left Courcy Castle just at eleven; it was only just past eleven, was it not, John? and——"

"Just past one, I think you mean," said the Honourable John, turning from the group and eyeing the signora through his glass. The signora gave him back his own, as the saying is, and more with it; so that the young nobleman was forced to avert his glance, and drop his glass.

"I say, Thorne," whispered he, "who the deuce is that on the sofa?"

"Dr. Stanhope's daughter," whispered back Mr. Thorne. "Signora Neroni, she calls herself."

"Whew-ew-ew!" whistled the Honourable John. "The devil she is! I have heard no end of stories about that filly. You must positively introduce me, Thorne; you positively must."

Mr. Thorne, who was respectability itself, did not quite like having a guest about whom the Honourable John De Courcy had heard no end of stories; but he couldn't help himself. He merely resolved that before he went to bed he would let his sister know somewhat of the history of the lady she was so willing to welcome. The innocence of Miss Thorne, at her time of life was perfectly charming; but even innocence may be dangerous.

"John may say what he likes," continued the countess, urging her excuses to Miss Thorne; "I am sure we were past the castle gate before twelve, weren't we, Margaretta?"

"Upon my word I don't know," said the Lady Margaretta, "for I was half asleep. But I do know that I was called sometime in the middle of the night, and was dressing myself before daylight."

Wise people, when they are in the wrong, always put themselves right by finding fault with the people against whom they have sinned. Lady De Courcy was a wise woman; and therefore, having treated Miss Thorne very badly by staying away till three o'clock, she assumed the offensive and attacked Mr. Thorne's roads. Her daughter, not less wise, attacked Miss Thorne's early hours. The art of doing this is among the most precious of those usually cultivated by persons who know how to live. There is no withstanding it. Who can go systematically to work, and having done battle with the primary accusation and settled that, then bring forward a counter-charge and support that also? Life is not long enough for such labours. A man in the right relies easily on his rectitude, and therefore goes about unarmed. His very strength is his weakness. A man in the wrong knows that he must look to his weapons; his very weakness is his strength. The one is never prepared for combat, the other is always ready. Therefore it is that in this world the man that is in the wrong almost invariably conquers the man that is in the right, and invariably despises him.

A man must be an idiot or else an angel, who after the age of forty shall attempt to be just to his neighbours. Many like the Lady Margaretta have learnt their lesson at a much earlier age. But this of course depends on the school in which they have been taught.

Poor Miss Thorne was altogether overcome. She knew very well that she had been ill-treated, and yet she found herself making apologies to Lady De Courcy. To do her ladyship justice, she received them very graciously, and allowed herself with her train of daughters to be led towards the lawn.

There were two windows in the drawing-room wide open for the countess to pass through; but she saw that there was a woman on a sofa, at the third window, and that that woman had, as it were, a following attached to her. Her ladyship therefore determined to investigate the woman. The De Courcys were hereditarily short sighted, and had been so for thirty centuries at least. So Lady De Courcy, who when she entered the family had adopted the family habits, did as her son had done before her, and taking her glass to investigate the Signora Neroni, pressed in among the gentlemen who surrounded the couch, and bowed slightly to those whom she chose to honour by her acquaintance.

In order to get to the window she had to pass close to the front of the couch, and as she did so she stared hard at the occupant. The occupant in return stared hard at the countess. The countess who since her countess-ship commenced had been accustomed to see all eyes, not royal, ducal or marquesal, fall before her own, paused as she went on, raised her eyebrows, and stared even harder than before. But she had now to do with one who cared little for countesses. It was, one may say, impossible for mortal man or woman to abash Madeline Neroni. She opened her large bright lustrous eyes wider and wider, till she seemed to be all eyes. She gazed up into the lady's face, not as though she did it with an effort, but as if she delighted in doing it. She used no glass to assist her effrontery, and needed none. The faintest possible smile of derision played round her mouth, and her nostrils were slightly dilated, as if in sure anticipation of her triumph. And it was sure. The Countess De Courcy, in spite of her thirty centuries and De Courcy castle, and the fact that Lord De Courcy was grand master of the ponies to the Prince of Wales, had not a chance with her. At first the little circlet of gold wavered in the countess's hand, then the hand shook, then the circlet fell, the countess's head tossed itself into the air, and

the countess's feet shambled out to the lawn. She did not however go so fast but what she heard the signora's voice, asking—

"Who on earth is that woman, Mr. Slope?"

"That is Lady De Courcy."

"Oh, ah. I might have supposed so. Ha, ha, ha. Well,
that's as good as a play."

It was as good as a play to any there who had eyes to
observe it, and wit to comment on what they observed.

But the Lady De Courcy soon found a congenial spirit on
the lawn. There she encountered Mrs. Proudie, and as Mrs.
Proudie was not only the wife of a bishop, but was also the
cousin of an earl, Lady De Courcy considered her to be the
fittest companion she was likely to meet in that assemblage.
They were accordingly delighted to see each other. Mrs. Proudie
by no means despised a countess, and as this countess lived in
the county and within a sort of extensive visiting distance of
Barchester, she was glad to have this opportunity of ingratiating
herself.

"My dear Lady De Courcy, I am so delighted," said she,
looking as little grim as it was in her nature to do. "I hardly
expected to see you here. It is such a distance, and then you
know, such a crowd."

"And such roads, Mrs. Proudie! I really wonder how the
people ever get about. But I don't suppose they ever do."

"Well, I really don't know; but I suppose not. The Thornes
don't, I know," said Mrs. Proudie. "Very nice person, Miss
Thorne, isn't she?"

"Oh, delightful, and so queer; I've known her these twenty
years. A great pet of mine is dear Miss Thorne. She is so very
strange, you know. She always makes me think of the Esquimaux
and the Indians. Isn't her dress quite delightful?"

"Delightful," said Mrs. Proudie; "I wonder now whether
she paints. Did you ever see such colour?"

"Oh, of course," said Lady De Courcy; "that is, I have no
doubt she does. But, Mrs. Proudie, who is that woman on the
sofa by the window? just step this way and you'll see her,
there——" and the countess led her to a spot where she could
plainly see the signora's well-remembered face and figure.

She did not however do so without being equally well seen
by the signora. "Look, look," said that lady to Mr. Slope, who
was still standing near to her; "see the high spiritualities and
temporalities of the land in league together, and all against poor
me. I'll wager my bracelet, Mr. Slope, against your next sermon,

that they've taken up their position there on purpose to pull me to pieces. Well, I can't rush to the combat, but I know how to protect myself if the enemy come near me."

But the enemy knew better. They could gain nothing by contact with the Signora Neroni, and they could abuse her as they pleased at a distance from her on the lawn.

"She's that horrid Italian woman, Lady De Courcy; you must have heard of her."

"What Italian woman?" said her ladyship, quite alive to the coming story; "I don't think I've heard of any Italian woman coming into the country. She doesn't look Italian either."

"Oh, you must have heard of her," said Mrs. Proudie. "No, she's not absolutely Italian. She is Dr. Stanhope's daughter—Dr. Stanhope, the prebendary; and she calls herself the Signora Neroni."

"Oh-h-h-h!" exclaimed the countess.

"I was sure you had heard of her," continued Mrs. Proudie. "I don't know anything about her husband. They do say that some man named Neroni is still alive. I believe she did marry such a man abroad, but I do not at all know who or what he was."

"Ah-h-h-h!" said the countess, shaking her head with much intelligence, as every additional "h" fell from her lips. "I know all about it now. I have heard George mention her. George knows all about her. George heard about her in Rome."

"She's an abominable woman, at any rate," said Mrs. Proudie.

"Insufferable," said the countess.

"She made her way into the palace once, before I knew anything about her; and I cannot tell you how dreadfully indecent her conduct was."

"Was it?" said the delighted countess.

"Insufferable," said the prelatess.

"But why does she lie on a sofa?" asked Lady De Courcy.

"She has only one leg," replied Mrs. Proudie.

"Only one leg!" said Lady De Courcy, who felt to a certain degree dissatisfied that the signora was thus incapacitated. "Was she born so?"

"Oh, no," said Mrs. Proudie,—and her ladyship felt somewhat recomforted by the assurance,—"she had two. But that Signor Neroni beat her, I believe, till she was obliged to have one amputated. At any rate, she entirely lost the use of it."

"Unfortunate creature!" said the countess, who herself knew something of matrimonial trials.

"Yes," said Mrs. Proudie; "one would pity her, in spite of her past bad conduct, if she now knew how to behave herself. But she does not. She is the most insolent creature I ever put my eyes on."

"Indeed she is," said Lady De Courcy.

"And her conduct with men is so abominable, that she is not fit to be admitted into any lady's drawing-room."

"Dear me!" said the countess, becoming again excited, happy, and merciless.

"You saw that man standing near her,—the clergyman with the red hair?"

"Yes, yes."

"She has absolutely ruined that man. The bishop, or I should rather take the blame on myself, for it was I,—I brought him down from London to Barchester. He is a tolerable preacher, an active young man, and I therefore introduced him to the bishop. That woman, Lady De Courcy, has got hold of him, and has so disgraced him, that I am forced to require that he shall leave the palace; and I doubt very much whether he won't lose his gown!"

"Why what an idiot the man must be!" said the countess.

"You don't know the intriguing villainy of that woman," said Mrs. Proudie, remembering her torn flounces.

"But you say she has only got one leg!"

"She is as full of mischief as tho' she had ten. Look at her eyes, Lady De Courcy. Did you ever see such eyes in a decent woman's head?"

"Indeed I never did, Mrs. Proudie."

"And her effrontery, and her voice; I quite pity her poor father, who is really a good sort of man."

"Dr. Stanhope, isn't he?"

"Yes, Dr. Stanhope. He is one of our prebendaries,—a good quiet sort of man himself. But I am surprised that he should let his daughter conduct herself as she does."

"I suppose he can't help it," said the countess.

"But a clergyman, you know, Lady De Courcy! He should at any rate prevent her from exhibiting in public, if he cannot induce her to behave at home. But he is to be pitied. I believe he has a desperate life of it with the lot of them. That apish-looking man there, with the long beard and the loose trousers,—he is the woman's brother. He is nearly as bad as she is. They are both of them infidels.''

"Infidels!" said Lady De Courcy, "and their father a prebendary!''

"Yes, and likely to be the new dean too," said Mrs. Proudie.

"Oh yes, poor dear Dr. Trefoil!" said the countess, who had once in her life spoken to that gentleman; "I was so distressed to hear it, Mrs. Proudie. And so Dr. Stanhope is to be the new dean! He comes of an excellent family, and I wish him success in spite of his daughter. Perhaps, Mrs. Proudie, when he is dean they'll be better able to see the error of their ways.''

To this Mrs. Proudie said nothing. Her dislike of the Signora Neroni was too deep to admit of her even hoping that that lady should see the error of her ways. Mrs. Proudie looked on the signora as one of the lost,—one of those beyond the reach of Christian charity, and was therefore able to enjoy the luxury of hating her, without the drawback of wishing her eventually well out of her sins.

Any further conversation between these congenial souls was prevented by the advent of Mr. Thorne, who came to lead the countess to the tent. Indeed, he had been desired to do so some ten minutes since; but he had been delayed in the drawing-room by the signora. She had contrived to detain him, to get him near to her sofa, and at last to make him seat himself on a chair close to her beautiful arm. The fish took the bait, was hooked, and caught, and landed. Within that ten minutes he had heard the whole of the signora's history in such strains as she chose to use in telling it. He learnt from the lady's own lips the whole of that mysterious tale to which the Honourable George had merely alluded. He discovered that the beautiful creature lying before him had been more sinned against than sinning. She had owned to him that she had been weak, confiding and indifferent to the world's opinion, and that she had therefore been ill-used, deceived and evil spoken of. She had spoken to him of her mutilated limb, her youth destroyed in its fullest bloom, her beauty robbed of its every charm, her life blighted, her hopes withered; and as she did so, a tear dropped from her eye to her cheek. She had told him of these things, and asked for his sympathy.

What could a good-natured genial Anglo-Saxon Squire Thorne do but promise to sympathise with her? Mr. Thorne did promise to sympathise; promised also to come and see the last of the Neros, to hear more of those tearful Roman days, of those light and innocent but dangerous hours which flitted by so fast on the shores of Como, and to make himself the confidant of the signora's sorrows.

We need hardly say that he dropped all idea of warning his sister against the dangerous lady. He had been mistaken; never so much mistaken in his life. He had always regarded that Honourable George as a coarse brutal-minded young man; now he was more convinced than ever that he was so. It was by such men as the Honourable George that the reputations of such women as Madeline Neroni were imperilled and damaged. He would go and see the lady in her own house; he was fully sure in his own mind of the soundness of his own judgment; if he found her, as he believed he should do, an injured well-disposed warm-hearted woman, he would get his sister Monica to invite her out to Ullathorne.

"No," said she, as at her instance he got up to leave her, and declared that he himself would attend upon her wants; "no, no, my friend; I positively put a veto upon your doing so. What, in your own house, with an assemblage round you such as there is here! Do you wish to make every woman hate me and every man stare at me? I lay a positive order on you not to come near me again to-day. Come and see me at home. It is only at home that I can talk; it is only at home that I really can live and enjoy myself. My days of going out, days such as these, are rare indeed. Come and see me at home, Mr. Thorne, and then I will not bid you to leave me."

It is, we believe, common with young men of five and twenty to look on their seniors—on men of, say, double their own age—as so many stocks and stones,—stocks and stones, that is, in regard to feminine beauty. There never was a greater mistake. Women, indeed, generally know better; but on this subject men of one age are thoroughly ignorant of what is the very nature of mankind of other ages. No experience of what goes on in the world, no reading of history, no observation of life, has any effect in teaching the truth. Men of fifty don't dance mazurkas, being generally too fat and wheezy; nor do they sit for the hour together on river banks at their mistresses' feet, being somewhat afraid of rheumatism. But for real true love, love at first sight, love to devotion, love that robs a man of his sleep, love that "will gaze an eagle blind," love that "will hear the lowest sound when the suspicious tread of theft is stopped," love that is "like a Hercules, still climbing trees in the Hesperides,"—we believe the best age is from forty-five to seventy; up to that, men are generally given to mere flirting.

At the present moment Mr. Thorne, *ætat.* fifty, was over head and ears in love at first sight with the Signora Madeline Vesey Neroni, *nata* Stanhope.

Nevertheless he was sufficiently master of himself to offer his arm with all propriety to Lady De Courcy, and the countess graciously permitted herself to be led to the tent. Such had been Miss Thorne's orders, as she had succeeded in inducing the bishop to lead old Lady Knowle to the top of the dining-room. One of the baronets was sent off in quest of Mrs. Proudie, and found that lady on the lawn not in the best of humours. Mr. Thorne and the countess had left her too abruptly; she had in vain looked around for an attendant chaplain, or even a stray curate; they were all drawing long bows with the young ladies at the bottom of the lawn, or finding places for their graceful co-toxophilites in some snug corner of the tent. In such position Mrs. Proudie had been wont in earlier days to fall back upon Mr. Slope; but now she could never fall back upon him again. She gave her head one shake as she thought of her lone position, and that shake was as good as a week deducted from Mr. Slope's longer sojourn in Barchester. Sir Harkaway Gorse, however, relieved her present misery, though his doing so by no means mitigated the sinning chaplain's doom.

And now the eating and drinking began in earnest. Dr. Grantly, to his great horror, found himself leagued to Mrs. Clantantram. Mrs. Clantantram had a great regard for the archdeacon, which was not cordially returned; and when she, coming up to him, whispered in his ear, "Come, archdeacon, I'm sure you won't begrudge an old friend the favour of your arm," and then proceeded to tell him the whole history of her roquelaure, he resolved that he would shake her off before he was fifteen minutes older. But latterly the archdeacon had not been successful in his resolutions; and on the present occasion Mrs. Clantantram stuck to him till the banquet was over.

Dr. Gwynne got a baronet's wife, and Mrs. Grantly fell to the lot of a baronet. Charlotte Stanhope attached herself to Mr. Harding in order to make room for Bertie, who succeeded in sitting down in the dining-room next to Mrs. Bold. To speak sooth, now that he had love in earnest to make, his heart almost failed him.

Eleanor had been right glad to avail herself of his arm, seeing that Mr. Slope was hovering nigh her. In striving to avoid that terrible Charybdis of a Slope she was in great danger of falling into an unseen Scylla on the other hand, that Scylla being Bertie Stanhope. Nothing could be more gracious than she was to Bertie. She almost jumped at his proffered arm. Charlotte perceived this from a distance, and triumphed in her heart; Bertie felt it, and was encouraged; Mr. Slope saw it, and glowered with jealousy. Eleanor and Bertie sat down to table in the dining-room; and as she took her seat at his right hand, she found that Mr. Slope was already in possession of the chair at her own.

As these things were going on in the dining-room, Mr. Arabin was hanging enraptured and alone over the signora's sofa; and Eleanor from her seat could look through the open door and see that he was doing so.

XXXVIII

The Bishop Sits Down to Breakfast, and the Dean Dies

The bishop of Barchester said grace over the well-spread board in the Ullathorne dining-room; and while he did so the last breath was flying from the dean of Barchester as he lay in his sick room in the deanery. When the bishop of Barchester raised his first glass of champagne to his lips, the deanship of Barchester was a good thing in the gift of the prime minister. Before the bishop of Barchester had left the table, the minister of the day was made aware of the fact at his country seat in Hampshire, and had already turned over in his mind the names of five very respectable aspirants for the preferment. It is at present only necessary to say that Mr. Slope's name was not among the five.

" 'Twas merry in the hall when the beards wagged all' "; and the clerical beards wagged merrily in the hall of Ullathorne that day. It was not till after the last cork had been drawn, the last speech made, the last nut cracked, that tidings reached and were whispered about that the poor dean was no more. It was well for the happiness of the clerical beards that this little delay took place, as otherwise decency would have forbidden them to wag at all.

But there was one sad man among them that day. Mr. Arabin's beard did not wag as it should have done. He had come there hoping the best, striving to think the best, about Eleanor; turning over in his mind all the words he remembered to have fallen from her about Mr. Slope, and trying to gather from them a conviction unfavourable to his rival. He had not exactly resolved to come that day to some decisive proof as to the widow's intention; but he had meant, if possible, to recultivate his friendship with Eleanor; and in his present frame of mind any such re-cultivation must have ended in a declaration of love.

He had passed the previous night alone at his new parsonage, and it was the first night that he had so passed. It had been dull and sombre enough. Mrs. Grantly had been right in saying that a priestess would be wanting at St. Ewold's. He had sat there alone with his glass before him, and then with his teapot, thinking about Eleanor Bold. As is usual in such meditations, he did little but blame her; blame her for liking Mr. Slope, and blame her for not liking him; blame her for her cordiality to himself, and blame her for her want of cordiality; blame her for being stubborn, headstrong, and passionate; and yet the more he thought of her the higher she rose in his affection. If only it should turn out, if only it could be made to turn out, that she had defended Mr. Slope, not from love, but on principle, all would be right. Such principle in itself would be admirable, loveable, womanly; he felt that he could be pleased to allow Mr. Slope just so much favour as that. But if—— And then Mr. Arabin poked his fire most unnecessarily, spoke crossly to his new parlour-maid who came in for the tea-things, and threw himself back in his chair determined to go to sleep. Why had she been so stiff-necked when asked a plain question? She could not but have known in what light he regarded her. Why had she not answered a plain question, and so put an end to his misery? Then, instead of going to sleep in his arm-chair, Mr. Arabin walked about the room as though he had been possessed.

On the following morning, when he attended Miss Thorne's behests, he was still in a somewhat confused state. His first duty had been to converse with Mrs. Clantantram, and that lady had found it impossible to elicit the slightest sympathy from him on the subject of her roquelaure. Miss Thorne had asked him whether Mrs. Bold was coming with the Grantlys; and the two names of

Bold and Grantly together had nearly made him jump from his seat.

He was in this state of confused uncertainty, hope, and doubt, when he saw Mr. Slope, with his most polished smile, handing Eleanor out of her carriage. He thought of nothing more. He never considered whether the carriage belonged to her or to Mr. Slope, or to any one else to whom they might both be mutually obliged without any concert between themselves. This sight in his present state of mind was quite enough to upset him and his resolves. It was clear as noonday. Had he seen her handed into a carriage by Mr. Slope at a church door with a white veil over her head, the truth could not be more manifest. He went into the house, and, as we have seen, soon found himself walking with Mr. Harding. Shortly afterwards Eleanor came up; and then he had to leave his companion, and either go about alone or find another. While in this state he was encountered by the archdeacon.

"I wonder," said Dr. Grantly, "if it be true that Mr. Slope and Mrs. Bold came here together. Susan says she is almost sure she saw their faces in the same carriage as she got out of her own."

Mr. Arabin had nothing for it but to bear his testimony to the correctness of Mrs. Grantly's eyesight.

"It is perfectly shameful," said the archdeacon; "or I should rather say, shameless. She was asked here as my guest; and if she be determined to disgrace herself, she should have feeling enough not to do so before my immediate friends. I wonder how that man got himself invited. I wonder whether she had the face to bring him."

To this Mr. Arabin could answer nothing, nor did he wish to answer anything. Though he abused Eleanor to himself, he did not choose to abuse her to any one else, nor was he well pleased to hear any one else speak ill of her. Dr. Grantly, however, was very angry, and did not spare his sister-in-law. Mr. Arabin therefore left him as soon as he could, and wandered back into the house.

He had not been there long, when the signora was brought in. For some time he kept himself out of temptation, and merely hovered round her at a distance; but as soon as Mr. Thorne had left her, he yielded himself up to the basilisk, and allowed himself to be made prey of.

It is impossible to say how the knowledge had been acquired, but the signora had a sort of instinctive knowledge that Mr.

Arabin was an admirer of Mrs. Bold. Men hunt foxes by the aid
of dogs, and are aware that they do so by the strong organ of
smell with which the dog is endowed. They do not, however, in
the least comprehend how such a sense can work with such
acuteness. The organ by which women instinctively, as it were,
know and feel how other women are regarded by men, and
how also men are regarded by other women, is equally strong,
and equally incomprehensible. A glance, a word, a motion,
suffices: by some such acute exercise of her feminine senses the
signora was aware that Mr. Arabin loved Eleanor Bold; and
therefore, by a further exercise of her peculiar feminine
propensities, it was quite natural for her to entrap Mr. Arabin
into her net.

The work was half done before she came to Ullathorne, and
when could she have a better opportunity of completing it? She
had had almost enough of Mr. Slope, though she could not quite
resist the fun of driving a very sanctimonious clergyman to
madness by a desperate and ruinous passion. Mr. Thorne had
fallen too easily to give much pleasure in the chase. His position
as a man of wealth might make his alliance of value, but as a
lover he was very second-rate. We may say that she regarded
him somewhat as a sportsman does a pheasant. The bird is so
easily shot, that he would not be worth the shooting were it not
for the very respectable appearance that he makes in a larder.
The signora would not waste much time in shooting Mr. Thorne,
but still he was worth bagging for family uses.

But Mr. Arabin was game of another sort. The signora was
herself possessed of quite sufficient intelligence to know that Mr.
Arabin was a man more than usually intellectual. She knew also,
that as a clergyman he was of a much higher stamp than Mr.
Slope, and that as a gentleman he was better educated than Mr.
Thorne. She would never have attempted to drive Mr. Arabin
into ridiculous misery as she did Mr. Slope, nor would she think
it possible to dispose of him in ten minutes as she had done with
Mr. Thorne.

Such were her reflections about Mr. Arabin. As to Mr.
Arabin, it cannot be said that he reflected at all about the
signora. He knew that she was beautiful, and he felt that she was
able to charm him. He required charming in his present misery,
and therefore he went and stood at the head of her couch. She
knew all about it. Such were her peculiar gifts. It was her nature
to see that he required charming, and it was her province to
charm him. As the Eastern idler swallows his dose of opium, as

the London reprobate swallows his dose of gin, so with similar desires and for similar reasons did Mr. Arabin prepare to swallow the charms of the Signora Neroni.

"Why an't you shooting with bows and arrows, Mr. Arabin?" said she, when they were nearly alone together in the drawing-room; "or talking with young ladies in shady bowers, or turning your talents to account in some way? What was a bachelor like you asked here for? Don't you mean to earn your cold chicken and champagne? Were I you, I should be ashamed to be so idle."

Mr. Arabin murmured some sort of answer. Though he wished to be charmed, he was hardly yet in a mood to be playful in return.

"Why, what ails you, Mr. Arabin?" said she, "here you are in your own parish; Miss Thorne tells me that her party is given expressly in your honour; and yet you are the only dull man at it. Your friend Mr. Slope was with me a few minutes since, full of life and spirits; why don't you rival him?"

It was not difficult for so acute an observer as Madeline Neroni to see that she had hit the nail on the head and driven the bolt home. Mr. Arabin winced visibly before her attack, and she knew at once that he was jealous of Mr. Slope.

"But I look on you and Mr. Slope as the very antipodes of men," said she. "There is nothing in which you are not each the reverse of the other, except in belonging to the same profession; and even in that you are so unlike as perfectly to maintain the rule. He is gregarious, you are given to solitude. He is active, you are passive. He works, you think. He likes women, you despise them. He is fond of position and power, and so are you, but for directly different reasons. He loves to be praised, you very foolishly abhor it. He will gain his rewards, which will be an insipid useful wife, a comfortable income, and a reputation for sanctimony. You will also gain yours."

"Well, and what will they be?" said Mr. Arabin, who knew that he was being flattered, and yet suffered himself to put up with it. "What will be my rewards?"

"The heart of some woman whom you will be too austere to own that you love, and the respect of some few friends which you will be too proud to own that you value."

"Rich rewards," said he; "but of little worth if they are to be so treated."

"Oh, you are not to look for such success as awaits Mr. Slope. He is born to be a successful man. He suggests to himself an object, and then starts for it with eager intention. Nothing will deter him from his pursuit. He will have no scruples, no fears, no hesitation. His desire is to be a bishop with a rising family, the wife will come first, and in due time the apron. You will see all this, and then——''

"Well, and what then?"

"Then you will begin to wish that you had done the same."

Mr. Arabin looked placidly out at the lawn, and resting his shoulder on the head of the sofa, rubbed his chin with his hand. It was a trick he had when he was thinking deeply; and what the signora said made him think. Was it not all true? Would he not hereafter look back, if not at Mr. Slope, at some others, perhaps not equally gifted with himself, who had risen in the world while he had lagged behind, and then wish that he had done the same?

"Is not such the doom of all speculative men of talent?" said she. "Do they not all sit rapt as you now are, cutting imaginary silken cords with their fine edges, while those not so highly tempered sever the every-day Gordian knots of the world's struggle, and win wealth and renown? Steel too highly polished, edges too sharp, do not do for this world's work, Mr. Arabin."

Who was this woman that thus read the secrets of his heart, and re-uttered to him the unwelcome bodings of his own soul? He looked full into her face when she had done speaking, and said, "Am I one of those foolish blades, too sharp and too fine to do a useful day's work?"

"Why do you let the Slopes of the world out-distance you?" said she. "Is not the blood in your veins as warm as his? does not your pulse beat as fast? Has not God made you a man, and intended you to do a man's work here, ay, and to take a man's wages also?"

Mr. Arabin sat ruminating and rubbing his face, and wondering why these things were said to him; but he replied nothing. The signora went on—

"The greatest mistake any man ever made is to suppose that the good things of the world are not worth the winning. And it is a mistake so opposed to the religion which you preach! Why does God permit his bishops one after another to have their five thousands and ten thousands a year if such wealth be bad and not worth having? Why are beautiful things given to us, and luxuries and pleasant enjoyments, if they be not intended to be used? They must be meant for some one, and what is good for a layman cannot surely be bad for a clerk. You try to despise these good things, but you only try; you don't succeed."

"Don't I?" said Mr. Arabin, still musing, and not knowing what he said.

"I ask you the question; do you succeed?"

Mr. Arabin looked at her piteously. It seemed to him as though he were being interrogated by some inner spirit of his own, to whom he could not refuse an answer, and to whom he did not dare to give a false reply.

"Come, Mr. Arabin, confess; do you succeed? Is money so contemptible? Is worldly power so worthless? Is feminine beauty a trifle to be so slightly regarded by a wise man?"

"Feminine beauty!" said he, gazing into her face, as though all the feminine beauty in the world were concentrated there. "Why do you say I do not regard it?"

"If you look at me like that, Mr. Arabin, I shall alter my opinion—or should do so, were I not of course aware that I have no beauty of my own worth regarding."

The gentleman blushed crimson, but the lady did not blush at all. A slightly increased colour animated her face, just so much so as to give her an air of special interest. She expected a compliment from her admirer, but she was rather grateful than otherwise by finding that he did not pay it to her. Messrs. Slope and Thorne, Messrs. Brown, Jones and Robinson, they all paid her compliments. She was rather in hopes that she would ultimately succeed in inducing Mr. Arabin to abuse her.

"But your gaze," said she, "is one of wonder, and not of admiration. You wonder at my audacity in asking you such questions about yourself."

"Well, I do rather," said he.

"Nevertheless I expect an answer, Mr. Arabin. Why were women made beautiful if men are not to regard them?"

"But men do regard them," he replied.

"And why not you?"

"You are begging the question, Madame Neroni."

"I am sure I shall beg nothing, Mr. Arabin, which you will not grant, and I do beg for an answer. Do you not as a rule think women below your notice as companions? Let us see. There is the widow Bold looking round at you from her chair this minute. What would you say to her as a companion for life?"

Mr. Arabin, rising from his position, leaned over the sofa and looked through the drawing-room door to the place where Eleanor was seated between Bertie Stanhope and Mr. Slope. She at once caught his glance, and averted her own. She was not pleasantly placed in her present position. Mr. Slope was doing

his best to attract her attention; and she was striving to prevent
his doing so by talking to Mr. Stanhope, while her mind was
intently fixed on Mr. Arabin and Madame Neroni. Bertie Stanhope endeavoured to take advantage of her favours, but he was
thinking more of the manner in which he would by-and-by throw
himself at her feet, than of amusing her at the present moment.

"There," said the signora. "She was stretching her beautiful neck to look at you, and now you have disturbed her. Well I
declare, I believe I am wrong about you; I believe that you do
think Mrs. Bold a charming woman. Your looks seem to say so;
and by her looks I should say that she is jealous of me. Come,
Mr. Arabin, confide in me, and if it is so, I'll do all in my power
to make up the match."

It is needless to say that the signora was not very sincere in
her offer. She was never sincere on such subjects. She never
expected others to be so, nor did she expect others to think her
so. Such matters were her playthings, her billiard table, her
hounds and hunters, her waltzes and polkas, her picnics and
summer-day excursions. She had little else to amuse her, and
therefore played at love-making in all its forms. She was now
playing at it with Mr. Arabin, and did not at all expect the
earnestness and truth of his answer.

"All in your power would be nothing," said he; "for Mrs.
Bold is, I imagine, already engaged to another."

"Then you own the impeachment yourself."

"You cross-question me rather unfairly," he replied, "and
I do not know why I answer you at all. Mrs. Bold is a very
beautiful woman, and as intelligent as beautiful. It is impossible
to know her without admiring her."

"So you think the widow a very beautiful woman?"

"Indeed I do."

"And one that would grace the parsonage of St. Ewold's."

"One that would grace any man's house."

"And you really have the effrontery to tell me this," said
she; "to tell me, who, as you very well know, set up to be a
beauty myself, and who am at this very moment taking such an
interest in your affairs, you really have the effrontery to tell me
that Mrs. Bold is the most beautiful woman you know."

"I did not say so," said Mr. Arabin; "you are more
beautiful——"

"Ah, come now, that is something like. I thought you could
not be so unfeeling."

"You are more beautiful, perhaps more clever."

"Thank you, thank you, Mr. Arabin. I knew that you and I should be freinds."

"But——"

"Not a word further. I will not hear a word further. If you talk till midnight, you cannot improve what you have said."

"But Madame Neroni, Mrs. Bold——"

"I will not hear a word about Mrs. Bold. Dread thoughts of strychnine did pass across my brain, but she is welcome to the second place."

"Her place——"

"I won't hear anything about her or her place. I am satisfied, and that is enough. But Mr. Arabin, I am dying with hunger; beautiful and clever as I am, you know I cannot go to my food, and yet you do not bring it to me."

This at any rate was so true as to make it necessary that Mr. Arabin should act upon it, and he accordingly went into the dining-room and supplied the signora's wants.

"And yourself?" said she.

"Oh," said he, "I am not hungry; I never eat at this hour."

"Come, come, Mr. Arabin, don't let love interfere with your appetite. It never does with mine. Give me half a glass more champagne, and then go to the table. Mrs. Bold will do me an injury if you stay talking to me any longer."

Mr. Arabin did as he was bid. He took her plate and glass from her, and going into the dining-room, helped himself to a sandwich from the crowded table and began munching it in a corner.

As he was doing so, Miss Thorne, who had hardly sat down for a moment, came into the room, and seeing him standing, was greatly distressed.

"Oh, my dear Mr. Arabin," said she, "have you never sat down yet? I am so distressed. You of all men too."

Mr. Arabin assured her that he had only just come into the room.

"That is the very reason why you should lose no more time. Come, I'll make room for you. Thank'ee, my dear," she said, seeing that Mrs. Bold was making an attempt to move from her chair, "but I would not for worlds see you stir, for all the ladies would think it necessary to follow. But, perhaps, if Mr. Stanhope has done—just for a minute, Mr. Stanhope—till I can get another chair."

And so Bertie had to rise to make way for his rival. This he did, as he did everything, with an air of good-humoured pleasantry which made it impossible for Mr. Arabin to refuse the proffered seat.

"His bishopric let another take," said Bertie; the quotation being certainly not very appropriate, either for the occasion or the person spoken to. "I have eaten and am satisfied; Mr. Arabin, pray take my chair. I wish for your sake that it really was a bishop's seat."

Mr. Arabin did sit down, and as he did so, Mrs. Bold got up as though to follow her neighbour.

"Pray, pray don't move," said Miss Thorne, almost forcing Eleanor back into her chair. "Mr. Stanhope is not going to leave us. He will stand behind you like a true knight as he is. And now I think of it, Mr. Arabin, let me introduce you to Mr. Slope. Mr. Slope, Mr. Arabin." And the two gentlemen bowed stiffly to each other across the lady whom they both intended to marry, while the other gentleman who also intended to marry her stood behind, watching them.

The two had never met each other before, and the present was certainly not a good opportunity for much cordial conversation, even if cordial conversation between them had been possible. As it was, the whole four who formed the party seemed as though their tongues were tied. Mr. Slope, who was wide awake to what he hoped was his coming opportunity, was not much concerned in the interest of the moment. His wish was to see Eleanor move, that he might pursue her. Bertie was not exactly in the same frame of mind; the evil day was near enough; there was no reason why he should precipitate it. He had made up his mind to marry Eleanor Bold if he could, and was resolved to-day to take the first preliminary step towards doing so. But there was time enough before him. He was not going to make an offer of marriage over the table-cloth. Having thus good-naturedly made way for Mr. Arabin, he was willing also to let him talk to the future Mrs. Stanhope as long as they remained in their present position.

Mr. Arabin, having bowed to Mr. Slope, began eating his food without saying a word further. He was full of thought, and though he ate he did so unconsciously.

But poor Eleanor was the most to be pitied. The only friend on whom she thought she could rely, was Bertie Stanhope, and he, it seemed, was determined to desert her. Mr. Arabin did not attempt to address her. She said a few words in reply to some remarks from Mr. Slope, and then feeling the situation too much for her, started from her chair in spite of Miss Thorne, and hurried from the room. Mr. Slope followed her, and young Stanhope lost the occasion.

Madeline Neroni, when she was left alone, could not help pondering much on the singular interview she had had with this singular man. Not a word that she had spoken to him had been intended by her to be received as true, and yet he had answered her in the very spirit of truth. He had done so, and she had been aware that he had so done. She had wormed from him his secret; and he, debarred as it would seem from man's usual privilege of lying, had innocently laid bare his whole soul to her. He loved Eleanor Bold, but Eleanor was not in his eye so beautiful as herself. He would fain have Eleanor for his wife, but yet he had acknowledged that she was the less gifted of the two. The man had literally been unable to falsify his thoughts when questioned, and had been compelled to be true *malgrè lui*, even when truth must have been so disagreeable to him.

This teacher of men, this Oxford pundit, this double-distilled quintessence of university perfection, this writer of religious treatises, this speaker of ecclesiastical speeches, had been like a child in her hands; she had turned him inside out, and read his very heart as she might have done that of a young girl. She could not but despise him for his facile openness, and yet she liked him for it too. It was a novelty to her, a new trait in a man's character. She felt also that she could never so completely make a fool of him as she did of the Slopes and Thornes. She felt that she never could induce Mr. Arabin to make protestations to her that were not true, or to listen to nonsense that was mere nonsense.

It was quite clear that Mr. Arabin was heartily in love with Mrs. Bold, and the signora, with very unwonted good nature, began to turn it over in her mind whether she could not do him a good turn. Of course Bertie was to have the first chance. It was an understood family arrangement that her brother was, if possible, to marry the widow Bold. Madeline knew too well his necessities and what was due to her sister to interfere with so excellent a plan, as long as it might be feasible. But she had strong suspicion that it was not feasible. She did not think it likely that Mrs. Bold would accept a man in her brother's position, and she had frequently said so to Charlotte. She was inclined to believe Mr. Slope had more chance of success; and with her it would be a labour of love to rob Mr. Slope of his wife.

And so the signora resolved, should Bertie fail, to do a good-natured act for once in her life, and give up Mr. Arabin to the woman whom he loved.

XXXIX

The Lookalofts and the Greenacres

On the whole, Miss Thorne's provision for the amusement and feeding of the outer classes in the exoteric paddock was not unsuccessful.

Two little drawbacks to the general happiness did take place, but they were of a temporary nature, and apparent rather than real. The first was the downfall of young Harry Greenacre, and the other the uprise of Mrs. Lookaloft and her family.

As to the quintain, it became more popular among the boys on foot, than it would ever have been among the men on horseback, even had young Greenacre been more successful. It was twirled round and round till it was nearly twirled out of the ground; and the bag of flour was used with great gusto in powdering the backs and heads of all who could be coaxed within its vicinity.

Of course it was reported all through the assemblage that Harry was dead, and there was a pathetic scene between him and his mother when it was found that he had escaped scatheless from the fall. A good deal of beer was drunk on the occasion, and the quintain was "dratted" and "bothered," and very generally anathematised by all the mothers who had young sons likely to be placed in similar jeopardy. But the affair of Mrs. Lookaloft was of a more serious nature.

"I do tell 'ee plainly,—face to face,—she be there in madam's drawing-room; herself and Gussy, and them two walloping gals, dressed up to their very eyeses." This was said by a very positive, very indignant, and very fat farmer's wife, who was sitting on the end of a bench leaning on the handle of a huge cotton umbrella.

"But you didn't zee her, Dame Guffern?" said Mrs.

Greenacre, whom this information, joined to the recent peril undergone by her son, almost overpowered. Mr. Greenacre held just as much land as Mr. Lookaloft, paid his rent quite as punctually, and his opinion in the vestry-room was reckoned to be every whit as good. Mrs. Lookaloft's rise in the world had been wormwood to Mrs. Greenacre. She had no taste herself for the sort of finery which had converted Barleystubb farm into Rosebank, and which had occasionally graced Mr. Lookaloft's letters with the dignity of esquirehood. She had no wish to convert her own homestead into Violet Villa, or to see her goodman go about with a new-fangled handle to his name. But it was a mortal injury to her that Mrs. Lookaloft should be successful in her hunt after such honours. She had abused and ridiculed Mrs. Lookaloft to the extent of her little power. She had pushed against her going out of church, and had excused herself with all the easiness of equality. "Ah, dame, I axes pardon; but you be grown so mortal stout these times." She had inquired with apparent cordiality of Mr. Lookaloft, after "the woman that owned him," and had, as she thought, been on the whole able to hold her own pretty well against her aspiring neighbour. Now, however, she found herself distinctly put into a separate and inferior class. Mrs. Lookaloft was asked into the Ullathorne drawing-room merely because she called her house Rosebank, and had talked over her husband into buying pianos and silk dresses instead of putting his money by to stock farms for his sons.

Mrs. Greenacre, much as she reverenced Miss Thorne, and highly as she respected her husband's landlord, could not but look on this as an act of injustice done to her and hers. Hitherto the Lookalofts had never been recognised as being of a different class from the Greenacres. Their pretensions were all self-pretensions, their finery was all paid for by themselves and not granted to them by others. The local sovereigns of the vicinity, the district fountains of honour, had hitherto conferred on them the stamp of no rank. Hitherto their crinoline petticoats, late hours, and mincing gait had been a fair subject of Mrs. Greenacre's raillery, and this raillery had been a safety valve for her envy. Now, however, and from henceforward, the case would be very different. Now the Lookalofts would boast that their aspirations had been sanctioned by the gentry of the country; now they would declare with some show of truth that their claims to peculiar consideration had been recognised. They had sat as equal guests in the presence of bishops and baronets; they had been curtseyed to by Miss Thorne on her own drawing-room carpet; they were about to sit down to table in company with a live countess! Bab Lookaloft, as she had always been called by the young Greenacres in the days of their juvenile equality, might possibly sit next to the Honourable George, and that wretched Gussy might be permitted to hand a custard to the Lady Margaretta De Courcy.

The fruition of those honours, or such of them as fell to the lot of the envied family, was not such as should have caused much envy. The attention paid to the Lookalofts by the De Courcys was very limited, and the amount of entertainment which they received from the bishop's society was hardly in itself a recompense for the dull monotony of their day. But of what they endured Mrs. Greenacre took no account; she thought only of what she considered they must enjoy, and of the dreadfully exalted tone of living which would be manifested by the Rosebank family, as the consequence of their present distinction.

"But did 'ee zee 'em there, dame, did 'ee zee 'em there with your own eyes?" asked poor Mrs. Greenacre; still hoping that there might be some ground for doubt.

"And how could I do that, unless so be I was there myself?" asked Mrs. Guffern. "I didn't zet eyes on none of them this blessed morning, but I zee'd them as did. You know our John; well, he will be for keeping company with Betsey Rusk, madam's own maid, you know. And Betsey isn't none of your common kitchen wenches. So Betsey, she came out to our John, you know, and she's always vastly polite to me, is Betsey Rusk, I must say. So before she took so much as one turn with John, she told me every ha'porth that was going on up in the house."

"Did she now?" said Mrs. Greenacre.

"Indeed she did," said Mrs. Guffern.

"And she told you them people was up there in the drawing-room?"

"She told me she zee'd them come in,—that they was dressed finer by half nor any of the family, with all their neckses and buzoms stark naked as a born babby."

"The minxes!" exclaimed Mrs. Greenacre, who felt herself more put about by this than any other mark of aristocratic distinction which her enemies had assumed.

"Yes, indeed," continued Mrs. Guffern, "as naked as you please, while all the quality was dressed just as you and I be, Mrs. Greenacre."

"Drat their impudence," said Mrs. Greenacre, from whose

well-covered bosom all milk of human kindness was receding, as far as the family of the Lookalofts were concerned.

"So says I," said Mrs. Guffern; "and so says my goodman, Thomas Guffern, when he hear'd it. 'Molly,' says he to me, 'if ever you takes to going about o' mornings with yourself all naked in them ways, I begs you won't come back no more to the old house.' So says I, 'Thomas, no more I wull.' 'But,' says he, 'drat it, how the deuce does she manage with her rheumatiz, and she not a rag on her' ": and Mrs. Guffern laughed loudly as she thought of Mrs. Lookaloft's probable sufferings from rheumatic attacks.

"But to liken herself that way to folk that ha' blood in their veins," said Mrs. Greenacre.

"Well, but that warn't all neither that Betsey told. There they all swelled into madam's drawing-room, like so many turkey cocks, as much as to say, 'and who dare say no to us?' and Gregory was thinking of telling of 'em to come down here, only his heart failed him 'cause of the grand way they was dressed. So in they went; but madam looked at them as glum as death."

"Well now," said Mrs. Greenacre, greatly relieved, "so they wasn't axed different from us at all then?"

"Betsey says that Gregory says that madam wasn't a bit too well pleased to see them where they was, and that, to his believing, they was expected to come here just like the rest of us."

There was great consolation in this. Not that Mrs. Greenacre was altogether satisfied. She felt that justice to herself demanded that Mrs. Lookaloft should not only not be encouraged, but that she should also be absolutely punished. What had been done at that scriptural banquet, of which Mrs. Greenacre so often read the account to her family? Why had not Miss Thorne boldly gone to the intruder and said, "Friend, thou hast come up hither to high places not fitted to thee. Go down lower, and thou wilt find thy mates." Let the Lookalofts be treated at the present moment with ever so cold a shoulder, they would still be enabled to boast hereafter of their position, their aspiration, and their honour.

"Well, with all her grandeur, I do wonder that she be so mean," continued Mrs. Greenacre, unable to dismiss the subject. "Did you hear, goodman?" she went on, about to repeat the whole story to her husband who then came up. "There's dame Lookaloft and Bab and Gussy and the lot of 'em all sitting as grand as fivepence in madam's drawing-room, and they not axed no more nor you nor me. Did you ever hear tell the like o' that?"

"Well, and what for shouldn't they?" said Farmer Greenacre.

"Likening theyselves to the quality, as though they was estated folk, or the like o' that!" said Mrs. Guffern.

"Well, if they likes it and madam likes it, they's welcome for me," said the farmer. "Now I likes this place better, cause I be more at home like, and don't have to pay for them fine clothes for the missus. Every one to his taste, Mrs. Guffern, and if neighbour Lookaloft thinks that he has the best of it, he's welcome."

Mrs. Greenacre sat down by her husband's side to begin the heavy work of the banquet, and she did so in some measure with restored tranquillity, but nevertheless she shook her head at her gossip to show that in this instance she did not quite approve of her husband's doctrine.

"And I'll tell 'ee what, dames," continued he; "if so be that we cannot enjoy the dinner that madam gives us because Mother Lookaloft is sitting up there on a grand sofa, I think we ought all to go home. If we greet at that, what'll we do when true sorrow comes across us? How would you be now, dame, if the boy there had broke his neck when he got the tumble?"

Mrs. Greenacre was humbled and said nothing further on the matter. But let prudent men, such as Mr. Greenacre, preach as they will, the family of the Lookalofts certainly does occasion a good deal of heart-burning in the world at large.

It was pleasant to see Mr. Plomacy, as leaning on his stout stick he went about among the rural guests, acting as a sort of head constable as well as master of the revels. "Now, young 'un, if you can't manage to get along without that screeching, you'd better go to the other side of the twelve-acre field, and take your dinner with you. Come, girls, what do you stand there for, twirling of your thumbs? come out, and let the lads see you; you've no need to be so ashamed of your faces. Hello! there, who are you? how did you make your way in here?"

This last disagreeable question was put to a young man of about twenty-four, who did not, in Mr. Plomacy's eye, bear sufficient vestiges of a rural education and residence.

"If you please, your worship, Master Barrell the coachman let me in at the church wicket, 'cause I do be working mostly al'ays for the family."

"Then Master Barrell the coachman may let you out again," said Mr. Plomacy, not even conciliated by the magisterial dignity which had been conceded to him. "What's your name? and what trade are you, and who do you work for?"

"I'm Stubbs, your worship, Bob Stubbs; and—and—and——"

"And what's your trade, Stubbs?"

"Plaisterer, please your worship."

"I'll plaister you, and Barrell too; you'll just walk out of this 'ere field as quick as you walked in. We don't want no plaisterers; when we do, we'll send for 'em. Come, my buck, walk."

Stubbs the plasterer was much downcast at this dreadful edict. He was a sprightly fellow, and had contrived since his egress into the Ullathorne elysium to attract to himself a forest nymph, to whom he was whispering a plasterer's usual soft nothings, when he was encountered by the great Mr. Plomacy. It was dreadful to be thus dissevered from his dryad, and sent howling back to a Barchester pandemonium just as the nectar and ambrosia were about to descend on the fields of asphodel. He began to try what prayers would do, but city prayers were vain against the great rural potentate. Not only did Mr. Plomacy order his exit, but raising his stick to show the way which led to the gate that had been left in the custody of that false Cerberus Barrell, proceeded himself to see the edict of banishment carried out.

The goddess Mercy, however, the sweetest goddess that ever sat upon a cloud, and the dearest to poor frail erring man, appeared on the field in the person of Mr. Greenacre. Never was interceding goodness more welcome.

"Come, man," said Mr. Greenacre, "never stick at trifles such a day as this. I know the lad well. Let him bide at my axing. Madam won't miss what he can eat and drink, I know."

Now Mr. Plomacy and Mr. Greenacre were sworn friends. Mr. Plomacy had at his own disposal as comfortable a room as there was in Ullathorne House; but he was a bachelor, and alone there; and, moreover, smoking in the house was not allowed even to Mr. Plomacy. His moments of truest happiness were spent in a huge arm-chair in the warmest corner of Mrs. Greenacre's beautifully clean front kitchen. 'Twas there that the inner man dissolved itself, and poured itself out in streams of pleasant chat; 'twas there, and perhaps there only, that he could unburden himself from the ceremonies of life without offending the dignity of those above him, or incurring the familiarity of those below. 'Twas there that his long pipe was always to be found on the accustomed chimney board, not only permitted but encouraged.

Such being the state of the case, it was not to be supposed that Mr. Plomacy could refuse such a favour to Mr. Greenacre; but nevertheless he did not grant it without some further show of austere authority.

"Eat and drink, Mr. Greenacre! No. It's not what he eats and drinks; but the example such a chap shows, coming in where he's not invited—a chap of his age too. He too that never did a day's work about Ullathorne since he was born. Plaisterer! I'll plaister him!"

"He worked long enough for me, then, Mr. Plomacy. And a good hand he is at setting tiles as any in Barchester," said the other, not sticking quite to veracity, as indeed mercy never should. "Come, come, let him alone to-day, and quarrel with him to-morrow. You wouldn't shame him before his lass there?"

"It goes against the grain with me, then," said Mr. Plomacy. "And take care, you Stubbs, and behave yourself. If I hear a row I shall know where it comes from. I'm up to you Barchester journeymen; I know what stuff you're made of."

And so Stubbs went off happy, pulling at the forelock of his shock head of hair in honour of the steward's clemency, and giving another double pull at it in honour of the farmer's kindness. And as he went he swore within his grateful heart, that if ever Farmer Greenacre wanted a day's work done for nothing, he was the lad to do it for him. Which promise it was not probable that he would ever be called on to perform.

But Mr. Plomacy was not quite happy in his mind, for he thought of the unjust steward, and began to reflect whether he had not made for himself friends of the mammon of unrighteousness. This, however, did not interfere with the manner in which he performed his duties at the bottom of the long board; nor did Mr. Greenacre perform his the worse at the top on account of the good wishes of Stubbs the plasterer. Moreover, the guests did not think it anything amiss when Mr. Plomacy, rising to say grace, prayed that God would make them all truly thankful for the good things which Madam Thorne in her great liberality had set before them!

All this time the quality in the tent on the lawn were getting on swimmingly; that is, if champagne without restriction can enable quality folk to swim. Sir Harkaway Gorse proposed the health of Miss Thorne, and likened her to a blood race-horse, always in condition, and not to be tired down by any amount of work. Mr. Thorne returned thanks, saying he hoped his sister would always be found able to run when called upon, and then gave the health and prosperity of the De Courcy family. His sister was very much honoured by seeing so many of them at her poor board. They were all aware that important avocations made the absence of the earl necessary. As his duty to his prince had called him from his family hearth, he, Mr. Thorne, could not venture to regret that he did not see him at Ullathorne; but nevertheless he would venture to say—that was to express a wish—an opinion he meant to say—— And so Mr. Thorne became somewhat gravelled, as country gentlemen in similar circumstances usually do; but he ultimately sat down, declaring that he had much satisfaction in drinking the noble earl's health, together with that of the countess, and all the family of De Courcy castle.

And then the Honourable George returned thanks. We will not follow him through the different periods of his somewhat irregular eloquence. Those immediately in his neighbourhood found it at first rather difficult to get him on his legs, but much greater difficulty was soon experienced in inducing him to resume his seat. One of two arrangements should certainly be made in these days: either let all speech-making on festive occasions be utterly tabooed and made as it were impossible; or else let those who are to exercise the privilege be first subjected to a competing examination before the civil service examining commissioners. As it is now, the Honourable Georges do but little honour to our exertions in favour of British education.

In the dining-room the bishop went through the honours of the day with much more neatness and propriety. He also drank Miss Thorne's health, and did it in a manner becoming the bench which he adorned. The party there, was perhaps a little more dull, a shade less lively than that in the tent. But what was lost in mirth, was fully made up in decorum.

And so the banquets passed off at the various tables with great éclat and universal delight.

XL

Ullathorne Sports—Act II

"That which has made them drunk, has made me bold." 'Twas thus that Mr. Slope encouraged himself, as he left the dining-room in pursuit of Eleanor. He had not indeed seen in that room any person really intoxicated; but there had been a good deal of wine drunk, and Mr. Slope had not hesitated to take his share, in order to screw himself up to the undertaking which he had in hand. He is not the first man who has thought it expedient to call in the assistance of Bacchus on such an occasion.

Eleanor was out through the window, and on the grass before she perceived that she was followed. Just at that moment the guests were nearly all occupied at the tables. Here and there were to be seen a constant couple or two, who preferred their own sweet discourse to the jingle of glasses, or the charms of rhetoric which fell from the mouths of the Honourable George and the bishop of Barchester; but the grounds were as nearly vacant as Mr. Slope could wish them to be.

Eleanor saw that she was pursued, and as a deer, when escape is no longer possible, will turn to bay and attack the hounds, so did she turn upon Mr. Slope.

"Pray don't let me take you from the room," said she, speaking with all the stiffness which she knew how to use. "I have come out to look for a friend. I must beg of you, Mr. Slope, to go back."

But Mr. Slope would not be thus entreated. He had observed all day that Mrs. Bold was not cordial to him, and this had to a certain extent oppressed him. But he did not deduce from this any assurance that his aspirations were in vain. He saw that she was angry with him. Might she not be so because he had so long tampered with her feelings,—might it not arise from his having, as he knew was the case, caused her name to be bruited about in conjunction with his own, without having given her the opportunity of confessing to the world that henceforth their names were to be one and the same? Poor lady! He had within him a certain Christian conscience-stricken feeling of remorse on this head. It might be that he had wronged her by his tardiness. He had, however, at the present moment imbibed too much of Mr. Thorne's champagne to have any inward misgivings. He was right in repeating the boast of Lady Macbeth: he was not drunk; but he was bold enough for anything. It was a pity that in such a state he could not have encountered Mrs. Proudie.

"You must permit me to attend you," said he; "I could not think of allowing you to go alone."

"Indeed you must, Mr. Slope," said Eleanor still very stiffly; "for it is my special wish to be alone."

The time for letting the great secret escape him had already come. Mr. Slope saw that it must be now or never, and he was determined that it should be now. This was not his first attempt at winning a fair lady. He had been on his knees, looked unutterable things with his eyes, and whispered honeyed words before this. Indeed he was somewhat an adept at these things, and had only to adapt to the perhaps different taste of Mrs. Bold the well-remembered rhapsodies which had once so much gratified Olivia Proudie.

"Do not ask me to leave you, Mrs. Bold," said he with an impassioned look, impassioned and sanctified as well, with that sort of look which is not uncommon with gentlemen of Mr. Slope's school, and which may perhaps be called the tender-pious. "Do not ask me to leave you, till I have spoken a few words with which my heart is full; which I have come hither purposely to say."

Eleanor saw how it was now. She knew directly what it was she was about to go through, and very miserable the knowledge made her. Of course she could refuse Mr. Slope, and there would be an end of that, one might say. But there would not be an end of it as far as Eleanor was concerned. The very fact of Mr. Slope's making an offer to her would be a triumph to the archdeacon, and in a great measure a vindication of Mr. Arabin's conduct. The widow could not bring herself to endure with patience the idea that she had been in the wrong. She had defended Mr. Slope, she had declared herself quite justified in admitting him among her acquaintance, had ridiculed the idea of his considering himself as more than an acquaintance, and had resented the archdeacon's caution in her behalf: now it was about to be proved to her in a manner sufficiently disagreeable that the archdeacon had been right, and she herself had been entirely wrong.

"I don't know what you can have to say to me, Mr. Slope, that you could not have said when we were sitting at table just now"; and she closed her lips, and steadied her eyeballs, and looked at him in a manner that ought to have frozen him.

But gentlemen are not easily frozen when they are full of champagne, and it would not at any time have been easy to freeze Mr. Slope.

"There are things, Mrs. Bold, which a man cannot well say before a crowd; which perhaps he cannot well say at any time; which indeed he may most fervently desire to get spoken; and which he may yet find it almost impossible to utter. It is such things as these, that I now wish to say to you"; and then the tender-pious look was repeated, with a little more emphasis even than before.

Eleanor had not found it practicable to stand stock still before the dining-room window, and there receive his offer in full view of Miss Thorne's guests. She had therefore in self-defence walked on, and thus Mr. Slope had gained his object of walking with her. He now offered her his arm.

"Thank you, Mr. Slope, I am much obliged to you; but for the very short time that I shall remain with you I shall prefer walking alone."

"And must it be so short?" said he; "must it be—"

"Yes," said Eleanor, interrupting him; "as short as possible, if you please, sir."

"I had hoped, Mrs. Bold—I had hoped—"

"Pray hope nothing, Mr. Slope, as far as I am concerned; pray do not; I do not know, and need not know what hope you mean. Our acquaintance is very slight, and will probably remain so. Pray, pray let that be enough; there is at any rate no necessity for us to quarrel."

Mrs. Bold was certainly treating Mr. Slope rather cavalierly, and he felt it so. She was rejecting him before he had offered himself, and informed him at the same time that he was taking a great deal too much on himself to be so familiar. She did not even make an attempt.

> From such a sharp and waspish word as "no"
> To pluck the sting.

He was still determined to be very tender and very pious, seeing that in spite of all Mrs. Bold had said to him, he had not yet abandoned hope; but he was inclined also to be somewhat angry. The widow was bearing herself, as he thought, with too high a hand, was speaking of herself in much too imperious a tone. She had clearly no idea that an honour was being conferred on her. Mr. Slope would be tender as long as he could, but he began to think, if that failed, it would not be amiss if he also mounted himself for a while on his high horse. Mr. Slope could undoubtedly be very tender, but he could be very savage also, and he knew his own abilities.

"That is cruel," said he, "and unchristian too. The worst of us are all still bidden to hope. What have I done that you should pass on me so severe a sentence?" and then he paused a moment, during which the widow walked steadily on with measured step, saying nothing further.

"Beautiful woman," at last he burst forth; "beautiful woman, you cannot pretend to be ignorant that I adore you. Yes, Eleanor, yes, I love you. I love you with the truest affection which man can bear to woman. Next to my hopes of heaven are my hopes of possessing you." (Mr. Slope's memory here played him false, or he would not have omitted the deanery.) "How sweet to walk to heaven with you by my side, with you for my guide, mutual guides. Say, Eleanor, dearest Eleanor, shall we walk that sweet path together?"

Eleanor had no intention of ever walking together with Mr. Slope on any other path than that special one of Miss Thorne's which they now occupied; but as she had been unable to prevent the expression of Mr. Slope's wishes and aspirations, she resolved to hear him out to the end, before she answered him.

"Ah! Eleanor," he continued, and it seemed to be his idea that as he had once found courage to pronounce her Christian name, he could not utter it often enough. "Ah! Eleanor, will it not be sweet, with the Lord's assistance, to travel hand in hand through this mortal valley which his mercies will make pleasant to us, till hereafter we shall dwell together at the foot of his throne?" And then a more tenderly pious glance than ever beamed from the lover's eyes. "Ah! Eleanor—"

"My name, Mr. Slope, is Mrs. Bold," said Eleanor, who, though determined to hear out the tale of his love, was too much disgusted by his blasphemy to be able to bear much more of it.

"Sweetest angel, be not so cold," said he, and as he said it the champagne broke forth, and he contrived to pass his arm round her waist. He did this with considerable cleverness, for up to this point Eleanor had contrived with tolerable success to keep her distance from him. They had got into a walk nearly enveloped by shrubs, and Mr. Slope therefore no doubt considered that as they were now alone it was fitting that he should give her some outward demonstration of that affection of which he talked so much. It may perhaps be presumed that the same stamp of measures had been found to succeed with Olivia Proudie. Be this as it may, it was not successful with Eleanor Bold.

She sprang from him as she would have jumped from an adder, but she did not spring far; not, indeed, beyond arm's length; and then, quick as thought, she raised her little hand and dealt him a box on the ear with such right good will, that it sounded among the trees like a miniature thunder-clap.

And now it is to be feared that every well-bred reader of these pages will lay down the book with disgust, feeling that, after all, the heroine is unworthy of sympathy. She is a hoyden, one will say. At any rate she is not a lady, another will exclaim. I have suspected her all through, a third will declare; she has no idea of the dignity of a matron; or of the peculiar propriety which her position demands. At one moment she is romping with young Stanhope; then she is making eyes at Mr. Arabin; anon she comes to fisty-cuffs with a third lover; and all before she is yet a widow of two years' standing.

She cannot altogether be defended; and yet it may be averred that she is not a hoyden, not given to romping, nor prone to boxing. It were to be wished devoutly that she had not struck Mr. Slope in the face. In doing so she derogated from her dignity and committed herself. Had she been educated in Belgravia, had she been brought up by any sterner mentor than that fond father, had she lived longer under the rule of a husband, she might, perhaps, have saved herself from this great fault. As it was, the provocation was too much for her, the temptation to instant resentment of the insult too strong. She was too keen in the feeling of independence, a feeling dangerous for a young woman, but one in which her position peculiarly tempted her to indulge. And then Mr. Slope's face, tinted with a deeper dye than usual by the wine he had drunk, simpering and puckering itself with pseudo piety and tender grimaces, seemed specially to call for such punishment. She had, too, a true instinct as to the man; he was capable of rebuke in this way and in no other. To him the blow from her little hand was as much an insult as a blow from a man would have been to another. It went direct to his pride. He conceived himself lowered in his dignity, and personally outraged. He could almost have struck at her again in his rage. Even the pain was a great annoyance to him, and the feeling that his clerical character had been wholly disregarded, sorely vexed him.

There are such men; men who can endure no taint on their personal self-respect, even from a woman;—men whose bodies are to themselves such sacred temples, that a joke against them is desecration, and a rough touch downright sacrilege. Mr. Slope was such a man; and, therefore, the slap on the face that he got from Eleanor was, as far as he was concerned, the fittest rebuke which could have been administered to him.

But, nevertheless, she should not have raised her hand against the man. Ladies' hands, so soft, so sweet, so delicious to the touch, so grateful to the eye, so gracious in their gentle doings, were not made to belabour men's faces. The moment the deed was done Eleanor felt that she had sinned against all propriety, and would have given little worlds to recall the blow. In her first agony of sorrow she all but begged the man's pardon. Her next impulse, however, and the one which she obeyed, was to run away.

"I never, never will speak another word to you," she said, gasping with emotion and the loss of breath which her exertion and violent feelings occasioned her, and so saying she put foot to the ground and ran quickly back along the path to the house.

But how shall I sing the divine wrath of Mr. Slope, or how invoke the tragic muse to describe the rage which swelled the celestial bosom of the bishop's chaplain? Such an undertaking by no means befits the low-heeled buskin of modern fiction. The painter put a veil over Agamemnon's face when called on to depict the father's grief at the early doom of his devoted daughter. The god, when he resolved to punish the rebellious winds, abstained from mouthing empty threats. We will not attempt to tell with what mighty surgings of the inner heart Mr. Slope swore to revenge himself on the woman who had disgraced him, nor will we vainly strive to depict his deep agony of soul.

There he is, however, alone in the garden walk, and we must contrive to bring him out of it. He was not willing to come forth quite at once. His cheek was stinging with the weight of Eleanor's fingers, and he fancied that every one who looked at him would be able to see on his face the traces of what he had endured. He stood awhile, becoming redder and redder with rage. He stood, motionless, undecided, glaring with his eyes, thinking of the pains and penalties of Hades, and meditating how he might best devote his enemy to the infernal gods with all the passion of his accustomed eloquence. He longed in his heart to be preaching at her. 'Twas thus that he was ordinarily avenged of sinning mortal men and women. Could he at once have ascended his Sunday rostrum and fulminated at her such denunciations as his spirit delighted in, his bosom would have been greatly eased.

But how preach to Mr. Thorne's laurels, or how preach indeed at all in such a vanity fair as this now going on at Ullathorne? And then he began to feel a righteous disgust at the wickedness of the doings around him. He had been justly chastised for lending, by his presence, a sanction to such worldly lures. The gaiety of society, the mirth of banquets, the laughter of the young, and the eating and drinking of the elders were, for awhile, without excuse in his sight. What had he now brought down upon himself by sojourning thus in the tents of the heathen? He had consorted with idolaters round the altars of Baal; and therefore a sore punishment had come upon him. He then thought of the Signora Neroni, and his soul within him was full of sorrow. He had an inkling—a true inkling—that he was a wicked, sinful man; but it led him in no right direction; he could admit no charity in his heart. He felt debasement coming on him, and he longed to shake it off, to rise up in his stirrup, to mount to high places and great power, that he might get up into a mighty pulpit and preach to the world a loud sermon against Mrs. Bold.

There he stood fixed to the gravel for about ten minutes. Fortune favoured him so far that no prying eyes came to look upon him in his misery. Then a shudder passed over his whole frame; he collected himself, and slowly wound his way round to the lawn, advancing along the path and not returning in the direction which Eleanor had taken. When he reached the tent he found the bishop standing there in conversation with the master of Lazarus. His lordship had come out to air himself after the exertion of his speech.

"This is very pleasant—very pleasant, my lord, is it not?" said Mr. Slope with his most gracious smile, and pointing to the tent; "very pleasant. It is delightful to see so many persons enjoying themselves so thoroughly."

Mr. Slope thought he might force the bishop to introduce him to Dr. Gwynne. A very great example had declared and practised the wisdom of being everything to everybody, and Mr. Slope was desirous of following it. His maxim was never to lose a chance. The bishop, however, at the present moment was not very anxious to increase Mr. Slope's circle of acquaintance among his clerical brethren. He had his own reasons for dropping any marked allusion to his domestic chaplain, and he therefore made his shoulder rather cold for the occasion.

"Very, very," said he without turning round, or even deigning to look at Mr. Slope. "And therefore, Dr. Gwynne, I really think that you will find that the hebdomadal board will exercise as wide and as general an authority as at the present moment. I, for one, Dr. Gwynne——"

"Dr. Gwynne," said Mr. Slope, raising his hat, and resolving not to be outwitted by such an insignificant little goose as the bishop of Barchester.

The master of Lazarus also raised his hat and bowed very politely to Mr. Slope. There is not a more courteous gentleman in the Queen's dominions than the master of Lazarus.

"My lord," said Mr. Slope; "pray do me the honour of introducing me to Dr. Gwynne. The opportunity is too much in my favour to be lost."

The bishop had no help for it. "My chaplain, Dr. Gwynne," said he; "my present chaplain, Mr. Slope." He certainly made the introduction as unsatisfactory to the chaplain as possible, and by the use of the word present, seemed to indicate that Mr. Slope might probably not long enjoy the honour which he now held. But Mr. Slope cared nothing for this. He understood the innuendo, and disregarded it. It might probably come to pass that he would be in a situation to resign his chaplaincy before the bishop was in a situation to dismiss him from it. What need the future dean of Barchester care for the bishop, or for the bishop's wife? Had not Mr. Slope, just as he was entering Dr. Stanhope's carriage, received an all important note from Tom Towers of the *Jupiter*? had he not that note this moment in his pocket?

So disregarding the bishop, he began to open out a conversation with the master of Lazarus.

But suddenly an interruption came, not altogether unwelcome to Mr. Slope. One of the bishop's servants came up to his master's shoulder with a long, grave face, and whispered into the bishop's ear.

"What is it, John?" said the bishop.

"The dean, my lord; he is dead."

Mr. Slope had no further desire to converse with the master of Lazarus, and was very soon on his road back to Barchester.

Eleanor, as we have said, having declared her intention of

never holding further communication with Mr. Slope, ran hurriedly back towards the house. The thought, however, of what she had done grieved her greatly, and she could not abstain from bursting into tears. 'Twas thus she played the second act in that day's melodrame.

XLI

Mrs. Bold Confides Her Sorrow to Her Friend Miss Stanhope

When Mrs. Bold came to the end of the walk and faced the lawn, she began to bethink herself what she should do. Was she to wait there till Mr. Slope caught her, or was she to go in among the crowd with tears in her eyes and passion in her face? She might in truth have stood there long enough without any reasonable fear of further immediate persecution from Mr. Slope; but we are all inclined to magnify the bugbears which frighten us. In her present state of dread she did not know of what atrocity he might venture to be guilty. Had any one told her a week ago that he would have put his arm round her waist at this party of Miss Thorne's, she would have been utterly incredulous. Had she been informed that he would be seen on the following Sunday walking down the High Street in a scarlet coat and top-boots, she would not have thought such a phenomenon more improbable.

But this improbable iniquity he had committed; and now there was nothing she could not believe of him. In the first place it was quite manifest that he was tipsy; in the next place, it was to be taken as proved that all his religion was sheer hypocrisy; and finally the man was utterly shameless. She therefore stood watching for the sound of his footfall, not without some fear that he might creep out at her suddenly from among the bushes.

As she thus stood, she saw Charlotte Stanhope at a little distance from her walking quickly across the grass. Eleanor's handkerchief was in her hand, and putting it to her face so as to conceal her tears, she ran across the lawn and joined her friend.

"Oh, Charlotte," she said, almost too much out of breath to speak very plainly; "I am so glad I have found you."

"Glad you have found me!" said Charlotte, laughing: "that's a good joke. Why Bertie and I have been looking for you everywhere. He swears that you have gone off with Mr. Slope, and is now on the point of hanging himself."

"Oh, Charlotte, don't," said Mrs. Bold.

"Why, my child, what on earth is the matter with you!" said Miss Stanhope, perceiving that Eleanor's hand trembled on her own arm, and finding also that her companion was still half choked by tears. "Goodness heaven! something has distressed you. What is it? What can I do for you?"

Eleanor answered her only by a sort of spasmodic gurgle in her throat. She was a good deal upset, as people say, and could not at the moment collect herself.

"Come here, this way, Mrs. Bold; come this way, and we shall not be seen. What has happened to vex you so? What can I do for you? Can Bertie do anything?"

"Oh, no, no, no, no," said Eleanor. "There is nothing to be done. Only that horrid man——"

"What horrid man?" asked Charlotte.

There are some moments in life in which both men and women feel themselves imperatively called on to make a confidence; in which not to do so requires a disagreeable resolution and also a disagreeable suspicion. There are people of both sexes who never make confidences; who are never tempted by momentary circumstances to disclose their secrets; but such are generally dull, close, unimpassioned spirits, "gloomy gnomes, who live in cold dark mines." There was nothing of the gnome about Eleanor; and she therefore resolved to tell Charlotte Stanhope the whole story about Mr. Slope.

"That horrid man; that Mr. Slope," said she: "did you not see that he followed me out of the dining-room?"

"Of course I did, and was sorry enough; but I could not help it. I knew you would be annoyed. But you and Bertie managed it badly between you."

"It was not his fault nor mine either. You know how I disliked the idea of coming in the carriage with that man."

"I am sure I am very sorry if that has led to it."

"I don't know what has led to it," said Eleanor, almost crying again. "But it has not been my fault."

"But what has he done, my dear?"

"He's an abominable, horrid, hypocritical man, and it would serve him right to tell the bishop all about it."

"Believe me, if you want to do him an injury, you had far better tell Mrs. Proudie. But what did he do, Mrs. Bold?"

"Ugh!" exclaimed Eleanor.

"Well, I must confess he's not very nice," said Charlotte Stanhope.

"Nice!" said Eleanor. "He is the most fulsome, fawning, abominable man I ever saw. What business had he to come to me?—I that never gave him the slightest tittle of encouragement—I that always hated him, though I did take his part when others ran him down."

"That's just where it is, my dear. He had heard that, and therefore fancied that of course you were in love with him."

This was wormwood to Eleanor. It was in fact the very thing which all her friends had been saying for the last month past; and which experience now proved to be true. Eleanor resolved within herself that she would never again take any man's part. The world with all its villainy, and all its ill nature, might wag as it liked; she would not again attempt to set crooked things straight.

"But what did he do, my dear?" said Charlotte, who was really rather interested in the subject.

"He—he—he—"

"Well—come, it can't have been anything so very horrid, for the man was not tipsy."

"Oh, I am sure he was," said Eleanor. "I am sure he must have been tipsy."

"Well, I declare I didn't observe it. But what was it, my love?"

"Why, I believe I can hardly tell you. He talked such horrid stuff that you never heard the like; about religion, and heaven, and love.—Oh, dear,—he is such a nasty man."

"I can easily imagine the sort of stuff he would talk. Well—and then—?"

"And then—he took hold of me."

"Took hold of you?"

"Yes—he somehow got close to me, and took hold of me—"

"By the waist?"

"Yes," said Eleanor shuddering.

"And then—"

"Then I jumped away from him, and gave him a slap on the face; and ran away along the path, till I saw you."

"Ha, ha, ha!" Charlotte Stanhope laughed heartily at the finale to the tragedy. It was delightful to her to think that Mr. Slope had had his ears boxed. She did not quite appreciate the feeling which made her friend so unhappy at the result of the interview. To her thinking, the matter had ended happily enough as regarded the widow, who indeed was entitled to some sort of triumph among her friends. Whereas to Mr. Slope would be due all those jibes and jeers which would naturally follow such an affair. His friends would ask him whether his ears tingled whenever he saw a widow; and he would be cautioned that beautiful things were made to be looked at, and not to be touched.

Such were Charlotte Stanhope's views on such matters; but she did not at the present moment clearly explain them to Mrs. Bold. Her object was to endear herself to her friend; and therefore, having had her laugh, she was ready enough to offer sympathy. Could Bertie do anything? Should Bertie speak to the man, and warn him that in future he must behave with more decorum? Bertie, indeed, she declared, would be more angry than any one else when he heard to what insult Mrs. Bold had been subjected.

"But you won't tell him?" said Mrs. Bold with a look of horror.

"Not if you don't like it," said Charlotte; "but considering everything, I would strongly advise it. If you had a brother, you know, it would be unnecessary. But it is very right that Mr. Slope should know that you have somebody by you that will, and can protect you."

"But my father is here."

"Yes, but it is so disagreeable for clergymen to have to quarrel with each other; and circumstanced as your father is just at this moment, it would be very inexpedient that there should be anything unpleasant between him and Mr. Slope. Surely you and Bertie are intimate enough for you to permit him to take your part."

Charlotte Stanhope was very anxious that her brother should at once on that very day settle matters with his future wife. Things had now come to that point between him and his father, and between him and his creditors, that he must either do so, or leave Barchester; either do that, or go back to his unwashed associates, dirty lodgings, and poor living at Carrara. Unless he could provide himself with an income, he must go to Carrara, or to ——. His father the prebendary had not said this in so many

words, but had he done so, he could not have signified it more
plainly.

Such being the state of the case, it was very necessary that
no more time should be lost. Charlotte had seen her brother's
apathy, when he neglected to follow Mrs. Bold out of the room,
with anger which she could hardly suppress. It was grievous to
think that Mr. Slope should have so distanced him. Charlotte felt
that she had played her part with sufficient skill. She had brought
them together and induced such a degree of intimacy, that her
brother was really relieved from all trouble and labour in the
matter. And moreover, it was quite plain that Mrs. Bold was
very fond of Bertie. And now it was plain enough also that he
had nothing to fear from his rival Mr. Slope.

There was certainly an awkwardness in subjecting Mrs.
Bold to a second offer on the same day. It would have been well
perhaps to have put the matter off for a week, could a week have
been spared. But circumstances are frequently too peremptory to
be arranged as we would wish to arrange them; and such was the
case now. This being so, could not this affair of Mr. Slope's be
turned to advantage? Could it not be made the excuse for bringing Bertie and Mrs. Bold into still closer connexion; into such
close connexion that they could not fail to throw themselves into
each other's arms? Such was the game which Miss Stanhope
now at a moment's notice resolved to play.

And very well she played it. In the first place, it was
arranged that Mr. Slope should not return in the Stanhopes'
carriage to Barchester. It so happened that Mr. Slope was already gone, but of that of course they knew nothing. The signora
should be induced to go first, with only the servants and her
sister, and Bertie should take Mr. Slope's place in the second
journey. Bertie was to be told in confidence of the whole affair,
and when the carriage was gone off with its first load, Eleanor
was to be left under Bertie's special protection, so as to insure
her from any further aggression from Mr. Slope. While the
carriage was getting ready, Bertie was to seek out that gentleman
and make him understand that he must provide himself with
another conveyance back to Barchester. Their immediate object
should be to walk about together in search of Bertie. Bertie, in
short, was to be the Pegasus on whose wings they were to ride
out of their present dilemma.

There was a warmth of friendship and cordial kindliness in
all this, that was very soothing to the widow; but yet, though she
gave way to it, she was hardly reconciled to doing so. It never

occurred to her, that now that she had killed one dragon, another was about to spring up in her path; she had no remote idea that she would have to encounter another suitor in her proposed protector, but she hardly liked the thought of putting herself so much into the hands of young Stanhope. She felt that if she wanted protection, she should go to her father. She felt that she should ask him to provide a carriage for her back to Barchester. Mrs. Clantantram she knew would give her a seat. She knew that she should not throw herself entirely upon friends whose friendship dated as it were but from yesterday. But yet she could not say "no," to one who was so sisterly in her kindness, so eager in her good nature, so comfortably sympathetic as Charlotte Stanhope. And thus she gave way to all the propositions made to her.

They first went into the dining-room, looking for their champion, and from thence to the drawing-room. Here they found Mr. Arabin, still hanging over the signora's sofa; or, rather, they found him sitting near her head, as a physician might have sat, had the lady been his patient. There was no other person in the room. The guests were some in the tent, some few still in the dining-room, some at the bows and arrows, but most of them walking with Miss Thorne through the park, and looking at the games that were going on.

All that had passed, and was passing between Mr. Arabin and the lady, it is unnecessary to give in detail. She was doing with him as she did with all others. It was her mission to make fools of men, and she was pursuing her mission with Mr. Arabin. She had almost got him to own his love for Mrs. Bold, and had subsequently almost induced him to acknowledge a passion for herself. He, poor man, was hardly aware what he was doing or saying, hardly conscious whether he was in heaven or hell. So little had he known of female attractions of that peculiar class which the signora owned, that he became affected with a kind of temporary delirium, when first subjected to its power. He lost his head rather than his heart, and toppled about mentally, reeling in his ideas as a drunken man does on his legs. She had whispered to him words that really meant nothing, but which coming from such beautiful lips, and accompanied by such lustrous glances, seemed to have a mysterious significance, which he felt though he could not understand.

In being thus be-sirened, Mr. Arabin behaved himself very differently from Mr. Slope. The signora had said truly, that the two men were the contrasts of each other; that the one was all for action, the other all for thought. Mr. Slope, when this lady laid upon his senses the overpowering breath of her charms, immediately attempted to obtain some fruition, to achieve some mighty triumph. He began by catching at her hand, and progressed by kissing it. He made vows of love, and asked for vows in return. He promised everlasting devotion, knelt before her, and swore that had she been on Mount Ida, Juno would have had no cause to hate the offspring of Venus. But Mr. Arabin uttered no oaths, kept his hand mostly in his trowsers pocket, and had no more thought of kissing Madame Neroni, than of kissing the Countess De Courcy.

As soon as Mr. Arabin saw Mrs. Bold enter the room, he blushed and rose from his chair; then he sat down again, and then again got up. The signora saw the blush at once, and smiled at the poor victim, but Eleanor was too much confused to see anything.

"Oh, Madeline," said Charlotte, "I want to speak to you particularly; we must arrange about the carriage, you know," and she stooped down to whisper to her sister. Mr. Arabin immediately withdrew to a little distance, and as Charlotte had in fact much to explain before she could make her new carriage arrangement intelligible, he had nothing to do but to talk to Mrs. Bold.

"We have had a very pleasant party," said he, using the tone he would have used had he declared that the sun was shining very brightly, or the rain falling very fast.

"Very," said Eleanor, who never in her life had passed a more unpleasant day.

"I hope Mr. Harding has enjoyed himself."

"Oh, yes, very much," said Eleanor, who had not seen her father since she parted from him soon after her arrival.

"He returns to Barchester to-night, I suppose."

"Yes, I believe so; that is, I think he is staying at Plumstead."

"Oh, staying at Plumstead," said Mr. Arabin.

"He came from there this morning. I believe he is going back, he didn't exactly say, however."

"I hope Mrs. Grantly is quite well."

"She seemed to be quite well. She is here; that is, unless she has gone away."

"Oh, yes, to be sure. I was talking to her. Looking very well indeed." Then there was a considerable pause; for Charlotte could not at once make Madeline understand why she was to be sent home in a hurry without her brother.

"Are you returning to Plumstead, Mrs. Bold?" Mr. Arabin merely asked this by way of making conversation, but he immediately perceived that he was approaching dangerous ground.

"No," said Mrs. Bold, very quietly; "I am going home to Barchester."

"Oh, ah, yes. I had forgotten that you had returned." And then Mr. Arabin, finding it impossible to say anything further, stood silent till Charlotte had completed her plans, and Mrs. Bold stood equally silent, intently occupied as it appeared in the arrangement of her rings.

And yet these two people were thoroughly in love with each other; and though one was a middle-aged clergyman, and the other a lady at any rate past the wishy-washy bread-and-butter period of life, they were as unable to tell their own minds to each other as any Damon and Phillis, whose united ages would not make up that to which Mr. Arabin had already attained.

Madeline Neroni consented to her sister's proposal, and then the two ladies again went off in quest of Bertie Stanhope.

XLII

Ullathorne Sports—Act III

And now Miss Thorne's guests were beginning to take their departure, and the amusement of those who remained was becoming slack. It was getting dark, and ladies in morning costumes were thinking that if they were to appear by candlelight they ought to readjust themselves. Some young gentlemen had been heard to talk so loud that prudent mammas determined to retire judiciously, and the more discreet of the male sex, whose libations had been moderate, felt that there was not much more left for them to do.

Morning parties, as a rule, are failures. People never know how to get away from them gracefully. A picnic on an island or a mountain or in a wood may perhaps be permitted. There is no master of the mountain bound by courtesy to bid you stay while in his heart he is longing for your departure. But in a private house or in private grounds a morning party is a bore. One is called on to eat and drink at unnatural hours. One is obliged to give up the day which is useful, and is then left without resource for the evening which is useless. One gets home fagged and *désœuvré,* and yet at an hour too early for bed. There is no comfortable resource left. Cards in these genteel days are among the things tabooed, and a rubber of whist is impracticable.

All this began now to be felt. Some young people had come with some amount of hope that they might get up a dance in the evening, and were unwilling to leave till all such hope was at an end. Others, fearful of staying longer than was expected, had ordered their carriages early, and were doing their best to go, solicitous for their servants and horses. The countess and her noble brood were among the first to leave, and as regarded the Hon. George, it was certainly time that he did so. Her ladyship was in a great fret and fume. Those horrid roads would, she was sure, be the death of her if unhappily she were caught in them by the dark night. The lamps she was assured were good, but no lamp could withstand the jolting of the roads of East Barsetshire. The De Courcy property lay in the western division of the county.

Mrs. Proudie could not stay when the countess was gone. So the bishop was searched for by the Revs. Messrs. Grey and Green, and found in one corner of the tent enjoying himself thoroughly in a disquisition on the hebdomadal board. He obeyed, however, the behests of his lady without finishing the sentence in which he was promising to Dr. Gwynne that his authority at Oxford should remain unimpaired; and the episcopal horses turned their noses towards the palatial stables. Then the Grantlys went. Before they did so, Mr. Harding managed to whisper a word into his daughter's ear. Of course, he said he would undeceive the Grantlys as to that foolish rumour about Mr. Slope.

"No, no, no," said Eleanor; "pray do not—pray wait till I see you. You will be home in a day or two, and then I will explain to you everything."

"I shall be home to-morrow," said he.

"I am so glad," said Eleanor. "You will come and dine with me, and then we shall be so comfortable."

Mr. Harding promised. He did not exactly know what there was to be explained, or why Dr. Grantly's mind should not be disabused of the mistake into which he had fallen; but nevertheless he promised. He owed some reparation to his daughter, and he thought that he might best make it by obedience.

And thus the people were thinning off by degrees, as Charlotte and Eleanor walked about in quest of Bertie. Their search might have been long, had they not happened to hear his voice. He was comfortably ensconced in the ha-ha, with his back to the sloping side, smoking a cigar, and eagerly engaged in conversation with some youngster from the further side of the county, whom he had never met before, who was also smoking under Bertie's pupilage, and listening with open ears to an account given by his companion of some of the pastimes of Eastern clime.

"Bertie, I am seeking you everywhere," said Charlotte. "Come up here at once."

Bertie looked up out of the ha-ha, and saw the two ladies before him. As there was nothing for him but to obey, he got up and threw away his cigar. From the first moment of his acquaintance with her he had liked Eleanor Bold. Had he been left to his own devices, had she been penniless, and had it then been quite out of the question that he should marry her, he would most probably have fallen violently in love with her. But now he could not help regarding her somewhat as he did the marble workshops at Carrara, as he had done his easel and palette, as he had done the lawyer's chambers in London; in fact, as he had invariably regarded everything by which it had been proposed to him to obtain the means of living. Eleanor Bold appeared before him, no longer as a beautiful woman, but as a new profession called matrimony. It was a profession indeed requiring but little labour, and one in which an income was insured to him. But nevertheless he had been as it were goaded on to it; his sister had talked to him of Eleanor, just as she had talked of busts and portraits. Bertie did not dislike money, but he hated the very thought of earning it. He was now called away from his pleasant cigar to earn it, by offering himself as a husband to Mrs. Bold. The work indeed was made easy enough; for in lieu of his having to seek the widow, the widow had apparently come to seek him.

He made some sudden absurd excuse to his auditor, and then throwing away his cigar, climbed up the wall of the ha-ha and joined the ladies on the lawn.

"Come and give Mrs. Bold an arm," said Charlotte, "while I set you on a piece of duty which, as a preux chevalier, you must immediately perform. Your personal danger will, I fear, be insignificant, as your antagonist is a clergyman."

Bertie immediately gave his arm to Eleanor, walking between her and his sister. He had lived too long abroad to fall into the Englishman's habit of offering each an arm to two ladies at the same time; a habit, by the bye, which foreigners regard as an approach to bigamy, or a sort of incipient Mormonism.

The little history of Mr. Slope's misconduct was then told to Bertie by his sister, Eleanor's ears tingling the while. And well they might tingle. If it were necessary to speak of the outrage at all, why should it be spoken of to such a person as Mr. Stanhope, and why in her own hearing? She knew she was wrong, and was unhappy and dispirited, and yet she could think of no way to extricate herself, no way to set herself right. Charlotte spared her as much as she possibly could, spoke of the whole thing as though Mr. Slope had taken a glass of wine too much, said that of course there would be nothing more about it, but that steps must be taken to exclude Mr. Slope from the carriage.

"Mrs. Bold need be under no alarm about that," said Bertie, "for Mr. Slope has gone this hour past. He told me that business made it necessary that he should start at once for Barchester."

"He is not so tipsy, at any rate, but what he knows his fault," said Charlotte. "Well, my dear, that is one difficulty over. Now I'll leave you with your true knight, and get Madeline off as quickly as I can. The carriage is here, I suppose, Bertie?"

"It has been here for the last hour."

"That's well. Good-bye, my dear. Of course you'll come in to tea. I shall trust to you to bring her, Bertie; even by force if necessary." And so saying, Charlotte ran off across the lawn, leaving her brother alone with the widow.

As Miss Stanhope went off, Eleanor bethought herself that, as Mr. Slope had taken his departure, there no longer existed any necessity for separating Mr. Stanhope from his sister Madeline, who so much needed his aid. It had been arranged that he should remain so as to preoccupy Mr. Slope's place in the carriage, and act as a social policeman to effect the exclusion of that disagreeable gentleman. But Mr. Slope had effected his own exclusion, and there was no possible reason now why Bertie should not go with his sister. At least Eleanor saw none, and she said as much.

"Oh, let Charlotte have her own way," said he. "She has arranged it, and there will be no end of confusion, if we make another change. Charlotte always arranges everything in our house; and rules us like a despot.''

"But the signora?'' said Eleanor.

"Oh, the signora can do very well without me. Indeed, she will have to do without me,'' he added, thinking rather of his studies in Carrara, than of his Barchester hymeneals.

"Why, you are not going to leave us?'' asked Eleanor.

It has been said that Bertie Stanhope was a man without principle. He certainly was so. He had no power of using active mental exertion to keep himself from doing evil. Evil had no ugliness in his eyes; virtue no beauty. He was void of any of those feelings which actuate men to do good. But he was perhaps equally void of those which actuate men to do evil. He got into debt with utter recklessness, thinking nothing as to whether the tradesmen would ever be paid or not. But he did not invent active schemes of deceit for the sake of extracting the goods of others. If a man gave him credit, that was the man's look-out; Bertie Stanhope troubled himself nothing further. In borrowing money he did the same; he gave people references to "his governor''; told them that the "old chap'' had a good income; and agreed to pay sixty per cent. for the accommodation. All this he did without a scruple of conscience; but then he never contrived active villainy.

In this affair of his marriage, it had been represented to him as a matter of duty that he ought to put himself in possession of Mrs. Bold's hand and fortune; and at first he had so regarded it. About her he had thought but little. It was the customary thing for men situated as he was to marry for money, and there was no reason why he should not do what others around him did. And so he consented. But now he began to see the matter in another light. He was setting himself down to catch this woman, as a cat sits to catch a mouse. He was to catch her, and swallow her up, her and her child, and her houses and land, in order that he might live on her instead of on his father. There was a cold, calculating, cautious cunning about this quite at variance with Bertie's character. The prudence of the measure was quite as antagonistic to his feelings as the iniquity.

And then, should he be successful, what would be the reward? Having satisfied his creditors with half of the widow's fortune, he would be allowed to sit down quietly at Barchester, keeping economical house with the remainder. His duty would be to rock the cradle of the late Mr. Bold's child, and his highest excitement a demure party at Plumstead rectory, should it ulti-

mately turn out that the archdeacon would be sufficiently reconciled to receive him.

There was very little in the programme to allure such a man
as Bertie Stanhope. Would not the Carrara workshop, or whatever worldly career fortune might have in store for him, would
not almost anything be better than this? The lady herself was
undoubtedly all that was desirable; but the most desirable lady
becomes nauseous when she has to be taken as a pill. He was
pledged to his sister, however, and let him quarrel with whom he
would, it behoved him not to quarrel with her. If she were lost to
him all would be lost that he could ever hope to derive henceforth from the paternal roof-tree. His mother was apparently
indifferent to his weal or woe, to his wants or his warfare. His
father's brow got blacker and blacker from day to day, as the old
man looked at his hopeless son. And as for Madeline—poor
Madeline, whom of all of them he liked the best,—she had
enough to do to shift for herself. No; come what might, he must
cling to his sister and obey her behests, let them be ever so stern;
or at the very least seem to obey them. Could not some happy
deceit bring him through in this matter, so that he might save
appearances with his sister, and yet not betray the widow to her
ruin? What if he made a confederate of Eleanor? 'Twas in this
spirit that Bertie Stanhope set about his wooing.

"But you are not going to leave Barchester?" asked Eleanor.

"I do not know," he replied; "I hardly know yet what I am
going to do. But it is at any rate certain that I must do something."

"You mean about your profession?" said she.

"Yes, about my profession, if you can call it one."

"And is it not one?" said Eleanor. "Were I a man, I know
none I should prefer to it, except painting. And I believe the one
is as much in your power as the other."

"Yes, just about equally so," said Bertie, with a little touch
of inward satire directed at himself. He knew in his heart that he
would never make a penny by either.

"I have often wondered, Mr. Stanhope, why you do not
exert yourself more," said Eleanor, who felt a friendly fondness
for the man with whom she was walking. "But I know it is very
impertinent in me to say so."

"Impertinent!" said he. "Not so, but much too kind. It is
much too kind in you to take any interest in so idle a scamp."

"But you are not a scamp, though you are perhaps idle; and
I do take an interest in you; a very great interest," she added, in
a voice which almost made him resolve to change his mind.

"And when I call you idle, I know you are only so for the present moment. Why can't you settle steadily to work here in Barchester?"

"And make busts of the bishop, dean and chapter? or perhaps, if I achieve a great success, obtain a commission to put up an elaborate tombstone over a prebendary's widow, a dead lady with a Grecian nose, a bandeau, and an intricate lace veil; lying of course on a marble sofa, from among the legs of which Death will be creeping out and poking at his victim with a small toasting-fork."

Eleanor laughed; but yet she thought that if the surviving prebendary paid the bill, the object of the artist as a professional man would, in a great measure, be obtained.

"I don't know about the dean and chapter and the prebendary's widow," said Eleanor. "Of course you must take them as they come. But the fact of your having a great cathedral in which such ornaments are required, could not but be in your favour."

"No real artist could descend to the ornamentation of a cathedral," said Bertie, who had his ideas of the high ecstatic ambition of art, as indeed all artists have, who are not in receipt of a good income. "Buildings should be fitted to grace the sculpture, not the sculpture to grace the building."

"Yes, when the work of art is good enough to merit it. Do you, Mr. Stanhope, do something sufficiently excellent, and we ladies of Barchester will erect for it a fitting receptacle. Come, what shall the subject be?"

"I'll put you in your pony chair, Mrs. Bold, as Dannecker put Ariadne on her lion. Only you must promise to sit for me."

"My ponies are too tame, I fear, and my broad-rimmed straw hat will not look so well in marble as the lace veil of the prebendary's wife."

"If you will not consent to that, Mrs. Bold, I will consent to try no other subject in Barchester."

"You are determined, then, to push your fortune in other lands?"

"I am determined," said Bertie, slowly and significantly, as he tried to bring up his mind to a great resolve; "I am determined in this matter to be guided wholly by you."

"Wholly by me!" said Eleanor, astonished at, and not quite liking, his altered manner.

"Wholly by you," said Bertie, dropping his companion's arm, and standing before her on the path. In their walk they had come exactly to the spot in which Eleanor had been provoked into slapping Mr. Slope's face. Could it be possible that this place was peculiarly unpropitious to her comfort? could it be possible that she should here have to encounter yet another amorous swain?

"If you will be guided by me, Mr. Stanhope, you will set yourself down to steady and persevering work, and you will be ruled by your father as to the place in which it will be most advisable for you to do so."

"Nothing could be more prudent, if only it were practicable. But now, if you will let me, I will tell you how it is that I will be guided by you, and why. Will you let me tell you?"

"I really do not know what you can have to tell."

"No,—you cannot know. It is impossible that you should. But we have been very good friends, Mrs. Bold, have we not?"

"Yes, I think we have," said she, observing in his demeanour an earnestness very unusual with him.

"You were kind enough to say just now that you took an interest in me, and I was perhaps vain enough to believe you."

"There is no vanity in that; I do so as your sister's brother— and as my own friend also."

"Well, I don't deserve that you should feel so kindly towards me," said Bertie; "but upon my word I am very grateful for it," and he paused awhile, hardly knowing how to introduce the subject that he had in hand.

And it was no wonder that he found it difficult. He had to make known to his companion the scheme that had been pre- pared to rob her of her wealth; he had to tell her that he intended to marry her without loving her, or else that he loved her without intending to marry her; and he had also to bespeak from her not only his own pardon, but also that of his sister, and induce Mrs. Bold to protest in her future communion with Charlotte that an offer had been duly made to her and duly rejected.

Bertie Stanhope was not prone to be very diffident of his own conversational powers, but it did seem to him that he was about to tax them almost too far. He hardly knew where to begin, and he hardly knew where he should end.

By this time Eleanor was again walking on slowly by his side, not taking his arm as she had heretofore done, but listening very intently for whatever Bertie might have to say to her.

"I wish to be guided by you," said he; "and, indeed, in this matter, there is no one else who can set me right."

"Oh, that must be nonsense," said she.

"Well, listen to me now, Mrs. Bold; and if you can help it, pray don't be angry with me."

"Angry!" said she.

"Oh, indeed you will have cause to be so. You know how very much attached to you my sister Charlotte is."

Eleanor acknowledged that she did.

"Indeed she is; I never knew her to love any one so warmly on so short an acquaintance. You know also how well she loves me?"

Eleanor now made no answer, but she felt the blood tingle in her cheek as she gathered from what he said the probable result of this double-barrelled love on the part of Miss Stanhope.

"I am her only brother, Mrs. Bold, and it is not to be wondered at that she should love me. But you do not yet know Charlotte,—you do not know how entirely the well-being of our family hangs on her. Without her to manage for us, I do not know how we should get on from day to day. You cannot yet have observed all this."

Eleanor had indeed observed a good deal of this; she did not however, now say so, but allowed him to proceed with his story.

"You cannot therefore be surprised that Charlotte should be most anxious to do the best for us all."

Eleanor said that she was not at all surprised.

"And she has had a very difficult game to play, Mrs. Bold—a very difficult game. Poor Madeline's unfortunate marriage and terrible accident, my mother's ill health, my father's absence from England, and last, and worst perhaps, my own roving, idle spirit have almost been too much for her. You cannot wonder if among all her cares one of the foremost is to see me settled in the world."

Eleanor on this occasion expressed no acquiescence. She certainly supposed that a formal offer was to be made, and could not but think that so singular an exordium was never before made by a gentleman in a similar position. Mr. Slope had annoyed her by the excess of his ardour. It was quite clear that no such danger was to be feared from Mr. Stanhope. Prudential motives alone actuated him. Not only was he about to make love because his sister told him, but he also took the precaution of explaining all this before he began. 'Twas thus, we may presume, that the matter presented itself to Mrs. Bold.

When he had got so far, Bertie began poking the gravel with a little cane which he carried. He still kept moving on, but very slowly, and his companion moved slowly by his side, not inclined to assist him in the task the performance of which appeared to be difficult to him.

"Knowing how fond she is of yourself, Mrs. Bold, cannot you imagine what scheme should have occurred to her?"

"I can imagine no better scheme, Mr. Stanhope, than the one I proposed to you just now."

"No," said he, somewhat lack-a-daisically; "I suppose that would be the best; but Charlotte thinks another plan might be joined with it.—She wants me to marry you."

A thousand remembrances flashed across Eleanor's mind all in a moment,—how Charlotte had talked about and praised her brother, how she had continually contrived to throw the two of them together, how she had encouraged all manner of little intimacies, how she had with singular cordiality persisted in treating Eleanor as one of the family. All this had been done to secure her comfortable income for the benefit of one of the family!

Such a feeling as this is very bitter when it first impresses itself on a young mind. To the old such plots and plans, such matured schemes for obtaining the goods of this world without the trouble of earning them, such long-headed attempts to convert "tuum" into "meum," are the ways of life to which they are accustomed. 'Tis thus that many live, and it therefore behoves all those who are well to do in the world to be on their guard against those who are not. With them it is the success that disgusts, not the attempt. But Eleanor had not yet learnt to look on her money as a source of danger; she had not begun to regard herself as fair game to be hunted down by hungry gentlemen. She had enjoyed the society of the Stanhopes, she had greatly liked the cordiality of Charlotte, and had been happy in her new friends. Now she saw the cause of all this kindness, and her mind was opened to a new phase of human life.

"Miss Stanhope," said she, haughtily, "has been contriving for me a great deal of honour, but she might have saved herself the trouble. I am not sufficiently ambitious."

"Pray don't be angry with her, Mrs. Bold," said he, "or with me either."

"Certainly not with you, Mr. Stanhope," said she, with considerable sarcasm in her tone. "Certainly not with you."

"No,—nor with her," said he, imploringly.

"And why, may I ask you, Mr. Stanhope, have you told me this singular story? For I may presume I may judge by your manner of telling it, that—that—that you and your sister are not exactly of one mind on the subject."

"No, we are not."

"And if so," said Mrs. Bold, who was now really angry with the unnecessary insult which she thought had been offered to her, "and if so, why has it been worth your while to tell me all this?"

"I did once think, Mrs. Bold,—that you—that you——"

The widow now again became entirely impassive, and would not lend the slightest assistance to her companion.

"I did once think that you perhaps might,—might have been taught to regard me as more than a friend."

"Never!" said Mrs. Bold, "never. If I have ever allowed myself to do anything to encourage such an idea, I have been very much to blame,—very much to blame indeed."

"You never have," said Bertie, who really had a good-natured anxiety to make what he said as little unpleasant as possible. "You never have, and I have seen for some time that I had no chance; but my sister's hopes ran higher. I have not mistaken you, Mrs. Bold, though perhaps she has."

"Then why have you said all this to me?"

"Because I must not anger her."

"And will not this anger her? Upon my word, Mr. Stanhope, I do not understand the policy of your family. Oh, how I wish I was at home!" And as she expressed the wish, she could restrain herself no longer, but burst out into a flood of tears.

Poor Bertie was greatly moved. "You shall have the carriage to yourself going home," said he; "at least you and my father. As for me I can walk, or for the matter of that it does not much signify what I do." He perfectly understood that part of Eleanor's grief arose from the apparent necessity of going back to Barchester in the carriage with her second suitor.   •

This somewhat mollified her. "Oh, Mr. Stanhope," said she, "why should you have made me so miserable? What will you have gained by telling me all this?"

He had not even yet explained to her the most difficult part of his proposition; he had not told her that she was to be a party to his little deception which he intended to play off upon his sister. This suggestion had still to be made, and as it was absolutely necessary, he proceeded to make it.

We need not follow him through the whole of his statement. At last, and not without considerable difficulty, he made Eleanor understand why he had let her into his confidence, seeing that he no longer intended her the honour of a formal offer. At last he made her comprehend the part which she was destined to play in this little family comedy.

But when she did understand it, she was only more angry with him than ever: more angry, not only with him, but with Charlotte also. Her fair name was to be bandied about between them in different senses, and each sense false. She was to be played off by the sister against the father; and then by the brother against the sister. Her dear friend Charlotte, with all her agreeable sympathy and affection, was striving to sacrifice her for the Stanhope family welfare; and Bertie, who, as he now proclaimed himself, was over head and ears in debt, completed the compliment of owning that he did not care to have his debts paid at so great a sacrifice of himself. Then she was asked to conspire together with this unwilling suitor, for the sake of making the family believe that he had in obedience to their commands done his best to throw himself thus away!

She lifted up her face when he had finished, and looking at him with much dignity, even through her tears, she said—

"I regret to say it, Mr. Stanhope; but after what has passed, I believe that all intercourse between your family and myself had better cease."

"Well, perhaps it had," said Bertie naïvely; "perhaps that will be better, at any rate for a time; and then Charlotte will think you are offended at what I have done."

"And now I will go back to the house, if you please," said Eleanor. "I can find my way by myself, Mr. Stanhope: after what has passed," she added, "I would rather go alone."

"But I must find the carriage for you, Mrs. Bold, and I must tell my father that you will return with him alone, and I must make some excuse to him for not going with you; and I must bid the servant put you down at your own house, for I suppose you will not now choose to see them again in the close."

There was a truth about this, and a perspicuity in making arrangements for lessening her immediate embarrassment, which had some effect in softening Eleanor's anger. So she suffered herself to walk by his side over the now deserted lawn, till they came to the drawing-room window. There was something about Bertie Stanhope which gave him, in the estimation of every one, a different standing from that which any other man would occupy under similar circumstances. Angry as Eleanor was, and great as was her cause for anger, she was not half as angry with him as she would have been with any one else. He was apparently so simple, so good-natured, so unaffected and easy to talk to, that she had already half-forgiven him before he was at the drawing-room window. When they arrived there, Dr. Stanhope was sitting nearly alone with Mr. and Miss Thorne; one or two other unfortunates were there, who from one cause or another were still delayed in getting away; but they were every moment getting fewer in number.

As soon as he had handed Eleanor over to his father, Bertie started off to the front gate, in search of the carriage, and there waited leaning patiently against the front wall, and comfortably smoking a cigar, till it came up. When he returned to the room Dr. Stanhope and Eleanor were alone with their hosts.

"At last, Miss Thorne," said he cheerily, "I have come to relieve you. Mrs. Bold and my father are the last roses of the very delightful summer you have given us, and desirable as Mrs. Bold's society always is, now at least you must be glad to see the last flowers plucked from the tree."

Miss Thorne declared that she was delighted to have Mrs. Bold and Dr. Stanhope still with her; and Mr. Thorne would have said the same, had he not been checked by a yawn, which he could not suppress.

"Father, will you give your arm to Mrs. Bold?" said Bertie: and so the last adieux were made, and the prebendary led out Mrs. Bold, followed by his son.

"I shall be home soon after you," said he, as the two got into the carriage.

"Are you not coming in the carriage?" said the father.

"No, no; I have some one to see on the road, and shall walk. John, mind you drive to Mrs. Bold's house first."

Eleanor looking out of the window, saw him with his hat in his hand, bowing to her with his usual gay smile, as though nothing had happened to mar the tranquillity of the day. It was many a long year before she saw him again. Dr. Stanhope hardly spoke to her on her way home; and she was safely deposited by John at her own hall-door, before the carriage drove into the close.

And thus our heroine played the last act of that day's melodrame.

XLIII

Mr. and Mrs. Quiverful Are Made Happy;
Mr. Slope Is Encouraged by the Press

Before she started for Ullathorne, Mrs. Proudie, careful soul, caused two letters to be written, one by herself and one by her lord, to the inhabitants of Puddingdale vicarage, which made happy the hearth of those within it.

As soon as the departure of the horses left the bishop's stable-groom free for other services, that humble denizen of the diocese started on the bishop's own pony with the two despatches. We have had so many letters lately that we will spare ourselves these. That from the bishop was simply a request that Mr. Quiverful would wait upon his lordship the next morning at 11 A.M.; and that from the lady was as simply a request that Mrs. Quiverful would do the same by her, though it was couched in somewhat longer and more grandiloquent phraseology.

It had become a point of conscience with Mrs. Proudie to urge the settlement of this great hospital question. She was resolved that Mr. Quiverful should have it. She was resolved that there should be no more doubt or delay, no more refusals and resignations, no more secret negotiations carried on by Mr. Slope on his own account in opposition to her behests.

"Bishop," she said, immediately after breakfast, on the morning of that eventful day, "have you signed the appointment yet?"

"No, my dear, not yet; it is not exactly signed as yet."

"Then do it," said the lady.

The bishop did it; and a very pleasant day indeed he spent at Ullathorne. And when he got home he had a glass of hot negus in his wife's sitting-room, and read the last number of the *Little Dorrit* of the day with great inward satisfaction. Oh, husbands, oh, my marital friends, what great comfort is there to be derived from a wife well obeyed!

Much perturbation and flutter, high expectation and renewed hopes, were occasioned at Puddingdale, by the receipt of these episcopal despatches. Mrs. Quiverful, whose careful ear caught the sound of the pony's feet as he trotted up to the vicarage kitchen door, brought them in hurriedly to her husband. She was at the moment concocting the Irish stew destined to satisfy the noonday wants of fourteen young birds, let alone the parent couple. She had taken the letters from the man's hands between the folds of her capacious apron, so as to save them from the contamination of the stew, and in this guise she brought them to her husband's desk.

They at once divided the spoil, each taking that addressed to the other. "Quiverful," said she with impressive voice, "you are to be at the palace at eleven tomorrow."

"And so are you, my dear," said he, almost gasping with the importance of the tidings: and then they exchanged letters.

"She'd never have sent for me again," said the lady, "if it wasn't all right!"

"Oh! my dear, don't be too certain," said the gentleman. "Only think if it should be wrong."

"She'd never have sent for me, Q., if it wasn't all right," again argued the lady. "She's stiff and hard and proud as piecrust, but I think she's right at bottom." Such was Mrs. Quiverful's verdict about Mrs. Proudie, to which in after times she always adhered. People when they get their income doubled usually think that those through whose instrumentality this little ceremony is performed are right at bottom.

"Oh Letty!" said Mr. Quiverful, rising from his well-worn seat.

"Oh Q.!" said Mrs. Quiverful: and then the two, unmindful of the kitchen apron, the greasy fingers, and the adherent Irish stew, threw themselves warmly into each other's arms.

"For heaven's sake don't let any one cajole you out of it again," said his wife.

"Let me alone for that," said the husband, with a look of almost fierce determination, pressing his fist as he spoke rigidly on his desk, as though he had Mr. Slope's head below his knuckles, and meant to keep it there.

"I wonder how soon it will be," said she.

"I wonder whether it will be at all," said he, still doubtful.

"Well, I won't say too much," said the lady. "The cup has

slipped twice before, and it may fall altogether this time; but I'll not believe it. He'll give you the appointment to-morrow. You'll find he will.''

"Heaven send he may," said Mr. Quiverful, solemnly. And who that considers the weight of the burden on this man's back, will say that the prayer was an improper one? There were fourteen of them—fourteen of them living—as Mrs. Quiverful had so powerfully urged in the presence of the bishop's wife. As long as promotion cometh from any human source, whether north or south, east or west, will not such a claim as this hold good, in spite of all our examination tests, *detur digniori*'s and optimist tendencies? It is fervently to be hoped that it may. Till we can become divine we must be content to be human, lest in our hurry for a change we sink to something lower.

And then the pair sitting down lovingly together, talked over all their difficulties, as they so often did, and all their hopes, as they so seldom were enabled to do.

"You had better call on that man, Q., as you come away from the palace," said Mrs. Quiverful, pointing to an angry call for money from the Barchester draper, which the post-man had left at the vicarage that morning. Cormorant that he was, unjust, hungry cormorant! When rumour first got abroad that the Quiverfuls were to go to the hospital, this fellow with fawning eagerness had pressed his goods upon the wants of the poor clergyman. He had done so, feeling that he should be paid from the hospital funds, and flattering himself that a man with fourteen children, and money wherewithal to clothe them, could not but be an excellent customer. As soon as the second rumour reached him, he applied for his money angrily.

And "the fourteen"—or such of them as were old enough to hope and discuss their hopes, talked over their golden future. The tall-grown girls whispered to each other of possible Barchester parties, of possible allowances for dress, of a possible piano— the one they had in the vicarage was so weather-beaten with the storms of years and children as to be no longer worthy of the name—of the pretty garden, and the pretty house. 'Twas of such things it most behoved them to whisper.

And the younger fry, they did not content themselves with whispers, but shouted to each other of their new play-ground beneath our dear ex-warden's well-loved elms, of their future own gardens, of marbles to be produced in the wished-for-city, and of the rumour which had reached them of a Barchester school.

'Twas in vain that their cautious mother tried to instil into their breasts the very feeling she had striven to banish from that of their father; 'twas in vain that she repeated to the girls that "there's many a slip 'twixt the cup and the lip"; 'twas in vain she attempted to make the children believe that they were to live at Puddingdale all their lives. Hopes mounted high and would not have themselves quelled. The neighbouring farmers heard the news, and came in to congratulate them. 'Twas Mrs. Quiverful herself who had kindled the fire, and in the first outbreak of her renewed expectations she did it so thoroughly, that it was quite past her power to put it out again.

Poor matron! good honest matron! doing thy duty in the state to which thou hast been called, heartily if not contentedly; let the fire burn on;—on this occasion the flames will not scorch; they shall warm thee and thine. 'Tis ordained that that husband of thine, that Q. of thy bosom, shall reign supreme for years to come over the bedesmen of Hiram's hospital.

And the last in all Barchester to mar their hopes, had he heard and seen all that passed at Puddingdale that day, would have been Mr. Harding. What wants had he to set in opposition to those of such a regiment of young ravens? There are fourteen of them living! with him at any rate, let us say, that that argument would have been sufficient for the appointment of Mr. Quiverful.

In the morning, Q. and his wife kept their appointments with that punctuality which bespeaks an expectant mind. The friendly farmer's gig was borrowed, and in that they went, discussing many things by the way. They had instructed the household to expect them back by one, and injunctions were given to the eldest pledge to have ready by that accustomed hour the remainder of the huge stew which the provident mother had prepared on the previous day. The hands of the kitchen clock came round to two, three, four, before the farmer's gig-wheels were again heard at the vicarage gate. With what palpitating hearts were the returning wanderers greeted!

"I suppose, children, you all thought we were never coming back any more?" said the mother, as she slowly let down her solid foot till it rested on the step of the gig. "Well, such a day as we've had!" and then leaning heavily on a big boy's shoulder, she stepped once more on terra firma.

There was no need for more than the tone of her voice to tell them that all was right. The Irish stew might burn itself to cinders now.

Then there was such kissing and hugging, such crying and laughing. Mr. Quiverful could not sit still at all, but kept walking from room to room, then out into the garden, then down the avenue into the road, and then back again to his wife. She, however, lost no time so idly.

"We must go to work at once, girls; and that in earnest. Mrs. Proudie expects us to be in the hospital house on the 15th of October."

Had Mrs. Proudie expressed a wish that they should all be there on the next morning, the girls would have had nothing to say against it.

"And when will the pay begin?" asked the eldest boy.

"To-day, my dear," said the gratified mother.

"Oh,—that is jolly," said the boy.

"Mrs. Proudie insisted on our going down to the house," continued the mother; "and when there I thought I might save a journey by measuring some of the rooms and windows; so I got a knot of tape from Bobbins. Bobbins is as civil as you please, now."

"I wouldn't thank him," said Letty the younger.

"Oh, it's the way of the world, my dear. They all do just the same. You might just as well be angry with the turkey cock for gobbling at you. It's the bird's nature." And as she enunciated to her bairns the upshot of her practical experience, she pulled from her pocket the portions of tape which showed the length and breadth of the various rooms at the hospital house.

And so we will leave her happy in her toils.

The Quiverfuls had hardly left the palace, and Mrs. Proudie was still holding forth on the matter to her husband, when another visitor was announced in the person of Dr. Gwynne. The master of Lazarus had asked for the bishop, and not for Mrs. Proudie, and therefore, when he was shown into the study, he was surprised rather than rejoiced to find the lady there.

But we must go back a little, and it shall be but a little, for a difficulty begins to make itself manifest in the necessity of disposing of all our friends in the small remainder of this one volume. Oh, that Mr. Longman would allow me a fourth! It should transcend the other three as the seventh heaven transcends all the lower stages of celestial bliss.

Going home in the carriage that evening from Ullathorne, Dr. Gwynne had not without difficulty brought round his friend the archdeacon to a line of tactics much less bellicose than that which his own taste would have preferred. "It will be unseemly in us to show ourselves in a bad humour: and moreover we have no power in this matter, and it will therefore be bad policy to act as though we had.'' 'Twas thus the master of Lazarus argued. "If," he continued, "the bishop be determined to appoint another to the hospital, threats will not prevent him, and threats should not be lightly used by an archdeacon to his bishop. If he will place a stranger in the hospital, we can only leave him to the indignation of others. It is probable that such a step may not eventually injure your father-in-law. I will see the bishop, if you will allow me,—alone." At this the archdeacon winced visibly; "yes, alone; for so I shall be calmer: and then I shall at any rate learn what he does mean to do in the matter."

The archdeacon puffed and blew, put up the carriage window and then put it down again, argued the matter up to his own gate, and at last gave way. Everybody was against him, his own wife, Mr. Harding, and Dr. Gwynne.

"Pray keep him out of hot water, Dr. Gwynne," Mrs. Grantly had said to her guest. "My dearest madam, I'll do my best," the courteous master had replied. 'Twas thus he did it; and earned for himself the gratitude of Mrs. Grantly.

And now we may return to the bishop's study.

Dr. Gwynne had certainly not foreseen the difficulty which here presented itself. He,—together with all the clerical world of England,—had heard it rumoured about that Mrs. Proudie did not confine herself to her wardrobes, still-rooms, and laundries; but yet it had never occurred to him that if he called on a bishop at one o'clock in the day, he could by any possibility find him closeted with his wife; or that if he did so, the wife would remain longer than necessary to make her curtsey. It appeared, however, as though in the present case Mrs. Proudie had no idea of retreating.

The bishop had been very much pleased with Dr. Gwynne on the preceding day, and of course thought that Dr. Gwynne had been as much pleased with him. He attributed the visit solely to compliment, and thought it an extremely gracious and proper thing for the master of Lazarus to drive over from Plumstead specially to call at the palace so soon after his arrival in the country. The fact that they were not on the same side either in politics or doctrines made the compliment the greater. The bishop, therefore, was all smiles. And Mrs. Proudie, who liked people with good handles to their names was also very well disposed to welcome the master of Lazarus.

"We had a charming party at Ullathorne, Master, had we not?" said she. "I hope Mrs. Grantly got home without fatigue."

Dr. Gwynne said that they had all been a little tired, but were none the worse this morning.

"An excellent person, Miss Thorne," suggested the bishop.

"And an exemplary Christian, I am told," said Mrs. Proudie.

Dr. Gwynne declared that he was very glad to hear it.

"I have not seen her Sabbath-day schools yet," continued the lady, "but I shall make a point of doing so before long."

Dr. Gwynne merely bowed at this intimation. He had heard something of Mrs. Proudie and her Sunday schools, both from Dr. Grantly and Mr. Harding.

"By the bye, Master," continued the lady, "I wonder whether Mrs. Grantly would like me to drive over and inspect her Sabbath-day school. I hear that it is most excellently kept."

Dr. Gwynne really could not say. He had no doubt Mrs. Grantly would be most happy to see Mrs. Proudie any day Mrs. Proudie would do her the honour of calling: that was, of course, if Mrs. Grantly should happen to be at home.

A slight cloud darkened the lady's brow. She saw that her offer was not taken in good part. This generation of unregenerated vipers was still perverse, stiffnecked, and hardened in their iniquity. "The archdeacon, I know," said she, "sets his face against these institutions."

At this Dr. Gwynne laughed slightly. It was but a smile. Had he given his cap for it he could not have helped it.

Mrs. Proudie frowned again. " 'Suffer little children, and forbid them not,' " said she. "Are we not to remember that, Dr. Gwynne? 'Take heed that ye despise not one of these little ones.' " Are we not to remember that, Dr. Gwynne?" And at each of these questions she raised at him her menacing forefinger.

"Certainly, madam, certainly," said the master, "and so does the archdeacon, I am sure, on week days as well as on Sundays."

"On week days you can't take heed not to despise them," said Mrs. Proudie, "because then they are out in the fields. On week days they belong to their parents, but on Sundays they ought to belong to the clergyman." And the finger was again raised.

The master began to understand and to share the intense disgust which the archdeacon always expressed when Mrs. Proudie's name was mentioned. What was he to do with such a woman as this? To take his hat and go would have been his natural resource; but then he did not wish to be foiled in his object.

"My lord," said he, "I wanted to ask you a question on business, if you could spare me one moment's leisure. I know I must apologise for so disturbing you; but in truth I will not detain you five minutes."

"Certainly, Master, certainly," said the bishop, "my time is quite yours,—pray make no apology, pray make no apology."

"You have a great deal to do just at the present moment, bishop. Do not forget how extremely busy you are at present," said Mrs. Proudie, whose spirit was now up; for she was angry with her visitor.

"I will not delay his lordship much above a minute," said the master of Lazarus, rising from his chair, and expecting that Mrs. Proudie would now go, or else that the bishop would lead the way into another room.

But neither event seemed likely to occur, and Dr. Gwynne stood for a moment silent in the middle of the room.

"Perhaps it's about Hiram's hospital?" suggested Mrs. Proudie.

Dr. Gwynne, lost in astonishment, and not knowing what else on earth to do, confessed that his business with the bishop was connected with Hiram's hospital.

"His lordship has finally conferred the appointment on Mr. Quiverful this morning," said the lady.

Dr. Gwynne made a simple reference to the bishop, and finding that the lady's statement was formally confirmed, he took his leave. "That comes of the reform bill," he said to himself as he walked down the bishop's avenue. "Well, at any rate the Greek play bishops were not so bad as that."

It has been said that Mr. Slope, as he started for Ullathorne, received a despatch from his friend, Mr. Towers, which had the effect of putting him in that high good-humour which subsequent events somewhat untowardly damped. It ran as follows. Its shortness will be its sufficient apology.

> My dear sir,—I wish you every success. I don't know that I can help you, but if I can, I will.
>   Yours ever,
>   T.T.
>   30/9/185—

There was more in this than in all Sir Nicholas Fitzwhiggin's flummery; more than in all the bishop's promises, even had they been ever so sincere; more than in any archbishop's good word, even had it been possible to obtain it. Tom Towers would do for him what he could.

Mr. Slope had from his youth upwards been a firm believer in the public press. He had dabbled in it himself ever since he had taken his degree, and regarded it as the great arranger and distributor of all future British terrestrial affairs whatever. He had not yet arrived at the age, an age which sooner or later comes to most of us, which dissipates the golden dreams of youth. He delighted in the idea of wresting power from the hands of his country's magnates, and placing it in a custody which was at any rate nearer to his own reach. Sixty thousand broad sheets dispersing themselves daily among his reading fellow-citizens, formed in his eyes a better depôt for supremacy than a throne at Windsor, a cabinet in Downing Street, or even an assembly at Westminster. And on this subject we must not quarrel with Mr. Slope, for the feeling is too general to be met with disrespect.

Tom Towers was as good, if not better than his promise. On the following morning the *Jupiter,* spouting forth public opinion with sixty thousand loud clarions, did proclaim to the world that Mr. Slope was the fitting man for the vacant post. It was pleasant for Mr. Slope to read the following lines in the Barchester news-room, which he did within thirty minutes after the morning train from London had reached the city.

"It is just now five years since we called the attention of our readers to the quiet city of Barchester. From that day to this, we have in no way meddled with the affairs of that happy ecclesiastical community. Since then, an old bishop has died there, and a young bishop has been installed; but we believe we did not do more than give some customary record of the interesting event. Nor are we now about to meddle very deeply in the affairs of the diocese. If any of the chapter feel a qualm of conscience on reading thus far, let it be quieted. Above all, let the mind of the new bishop be at rest. We are now not armed for war, but approach the reverend towers of the old cathedral with an olive-branch in our hands.

"It will be remembered that at the time alluded to, now five years past, we had occasion to remark on the state of a charity in Barchester called Hiram's hospital. We thought that it was maladministered, and that the very estimable and reverend gentleman who held the office of warden was somewhat too highly paid for duties which were somewhat too easily performed. This gentleman—and we say it in all sincerity and with no touch of sarcasm—had never looked on the matter in this light before. We do not wish to take praise to ourselves whether praise be due to us or not. But the consequence of our remark was, that the warden did look into the matter, and finding on so doing that he himself could come to no other opinion than that expressed by us, he very creditably threw up the appointment. The then bishop as creditably declined to fill the vacancy till the affair was put on a better footing. Parliament then took it up; and we have now the satisfaction of informing our readers that Hiram's hospital will be immediately re-opened under new auspices. Heretofore, provision was made for the maintenance of twelve old men. This will now be extended to the fair sex, and twelve elderly women, if any such can be found in Barchester, will be added to the establishment. There will be a matron; there will, it is hoped, be schools attached for the poorest of the children of the poor, and there will be a steward. The warden, for there will still be a warden, will receive an income more in keeping with the extent of the charity than that heretofore paid. The stipend we believe will be £450. We may add that the excellent house which the former warden inhabited will still be attached to the situation.

"Barchester hospital cannot perhaps boast a world-wide reputation; but as we adverted to its state of decadence, we think it right also to advert to its renaissance. May it go on and prosper. Whether the salutary reform which has been introduced within its walls has been carried as far as could have been desired, may be doubtful. The important question of the school appears to be somewhat left to the discretion of the new warden. This might have been made the most important part of the establishment, and the new warden, whom we trust we shall not offend by the freedom of our remarks, might have been selected with some view to his fitness as schoolmaster. But we will not now look a gift horse in the mouth. May the hospital go on and prosper! The situation of warden has of course been offered to the gentleman who so honourably vacated it five years since; but we are given to understand that he has declined it. Whether the ladies who have been introduced, be in his estimation too much for his powers of control, whether it be that the diminished income does not offer to him sufficient temptation to resume his old place, or that he has in the meantime assumed other clerical duties, we do not know. We are, however, informed that he has refused the offer, and that the situation has been accepted by Mr. Quiverful, the vicar of Puddingdale.

"So much we think is due to Hiram redivivus. But while

we are on the subject of Barchester, we will venture with all respectful humility to express our opinion on another matter, connected with the ecclesiastical polity of that ancient city. Dr. Trefoil, the dean, died yesterday. A short record of his death, giving his age, and the various pieces of preferment which he has at different times held, will be found in another column of this paper. The only fault we knew in him was his age, and as that is a crime of which we all hope to be guilty, we will not bear heavily on it. May he rest in peace! But though the great age of an expiring dean cannot be made matter of reproach, we are not inclined to look on such a fault as at all pardonable in a dean just brought to the birth. We do hope that the days of sexagenarian appointments are past. If we want deans, we must want them for some purpose. That purpose will necessarily be better fulfilled by a man of forty than by a man of sixty. If we are to pay deans at all, we are to pay them for some sort of work. That work, be it what it may, will be best performed by a workman in the prime of life. Dr. Trefoil, we see, was eighty when he died. As we have as yet completed no plan for pensioning superannuated clergymen, we do not wish to get rid of any existing deans of that age. But we prefer having as few such as possible. If a man of seventy be now appointed, we beg to point out to Lord —— that he will be past all use in a year or two, if indeed he be not so at the present moment. His lordship will allow us to remind him that all men are not evergreens like himself.

"We hear that Mr. Slope's name has been mentioned for this preferment. Mr. Slope is at present chaplain to the bishop. A better man could hardly be selected. He is a man of talent, young, active, and conversant with the affairs of the cathedral; he is moreover, we conscientiously believe, a truly pious clergyman. We know that his services in the city of Barchester have been highly appreciated. He is an eloquent preacher and a ripe scholar. Such a selection as this would go far to raise the confidence of the public in the present administration of church patronage, and would teach men to believe that from henceforth the establishment of our church will not afford easy couches to worn-out clerical voluptuaries."

Standing at a reading-desk in the Barchester news-room, Mr. Slope digested this article with considerable satisfaction. What was therein said as to the hospital was now comparatively matter of indifference to him. He was certainly glad that he had not succeeded in restoring to the place the father of that virago who had so audaciously outraged all decency in his person; and was so far satisfied. But Mrs. Proudie's nominee was appointed, and he was so far dissatisfied. His mind, however, was now soaring above Mrs. Bold or Mrs. Proudie. He was sufficiently conversant with the tactics of the *Jupiter* to know that the pith of the article would lie in the last paragraph. The place of honour was given to him, and it was indeed as honourable as even he could have wished. He was very grateful to his friend Mr. Towers, and with full heart looked forward to the day when he might entertain him in princely style at his own full-spread board in the deanery dining-room.

It had been well for Mr. Slope that Dr. Trefoil had died in the autumn. Those caterers for our morning repast, the staff of the *Jupiter,* had been sorely put to it for the last month to find a sufficiency of proper pabulum. Just then there was no talk of a new American president. No wonderful tragedies had occurred on railway trains in Georgia, or elsewhere. There was a dearth of broken banks, and a dead dean with the necessity for a live one was a godsend. Had Dr. Trefoil died in June, Mr. Towers would probably not have known so much about the piety of Mr. Slope.

And here we will leave Mr. Slope for a while in his triumph; explaining, however, that his feelings were not altogether of a triumphant nature. His rejection by the widow, or rather the method of his rejection, galled him terribly. For days to come he positively felt the sting upon his cheek, whenever he thought of what had been done to him. He could not refrain from calling her by harsh names, speaking to himself as he walked through the streets of Barchester. When he said his prayers, he could not bring himself to forgive her. When he strove to do so, his mind recoiled from the attempt, and in lieu of forgiving ran off in a double spirit of vindictiveness, dwelling on the extent of the injury he had received. And so his prayers dropped senseless from his lips.

And then the signora; what would he not have given to be able to hate her also? As it was, he worshipped the very sofa on which she was ever lying. And thus it was not all rose colour with Mr. Slope, although his hopes ran high.

XLIV

Mrs. Bold at Home

Poor Mrs. Bold, when she got home from Ullathorne on the evening of Miss Thorne's party, was very unhappy, and moreover, very tired. Nothing fatigues the body so much as weariness of spirit, and Eleanor's spirit was indeed weary.

Dr. Stanhope had civilly but not very cordially asked her in to tea, and her manner of refusal convinced the worthy doctor that he need not repeat the invitation. He had not exactly made himself a party to the intrigue which was to convert the late Mr. Bold's patrimoney into an income for his hopeful son, but he had been well aware what was going on. And he was well aware also, when he perceived that Bertie declined accompanying them home in the carriage, that the affair had gone off.

Eleanor was very much afraid that Charlotte would have darted out upon her, as the prebendary got out at his own door, but Bertie had thoughtfully saved her from this, by causing the carriage to go round by her own house. This also Dr. Stanhope understood, and allowed to pass by without remark.

When she got home, she found Mary Bold in the drawing-room with the child in her lap. She rushed forward, and, throwing herself on her knees, kissed the little fellow till she almost frightened him.

"Oh, Mary, I am so glad you did not go. It was an odious party."

Now the question of Mary's going had been one greatly mooted between them. Mrs. Bold, when invited, had been the guest of the Grantlys, and Miss Thorne, who had chiefly known Eleanor at the hospital or at Plumstead rectory, had forgotten all about Mary Bold. Her sister-in-law had implored her to go under her wing, and had offered to write to Miss Thorne, or to call on her. But Miss Bold had declined. In fact, Mr. Bold had not been very popular with such people as the Thornes, and his sister would not go among them unless she were specially asked to do so.

"Well then," said Mary, cheerfully, "I have the less to regret."

"You have nothing to regret; but oh! Mary, I have—so much—so much";—and then she began kissing her boy, whom her caresses had aroused from his slumbers. When she raised her head, Mary saw that the tears were running down her cheeks.

"Good heavens, Eleanor, what is the matter? what has happened to you?—Eleanor—dearest Eleanor—what is the matter?" and Mary got up with the boy still in her arms.

"Give him to me—give him to me," said the young mother. "Give him to me, Mary," and she almost tore the child out of her sister's arms. The poor little fellow murmured somewhat at the disturbance, but nevertheless nestled himself close into his mother's bosom.

"Here, Mary, take the cloak from me. My own, own darling, darling, darling jewel. You are not false to me. Everybody else is false; everybody else is cruel. Mamma will care for nobody, nobody, nobody, but her own, own, own little man"; and she again kissed and pressed the baby, and cried till the tears ran down over the child's face.

"Who has been cruel to you, Eleanor?" said Mary. "I hope I have not."

Now, in this matter, Eleanor had great cause for mental uneasiness. She could not certainly accuse her loving sister-in-law of cruelty; but she had to do that which was more galling; she had to accuse herself of imprudence against which her sister-in-law had warned her. Miss Bold had never encouraged Eleanor's acquaintance with Mr. Slope, and she had positively discouraged the friendship of the Stanhopes as far as her usual gentle mode of speaking had permitted. Eleanor had only laughed at her, however, when she said that she disapproved of married women who lived apart from their husbands, and suggested that Charlotte Stanhope never went to church. Now, however, Eleanor must either hold her tongue, which was quite impossible, or confess herself to have been utterly wrong, which was nearly equally so. So she staved off the evil day by more tears, and consoled herself by inducing little Johnny to rouse himself sufficiently to return her caresses.

"He is a darling—as true as gold. What would mamma do

without him? Mamma would lie down and die if she had not her own Johnny Bold to give her comfort." This and much more she said of the same kind, and for a time made no other answer to Mary's inquiries.

This kind of consolation from the world's deceit is very common.

Mothers obtain it from their children, and men from their dogs. Some men even do so from their walking-sticks, which is just as rational. How is it that we can take joy to ourselves in that we are not deceived by those who have not attained the art to deceive us? In a true man, if such can be found, or a true woman, much consolation may indeed be taken.

In the caresses of her child, however, Eleanor did receive consolation; and may ill befall the man who would begrudge it to her. The evil day, however, was only postponed. She had to tell her disagreeable tale to Mary, and she had also to tell it to her father. Must it not, indeed, be told to the whole circle of her acquaintance before she could be made to stand all right with them? At the present moment there was no one to whom she could turn for comfort. She hated Mr. Slope; that was a matter of course, in that feeling she revelled. She hated and despised the Stanhopes; but that feeling distressed her greatly. She had, as it were, separated herself from her old friends to throw herself into the arms of this family; and then how had they intended to use her? She could hardly reconcile herself to her own father, who had believed ill of her. Mary Bold had turned Mentor. That she could have forgiven had the Mentor turned out to be in the wrong; but Mentors in the right are not to be pardoned. She could not hate the archdeacon; and now she hated him worse than ever, for she must in some sort humble herself before him. She hated her sister, for she was part and parcel of the archdeacon. And she would have hated Mr. Arabin if she could. He had pretended to regard her, and yet before her face he had hung over that Italian woman as though there had been no beauty in the world but hers—no other woman worth a moment's attention. And Mr. Arabin would have to learn all this about Mr. Slope! She told herself that she hated him, and she knew that she was lying to herself as she did so. She had no consolation but her baby, and of that she made the most. Mary, though she could not surmise what it was that had so violently affected her sister-in-law, saw at once that her grief was too great to be kept under control, and waited patiently till the child should be in his cradle.

"You'll have some tea, Eleanor," she said.

"Oh, I don't care," said she; though in fact she must have been very hungry, for she had eaten nothing at Ullathorne.

Mary quietly made the tea, and buttered the bread, laid aside the cloak, and made things look comfortable.

"He's fast asleep," said she, "you're very tired; let me take him up to bed."

But Eleanor would not let her sister touch him. She looked wistfully at her baby's eyes, saw that they were lost in the deepest slumber, and then made a sort of couch for him on the sofa. She was determined that nothing should prevail upon her to let him out of her sight that night.

"Come, Nelly," said Mary, "don't be cross with me. I at least have done nothing to offend you."

"I an't cross," said Eleanor.

"Are you angry then? Surely you can't be angry with me."

"No, I an't angry; at least not with you."

"If you are not, drink the tea I have made for you. I am sure you must want it."

Eleanor did drink it, and allowed herself to be persuaded. She ate and drank, and as the inner woman was recruited she felt a little more charitable towards the world at large. At last she found words to begin her story, and before she went to bed, she had made a clean breast of it and told everything—everything, that is, as to the lovers she had rejected: of Mr. Arabin she said not a word.

"I know I was wrong," said she, speaking of the blow she had given to Mr. Slope; "but I didn't know what he might do, and I had to protect myself."

"He richly deserved it," said Mary.

"Deserved it!" said Eleanor, whose mind as regarded Mr. Slope was almost bloodthirsty. "Had I stabbed him with a dagger, he would have deserved it. But what will they say about it at Plumstead?"

"I don't think I should tell them," said Mary. Eleanor began to think that she would not.

There could have been no kinder comforter than Mary Bold. There was not the slightest dash of triumph about her when she heard of the Stanhope scheme, nor did she allude to her former opinion when Eleanor called her late friend Charlotte a base, designing woman. She re-echoed all the abuse that was heaped on Mr. Slope's head, and never hinted that she had said as much before. "I told you so, I told you so!" is the croak of a true Job's comforter. But Mary, when she found her friend lying in her sorrow and scraping herself with potsherds, forbore to argue and to exult. Eleanor acknowledged the merit of the forbearance, and at length allowed herself to be tranquilised.

On the next day she did not go out of the house. Barchester she thought would be crowded with Stanhopes and Slopes; perhaps also with Arabins and Grantlys. Indeed there was hardly any one among her friends whom she could have met, without some cause of uneasiness.

In the course of the afternoon she heard that the dean was dead; and she also heard that Mr. Quiverful had been finally appointed to the hospital.

In the evening her father came to her, and then the story, or as much of it as she could bring herself to tell him, had to be repeated. He was not in truth much surprised at Mr. Slope's effrontery; but he was obliged to act as though he had been, to save his daughter's feelings. He was, however, anything but skilful in his deceit, and she saw through it.

"I see," said she, "that you think it only in the common course of things that Mr. Slope should have treated me in this way." She had said nothing to him about the embrace, nor yet of the way in which it had been met.

"I do not think it at all strange," said he, "that any one should admire my Eleanor."

"It is strange to me," said she, "that any man should have so much audacity, without ever having received the slightest encouragement."

To this Mr. Harding answered nothing. With the archdeacon it would have been the text for a rejoinder, which would not have disgraced Bildad the Shuhite.

"But you'll tell the archdeacon?" asked Mr. Harding.

"Tell him what?" said she sharply.

"Or Susan?" continued Mr. Harding. "You'll tell Susan; you'll let them know that they wronged you in supposing that this man's addresses would be agreeable to you?"

"They may find that out their own way," said she; "I shall not ever willingly mention Mr. Slope's name to either of them."

"But I may."

"I have no right to hinder you from doing anything that may be necessary to your own comfort, but pray do not do it for my sake. Dr. Grantly never thought well of me, and never will. I don't know now that I am even anxious that he should do so."

And then they went to the affair of the hospital. "But is it true, papa?"

"What, my dear? said he. "About the dean? Yes, I fear quite true. Indeed I know there is no doubt about it."

"Poor Miss Trefoil. I am so sorry for her. But I did not mean that," said Eleanor. "But about the hospital, papa?"

"Yes, my dear. I believe it is true that Mr. Quiverful is to have it."

"Oh, what a shame!"

"No, my dear, not at all, not at all a shame: I am sure I hope it will suit him."

"But, papa, you know it is a shame. After all your hopes, all your expectations to get back to your old house, to see it given away in this way to a perfect stranger!"

"My dear, the bishop had a right to give it to whom he pleased."

"I deny that, papa. He had no such right. It is not as though you were a candidate for a new piece of preferment. If the bishop has a grain of justice—"

"The bishop offered it to me on his terms, and as I did not like the terms, I refused it. After that, I cannot complain."

"Terms! He had no right to make terms."

"I don't know about that; but it seems he had the power. But to tell you the truth, Nelly, I am as well satisfied as it is. When the affair became the subject of angry discussion, I thoroughly wished to be rid of it altogether."

"But you did want to go back to the old house, papa. You told me so yourself."

"Yes, my dear, I did. For a short time I did wish it. And I was foolish in doing so. I am getting old now; and my chief worldly wish is for peace and rest. Had I gone back to the hospital, I should have had endless contentions with the bishop, contentions with his chaplain, and contentions with the archdeacon. I am not up to this now, I am not able to meet such troubles; and therefore I am not ill-pleased to find myself left to the little church of St. Cuthbert's. I shall never starve," added he, laughing, "as long as you are here."

"But will you come and live with me, papa?" she said earnestly, taking him by both his hands. "If you will do that, if you will promise that, I will own that you are right."

"I will dine with you to-day at any rate."

"No, but live here altogether. Give up that close, odious little room in High Street."

"My dear, it's a very nice little room; and you are really quite uncivil."

"Oh, papa, don't joke. It's not a nice place for you. You say you are growing old, though I am sure you are not."

"Am not I, my dear?"

"No, papa, not old—not to say old. But you are quite old enough to feel the want of a decent room to sit in. You know how lonely Mary and I are here. You know nobody ever sleeps in the big front bed-room. It is really unkind of you to remain up there alone, when you are so much wanted here."

"Thank you, Nelly—thank you. But, my dear—"

"If you had been living here, papa, with us, as I really think you ought to have done, considering how lonely we are, there would have been none of all this dreadful affair about Mr. Slope."

Mr. Harding, however, did not allow himself to be talked over into giving up his own and only little *pied à terre* in the High Street. He promised to come and dine with his daughter, and stay with her, and visit her, and do everything but absolutely live with her. It did not suit the peculiar feelings of the man to tell his daughter that though she had rejected Mr. Slope, and been ready to reject Mr. Stanhope, some other more favoured suitor would probaby soon appear; and that on the appearance of such a suitor the big front bed-room might perhaps be more frequently in requisition than at present. But doubtless such an idea crossed his mind, and added its weight to the other reasons which made him decide on still keeping the close, odious little room in High Street.

The evening passed over quietly and in comfort. Eleanor was always happier with her father than with any one else. He had not, perhaps, any natural taste for baby-worship, but he was always ready to sacrifice himself, and therefore made an excellent third in a trio with his daughter and Mary Bold in singing the praises of the wonderful child.

They were standing together over their music in the evening, the baby having again been put to bed upon the sofa, when the servant brought in a very small note in a beautiful pink envelope. It quite filled the room with perfume as it lay upon the small salver. Mary Bold and Mrs. Bold were both at the piano, and Mr. Harding was sitting close to them, with the violoncello between his legs; so that the elegancy of the epistle was visible to them all.

"Please, ma'am, Dr. Stanhope's coachman says he is to wait for an answer," said the servant.

Eleanor got very red in the face as she took the note in her hand. She had never seen the writing before. Charlotte's epistles, to which she was well accustomed, were of a very different style and kind. She generally wrote on large note-paper; she twisted up her letters into the shape and sometimes into the size of cocked hats; she addressed them in a sprawling manly hand, and not unusually added a blot or a smudge, as though such were her own peculiar sign-manual. The address of this note was written in a beautiful female hand, and the gummed wafer bore on it an impress of a gilt coronet. Though Eleanor had never seen such a one before, she guessed that it came from the signora. Such epistles were very numerously sent out from any house in which the signora might happen to be dwelling, but they were rarely addressed to ladies. When the coachman was told by the lady's maid to take the letter to Mrs. Bold, he openly expressed his opinion that there was some mistake about it. Whereupon the lady's maid boxed the coachman's ears. Had Mr. Slope seen in how meek a spirit the coachman took the rebuke, he might have learnt a useful lesson, both in philosophy and religion.

The note was as follows. It may be taken as a faithful promise that no further letter whatever shall be transcribed at length in these pages.

My dear Mrs. Bold,—May I ask you, as a great favour, to call on me to-morrow? You can say what hour will best suit you; but quite early, if you can. I need hardly say that if I could call upon you I should not take this liberty with you.

I partly know what occurred the other day, and I promise you that you shall meet with no annoyance if you will come to me. My brother leaves us for London to-day; from thence he goes to Italy.

It will probably occur to you that I should not thus intrude on you, unless I had that to say to you which may be of considerable moment. Pray therefore excuse me, even if you do not grant my request, and believe me,

Very sincerely yours,
M. VESEY NERONI.

Thursday Evening.

The three of them sat in consultation on this epistle for some ten or fifteen minutes, and then decided that Eleanor should write a line saying that she would see the signora the next morning, at twelve o'clock.

XLV

The Stanhopes at Home

We must now return to the Stanhopes, and see how they behaved themselves on their return from Ullathorne.

Charlotte, who came back in the first homeward journey with her sister, waited in palpitating expectation till the carriage drove up to the door a second time. She did not run down or stand at the window, or show in any outward manner that she looked for anything wonderful to occur; but, when she heard the carriage-wheels, she stood up with erect ears, listening for Eleanor's footfall on the pavement or the cheery sound of Bertie's voice welcoming her in. Had she heard either, she would have felt that all was right; but neither sound was there for her to hear. She heard only her father's slow step, as he ponderously let himself down from the carriage, and slowly walked along the hall, till he got into his own private room on the ground floor. "Send Miss Stanhope to me," he said to the servant.

"There's something wrong now," said Madeline, who was lying on her sofa in the back drawing-room.

"It's all up with Bertie," replied Charlotte. "I know, I know," she said to the servant, as he brought up the message. "Tell my father I will be with him immediately."

"Bertie's wooing has gone astray," said Madeline; "I knew it would."

"It has been his own fault then. She was ready enough, I am quite sure," said Charlotte, with that sort of ill-nature which is not uncommon when one woman speaks of another.

"What will you say to him now?" By 'him,' the signora meant their father.

"That will be as I find him. He was ready to pay two hundred pounds for Bertie, to stave off the worst of his creditors, if this marriage had gone on. Bertie must now have the money instead, and go and take his chance."

"Where is he now?"

"Heaven knows! smoking in the bottom of Mr. Thorne's ha-ha, or philandering with some of those Miss Chadwicks. Nothing will ever make an impression on him. But he'll be furious if I don't go down."

"No; nothing ever will. But don't be long, Charlotte, for I want my tea."

And so Charlotte went down to her father. There was a very black cloud on the old man's brow; blacker than his daughter could ever yet remember to have seen there. He was sitting in his own arm-chair, not comfortably over the fire, but in the middle of the room, waiting till she should come and listen to him.

"What has become of your brother?" he said, as soon as the door was shut.

"I should rather ask you," said Charlotte. "I left you both at Ullathorne, when I came away. What have you done with Mrs. Bold?"

"Mrs. Bold! nonsense. The woman has gone home as she ought to do. And heartily glad I am that she should not be sacrificed to so heartless a reprobate."

"Oh, papa!"

"A heartless reprobate! Tell me now where he is, and what he is going to do. I have allowed myself to be fooled between you. Marriage, indeed! Who on earth that has money, or credit, or respect in the world to lose, would marry him?"

"It is no use your scolding me, papa. I have done the best I could for him and you."

"And Madeline is nearly as bad," said the prebendary, who was in truth very, very angry.

"Oh, I suppose we are all bad," replied Charlotte.

The old man emitted a huge leonine sigh. If they were all bad, who had made them so? If they were unprincipled, selfish, and disreputable, who was to be blamed for the education which had so injurious an effect?

"I know you'll ruin me among you," said he.

"Why, papa, what nonsense that is. You are living within your income this minute, and if there are any new debts, I don't know of them. I am sure there ought to be none, for we are dull enough here."

"Are those bills of Madeline's paid?"

"No, they are not. Who was to pay them?"

"Her husband may pay them."

"Her husband! would you wish me to tell her you say so? Do you wish to turn her out of your house?"

"I wish she would know how to behave herself."

"Why, what on earth has she done now? Poor Madeline! To-day is only the second time she has gone out since we came to this vile town."

He then sat silent for a time, thinking in what shape he would declare his resolve. "Well, papa," said Charlotte, "shall I stay here, or may I go up-stairs and give mamma her tea?"

"You are in your brother's confidence. Tell me what he is going to do?"

"Nothing, that I am aware of."

"Nothing—nothing! nothing but eat and drink, and spend every shilling of my money he can lay his hands upon. I have made up my mind, Charlotte. He shall eat and drink no more in this house."

"Very well. Then I suppose he must go back to Italy."

"He may go where he pleases."

"That's easily said, papa; but what does it mean? You can't let him——"

"It means this," said the doctor, speaking more loudly than was his wont, and with wrath flashing from his eyes; "that as sure as God rules in heaven, I will not maintain him any longer in idleness."

"Oh, ruling in heaven!" said Charlotte. "It is no use talking about that. You must rule him here on earth; and the question is, how you can do it. You can't turn him out of the house penniless, to beg about the street."

"He may beg where he likes."

"He must go back to Carrara. That is the cheapest place he can live at, and nobody there will give him credit for above two or three hundred pauls. But you must let him have the means of going."

"As sure as——"

"Oh, papa, don't swear. You know you must do it. You were ready to pay two hundred pounds for him if this marriage came off. Half that will start him to Carrara."

"What? give him a hundred pounds!"

"You know we are all in the dark, papa," said she, thinking it expedient to change the conversation. "For anything we know, he may be at this moment engaged to Mrs. Bold."

"Fiddlestick," said the father, who had seen the way in which Mrs. Bold had got into the carriage, while his son stood apart without even offering her his hand.

"Well, then, he must go to Carrara," said Charlotte.

Just at this moment the lock of the front door was heard, and Charlotte's quick ears detected her brother's cat-like step in the hall. She said nothing, feeling that for the present Bertie had better keep out of her father's way. But Dr. Stanhope also heard the sound of the lock.

"Who's that?" he demanded. Charlotte made no reply, and he asked again, "Who is that that has just come in? Open the door. Who is it?"

"I suppose it is Bertie."

"Bid him to come here," said the father. But Bertie, who was close to the door and heard the call, required no further bidding, but walked in with a perfectly unconcerned and cheerful air. It was this peculiar *insouciance* which angered Dr. Stanhope, even more than his son's extravagance.

"Well, sir?" said the doctor.

"And how did you get home, sir, with your fair companion?" said Bertie. "I suppose she is not up-stairs, Charlotte?"

"Bertie," said Charlotte, "papa is in no humour for joking. He is very angry with you."

"Angry!" said Bertie, raising his eyebrows, as though he had never yet given his parent cause for a single moment's uneasiness.

"Sit down, if you please, sir," said Dr. Stanhope very sternly, but not now very loudly. "And I'll trouble you to sit down too, Charlotte. Your mother can wait for her tea a few minutes."

Charlotte sat down on the chair nearest to the door, in somewhat of a perverse sort of manner; as much as though she would say—Well, here I am; you shan't say I don't do what I am bid; but I'll be whipped if I give way to you. And she was determined not to give way. She too was angry with Bertie; but she was not the less ready on that account to defend him from his father. Bertie also sat down. He drew his chair close to the library-table upon which he put his elbow, and then resting his face comfortably on one hand, he began drawing little pictures on a sheet of paper with the other. Before the scene was over he had completed admirable figures of Miss Thorne, Mrs. Proudie, and Lady De Courcy, and begun a family piece to comprise the whole set of the Lookalofts.

"Would it suit you, sir," said the father, "to give me some idea as to what your present intentions are?—what way of living you propose to yourself?"

"I'll do anything you can suggest, sir," replied Bertie.

"No, I shall suggest nothing further. My time for suggesting has gone by. I have only one order to give, and that is, that you leave my house."

"To-night?" said Bertie; and the simple tone of the question left the doctor without any adequately dignified method of reply.

"Papa does not quite mean to-night," said Charlotte, "at least I suppose not."

"To-morrow, perhaps," suggested Bertie.

"Yes, sir, to-morrow," said the doctor. "You shall leave this to-morrow."

"Very well, sir. Will the 4:30 P.M. train be soon enough?" and Bertie, as he asked, put the finishing touch to Miss Thorne's high-heeled boots.

"You may go how and when and where you please, so that you leave my house to-morrow. You have disgraced me, sir; you have disgraced yourself, and me, and your sisters."

"I am glad at least, sir, that I have not disgraced my mother," said Bertie.

Charlotte could hardly keep her countenance; but the doctor's brow grew still blacker than ever. Bertie was executing his *chef d'œuvre* in the delineation of Mrs. Proudie's nose and mouth.

"You are a heartless reprobate, sir; a heartless, thankless, good-for-nothing reprobate. I have done with you. You are my son—that I cannot help; but you shall have no more part or parcel in me as a child, nor I in you as your father."

"Oh, papa, papa! you must not, shall not say so," said Charlotte.

"I will say so, and do say so," said the father, rising from his chair. "And now leave the room, sir."

"Stop, stop," said Charlotte; "why don't you speak, Bertie? why don't you look up and speak? It is your manner that makes papa so angry."

"He is perfectly indifferent to all decency, to all propriety," said the doctor; and then he shouted out, "Leave the room, sir! Do you hear what I say?"

"Papa, papa, I will not let you part so. I know you will be sorry for it." And then she added, getting up and whispering into his ear, "Is he only to blame? Think of that. We have made our own bed, and, such as it is, we must lie on it. It is no use for us to quarrel among ourselves," and as she finished her whisper Bertie finished off the countess's bustle, which was so well done that it absolutely seemed to be swaying to and fro on the paper with its usual lateral motion.

"My father is angry at the present time," said Bertie, looking up for a moment from his sketches, "because I am not going to marry Mrs. Bold. What can I say on the matter? It is true that I am not going to marry her. In the first place——"

"That is not true, sir," said Dr. Stanhope; "but I will not argue with you."

"You were angry just this moment because I would not speak," said Bertie, going on with a young Lookaloft.

"Give over drawing," said Charlotte, going up to him and taking the paper from under his hand. The caricatures, however, she preserved, and showed them afterwards to the friends of the Thornes, the Proudies, and De Courcys. Bertie, deprived of his occupation, threw himself back in his chair and waited further orders.

"I think it will certainly be for the best that Bertie should leave this at once, perhaps to-morrow," said Charlotte, "but pray, papa, let us arrange some scheme together."

"If he will leave this to-morrow, I will give him £10, and he shall be paid £5 a month by the banker at Carrara as long as he stays permanently in that place."

"Well, sir! it won't be long," said Bertie; "for I shall be starved to death in about three months."

"He must have marble to work with," said Charlotte.

"I have plenty there in the studio to last me three months," said Bertie. "It will be no use attempting anything large in so limited a time; unless I do my own tombstone."

Terms, however, were ultimately come to, somewhat more liberal than those proposed, and the doctor was induced to shake hands with his son, and bid him good night. Dr. Stanhope would not go up to tea, but had it brought to him in his study by his daughter.

But Bertie went up-stairs and spent a pleasant evening. He finished the Lookalofts, greatly to the delight of his sisters, though the manner of portraying their *décolleté* dresses was not the most refined. Finding how matters were going, he by degrees allowed it to escape from him that he had not pressed his suit upon the widow in a very urgent way.

"I suppose, in point of fact, you never proposed at all?" said Charlotte.

"Oh, she understood that she might have me if she wished," said he.

"And she didn't wish," said the signora.

"You have thrown me over in the most shameful manner," said Charlotte. "I suppose you told her about my little plan?"

"Well, it came out somehow; at least the most of it."

"There's an end of that alliance," said Charlotte; "but it doesn't matter much. I suppose we shall all be back at Como soon."

"I am sure I hope so," said the signora; "I'm sick of the sight of black coats. If that Mr. Slope comes here any more, he'll be the death of me."

"You've been the ruin of him, I think," said Charlotte.

"And as for a second black-coated lover of mine, I am going to make a present of him to another lady with most singular disinterestedness."

The next day, true to his promise, Bertie packed up and went off by the 4:30 P.M. train, with £20 in his pocket, bound for the marble quarries of Carrara. And so he disappears from our scene.

At twelve o'clock on the day following that on which Bertie went, Mrs. Bold, true also to her word, knocked at Dr. Stanhope's door with a timid hand and palpitating heart. She was at once shown up to the back drawing-room, the folding doors of which were closed, so that in visiting the signora Eleanor was not necessarily thrown into any communion with those in the front room. As she went up the stairs, she saw none of the family, and was so far saved much of the annoyance which she had dreaded.

"This is very kind of you, Mrs. Bold; very kind, after what has happened," said the lady on the sofa with her sweetest smile.

"You wrote in such a strain that I could not but come to you."

"I did, I did; I wanted to force you to see me."

"Well, signora; I am here."

"How cold you are to me. But I suppose I must put up with that. I know you think you have reason to be displeased with us all. Poor Bertie! if you knew all, you would not be angry with him."

"I am not angry with your brother—not in the least. But I hope you did not send for me here to talk about him."

"If you are angry with Charlotte, that is worse; for you have no warmer friend in all Barchester. But I did *not* send for you to talk about this,—pray bring your chair nearer, Mrs. Bold, so that I may look at you. It is so unnatural to see you keeping so far off from me."

Eleanor did as she was bid, and brought her chair close to the sofa.

"And now, Mrs. Bold, I am going to tell you something which you may perhaps think indelicate; but yet I know that I am right in doing so."

Hereupon Mrs. Bold said nothing, but felt inclined to shake in her chair. The signora, she knew, was not very particular, and that which to her appeared to be indelicate might to Mrs. Bold appear to be extremely indecent.

"I believe you know Mr. Arabin?"

Mrs. Bold would have given the world not to blush, but her blood was not at her own command. She did blush up to her forehead, and the signora, who had made her sit in a special light in order that she might watch her, saw that she did so.

"Yes,—I am acquainted with him. That is, slightly. He is an intimate friend of Dr. Grantly, and Dr. Grantly is my brother-in-law."

"Well; if you know Mr. Arabin, I am sure you must like him. I know and like him much. Everybody that knows him must like him."

Mrs. Bold felt it quite impossible to say anything in reply to this. Her blood was rushing about her body she knew not how or why. She felt as though she were swinging in her chair; and she knew that she was not only red in the face, but also almost suffocated with heat. However, she sat still and said nothing.

"How stiff you are with me, Mrs. Bold," said the signora; "and I the while am doing for you all that one woman can do to serve another."

A kind of thought came over the widow's mind that perhaps the signora's friendship was real, and that at any rate it could not hurt her; and another kind of thought, a glimmering of a thought, came to her also,—that Mr. Arabin was too precious to be lost. She despised the signora; but might she not stoop to conquer? It should be but the smallest fraction of a stoop!

"I don't want to be stiff," she said, "but your questions are so very singular."

"Well, then, I will ask you one more singular still," said Madeline Neroni, raising herself on her elbow and turning her own face full upon her companion's. "Do you love him, love him with all your heart and soul, with all the love your bosom can feel? For I can tell you that he loves you, adores you, worships you, thinks of you and nothing else, is now thinking of you as he attempts to write his sermon for next Sunday's preaching. What would I not give to be loved in such a way by such a man, that is, if I were an object fit for any man to love!"

Mrs. Bold got up from her seat and stood speechless before the woman who was now addressing her in this impassioned way. When the signora thus alluded to herself, the widow's heart was softened, and she put her own hand, as though caressingly, on that of her companion which was resting on the table. The signora grasped it and went on speaking.

"What I tell you is God's own truth; and it is for you to use it as may be best for your own happiness. But you must not betray me. He knows nothing of this. He knows nothing of my knowing his inmost heart. He is simple as a child in these matters. He told me his secret in a thousand ways because he could not dissemble; but he does not dream that he has told it. You know it now, and I advise you to use it."

Eleanor returned the pressure of the other's hand with an infinitesimal *soupçon* of a squeeze.

"And remember," continued the signora, "he is not like other men. You must not expect him to come to you with vows and oaths and pretty presents, to kneel at your feet, and kiss your shoe-strings. If you want that, there are plenty to do it; but he won't be one of them." Eleanor's bosom nearly burst with a sigh; but Madeline, not heeding her, went on. "With him, yea will stand for yea, and nay for nay. Though his heart should break for it, the woman who shall reject him once, will have rejected him once and for all. Remember that. And now, Mrs. Bold, I will not keep you, for you are fluttered. I partly guess what use you will make of what I have said to you. If ever you are a happy wife in that man's house, we shall be far away; but I shall expect you to write me one line to say that you have forgiven the sins of the family."

Eleanor half whispered that she would, and then, without uttering another word, crept out of the room, and down the stairs, opened the front door for herself without hearing or seeing any one, and found herself in the close.

It would be difficult to analyse Eleanor's feelings as she

walked home. She was nearly stupefied by the things that had been said to her. She felt sore that her heart should have been so searched and riddled by a comparative stranger, by a woman whom she had never liked and never could like. She was mortified that the man whom she owned to herself that she loved should have concealed his love from her and shown it to another. There was much to vex her proud spirit. But there was, nevertheless, an under-stratum of joy in all this which buoyed her up wondrously. She tried if she could disbelieve what Madame Neroni had said to her; but she found that she could not. It was true; it must be true. She could not, would not, did not doubt it.

On one point she fully resolved to follow the advice given her. If it should ever please Mr. Arabin to put such a question to her as that suggested, her "yea" should be "yea." Would not all her miseries be at an end, if she could talk of them to him openly, with her head resting on his shoulder?

XLVI

Mr. Slope's Parting Interview with the Signora

On the following day the signora was in her pride. She was dressed in her brightest of morning dresses, and had quite a *levée* round her couch. It was a beautifully bright October afternoon; all the gentlemen of the neighbourhood were in Barchester, and those who had the entry of Dr. Stanhope's house were in the signora's back drawing-room. Charlotte and Mrs. Stanhope were in the front room, and such of the lady's squires as could not for the moment get near the centre of attraction had to waste their fragrance on the mother and sister.

The first who came and the last to leave was Mr. Arabin. This was the second visit he had paid to Madame Neroni since he had met her at Ullathorne. He came he knew not why, to talk about he knew not what. But, in truth, the feelings which now troubled him were new to him, and he could not analyse them. It may seem strange that he should thus come dangling about Madame Neroni because he was in love with Mrs. Bold; but it was nevertheless the fact; and though he could not understand why he did so, Madame Neroni understood it well enough.

She had been gentle and kind to him, and had encouraged his staying. Therefore he stayed on. She pressed his hand when he first greeted her, she made him remain near her; and whispered to him little nothings. And then her eye, brilliant and bright, now mirthful, now melancholy, and invincible in either way! What man with warm feelings, blood unchilled, and a heart not guarded by a triple steel of experience could have withstood those eyes! The lady, it is true, intended to do him no mortal injury; she merely chose to inhale a slight breath of incense before she handed the casket over to another. Whether Mrs. Bold would willingly have spared even so much is another question.

. And then came Mr. Slope. All the world now knew that Mr. Slope was a candidate for the deanery, and that he was generally considered to be the favourite. Mr. Slope, therefore, walked rather largely upon the earth. He gave to himself a portly air, such as might become a dean, spoke but little to other clergymen, and shunned the bishop as much as possible. How the meagre little prebendary, and the burly chancellor, and all the minor canons and vicars choral, ay, and all the choristers too, cowered and shook and walked about with long faces when they read or heard of that article in the *Jupiter*. Now were coming the days when nothing would avail to keep the impure spirit from the cathedral pulpit. That pulpit would indeed be his own. Precentors, vicars, and choristers might hang up their harps on the willows. Ichabod! Ichabod! the glory of their house was departing from them.

Mr. Slope, great as he was with embryo grandeur, still came to see the signora. Indeed, he could not keep himself away. He dreamed of that soft hand which he had kissed so often, and of that imperial brow which his lips had once pressed, and he then dreamed also of further favours.

And Mr. Thorne was there also. It was the first visit he had ever paid to the signora, and he made it not without due preparation. Mr. Thorne was a gentleman usually precise in his dress, and prone to make the most of himself in an unpretending way. The grey hairs in his whiskers were eliminated perhaps once a month; those on his head were softened by a mixture which we will not call a dye; it was only a wash. His tailor lived in St. James's Street, and his bootmaker at the corner of that street and Piccadilly. He was particular in the article of gloves, and the getting up of his shirts was a matter not lightly thought of in the Ullathorne laundry. On the occasion of the present visit he had rather overdone his usual efforts, and caused some little uneasiness to his sister, who had not hitherto received very cordially the proposition for a lengthened visit from the signora at Ullathorne.

There were others also there—young men about the city who had not much to do, and who were induced by the lady's charms to neglect that little; but all gave way to Mr. Thorne, who was somewhat of a grand signor, as a country gentleman always is in a provincial city.

"Oh, Mr. Thorne, this is so kind of you!" said the signora. "You promised to come; but I really did not expect it. I thought you country gentlemen never kept your pledges."

"Oh, yes, sometimes," said Mr. Thorne, looking rather sheepish, and making his salutations a little too much in the style of the last century.

"You deceive none but your consti—stit—stit; what do you call the people that carry you about in chairs and pelt you with eggs and apples when they make you a member of Parliament?"

"One another also, sometimes, signora," said Mr. Slope, with a deanish sort of smirk on his face. "Country gentlemen do deceive one another sometimes, don't they, Mr. Thorne?"

Mr. Thorne gave him a look which undeaned him completely for the moment; but he soon remembered his high hopes, and recovering himself quickly, sustained his probable coming dignity by a laugh at Mr. Thorne's expense.

"I never deceive a lady, at any rate," said Mr. Thorne; "especially when the gratification of my own wishes is so strong an inducement to keep me true, as it now is."

Mr. Thorne went on thus awhile with antediluvian grimaces and compliments which he had picked up from Sir Charles Grandison, and the signora at every grimace and at every bow smiled a little smile and bowed a little bow. Mr. Thorne, however, was kept standing at the foot of the couch, for the new dean sat in the seat of honour near the table. Mr. Arabin the while was standing with his back to the fire, his coat tails under his arms, gazing at her with all his eyes—not quite in vain, for every now and again a glance came up at him, bright as a meteor out of heaven.

"Oh, Mr. Thorne, you promised to let me introduce my

little girl to you. Can you spare a moment?—will you see her now?''

Mr. Thorne assured her that he could, and would see the young lady with the greatest pleasure in life. "Mr. Slope, might I trouble you to ring the bell?'' said she; and when Mr. Slope got up she looked at Mr. Thorne and pointed to the chair. Mr. Thorne, however, was much too slow to understand her, and Mr. Slope would have recovered his seat had not the signora, who never chose to be unsuccessful, somewhat summarily ordered him out of it.

"Oh, Mr. Slope, I must ask you to let Mr. Thorne sit here just for a moment or two. I am sure you will pardon me. We can take a liberty with you this week. Next week, you know, when you move into the dean's house, we shall be afraid of you.''

Mr. Slope, with an air of much indifference, rose from his seat, and, walking into the next room, became greatly interested in Mrs. Stanhope's worsted work.

And then the child was brought in. She was a little girl, about eight years of age, like her mother, only that her enormous eyes were black, and her hair quite jet. Her complexion, too, was very dark, and bespoke her foreign blood. She was dressed in the most outlandish and extravagant way in which clothes could be put on a child's back. She had great bracelets on her naked little arms, a crimson fillet braided with gold round her head, and scarlet shoes with high heels. Her dress was all flounces, and stuck out from her as though the object were to make it lie off horizontally from her little hips. It did not nearly cover her knees; but this was atoned for by a loose pair of drawers, which seemed made throughout of lace; then she had on pink silk stockings. It was thus that the last of the Neros was habitually dressed at the hour when visitors were wont to call.

"Julia, my love,'' said the mother—Julia was ever a favourite name with the ladies of that family. "Julia, my love, come here. I was telling you about the beautiful party poor mamma went to. This is Mr. Thorne; will you give him a kiss, dearest?''

Julia put up her face to be kissed, as she did to all her mother's visitors; and then Mr. Thorne found that he had got her, and, which was much more terrific to him, all her finery, into his arms. The lace and starch crumpled against his waistcoat and trowsers, the greasy black curls hung upon his cheek, and one of the bracelet clasps scratched his ear. He did not at all know how to hold so magnificent a lady, nor holding her what to do with her. However, he had on other occasions been compelled to fondle little nieces and nephews, and now set about the task in the mode he always had used.

"Diddle, diddle, diddle, diddle," said he, putting the child on one knee, and working away with it as though he were turning a knife-grinder's wheel with his foot.

"Mamma, mamma," said Julia crossly, "I don't want to be diddle diddled. Let me go, you naughty old man, you."

Poor Mr. Thorne put the child down quietly on the ground, and drew back his chair; Mr. Slope, who had returned to the pole star that attracted him, laughed aloud; Mr. Arabin winced and shut his eyes; and the signora pretended not to hear her daughter.

"Go to Aunt Charlotte, lovey," said the mamma, "and ask her if it is time for you to go out."

But little Miss Julia, though she had not exactly liked the nature of Mr. Thorne's attention, was accustomed to be played with by gentlemen, and did not relish the idea of being sent so soon to her aunt.

"Julia, go when I tell you, my dear." But Julia still went pouting about the room. "Charlotte, do come and take her," said the signora. "She must go out; and the days get so short now." And thus ended the much-talked of interview between Mr. Thorne and the last of the Neros.

Mr. Thorne recovered from the child's crossness sooner than from Mr. Slope's laughter. He could put up with being called an old man by an infant, but he did not like to be laughed at by the bishop's chaplain, even though that chaplain was about to become a dean. He said nothing, but he showed plainly enough that he was angry.

The signora was ready enough to avenge him. "Mr. Slope," said she, "I hear that you are triumphing on all sides."

"How so?" said he, smiling. He did not dislike being talked to about the deanery, though, of course, he strongly denied the imputation.

"You carry the day both in love and war." Mr. Slope hereupon did not look quite so satisfied as he had done.

"Mr. Arabin," continued the signora, "don't you think Mr. Slope is a very lucky man?"

"Not more so than he deserves, I am sure," said Mr. Arabin.

"Only think, Mr. Thorne, he is to be our new dean; of course we all know that."

"Indeed, Signora," said Mr. Slope, "we all know nothing about it. I can assure you I myself——"

"He *is* to be the new dean—there is no manner of doubt of it, Mr. Thorne."

"Hum!" said Mr. Thorne.

"Passing over the heads of old men like my father and Archdeacon Grantly——"

"Oh—oh!" said Mr. Slope.

"The archdeacon would not accept it," said Mr. Arabin; whereupon Mr. Slope smiled abominably, and said, as plainly as a look could speak, that the grapes were sour.

"Going over all our heads," continued the signora, "for, of course, I consider myself one of the chapter."

"If I am ever dean," said Mr. Slope—"that is, were I ever to become so, I should glory in such a canoness."

"Oh, Mr. Slope, stop; I haven't half done. There is another canoness for you to glory in. Mr. Slope is not only to have the deanery, but a wife to put in it."

Mr. Slope again looked disconcerted.

"A wife with a large fortune too. It never rains but it pours, does it, Mr. Thorne?"

"No, never," said Mr. Thorne, who did not quite relish talking about Mr. Slope and his affairs.

"When will it be, Mr. Slope?"

"When will what be?" said he.

"Oh! we know when the affair of the dean will be: a week will settle that. The new hat, I have no doubt, has been already ordered. But when will the marriage come off?"

"Do you mean mine or Mr. Arabin's?" said he, striving to be facetious.

"Well, just then I meant yours, though, perhaps, after all, Mr. Arabin's may be first. But we know nothing of him. He is too close for any of us. Now all is open and above board with you; which, by the bye, Mr. Arabin, I beg to tell you I like much the best. He who runs can read that Mr. Slope is a favoured lover. Come, Mr. Slope, when is the widow to be made Mrs. Dean?"

To Mr. Arabin this badinage was peculiarly painful, and yet he could not tear himself away and leave it. He believed, still believed with that sort of belief which the fear of a thing engenders, that Mrs. Bold would probably become the wife of Mr. Slope. Of Mr. Slope's little adventure in the garden he knew nothing. For aught he knew, Mr. Slope might have had an adventure of quite a different character. He might have thrown himself at the widow's feet, been accepted, and then returned to town a jolly, thriving wooer. The signora's jokes were bitter enough to Mr. Slope, but they were quite as bitter to Mr. Arabin. He still stood leaning against the fire-place, fumbling with his hands in his trowsers pockets.

"Come, come, Mr. Slope, don't be so bashful," continued the signora. "We all know that you proposed to the lady the other day at Ullathorne. Tell us with what words she accepted you. Was it with a simple 'yes,' or with two 'no no's,' which make an affirmative? or did silence give consent? or did she speak out with that spirit which so well becomes a widow, and say openly, 'By my troth, sir, you shall make me Mrs. Slope as soon as it is your pleasure to do so'?"

Mr. Slope had seldom in his life felt himself less at his ease. There sat Mr. Thorne, gazing at him with all his eyes. There round the door between the two rooms were clustered a little group of people, including Miss Stanhope and the Rev. Messrs. Gray and Green, all listening to his discomfiture. He knew that it depended solely on his own wit whether or no he could throw the joke back upon the lady. He knew that it stood him to do so if he possibly could; but he had not a word. " 'Tis conscience that makes cowards of us all." He felt on his cheek the sharp points of Eleanor's fingers, and did not know who might have seen the blow, who might have told the tale to this pestilent woman who took such delight in jeering him. He stood there, therefore, red as a carbuncle and mute as a fish; grinning just sufficiently to show his teeth; an object of pity.

But the signora had no pity; she knew nothing of mercy. Her present object was to put Mr. Slope down, and she was determined to do it thoroughly, now that she had him in her power.

"What, Mr. Slope, no answer? Why it can't possibly be that the woman has been fool enough to refuse you? She can't surely be looking out after a bishop. But I see how it is, Mr. Slope. Widows are proverbially cautious. You should have let her alone till the new hat was on your head; till you could show her the key of the deanery."

"Signora," said he at last, trying to speak in a tone of dignified reproach, "you really permit yourself to talk on solemn subjects in a very improper way."

"Solemn subjects—what solemn subject? Surely a dean's hat is not such a solemn subject."

"I have no aspirations such as those you impute to me. Perhaps you will drop the subject."

"Oh, certainly, Mr. Slope; but one word first. Go to her

again with the prime minister's letter in your pocket. I'll wager my shawl to your shovel she does not refuse you then.''

"I must say, signora, that I think you are speaking of the lady in a very unjustifiable manner.''

"And one other piece of advice, Mr. Slope; I'll only offer you one other''; and then she commenced singing—

> "It's gude to be merry and wise, Mr. Slope;
>   It's gude to be honest and true;
>   It's gude to be off with the old love—Mr. Slope,
>   Before you are on with the new.—
> "Ha, ha, ha!''

And the signora, throwing herself back on her sofa, laughed merrily. She little recked how those who heard her would, in their own imaginations, fill up the little history of Mr. Slope's first love. She little cared that some among them might attribute to her the honour of his earliest admiration. She was tired of Mr. Slope and wanted to get rid of him; she had ground for anger with him, and she chose to be revenged.

How Mr. Slope got out of that room he never himself knew. He did succeed ultimately, and probably with some assistance, in getting his hat and escaping into the air. At last his love for the signora was cured. Whenever he again thought of her in his dreams, it was not as of an angel with azure wings. He connected her rather with fire and brimstone, and though he could still believe her to be a spirit, he banished her entirely out of heaven, and found a place for her among the infernal gods. When he weighed in the balance, as he not seldom did, the two women to whom he had attached himself in Barchester, the pre-eminent place in his soul's hatred was usually allotted to the signora.

XLVII

The Dean Elect

During the entire next week Barchester was ignorant who was to be its new dean on Sunday morning. Mr. Slope was decidedly the favourite; but he did not show himself in the cathedral, and then he sank a point or two in the betting. On Monday, he got a scolding from the bishop in the hearing of the servants, and down he went till nobody would have him at any price; but on Tuesday he received a letter, in an official cover, marked private, by which he fully recovered his place in the public favour. On Wednesday, he was said to be ill, and that did not look well; but on Thursday morning he went down to the railway station, with a very jaunty air; and when it was ascertained that he had taken a first-class ticket for London, there was no longer any room for doubt on the matter.

While matters were in this state of ferment at Barchester, there was not much mental comfort at Plumstead. Our friend the archdeacon had many grounds for inward grief. He was much displeased at the result of Dr. Gwynne's diplomatic mission to the palace, and did not even scruple to say to his wife that had he gone himself, he would have managed the affair much better. His wife did not agree with him, but that did not mend the matter.

Mr. Quiverful's appointment to the hospital was, however, a *fait accompli*, and Mr. Harding's acquiescence in that appointment was not less so. Nothing would induce Mr. Harding to make a public appeal against the bishop; and the Master of Lazarus quite approved of his not doing so.

"I don't know what has come to the Master," said the archdeacon over and over again. "He used to be ready enough to

588

stand up for his order.''

"My dear archdeacon,'' Mr. Grantly would say in reply, "what is the use of always fighting? I really think the Master is right.'' The Master, however, had taken steps of his own, of which neither the archdeacon nor his wife knew anything.

Then Mr. Slope's successes were henbane to Dr. Gantly; and Mrs. Bold's improprieties were as bad. What would be all the world to Archdeacon Grantly if Mr. Slope should become Dean of Barchester and marry his wife's sister! He talked of it, and talked of it till he was nearly ill. Mrs. Grantly almost wished that the marriage was done and over, so that she might hear no more about it.

And there was yet another ground of misery which cut him to the quick, nearly as closely as either of the others. That paragon of a clergyman, whom he had bestowed upon St. Ewold's, that college friend of whom he had boasted so loudly, that ecclesiastical knight before whose lance Mr. Slope was to fall and bite the dust, that worthy bulwark of the church as it should be, that honoured representative of Oxford's best spirit, was—so at least his wife had told him half a dozen times—misconducting himself!

Nothing had been seen of Mr. Arabin at Plumstead for the last week, but a good deal had, unfortunately, been heard of him. As soon as Mrs. Grantly had found herself alone with the archdeacon, on the evening of the Ullathorne party, she had expressed herself very forcibly as to Mr. Arabin's conduct on that occasion. He had, she declared, looked and acted and talked very unlike a decent parish clergyman. At first the archdeacon had laughed at this, and assured her that she need not trouble herself; that Mr. Arabin would be found to be quite safe. But by degrees he began to find that his wife's eyes had been sharper than his own. Other people coupled the signora's name with that of Mr. Arabin. The meagre little prebendary who lived in the close, told him to a nicety how often Mr. Arabin had visited at Dr. Stanhope's, and how long he had remained on the occasion of each visit. He had asked after Mr. Arabin at the cathedral library, and an officious little choral had offered to go and see whether he could be found at Dr. Stanhope's. Rumour, when she has contrived to sound the first note on her trumpet, soon makes a loud peal audible enough. It was too clear that Mr. Arabin had succumbed to the Italian woman, and that the archdeacon's credit would suffer fearfully if something were not done to

rescue the brand from the burning. Besides, to give the archdeacon his due, he was really attached to Mr. Arabin, and grieved
greatly at his backsliding.

They were sitting, talking over their sorrows, in the drawing-
room before dinner on the day after Mr. Slope's departure for
London; and on this occasion Mrs. Grantly spoke out her mind
freely. She had opinions of her own about parish clergymen, and
now thought it right to give vent to them.

"If you would have been led by me, archdeacon, you
would never have put a bachelor into St. Ewold's."

"But, my dear, you don't mean to say that all bachelor
clergymen misbehave themselves."

"I don't know that clergymen are so much better than other
men," said Mrs. Grantly. "It's all very well with a curate whom
you have under your own eye, and whom you can get rid of if he
persists in improprieties."

"But Mr. Arabin was a fellow, and couldn't have had a
wife."

"Then I would have found some one who could."

"But, my dear, are fellows never to get livings?"

"Yes, to be sure they are, when they get engaged. I never
would put a young man into a living unless he were married, or
engaged to be married. Now here is Mr. Arabin. The whole
responsibility lies upon you."

"There is not at this moment a clergyman in all Oxford
more respected for morals and conduct than Arabin."

"Oh, Oxford!" said the lady, with a sneer. "What men
choose to do at Oxford, nobody ever hears of. A man may do
very well at Oxford who would bring disgrace on a parish; and,
to tell you the truth, it seems to me that Mr. Arabin is just such a
man."

The archdeacon groaned deeply, but he had no further
answer to make.

"You really must speak to him, archdeacon. Only think
what the Thornes will say if they hear that their parish clergyman
spends his whole time philandering with this woman."

The archdeacon groaned again. He was a courageous man,
and knew well enough how to rebuke the younger clergymen of
the diocese, when necessary. But there was that about Mr.
Arabin which made the doctor feel that it would be very difficult
to rebuke him with good effect.

"You can advise him to find a wife for himself, and he will
understand well enough what that means," said Mrs. Grantly.

The archdeacon had nothing for it but groaning. There was Mr. Slope; he was going to be made dean; he was going to take a wife; he was about to achieve respectability and wealth; an excellent family mansion, and a family carriage; he would soon be among the comfortable *élite* of the ecclesiastical world of Barchester; whereas his own *protégé*, the true scion of the true church, by whom he had sworn, would be still but a poor vicar, and that with a very indifferent character for moral conduct! It might be all very well recommending Mr. Arabin to marry, but how would Mr. Arabin when married support a wife!

Things were ordering themselves thus in Plumstead drawing-room when Dr. and Mrs. Grantly were disturbed in their sweet discourse by the quick rattle of a carriage and pair of horses on the gravel sweep. The sound was not that of visitors, whose private carriages are generally brought up to country-house doors with demure propriety, but betokened rather the advent of some person or persons who were in a hurry to reach the house, and had no intention of immediately leaving it. Guests invited to stay a week, and who were conscious of arriving after the first dinner bell, would probably approach in such a manner. So might arrive an attorney with the news of a granduncle's death, or a son from college with all the fresh honours of a double first. No one would have had himself driven up to the door of a country house in such a manner who had the slightest doubt of his own right to force an entry.

"Who is it?" said Mrs. Grantly, looking at her husband.

"Who on earth can it be?" said the archdeacon to his wife. He then quietly got up and stood with the drawing-room door open in his hand. "Why, it's your father!"

It was indeed Mr. Harding, and Mr. Harding alone. He had come by himself in a post-chaise with a couple of horses from Barchester, arriving almost after dark, and evidently full of news. His visits had usually been made in the quietest manner; he had rarely presumed to come without notice, and had always been driven up in a modest old green fly, with one horse, that hardly made itself heard as it crawled up to the hall-door.

"Good gracious, Warden, is it you?" said the archdeacon, forgetting in his surprise the events of the last few years. "But come in; nothing the matter, I hope."

"We are very glad you are come, papa," said his daughter. "I'll go and get your room ready at once."

"I an't warden, archdeacon," said Mr. Harding. "Mr. Quiverful is warden."

"Oh, I know, I know," said the archdeacon, petulantly. "I forgot all about it at the moment. Is anything the matter?"

"Don't go this moment, Susan," said Mr. Harding; "I have something to tell you."

"The dinner bell will ring in five minutes," said she.

"Will it?" said Mr. Harding. "Then, perhaps, I had better wait." He was big with news which he had come to tell, but which he knew could not be told without much discussion. He had hurried away to Plumstead as fast as two horses could bring him; and now, finding himself there, he was willing to accept the reprieve which dinner would give him.

"If you have anything of moment to tell us," said the archdeacon, "pray let us hear it at once. Has Eleanor gone off?"

"No, she has not," said Mr. Harding, with a look of great displeasure.

"Has Slope been made dean?"

"No, he has not; but—"

"But what?" said the archdeacon, who was becoming very impatient.

"They have—"

"They have what?" said the archdeacon.

"They have offered it to me," said Mr. Harding, with a modesty which almost prevented his speaking.

"Good heavens!" said the archdeacon, and sank back exhausted in an easy-chair.

"My dear, dear father," said Mrs. Grantly, and threw her arms round her father's neck.

"So I thought I had better come out and consult with you at once," said Mr. Harding.

"Consult!" shouted the archdeacon. "But, my dear Harding, I congratulate you with my whole heart—with my whole heart; I do indeed. I never heard anything in my life that gave me so much pleasure"; and he got hold of both his father-in-law's hands, and shook them as though he were going to shake them off, and walked round and round the room, twirling a copy of the *Jupiter* over his head, to show his extreme exultation.

"But—" began Mr. Harding.

"But me no buts," said the archdeacon. "I never was so happy in my life. It was just the proper thing to do. Upon my honour, I'll never say another word against Lord —— the longest day I have to live."

"That's Dr. Gwynne's doing, you may be sure," said Mrs.

Grantly, who greatly liked the Master of Lazarus, he being an orderly married man with a large family.

"I suppose it is," said the archdeacon.

"Oh, papa, I am so truly delighted!" said Mrs. Grantly, getting up and kissing her father.

"But, my dear," said Mr. Harding.—It was all in vain that he strove to speak; nobody would listen to him.

"Well, Mr. Dean," said the archdeacon, triumphing; "the deanery gardens will be some consolation for the hospital elms. Well, poor Quiverful! I won't begrudge him his good fortune any longer."

"No, indeed," said Mrs. Grantly. "Poor woman, she has fourteen children. I am sure I am very glad they have got it."

"So am I," said Mr. Harding.

"I would give twenty pounds," said the archdeacon, "to see how Mr. Slope will look when he hears it." The idea of Mr. Slope's discomfiture formed no small part of the archdeacon's pleasure.

At last Mr. Harding was allowed to go up-stairs and wash his hands, having, in fact, said very little of all that he had come out to Plumstead on purpose to say. Nor could anything more be said till the servants were gone after dinner. The joy of Dr. Grantly was so uncontrollable that he could not refrain from calling his father-in-law Mr. Dean before the men; and therefore it was soon matter of discussion in the lower regions how Mr. Harding, instead of his daughter's future husband, was to be the new dean, and various were the opinions on the matter. The cook and the butler, who were advanced in years, thought that it was just as it should be; but the footman and lady's maid, who were younger, thought it was a great shame that Mr. Slope should lose his chance.

"He's a mean chap all the same," said the footman; "and it an't along of him that I says so. But I always did admire the missus's sister; and she'd well become the situation."

While these were the ideas down-stairs, a very great difference of opinion existed above. As soon as the cloth was drawn and the wine on the table, Mr. Harding made for himself an opportunity of speaking. It was, however, with much inward troubling that he said:—

"It's very kind of Lord ——,very kind, and I feel it deeply, most deeply. I am, I must confess, gratified by the offer—"

"I should think so," said the archdeacon.

"But, all the same, I am afraid that I can't accept it."

The decanter almost fell from the archdeacon's hand upon the table; and the start he made was so great as to make his wife jump up from her chair. Not accept the deanship! If it really ended in this, there would be no longer any doubt that his father-in-law was demented. The question now was whether a clergyman with low rank, and preferment amounting to less than £200 a year, should accept high rank, £1200 a year, and one of the most desirable positions which his profession had to afford!

"What!" said the archdeacon, gasping for breath, and staring at his guest as though the violence of his emotion had almost thrown him into a fit.

"What!"

"I do not find myself fit for new duties," urged Mr. Harding.

"New duties! what duties?" said the archdeacon, with unintended sarcasm.

"Oh, papa," said Mrs. Grantly, "nothing can be easier than what a dean has to do. Surely you are more active than Dr. Trefoil."

"He won't have half as much to do as he has at present," said Dr. Grantly.

"Did you see what the *Jupiter* said the other day about young men?"

"Yes; and I saw that the *Jupiter* said all that it could to induce the appointment of Mr. Slope. Perhaps you would wish to see Mr. Slope made dean."

Mr. Harding made no reply to this rebuke, though he felt it strongly. He had not come over to Plumstead to have further contention with his son-in-law about Mr. Slope, so he allowed it to pass by.

"I know I cannot make you understand my feeling," he said, "for we have been cast in different moulds. I may wish that I had your spirit and energy and power of combating; but I have not. Every day that is added to my life increases my wish for peace and rest."

"And where on earth can a man have peace and rest if not in a deanery?" said the archdeacon.

"People will say that I am too old for it."

"Good heavens! people! what people? What need you care for any people?"

"But I think myself I am too old for any new place."

"Dear papa," said Mrs. Grantly, "men ten years older than you are appointed to new situations day after day."

"My dear," said he, "it is impossible that I should make you understand my feelings, nor do I pretend to any great virtue in the matter. The truth is, I want the force of character which might enable me to stand against the spirit of the times. The call on all sides now is for young men, and I have not the nerve to put myself in opposition to the demand. Were the *Jupiter*, when it hears of my appointment, to write article after article, setting forth my incompetency, I am sure it would cost me my reason. I ought to be able to bear with such things, you will say. Well, my dear, I own that I ought. But I feel my weakness, and I know that I can't. And, to tell you the truth, I know no more than a child what the dean has to do."

"Pshaw!" exclaimed the archdeacon.

"Don't be angry with me, archdeacon: don't let us quarrel about it, Susan. If you knew how keenly I feel the necessity of having to disoblige you in this matter, you would not be angry with me."

This was a dreadful blow to Dr. Grantly. Nothing could possibly have suited him better than having Mr. Harding in the deanery. Though he had never looked down on Mr. Harding on account of his recent poverty, he did fully recognise the satisfaction of having those belonging to him in comfortable positions. It would be much more suitable that Mr. Harding should be dean of Barchester than vicar of St. Cuthbert's and precentor to boot. And then the great discomfiture of that arch enemy of all that was respectable in Barchester, of that new low-church clerical *parvenu* that had fallen amongst them, that alone would be worth more, almost, than the situation itself. It was frightful to think that such unhoped-for good fortune should be marred by the absurd crotchets and unwholesome hallucinations by which Mr. Harding allowed himself to be led astray. To have the cup so near his lips and then to lose the drinking of it, was more than Dr. Grantly could endure.

And yet it appeared as though he would have to endure it. In vain he threatened and in vain he coaxed. Mr. Harding did not indeed speak with perfect decision of refusing the proffered glory, but he would not speak with anything like decision of accepting it. When pressed again and again, he would again and again allege that he was wholly unfitted to new duties. It was in vain that the archdeacon tried to insinuate, though he could not plainly declare, that there were no new duties to perform. It was in vain he hinted that in all cases of difficulty he, the archdeacon, was willing and able to guide a weak-minded dean. Mr. Harding seemed to have a foolish idea, not only that there were new duties to do, but that no one should accept the place who was not himself prepared to do them.

The conference ended in an understanding that Mr. Harding should at once acknowledge the letter he had received from the minister's private secretary, and should beg that he might be allowed two days to make up his mind; and that during those two days the matter should be considered.

On the following morning the archdeacon was to drive Mr. Harding back to Barchester.

XLVIII

Miss Thorne Shows Her Talent at Match-making

On Mr. Harding's return to Barchester from Plumstead, which was effected by him in due course in company with the archdeacon, more tidings of a surprising nature met him. He was, during the journey, subjected to such a weight of unanswerable argument, all of which went to prove that it was his bounden duty not to interfere with the paternal government that was so anxious to make him a dean, that when he arrived at the chemist's door in High Street, he hardly knew which way to turn himself in the matter. But, perplexed as he was, he was doomed to further perplexity. He found a note there from his daughter begging him most urgently to come to her immediately. But we must again go back a little in our story.

Miss Thorne had not been slow to hear the rumours respecting Mr. Arabin, which had so disturbed the happiness of Mrs. Grantly. And she, also, was unhappy to think that her parish clergyman should be accused of worshipping a strange goddess.

She, also, was of opinion, that rectors and vicars should all be married, and with that good-natured energy which was characteristic of her, she put her wits to work to find a fitting match for Mr. Arabin. Mrs. Grantly, in this difficulty, could think of no better remedy than a lecture from the archdeacon. Miss Thorne thought that a young lady, marriageable, and with a dowry, might be of more efficacy. In looking through the catalogue of her unmarried friends, who might possibly be in want of a husband, and might also be fit for such promotion as a country parsonage affords, she could think of no one more eligible than Mrs. Bold; and, consequently, losing no time, she went into Barchester on the day of Mr. Slope's discomfiture, the same day that her brother had had his interesting interview with the last of the Neros, and invited Mrs. Bold to bring her nurse and baby to Ullathorne and make them a protracted visit.

Miss Thorne suggested a month or two, intending to use her influence afterwards in prolonging it so as to last out the winter, in order that Mr. Arabin might have an opportunity of becoming fairly intimate with his intended bride. "We'll have Mr. Arabin too," said Miss Thorne to herself; "and before the spring they'll know each other; and in twelve or eighteen months' time, if all goes well, Mrs. Bold will be domiciled at St. Ewold's"; and then the kind-hearted lady gave herself some not undeserved praise for her matchmaking genius.

Eleanor was taken a little by surprise, but the matter ended in her promising to go to Ullathorne for at any rate a week or two; and on the day previous to that on which her father drove out to Plumstead, she had had herself driven out to Ullathorne.

Miss Thorne would not perplex her with her embryo lord on that same evening, thinking that she would allow her a few hours to make herself at home; but on the following morning Mr. Arabin arrived. "And now," said Miss Thorne to herself, "I must contrive to throw them in each other's way." That same day, after dinner, Eleanor, with an assumed air of dignity which she could not maintain, with tears that she could not suppress, with a flutter which she could not conquer, and a joy which she could not hide, told Miss Thorne that she was engaged to marry Mr. Arabin, and that it behoved her to get back home to Barchester as quick as she could.

To say simply that Miss Thorne was rejoiced at the success of the scheme, would give a very faint idea of her feelings on the occasion. My readers may probably have dreamt before now that they have had before them some terribly long walk to accomplish, some journey of twenty or thirty miles, an amount of labour frightful to anticipate, and that immediately on starting they have ingeniously found some accommodating short cut which has brought them without fatigue to their work's end in five minutes. Miss Thorne's waking feelings were somewhat of the same nature. My readers may perhaps have had to do with children, and may on some occasion have promised to their young charges some great gratification intended to come off, perhaps at the end of the winter, or at the beginning of summer. The impatient juveniles, however, will not wait, and clamorously demand their treat before they go to bed. Miss Thorne had a sort of feeling that her children were equally unreasonable. She was like an inexperienced gunner, who has ill calculated the length of the train that he has laid. The gunpowder exploded much too soon, and poor Miss Thorne felt that she was blown up by the strength of her own petard.

Miss Thorne had had lovers of her own, but they had been gentlemen of old-fashioned and deliberate habits. Miss Thorne's heart also had not always been hard, though she was still a virgin spinster; but it had never yielded in this way at the first assault. She had intended to bring together a middle-aged studious clergyman, and a discreet matron who might possibly be induced to marry again; and in doing so she had thrown fire among tinder. Well, it was all as it should be, but she did feel perhaps a little put out by the precipitancy of her own success; and perhaps a little vexed at the readiness of Mrs. Bold to be wooed.

She said, however, nothing about it to any one, and ascribed it all to the altered manners of the new age. Their mothers and grandmothers were perhaps a little more deliberate; but it was admitted on all sides that things were conducted very differently now than in former times. For aught Miss Thorne knew of the matter, a couple of hours might be quite sufficient under the new régime to complete that for which she in her ignorance had allotted twelve months.

But we must not pass over the wooing so cavalierly. It has been told, with perhaps tedious accuracy, how Eleanor disposed of two of her lovers at Ullathorne; and it must also be told with equal accuracy, and if possible with less tedium, how she encountered Mr. Arabin.

It cannot be denied that when Eleanor accepted Miss Thorne's invitation, she remembered that Ullathorne was in the parish of

St. Ewold's. Since her interview with the signora she had done little else than think about Mr. Arabin, and the appeal that had been made to her. She could not bring herself to believe or try to bring herself to believe, that what she had been told was untrue. Think of it how she would, she could not but accept it as a fact that Mr. Arabin was fond of her; and then when she went further, and asked herself the question, she could not but accept it as a fact also that she was fond of him. If it were destined for her to be the partner of his hopes and sorrows, to whom could she look for friendship so properly as to Miss Thorne? This invitation was like an ordained step towards the fulfilment of her destiny, and when she also heard that Mr. Arabin was expected to be at Ullathorne on the following day, it seemed as though all the world were conspiring in her favour. Well, did she not deserve it? In that affair of Mr. Slope, had not all the world conspired against her?

She could not, however, make herself easy and at home. When in the evening after dinner Miss Thorne expatiated on the excellence of Mr. Arabin's qualities, and hinted that any little rumour which might be ill-naturedly spread abroad concerning him really meant nothing, Mrs. Bold found herself unable to answer. When Miss Thorne went a little further and declared that she did not know a prettier vicarage-house in the county than St. Ewold's, Mrs. Bold remembering the projected bow-window and the projected priestess still held her tongue; though her eyes tingled with the conviction that all the world knew that she was in love with Mr. Arabin. Well; what would that matter if they could only meet and tell each other what each now longed to tell?

And they did meet. Mr. Arabin came early in the day, and found the two ladies together at work in the drawing-room. Miss Thorne, who had she known all the truth would have vanished into the air at once, had no conception that her immediate absence would be a blessing, and remained chatting with them till luncheon-time. Mr. Arabin could talk about nothing but the Signora Neroni's beauty, would discuss no people but the Stanhopes. This was very distressing to Eleanor, and not very satisfactory to Miss Thorne. But yet there was evidence of innocence in his open avowal of admiration.

And then they had lunch, and then Mr. Arabin went out on parish duty, and Eleanor and Miss Thorne were left to take a walk together.

"Do you think the Signora Neroni is so lovely as people say?" Eleanor asked as they were coming home.

"She is very beautiful certainly, very beautiful," Miss Thorne answered; "but I do not know that any one considers her lovely. She is a woman all men would like to look at; but few I imagine would be glad to take her to their hearths, even were she unmarried and not afflicted as she is."

There was some little comfort in this. Eleanor made the most of it till she got back to the house. She was then left alone in the drawing-room, and just as it was getting dark Mr. Arabin came in.

It was a beautiful afternoon in the beginning of October, and Eleanor was sitting in the window to get the advantage of the last daylight for her novel. There was a fire in the comfortable room, but the weather was not cold enough to make it attractive; and as she could see the sun set from where she sat, she was not very attentive to her book.

Mr. Arabin when he entered stood awhile with his back to the fire in his usual way, merely uttering a few common-place remarks about the beauty of the weather, while he plucked up courage for more interesting converse. It cannot probably be said that he had resolved then and there to make an offer to Eleanor. Men we believe seldom make such resolves. Mr. Slope and Mr. Stanhope had done so, it is true; but gentlemen generally propose without any absolutely defined determination as to their doing so. Such was now the case with Mr. Arabin.

"It is a lovely sunset," said Eleanor, answering him on the dreadfully trite subject which he had chosen.

Mr. Arabin could not see the sunset from the hearth-rug, so he had to go close to her.

"Very lovely," said he, standing modestly so far away from her as to avoid touching the flounces of her dress. Then it appeared that he had nothing further to say; so after gazing for a moment in silence at the brightness of the setting sun, he returned to the fire.

Eleanor found that it was quite impossible for herself to commence a conversation. In the first place she could find nothing to say; words, which were generally plenty enough with her, would not come to her relief. And, moreover, do what she would, she could hardly prevent herself from crying.

"Do you like Ullathorne?" said Mr. Arabin, speaking from the safely distant position which he had assumed on the hearth-rug.

"Yes, indeed, very much!"

"I don't mean Mr. and Miss Thorne. I know you like them; but the style of the house. There is something about old-fashioned mansions, built as this is, and old-fashioned gardens, that to me is especially delightful."

"I like everything old-fashioned," said Eleanor; "old-fashioned things are so much the honestest."

"I don't know about that," said Mr. Arabin, gently laughing. "That is an opinion on which very much may be said on either side. It is strange how widely the world is divided on a subject which so nearly concerns us all, and which is so close beneath our eyes. Some think that we are quickly progressing towards perfection, while others imagine that virtue is disappearing from the earth."

"And you, Mr. Arabin, what do you think?" said Eleanor. She felt somewhat surprised at the tone which his conversation was taking, and yet she was relieved at his saying something which enabled herself to speak without showing her own emotion.

"What do I think, Mrs. Bold?" and then he rumbled his money with his hands in his trowsers pockets, and looked and spoke very little like a thriving lover. "It is the bane of my life that on important subjects I acquire no fixed opinion. I think, and think, and go on thinking; and yet my thoughts are running ever in different directions. I hardly know whether or no we do lean more confidently than our fathers did on those high hopes to which we profess to aspire."

"I think the world grows more worldly every day," said Eleanor.

"That is because you see more of it than when you were younger. But we should hardly judge by what we see,—we see so very very little." There was then a pause for a while, during which Mr. Arabin continued to turn over his shillings and half-crowns. "If we believe in Scripture, we can hardly think that mankind in general will now be allowed to retrograde."

Eleanor, whose mind was certainly engaged otherwise than on the general state of mankind, made no answer to this. She felt thoroughly dissatisfied with herself. She could not force her thoughts away from the topic on which the signora had spoken to her in so strange a way, and yet she knew that she could not converse with Mr. Arabin in an unrestrained natural tone till she did so. She was most anxious not to show to him any special emotion, and yet she felt that if he looked at her he would at once see that she was not at ease.

But he did not look at her. Instead of doing so, he left the fire-place and began walking up and down the room. Eleanor took up her book resolutely; but she could not read, for there was a tear in her eye, and do what she would it fell on her cheek. When Mr. Arabin's back was turned to her she wiped it away; but another was soon coursing down her face in its place. They would come; not a deluge of tears that would have betrayed her at once, but one by one, single monitors. Mr. Arabin did not observe her closely, and they passed unseen.

Mr. Arabin, thus pacing up and down the room, took four or five turns before he spoke another word, and Eleanor sat equally silent with her face bent over her book. She was afraid that her tears would get the better of her, and was preparing for an escape from the room, when Mr. Arabin in his walk stood opposite to her. He did not come close up, but stood exactly on the spot to which his course brought him, and then, with his hands under his coat tails, thus made his confession.

"Mrs. Bold," said he, "I owe you retribution for a great offence of which I have been guilty towards you." Eleanor's heart beat so that she could not trust herself to say that he had never been guilty of any offence. So Mr. Arabin thus went on.

"I have thought much of it since, and I am now aware that I was wholly unwarranted in putting to you a question which I once asked you. It was indelicate on my part, and perhaps unmanly. No intimacy which may exist between myself and your connexion, Dr. Grantly, could justify it. Nor could the acquaintance which existed between ourselves." This word acquaintance struck cold on Eleanor's heart. Was this to be her doom after all? "I therefore think it right to beg your pardon in a humble spirit, and I now do so."

What was Eleanor to say to him? She could not say much, because she was crying, and yet she must say something. She was most anxious to say that something graciously, kindly, and yet not in such a manner as to betray herself. She had never felt herself so much at a loss for words.

"Indeed I took no offence, Mr. Arabin."

"Oh, but you did! And had you not done so, you would not have been yourself. You were as right to be offended, as I was wrong so to offend you. I have not forgiven myself, but I hope to hear that you forgive me."

She was now past speaking calmly, though she still continued to hide her tears, and Mr. Arabin, after pausing a moment in vain for her reply, was walking off towards the door. She felt that she could not allow him to go unanswered without grievously sinning against all charity; so, rising from her seat, she gently touched his arm and said: "Oh, Mr. Arabin, do not go till I speak to you! I do forgive you. You know that I forgive you."

He took the hand that had so gently touched his arm, and then gazed into her face as if he would peruse there, as though written in a book, the whole future destiny of his life; and as he did so, there was a sober sad seriousness in his own countenance, which Eleanor found herself unable to sustain. She could only look down upon the carpet, let her tears trickle as they would, and leave her hand within his.

It was but for a minute that they stood so, but the duration of that minute was sufficient to make it ever memorable to them both. Eleanor was sure now that she was loved. No words, be their eloquence what it might, could be more impressive than that eager, melancholy gaze.

Why did he look so into her eyes? Why did he not speak to her? Could it be that he looked for her to make the first sign?

And he, though he knew but little of women, even he knew that he was loved. He had only to ask and it would be all his own, that inexpressible loveliness, those ever speaking but yet now mute eyes, that feminine brightness and eager loving spirit which had so attracted him since first he had encountered it at St. Ewold's. It might, must all be his own now. On no other supposition was it possible that she should allow her hand to remain thus clasped within his own. He had only to ask. Ah! but that was the difficulty. Did a minute suffice for all this? Nay, perhaps it might be more than a minute.

"Mrs. Bold—" at last he said, and then stopped himself.

If he could not speak, how was she to do so? He had called her by her name, the same name that any merest stranger would have used! She withdrew her hand from his, and moved as though to return to her seat. "Eleanor!" he then said, in his softest tone, as though the courage of a lover were as yet but half assumed, as though he were still afraid of giving offence by the freedom which he took. She looked slowly, gently, almost piteously up into his face. There was at any rate no anger there to deter him.

"Eleanor!" he again exclaimed; and in a moment he had her clasped to his bosom. How this was done, whether the doing was with him or her, whether she had flown thither conquered by the tenderness of his voice, or he with a violence not likely to give offence had drawn her to his breast, neither of them knew; nor can I declare. There was now that sympathy between them which hardly admitted of individual motion. They were one and the same,—one flesh,—one spirit,—one life.

"Eleanor, my own Eleanor, my own, my wife!" She ventured to look up at him through her tears, and he, bowing his face down over hers, pressed his lips upon her brow; his virgin lips, which since a beard first grew upon his chin, had never yet tasted the luxury of a woman's cheek.

She had been told that her yea must be yea, or her nay, nay; but she was called on for neither the one nor the other. She told Miss Thorne that she was engaged to Mr. Arabin, but no such words had passed between them, no promises had been asked or given.

"Oh, let me go," said she; "let me go now. I am too happy to remain,—let me go, that I may be alone." He did not try to hinder her; he did not repeat the kiss; he did not press another on her lips. He might have done so had he been so minded. She was now all his own. He took his arm from round her waist, his arm that was trembling with a new delight, and let her go. She fled like a roe to her own chamber, and then, having turned the bolt, she enjoyed the full luxury of her love. She idolised, almost worshipped this man who had so meekly begged her pardon. And he was now her own. Oh, how she wept and cried and laughed, as the hopes and fears and miseries of the last few weeks passed in remembrance through her mind.

Mr. Slope! That any one should have dared to think that she who had been chosen by him could possibly have mated herself with Mr. Slope! That they should have dared to tell him, also, and subject her bright happiness to such needless risk! And then she smiled with joy as she thought of all the comforts she could give him; not that he cared for comfort, but that it would be so delicious for her to give.

She got up and rang for her maid that she might tell her little boy of his new father; and in her own way she did tell him. She desired her maid to leave her, in order that she might be alone with her child; and then, while he lay sprawling on the bed, she poured forth the praises, all unmeaning to him, of the man she had selected to guard his infancy.

She could not be happy, however, till she had made Mr. Arabin take the child to himself, and thus, as it were, adopt him as his own. The moment the idea struck her she took the baby up in her arms, and opening her door, ran quickly down to the drawing-room. She at once found, by his step still pacing on the floor, that he was there; and a glance within the room told her that he was alone. She hesitated a moment, and then hurried in with her precious charge.

Mr. Arabin met her in the middle of the room. "There," said she, breathless with her haste; "there, take him—take him and love him."

Mr. Arabin took the little fellow from her, and kissing him again and again, prayed God to bless him. "He shall be all as my own—all as my own," said he. Eleanor, as she stooped to take back her child, kissed the hand that held him, and then rushed back with her treasure to her chamber.

It was thus that Mr. Harding's younger daughter was won for the second time. At dinner neither she nor Mr. Arabin were very bright, but their silence occasioned no remark. In the drawing-room, as we have before said, she told Miss Thorne what had occurred. The next morning she returned to Barchester, and Mr. Arabin went over with his budget of news to the archdeacon. As Doctor Grantly was not there, he could only satisfy himself by telling Mrs. Grantly how that he intended himself the honour of becoming her brother-in-law. In the ecstasy of her joy at hearing such tidings, Mrs. Grantly vouchsafed him a warmer welcome than any he had yet received from Eleanor.

"Good heavens!" she exclaimed—it was the general exclamation of the rectory. "Poor Eleanor! Dear Eleanor! What a monstrous injustice has been done her!—Well, it shall all be made up now." And then she thought of the signora. "What lies people tell," she said to herself.

But people in this matter had told no lies at all.

XLIX

The Belzebub Colt

When Miss Thorne left the dining-room, Eleanor had formed no intention of revealing to her what had occurred; but when she was seated beside her hostess on the sofa the secret dropped from her almost unawares. Eleanor was but a bad hypocrite, and she found herself quite unable to continue talking about Mr. Arabin as though he were a stranger, while her heart was full of him. When Miss Thorne, pursuing her own scheme with discreet zeal, asked the young widow whether, in her opinion, it would not be a good thing for Mr. Arabin to get married, she had nothing for it but to confess the truth. "I suppose it would," said Eleanor, rather sheepishly. Whereupon Miss Thorne amplified on the idea. "Oh, Miss Thorne," said Eleanor, "he is going to be married: I am engaged to him."

Now Miss Thorne knew very well that there had been no such engagement when she had been walking with Mrs. Bold in the morning. She had also heard enough to be tolerably sure that there had been no preliminaries to such an engagement. She was, therefore, as we have before described, taken a little by surprise. But, nevertheless, she embraced her guest, and cordially congratulated her.

Eleanor had no opportunity of speaking another word to Mr. Arabin that evening, except such words as all the world might hear; and these, as may be supposed, were few enough. Miss Thorne did her best to leave them in privacy; but Mr. Thorne, who knew nothing of what had occurred, and another guest, a friend of his, entirely interfered with her good intentions. So poor Eleanor had to go to bed without one sign of affection. Her state, nevertheless, was not to be pitied.

The next morning she was up early. It was probable, she thought, that by going down a little before the usual hour of breakfast, she might find Mr. Arabin alone in the dining-room. Might it not be that he also would calculate that an interview would thus be possible? Thus thinking, Eleanor was dressed a full hour before the time fixed in the Ullathorne household for morning prayers. She did not at once go down. She was afraid to seem to be too anxious to meet her lover; though, heaven knows, her anxiety was intense enough. She therefore sat herself down at her window, and repeatedly looking at her watch, nursed her child till she thought she might venture forth.

When she found herself at the dining-room door, she stood a moment, hesitating to turn the handle; but when she heard Mr. Thorne's voice inside she hesitated no longer. Her object was defeated, and she might now go in as soon as she liked without the slightest imputation on her delicacy. Mr. Thorne and Mr. Arabin were standing on the hearth-rug, discussing the merits of the Belzebub colt; or rather, Mr. Thorne was discussing, and Mr. Arabin was listening. That interesting animal had rubbed the stump of his tail against the wall of his stable, and occasioned much uneasiness to the Ullathorne master of the horse. Had Eleanor but waited another minute, Mr. Thorne would have been in the stables.

Mr. Thorne, when he saw his lady guest, repressed his anxiety. The Belzebub colt must do without him. And so the three stood, saying little or nothing to each other, till at last the master of the house, finding that he could no longer bear his present state of suspense respecting his favourite young steed, made an elaborate apology to Mrs. Bold, and escaped. As he shut the door behind him, Eleanor almost wished that he had remained. It was not that she was afraid of Mr. Arabin, but she hardly yet knew how to address him.

He, however, soon relieved her from her embarrassment. He came up to her, and taking both her hands in his, he said: "So, Eleanor, you and I are to be man and wife. Is it so?"

She looked up into his eyes, and her lips formed themselves into a single syllable. She uttered no sound, but he could read the affirmative plainly in her face.

"It is a great trust," said he; "a very great trust."

"It is—it is," said Eleanor, not exactly taking what he had said in the sense that he had meant. "It is a very, very great trust, and I will do my utmost to deserve it."

"And I also will do my utmost to deserve it," said Mr. Arabin, very solemnly. And then, winding his arm round her waist, he stood there gazing at the fire, and she with her head leaning on his shoulder, stood by him, well satisfied with her position. They neither of them spoke, or found any want of speaking. All that was needful for them to say had been said. The yea, yea, had been spoken by Eleanor in her own way—and that way had been perfectly satisfactory to Mr. Arabin.

And now it remained to them each to enjoy the assurance of the other's love. And how great the luxury is! How far it surpasses any other pleasure which God has allowed to his creatures! And to a woman's heart how doubly delightful!

When the ivy has found its tower, when the delicate creeper has found its strong wall, we know how the parasite plants grow and prosper. They were not created to stretch forth their branches alone, and endure without protection the summer's sun and the winter's storm. Alone they but spread themselves on the ground, and cower unseen in the dingy shade. But when they have found their firm supporters, how wonderful is their beauty; how all pervading and victorious! What is the turret without its ivy, or the high garden-wall without the jasmine which gives it its beauty and fragrance? The hedge without the honeysuckle is but a hedge.

There is a feeling still half existing, but now half conquered by the the force of human nature, that a woman should be ashamed of her love till the husband's right to her compels her to acknowledge it. We would fain preach a different doctrine. A woman should glory in her love; but on that account let her take the more care that it be such as to justify her glory.

Eleanor did glory in hers, and she felt, and had cause to feel, that it deserved to be held as glorious. She could have stood there for hours with his arm round her, had fate and Mr. Thorne permitted it. Each moment she crept nearer to his bosom, and felt more and more certain that there was her home. What now to her was the archdeacon's arrogance, her sister's coldness, or her dear father's weakness? What need she care for the duplicity of such friends as Charlotte Stanhope? She had found the strong shield that should guard her from all wrongs, the trusty pilot that should henceforward guide her through the shoals and rocks. She would give up the heavy burden of her independence, and once more assume the position of a woman, and the duties of a trusting and loving wife.

And he, too, stood there fully satisfied with his place. They were both looking intently on the fire, as though they could read there their future fate, till at last Eleanor turned her face towards his. "How sad you are," she said, smiling; and indeed his face was, if not sad, at least serious. "How sad you are, love!"

"Sad," said he, looking down at her; "no, certainly not sad." Her sweet loving eyes were turned towards him, and she smiled softly as he answered her. The temptation was too strong even for the demure propriety of Mr. Arabin, and, bending over her, he pressed his lips to hers.

Immediately after this, Mr. Thorne appeared, and they were both delighted to hear that the tail of the Belzebub colt was not materially injured.

It had been Mr. Harding's intention to hurry over to Ullathorne as soon as possible after his return to Barchester, in order to secure the support of his daughter in his meditated revolt against the archdeacon as touching the deanery; but he was spared the additional journey by hearing that Mrs. Bold had returned unexpectedly home. As soon as he had read her note he started off, and found her waiting for him in her own house.

How much each of them had to tell the other, and how certain each was that the story which he or she had to tell would astonish the other!

"My dear, I am so anxious to see you," said Mr. Harding, kissing his daughter.

"Oh, papa, I have so much to tell you!" said the daughter, returning the embrace.

"My dear, they have offered me the deanery!" said Mr. Harding, anticipating by the suddenness of the revelation the tidings which Eleanor had to give to him.

"Oh, papa," said she, forgetting her own love and happiness in her joy at the surprising news; "oh, papa, can it be possible? Dear papa, how thoroughly, thoroughly happy that makes me!"

"But, my dear, I think it best to refuse it."

"Oh, papa!"

"I am sure you will agree with me, Eleanor, when I

explain it to you. You know, my dear, how old I am. If I live, I——"

"But, papa, I must tell you about myself."

"Well, my dear."

"I do so wonder how you'll take it."

"Take what?"

"If you don't rejoice at it, if it doesn't make you happy, if you don't encourage me, I shall break my heart."

"If that be the case, Nelly, I certainly will encourage you."

"But I fear you won't. I do so fear you won't. And yet you can't but think I am the most fortunate woman living on God's earth."

"Are you, dearest? Then I certainly will rejoice with you. Come, Nelly, come to me, and tell me what it is."

"I am going——"

He led her to the sofa, and seating himself beside her, took both her hands in his. "You are going to be married, Nelly. Is not that it?"

"Yes," she said, faintly. "That is if you will approve," and then she blushed as she remembered the promise which she had so lately volunteered to him, and which she had so utterly forgotten in making her engagement with Mr. Arabin.

Mr. Harding thought for a moment who the man could be whom he was to be called upon to welcome as his son-in-law. A week since he would have had no doubt whom to name. In that case he would have been prepared to give his sanction, although he would have done so with a heavy heart. Now he knew that at any rate it would not be Mr. Slope, though he was perfectly at a loss to guess who could possibly have filled the place. For a moment he thought that the man might be Bertie Stanhope, and his very soul sank within him.

"Well, Nelly?"

"Oh, papa, promise to me that, for my sake, you will love him."

"Come, Nelly, come; tell me who it is."

"But will you love him, papa?"

"Dearest, I must love any one that you love." Then she turned her face to his, and whispered into his ear the name of Mr. Arabin.

No man that she could have named could have more surprised or more delighted him. Had he looked round the world for a son-in-law to his taste, he could have selected no one whom he would have preferred to Mr. Arabin. He was a clergyman; he held a living in the neighbourhood; he was of a set to which all Mr. Harding's own partialities most closely adhered; he was the great friend of Dr. Grantly; and he was, moreover, a man of whom Mr. Harding knew nothing but what he approved. Nevertheless, his surprise was so great as to prevent the immediate expression of his joy. He had never thought of Mr. Arabin in connection with his daughter; he had never imagined that they had any feeling in common. He had feared that his daughter had been made hostile to clergymen of Mr. Arabin's stamp by her intolerance of the archdeacon's pretensions. Had he been put to wish, he might have wished for Mr. Arabin for a son-in-law; but had he been put to guess, the name would never have occurred to him.

"Mr. Arabin!" he exclaimed; "impossible!"

"Oh, papa, for heaven's sake don't say anything against him! If you love me, don't say anything against him. Oh, papa, it's done, and mustn't be undone—oh, papa!"

Fickle Eleanor! where was the promise that she would make no choice for herself without her father's approval? She had chosen, and now demanded his acquiescence. "Oh, papa, isn't he good? isn't he noble? isn't he religious, highminded, everything that a good man possibly can be?" and she clung to her father, beseeching him for his consent.

"My Nelly, my child, my own daughter! He is; he is noble and good and highminded; he is all that a woman can love and a man admire. He shall be my son, my own son. He shall be as close to my heart as you are. My Nelly, my child, my happy, happy child!"

We need not pursue the interview any further. By degrees they returned to the subject of the new promotion. Eleanor tried to prove to him, as the Grantlys had done, that his age could be no bar to his being a very excellent dean; but those arguments had now even less weight on him than before. He said little or nothing, but sat meditative. Every now and then he would kiss his daughter, and say "yes," or "no," or "very true," or "well, my dear, I can't quite agree with you there," but he could not be got to enter sharply into the question of "to be, or not to be" dean of Barchester. Of her and her happiness, of Mr. Arabin and his virtues, he would talk as much as Eleanor desired; and, to tell the truth, that was not a little; but about the deanery he would now say nothing further. He had got a new idea into his head— Why should not Mr. Arabin be the new dean?

L

The Archdeacon Is Satisfied with the State of Affairs

The archdeacon, in his journey into Barchester, had been assured by Mr. Harding that all their prognostications about Mr. Slope and Eleanor were groundless. Mr. Harding, however, had found it very difficult to shake his son-in-law's faith in his own acuteness. The matter had, to Dr. Grantly, been so plainly corroborated by such patent evidence, borne out by such endless circumstances, that he at first refused to take as true the positive statement which Mr. Harding made to him of Eleanor's own disavowal of the impeachment. But at last he yielded in a qualified way. He brought himself to admit that he would at the present regard his past convictions as a mistake; but in doing this he so guarded himself, that if, at any future time, Eleanor should come forth to the world as Mrs. Slope, he might still be able to say: "There, I told you so. Remember what you said and what I said; and remember also for coming years, that I was right in this matter,—as in all others."

He carried, however, his concession so far as to bring himself to undertake to call at Eleanor's house, and he did call accordingly, while the father and daughter were yet in the middle of their conference. Mr. Harding had had so much to hear and to say that he had forgotten to advertise Eleanor of the honour that awaited her, and she heard her brother-in-law's voice in the hall, while she was quite unprepared to see him.

"There's the archdeacon," she said, springing up.

"Yes, my dear. He told me to tell you that he would come and see you; but, to tell the truth, I had forgotten all about it."

Eleanor fled away, regardless of all her father's entreaties. She could not now, in the first hours of her joy, bring herself to bear all the archdeacon's retractions, apologies, and congratulations.

He would have so much to say, and would be so tedious in saying it; consequently, the archdeacon, when he was shown into the drawing-room, found no one there but Mr. Harding.

"You must excuse Eleanor," said Mr. Harding.

"Is anything the matter?" asked the doctor, who at once anticipated that the whole truth about Mr. Slope had at last come out.

"Well, something is the matter. I wonder now whether you will be much surprised?"

The archdeacon saw by his father-in-law's manner that after all he had nothing to tell him about Mr. Slope. "No," said he, "certainly not—nothing will ever surprise me again." Very many men now-a-days, besides the archdeacon, adopt or affect to adopt the *nil admirari* doctrine; but nevertheless, to judge from their appearance, they are just as subject to sudden emotions as their grandfathers and grandmothers were before them.

"What do you think Mr. Arabin has done?"

"Mr. Arabin! It's nothing about that daughter of Stanhope's, I hope?"

"No, not that woman," said Mr. Harding, enjoying his joke in his sleeve.

"Not that woman! Is he going to do anything about any woman? Why can't you speak out if you have anything to say? There is nothing I hate so much as these sort of mysteries."

"There shall be no mystery with you, archdeacon; though of course, it must go no further at present!"

"Well."

"Except Susan. You must promise me you'll tell no one else."

"Nonsense!" exclaimed the archdeacon, who was becoming angry in his suspense. "You can't have any secret about Mr. Arabin."

"Only this—that he and Eleanor are engaged."

It was quite clear to see, by the archdeacon's face, that he did not believe a word of it. "Mr. Arabin! It's impossible!"

"Eleanor, at any rate, has just now told me so."

"It's impossible," repeated the archdeacon.

"Well, I can't say I think it impossible. It certainly took me by surprise; but that does not make it impossible."

"She must be mistaken."

Mr. Harding assured him that there was no mistake; that he would find, on returning home, that Mr. Arabin had been at Plumstead with the express object of making the same declaration, that even Miss Thorne knew all about it; and that, in fact, the thing was as clearly settled as any such arrangement between a lady and a gentleman could well be.

"Good heavens!" said the archdeacon, walking up and down Eleanor's drawing-room. "Good heavens! Good heavens!"

Now, these exclamations certainly betokened faith. Mr. Harding properly gathered from it that, at last, Dr. Grantly did believe the fact. The first utterance clearly evinced a certain amount of distaste at the information he had received; the second, simply indicated surprise; in the tone of the third, Mr. Harding fancied that he could catch a certain gleam of satisfaction.

The archdeacon had truly expressed the workings of his mind. He could not but be disgusted to find how utterly astray he had been in all his anticipations. Had he only been lucky enough to have suggested this marriage himself when he first brought Mr. Arabin into the country, his character for judgment and wisdom would have received an addition which would have classed him at any rate next to Solomon. And why had he not done so? Might he not have foreseen that Mr. Arabin would want a wife in his parsonage? He had foreseen that Eleanor would want a husband; but should he not also have perceived that Mr. Arabin was a man much more likely to attract her than Mr. Slope? The archdeacon found that he had been at fault, and of course could not immediately get over his discomfiture.

Then his surprise was intense. How sly this pair of young turtle doves had been with him. How egregiously they had hoaxed him. He had preached to Eleanor against her fancied attachment to Mr. Slope, at the very time that she was in love with his own protégé, Mr. Arabin; and had absolutely taken that same Mr. Arabin into his confidence with reference to his dread of Mr. Slope's alliance. It was very natural that the archdeacon should feel suprise.

But there was also great ground for satisfaction. Looking at the match by itself, it was the very thing to help the doctor out of his difficulties. In the first place, the assurance that he should never have Mr. Slope for his brother-in-law, was in itself a great comfort. Then Mr. Arabin was, of all men, the one with whom it would best suit him to be so intimately connected. But the crowning comfort was the blow which this marriage would give to Mr. Slope. He had now certainly lost his wife; rumour was beginning to whisper that he might possibly lose his position in the palace; and if Mr. Harding would only be true, the great danger of all would be surmounted. In such case it might be expected that Mr. Slope would own himself vanquished, and take himself altogether away from Barchester. And so the archdeacon would again be able to breathe pure air.

"Well, well," said he. "Good heavens! good heavens!" and the tone of the fifth exclamation made Mr. Harding fully aware that content was reigning in the archdeacon's bosom.

And then slowly, gradually, and craftily, Mr. Harding propounded his own new scheme. Why should not Mr. Arabin be the new dean?

Slowly, gradually, and thoughtfully Dr. Grantly fell into his father-in-law's views. Much as he liked Mr. Arabin, sincere as was his admiration for that gentleman's ecclesiastical abilities, he would not have sanctioned a measure which would rob his father-in-law of his fairly earned promotion, were it at all practicable to induce his father-in-law to accept the promotion which he had earned. But the archdeacon had, on a former occasion, received proof of the obstinacy with which Mr. Harding could adhere to his own views in opposition to the advice of all his friends. He knew tolerably well that nothing would induce the meek, mild man before him to take the high place offered to him, if he thought it wrong to do so. Knowing this he also said to himself more than once: "Why should not Mr. Arabin be Dean of Barchester?" It was at last arranged between them that they would together start to London by the earliest train on the following morning, making a little *détour* to Oxford on their journey. Dr. Gwynne's counsels, they imagined, might perhaps be of assistance to them.

These matters settled, the archdeacon hurried off, that he might return to Plumstead and prepare for his journey. The day was extremely fine, and he came into the city in an open gig. As he was driving up the High Street he encountered Mr. Slope at a crossing. Had he not pulled up rather sharply, he would have run over him. The two had never spoken to each other since they had met on a memorable occasion in the bishop's study. They did not speak now; but they looked each other full in the face, and Mr. Slope's countenance was as impudent, as triumphant, as defiant as ever. Had Dr. Grantly not known to the contrary, he would have imagined that his enemy had won the deanship, the wife, and all the rich honours, for which he had been striving. As it was, he had lost everything that he had in the world, and had just received his *congé* from the bishop.

In leaving the town the archdeacon drove by the well-remembered entrance of Hiram's hospital. There, at the gate, was a large, untidy, farmer's wagon, laden with untidy-looking furniture; and there, inspecting the arrival, was good Mrs. Quiverful—not dressed in her Sunday best—not very clean in her apparel—not graceful as to her bonnet and shawl; or, indeed with many feminine charms as to her whole appearance. She was busy at domestic work in her new house, and had just ventured out, expecting to see no one on the arrival of the family chattels. The archdeacon was down upon her before she knew where she was.

Her acquaintance with Dr. Grantly or his family was very slight indeed. The archdeacon, as a matter of course, knew every clergyman in the archdeaconry, it may almost be said in the diocese, and had some acquaintance, more or less intimate, with their wives and families. With Mr. Quiverful he had been concerned on various matters of business; but of Mrs. Q. he had seen very little. Now, however, he was in too gracious a mood to pass her by unnoticed. The Quiverfuls, one and all, had looked for the bitterest hostility from Dr. Grantly; they knew his anxiety that Mr. Harding should return to his old home at the hospital, and they did not know that a new home had been offered to him at the deanery. Mrs. Quiverful was therefore not a little surprised and not a little rejoiced also, at the tone in which she was addressed.

"How do you do, Mrs. Quiverful?—how do you do?" said he, stretching his left hand out of the gig, as he spoke to her. "I am very glad to see you employed in so pleasant and useful a manner; very glad indeed."

Mrs. Quiverful thanked him, and shook hands with him, and looked into his face suspiciously. She was not sure whether the congratulations and kindness were or were not ironical.

"Pray tell Mr. Quiverful from me," he continued, "that I am rejoiced at his appointment. It's a comfortable place, Mrs. Quiverful, and a comfortable house, and I am very glad to see you in it. Good-bye—good-bye." And he drove on, leaving the lady well pleased and astonished at his good-nature. On the whole things were going well with the archdeacon, and he could afford to be charitable to Mrs. Quiverful. He looked forth from his gig smilingly on all the world, and forgave every one in Barchester their sins, excepting only Mrs. Proudie and Mr. Slope. Had he seen the bishop, he would have felt inclined to pat even him kindly on the head.

He determined to go home by St. Ewold's. This would take him some three miles out of his way; but he felt that he could not leave Plumstead comfortably without saying one word of good fellowship to Mr. Arabin. When he reached the parsonage the vicar was still out; but, from what he had heard, he did not doubt that he would meet him on the road between their two houses. He was right in this, for about halfway home, at a narrow turn, he came upon Mr. Arabin, who was on horseback.

"Well, well, well, well"; said the archdeacon, loudly, joyously, and with supreme good humour; "well, well, well, well; so, after all, we have no further cause to fear Mr. Slope."

"I hear from Mrs. Grantly that they have offered the deanery to Mr. Harding," said the other.

"Mr. Slope has lost more than the deanery, I find," and then the archdeacon laughed jocosely. "Come, come, Arabin, you have kept your secret well enough. I know all about it now."

"I have had no secret, archdeacon," said the other with a quiet smile. "None at all—not for a day. It was only yesterday that I knew my own good fortune, and to-day I went over to Plumstead to ask your approval. From what Mrs. Grantly has said to me, I am led to hope that I shall have it."

"With all my heart, with all my heart," said the archdeacon cordially, holding his friend fast by the hand. "It's just as I would have it. She is an excellent young woman; she will not come to you empty-handed; and I think she will make you a good wife. If she does her duty by you as her sister does by me, you'll be a happy man; that's all I can say." And as he finished speaking, a tear might have been observed in each of the doctor's eyes.

Mr. Arabin warmly returned the archdeacon's grasp, but he said little. His heart was too full for speaking, and he could not express the gratitude which he felt. Dr. Grantly understood him as well as though he had spoken for an hour.

"And mind, Arabin," said he, "no one but myself shall tie the knot. We'll get Eleanor out to Plumstead, and it shall come off there. I'll make Susan stir herself, and we'll do it in style. I must be off to London to-morrow on special business. Harding goes with me. But I'll be back before your bride has got her wedding dress ready." And so they parted.

On his journey home the archdeacon occupied his mind with preparations for the marriage festivities. He made a great resolve that he would atone to Eleanor for all the injury he had done her by the munificence of his future treatment. He would show her what was the difference in his eyes between a Slope and an Arabin. On one other thing also he decided with a firm mind; if the affair of the dean should not be settled in Mr.

Arabin's favour, nothing should prevent him putting a new front and bow-window in the dining-room at St. Ewold's parsonage.

"So we're sold after all, Sue," said he to his wife, accosting her with a kiss as soon as he entered his house. He did not call his wife Sue above twice or thrice in a year, and these occasions were great high days.

"Eleanor has had more sense than we gave her credit for," said Mrs. Grantly.

And there was great content in Plumstead rectory that evening; and Mrs. Grantly promised her husband that she would now open her heart, and take Mr. Arabin into it. Hitherto she had declined to do so.

LI

Mr. Slope Bids Farewell to the Palace and Its Inhabitants

We must now take leave of Mr. Slope, and of the bishop also, and of Mrs. Proudie. These leave-takings in novels are as disagreeable as they are in real life; not so sad, indeed, for they want the reality of sadness; but quite as perplexing, and generally less satisfactory. What novelist, what Fielding, what Scott, what George Sand, or Sue, or Dumas, can impart an interest to the last chapter of his fictitious history? Promises of two children and superhuman happiness are of no avail, nor assurance of extreme respectability carried to an age far exceeding that usually allotted to mortals. The sorrows of our heroes and heroines, they are your delight, oh public! their sorrows, or their sins, or their absurdities; not their virtues, good sense, and consequent rewards. When we begin to tint our final pages with *couleur de rose*, as in accordance with fixed rule we must do, we altogether extinguish our own powers of pleasing. When we become dull we offend your intellect; and we must become dull or we should offend your taste. A late writer, wishing to sustain his interest to the last page, hung his hero at the end of the third volume. The consequence was, that no one would read his novel. And who can apportion out and dovetail his incidents, dialogues, characters, and descriptive morsels, so as to fit them all exactly into 439 pages, without either compressing them unnaturally, or extending them artificially at the end of his labour? Do I not myself know that I am at this moment in want of a dozen pages, and that I am sick with cudgelling my brains to find them? And then when everything is done, the kindest-hearted critic of them all invariably twits us with the incompetency and lameness of our conclusion. We have either become idle and neglected it, or tedious and over-laboured it. It is insipid or unnatural, overstrained or imbecile. It means nothing, or attempts too much. The last scene of all, as all last scenes we fear must be,

> Is second childishness, and mere oblivion,
> Sans teeth, sans eyes, sans taste, sans everything.

I can only say that if some critic, who thoroughly knows his work, and has laboured on it till experience has made him perfect, will write the last fifty pages of a novel in the way they should be written, I, for one, will in future do my best to copy the example. Guided by my own lights only, I confess that I despair of success.

For the last week or ten days, Mr. Slope had seen nothing of Mrs. Poudie, and very little of the bishop. He still lived in the palace, still went through his usual routine work; but the confidential doings of the diocese had passed into other hands. He had seen this clearly and marked it well; but it had not much disturbed him. He had indulged in other hopes till the bishop's affairs had become dull to him, and he was aware that, as regarded the diocese, Mrs. Proudie had checkmated him. It has been explained, in the beginning of these pages, how three or four were contending together as to who, in fact, should be bishop of Barchester. Each of these had now admitted to himself (or boasted to herself) that Mrs. Proudie was victorious in the struggle. They had gone through a competitive examination of considerable severity, and she had come forth the winner, *facile princeps*. Mr. Slope had, for a moment, run her hard, but it was only for a moment. It had become, as it were, acknowledged that Hiram's hospital should be the testing point between them, and now Mr. Quiverful was already in the hospital, the proof of Mrs. Proudie's skill and courage.

All this did not break down Mr. Slope's spirit, because he had other hopes. But, alas, at last there came to him a note from his friend Sir Nicholas, informing him that the deanship was disposed of. Let us give Mr. Slope his due. He did not lie prostrate under this blow, or give himself up to vain lamentations; he did not henceforward despair of life, and call upon gods above and gods below to carry him off. He sat himself down in his chair, counted out what monies he had in hand for present purposes, and what others were coming in to him, bethought himself as to the best sphere for his future exertions, and at once wrote off a letter to a rich sugar-refiner's wife in Baker Street, who, as he well knew, was much given to the entertainment and encouragement of serious young evangelical clergymen. He was again, he said, "upon the world, having found the air of a cathedral town, and the very nature of cathedral services, uncongenial to his spirit"; and then he sat awhile, making firm resolves as to his manner of parting from the bishop, and also as to his future conduct.

At last he rose, and twitched his mantle blue (black),
To-morrow to fresh woods and pastures new.

Having received a formal command to wait upon the bishop, he rose and proceeded to obey it. He rang the bell and desired the servant to inform his master that if it suited his lordship, he, Mr. Slope, was ready to wait upon him. The servant, who well understood that Mr. Slope was no longer in the ascendant, brought back a message, saying that "his lordship desired that Mr. Slope would attend him immediately in his study." Mr. Slope waited about ten minutes more to prove his independence, and then he went into the bishop's room. There, as he had expected, he found Mrs. Proudie, together with her husband.

"Hum, ha,—Mr. Slope, pray take a chair," said the gentleman bishop.

"Pray be seated, Mr. Slope," said the lady bishop.

"Thank ye, thank ye," said Mr. Slope, and walking round to the fire, he threw himself into one of the arm-chairs that graced the hearth-rug.

"Mr. Slope," said the bishop, "it has become necessary that I should speak to you definitively on a matter that has for some time been pressing itself on my attention."

"May I ask whether the subject is in any way connected with myself?" said Mr. Slope.

"It is so,—certainly,—yes, it certainly is connected with yourself, Mr. Slope."

"Then, my lord, if I may be allowed to express a wish, I would prefer that no discussion on the subject should take place between us in the presence of a third person."

"Don't alarm yourself, Mr. Slope," said Mrs. Proudie, "no discussion is at all necessary. The bishop merely intends to express his own wishes."

"I merely intend, Mr. Slope, to express my own wishes,—no discussion will be at all necessary," said the bishop, reiterating his wife's words.

"That is more, my lord, than we any of us can be sure of," said Mr. Slope; "I cannot, however, force Mrs. Proudie to leave the room; nor can I refuse to remain here if it be your lordship's wish that I should do so."

"It is his lordship's wish, certainly," said Mrs. Proudie.

"Mr. Slope," began the bishop, in a solemn, serious voice, "it grieves me to have to find fault. It grieves me much to have to find fault with a clergyman; but especially so with a clergyman in your position."

"Why, what have I done amiss, my lord?" demanded Mr. Slope, boldly.

"What have you done amiss, Mr. Slope?" said Mrs. Proudie, standing erect before the culprit, and raising that terrible forefinger. "Do you dare to ask the bishop what you have done amiss? does not your conscience——"

"Mrs. Proudie, pray let it be understood, once and for all, that I will have no words with you."

"Ah, sir, but you will have words," said she, "you must have words. Why have you had so many words with that Signora Neroni? Why have you disgraced yourself, you a clergyman too, by constantly consorting with such a woman as that,—with a married woman—with one altogether unfit for a clergyman's society?"

"At any rate, I was introduced to her in your drawing-room," retorted Mr. Slope.

"And shamefully you behaved there," said Mrs. Proudie, "most shamefully. I was wrong to allow you to remain in the house a day after what I then saw. I should have insisted on your instant dismissal."

"I have yet to learn, Mrs. Proudie, that you have the power to insist either on my going from hence or on my staying here."

"What!" said the lady; "I am not to have the privilege of saying who shall and who shall not frequent my own drawing-room! I am not to save my servants and dependents from having their morals corrupted by improper conduct! I am not to save my own daughters from impurity! I will let you see, Mr. Slope, whether I have the power or whether I have not. You will have the goodness to understand that you no longer fill any situation about the bishop; and as your room will be immediately wanted in the palace for another chaplain, I must ask you to provide yourself with apartments as soon as may be convenient for you."

"My lord," said Mr. Slope, appealing to the bishop, and so turning his back completely on the lady, "will you permit me to ask that I may have from your own lips any decision that you may have come to on this matter?"

"Certainly, Mr. Slope, certainly," said the bishop; "that is but reasonable. Well, my decision is that you had better look for some other preferment. For the situation which you have lately held I do not think that you are well suited."

"And what, my lord, has been my fault?"

"That Signora Neroni is one fault," said Mrs. Proudie; "and a very abominable fault she is; very abominable and very disgraceful. Fie, Mr. Slope, fie! You an evangelical clergyman indeed!"

"My lord, I desire to know for what fault I am turned out of your lordship's house?"

"You hear what Mrs. Proudie says," said the bishop.

"When I publish the history of this transaction, my lord, as I decidedly shall do in my own vindication, I presume you will not wish me to state that you have discarded me at your wife's bidding—because she has objected to my being acquainted with another lady, the daughter of one of the prebendaries of the chapter?"

"You may publish what you please, sir," said Mrs. Proudie. "But you will not be insane enough to publish any of your doings in Barchester. Do you think I have not heard of your kneelings at that creature's feet—that is if she has any feet—and of your constant slobbering over her hand? I advise you to beware, Mr. Slope, of what you do and say. Clergymen have been unfrocked for less than what you have been guilty of."

"My lord, if this goes on I shall be obliged to indict this woman—Mrs. Proudie I mean—for defamation of character."

"I think, Mr. Slope, you had better now retire," said the bishop. "I will enclose to you a cheque for any balance that may be due to you; and, under the present circumstances, it will of course be better for all parties that you should leave the palace at the earliest possible moment. I will allow you for your journey back to London, and for your maintenance in Barchester for a week from this date.''

''If, however, you wish to remain in this neighbourhood,'' said Mrs. Proudie, ''and will solemnly pledge yourself never again to see that woman, and will promise also to be more circumspect in your conduct, the bishop will mention your name to Mr. Quiverful, who now wants a curate at Puddingdale. The house is, I imagine, quite sufficient for your requirements: and there will moreover be a stipend of fifty pounds a year.''

''May God forgive you, madam, for the manner in which you have treated me,'' said Mr. Slope, looking at her with a very heavenly look; ''and remember this, madam, that you yourself may still have a fall''; and he looked at her with a very worldly look. ''As to the bishop, I pity him!'' And so saying, Mr. Slope left the room. Thus ended the intimacy of the Bishop of Barchester with his first confidential chaplain.

Mrs. Proudie was right in this; namely, that Mr. Slope was not insane enough to publish to the world any of his doings in Barchester. He did not trouble his friend Mr. Towers with any written statement of the iniquity of Mrs. Proudie, or the imbecility of her husband. He was aware that it would be wise in him to drop for the future all allusions of his doings in the cathedral city. Soon after the interview just recorded, he left Barchester, shaking the dust off his feet as he entered the railway carriage; and he gave no longing lingering look after the cathedral towers, as the train hurried him quickly out of their sight.

It is well known that the family of the Slopes never starve: they always fall on their feet like cats, and let them fall where they will, they live on the fat of the land. Our Mr. Slope did so. On his return to town he found that the sugar-refiner had died, and that his widow was inconsolable: or, in other words, in want of consolation. Mr. Slope consoled her, and soon found himself settled with much comfort in the house in Baker Street. He possessed himself, also, before long, of a church in the vicinity of the New Road, and became known to fame as one of the most eloquent preachers and pious clergymen in that part of the metropolis. There let us leave him.

Of the bishop and his wife very little further need be said. From that time forth nothing material occurred to interrupt the even course of their domestic harmony. Very speedily, a further vacancy on the bench of bishops gave to Dr. Proudie the seat in the House of Lords, which he at first so anxiously longed for. But by this time he had become a wiser man. He did certainly take his seat, and occasionally registered a vote in favour of Government views on ecclesiastical matters. But he had thoroughly learnt that his proper sphere of action lay in close contiguity with Mrs. Proudie's wardrobe. He never again aspired to disobey, or seemed even to wish for autocratic diocesan authority. If ever he thought of freedom, he did so, as men think of the millennium, as of a good time which may be coming, but which nobody expects to come in their day. Mrs. Proudie might be said still to bloom, and was, at any rate, strong; and the bishop had no reason to apprehend that he would be speedily visited with the sorrows of a widower's life.

He is still Bishop of Barchester. He has so graced that throne, that the Government has been averse to translate him, even to higher dignities. There may he remain, under safe pupilage, till the new-fangled manners of the age have discovered him to be superannuated, and bestowed on him a pension. As for Mrs. Proudie, our prayers for her are that she may live for ever.

LII

The New Dean Takes Possession of the Deanery, and the New Warden of the Hospital

Mr. Harding and the archdeacon together made their way to Oxford, and there, by dint of cunning argument, they induced the Master of Lazarus also to ask himself this momentous question: "Why should not Mr. Arabin be Dean of Barchester?" He of course, for a while tried his hand at persuading Mr. Harding that he was foolish, over-scrupulous, self-willed, and weak-minded; but he tried in vain. If Mr. Harding would not give way to Dr. Grantly, it was not likely he would give way to Dr. Gwynne; more especially now that so admirable a scheme as that of inducting Mr. Arabin into the deanery had been set on foot. When the master found that his eloquence was vain, and heard also that Mr. Arabin was about to become Mr. Harding's son-in-law, he confessed that he also would, under such circumstances, be glad to see his old friend and protégé, the fellow of his college, placed in the comfortable position that was going a-begging.

'It might be the means, you know, Master, of keeping Mr. Slope out,'' said the archdeacon with grave caution.

"He has no more chance of it,'' said the master, ''than our college chaplain. I know more about it than that.''

Mrs. Grantly had been right in her surmise. It was the Master of Lazarus who had been instrumental in representing in high places the claims which Mr. Harding had upon the Government, and he now consented to use his best endeavours towards getting the offer transferred to Mr. Arabin. The three of them went on to London together, and there they remained a week, to the great disgust of Mrs. Grantly, and most probably also of Mrs. Gwynne. The minister was out of town in one direction, and his private secretary in another. The clerks who remained could do nothing in such a matter as this, and all was difficulty and confusion. The two doctors seemed to have plenty to do; they bustled here and they bustled there, and complained at their club in the evenings that they had been driven off their legs; but Mr. Harding had no occupation. Once or twice he suggested that he might perhaps return to Barchester. His request, however, was peremptorily refused, and he had nothing for it but to while away his time in Westminster Abbey.

At length an answer from the great man came. The Master of Lazarus had made his proposition through the Bishop of Belgravia. Now this bishop, though but newly gifted with his diocesan honours, was a man of much weight in the clerico-political world. He was, if not as pious, at any rate as wise as St. Paul, and had been with so much effect all things to all men, that though he was great among the dons of Oxford, he had been selected for the most favourite seat on the bench by a Whig Prime Minister. To him Dr. Gwynne had made known his wishes and his arguments, and the bishop had made them known to the Marquis of Kensington Gore. The marquis, who was Lord High Steward of the Pantry Board, and who by most men was supposed to hold the highest office out of the cabinet, trafficked much in affairs of this kind. He not only suggested the arrangement to the minister over a cup of coffee, standing on a drawing-room rug in Windsor Castle, but he also favourably mentioned Mr. Arabin's name in the ear of a distinguished person.

And so the matter was arranged. The answer of the great man came, and Mr. Arabin was made Dean of Barchester. The three clergymen who had come up to town on this important mission dined together with great glee on the day on which the news reached them. In a silent, decent, clerical manner, they toasted Mr. Arabin with full bumpers of claret. The satisfaction of all of them was supreme. The Master of Lazarus had been successful in his attempt, and success is dear to us all. The archdeacon had trampled upon Mr. Slope, and had lifted to high honours the young clergyman whom he had induced to quit the retirement and comfort of the university. So at least the archdeacon thought; though, to speak sooth, not he, but circumstances, had trampled on Mr. Slope. But the satisfaction of Mr. Harding was, of all, perhaps, the most complete. He laid aside his usual melancholy manner, and brought forth little quiet jokes from the inmost mirth of his heart; he poked his fun at the archdeacon about Mr. Slope's marriage, and quizzed him for his improper love for Mrs. Proudie. On the following day they all returned to Barchester.

It was arranged that Mr. Arabin should know nothing of what had been done till he received the minister's letter from the hands of his embryo father-in-law. In order that no time might be lost, a message had been sent to him by the preceding night's post, begging him to be at the deanery at the hour that the train from London arrived. There was nothing in this which surprised Mr. Arabin. It had somehow got about through all Barchester that Mr. Harding was the new dean, and all Barchester was prepared to welcome him with pealing bells and full hearts. Mr. Slope had certainly had a party; there had certainly been those in Barchester who were prepared to congratulate him on his promotion with assumed sincerity, but even his own party was not broken-hearted by his failure. The inhabitants of the city, even the high-souled ecstatic young ladies of thirty-five, had begun to comprehend that their welfare, and the welfare of the place, was connected in some mysterious manner with daily chants and bi-weekly anthems. The expenditure of the palace had not added much to the popularity of the bishop's side of the question; and, on the whole, there was a strong reaction. When it became known to all the world that Mr. Harding was to be the new dean, all the world rejoiced heartily.

Mr. Arabin, we have said, was not surprised at the sum-

mons which called him to the deanery. He had not as yet seen
Mr. Harding since Eleanor had accepted him, nor had he seen
him since he had learnt his future father-in-law's preferment.
There was nothing more natural, more necessary, than that they
should meet each other at the earliest possible moment. Mr.
Arabin was waiting in the deanery parlour when Mr. Harding
and Dr. Grantly were driven up from the station.

There was some excitement in the bosoms of them all, as
they met and shook hands; by far too much to enable either of
them to begin his story and tell it in a proper equable style of
narrative. Mr. Harding was some minutes quite dumbfounded,
and Mr. Arabin could only talk in short, spasmodic sentences
about his love and good fortune. He slipped in, as best he could,
some sort of congratulations about the deanship, and then went
on with his hopes and fears,—hopes that he might be received as
a son, and fears that he hardly deserved such good fortune. Then
he went back to the dean; it was the most thoroughly satisfactory
appointment, he said, of which he had ever heard.

"But! but! but—" said Mr. Harding; and then failing to get
any further, he looked imploringly at the archdeacon.

"The truth is, Arabin," said the doctor, "that, after all,
you are not destined to be son-in-law to a dean. Nor am I either:
more's the pity."

Mr. Arabin looked at him for explanation. "Is not Mr.
Harding to be the new dean?"

"It appears not," said the archdeacon. Mr. Arabin's face
fell a little, and he looked from one to the other. It was plainly to
be seen from them both that there was no cause of unhappiness
in the matter, at least not of unhappiness to them; but there was
as yet no elucidation of the mystery.

"Think how old I am," said Mr. Harding imploringly.

"Fiddlestick!" said the archdeacon.

"That's all very well, but it won't make a young man of
me," said Mr. Harding.

"And who is to be dean?" asked Mr. Arabin.

"Yes, that's the question," said the archdeacon. "Come,
Mr. Precentor, since you obstinately refuse to be anything else,
let us know who is to be the man. He has got the nomination in
his pocket."

With eyes brim full of tears Mr. Harding pulled out the letter
and handed it to his future son-in-law. He tried to make a little
speech but failed altogether. Having given up the document, he
turned round to the wall, feigning to blow his nose and then sat

himself down on the old dean's dingy horse-hair sofa. And here
we find it necessary to bring our account of the interview to an
end.

Nor can we pretend to describe the rapture with which Mr.
Harding was received by his daughter. She wept with grief and
wept with joy; with grief that her father should, in his old age,
still be without the rank and worldly position, which, according
to her ideas, he had so well earned; and with joy in that he, her
darling father, should have bestowed on that other dear one the
good things of which he himself would not open his hand to take
possession. And here Mr. Harding again showed his weakness.
In the *mêlée* of this exposal of their loves and reciprocal affection,
he found himself unable to resist the entreaties of all parties that
the lodgings in the High Street should be given up. Eleanor
would not live in the deanery, she said, unless her father lived
there also. Mr. Arabin would not be dean, unless Mr. Harding
would be co-dean with him. The archdeacon declared that his
father-in-law should not have his own way in everything, and
Mrs. Grantly carried him off to Plumstead, that he might remain
there till Mr. and Mrs. Arabin were in a state to receive him in
their own mansion.

Pressed by such arguments as these, what could a weak old
man do but yield?

But there was yet another task which it behoved Mr. Harding to do before he could allow himself to be at rest. Little has
been said in these pages of the state of those remaining old men
who have lived under his sway at the hospital. But not on this
account must it be presumed that he had forgotten them, or that
in their state of anarchy and in their want of due government he
had omitted to visit them. He visited them constantly, and had
latterly given them to understand that they would soon be required to subscribe their adherence to a new master. There were
now but five of them, one of them having been but quite lately
carried to his rest,—but five of the full number, which had
hitherto been twelve, and which was now to be raised to twenty-
four, including women. Of these old Bunce who for many years
had been the favourite of the late warden, was one; and Abel
Handy, who had been the humble means of driving that warden
from his home, was another.

Mr. Harding now resolved that he himself would introduce
the new warden to the hospital. He felt that many circumstances
might conspire to make the men receive Mr. Quiverful with
aversion and disrespect; he felt also that Mr. Quiverful might

himself feel some qualms of conscience if he entered the hospital
with an idea that he did so in hostility to his predecessor. Mr.
Harding therefore determined to walk in, arm in arm with Mr.
Quiverful, and to ask from these men their respectful obedience
to their new master.

On returning to Barchester, he found that Mr. Quiverful had
not yet slept in the hospital house, or entered on his new duties.
He accordingly made known to that gentleman his wishes, and
his proposition was not rejected.

It was a bright clear morning, though in November, that
Mr. Harding and Mr. Quiverful, arm in arm, walked through the
hospital gate. It was one trait in our old friend's character that he
did nothing with parade. He omitted, even in the more important
doings of his life, that sort of parade by which most of us deem
it necessary to grace our important doings. We have house-
warmings, christenings, and gala days; we keep, if not our own
birthdays, those of our children; we are apt to fuss ourselves if
called upon to change our residences, and have, almost all of us,
our little state occasions. Mr. Harding had no state occasions.
When he left his old house, he went forth from it with the same
quiet composure as though he were merely taking his daily walk;
and now that he re-entered it with another warden under his
wing, he did so with the same quiet step and calm demeanour. He
was a little less upright than he had been five years, nay, it was
now nearly six years ago; he walked perhaps a little slower; his
footfall was perhaps a thought less than firm; otherwise one
might have said that he was merely returning with a friend under
his arm.

This friendliness was everything to Mr. Quiverful. To him,
even in his poverty, the thought that he was supplanting a
brother clergyman so kind and courteous as Mr. Harding, had
been very bitter. Under his circumstances it had been impossible
for him to refuse the proffered boon; he could not reject the
bread that was offered to his children, or refuse to ease the heavy
burden that had so long oppressed that poor wife of his; nevertheless, it had been very grievous to him to think that in going
to the hospital he might encounter the ill will of his brethren in
the diocese. All this Mr. Harding had fully comprehended. It
was for such feelings as these, for the nice comprehension of
such motives, that his heart and intellect were peculiarly fitted. In
most matters of wordly import the archdeacon set down his
father-in-law as little better than a fool. And perhaps he was
right. But in some other matters, equally important if they be

rightly judged, Mr. Harding, had he been so minded, might with as much propriety have set down his son-in-law for a fool. Few men, however, are constituted as was Mr. Harding. He had that nice appreciation of the feelings of others which belongs of right exclusively to women.

Arm in arm they walked into the inner quadrangle of the building, and there the five old men met them. Mr. Harding shook hands with them all, and then Mr. Quiverful did the same. With Bunce Mr. Harding shook hands twice, and Mr. Quiverful was about to repeat the same ceremony, but the old man gave him no encouragement.

"I am very glad to know that at last you have a new warden," said Mr. Harding in a very cheery voice.

"We be very old for any change," said one of them; "but we do suppose it be all for the best."

"Certainly—certainly it is for the best," said Mr. Harding. "You will again have a clergyman of your own church under the same roof with you, and a very excellent clergyman you will have. It is a great satisfaction to me to know that so good a man is coming to take care of you, and that it is no stranger, but a friend of my own, who will allow me from time to time to come in and see you."

"We be very thankful to your reverence," said another of them.

"I need not tell you, my good friends," said Mr. Quiverful, "how extremely grateful I am to Mr. Harding for his kindness to me,—I must say his uncalled for, unexpected kindness."

"He be always very kind," said a third.

"What I can do to fill the void which he left here, I will do. For your sake and my own I will do so, and especially for his sake. But to you who have known him, I can never be the same well-loved friend and father that he has been."

"No, sir, no," said old Bunce, who hitherto had held his peace; "no one can be that. Not if the new bishop sent a hangel to us out of heaven. We doesn't doubt you'll do your best, sir, but you'll not be like the old master; not to us old ones."

"Fie, Bunce, fie! how dare you talk in that way?" said Mr. Harding; but as he scolded the old man he still held him by his arm, and pressed it with warm affection.

There was no getting up any enthusiasm in the matter. How could five old men tottering away to their final resting-place be enthusiastic on the reception of a stranger? What could Mr. Quiverful be to them, or they to Mr. Quiverful? Had Mr. Harding indeed come back to them, some last flicker of joyous light might have shone forth on their aged cheeks: but it was in vain to bid them rejoice because Mr. Quiverful was about to move his fourteen children from Puddingdale into the hospital house. In reality they did no doubt receive advantage, spiritual as well as corporal; but this they could neither anticipate nor acknowledge.

It was a dull affair enough, this introduction of Mr. Quiverful; but still it had its effect. The good which Mr. Harding intended did not fall to the ground. All the Barchester world, including the five old bedesmen, treated Mr. Quiverful with the more respect, because Mr. Harding had thus walked in arm in arm with him, on his first entrance to his duties.

And here in their new abode we will leave Mr. and Mrs. Quiverful and their fourteen children. May they enjoy the good things which Providence has at length given to them!

LIII

Conclusion

The end of a novel, like the end of a children's dinner-party, must be made up of sweetmeats and sugar-plums. There is now nothing else to be told but the gala doings of Mr. Arabin's marriage, nothing more to be described than the wedding dresses, no further dialogue to be recorded than that which took place between the archdeacon who married them, and Mr. Arabin and Eleanor who were married. "Wilt thou have this woman to thy wedded wife," and "Wilt thou have this man to thy wedded husband, to live together according to God's ordinance?" Mr. Arabin and Eleanor each answered, "I will." We have no doubt that they will keep their promises; the more especially as the Signora Neroni has left Barchester before the ceremony was performed.

Mrs. Bold had been somewhat more than two years a widow before she was married to her second husband, and little

Johnny was then able with due assistance to walk on his own legs into the drawing-room to receive the salutations of the assembled guests. Mr. Harding gave away the bride, the archdeacon performed the service, and the two Miss Grantlys, who were joined in their labours by other young ladies of the neighbourhood, performed the duties of bridesmaids with equal diligence, and grace. Mrs. Grantly superintended the breakfast and bouquets, and Mary Bold distributed the cards and cake. The archdeacon's three sons had also come home for the occasion. The eldest was great with learning, being regarded by all who knew him as a certain future double first. The second, however, bore the palm on this occasion, being resplendent in a new uniform. The third was just entering the university, and was probably the proudest of the three.

But the most remarkable feature in the whole occasion was the excessive liberality of the archdeacon. He literally made presents to everybody. As Mr. Arabin had already moved out of the parsonage of St. Ewold's, that scheme of elongating the dining-room was of course abandoned; but he would have refurnished the whole deanery had he been allowed. He sent down a magnificent piano by Erard, gave Mr. Arabin a cob which any dean in the land might have been proud to bestride, and made a special present to Eleanor of a new pony chair that had gained a prize in the Exhibition. Nor did he even stay his hand here; he bought a set of cameos for his wife, and a sapphire bracelet for Miss Bold; showered pearls and workboxes on his daughters, and to each of his sons he presented a cheque for £20. On Mr. Harding he bestowed a magnificent violoncello with all the new-fashioned arrangements and expensive additions, which, on account of these novelties, that gentleman could never use with satisfaction to his audience or pleasure to himself.

Those who knew the archdeacon well, perfectly understood the cause of his extravagance. 'Twas thus that he sang his song of triumph over Mr. Slope. This was his pæan, his hymn of thanksgiving, his loud oration. He had girded himself with his sword, and gone forth to the war; now he was returning from the field laden with the spoils of the foe. The cob and the cameos, the violoncello and the pianoforte, were all as it were trophies reft from the tent of his now conquered enemy.

The Arabins after their marriage went abroad for a couple of months, according to the custom in such matters now duly established, and then commenced their deanery life under good auspices. And nothing can be more pleasant than the present arrangement of ecclesiastical affairs in Barchester. The titular bishop never interfered, and Mrs. Proudie no† often. Her sphere is more extended, more noble, and more suited to her ambition than that of a cathedral city. As long as she can do what she pleases with the diocese, she is willing to leave the dean and chapter to themselves. Mr. Slope tried his hand at subverting the old-established customs of the close, and from his failure she has learnt experience. The burly chancellor and meagre little prebendary are not teased by any application respecting Sabbath-day schools, the dean is left to his own dominions, and the intercourse between Mrs. Proudie and Mrs. Arabin is confined to a yearly dinner given by each to the other. At these dinners Dr. Grantly will not take part; but he never fails to ask for and receive a full account of all that Mrs. Proudie either does or says.

His ecclesiastical authority has been greatly shorn since the palmy days in which he reigned supreme as mayor of the palace to his father, but nevertheless such authority as is now left to him he can enjoy without interference. He can walk down the High Street of Barchester without feeling that those who see him are comparing his claims with those of Mr. Slope. The intercourse between Plumstead and the deanery is of the most constant and familiar description. Since Eleanor has been married to a clergyman, and especially to a dignitary of the church, Mrs. Grantly has found many more points of sympathy with her sister; and on a coming occasion, which is much looked forward to by all parties, she intends to spend a month or two at the deanery. She never thought of spending a month in Barchester when little Johnny Bold was born!

The two sisters do not quite agree on matters of church doctrine, though their differences are of the most amicable description. Mr. Arabin's church is two degrees higher than that of Mrs. Grantly. This may seem strange to those who will remember that Eleanor was once accused of partiality to Mr. Slope; but it is no less the fact. She likes her husband's silken vest, she likes his adherence to the rubric, she specially likes the eloquent philosophy of his sermons, and she likes the red letters in her own prayer-book. It must not be presumed that she has a taste for candles, or that she is at all astray about the real presence; but she has an inkling that way. She sent a handsome subscription towards certain very heavy ecclesiastical legal expenses which have lately been incurred in Bath, her name of course not appearing; she assumes a smile of gentle ridicule when the Archbishop of

Canterbury is named, and she has put up a memorial window in the cathedral.

Mrs. Grantly, who belongs to the high- and dry-church, the high church as it was some fifty years ago, before tracts were written and young clergyman took upon themselves the highly meritorious duty of cleaning churches, rather laughs at her sister. She shrugs her shoulders, and tells Miss Thorne that she supposes Eleanor will have an oratory in the deanery before she has done. But she is not on that account a whit displeased. A few high church vagaries do not, she thinks, sit amiss on the shoulders of a young dean's wife. It shows at any rate that her heart is in the subject; and it shows moreover that she is removed, wide as the poles asunder, from that cesspool of abomination in which it was once suspected that she would wallow and grovel. Anathema maranatha! Let anything else be held as blessed, so that that be well cursed. Welcome kneelings and bowings, welcome matins and complines, welcome bell, book, and candle, so that Mr. Slope's dirty surplices and ceremonial Sabbaths be held in due execration!

If it be essentially and absolutely necessary to choose between the two, we are inclined to agree with Mrs. Grantly that the bell, book, and candle are the lesser evil of the two. Let it however be understood that no such necessity is admitted in these pages.

Dr. Arabin (we suppose he must have become a doctor when he became a dean) is more moderate and less outspoken on doctrinal points than his wife, as indeed in his station it behoves him to be. He is a studious, thoughtful, hard-working man. He lives constantly at the deanery, and preaches nearly every Sunday. His time in spent in sifting and editing old ecclesiastical literature, and in producing the same articles new. At Oxford he is generally regarded as the most promising clerical ornament of the age. He and his wife live together in perfect mutual confidence. There is but one secret in her bosom which he has not shared. He has never yet learned how Mr. Slope had his ears boxed.

The Stanhopes soon found that Mr. Slope's power need no longer operate to keep them from the delight of their Italian villa. Before Eleanor's marriage they had all migrated back to the shores of Como. They had not been resettled long before the signora received from Mrs. Arabin a very pretty though very short epistle, in which she was informed of the fate of the writer. This letter was answered by another, bright, charming, and witty, as the signora's letters always were; and so ended the friendship between Eleanor and the Stanhopes.

One word of Mr. Harding and we have done.

· He is still Precentor of Barchester, and still pastor of the little church of St. Cuthbert's. In spite of what he has so often said himself, he is not even yet an old man. He does such duties as fall to his lot well and conscientiously, and is thankful that he has never been tempted to assume others for which he might be less fitted.

The Author now leaves him in the hands of his readers; not as a hero, not as a man to be admired and talked of, not as a man who should be toasted at public dinners and spoken of with conventional absurdity as a perfect divine, but as a good man without guile, believing humbly in the religion which he has striven to teach, and guided by the precepts which he has striven to learn.

Bibliography

Works by Anthony Trollope

The Macdermots of Ballycloran. 3 vols. London: Newby, 1847.

The Kellys and the O'Kellys; or Landlords and Tenants. 3 vols. London: Colburn, 1848.

La Vendée: An Historical Romance. 3 vols. London: Colburn, 1850.

The Warden. London: Longman, 1855.

Barchester Towers. 3 vols. London: Longman, 1857.

The Three Clerks. 3 vols. London: Bentley, 1858.

Doctor Thorne. 3 vols. London: Chapman & Hall, 1858.

The Bertrams. 3 vols. London: Chapman & Hall, 1859.

The West Indies and the Spanish Main. London: Chapman & Hall, 1859.

Castle Richmond. 3 vols. London: Chapman & Hall, 1860.

Framley Parsonage. 3 vols. London: Smith, Elder, 1861.

Tales of All Countries. London: Chapman & Hall, 1861.

Orley Farm. 2 vols. London: Chapman & Hall, 1862.

North America. 2 vols. London: Chapman & Hall, 1862.

Tales of All Countries: Second Series. London: Chapman & Hall, 1863.

Rachel Ray. 2 vols. London: Chapman & Hall, 1863.

The Small House at Allington. 2 vols. London: Smith, Elder, 1864.

Can You Forgive Her? 2 vols. London: Chapman & Hall, 1864.

Miss Mackenzie. 2 vols. London: Chapman & Hall, 1865.

Hunting Sketches. London: Chapman & Hall, 1865.

The Belton Estate. 3 vols. London: Chapman & Hall, 1866.

Travelling Sketches. London: Chapman & Hall, 1866.

Clergymen of the Church of England. London: Chapman & Hall, 1866.

Nina Balatka. 2 vols. Edinburgh & London: Blackwood, 1867.

The Last Chronicle of.Barset. 2 vols. London: Smith, Elder, 1867.

The Claverings. 2 vols. London: Smith, Elder, 1867.

Lotta Schmidt: And Other Stories. London: Strahan, 1867.

Linda Tressel. 2 vols. Edinburgh & London: Blackwood, 1868.

Phineas Finn: The Irish Member. 2 vols. London: Virtue, 1869.

He Knew He Was Right. 2 vols. London: Strahan, 1869.

The Vicar of Bullhampton. London: Bradbury, Evans, 1870.

An Editor's Tales. London: Strahan, 1870.

The Struggles of Brown, Jones and Robinson. London: Smith, Elder, 1870.

The Commentaries of Cæsar. Edinburgh & London: Blackwood, 1870.

Sir Harry Hotspur of Humblethwaite. London: Hurst & Blackett, 1871.

Ralph the Heir. 3 vols. London: Hurst & Blackett, 1871.

The Golden Lion of Granpère. London: Tinsley, 1872.

The Eustace Diamonds. 3 vols. London: Chapman & Hall, 1873.

Australia and New Zealand. 2 vols. London: Chapman & Hall, 1873.

Phineas Redux. 2 vols. London: Chapman & Hall, 1874.

Lady Anna. 2 vols. London: Chapman & Hall, 1874.

Harry Heathcote of Gangoil: A Tale of Australian Bush Life. London: Sampson Low, 1874.

The Way We Live Now. 2 vols. London: Chapman & Hall, 1875.

The Prime Minister. 4 vols. London: Chapman & Hall, 1876.

The American Senator. 3 vols. London: Chapman & Hall, 1877.

South Africa. 2 vols. London: Chapman & Hall, 1878.

Is He Popenjoy? 3 vols. London: Chapman & Hall, 1878.

How the "Mastiffs" Went to Iceland. London: Virtue, 1878.

An Eye for an Eye. 2 vols. London: Chapman & Hall, 1879.

Thackeray. London: Macmillan, 1879.

John Caldigate. 3 vols. London: Chapman & Hall, 1879.

Cousin Henry. 2 vols. London: Chapman & Hall, 1879.

The Duke's Children. 3 vols. London: Chapman & Hall, 1880.

The Life of Cicero. 2 vols. London: Chapman & Hall, 1880.

Dr. Wortle's School. 2 vols. London: Chapman & Hall, 1881.

Ayala's Angel. 3 vols. London: Chapman & Hall, 1881.

Why Fran Frohmann Raised Her Prices: And Other Stories. London: Isbister, 1882.

Lord Palmerston. London: Isbister, 1882.

Kept in the Dark. 2 vols. London: Chatto & Windus, 1882.

Marion Fay. 3 vols. London: Chapman & Hall, 1882.

The Fixed Period. 2 vols. Edinburgh & London: Blackwood, 1882.

Mr. Scarborough's Family. 3 vols. London: Chatto & Windus, 1883.

The Landleaguers. 3 vols. London: Chatto & Windus, 1883.

An Autobiography. 2 vols. Edinburgh & London: Blackwood, 1883.

An Old Man's Love. 2 vols. Edinburgh & London: Blackwood, 1884.

The Noble Jilt. London: Constable, 1923.

London Tradesmen. London: Mathews & Marrot, 1927.

Did He Steal It? Princeton: Princeton University Library, 1952.

The New Zealander, ed. N. John Hall. Oxford: Clarendon Press, 1972.

Miscellaneous Essays and Reviews. New York: Arno Press, 1981.

Writings for Saint Paul's Magazine. New York: Arno Press, 1981.

Collected Short Stories. New York: Arno Press, 1981.

The Letters of Anthony Trollope, ed. N. John Hall. 2 vols. Stanford: Stanford University Press, 1983.

Biography and Bibliography

Escott, T.H.S. *Anthony Trollope: His Work, Associates and Literary Originals*. London: John Lane, 1913.

Olmsted, John Charles, and Jeffrey Egan Welch. *The Reputation of Trollope: An Annotated Bibliography 1925–1975*. New York and London: Garland, 1978.

Pope Hennessy, James. *Anthony Trollope*. Boston: Little, Brown, 1971.

Sadleir, Michael. *Trollope: A Bibliography*. London: Constable, 1928; rpt. London: Dawsons, 1964.

———. *Trollope: A Commentary*. London: Constable, 1927; 3rd edn, rpt. London: Oxford University Press, 1961.

Snow, C.P. *Trollope: His Life and Art*. London: Macmillan, 1975.

Stebbins, Lucy, and Richard Poate Stebbins. *The Trollopes: The Chronicle of a Writing Family*. New York: Columbia University Press, 1945.

Super, R.H. *Trollope in the Post Office*. Ann Arbor: University of Michigan Press, 1981.

Selected Criticism

apRoberts, Ruth. *Trollope: Artist and Moralist*. London: Chatto & Windus, 1971.

Booth, Bradford A. *Anthony Trollope: Aspects of His Life and Art*. Bloomington, Ind.: Indiana University Press, 1958.

Cockshut, A.O.J. *Anthony Trollope: A Critical Study*. London: Collins, 1955.

Davies, Hugh Sykes. *Trollope*. Writers and Their Work, No. 118. London: Longmans Green, 1960.

Edwards, P.D. *Anthony Trollope: His Art and Scope*. St. Lucia: University of Queensland Press, 1977.

Gerould, Winifred Gregory, and James Thayer Gerould. *A Guide to Trollope*. Princeton: Princeton University Press, 1948.

Hall, N. John. *Trollope and His Illustrators*. London: Macmillan, 1980.

———, ed. *The Trollope Critics*. London: Macmillan, 1981.

———, and Donald D. Stone, eds. *Nineteenth-Century Fiction: Anthony Trollope, 1882-1982 (Special Issue)* (December 1982).

Halperin, John. *Trollope and Politics: A Study of the Pallisers and Others*. London: Macmillan, 1977.

———, ed. *Trollope Centenary Essays*. London: Macmillan, 1982.

Harvey, Geoffrey. *The Art of Anthony Trollope*. New York: St. Martin's Press, 1980.

Kendrick, Walter. *The Novel-Machine: The Theory and Fiction of Anthony Trollope*. Baltimore: Johns Hopkins University Press, 1980.

Kincaid, James R. *The Novels of Anthony Trollope*. Oxford: Clarendon Press, 1977.

Lansbury, Coral. *The Reasonable Man: Trollope's Legal Fiction*. Princeton: Princeton University Press, 1981.

McMaster, Juliet. *Trollope's Palliser Novels: Theme and Pattern*. London: Macmillan, 1978.

Overton, Bill. *The Unofficial Trollope*. Brighton: Harvester Press, 1982.

Polhemus, Robert M. *The Changing World of Anthony Trollope*. Berkeley and Los Angeles: University of California Press, 1968.

Pollard, Arthur. *Anthony Trollope*. London: Routledge & Kegan Paul, 1978.

Skilton, David. *Trollope and His Contemporaries: A Study in the Theory and Conventions of Mid-Victorian Fiction*. London: Longman, 1972.

Smalley, Donald, ed. *Trollope: The Critical Heritage*. London: Routledge & Kegan Paul; New York: Barnes & Noble, 1969.

Terry, R.C. *Anthony Trollope: The Artist in Hiding*. London: Macmillan, 1977.

Tracy, Robert. *Trollope's Later Novels*. Berkeley, Los Angeles, and London: University of California Press, 1978.

Wright, Andrew. *Anthony Trollope: Dream and Art*. London: Macmillan Press, 1983.

• A BANTAM CLASSIC • A BANTAM CLASSIC • A BANTA

Bantam Classics bring you the world's greatest literature—books that have stood the test of time—at specially low prices. These beautifully designed books will be proud additions to your bookshelf. You'll want all these time-tested classics for your own reading pleasure.

☐	21137	**PERSUASION** Jane Austen	$2.95
☐	21051	**DAVID COPPERFIELD** Charles Dickens	$2.50
☐	21148	**DRACULA** Bram Stoker	$1.95
☐	21044	**FRANKENSTEIN** Mary Shelley	$1.50
☐	21171	**ANNA KARENINA** Leo Tolstoy	$2.95
☐	21035	**THE DEATH OF IVAN ILYICH** Leo Tolstoy	$1.95
☐	21163	**THE BROTHERS KARAMAZOV** Fyodor Dostoevsky	$2.95
☐	21175	**CRIME AND PUNISHMENT** Fyodor Dostoevsky	$2.50
☐	21136	**THE IDIOT** Fyodor Dostoevsky	$3.50
☐	21166	**CANDIDE** Voltaire	$2.25
☐	21130	**THE COUNT OF MONTE CRISTO** Alexandre Dumas	$2.95
☐	21118	**CYRANO DE BERGERAC** Edmond Rostand	$1.75
☐	21048	**SILAS MARNER** George Eliot	$1.75
☐	21089	**FATHERS AND SONS** Ivan Turgenev	$1.95
☐	21032	**THE HUNCHBACK OF NOTRE DAME** Victor Hugo	$1.95
☐	21101	**MADAME BOVARY** Gustave Flaubert	$2.50
☐	21059	**THE TURN OF THE SCREW AND OTHER SHORT FICTION** Henry James	$1.95

Prices and availability subject to change without notice.

Buy them at your local bookstore or use this handy coupon for ordering:

Bantam Books, Inc., Dept. CL, 414 East Golf Road, Des Plaines, Ill. 60016

Please send me the books I have checked above. I am enclosing $_____ (please add $1.25 to cover postage and handling). Send check or money order —no cash or C.O.D.'s please.

Mr/Mrs/Miss_____

Address_____

City_____ State/Zip_____

CL—7/84

Please allow four to six weeks for delivery. This offer expires 1/85.

• A BANTAM CLASSIC • A BANTAM CLASSIC • A BANTA

Bantam Classics bring you the world's greatest literature—books that have stood the test of time—at specially low prices. These beautifully designed books
will be proud additions to your bookshelf. You'll
want all these time-tested classics for your own
reading pleasure.

Titles by Charles Dickens

☐ 21123	**THE PICKWICK PAPERS** Charles Dickens	$4.95
☐ 21108	**BLEAK HOUSE** Charles Dickens	$3.95
☐ 21086	**NICHOLAS NICKLEBY** Charles Dickens	$4.50
☐ 21051	**DAVID COPPERFIELD** Charles Dickens	$2.50
☐ 21113	**GREAT EXPECTATIONS** Charles Dickens	$2.50
☐ 21106	**A TALE OF TWO CITIES** Charles Dickens	$1.95
☐ 21016	**HARD TIMES** Charles Dickens	$1.95

Titles by Thomas Hardy:

☐ 21152	**JUDE THE OBSCURE**	$2.75
☐ 21024	**THE MAYOR OF CASTERBRIDGE**	$1.95
☐ 21080	**THE RETURN OF THE NATIVE**	$1.95
☐ 21168	**TESS OF THE D'URBERVILLES**	$2.95
☐ 21131	**FAR FROM THE MADDENING CROWD**	$2.75

☐ 21059	**THE TURN OF THE SCREW AND OTHER SHORT FICTION** Henry James	$1.95
☐ 21021	**WUTHERING HEIGHTS** Emily Bronte	$1.75
☐ 21149	**LADY CHATTERLY'S LOVER** D. H. Lawrence	$2.75
☐ 21159	**EMMA** Jane Austen	$1.95

Prices and availability subject to change without notice.

Buy them at your local bookstore or use this handy coupon for ordering:

Bantam Books, Inc., Dept. CL3, 414 East Golf Road, Des Plaines, Ill. 60016

Please send me the books I have checked above. I am enclosing $_____
(please add $1.25 to cover postage and handling). Send check or money order
—no cash or C.O.D.'s please.

Mr/Mrs/Miss _____

Address_____

City_____ State/Zip_____

CL3—7/84

Please allow four to six weeks for delivery. This offer expires 1/85.

• A BANTAM CLASSIC • A BANTAM CLASSIC • A BANTA

These books have been bestsellers for generations of readers. Bantam Classics now bring you the world's greatest literature in specially low-priced editions. From the American epic Moby Dick to Dostoevsky's towering works, you'll want all these time-tested classics for your own.

☐	21138	**THE HOUSE OF MIRTH** Edward Wharton	$2.25
☐	21133	**THE DIVINE COMEDY: PURGATORIO** Dante (trans. by Allen Mandelbaum)	$2.50
☐	21041	**THE AENEID** Virgil (trans. by Allen Mandelbaum)	$2.95
☐	21005	**THE CALL OF THE WILD and WHITE FANG** Jack London	$1.75
☐	21166	**CANDIDE** Voltaire	$2.25
☐	21082	**THE CANTERBURY TALES** Geoffrey Chaucer	$2.95
☐	21130	**THE COUNT OF MONTE CRISTO** Alexander Dumas	$2.95
☐	21175	**CRIME AND PUNISHMENT** Fyodor Dostoevsky	$2.50
☐	21134	**THE SECRET AGENT** Joseph Conrad	$2.95
☐	21088	**HEART OF DARKNESS & THE SECRET SHARER** Joseph Conrad	$1.75
☐	21007	**MOBY DICK** Herman Melville	$1.95
☐	21021	**WUTHERING HEIGHTS** Emily Bronte	$1.75
☐	21117	**KIM** Rudyard Kipling	$2.25
☐	21115	**LITTLE WOMEN** Louisa May Alcott	$2.95
☐	21077	**CAPTAINS COURAGEOUS** Rudyard Kipling	$1.50
☐	21067	**KIDNAPPED** Robert Louis Stevenson	$1.50
☐	21079	**THE ADVENTURES OF HUCKLEBERRY FINN** Mark Twain	$1.75

Prices and availability subject to change without notice.

Buy them at your local bookstore or use this handy coupon for ordering:

Bantam Books, Inc., Dept. CL4, 414 East Golf Road, Des Plaines, Ill. 60016

Please send me the books I have checked above. I am enclosing $_____ (please add $1.25 to cover postage and handling). Send check or money order —no cash or C.O.D.'s please.

Mr/Mrs/Miss _____

Address_____

City_____ State/Zip_____

CL4—7/84

Please allow four to six weeks for delivery. This offer expires 1/85.

SPECIAL
MONEY SAVING
OFFER

Now you can have an up-to-date listing of Bantam's hundreds of titles plus take advantage of our unique and exciting bonus book offer. A special offer which gives you the opportunity to purchase a Bantam book for only 50¢. Here's how!

By ordering any five books at the regular price per order, you can also choose any other single book listed (up to a $4.95 value) for just 50¢. Some restrictions do apply, but for further details why not send for Bantam's listing of titles today!

Just send us your name and address plus 50¢ to defray the postage and handling costs.

BANTAM BOOKS, INC.
Dept. FC, 414 East Golf Road, Des Plaines, Ill 60016

Mr./Mrs./Miss/Ms. _____
                        (please print)

Address _____

City_____ State_____ Zip_____

FC—3/84

"Dave took me to Denny's for dinner," Ali answered. "And you're right. It was late when I got home. Anything in the paper?"

"Lots," Edie replied. "Help yourself."

Ali settled onto the couch and picked up one of the other papers where Monique Ragsdale's death, under suspicious circumstances, was front-page news. Her relationship to network executive Paul Grayson, who had been murdered two days earlier, was laid out in tabloid-worthy detail. The cops were cagey. The public information officer mentioned that detectives had identified several people of interest in the case but that no arrests had been made at this time.

Edie was evidently reading something similar. "I'm assuming you're one of the 'persons of interest'?"

"Who else?" Ali responded. She said nothing more.

When the first cup of coffee was gone, she called room service and ordered breakfast for two along with more coffee—a full pot this time. Then, with Edie still preoccupied with the hard-copy newspapers, Ali booted up her computer.

Dear Babe,

My name is Adele Richardson. I used to watch you when you were on the news here in L.A. and I've been a fan of cutlooseblog.com from the time you started it. And I'm sure you know the reason. Something very similar happened to me. Not the job thing but a very similar marriage disaster. Over the months I've admired the way you've picked yourself up and gone on, reaching out to help others along the way. In fact, I think it's safe to say that you're one of my heroes. And, because of you, I've started reading other blogs as well. Who knows? Maybe you've turned me into an addict. Are there twelve-step programs for people addicted to reading blogs?

Anyway, I read your last post and I'm smart enough to read between the lines. As long as you're caught up in any kind of legal proceedings, I'm sure your attorney won't let you do any posting. But I'm also selfish enough to miss having cutloose as part of my morning routine. So I'm writing to you today with a proposition. Maybe you'll think I'm being too forward. If so, all you have to do is press the delete button.

I was a journalism major in college. Then, during my senior year, I got engaged and realized that for me, marriage and kids and a career in journalism just wasn't going to work, so I switched over to elementary education. I've been teaching third grade in Escondido for the past fifteen years. It turns out that marriage and elementary education didn't work out very well, either, but how was I to know?

So here's the nervy part. Unlike you, I'm not famous, but I am a survivor. My husband ended up getting caught up in online gambling. We lost everything, including the house, our savings, and most of my retirement account as well. I'm divorced now. Slowly but surely I'm rebuilding my life—just as you're rebuilding yours.

Sometimes one of the bloggers I read needs to take a break to go on vacation or to have a *baby or even because there's some kind of health crisis. A lot of the time, they just put their blog on hiatus for a while and then go back to writing it when they're good and ready. Others invite guest bloggers to sit in and take over for them in the meantime. That way, regular readers don't get out of the habit of checking the site every day.*

And that's why I'm writing to you today—to see if you'd like me to be your guest blogger for the next little while—until you're able to come back. Yes, I suppose I could just kick over the traces and start my own blog, but I've followed what you do on cutloose, and I'd really like to make a contribution and help you.

I'm assuming you can see from this that I'm not exactly illiterate. From reading your blogs, I know we share similar opinions on many issues, although you probably can't tell that from what I've written here. (I do have an unfair advantage, since, through reading your columns, I know you far better than you know me.)

You don't have to answer right now. In fact, you don't have to answer at all, but if you'd like to have me do a couple of sample blog postings for you, I'd be glad to audition. Let me know.

ADELE RICHARDSON, AKA LEDA

Ali was touched by Adele's offer. She was also provoked by it. Based on Victor's advice, she had announced she was putting cutloose aside for the time being, and Adele was responding to that in a kind and supportive fashion. But included in that kindness was an implicit agreement with Victor's take on things—that Ali Reynolds needed to sit down and shut up. This morning that didn't seem likely.

> Dear Adele/Leda,
> Thank you for your kind offer. I've been rethinking my position. In the past I've used cutloose as a way of responding to and dealing with events that were going on in my life at the time. As you so correctly pointed out, the legal ramifications occurring in my life right now make that difficult since there are things happening— the things that are most important to me—that I won't be able to discuss. But I don't think I can walk away from cutloose entirely.
>
> From your note, I see you have an interesting perspective about having had your life blow up and figuring out a way to move on afterward. And that's the whole point of cutlooseblog. com—to support women who find themselves in those difficult circumstances. So do send me your comments, and I'll be glad to post them, but for right now, cutloose is back in business, and I'd better go to work.
>
> BABE

About then room service showed up. Edie let the waiter and his serving cart into the room. "Shall I see if April's ready for breakfast?" Edie asked.

Ali had ordered a fruit plate along with a basket of pastries. "I'm sure there'll be plenty," she said.

Edie bustled off down the hall. She returned a few minutes later with a puffy-eyed April in tow. Her hair was in disarray, and she was wrapped in a terry-cloth robe that once again didn't quite cover her middle. The faint odor of cigarette smoke entered the room when April did.

"Thanks for waking me," she said, helping herself to a coffee cup and a plate of pastries. "The baby was jumping around all night. I hardly got any sleep at all, but now I'm starving."

April had been starving the day before, too. Ali remembered how, while she was pregnant with Chris, she'd also been hungry all the time. "Help yourself," she said.

Settling into the room's only armchair, April set her coffee on a nearby end table and perched a loaded plate on her belly. "The cops said I won't be able to go back to the house until they're done with it," she announced, buttering a blueberry muffin. "They say it's a crime scene. I thought Mom just fell down the stairs, but they're thinking she was pushed."

Ali simply nodded.

"One of my friends, Cindy, runs a shop called Motherhood in Bloom," April continued. "I thought I'd call her later this morning to see if she can bring some stuff by here—underwear, bras, and some new maternity clothes. I've got to have something to wear. And what about colors? I don't have anything in black. Or should I wear navy? Would that be better?"

Ali and her mother exchanged glances. As far as Ali

was concerned, April's preoccupation with her wardrobe seemed very cold-blooded. Edie was the one who answered. "For the services, you mean?" she asked.

April nodded. "And for interviews, too," she said. "Last night at the hospital I happened to run into someone named Sheila Rosenburg. She wants to set up an interview with me."

Happened to run into her? Ali thought. *That was no accident.* "An interview for Court TV?" she asked.

April nodded again. "You know Sheila then?"

Ali had flat-out refused Sheila Rosenburg's offer of an interview, and she hoped April would do the same, but it wasn't Ali's place to tell her so. *It's April's decision, not mine,* she reminded herself.

"I know of Sheila Rosenburg," Ali answered aloud, "but I don't know her personally. I'm concerned that she'll try to turn your mother's death and Paul's into some kind of media circus."

April seemed unconcerned. "Some people pay for interviews," April replied, reaching for another pastry. "And she said she knew of an author who might be able to get me a book contract—you know, so I can write about all this while it's going on, sort of like a diary or a journal. She said people are really interested in true crime. It might even end up being a best-seller. I wouldn't have to do the actual writing, either, since I'm not that good at it. My name would be on the cover of the book, but the publisher would hire somebody else to do that part of it, a ghostwriter, she called it."

Ali was appalled. Shocked and appalled, but her mother was the one who spoke up.

"Are you sure you want to do that?" Edie asked. "I know this is all happening to you, April, but it's also happening to your baby. It's going to be part of Sonia Marie's history, too. Do you want to bring a child into the world with that kind of notoriety?"

It's also happening to me, Ali thought, but there didn't seem to be any point in mentioning it. April was totally absorbed in her own concerns.

"Maybe not," April agreed, "but I think I'm going to need the money."

"Surely we'll be able to work something out so you won't have to lay all our lives bare for the world to see," Ali said.

"I hope so," April said. She stood up. "I'd better go make that call. Those detectives said they'd be by to see me later this morning, too. I'd like to have some clean clothes to wear before they get here."

April went out and closed the door behind her.

"Whoa!" Edie Larson said. "That girl is a lot tougher than she looks."

Ali nodded. "Maybe she's a chip off her mother's block."

"And smoking while she's pregnant?" Edie shook her head.

At that juncture Edie's cell phone rang with a call from Bob Larson back in Sedona. While Edie brought her husband up to date, Ali's phone rang, too. It was Chris.

"Sorry I was so cranky last night," he said. "I felt like you were leaving me out of everything."

"I'm sorry, too," she said.

"So do you want me to come out there or not?"

"Not right now," she said. "I'll probably need you to come over later, but for now I think Grandma and I have things under control."

"All right then," he said. "But remember, keep me posted."

Edie was still chatting on the phone, so Ali returned to her computer.

> Ms. Reynolds,
> *You fired my uncle yesterday without giving him even so much as a day's notice much less two weeks. And then you have the gall to say you have no idea what you could have done or whether or not you should apologize? How dare you?*
>
> ANDREA MORALES

But I didn't fire anyone, Ali thought. *What the hell is this woman raving about?*

Then, sitting staring at the words on the computer screen, Ali had a sudden flash of memory. She remembered coming home late one night to find the house alive with the smells of cooking meat and masa. Following her nose and the sound of voices and laughter to the brightly lit kitchen, Ali had found Elvira and several others, women and girls both, clustered in the kitchen busily making dozens of tamales in advance of Paul's annual Cinco de Mayo celebration. One of the women had been Jesus Sanchez's wife, Clemencia. Had one of those girls been his niece, perhaps? Ali had a dim memory that one of them had been named Andrea, but she wasn't sure.

Still puzzled, Ali sent off a four-word reply:

Dear Andrea,
Who is your uncle?

REGARDS,
ALI REYNOLDS

Ali worked her way through a long list of well-wishing e-mails, most of them begging her not to abandon her blog. Because many of the notes touched on Paul Grayson's death, she didn't post any of them but answered each one directly with the same kind of non-engagement strategy she had employed earlier. It was gratifying to know that her readers were as reluctant to give up on her as she was on them. Finally, she turned to write her response.

CUTLOOSEBLOG.COM
Sunday, September 18, 2005

In my last post I said I was going to step away from cutloose for a time, but it turns out that was a lie. I don't want to step away. I've heard from many of you this morning. Most have wished me well and urged me not to abandon ship. So I'm not going to.

I've been doing this for more than six months now—yes, last week was my half-year blogiversary. In the past, there has always been a sense of immediacy to what I've written. My posts have offered me a way to examine things that were going on in my life. I've been amazed to learn that what I've written has resonated with so many people, some of whom have shared similar experiences.

This morning one of my fans wrote and offered to stand in for me for as long as necessary. While I appreciate Leda's kind offer, hearing from her brought me up short and made me realize I'm unwilling to give up my forum. So cutlooseblog is back. For right now, there are things I simply won't be able to discuss. I probably won't be able to post comments from you regarding those issues, either, and I beg your understanding in that regard.

But there is something I can say. My mother is sitting right here beside me as I write this. We're in a hotel room several hundred miles away from both our homes, away from her business and from her husband, my father, who is working two jobs—his and hers—to keep their restaurant afloat while she's here backstopping me—her daughter. Their daughter.

So this post is for parents—for my parents and for all those other parents out there—the ones who stick with their offspring through thick and thin; who don't turn their backs on their children no matter what; who realize that regardless of how old their kids may be, their children are still their children.

Thanks, Mom and Dad. You're the greatest.

Posted 11:10 A.M., September 18, 2005 by Babe

By the time she finished writing her post, there were several new e-mails. The third one of those was from her old fan Velma.

> *Dear Babe,*
> *When I first started reading cutloose, I didn't*
> *even know what a blog was. Now I read several of*
> *them. One of the ones I read daily, besides yours,*
> *is called socalcopshop. It talks about stuff going*
> *on here in the L.A. area that hardly ever makes it*
> *into the regular papers. You might want to check*
> *out this morning's post. Do you know this guy?*
> *Can you sue him?*
>
> VELMA T IN LAGUNA

Even as Ali searched for the Web site, she had an inkling of what she would find there, and she wasn't disappointed. The moment she saw the headline, her heart sank.

BLACK WIDOW OF ROBERT LANE RIDES AGAIN

Alison Reynolds, already a person of interest in the grisly homicide of her estranged network executive husband, Paul Grayson, is now the target of a new police investigation as police look into the mysterious death of the woman who, had she and he both lived, would have become Paul Grayson's new mother-in-law. Monique Ragsdale, now deceased, was the mother of April Anne Gaddis, Mr. Grayson's intended bride, whom he was scheduled to marry in a ceremony at his Robert Lane mansion early yesterday afternoon.

Sources close to the investigation state that the two women may have clashed during a meeting earlier in the day, prior to Ms. Ragsdale's fatal plunge down the stairway of the house formerly owned by Ms. Reynolds and her husband. Rather than the site of a joyous celebration, the house is now surrounded by crime scene tape as investigators attempt to get to the bottom of what happened.

Mr. Grayson disappeared from a pre-wedding bachelor party on Thursday night. His bound body was found later near the wreckage of a vehicle that had been left on the train tracks west of Palm Springs.

At least one anonymous source claimed that because divorce proceedings between Mr. Grayson and Ms. Reynolds were never finalized, she is allegedly her husband's sole heir, leaving his pregnant fiancée unprovided for. This was supposedly the basis for the alleged confrontation between Ms. Reynolds and Ms. Ragsdale.

Messy divorce proceedings between Ms. Reynolds and her estranged husband have played out in a very public fashion after she was fired from her position as an evening newscaster by the local affiliate of her husband's network. For the past six months she has vented her side of the story as an ongoing saga in posts to a feminist-leaning Web blog called cutlooseblog.com.

In that same six-month period, Ms. Reynolds has been questioned as part of four separate homicide investigations. In two of those she has been exonerated and the cases are considered closed. The other two are still under active investigation, one by the LAPD and the other by the Riverside County Sheriff's Department.

In view of Ms. Reynolds's mounting legal difficulties, her blog has reportedly gone on hiatus.

Posted 7:55 A.M., LMB

No, it hasn't, Ali thought to herself. *Cutloose is definitely back.*

Ali scanned back through the post. There were enough journalistic weasel words—"alleged," "supposed," "reportedly"—along with the ever-so-useful anonymous sources routine, that the article probably wasn't actionable. So, no, Velma, I probably can't sue this guy. As for the signature? LMB. There was no additional information about him available, but Ali had a suspicion that he and the guy who had sent her the poison-pen note earlier, Lance-a-lot, were one and the same.

She looked back through her discarded mail. Sure enough, his address was still there. She started to send him a terse note about publishing unfounded speculation, then she changed her mind. Instead, Ali deleted her half-written e-mail and permanently deleted his e-mail address as well. If Lance-a-lot wanted attention, he sure as hell wasn't going to get it from her.

Ali was disheartened to know, however, that his cutesy pet name for her, Black Widow, was out. Even though the man's allegations were groundless, she understood that other media outlets would most likely pick up on Lance's lead and run with it.

Ali was about to turn off the computer to go shower and dress when another e-mail popped up. Ali recognized the address—Andrea Morales.

There were only two words in Andrea's message:

Jesus Sanchez.

So she was right, this Andrea was that Andrea— the one from the kitchen tamale-making project. But what was this about someone firing Jesus? It made no sense. It was his TLC that kept the grounds of the Robert Lane mansion in pristine order. Why would anyone fire him? Ali sent off yet another immediate reply.

Dear Andrea,
Please believe me that I know nothing about this.
Your uncle's work for us has always been more
than satisfactory.
Below you'll find my relevant contact
information.
Give me a call at your earliest convenience so
we can discuss this and sort it out. Thank you.

REGARDS,
ALI REYNOLDS

Ali slammed shut her computer and started into the bathroom. "What's going on?" Edie asked.

"I'm going to shower and get dressed," Ali said. "Somebody fired the gardener yesterday, and Jesus's niece thinks it's my fault."

"I'm not surprised," Edie replied. "You're as bad as George Bush. It looks like everything is your fault."

Yes, Ali thought. *Isn't that the truth.*

A few minutes later, dressed but with a towel wrapped around her wet hair, Ali hurried down the hall to April's room and knocked on the door. A young woman Ali had never met before opened the door. The room was strewn with a collection of clothing and garment bags. April stood in front of a mirror wearing a full-length navy blue maternity smock complete with wide pleats, a white Peter Pan collar, and matching white cuffs.

"This is my friend Cindy Durbin," April explained. "Even though it's Sunday and she's supposed to be off work, she brought over some clothes for me to try on. What do you think?" April turned in front of the mirror. "Is this too retro?"

Ali nodded curtly in Cindy's direction. The outfit was retro, all right. It looked like it could have stepped right out of Lucille Ball's 1950s costume closet for the old *I Love Lucy* shows that were still in perpetual reruns on TV Land.

"It's fine," Ali said.

April turned from the mirror and studied Ali's face, which must have betrayed some of her roiling feelings. "What's wrong?" April asked.

"Someone fired Jesus Sanchez, the gardener, yesterday," Ali said. "Did you do it?"

"No," April responded. "Mom did. His salary and the cook's both came out of what Paul kept in petty cash. Other than my credit cards, that's the only real money I have right now. Mother said I couldn't afford to keep paying them because I'd run out of money that much sooner. She said she'd take care of getting rid of them for me so I wouldn't have to do it. Why, did we do something wrong?"

Yes, you did something wrong, Ali thought, but there didn't seem much point in discussing it.

"Never mind," she said. "I'll fix it. What's the cook's name?"

"Henrietta, I think," April said. "Henrietta Jackson."

"Where does she live? How long had she worked for you? Do you have a phone number for her?"

"No. Paul probably had that information, but I don't. It would be in his office."

And that's locked up behind a wall of crime scene tape, Ali thought. *How convenient.*

"That's all right," she said. "I'll find her."

"Why?" April asked. "What are you going to do?"

"I'm going to hire them back," Ali replied. "Or, if nothing else, I'll at least offer them severance pay."

"But who's going to pay it?" April objected. "I can't."

"Then I guess I will," Ali said.

With that, she stalked out of the room and slammed the door shut behind her.

{ CHAPTER 11 }

With her temper flaring, Ali stormed back into the room she was sharing with her mother, where she was surprised to find Edie seated at the desk in front of Ali's open laptop. Dave Holman had arrived and taken over the easy chair. He was also finishing up the leavings from their breakfast cart.

"No breakfast buffet at Motel 6," he explained, polishing off the last remaining croissant. "Who lit a fire under you?"

"Monique Ragsdale fired both the cook and the gardener yesterday to keep April from spending some of her precious stash of cash. She sent them packing and blamed it all on me."

"So?" Dave said.

"We're going to find them and hire them back."

"But they can't go back to the house," Dave objected. "The place is a crime scene."

"The fact that it's a crime scene isn't their fault," Ali replied. "If nothing else, I can offer them severance pay. Did anyone call?"

Edie nodded and handed Ali her cell phone. "Andrea Morales," Edie said. "She wants you to call her back."

"The gardener's niece," Ali explained as she scrolled through her received calls and punched the appropriate number.

"Andrea?" Ali asked.

"Yes."

"This is all a terrible misunderstanding. Your uncle

never should have been fired in the first place. Is it possible for you to put me in touch with him?"

"Why?" Andrea asked bluntly.

"Because I want to offer him severance pay at least and possibly his job back," Ali answered. "There's some confusion with my husband's estate at the moment. The right hand doesn't necessarily know what the left hand is doing."

"The woman who fired him knew perfectly well what she was doing," Andrea countered. "She told him he should get his stuff together and get the hell out. She said you were the boss now, and that you didn't want to pay him anymore."

"But I will pay him," Ali insisted. "Can you put me in touch with him?"

"My uncle's English isn't so good," Andrea said. "He'll need someone to translate."

"Would you?"

"I guess," Andrea agreed.

"So where is he?"

"Here," she said. "Well, a few blocks away."

"Where's here?" Ali asked.

Andrea didn't answer the question directly. "Let me ask him if he wants to talk to you. I'll call you back."

Ali hung up and turned to face Dave. "Now how do I find Henrietta Jackson?"

"Who's she? The cook?" Dave asked.

Ali nodded.

"And that's all the information you have on her—just her name? No address? No phone number?"

"Paul probably had more information than that, but it would be in his office and—"

"And the house is a crime scene," Dave finished for her.

"Exactly."

Dave busied himself with making phone calls, but Ali didn't listen to what he was doing. She was thinking about Paul Grayson. She had always had her own money, but Paul had handled the bill paying for everything, including the household accounts. She had never realized until today that the help had been paid in cash. Despite the fact that they had been in this country for years, it probably meant that either Jesus or his wife, Clemencia Sanchez, or both of them were illegals, living and working beneath the INS radar.

For the first time Ali wondered about Elvira Jimenez, Paul's former cook. Was the same true for her? Was she, too, working without proper papers? And what had happened to her? After years of working in the household, why had she been let go? And what about Henrietta? The woman's distinctive accent placed her as being from somewhere in the southern United States. She certainly wasn't an undocumented immigrant, so was she working in an underground economy simply to avoid paying taxes? And if Ali did manage to find Jesus and Henrietta and offer them their jobs back, what kind of liability would she be incurring?

"Your cook has no driver's license as far as I can find," Dave announced a few minutes later. "At least, she doesn't have a California driver's license."

"How did you do that?"

"I know people who know people," he said.

"What about Jesus Sanchez? Could you find him?"

"I thought his niece was going to put you in touch with him."

"What if she doesn't? What if I need to find him on my own?"

A moment later, when Ali's phone rang, her concern about locating Jesus Sanchez proved entirely accurate. "My uncle doesn't want to see you," Andrea Morales announced.

"I just want to talk to him," Ali began.

"He doesn't want to talk to you," Andrea returned forcefully. "He said no, and that means no." With that, she hung up.

Ali was stunned. Because of Jesus's limited English skills and because Ali spoke only rudimentary Spanish, communications between the two of them had always been minimal at best. As far as Ali knew, however, there had never been any kind of ill will.

"Andrea Morales," Dave was saying into his phone as Ali put down hers. "You've dozens? Give me the addresses."

Minutes later, though, armed with a phone book and the list of addresses, Dave was able to match one specific Andrea Morales with the received call number logged into Ali's cell phone. "There you are," he said triumphantly. "Andrea and Miguel Morales, two-twenty-four South Sixth, Pico Gardens."

Ali knew from her days on the news desk that Pico Gardens had a reputation for being a center of gang-related activities. It was also known as a haven for newly arrived illegal aliens.

"Let's go," Ali said. She went over to the wall safe,

opened it, and removed both her Glock and the small-of-back holster she had purchased to carry it.

"Go where?" Dave asked. He eyed her weapon uneasily. "And is that really necessary?"

"In Pico Gardens?" Ali returned. "Yes. If a couple of gringos are going there, being armed is probably the only sensible idea. Andrea told me that Jesus lives somewhere nearby—within a few blocks of where she and her husband live. Jesus drives an old blue van. If it's parked on the street, I'll recognize it."

"It didn't sound as though Jesus is eager to talk to you," Dave pointed out.

"Doesn't matter," Ali said. "I want to talk to him." Ali turned to her mother. "Are you coming along?" she asked.

"I don't think so," Edie said. "If you don't mind, I think I'll hang around here. I'll use your computer to surf the Net."

The idea of her mother, Edie Larson, "surfing the Net" was still strange to Ali. Amazing even. "Be my guest," she said.

"I'll also look in on April from time to time," Edie added. "Just to make sure she's okay."

When Dave and Ali left the hotel, they attempted the back door exit that had worked flawlessly for them the day before, but the media folks had wised up. A reporter, one lowly enough to be relegated to hanging around by the reeking kitchen Dumpster, and her equally low-on-the-totem-pole photographer were lying in wait just outside the door.

"Hey, Ms. Reynolds," the reporter called, holding

her microphone aloft and rushing up to the car. "Is it true you've been brought in for questioning in two homicide cases? Do you have any comment?"

Of course I don't have a comment, Ali thought. She said nothing as Dave opened the door on his Nissan. It was too bad they hadn't taken her Cayenne on this trip. Now the media would have information on what had previously been their stealth vehicle.

The photographer focused his camera on Dave. "Out of my way," he said with a snarl, but the photographer didn't take the hint. He was still snapping away as Dave scrambled into the driver's seat and slammed the door shut behind him.

"What jackasses!" he exclaimed. "Were you ever that bad?"

"I don't think so," Ali said. *I hope not,* she thought.

The reporter and photographer were legging it for the front of the building and, presumably, some vehicle, when Dave peeled out of the back driveway and bounced over the edge of the curb into the street.

"Are they going to catch us?" Ali asked.

"Not if I can help it," Dave returned. "Now which way?"

Without her GPS or a detailed map to rely on, Ali had to think for a moment before she was able to get her bearings and direct him onto the southbound ramp of the 405 and from there onto the 10.

"How's your Spanish?" Ali asked as they sped down the freeway.

"I speak menu Spanish fairly well. Why?"

"Because Jesus speaks almost no English and I speak almost no Spanish."

"Maybe his niece, Andrea Whatever, would translate for us."

"I doubt that," Ali said. She picked up her cell phone and scrolled through her phone book until she located the name Duarte.

During her time as a newscaster in L.A., one of Ali's PR roles had been serving as the station's goodwill ambassador to the cancer community. Because of her own tragic history with Dean's death from cancer, she had been a likely and willing candidate. She had served on boards and walked in Races for the Cure and Relays for Life. But she had also done a lot of hands-on caregiving, work that had nothing to do with public relations and never made it into the news. One such case had been a three-year-old leukemia patient named Alonso Duarte.

Lonso's father, Eduardo, had worked at Ali's television station in the capacity of janitor. His wife, Rosa, had worked as a maid for a series of hotels. Once Lonso was diagnosed, the station had broadcast a series of stories about his battle and about his family's plight as well. They had helped raise money to fill in the gap between the bills and what medical insurance actually paid. The station's official involvement had eventually ended, but Ali had remained a part of the family's support system during Lonso's many hospitalizations and chemo treatments. The last Ali had heard, the boy had been in remission for four years.

Eddie Duarte had been working at the station the night Ali had been let go. He, of all people, had been drafted to carry her box of personal possessions out to her car. At the time he had offered to testify on her behalf in any wrongful dismissal suit. Since negotiations on that score were still pending, Eddie's testimony in the matter had so far been unnecessary. As far as Ali knew he was still on the station's payroll, but since he was a nighttime janitor, she worried about calling during the morning hours and waking him. But she did it anyway—called him and woke him.

"Ali," he said, when he finally realized who she was. "So good to hear from you. How are you? I heard about your husband. I'm so sorry."

Sorry for what? Ali wondered. *Sorry because Paul's dead or sorry because he was such a jerk?*

"Thank you," she said. "How is Rosa? How's Lonso?"

"Rosa's fine and Lonso's great. He even got to play peewee league this year—second base."

For a child who had been hovering at death's door five years earlier, this seemed like nothing short of a miracle.

"But what about you?" he asked. "I don't work for the station anymore. I got hired on with another company. If you need me to testify . . ."

"We may still need you to do that, but right now, I need something else," Ali said.

"Name it," Eddie said.

"I'm trying to find my old gardener," Ali said. "There's been a misunderstanding. I need to hire him back, but I don't speak enough Spanish."

"You need me to translate?" Eddie asked.

"Yes," Ali said. "Please."

"Where? When?"

"Soon," Ali said. "As soon as possible. But I'm not

sure where. He lives somewhere in Pico Gardens, but we're not there yet, and I don't have an address."

"The only place I know there is that old Linda Vista Hospital, the abandoned hospital they use for movies and TV shows," Eddie said. "I could meet you there— out front in the parking lot. It'll take me about forty-five minutes to get there."

"Great," Ali said. "Maybe by then we'll have found him."

"Who's Eddie?" Dave asked.

"Long story," Ali returned. "A very long story."

With Ali on the phone and Dave preoccupied with dodging other drivers, they were in the wrong lane and had missed the fork onto I-10 East. Half an hour after leaving the tony environs of Wilshire Boulevard, they were driving around the desolate, graffiti-marred streets of Boyle Heights. It was a neighborhood of houses that had been built in the early part of the twentieth century and were somehow still holding together. Some of them appeared to be in reasonably decent shape. Others were little more than crumbling wrecks.

They started by locating the Morales household on Sixth and then circled out from there, searching for Jesus Sanchez's van. As they turned up South Chicago, Ali pointed. "There it is," she announced. "That's his van."

The aging, much-dented Aerostar was parked in the driveway of a decrepit duplex.

"Now that we know where to find Jesus, let's go back to the hospital parking lot and wait for my interpreter to show up."

"What if he doesn't?"

"Don't worry. Eddie will be here."

Once they were parked and waiting, Ali told Dave the Eddie Duarte story from beginning to end. She was just finishing when her phone rang.

"You're not going to believe this," Edie Larson said. "If I weren't down here in the lobby seeing it with my own eyes, I wouldn't believe it myself."

Ali switched her phone to "speaker" so Dave could hear both sides of the conversation. "Seeing what?" she asked. "What's going on?"

"Lights, camera, action," Edie replied grimly. "April is down here in the lobby in a blue and white maternity outfit with perfect makeup and perfect hair. She's doing a sit-down interview with some young woman with very long blond hair and an astonishingly short skirt. I saw the logo on one of the cameras. It said Court TV."

"The blonde would be Sheila Rosenburg," Ali said. "So April is doing the interview after all."

"And against our advice," Edie added. "But there's more. I told you when you left that I was going to go check on her and see if she needed anything. Only when I opened my door, there was a man coming out of her room, so I ducked back inside ours. He was a young man, by the way, a very good-looking young man."

"Probably one of her friends," Ali said.

"That's what I thought right up until he kissed her good-bye," Edie returned. "Believe me, it was a lot more than a 'just friends' kiss. But when he turned away from her, I recognized him. I had seen him before."

"Where?" Ali asked.

"On his Web site."

Ali felt like she was bumbling around in the dark. "What Web site?" she asked.

"Ever since you told me about all that Sumo Sudoku nonsense, I've been curious about it," Edie answered. "I mean, why would Paul and April want to have a bunch of supposedly brainy bodybuilders cluttering up their wedding day? In my experience, weddings are stressful enough without having a film crew and extra people mucking around under hand and foot at the same time. So this morning, I looked up some Sumo Sudoku Web sites and that's where I found him. The guy's name is Tracy McLaughlin."

Ali was stunned. "You're saying you think April has been messing around with Tracy McLaughlin? Are you kidding?"

"I'm not kidding," Edie replied. "Do you know if there's been a paternity test?"

Ali remembered how pleased Paul had been when he learned April was pregnant—pleased and excited.

"I have no idea," Ali said.

"If there hasn't been one, there probably should be," Edie said. "As Paul's executor, if you're going to be forced into setting up a trust fund for Paul's supposed catch colt, you'd best be sure the baby is really his."

Edie Larson had always been a keen observer of human behavior. One of the spooky things about Ali's mother, something that had always left her daughter more than slightly mystified, was her innate ability to see through things that went over other people's heads. Aunt Evelyn, Edie's twin sister, had always claimed that Edie had eyes in the back of her head. As a child, Ali had believed it was true. Maybe it still was, but this seemed like too much.

"Based on seeing the man in a hotel hallway, you're convinced Sonia Marie is really Tracy McLaughlin's baby rather than Paul's?" Ali asked.

"I'd bet money on it," Edie declared. "You should have seen the little love tap and the kiss the man laid on April's tummy as he was saying good-bye. That was a daddy-style maneuver if I've ever seen one."

That meant Paul was cheating on Ali with April, and April was cheating on Paul with Tracy McLaughlin. This was, Ali supposed, entirely predictable.

"What goes around comes around," she said. "So what do we know about Tracy McLaughlin?"

"Only what was on his Web site, and I've got his bio right here," Edie replied. "Says he came to Hollywood from Des Moines, Iowa, determined to be a stuntman. He ended up in a stunt that went bad and spent the next six months in a full body cast. When he got out of the cast, he went into bodybuilding to regain his strength. He worked puzzles while he was laid up and invented Sumo Sudoku once he got better as a way of proving to people that he had recovered completely. But that's not all."

"What's not all?" Ali asked.

"You'll never guess who put up a major part of the capital to get Sumo Sudoku off the ground."

"Paul?"

"You've got it. He's one of the original investors in the organization. There are ten people who put up big bucks to get it started. I don't recognize any of the other names, but you may. I think that's why they were holding the Sumo Sudoku tournament at the house on the same day as the wedding. I'm sure Paul knew there would be lots of media coverage. That way the tournament would generate lots of interest . . ."

"And lots of buzz," Ali finished. "In this town, buzz is everything. Once something is the current 'in' thing, then it's everybody's 'in' thing. Get one appearance on *Jay Leno* and you're on your way."

A gray Chevrolet Impala pulled up and stopped beside Dave's Nissan. "I've gotta go, Mom," Ali said. "My translator is here."

Leaving the Chevy idling, Eddie Duarte hurried over to Ali's door, reached in, and gave her a swift hug.

"Thank you for coming," she said.

"No problem," Eddie returned. "Now, where's this guy you need me to talk to?"

With Eddie following in his Chevy, Dave and Ali drove back to South Chicago Street, where Jesus Sanchez's distinctive blue van was still parked in the driveway. Dave drove half a block beyond the Sanchez house and then stopped in a parking spot that was large enough for both his Nissan and Eddie's Impala. Before they could open their doors, however, a big unmarked Crown Victoria came careening around the corner and grabbed the spot just behind Eddie. Dave watched in his mirror as two people exited the vehicle and hurried past the van and into the fenced yard.

"Hey," Dave began. "I think I know them. Aren't they the two homicide detectives who came to the hospital to talk to April last night?"

Ali turned and looked. Sure enough, Detectives Tim Hubbard and Rosalie Martin hurried up onto the duplex's shaded front porch and rang the bell. "They talked to me, too," Ali said. "What are they doing here?"

"Same thing we are," Dave replied. "Looking for answers."

"Which means we're too late then," Ali said.

"Looks like," Dave agreed. "They'll recognize you. You stay where you are, and I'll let your friend Eddie know what's going on."

While Ali watched, the two detectives tried ringing a doorbell. Then they knocked—and knocked some more. Finally a woman Ali recognized to be Jesus's wife, Clemencia, came to the door and slipped out onto the porch. She stood there talking to the two detectives for several long minutes, alternately shaking her head and gesturing. A little later, an LAPD patrol car pulled up as well. A young Hispanic officer exited the vehicle and hurried up onto the porch, where he joined in the conversation.

By then Dave had returned. "The new guy is probably here to translate," Dave muttered. "That means they have the same language problem we do."

They waited and watched for another fifteen minutes. Finally, the clearly frustrated detectives and the patrolman stepped off the porch and returned to their two separate vehicles. As they drove away, Dave let out a sigh of relief.

"If Jesus is there, he refused to come out and talk to them, and they didn't go in after him. That means Hubbard and Martin were only here on a fishing expedition, and they went away empty-handed. If they'd had enough for a search warrant, it would have been a different story."

"Let's go then," Ali said, opening her door. "I know

Clemencia. At least I've met her. Maybe she'll talk to me."

Dave Holman didn't budge. "Are you coming or not?" Ali asked.

"You and Eddie go on ahead," Dave said. "And you'd better make it quick. If Hubbard and Martin come back with a warrant, this may be your only chance."

"And what are you going to do?" Ali asked.

"I'll let you know if it works," Dave replied.

Ali scrambled out of the Nissan and motioned for Eddie Duarte to join her. A moment later, they were standing on the porch in front of a sun-bleached mahogany door. Ali pressed the doorbell, but there was no answering ring from inside. While she waited, Ali edged over to one of the windows. The curtains had been pulled shut, but there was enough of a space left between them that Ali was able to see into the living room, where a stack of taped cardboard boxes and a collection of mismatched luggage gave evidence of hurried packing. Apparently Jesus and Clemencia Sanchez were headed out of Dodge.

Convinced the doorbell wasn't in working order, Ali tried knocking instead. Nothing happened then, either.

"Her name is Clemencia," Ali told Eddie. "Call out to her. Tell her we know she's inside. Tell her I'm here. Say I need to talk to her and that we aren't going away until I do—that we'll stay here all afternoon if necessary. Tell her that the neighbors already saw the cops come and go, and they're watching us now."

It was several long minutes before Clemencia Sanchez finally came to the door. She pulled it open slightly and then slipped outside. The look she leveled in Ali's direction was nothing short of venomous.

"What do you want?" she demanded.

"Where's Jesus?" Ali returned. "I need to talk to him."

Ali knew for sure that Clemencia understood that much English, but the woman deliberately turned away from her, looking instead to Eddie as though she expected understanding from him rather than a translation, which he nonetheless provided.

"He's gone," Clemencia answered. "He went away."

"Gone where?" Ali asked.

Clemencia shrugged. "It doesn't matter. He isn't coming back."

"But I want to give him his job back," Ali said. "He should never have been fired in the first place. It was a mistake."

Unimpressed, Clemencia shrugged again. Ali tried another tack.

"The cops that were here before. What did they want?"

Clemencia's dark eyes sparked with sudden fury. Her nostrils flared. "Jesus knew they would come for him, and they did. That's why he left, thank God. He went away before they got here."

"But why would they come for him?" Ali asked.

"Because that awful woman fired him," Clemencia said in a barrage of angry Spanish. "You wanted him gone, but she was the one who did the dirty work for you. And when he was ready to leave and went to turn in his keys, there she was—at the bottom of the stairs."

"Monique had already fallen before Jesus left? Why didn't he call for help?"

"Because he thought she was already dead," Clemencia answered. "It looked to him like she was dead. And Jesus knew what the cops would think—that since she fired him, he killed her. He dropped his key ring, and he's sure they found it. They'll find his fingerprints there, too, and they'll blame him." For the first time, Clemencia's fury seemed to dissolve into something closer to despair. She stopped speaking and blinked back tears.

At the time the EMTs had been moving Monique to the gurney, Ali had been too busy to pay any attention to the key ring. She had been focused instead on the phone. But she remembered it now. And she knew, just as the detectives had, that the keys had belonged to Jesus Sanchez because his name had been on the ring as well. Paul Grayson had been a great one for wielding his P-Touch labeler. Everyone who had access to the house or the grounds, Ali included, had been issued appropriate sets of keys with their names clearly visible.

She also understood why Jesus had chosen to disappear. She knew full well that the U.S. Constitution aside, all men are *not* created equal. Hispanics or blacks accused of crimes often found themselves on an entirely different legal track than Anglos did—one with an automatic presumption of guilt rather than innocence. In fact, she thought wryly, the same thing held true when media babes ended up accused of crimes they may not have committed.

"I'd like to help," Ali said quietly.

Without needing or waiting for Eddie to translate, Clemencia replied, "Why?"

"Because I know what it feels like to be suspected of doing something you haven't done," Ali said. She scrounged in her purse until she found one of Victor's cards. She handed it over. "If Jesus wants an attorney, have him call this man."

Clemencia studied the gold-embossed card, then handed it back. "We could not afford someone like this," she said.

Just then Ali remembered Velma T's nephew. Maybe Jesus and Clemencia wouldn't find him quite as daunting. "There's another man I could recommend then," Ali said. "I'll forward his information to your niece, Andrea."

"But still . . ." Clemencia objected. "We can't afford to pay for any attorney."

"I can afford it," Ali said. "And I will. Be sure to tell Jesus that when you talk to him. And be sure he knows that if he wants it, he still has a job."

With that, she turned and walked away.

{ CHAPTER 12 }

Eddie Duarte stayed on the porch for several minutes after Ali returned to the car and while she was giving Dave a brief summary of what had transpired.

"You gave Jesus Sanchez Victor Angeleri's card?" he

asked incredulously. "Who's going to pay the bill? I'd hate to think what his hourly billable rate is."

"She didn't take it," Ali said. "But I'll pay for whatever attorney they do hire."

"So now you're setting out to save the world?"

"Only the parts of it I've screwed up," Ali responded.

"Excuse me," Dave returned. "As far as I can tell, you had nothing at all to do with the fact that Monique Ragsdale took a header down those stairs."

"No, but if it turns out she was pushed—"

"She was," Dave interjected.

"You know that for sure?" Ali asked.

Dave nodded. "I have a source who confirmed it as a suspected homicide while you were busy with Clemencia."

"Then whoever's responsible is probably connected to me as well," Ali asserted. "And if Jesus is being wrongly blamed for what happened to her? Well, I'm connected to him, too."

"I hope your husband left you a ton of money then," Dave said. "It sounds like you're going to need it."

Eddie Duarte approached Ali's side of the car and tapped on the window. She rolled it down.

"What did Clemencia say after I left?" Ali asked.

Eddie frowned. "She told me that you're as evil as your husband."

That revelation hurt Ali's feelings. Personally, she had to agree about Paul—he was evil—but Ali didn't like being tarred with the same brush.

"I told her I knew you were a good person," Eddie continued. "And that if you said you would do something, you would do it. I'm not sure she believed me, though."

Why would she? Ali thought. "Thank you for saying that, Eddie, and thank you for coming," she added. "I really appreciate your help."

"Not that it did much good," Eddie said dejectedly and, offering a good-bye wave, returned to his car.

"Where to now?" Dave asked. "Back to the hotel?"

Ali nodded.

"How did you find out Monique's death is now classified as a homicide?" Ali asked. "Who told you?"

"Ken Nickerson is one of my good old buddies from the Marines. We served together in Iraq. Now he works for LAPD."

"Ken's the one who got you Andrea Morales's address information?" Ali asked.

"That's right. While you were talking to Clemencia, I called him up and asked him straight out if they had autopsy results back on Monique Ragsdale, and they did."

"Already?" Ali asked.

Dave nodded. "Preliminary," he said. "It may be Sunday, but since it's a high-profile case, the guys over on North Mission Road really got their rears in gear on this one."

"And?" Ali asked.

"Bruising on her arms and on her back. Defensive wounds and definite signs of a struggle. No sexual assault. They took scrapings from under her nails. There could be identifiable DNA found in those. The real problem for Jesus Sanchez is that the cops found something at the crime scene that links him to Monique's death."

"I know," Ali said. "Keys with his name on them. I saw them, too. According to what Jesus told Clemencia, after he was let go, he came to the house to turn in his keys. That's when he found Monique at the bottom of the stairs. I'm sure he was upset at seeing her like that, and I don't blame him. I know how I felt when we found her later on. He must have panicked and dropped his keys. Later on, when he realized what had happened, he knew the cops would find them and come looking for him—which they did. That's probably why he took off."

"The big question is, were the keys under the victim or were they beside her?" Dave asked. "If they were under, it means the keys and Jesus were probably there either before she fell or at the same time. In that case, things are looking pretty grim for poor old Jesus. If the keys were found nearby, they could have been dropped at the same time or either before or after the fact."

Ali thought about that. "I don't know," she said finally. "I don't remember seeing them until after the EMTs put Monique on the stretcher. It could be they were right there in plain sight the whole time, and we just didn't notice them."

"One way or the other, why is it you think it's your responsibility to hire a defense attorney for Mr. Sanchez?"

"Shut up and drive," Ali returned.

The fact that Dave Holman did so made Ali like him better.

"And that's not all," he said a few minutes later.

"There's more?"

"Actually, yes. It turns out your Sumo Sudoku pal's Web site bio didn't tell the whole story."

"What did he leave out?"

"That when he was eighteen he went to prison for grand theft auto. It's not the kind of thing somebody puts on a résumé when he's out trolling for well-heeled investors."

"What if Paul suspected something was going on between April and Tracy? What if he started looking into McLaughlin's background and found out some of this stuff?" Ali asked.

"Sounds like possible motive to me," Dave said.

"Except the cops aren't looking in that direction."

"Not yet," Dave said. "But there's no reason we can't point them that way."

Without missing the critical merge, it didn't take nearly as long to get back to the hotel as it had taken to drive to Pico Gardens. "Are you coming up?" Ali asked, as they drove up to the entrance.

"I think I'll take a pass," Dave said. "I want to go back to my place and call my kids. I try to talk to them on Sunday afternoons."

"Just drop me at the front door then," Ali said. "At this point I don't care if the lobby is teeming with reporters. I'm tired of sneaking around. I'll just brazen it out."

"Good girl," Dave said. "I'm glad to hear it. Maybe you can afford to keep handing over those terrific tips. I can't."

The hotel lobby was completely devoid of reporters as Ali made her way upstairs, leading her to conclude that something more interesting must have turned up as fodder for that evening's news broadcasts. Back in the room she was surprised to find her mother wasn't there. Ali tried calling Edie's cell phone. When the call went to voice mail, Ali hung up. Maybe Edie had decided to take advantage of being in L.A. by going to a movie. Edie preferred what her husband called "arty" films to his shoot-'em-ups, but the former seldom made it to the screens of Sedona's single multiplex.

Kicking off her tennies, Ali returned her Glock to the safe and raided the honor bar for a Diet Sprite. While there she noticed something odd. Her mother carried her daily allocation of vitamins in a series of ziplock sandwich bags, which she carefully saved each day, packing them away for future use. One of those plastic bags lay in the armoire next to the TV remote. It contained a single cigarette butt.

Ali picked up the bag and examined the contents. The filtered stub was unremarkable in every way. There was no lipstick residue that might indicate that whoever had smoked it was a female. For Edie, a lifelong vociferous nonsmoker, to see fit to keep the remains of a cigarette in what was a clearly designated nonsmoking room could only mean Edie was playing detective in her own right.

Replacing the bag, Ali took her soda to the couch, sat down, picked up her computer, logged on, and googled Richard Dahlgood, Velma T's nephew. There were several hits, all of them concerning appearances in state and federal courts on behalf of various clients. From everything Ali was able to glean from those reports, Dahlgood seemed like the real deal.

The first e-mail she sent was to Velma T in Laguna.

> Dear Velma,
> A friend of mine may well be in need of your
> nephew's services. Please let him know that if
> he is contacted in regard to defending someone
> named Jesus Sanchez, he should be in touch with
> me so arrangements can be made for handling
> any necessary retainer. My contact phone number
> is listed below.
>
> ALI

Next Ali wrote to Andrea Morales.

> Dear Andrea,
> I spoke to your aunt, Clemencia Sanchez,
> earlier today. It seems likely that your uncle,
> Jesus, may require the services of a defense
> attorney. A friend of mine has recommended
> someone named Richard Dahlgood. Although I
> don't know the man personally, he does appear
> to have a considerable defense practice here in
> the L.A. area. His contact information is listed
> below.
>   If your aunt and uncle are interested in
> engaging Mr. Dahlgood's services, please let me
> know so I can make arrangements for payment
> of any required retainer. Also, please let your
> uncle know that he is back on my payroll at the
> moment regardless of whether or not he is able
> to return to work. Also tell him the house on

Robert Lane is currently off-limits to all of us
due to the ongoing police investigation. I will
need to know where his pay envelopes should be
delivered.

Also, if he has any information concerning the
whereabouts of Henrietta Jackson, the cook who
was fired along with him, or of my former cook,
Elvira Jimenez, I would appreciate knowing how
to reach them. I'm concerned that Elvira may
have been let go under circumstances similar to
what happened to your uncle.

REGARDS,
ALI REYNOLDS

Several readers weighed in on Ali's legal issues.
Those she responded to briefly and let go. Several others addressed her earlier post about her mother.

Dear Babe,
I read several blogs a day and have been a fan
of yours for some time. Not all mothers are
created equal. You're lucky. Your mother sounds
wonderful. Mine was poison. I'm glad she's dead.

ALMA

That one Ali posted. As she kept reading, she found
that the people who had written in were divided almost
fifty-fifty on either side of the good mother/bad mother
spectrum. By the time she had worked her way through
that set of correspondence and added several more

posts, Ali found herself agreeing with Alma's assessment. Ali Reynolds really was lucky.

As the afternoon waned, Ali realized she was hungry. Edie had not yet returned. Ali tried calling her mother's cell again—to no avail. Once again the call went straight to voice mail. Just to be sure, Ali checked her own phone to see if she had missed receiving a message. She hadn't. She checked the room phone for messages as well. No luck. Finally she called down to the desk. Edie hadn't left a note there, either. And then, just to cover all the bases, she tried April's phones, too, both her room and her cell. Again, no answer.

Feeling the first inkling of concern, Ali transferred over to the bell captain. "This is Ali Reynolds," she said.

Her reputation for generous tipping had preceded her. For Ali Reynolds no ticket number was required. "Right, Ms. Reynolds," the bell captain said at once. "Would you like me to have your vehicle brought around to the back?"

"No," she said. "I'm actually calling about my mother's vehicle. Is it there?"

"Do you have the valet number for that one?"

"No," Ali replied. "It's a white Oldsmobile Alero with Arizona plates."

"Oh, that one," he said. "It was self-parked. She left like she was headed to a fire sometime right around one. It was busy, and we were totally backed up here. She was in such a hurry that she almost ran down one of my guys."

"Was she alone?"

"As far as I know."

Off the phone, Ali tried to imagine where Edie

would have been going in such a hurry. As an out-of-town driver, she wasn't familiar with the L.A. area. Wherever it was, it was likely she would have needed detailed directions. If she hadn't asked one of the parking valets for help, maybe she had done so online.

Ali returned to her computer and checked out the search page, looking for the most recent searches. She expected to find a listing for MapQuest or one of the other online map providers. What she found instead was a list of several Iowa-based searches, including one for the *Des Moines Register*. Iowa. Tracy McLaughlin had been sent up for grand theft auto in Iowa.

Ali grabbed her phone and dialed Dave.

"What's up?" he asked.

"We may have a problem," Ali said. "I can't find my mother, and I'm pretty sure she's been playing detective. While I was gone, she was looking up something in the *Des Moines Register*."

"Smart woman," Dave said. "She must have been tracking Tracy McLaughlin, too."

"She may be smart, but she's also not here," Ali said. "At the hotel."

"Where'd she go?"

"That's what I'm trying to tell you. I have no idea. The parking valet said she left in a hell of a hurry, but she didn't leave a note, and she's not answering her cell."

"How long has she been gone?"

"She left the hotel a little after one," Ali replied.

"Have you called your dad?" Dave asked. "Maybe she's called him."

"I can check," Ali said.

"Good. You do that," Dave said. "In the meantime, I'm on my way. I'll be there as soon as I can."

Ali was waiting at the hotel entrance when Dave pulled into the driveway in his Nissan. "Well?" he asked as she settled into the passenger seat.

"Dad hasn't heard from her," Ali reported. "His first thought was that she'd probably gone to see a bargain matinee. That was my idea, too, but the movie would be over by now. Dad's worried, and so am I. Should I call the cops and report her missing?"

Dave shook his head. "It won't make any difference. They're not going to go looking for her right now anyway. We're better off looking ourselves. Where do you think she might have gone?"

"Mom's from out of town," Ali replied. "She doesn't really know her way around L.A. The only map she has in the Alero is that big atlas. I know she used Map-Quest directions to get to the hotel, but there were no MapQuest searches on my computer."

"So wherever she went, if she drove herself, she must have known where she was going," Dave concluded.

Ali nodded. "Right. And the only two familiar places I know about for sure are the hospital and the house on Robert Lane. If April went into labor, she could have gone to Cedars-Sinai. I'm pretty sure that's where Mom said April plans to deliver. But it's possible she might have gone to the house for some strange reason, too."

Dave put the Nissan in gear. "The hospital isn't going to tell us anything. Let's try the house first. Have you tried calling April?"

"I did," Ali told him. "Both her room and her cell. No answer."

"Try again, just in case."

Once again both of April's phones went to voice mail. Ali tried Edie's phone again with the same result. By then Ali was feeling the first tinge of real panic.

When they reached the house on Robert Lane, they found it deserted. Crime scene tape was still draped across the front door, warning people not to enter. There was no sign of Edie's Oldsmobile anywhere and no sign of any other vehicles, either.

"She's not here," Ali concluded. "And I'm beginning to get a bad feeling about this—a really bad feeling."

"Don't worry," Dave said. "Not yet. I'm sure she's fine. Let's try the hospital next."

At Cedars-Sinai, Dave drove through the parking garages, prowling the stalls and searching for the Alero, while Ali went inside to the patient information desk and tried to bluff her way into finding out whether or not a patient named April Gaddis had been admitted. It was like banging her head on a brick wall. No one would tell her anything. Period. When Ali caught up with Dave again, she learned that his garage search had been equally fruitless.

"Back to the hotel then?" Dave asked.

"I guess," Ali said. "Is it time?"

"Time for what?" Dave returned.

"To call Missing Persons?"

"After less than five hours?" Dave responded. "Believe me, they'll laugh you off the phone. At this point they probably wouldn't even bother taking a report. Your mother's an adult. Adults are allowed to disappear whenever they want to. They can and do. Let's go back to the hotel and wait a while longer. Maybe she'll turn up. Besides, since the hotel was where you last spoke to her, that's a reasonable place to try picking up her trail. Didn't you say she was watching an interview at the time?"

Ali nodded. "Yes. The one with Sheila Rosenburg from Court TV."

"Since April and your mother are both among the missing," Dave suggested, "there's always a possibility that they're together. What if your mother and April are doing something perfectly harmless? Maybe once the interview was over they decided to go shopping. After all, April's expecting a baby. Maybe your mom wanted to get her something nice."

Ali shot that idea down without a moment's hesitation. "Mom hates shopping," she said.

"All right then," Dave said. "Let's track down this Sheila person. Maybe one or the other of them would have mentioned to her where they were going or what they planned to do next."

"Maybe," Ali agreed, but she didn't think the idea sounded very promising.

Back at the hotel Ali was relieved to find that the media were still absent. Up on the seventh floor and on the way down the hallway from the elevator, Ali stopped off just long enough to tap on April's door. There was no answer. Ali was in the process of unlocking the door to her own room when her phone rang. The number showing in the readout was her parents' home number in Sedona.

"Hello," Ali said.

"Did you find her?" Bob Larson demanded.

"No," Ali said. "Not yet. We're still looking."

"Well, I just got off the phone with Chris, and we've made up our minds," Bob said. "We've got a contingency plan all lined up. I've found a substitute short-order cook who'll come in and cover for me, and Chris is going to leave his conference early and call for a substitute, too. Kip will stay here and look after Samantha. Once we get the details squared away, we'll throw our stuff in my car and be under way."

"Under way where?" Ali asked. "You mean you're coming here?"

"Of course I'm coming there," Bob said determinedly. "My wife is missing. Do you think I'm just going to sit around on my butt and twiddle my thumbs?"

The idea of her father and Chris driving across the desert in Bob's doddering Bronco seemed downright ludicrous. When it came to dependability, Chris's far newer Prius would have been a better choice.

"Dad," Ali reasoned. "Are you sure you want to do that? I mean, she isn't officially missing."

"You haven't reported it?"

"Dave said it's too soon. No one will pay any attention."

"I'm paying attention," Bob Larson countered. "Your mother's as dependable as the day is long. She wouldn't run off somewhere without letting one of us know. She just wouldn't."

That, of course, was Ali's opinion, too. Leaving without a word was totally out of character for Edie even if that assessment wouldn't carry much weight with the LAPD.

"Do what you need to do," Ali said at last.

"I was planning on it all along," Bob said with a

growl. "Chris and I had already discussed it. And don't think I'm asking for permission, either."

"Of course not," Ali agreed. "But I'm glad you're not coming alone."

"Me, too," Bob said. "I'm not as young as I used to be."

Once Bob was off the phone, Ali called down to the desk. She made arrangements for April to be moved out of the more expensive two-room suite to one room and then reserved two more rooms as well—one for her parents and another for Chris. At this rate, she'd soon be occupying the whole floor. It was just as well that Dave was bunking at Motel 6.

A chastened Ali let Dave into her room, where he immediately appropriated her computer and hunkered down over it. "What was she using to search?" he asked.

"Google."

"Good. I'll see if I can track down her search history. In the meantime, see if you can locate that Sheila person from Court TV."

Ali had to bite her lip. She had already gone over her mother's search history, but she kept her mouth shut and began looking for Sheila's number. Before she found it, however, the phone rang.

"Ms. Reynolds?"

"Yes."

"My name's Richard Dahlgood. I understand you're a good friend of my aunt Velma's."

That wasn't entirely true, but it was close enough.

"Yes," Ali said. "I do know her."

"I've just had a very strange phone call from someone named Andrea Morales," Dahlgood continued.

"She said her uncle might possibly be in need of legal representation in a criminal matter and that, if I took him on, you would be responsible for any expenses that were incurred."

"Yes," Ali said. "That's correct."

"So you know who this person is then, what he might be accused of, and all that?"

"I do."

"I have to say, Ms. Reynolds, it's very unusual for someone to assume someone else's legal obligations in this fashion."

"Unusual but not out of the question."

"No, but I would have to have a signed authorization from my client—once I meet him, that is—giving you permission to have access to the bill. Billing information is also highly confidential."

By then Ali had had it up to here with her bevy of attorneys, all of them standing around with their hands out.

"Please tell Ms. Morales that her understanding is correct and that if she makes arrangements for the client to meet with you, you'll come prepared with whatever paperwork is necessary for me to handle the bill."

"If it's a criminal charge, the costs could be considerable," Dahlgood warned.

Not nearly as considerable as Victor Angeleri's, Ali thought as she ended the call.

Finally Dave set Ali's computer aside. "There's nothing here," he said. "How about if I go downstairs and see if I can make friends with hotel security. Maybe their surveillance tapes will show us something. Are you all right holding down the fort here?"

Ali nodded. "I'll be fine," she said.

He went out, leaving Ali alone. She sat still for a few minutes. then ended up pacing. Her third pass across the room brought her face-to-face with the television armoire and the baggie with the cigarette butt. She picked it up and looked at it.

Suddenly, remembering the hint of stale cigarette smoke in April's room, that cigarette butt made a whole lot more sense to her.

Her mother had been telling her about seeing April and Tracy McLaughlin sharing a romantic interlude in the hallway. And her next comment had been something about doing a paternity test. Maybe the cigarette butt had belonged to Tracy McLaughlin. Maybe Edie hoped enough genetic material could be located on the filter to develop a DNA profile to prove for certain whether or not Tracy McLaughlin was the father of April's unborn child.

Grabbing her cell phone and room key, Ali dashed out of the room and hurried down to the lobby. She found Dave Holman and a uniformed security guard closeted in a windowless room behind the front desk, where they were surveying a bank of security monitors.

Dave was surprised to see her. "What are you doing here?" he asked.

For an answer, she waved the baggie in front of him. "What's that?"

"Evidence, most likely," Ali replied. "At least it's evidence as far as my mother is concerned. I told you Mom was playing detective. I'm guessing this cigarette butt belongs to Tracy McLaughlin, and she thought we could use it as part of a paternity test."

Dave took the bag from her hand and held it up to the light. "It could mean a whole lot more than that."

"What?"

"Tracy's a convicted felon, and a vehicle theft was involved in your husband's murder. Tracy had a business connection with Paul Grayson, but he also has a possibly illicit relationship with Paul's bride-to-be. This is sounding like a whole lot of motive to me."

"But how does the cigarette play into this?" Ali asked.

"The duct tape. Didn't you tell me your husband was bound with duct tape?"

Ali nodded. "That's what I was told, but I saw it, too. Not the tape itself, but the marks it left on his face. Why?"

"Most bad guys still haven't figured out that using duct tape in the commission of a crime is a really bad idea. Glue from the tape almost always captures the criminal's DNA right along with the victim's. Say somebody tears the tape with their teeth. They also leave behind traces of their saliva. And there's DNA in the tiny pieces of skin that slough off the bad guy and onto the tape as it's being applied. If the duct tape used on Paul hasn't already been examined for DNA evidence, you can bet it will be. Crime labs can usually find DNA evidence. The big problem comes when it's time to match that evidence to a known perpetrator, and that's what Edie may have given us."

"Since Tracy's been in prison, won't they have a record of his DNA profile?" Ali asked.

"Not necessarily," Dave said. "For one thing, those

databases are relatively new. McLaughlin could well have been let go without having to leave a sample."

Ali looked at the cigarette again. "When Mom grabbed this, she wasn't thinking about the possibility that McLaughlin might be a killer. She was thinking about the baby."

"And from the looks of things, I'd say she gave him hell about it, too."

Ali was dismayed. "She did? When?"

"Down in the lobby. After the interview. It's on one of the security tapes. Come take a look."

Dave led Ali over to the monitors. On one of them, Ali saw a frozen image of her mother, standing flat-footed, hands on her hips, glaring up into Tracy McLaughlin's face. The security guard pressed one of the controls. Suddenly Edie Larson was in motion. Her mouth moved. Her hands gestured furiously. No words could be heard, but then, they didn't need to be.

Ali knew her mother. Edie had never been one to hold back on delivering her opinions. Here she was giving a suspected killer a piece of her mind.

Watching the video sent a surge of fear through Ali's body. She had done the same thing once—she had bearded a suspected killer long before anyone else had tumbled to what had happened. In the process Ali had put herself in harm's way and had come closer to dying that day than she cared to remember. Now Edie Larson had done the same thing—put herself in harm's way.

"What now?" she asked.

"I think it's time to file that missing person's report," Dave said.

{ CHAPTER 13 }

Upstairs, the first call Ali made was to Missing Persons at LAPD—with predictable results. Carolyn Little, the Missing Persons cop Ali had spoken to on Friday, wasn't available on weekends, and no other officer came on the line, either. Instead, an indifferent clerk with minimal typing skills and an even smaller sense of urgency took the information on the disappearance of Edie Larson.

"You be sure to let us know if Ms. Larson turns up, now," the clerk said cheerily when she finished. "If we don't hear from you by this time tomorrow, an officer should be in touch. If not tomorrow, then the day after." Click.

Ali flung down the phone. "So much for getting any help from LAPD," she muttered.

"What did you expect?" Dave asked.

Shaking her head in disgust, Ali dialed the number she had for the Riverside Sheriff's Department. If she had reached the younger detective, she might have achieved better results, but at seven o'clock on a Sunday evening, talking with Detective Sims was the best she could do. He was a long way from sympathetic.

"I'm a homicide detective," he said. "If you've got a missing person on your end, you need to call LAPD."

"We already did that," Ali told him. "They're not exactly interested."

"Why should I be?"

"Because we think my mother's disappearance may have something to do with my husband's homicide and with one of my husband's acquaintances—a guy named Tracy McLaughlin."

"What about him?" Sims asked.

The way Sims asked the question made it clear McLaughlin was already a known entity, but Ali wasn't eager to give up any additional information without first having some assurances from the detective that he would intercede with the LAPD on Edie Larson's behalf.

"You know Tracy McLaughlin went to prison for car theft?" Ali asked.

"That's what I like about all you hotshot media types," Detective Sims grumbled. "You think that just because we're cops, we must be too dumb to wipe our own butts. Of course I know McLaughlin got sent up for grand theft auto. Served five and a half years. In a homicide involving a stolen vehicle, don't you think that's the kind of thing that would have come to our attention once we started investigating your husband's friends and associates? And what the hell does that have to do with the fact that your mother has apparently taken a powder?"

"My mother's a responsible person," Ali returned. "She wouldn't leave of her own volition without letting one of us know. I talked to her shortly before she disappeared. She said she thought Tracy McLaughlin was somehow involved with April Gaddis, my husband's fiancée."

"Talk about yesterday's news," Sims returned dismissively. "Of course they were involved. April and Tracy have been friends for years. According to what April told us earlier, she was the one who brought

Sumo Sudoku to your husband's attention in the first place."

Being friends and having a romantic encounter in a hotel hallway were two entirely different things, but Ali suspected that if she hinted at a possible romantic connection between April and Tracy, Detective Sims would most likely discount that as well.

"Before my mother left she was involved in a verbal confrontation with Tracy McLaughlin. We saw that on a security tape. She also collected a cigarette butt and left it in a plastic bag," Ali continued. "Dave Holman and I believe that may have come from Tracy McLaughlin as well. If DNA from that could be linked to the duct tape found on my husband—"

"Who says there was duct tape?" Detective Sims demanded. "How would you know about that?"

"I saw it, remember?" Ali reminded him. "When I identified the body. I'm no expert, but the marks I saw on his face certainly looked like they could have come from duct tape."

"Oh," Sims said. "I see."

"So are you checking the duct tape for DNA evidence?" Ali insisted.

"Of course we're checking it," Sims replied with an impatient snarl. "But this isn't exactly *CSI Miami*. In our neck of the woods it generally takes a while for our people to develop a DNA profile. We don't try to get the job done in sixty minutes minus commercials, so don't expect us to have lab results tomorrow or next week or even next month. We're also required to maintain chains of evidence. If and when we decide we need a DNA sample from Mr. McLaughlin, you can be sure we'll be able to obtain one on our own without help from either you or your mother. In the meantime, we have leads and we're working them. Now, if you don't mind, this is supposed to be my day off."

With that Sims hung up, leaving Ali holding the phone.

"What?" Dave asked.

"I don't think Detective Sims is going to help us find Mom or Tracy McLaughlin," Ali said.

"If we can't go through official channels, we'll have to try some unofficial ones," Dave said, reaching for his phone.

"Your pal at LAPD?"

Dave nodded. "If he's home. He said something about going camping on his days off."

While Dave worked his phone, Ali stood in the middle of the room, holding her cell phone and thinking. She remembered something Helga had said the day before as Victor had been driving them from the hotel to Robert Lane. Scrolling through her cell's phone book, Ali located Helga Myerhoff's number and dialed it.

"Yesterday, when you were talking to me about April Gaddis," Ali said, "I seem to remember that you mentioned something about her wanting to be a Pilates instructor."

"Yes," Helga answered. "That's right."

"And that some of her friends weren't exactly nice people?" Ali pressed.

"Bit of an understatement," Helga replied. "Have you ever heard of The Body Shop in Century City?"

"Car repairs?" Ali asked.

"Not exactly," Helga said with a snort. "Although

it's located in a building that once held an auto dealership, it's got nothing at all to do with cars. It's a twenty-four-hour upscale fitness club where network bigwigs and wannabe bigwigs can mix and mingle, see and be seen. It's also one of the hot, in-crowd places at the moment. Supposedly the gym comes complete with one-on-one personal trainers, an organic juice bar, and with personal chefs available upon request. More than that, though, it also operates as a convenient pickup joint. That's where April first met Paul, by the way. She worked there as a receptionist."

Makes sense, Ali thought. For an undereducated and beautiful young woman like April Gaddis, who was also ambitious and determinedly upwardly mobile, The Body Shop sounded like the perfect manhunt launching pad.

"The Body Shop's biggest appeal is that it's both respectable and edgy," Helga continued. "As you already know, some of Hollywood's best-known heavy hitters are afflicted with complicated substance-abuse issues. For these relatively respectable guys, it's a lot more convenient if they can meet up with their drug supplier at some fashionable watering hole rather than having to buy their next hit from a street dealer at some dingy intersection in L.A."

"What about Tracy McLaughlin?" Ali asked.

"The Sumo Sudoku guy?" Helga asked. "The one in the kilt?"

"That's the one," Ali said. "Did he work there, too?"

"He may have," Helga said. "I don't know for sure, but I'll tell you this. I liked looking at the guy. He might be a bit young for me, but I wouldn't mind taking him home for a day or two to check out whatever it is he keeps under that kilt."

Ali was glad that Dave wasn't hearing Helga's part of the conversation.

"Why all this sudden interest in Tracy McLaughlin?" Helga asked. "What's going on?"

"My mother's missing," Ali said. "This morning she witnessed what looked to her like a bit of hanky-panky going on between April and Tracy. Early this afternoon one of the hotel security cameras recorded a confrontation between McLaughlin and my mom, but by the time I got back to the hotel to talk to her about it, she was gone—not just from our room, but from the hotel, too. The parking attendant told us he saw her peel out of the hotel garage sometime after one. I've tried calling her. No answer, and she hasn't called me back, either."

"Have you reported her missing?"

"Yes," Ali said. "Not that it did much good. No one at LAPD is particularly interested."

"So what can I do to help?" Helga asked.

"When you were doing your investigation of Paul, did Tracy McLaughlin's name come up?"

"I remember looking into the Sumo Sudoku thing because S and S Enterprises was one of your husband's newer business ventures. That name could have been mentioned, but I don't remember it in particular. I'd have to check with one of my investigators—and I probably won't be able to talk to him until tomorrow. Is there anything I can do in the meantime—anything I can do tonight?"

"I don't know," Ali said. "I can't really think straight right now."

"If you come up with something you need," Helga said, "don't hesitate to call. Have you told Victor?"

"Not yet," Ali said.

"I'll call him," Helga said. "He'll want to know what's going on."

Ali put down the phone. Dave had finished a series of calls and was once again hunkered over her computer.

"Google S and S Enterprises here in L.A.," Ali told him. "See what you get."

"S and S Enterprises holds all rights to Worldwide Sumo Sudoku," Dave said a few minutes later. "S and S was incorporated back in April with Paul Grayson named as executive director and CEO."

That announcement hit Ali hard. She had left Robert Lane early in March. No doubt negotiations for S and S Enterprises had been well under way long before Ali's departure, but she had known nothing about it. Sumo Sudoku had never been mentioned. In the scheme of Paul's betrayals, this one seemed relatively small, but it was a betrayal nonetheless.

"Who else is on the board of directors?" Ali asked.

"Guy by the name of Jake Maxwell," Dave replied.

"He worked with Paul at the network," Ali explained. "I always thought of him more as a rival than a friend, but there are lots of shifting loyalties in television, and things change. Jake showed up at court last week when the divorce was supposed to be final. He came there to back Paul up. He was also the official host of Paul's bachelor party from the night before."

Dave was still studying the computer screen. "This is interesting," he said. "S and S leases all the RVs that the various teams use. In other words, all the Sumo

Sudoku guys are ultimately employees of S and S, but they're hoping to create team rivalries that will attract media attention."

"Sort of like professional wrestling?" Ali suggested.

Dave nodded. "Just about that real. According to this, the company was incorporated with the stated intention of obtaining coverage for the sport on one or the other of the sports-oriented cable channels. No doubt that's why they scheduled the filming around Paul's wedding—to garner additional media attention."

"And that's why they went forward with the shoot anyway, even though Paul was dead," Ali added. "That's how the business works. The show must go on no matter what."

"I'll say," Dave agreed.

"So let's go see him," Ali said.

"Go see who?"

"Jake," Ali said. "Jake Maxwell. The person we really need to see is Tracy, but we don't have any idea where to find him, so Jake is our next best choice."

"I've got a call in for Tracy's vehicle records," Dave said. "I'm waiting for someone to get back to me."

"Fine," Ali replied. "But in the meantime, since Jake is clearly part of all this, maybe he can point us in the right direction."

"Where do we find him?"

Ali picked up her purse. "He and his wife, Roseanne, live out in Westlake Village."

"Where's that?" Dave asked.

"Not that far. Out the 101."

"Do we need to call first?" Dave asked.

"I think we'll just show up," Ali returned. "And we're probably better off if I drive."

"Amen to that," Dave said. "You drive. I'll handle the phones."

They left the hotel a few minutes later and headed for the 405 with Ali behind the wheel of her Cayenne.

"Have you had anything to eat since breakfast?" Dave asked as they went.

Thinking about her mother, Ali shook her head. "I'm not hungry," she said.

"Too bad," Dave said. "Edie would want you to eat, and we're eating. Pull up at the next Burger King you see."

Ali did as she was told, and much as she didn't want to admit it, eating a Whopper did help. Back in the car, Sunday evening traffic turned what should have been a forty-minute drive into an hour and ten, most of which Ali drove in silence.

"What's going on?" Dave asked finally. "Worried about your mom?"

"That," Ali said, "and trying to get over being pissed off."

"What about?"

"This whole S and S Enterprises thing," she returned. "Obviously it was going on long before I left home last March. That kind of stuff doesn't happen in a day or even a month, but I didn't know a thing about it even though Jake and Roseanne Maxwell did."

"So?"

"Once I was in Sedona, Roseanne sent me a sugar-coated e-mail in which she pretended like she and I were the very best of friends and she thought Paul was a cad, while at the same time Jake and Paul were starting a business together. I'll never forget her cutesy little message. She kept harping on how awful it was that I was reduced to living in a trailer and having to wait tables for a living. She even offered me a place to stay—in their newly remodeled casita."

"I take it you turned her down."

"Do you think?" Ali asked with a curt nod. "But now it grates on me that I have to go see this woman and make nice with her when what I'd really like to do is smack her upside the head."

"We're doing this for your mother," Dave reminded her. "Stay cool."

Ali had no difficulty driving them to Jake and Roseanne's sprawling, ranch-style house built on a grassy hillside outside Thousand Oaks. At the bottom end of the long, paved driveway, an ornamental iron gate blocked the way. Ali pressed a button and a disembodied voice spoke to them through an intercom attached to the gatepost. Half a minute later, the gate swung open.

Jake Maxwell himself stepped through the tall front door and came out into the circular parking area to meet them.

"Ali," he gushed, taking her hand in both of his. "What an unexpected pleasure. How good to see you, although I can't imagine what you're going through right now."

And you don't know the half of it, Ali thought.

When Dave emerged from the far side of the car, Jake frowned slightly. "And who's this?" he added.

"Dave Holman is a friend of mine," Ali replied without any further explanation. "We have some questions for you."

"What kind of questions?" Jake asked.

"About S and S Enterprises," Ali returned. "And about a guy named Tracy McLaughlin."

Jake glanced warily from Ali to Dave and back again. It was something that wouldn't have been apparent over a phone line. Clearly Jake had been caught off guard. Ali was glad they'd put good manners aside and hadn't called in advance to warn Jake of their impending arrival.

"What about Tracy McLaughlin?" Jake asked.

"We were wondering if you knew where we could find him," Ali said casually. "A few loose ends came up after the shoot ended yesterday. I wanted to ask him about them."

"What things?"

Before Ali could answer, the door behind Jake opened. A woman wearing a pair of tight pedal pushers tottered out onto the front porch on a pair of very high heels. She was carrying a tall goblet filled with red wine.

"Didn't know we had company," she said, coming to an uncertain stop and standing, weaving, with one hand poised on her hip. "I just told Kimball to open another bottle," she said. "Anybody want to join me for a little drinky-poo?"

Kimball (Ali had no idea if Kimball was the man's first or last name) was a professionally trained butler with a British accent and an imperious air who had been Jake Maxwell's aide-de-camp for as long as Ali could remember.

Ali stared. Whoever this smashed young woman

was, she sure as hell wasn't Roseanne Maxwell. And why she felt free to order Kimball around was another issue entirely.

"Go back inside, Amber," Jake said brusquely. "Can't you see I'm busy?"

Amber pouted. "I was just trying to be hosp . . . hosp . . ." she began before finally subsiding into tongue-tied silence.

"Hospitable," Jake finished for her impatiently. "Now do as I said. Go back inside and wait."

As in "Sit!" and "Stay!" Ali thought.

Without another word, the woman staggered back into the house, slamming the door behind her. Jake looked back at Ali.

"One of Roseanne's friends," he explained unconvincingly. "She's staying here while she's waiting for her new house to close. I'm afraid she had a bit too much wine with dinner. But I'm forgetting my manners. Won't you come in?"

Amber's appearance had fueled Ali's curiosity. Based on her own unfortunate marital experience, nothing short of a loaded weapon would have kept her from accepting Jake's rather halfhearted invitation.

"Thank you so much," Ali said, and headed for the door, leaving both Dave Holman and Jake to trail along behind her.

She saw signs of change the moment she stepped inside the entryway. For years a flattering oil portrait of Roseanne Maxwell had held sway just inside their front door. That painting was no longer there. Instead, a large rectangle of slightly lighter cream paint showed where the painting had once hung. Over the massive river-rock fireplace another painting—an unframed canvas Ali recalled as featuring a modern rendition of what appeared to be sunflowers—was also missing from its place of honor. Amber was nowhere to be seen, but from some distant corner of the house came the muffled sound of a television drama.

"Don't tell me Roseanne isn't home," Ali exclaimed. "She was really kind to me last spring when everything was so awful. I wanted to thank her."

"She's in New York right now," Jake said a little too quickly. "She went with one of her friends. They're busy buying next year's clothes and taking in a couple of shows."

"Do let her know I'm sorry we missed her," Ali said. "If she returns before I leave, we'll have to have lunch."

"Of course, of course," Jake murmured. "Now, can I get you something?"

Dave shook his head. "No, thanks," he replied.

"Some ice water would be nice," Ali said.

While Jake summoned his majordomo and issued the drink order, Ali examined her surroundings. Two pieces of Dale Chihuly blown glass were missing from the ebony sideboard in the dining room. Their absence along with the missing paintings led Ali to only one conclusion. Most people don't pack their precious artwork when they go off on a weeklong shopping excursion. Roseanne's departure had to be more serious than that.

Kimball appeared, bearing a silver drinks tray complete with an ice bucket, a collection of Baccarat crystal glasses, Voss bottled water, a decanter of wine, and a bottle of Oban single-malt scotch. With a slight bow, he deposited the tray on a side table. Then, without bothering to ask, he poured Jake a rocks glass with a tall, two-finger scotch. Meantime, Jake settled himself comfortably on a nearby love seat and crossed his legs, revealing a pair of very expensive Italian loafers.

"So what's all this about Tracy McLaughlin?" he asked.

He was trying so hard to be nonchalant and casual that an imp got into Ali Reynolds. She decided to go for the gold.

"I suppose you've heard about Paul's will?" she asked.

"Yes," Jake said with a thoughtful nod. "I heard that you got left holding the bag. It's got to be really tough, dealing with a complicated mess like that. And then, with everything else, to have April's mother fall down the stairs . . ."

"It's been tough, all right," Ali agreed. "And it's likely to get even tougher. Dave and I have reason to believe that the child April is carrying might not be Paul's after all. Since you and Paul were so close, I was wondering if you'd have any insight into that?"

Jake's face registered astonishment. "If it's not Paul's, whose baby is it?"

"She," Ali corrected. "The baby is a she. But that's what we're trying to determine—the identity of the baby's father. It's also why we're looking for Tracy McLaughlin."

Jake allowed himself a generous slug of neat Oban. "You're thinking Tracy might be the baby's father?" he asked.

"It's possible," Ali said. "So what can you tell us about him?"

Jake peered into his glass, studying the contents. "I suppose you know that he had a bit of a rough start."

"As in being sent to prison for grand theft auto," Ali returned. "Yes, we're aware of that."

"After he got out, he came out to California, where he eventually developed this Sumo Sudoku idea. And it was a great idea—he got a trademark on it and everything. Unfortunately, at the same time, Tracy was also developing a bit of a gambling problem. Finally, he was in so deep that Paul and I bought him out. We gave him enough of an advance to pay off his debts. After he's earned that back, he'll get royalties."

"Which is how the guy who invented the whole thing ends up doing grunt labor," Ali said. "That's why he wears a kilt, lugs rocks around, and drives a leased RV."

"Something like that," Jake said.

"So is Tracy mad about that—about losing control of his brainchild to someone else?" Dave asked.

"I don't think so," Jake answered. "He wanted his debts paid off a lot more than he wanted to run things."

"What if Sumo Sudoku happens to get picked up by one of the sports networks?" Ali asked. "What happens then? Would Tracy make money?"

"We'd all make money."

"Which is why," Ali said, "even with Paul dead, April was determined to go forward with the shoot."

Jake sipped his scotch. "I suppose," he said. "But I still don't see what makes you think the baby might be

Tracy's. I mean, I've never seen any evidence of them hanging out together."

"How did Tracy get hooked up with you and Paul to begin with?" Ali asked.

"Touché," Jake said after a pause. "Now that you mention it, I guess April was the one who introduced us."

Somehow Ali didn't find that the least bit surprising.

"Do you have any idea where Tracy McLaughlin lives?" Dave asked. "We'd like to talk to him if at all possible, the sooner the better."

"No idea," Jake answered. "None at all. He lives a pretty marginal lifestyle, if you know what I mean."

"So he's still gambling?" Dave asked.

"I suppose."

"And he's still broke?"

"Most likely."

"But he would need a place to park that huge rig of his. And since your name is on the lease of that very valuable piece of equipment, I would imagine you'd know where that secret parking place might be."

"Sorry," Jake said. "I have no idea."

It was a simple answer, but as soon as Ali heard it, she knew it was a lie.

"Does he have another vehicle?" Ali asked. "Something a little smaller and easier to park?"

"Probably," Jake answered, "but I'm not sure what."

"So you just turn these guys loose with your leased RVs and don't pay any attention to where they go or what they do with them?"

"Their contracts dictate that they have to be out in public doing events for a set number of hours per week, mostly up and down the West Coast. Some of the contests we set up—like the shoot at the house yesterday. Some of the others are just pickup games—on the beach, in parks, wherever. But with the advertising on the RVs, our guys are doing their job wherever they are, even when they're just driving up and down the Five. After all, name familiarity is the name of the game."

"So you're still moving forward with this Sumo Sudoku thing?" Ali asked.

"Of course," Jake replied with absolute confidence. "There's no reason not to."

There might be, Ali thought. *I'm your new partner and I may not be quite as interested in it as Paul was.*

Amber, her empty wineglass in hand, meandered into the living room from somewhere else in the house. "Oh," she blurted vaguely, looking at Ali and Dave. "Are you still here?"

Ali took the hint and stood up. Dave followed suit while Amber staggered toward the drinks tray. Clearly the woman had had more than enough, but that didn't keep her from refilling her glass.

"Amber," Jake said warningly.

"What?" Amber seemed defiant. She dropped onto a sofa, slopping a splotch of vivid red wine onto the white silk. "What?" she said again.

Jake shook his head wearily and said nothing. Obviously Amber was a bit of a handful.

"We'll be going then," Ali said. She walked as far as the door before pausing and turning back toward their host. "When did you say Roseanne will be back?" she asked.

"I'm not sure," Jake said uneasily. "This week sometime. It was pretty open-ended. You'll let us know when the funeral is, won't you?" he asked. "She'll want to be home for that."

"I'm sure she will," Ali agreed. "Tell Roseanne I'll give her a call as soon as the services are scheduled."

Outside, the sun was down. The warm September evening had cooled under a blanket of damp marine air that had rolled in off the Pacific.

"What now?" Dave asked as they climbed into the Cayenne and buckled up.

"I'm not sure," Ali said.

She put the car in gear and drove to the bottom of the driveway. The gate opened and closed, letting them back onto the roadway. Ali drove a hundred yards or so up the road and pulled off into the approach to yet another driveway.

"What on earth are you doing?" Dave asked.

"Wait," Ali said. "Let's see what happens."

Less than a minute later, the gate to the Maxwells' place swung open and a silver Jaguar XJ convertible with the top down nosed out of the driveway and onto the road.

"Bingo," Ali said. "There he is."

"What are you going to do?"

"We're going to follow him," Ali said, putting the Cayenne in gear and pulling out well behind the Jag. "I'm guessing he'll lead us straight to Tracy McLaughlin."

"God help me," Dave groaned. "Do you know anything at all about pursuit driving?"

"Not a thing," she answered. "But I know a lot more about California drivers than you do, so you watch him and I'll drive."

Both of which were easier said than done.

Ali raced through two lights that were in the process of turning red in an effort to keep Maxwell's Jaguar in sight as he turned onto the 101 and headed back toward the city. By the time Ali merged onto the freeway, he was in the far left lane and passing everything in sight. Ali headed for the left lane as well.

"We'll never catch him," Dave protested. "Or else we'll be killed."

"We'll catch him, all right," Ali said determinedly. "And with all this traffic, he'll never know it's us."

She managed to stick with the speeding Jag for the next hair-raising ten minutes or so until Maxwell finally swerved back into the far right-hand lane and onto the Fallbrook Avenue exit. Dodging through traffic, Ali followed suit, making it onto the ramp with bare inches to spare. Once there, she slowed and dropped back far enough to allow another car to merge in ahead of them at the light.

Back on surface streets it was easier to keep the Jag in sight while maintaining a safe distance. A mile and a half later, Jake Maxwell turned into a well-lit commercial parking lot.

"Geez!" Dave grumbled. "This guy has spent the last half hour driving like a bat out of hell and endangering life and limb. And for what? To go to Wal-Mart? What's he going to do, buy a loaf of bread or a gallon of milk?"

But instead of turning up the aisle of parked vehicles that would have led toward the store's main entrance, the Jag turned left and headed off across the outermost boundary of the parking lot, stopping at last in a far corner of the property where several hulking motor homes and campers had pulled up and parked for the night. The fluorescent glow of the parking lot lights revealed that one of the assembled RVs sported a more-than-life-sized portrait of a smiling Tracy McLaughlin wearing his distinctive Sumo Sudoku kilt. Hooked onto a tow bar behind it was a spanking-new Honda Element with the paper temporary plate still in its back window.

Dave stifled his series of complaints and sat bolt upright. "I'll be damned!" he exclaimed with undisguised admiration. "I don't believe it. You were right all along. Maxwell led us straight to Tracy."

"Yes, he did," Ali agreed. "Now what?"

"Pull over, park, and kill your lights and engine," Dave directed. "We're going to hide and watch."

{ CHAPTER 14 }

So what's Jake Maxwell's deal?" Dave asked as they waited in the parking lot. "When you're doing a homicide investigation, you always go after the first person who lies. So how come Jake told us he had no idea how to get hold of Tracy when he obviously did?"

"And why didn't he just call him?" Ali asked.

"That's easy," Dave replied. "I'm guessing he's worried about leaving a phone record trail."

"He lied about Roseanne, too," Ali said.

"That's his wife?" Dave asked.

Ali nodded. "She may be shopping in New York, but

I doubt it. Several important pieces of artwork—valuable pieces—are missing from Jake's walls and shelves. That tells me something's up between him and Roseanne that has nothing to do with next year's wardrobe and a whole lot to do with his pal Amber."

Learning that Roseanne Maxwell had most likely joined the ranks of Hollywood's cast-off and obsolete wives should have elicited more sympathy from Ali, but she couldn't summon it. The condescending comments Roseanne had e-mailed to Ali months earlier still rankled too much.

"Can you reach Roseanne?" Dave asked.

"Maybe," Ali replied. "I used to have her phone numbers and her e-mail address in my database, and they may still be in my computer back at the hotel. The problem is, that was months ago. If everything else has changed, her numbers may have changed as well."

"When you have a chance, try getting in touch with her," Dave said. "She may be able to help us."

The door to Tracy's RV opened. Jake emerged and slammed the door shut behind him. He stood for a few seconds as if undecided about something, then hurried back to his Jag. He peeled out of the parking place so fast that the car wobbled dangerously and almost careened into one of the parked RVs before he got the vehicle back under control.

"How much do you think he had to drink?" Dave asked.

"I don't know," Ali returned. "I doubt the scotch we saw him drink was the first he'd had this evening."

"I doubt that, too," Dave agreed. "And he's obviously

of the opinion that speed limits are posted for advisory purposes only. Let's make his life a little more interesting, shall we?"

With that Dave picked up his phone. "Yes," he said when someone answered. "I'm at the Wal-Mart here on Fallbrook Avenue. A guy just took off out of the parking lot in a silver Jaguar XJ," Dave said. "He's heading back toward Highway 101 and driving like a maniac. Almost smashed into a parked RV on his way out of the lot. The way he's driving, he may be drunk."

After repeating the Jag's plate information and leaving his cell phone number, Dave closed his phone with a grin. "Let's hear it for the California Highway Patrol," he said. "Considering the mood Jake's in at the moment, any interaction with cops should prove interesting to all concerned. In the meantime, let's go have a chat with Tracy McLaughlin."

"What about?" Ali asked.

"Let's start with your mother," Dave suggested. "Again, the one thing we need to establish is if he's lying to us or telling the truth. That means we ask him questions where we already know the answers."

"Like whether or not he spoke to my mother?"

"For starters," Dave said. "And you take the lead. Tracy's an ex-con, which means he probably thinks of himself as a cool macho dude. He's likely to underestimate you and say more than he should. Try to be conversational with him and get him to talk."

"You mean sort of like what I did for years when I was conducting television interviews?" Ali asked.

Dave looked chagrined. "I suppose so," he returned. "Something like that. Sorry."

They approached the RV with Dave staying in the background. As Ali mounted the steps and knocked, she noticed a hint of cigarette smoke lingering in the outside air. It reminded her of the smoke she had smelled in the hotel hallway the night before.

"Who is it?" an invisible voice demanded.

"Ali Reynolds," she replied. "I'm Paul Grayson's wife . . . his widow actually," she corrected. "We met yesterday morning before the Sumo Sudoku shoot. I was having coffee with April Gaddis out on the terrace at the house on Robert Lane."

After a few minutes, the door opened, allowing more secondhand smoke to spill outside. Tracy McLaughlin's hulking figure stood backlit in the doorway. He held the burning stub of a cigarette in one hand and a beer in the other.

"That's right," Tracy said. "I remember you now. What do you want?"

"I'm looking for my mother," Ali said at once.

"Your mother," he repeated belligerently. "Who the hell's your mother?"

It had not been Jake Maxwell's first scotch, and this was not Tracy McLaughlin's first beer.

"Let me give you a hint," Ali said. "Her name's Edie Larson. She's in her early sixties. Gray hair. Wears glasses and a hearing aid. She's gone missing."

"Name doesn't ring a bell," Tracy muttered. "There are lots of women like that. I'm afraid I don't know your mother from a hole in the ground."

"That's funny," Ali said. "I could have sworn I saw a hotel security surveillance tape where you were talking with her earlier this afternoon—arguing with her, in fact. She seemed to be quite upset about something. The digital readout on the video shows that the confrontation happened shortly before she disappeared."

Dave emerged from the shadows.

"Who are you?" Tracy demanded when Dave came into view.

"A friend of Edie's," Dave replied. "And we have reason to believe Edie had pegged you as possibly being the father of April Gaddis's baby."

"Well, she's wrong about that," Tracy McLaughlin declared. "Besides, it wasn't any of her business to begin with. I tried to tell that crazy old woman that she had it all wrong and to get off my case, but she wouldn't listen."

"So you're claiming you're not the father of April's baby after all?" Ali asked.

"I'm saying you're talking to the wrong person. You should be asking April about this, not me."

"But you're saying the baby might not be Paul's?"

"I didn't say that."

"What are you saying?"

"It's complicated."

"It's not complicated at all," Ali said firmly. "Either the baby is Paul's or she's not. And if she isn't, she won't be eligible to receive monies from his estate."

"So what does any of this have to do with me?"

"What it has to do with is fraud," Ali replied. "And with whether or not you're a co-conspirator."

"I don't know anything," Tracy insisted. "I haven't done anything."

"What about this afternoon?" Ali asked.

"What about it?"

"What happened after you saw my mother?"

"I left the hotel."

"Where did you go?"

"A couple of places," he said.

Dave moved closer. "Ms. Reynolds isn't a police officer," he said. "But I am. At this point you're not being charged with anything, Mr. McLaughlin, so it might be smart for you to cooperate. If you have an alibi for this afternoon—a verifiable alibi—you might want to give it to us before things get any more complicated."

"What do you want from me?"

"We want you to tell us about what you did this afternoon. All of it."

"Do I need an attorney?" Tracy asked.

"Not right now," Dave said. "That's what I told you a minute ago. At the moment, finding Ali's mother is our highest priority. Compared to that, everything else takes a backseat."

Tracy had tossed one cigarette butt aside. Now he paused long enough to light another smoke. "I knew April was going to be doing that Court TV interview," he said at last. "I wanted to see how it worked out. You see, that same woman has been in touch with me—"

"Sheila Rosenburg?" Ali asked.

Tracy nodded. "She's been talking to all of April's friends. And that's what April and I are—friends."

What kind of friends? Ali wondered, although she thought she knew.

"Anyway," Tracy continued, "I wanted to see what the interview would be like—if the reporter would be on April's case and accusing her of something or other—before I agreed to do one myself. So I came into the lobby and was watching everything that was going on when that woman—your mother—showed up and started giving me a hard time and causing a scene. I left before anyone had a chance to call security."

"Why was that?" Ali asked.

"It just seemed like a good idea to get the hell out of there before there was any trouble. Besides, I didn't want to disrupt what April was doing."

"You still haven't told us where you went," Dave said. "We need names and addresses. We also need the names of any people who might have seen you there."

Tracy's reluctance to discuss the matter was obvious in the sullen way he sucked on his cigarette and said nothing.

"We've been told that you had a bad enough gambling habit that you had to sell your Sumo Sudoku idea to the highest bidder," Dave said. "Men can change, but they seldom do. So what's the story here, Tracy? Are you back in the game again? Did you spend the afternoon at a casino someplace? Or was it somewhere less obvious—like an illegal card room, maybe? And how deep are they into you again? In some circles, gambling on credit can be a very dangerous undertaking."

The look of surprise that flashed over Tracy's face made it clear Dave had nailed him. "Where's the card room?" Dave asked.

"Upstairs over a strip club on Santa Monica called the Pink Swan," Tracy answered. "I was there all afternoon. I got there about two, and then came directly here."

Ali remembered the name from newspaper accounts about Paul's death. She also remembered Helga's account of the health club called The Body Shop. She wondered if the Pink Swan was a step up or a step down.

"The Pink Swan," she mused. "Isn't that where Paul's bachelor party was held?"

Tracy nodded. "I believe so."

"You weren't at the bachelor party?"

"No."

"Why not?"

"Because I wasn't invited," Tracy answered. "I mean, Paul and I had a business relationship but we weren't really buddies or anything."

"Especially since it sounds to me as if you used to screw around with his bride-to-be," Ali put in.

Tracy looked at her, but he didn't bother denying it.

"This Pink Swan place," Dave persisted. "Would they have you on this afternoon's surveillance tapes? Would we be able to see what time you arrived there and when you left?"

"That's the whole point of a place like the Pink Swan," Tracy said. "There are no surveillance tapes."

A piece of the puzzle fell into place. If the Pink Swan was a surveillance-free zone, Ali realized, that might explain why no one had any record of Paul's exit from there. And who had been in charge of choosing the venue for the bachelor party? Presumably Jake Maxwell.

A pair of matching RVs nosed into the aisle and parked side by side directly across from Tracy McLaughlin's. Once the newly arrived vehicles were in place, several people exited. Laughing and talking, they set off across the parking lot toward the store entrance.

Tracy glanced at his watch. "Look," he said impatiently, "I'm tired. I had a big match today, and I have another one early tomorrow morning. Could we do this some other time?"

"My mother's missing now," Ali insisted. "What did Jake Maxwell want when he came here a little while ago?"

"It was just a scheduling glitch," he said. "One of the other guys canceled a match. Jake was hoping I could step in for him."

"So when Jake has a problem, he comes to you with it?" Dave asked.

Tracy nodded.

"Why didn't he call? You do have a cell, don't you?"

Tracy shrugged. "Maybe he wanted to get out of the house for a while."

"And maybe he didn't want there to be a record of his calling you," Dave suggested.

"Look," Tracy said, "I'm here, minding my own business, not bothering anyone—"

"Is that what you were doing when you spent last night in April's room?" Ali asked. "Minding your own business?"

Clearly her pointed question surprised Tracy McLaughlin. He didn't deny that, either.

"I already told you we were friends," he said. "That's what she needed last night—a friend." He tossed his dying cigarette out into the parking lot. Ali scurried down the stairs. She retrieved the smoldering butt, ground it out, and put it in her pocket.

"What are you doing?" Tracy demanded.

"You said you weren't the baby's father," she said.

"It may take a few weeks to get a real answer, but your DNA should prove it one way or the other."

"I didn't give you permission to take that," Tracy began. He started down the stairs after her, but Dave stepped up and blocked his way.

"I'm not a police officer," she said. "You tossed your trash out into a public parking lot. If I want to clean up your litter, that's my call, not yours. And if I'm willing to pay for a paternity test, that's my call, too."

Ali stepped around to the back of the Honda and studied the temporary plate. "While we're at it," she added, "tell us about this vehicle. I see you just bought it—on Friday. But I was under the impression you were having a tough time financially. So where'd the money come from for a new car?"

"That's none of your business," Tracy said. "I want you to leave now, before I have to call the cops."

"I already told you," Dave said. "I am a cop."

"More cops then," Tracy said.

"By all means, call away," Ali said. "With everything that's gone on the past few days, I think they'll be interested in hearing what we all have to say."

Without another word, Tracy McLaughlin returned to his RV, slamming the door shut behind him.

"The DNA thing certainly got a reaction," Dave observed. "Now what? Back to the hotel?"

"Sure," Ali said, but once she was behind the wheel, she steered away from the entrance to the parking lot and tucked the Cayenne in among the vehicles parked near the front of the store.

"What now?" Dave asked.

"Let's just watch for a while and see if he stays

put," Ali answered. "It worked once with Jake Maxwell. Maybe it'll work again with Tracy."

And it did. Less than twenty minutes later, a dark-colored Ford Windstar minivan pulled into the lot. It stopped next to Tracy's RV. The Cayenne was parked too far away for Ali and Dave to be able to make out exactly what was happening.

"Stay here," Dave said. "I'll try to get closer."

While he was out of the car, Ali's cell phone rang. "Any sign of your mother?" Bob Larson asked. Ali heard the edge of panic in her father's voice.

"Not so far," Ali returned.

"Damn," Bob muttered. "I've got a really bad feeling about this."

Ali did, too, but she didn't want to say so. "We'll find her," Ali told her father with far more confidence than she felt. *We've got to!*

As the call ended Dave ducked into the passenger seat and then leaned back, breathing a sigh of apparent relief. "Thank God they didn't see me," he said, "but now we know how they do it."

"Do what?"

"How Sumo Sudoku can support all those very expensive RVs."

"What are you talking about?" Ali asked.

"The sudoku thing is probably nothing but an elaborate cover. I'm guessing they're really using the RVs as part of a drug distribution network, transporting drugs up and down the West Coast with their cargoholds full of something besides those round granite rocks. I'm betting they're moving heroin or else coke. They just unloaded a bunch of stuff from Tracy's RV and stuck it in the minivan. My guess is that Jake Maxwell came racing over here tonight to let Tracy know that we had been nosing around and that they needed to make arrangements to get rid of the goods sooner rather than later."

"Are you telling me Jake Maxwell and Paul got involved in some kind of drug-smuggling group?" Ali asked.

"That's how it looks."

By then the load transfer was finished and the van was pulling away from Tracy's RV. "They're leaving," Ali said. "Shouldn't we follow them?"

As Ali reached for the key, Dave caught her hand in midair and kept her from turning the key in the ignition.

"Absolutely not!" he declared. "There were three of them at least. Four counting McLaughlin. That means we'd be outmanned—no offense—and probably outgunned, too. This is way more than you and I can handle on our own."

"We call the cops then?"

"No," Dave said.

Ali was exasperated. "You mean we're just going to let them get away?"

"For right now," Dave answered. "If we've stumbled onto a big-time drug-smuggling program, you've got to understand these people aren't to be trifled with. You try bluffing guys like that or crossing them, and they'll blow you away without a second thought. From the looks of it, this could be a very big operation, which means we're going to have to go higher up the food chain than the local LAPD cop shop."

"What do you mean?"

"Once I get back to the hotel, I'll call in the Marines."

"The Marines?" Ali repeated.

"One Marine in particular—Ezekiel Washington, if I can find him. 'Easy' for short," Dave added. "When he's not deployed with the reserves, he works for the DEA here in L.A. Once they get wind of this, they're going to want to take down the whole thing—not just Tracy McLaughlin and the guys loading the van."

They were on the 101 by then. For a while Ali drove in thoughtful silence. What Dave had said about drug dealers killing people without compunction had hit her hard. "Do you think my mother's somehow mixed up with this drug business?" she asked finally.

"She may have blundered into it the same way we did," Dave replied somberly.

Ali felt her stomach clutch. "We'll be lucky to see her alive, won't we?"

As the hours had worn on, Ali had managed to keep her worst fear at bay. Now, having spoken it aloud, she felt like she was drowning in self-reproach. Whatever befell Edie Larson would be all Ali's fault. If she hadn't let herself be bamboozled into marrying Paul Grayson in the first place, none of this would have happened. It was bad enough to learn that he'd been unfaithful to her. That much she had somehow suspected, and having it verified hadn't been all that much of a shock. But for him to have been involved in the drug trade, too? That was way beyond anything she had ever thought Paul capable of, but then she guessed she hadn't known him nearly as well as she thought she had.

Blaming herself and agonizing about her mother

accomplished nothing, so she forced herself to turn back to the McLaughlin interview.

"What about the Pink Swan?" she asked.

"If it's a topless place with illegal gambling and they don't do surveillance tapes, that means they appeal to a clientele with plenty to hide."

"It's also the place where Jake hosted Paul's bachelor party."

"I'll turn Easy on to that, too. But from the sound of it, the Pink Swan is probably already on the DEA's radar."

"And then there's Roseanne," Ali added thoughtfully. "I wonder about her."

"Maxwell's wife?"

Ali nodded. "If I didn't know what was going on, I wonder if Roseanne did."

"Too bad we don't know where to find her."

"Maybe somebody does," Ali said determinedly. She passed Dave her phone. "Punch the green button. That'll give you my list of made calls. Look for Helga Myerhoff."

"Your divorce lawyer?" Dave asked. "How come?"

"She specializes in high-profile divorce cases. If Roseanne and Jake are splitting the sheets, you can figure there's a lawyer involved—or a whole bevy of them. Helga's more likely than anyone else to know which ones."

Dave found the number, pressed it, and then handed the phone to Ali.

"I didn't know they were getting a divorce," Helga said, once Ali had said her piece. "But I can't say I'd be surprised."

"Because Jake's involved with another woman?" Ali asked.

"Because they're broke," Helga returned. "Relatively speaking, of course."

Jake Maxwell hadn't looked broke earlier that evening. Anything but.

"Even in somewhat straitened circumstances, however," Helga continued, "everyone I know would have been panting after Roseanne Maxwell and hoping to land her as a client."

"How can Jake Maxwell be broke?" Ali asked.

"Lost his job, bad investments, gambling?" Helga said. "Take your pick. There are lots of ways to go broke in this town."

"You're saying Jake lost his job?" Ali asked.

"You didn't know that? It happened several months ago now—some kind of corporate job consolidation move. Paul and Jake ended up going head-to-head for the same job. Paul got the job—Jake Maxwell got a golden handshake. That's why I was a little surprised when he showed up at court on Friday to be in Paul's corner, but then sometimes people turn out to be better than you think they are."

Or worse, Ali thought.

"Getting back to Roseanne," Helga finished. "I do have some connections. If she's holed up somewhere, someone I know will be able to find her."

"Thanks."

"Victor wanted you to call. Have you talked to him yet?"

"No."

"If you're driving all over hell and gone, you should

probably let him know from you exactly what you're up to."

Ali knew what Victor would say—stay put; don't talk to anyone; let the cops look for her mother.

"I'll call him," Ali agreed. *Eventually.*

Once off the phone, she recounted to Dave every-thing that had been said. "Makes sense," he said. "If Jake was needing to make some quick cash, someone may have made him an offer he couldn't refuse."

"But Paul wasn't broke," Ali returned. "Why would he be mixed up in it?"

Dave shook his head. "I have no idea."

By then they were pulling into the hotel entrance. "Do you want me to come up?" Dave asked.

"No," she said. "Dad and Chris will be here soon. I'm going to take a shower and put my feet up for a few minutes. I may even try closing my eyes."

"Good idea," Dave said. He hopped out of the Cay-enne and headed for his own car.

Ali handed her car keys over to the parking valet and headed straight into the lobby. If there were reporters waiting there, she'd tough her way through them.

Opening the door to her room Ali hoped, through some miracle, Edie would be there waiting for her, but of course she wasn't. The room was empty—dark and empty. Ali slipped off her shoes, sank onto the couch, and, as promised, rested her feet on the coffee table. She had spent the last hours busily doing something—playing detective and trying to find her mother. Now, in the quiet stillness, the awful reality began to sink in. Perhaps Edie really was lost to her—lost to all of them. Perhaps there would be no more of Edie's steaming,

soft-centered homemade sweet rolls at Sedona's Sugar
Loaf Café. Perhaps Ali would never again sit over a hot
cup of coffee, listening to and often disregarding her
mother's good advice. Perhaps she would never again
witness one of her parents' never-ending rounds of
good-natured teasing.

It was that realization—that losing her mother would
be harder on Bob Larson than on anyone else—which
finally goaded Ali to action. She picked up her computer and logged on.

CUTLOOSEBLOG.COM
Sunday, September 18, 2005

My mother is missing. Edie Darlene Larson, age
61, of Sedona, Arizona, disappeared from a hotel
lobby in L.A. early this afternoon. She was last
seen driving away from the Westwood Hotel on
Wilshire in her white 2003 Oldsmobile Alero.
Edie is five foot seven, has medium-length gray
hair, fair skin, and weighs approximately 140
pounds. She also wears two hearing aids. (She'll
kill me for printing that.) Anyone with information about Edie should contact LAPD's Missing
Persons Unit—and me!
    Posted 10:23 P.M., September 18, 2005 by Babe

There was far more she wanted to say, would have
said, but this was a case where less was more. She
deliberately made no mention of Edie's encounter with
Tracy McLaughlin. If, as Dave suspected, this whole

thing was tied to a drug-smuggling ring, it was better to leave that out. Ali stripped off her clothes and was about to step into the shower when her cell phone rang. Grabbing it off the counter, she was amazed to see her mother's name in the caller ID readout.

Sick with relief, Ali shouted into the phone, "Mom! Is that you? Are you all right? Where are you?"

Except there was no answer. Ali could hear a rustling sound and distant voices, but no one was talking directly to her. Maybe it was just a bad connection. Frustrated, Ali punched the volume button on the side of her phone. "Mom. Can you hear me?" she called again.

There was more rustling and then she heard her mother's voice. "What in the world do you think you're doing?"

"I'm trying to talk to you," Ali answered. "Where are you? What's going on?"

Someone else—another woman—was speaking in the background. Ali could hear the voice but not clear enough to make out any of the individual words.

"You need to let me go," Edie said clearly and firmly. "This is stupid. It makes no sense."

That's when Ali realized she was listening in on what people at the Sugar Loaf called Edie's infamous "bra calls." Because that's where Edie Larson always carried her phone—in her bra. At work her apron pockets usually overflowed with order pads and pencils. When she had added a cell phone into the mix, it hadn't worked, so she had opted for stowing her phone in the only other available spot—tucked inside her bra. Because Edie didn't always remember to activate her key guard, she occasionally made accidental calls, burning up min-

utes and inadvertently revealing all kinds of mundane
details of life in a restaurant to several different hapless
recipients.

Ali knew at once, however, that this call was no
accident. Whoever was with Edie had no idea she was
in possession of a cell phone. They also had no idea she
had figured out a way to signal for help. And instead of
dialing 911, Edie had simply punched "send."

There was a murmured answer in response to
her mother's comment, but nothing Ali could make
out.

"Why are you doing this?" Edie demanded, sounding more agitated. "Where are we? In a basement somewhere?"

So her mother had been blindfolded or maybe even
unconscious. She had no idea where she was, and she
was being held there against her will.

Ali strained to hear the other woman's response, but
it was totally inaudible.

Then Ali heard her mother's voice again. "Untie
me," she said. "Let me go. I'm sure we can sort all this
out."

There was a momentary pause followed by a burst
of outrage. "We're not going to sort it out. We're not
sorting anything. Stop telling me what to do, damn it!
Just stop it!"

And now that Ali heard the voice clearly, she knew
whose it was—April's. The voice belonged to April Gaddis. How could that be?

"Please, April," Edie said aloud. "Be reasonable."

But April had evidently moved beyond reason. "Shut
up!" she screamed. "Shut the hell up!"

April's shout was followed by the sounds of a brief struggle complete with lots more rustling and a sharp clatter. In her mind's eye, Ali imagined the phone falling out of Edie's bra and skittering across some hard surface. In her ears, the noise was deafening, but Edie's attacker didn't seem to notice. There were other sounds, too—the horrifying thumps of something heavy landing on human flesh. Knowing her mother was most likely bound and helpless, Ali cringed at each one. At last the struggle ended in a terrible groan and a spate of ragged breathing.

"There now," April said very clearly. "Maybe now you'll finally shut the hell up and stay where I put you."

Ali heard a door slam shut followed by an awful silence on the other end of the line. By some miracle the call was still connected.

"Mother?" Ali called. "Are you there? Can you hear me?"

But of course there was no reply. If Edie Larson was even still conscious, she couldn't hear her daughter's voice.

For a moment longer Ali stared at the phone in an agony of indecision. The phone in her hand was her only connection to her mother, but where was she? If Ali dialed 911 on her room phone, what would she say to them? "My mother's been attacked somewhere in L.A. I have no idea where." Or, was it possible there was an emergency operator somewhere who could trace the call between Ali's cell phone and wherever it was her mother was being held, injured, perhaps, or maybe even unconscious? But how long would that take? And even if Ali managed to maintain the connection for a while, could she keep it going long enough? What would happen when Edie's phone ran out of battery power and turned itself off?

Closing her eyes, Ali tried to decide what to do. Wherever April had taken Edie, it had to be a place to which April had ready access. And Edie had mentioned something about a basement. This was California, an area where basements weren't all that common, but Ali knew where there was at least one basement—a huge one—in the bottom of the house on Robert Lane.

More than half of the space had been and still was devoted to Paul's extensive wine collection, but there had been several other rooms as well, including a decommissioned redwood-lined sauna that Paul had considered turning into a safe room. Thinking about the way the heavy door had slammed shut behind April as she'd left, Ali had the sudden sense that she knew the answer. She wasn't confident enough in her idea that she was willing to place an emergency call based on it, but she did know for sure that there wasn't a moment to lose.

With the call still connected and on speaker, Ali dressed and strapped on her Glock. She paused only long enough to call for her car before grabbing for her purse.

Riding down in the elevator, Ali realized that taking on someone as seemingly deranged as April all by herself was nothing short of stupid. Once more she considered ending the one call and dialing 911. But again, what would she tell them? *Let's see. How about:* "My mother's been attacked by my dead husband's pregnant fiancée who may or may not be holding her prisoner somewhere in my *house on Robert Lane"*? Did that sound like a call emergency operators were likely to take seriously? And even if they did, if April had come unhinged, what would she do if a bunch of cop cars came screaming into the yard? With Edie possibly injured and alone in the house with April, that was a risk Ali wasn't prepared to take.

While she was riding down in the elevator, the call ended on its own. Either her mother's phone had run out of power, or Ali's had simply lost the signal. Frustrated, Ali tried calling Dave. He didn't answer, so she left a terse message.

"On my way to the house. I think April's there, but I'm not sure. I also think she's lost it. Wherever she is, I believe she's holding Mom prisoner. Call me as soon as you get this message. Please."

Scrambling into the Cayenne, Ali rammed it into gear. Heading for the house, she was reasonably confident that in a fair fight—a one-on-one altercation—she would be able to take April.

And I have no intention of fighting fair, Ali told herself grimly. *None whatsoever!*

{ CHAPTER 15 }

Ali should have been pulled over a dozen times between the hotel and the house. She drove at breakneck speeds, passing like a maniac, going through lights that were already turning red. She almost hoped she could provoke an observant traffic cop into following her. Maybe having cops there was a good idea after all, and that was one way to summon some police presence without having to explain her soap opera existence to some emergency operator. But it didn't happen. When Ali finally sped through the broken gate and pulled to a stop in the paved driveway, she was still on her own. Dave hadn't called her back, and she couldn't take the time to call him again.

It's now or never, she told herself.

Before Ali ever stepped out of the car, she considered drawing her Glock but decided against it. Her plan was to try talking first. The Glock would come into play only as a last resort.

Ali was disappointed to find no sign of April's bright red Volvo there in the driveway, and no sign of Edie Larson's Olds, either. It was possible both cars were parked in the spacious five-car garage. Maybe that was where they had been parked when Ali and Dave had come to the house earlier and decided no one was there. It was also possible, Ali realized, that she was wrong and there was no one at the house now, either.

Hurrying up onto the porch, Ali reached past a tangle of crime scene tape and tried the front door. It was locked. Ali headed for the back of the house, wondering as she went if the alarm system had ever been reengaged. She tried the slider from the pool patio into the family room. No luck. That was locked, too. Finally she tried the door into the kitchen. The knob turned easily in her hand.

"I wondered how long it would take you to get here," April said.

Ali stopped just inside the door. April was across the room, seated on a chair at the kitchen table. A pistol Ali recognized as one of Paul's lay nearby on the tabletop, well within April's reach. Ali knew that had she come into the house with her own weapon drawn, they both might have died in a hail of gunfire.

"What's going on?" Ali demanded. "What have you done to my mother?"

"She kept trying to tell me what to do. I got sick of it. So I decided to show her a thing or two."

"My mother told you what to do so you're holding her prisoner in the basement? Are you nuts?"

"Maybe," April conceded. "Maybe a little."

Ali took a step into the room. As soon as she did, April picked up the gun and pointed it in Ali's direction. "Don't come any closer," she said. "Put your hands behind your head and stay where you are."

"Is my mother hurt?" Ali asked.

"I didn't hit her that hard," April said. "I was tired of listening to her. I just wanted her to shut up."

"I asked you if my mother's all right."

"She's still breathing, if that's what you want to know," April allowed. "I came upstairs to get more duct tape. When I went back down, I found her phone. I heard it ringing. Someone named Bobby called—whoever that is."

Bobby was Robert Larson, Ali's father, although Edie hardly ever called her husband by that pet name to his face.

"And that's when I saw Edie had called you," April continued.

"You're right," Ali agreed. "She did call me, and I

heard everything that was said between you, April. All of it. And when she mentioned being in a basement, I knew you had to be holding her here at the house. But why? What do you think you're doing? What's this all about? Whatever it is, we've got to put a stop to it."

"We?" April returned bitterly. "There you go doing the same thing your mother did—ordering me around, telling me what to do. Why does everyone think they can get away with that? It's been that way all my life. It's like people think that just because someone is pretty they're also stupid. I'm not, you know."

"What exactly did my mother tell you to do?" Ali asked.

"She told me to stop smoking—like I was in junior high. She sounded just like my mother. Exactly like my mother. It was like a flashback or something."

"So your mother was always ordering you around, too?" Ali asked the question more to sustain the conversation than anything else. She knew she needed to keep April talking while she figured out what to do next.

"Are you kidding?" April demanded. "Don't try to tell me you didn't notice. She was the worst one of all—talking to the lawyers, firing the cook and the gardener, acting like it was her house and her life instead of mine."

For the first time it occurred to Ali that April herself might have been responsible for her mother's fatal plunge down the stairs.

"Your mother was trying to look out for you," Ali said reasonably. "For you and your baby both."

"Screw the baby," April said. "I never even wanted a damned baby. I never should have told Paul about it in the first place. He's the one who talked me into keeping it. If it had been up to me, I would have had an abortion just like I did those other times. But as soon as Paul knew about it, he was wild to get married, have the baby and everything."

April's words hit Ali hard. She remembered that she and Paul had talked some about having kids shortly after they married, but Chris was already a teenager by then. Ali had been happy with the way her career was going. She hadn't wanted to start the motherhood program over again, especially knowing full well that no matter how much paid help she'd have had, most of the responsibility for the new arrival would fall to her. She had already raised one only child. She hadn't wanted to do that again, but she certainly hadn't wanted to have two more children, either. So she hadn't exactly said no to Paul, but she hadn't ever stopped taking her birth control pills, either. The upshot of that had been that Paul had resented Chris—resented everything about Chris—and had never really accepted him.

Once Ali had learned about April, she had moved out of the house. In the months since then, she had blamed Paul for everything that had been wrong with their marriage. Now, though, standing with her fingers locked around the back of her neck, facing her husband's armed mistress across an expanse of kitchen, Ali Reynolds came face-to-face with her own culpability. For the first time she had to admit that it had taken two people to destroy her marriage—three, counting April.

But that wasn't the real issue here. The real bottom line had to do with April and her gun. If she had gone totally off her rocker, was anyone going to come out of this confrontation alive?

"You killed your mother?" Ali asked.

"What if I did?" April replied. "It was an accident. We were arguing in the upstairs hallway. It got physical. I pushed her and down she went."

April's dispassionate confession was calm, conversational, and utterly chilling.

"But she was still alive when she landed," Ali argued. "She was still alive hours later when we found her. Why didn't you try to help her? Why didn't you call for an ambulance?"

"Because I didn't want to help her," April returned. "Because I was tired of having her scream at me. I just left her where she was and went shopping. I figured someone else would find her eventually, and I was right."

"My mother never screamed at you," Ali said.

"No," April agreed. "But every time I was around her, she kept telling me what I should and shouldn't be doing for the baby. Smoking is bad for the baby. Drinking is bad. Eating spicy food is bad. Coffee is bad. I'm sick and tired of the damned baby. She's not even born yet, and even Sonia Marie gets to tell me what to do."

She really is crazy, Ali thought. *Totally nuts!*

"How did my mother get here to the house?" Ali asked.

"She figured it out," April said.

"Figured what out?"

"About my mother. She came to my room after the interview while I was changing clothes. She saw the scratches on my arms and asked me about them, so I decided to get rid of her, too. And since she liked the baby so much, I used the baby against her. I came here to the house and then I called Edie. I told her where I was and that I needed her to come quick and pick me up because my contractions had started. Worked like a charm. She couldn't get here fast enough. She was surprised when I pulled the gun on her, though. I think she thought I was kidding. I wasn't."

So Edie's ability to see through people was what had gotten her in trouble.

"My arms are getting tired," Ali said. "My hands are going to sleep. Can I put them down now?"

"Stay on that side of the room then," April ordered. "Over against the sink. Don't come any closer."

"What about Paul?" Ali asked, changing the subject ever so slightly. "Did he ever tell you what to do?"

"Sort of," April admitted. "I didn't mind that much because he was nice about it, at least at first. It got worse after I moved in here. That's when I really noticed it. He started sounding more and more like my mother. He was closer to her age, you know—closer to hers than he was to mine."

"You killed him, too, then?" Ali asked.

"Of course I didn't kill him," April said indignantly. "I keep telling you, I'm not stupid. Why would I kill Paul when we weren't married and he hadn't even signed his new will yet? That makes no sense."

"I thought you didn't know whether or not he had signed it."

"There are a lot of things I know that people don't think I know," April returned with a grim smile. "That's the one nice thing about people thinking I'm stupid. They always underestimate me."

April had already nonchalantly admitted to one murder, and Ali knew she had most likely attempted another. Given that, when she denied having been involved in Paul Grayson's death, Ali had to concede there was a possibility April was telling the truth.

"So what are you going to do now?" Ali asked.

"What do you mean?"

"You've admitted to me that you killed your own mother. You've attacked mine, and you're holding her prisoner. You're holding me at gunpoint. How is this all going to end, April? Do you have a plan?"

"Not really," April said with a shrug of her shoulders. "After everything that's happened, I really don't care that much one way or the other."

To Ali's ear, that sounded very much like an implied suicide threat. Dealing with someone in that distraught state who was also armed with a lethal weapon was a very bad idea.

"What if I've called the cops?" Ali asked.

April shrugged again. "If you had, they'd be here by now."

"What if I've called someone else?"

"You're bluffing."

"Tell me about Tracy McLaughlin."

"What about him? He's a friend of mine and a lot closer to my age than anybody else around here."

"How good a friend?" Ali asked.

"That's what your mother wanted to know, too," April said bitterly. "She even asked me if Trace was the father of my baby. Of course he isn't. You think I'm dumb enough to try passing somebody else's baby off as Paul's? What if he'd asked for a paternity test? What do you think would have happened to me then? If the baby wasn't his, I would have been out in the cold, just like I am anyway. So what does it matter?"

"Look," Ali said, trying to sound reassuring. "Let's go down to the basement and check on my mother. Once I'm sure she's all right, we can work together to figure out what's best for you and for your baby."

"You still don't get it, do you?" April said. "It's over."

"What's over?"

"There's not going to be a baby. I'm going to end this whole thing today. Now. What kind of a life would Sonia Marie have with her father dead and me in prison? Even if the cops arrest Jesus Sanchez, sooner or later they're going to figure out what really happened, the same way your mother did. Then they'll come after me. What's the point?"

"You might be in prison, but the baby would be alive."

"Somehow I don't think that's much of a favor. I already told you, there isn't going to be a baby. Come to think of it, maybe I'll burn this house down while I'm at it. That would be pretty funny, wouldn't it? If you're gone and I'm gone and the baby's gone, who gets Paul's money then?" April's question trailed off in a mirthless giggle.

Before Ali could attempt an answer, her phone rang. She pulled it out of her pocket. A glance at the caller ID window told her it was Dave calling.

"It's my father," Ali said to April. "I need to take this call. Otherwise he might come here looking for me."

April nodded. "All right," she said. "Answer it."

Ali pressed the "talk" button.

"Hi, Dad," she said with forced cheerfulness. "How close are you?"

"Dad!" Dave repeated. "I'm not your father. It's Dave, for God's sake. Don't you ever check the caller ID before you answer? And what the hell do you mean, going over to the house all by yourself?—"

"No," Ali said calmly, interrupting his angry outburst. "We still haven't found her. I called in a report to Missing Persons, but I haven't gone to the cops directly. If you want to, that's up to you."

"What's going on—" Dave stopped abruptly, and then seemed to tumble. "I see," he said. "It's April, isn't it? I'm almost at the house now, just turning up the hill. I'll be there in a matter of minutes."

Somehow Dave Holman was managing to sort through what Ali was saying and arrive at what she needed him to hear. *God bless this man!* she thought.

"Yes, Dad," Ali said. "It's a very nice hotel. Don't worry. You'll be able to get something to eat. Even if the kitchen is closed when you get there, they have twenty-four-hour room service."

"The kitchen, then," Dave said. "You want me to come to the kitchen. Is she armed?"

"Absolutely," Ali answered. "We'll find her, Dad," she added less vehemently. "I know we will."

"When you see me, try to create a diversion. Or else I will."

"Okay, Pops," Ali said. "See you soon."

She ended the call.

"Turn the phone off and put it on the counter," April said. "You're not taking any more calls."

Ali put the phone down.

"Still," April added wistfully, "it must be nice having a whole family you can call on and have them come riding to the rescue at a moment's notice."

Ali was still standing just to the right of the door. The kitchen window was behind her. If Dave approached the kitchen from that direction, April would see him, and she'd have a shot at both of them. If Ali could manage to distance herself from the door, April's attention would be split.

"You do have that kind of family," Ali said. "You've had it all along. That's what my mother was trying to do—help you. Your mother was doing the same thing. They were both trying to give you some hard-won advice to help you through this terrible time."

As she spoke, Ali moved past the sink, but April noticed.

"Where do you think you're going?" she demanded. "I told you to stay there."

Ali's heart pounded in her chest. Summoning as much nonchalance as she could muster, she reached up in the cupboard and took down a glass.

"I'm thirsty," Ali said. "I need a drink of water. Do you want some?"

April shook her head.

Taking that as permission, Ali proceeded over to the fridge, where she used the door dispenser to fill the glass with both ice and water. She was relieved to see that April's attention remained focused on her. Unfortunately, so did the gun. Ali's move to the fridge meant she was closer to the weapon now, as well. The barrel seemed immense. And it must have been heavy, too.

April's hand seemed to tremble as she tried to hold it steady.

Ali took a deep breath. If she attempted to reason with April, what were the chances she'd simply provoke the disturbed woman that much more? And how much longer would it take for Dave to get here? And when all hell broke loose, where in this high-tech granite and stainless steel kitchen would she look for cover? Ali was far more accustomed to dealing with the world through words than she was with weapons.

"Please, April," she said. "This is pointless. Put the gun down."

As Ali had feared, April did the exact opposite. Rather than putting the pistol down, she raised it and pointed it toward herself. Out of the corner of her eye, Ali caught a hint of movement at the kitchen door. Dave was there. He had approached from the opposite side without passing the window and without being seen while April's life hung in the balance.

Dropping the glass, Ali sprang forward. She reached across the table and slammed one closed fist into April's wrist. At the same time she straight-armed April in the chest with her other arm. Caught off guard and off balance, April spilled backward. The gun exploded with a roar. So did one of the glass pendant light fixtures over the counter. April landed on her back with a grunt. The force of the fall was enough that the gun bounced out of her hand and went spinning across the floor, where it came to rest against the base of the dishwasher. While April struggled to right herself, Ali scrambled after the gun.

"Ali," Dave was shouting. "Are you okay? Did she get you?"

Holding the pistol in one hand and shaking her head, Ali struggled to her feet as Dave helped April to hers. April was crying. There was blood on her face from what looked like a series of jagged cuts, but not from a self-inflicted gunshot wound. That meant Ali's desperate measure had succeeded.

"Why didn't you just let me do it?" April demanded tearfully. "Why can't you people just leave me alone? Why don't you mind your own business?"

It was a moment or two before Ali could find her own voice. Trembling, she examined her body and was more than half surprised to find no gaping wounds.

"I'm okay," she managed at last. "At least I think I am."

In the background now, she could hear the sound of approaching sirens. So Dave had called for backup. He just hadn't waited for reinforcements to arrive before coming to the door. For that Ali was incredibly grateful.

Without another word, Ali left April's gun on the counter and raced for the stairs that led to the basement. She dashed past Paul's loaded wine racks and through the media room. Just as she expected, she found Edie in the decommissioned sauna—duct-taped to the slats of the wooden bench. Another piece of duct tape covered her mouth. Her eyes were wide open.

Cringing, Ali peeled the tape off her mother's mouth, removing a good deal of skin along with it.

"Are you all right?" Ali asked.

"Just let me at that little nutcase," Edie replied. "I'll tear her limb from limb. Did I hear gunshots?"

Ali nodded while she struggled to loosen Edie's other restraints, starting with her arms. "You did hear gunshots," Ali said. "One, at least. Fortunately she missed. Dave is upstairs with her, waiting for the cops to get here. If they're not here already, they will be any minute. Are you all right?"

"I'm more mad than hurt," Edie replied. "She gave me a good crack on the back of the head. I was out for a while, and my head hurts like crazy. What in the world is the matter with that girl?"

There was no way to answer that question.

As Ali worked to free her mother from her restraints, footsteps pounded across the kitchen and down the stairs. "Where are you?" Dave demanded.

"Down the hall," Ali called back. "In the sauna."

Dave's anxious face appeared in the doorway a moment later. "Is Edie here? Is she okay?"

With the last of the tape removed, Edie tried to get to her feet. She stood briefly, but even with Ali helping her, she swayed a little and sat back down abruptly. "I guess I'm still a little woozy," she said.

"An ambulance is already on the way," Dave said.

"What's going on upstairs?" Ali asked.

"When April saw the uniforms, she fought the cops tooth and nail, but they have her in custody now. They're putting her in a patrol car or an ambulance."

A uniformed cop showed up in the sauna just then, followed immediately by two more. "Is the other lady all right?" one of them asked.

"I'll be a whole lot better once you get me out of here," Edie Larson said, rising again. "I never have liked saunas. They make me feel claustrophobic."

For good reason, Ali thought.

"Ma'am," one of the cops said. He didn't look to be much older than Chris. "Are you sure you should be moving around like this? Wouldn't you be better off sitting back down and waiting here for the EMTs to come take a look at you?"

"Young man," Edie said firmly, "I'm not staying in this room for another minute. Now either help me out of here or else get out of the way so I can do it on my own." With that, Edie turned to Ali. "Call your father," she ordered. "Let him know I'm all right. If you've told him about any of this, he's probably worried sick."

That was when Ali knew for sure Edie was all right.

As the clutch of uniformed officers helped Edie out of the sauna and down the hall, Dave handed Ali his phone. "Call your dad," he said.

Bob and Chris had arrived at the hotel by then, and they were jubilant when they heard the news. "I can't believe you and Dave pulled it off!" Bob Larson exclaimed.

Ali gave Dave a sideways look. "I can't, either," she said. "But we did."

"And everybody's all right?"

"They're taking Mom to an ER to be checked out. She has a nasty lump on her head and was a little shaky on her feet. She may have a slight concussion."

"Which hospital?"

"Cedars-Sinai," Ali answered. "Ask Chris. He'll know how to get there."

"What about you?" Bob asked.

"I'm fine," Ali said. And she had been fine while she

was helping her mother. But now she could feel tears welling up in her eyes as she spoke to her father. "I'll talk to you later."

She handed the phone over to Dave, trying to dodge his questioning glance as she did so, trying not to let him see that her hands were shaking and her knees knocking. Ali sank down on the redwood bench, and Dave sat down beside her.

"You're not fine," he said, wrapping a comforting arm around her shoulder. "You're not fine at all."

{ CHAPTER 16 }

They sat together for some time, with Ali simply leaning into Dave's shoulder and gathering her strength. "Thank you," she said at last. "Thank you for being here and thank you for listening to what I meant as opposed to what I said."

"You're welcome," he said. "Better now?"

She nodded.

"Good," he said, "because it's about time to go back upstairs and give another statement."

"And call Victor again?"

"I think we can pass on calling Victor this time."

The officer who took Ali's statement was one of the Eagle Scout–looking uniforms who had helped Edie make her way back upstairs.

"So this whole thing came about because your

mother and this April Gaddis had some kind of disagreement?"

"Evidently," Ali said.

"And what exactly is your relationship to the perpetrator—or your mother's, for that matter?"

Ali sighed. "April Gaddis is my dead husband's mistress. My dead husband's pregnant mistress. They were
supposed to get married yesterday, but he was murdered early Friday morning and died before our divorce
became final."

The young man frowned. Concentrating as he
wrote, he made no comment about Ali's very complicated life, and Ali greatly appreciated his lack of editorial input.

"And the cause of the difficulty between April and
your mother?" he continued.

"Mom tried to tell April she shouldn't be smoking
when she's pregnant."

"Makes sense to me," the young cop said. His name
was Rich Green, and maybe he really was an Eagle
Scout.

Officer Green took the information from both Ali
and Dave in a methodical manner. He was thorough.
He was patient. He was also slow as Christmas. By the
time he finally finished, Ali was ready to strangle him.

"So where did they take April?" Ali asked when
the ordeal was finally over. "And what about my
mother?"

"They were both supposed to be transported to
Cedars-Sinai," Officer Green told them. "But I believe
your mother decided against going at the last moment.
Said she had a perfectly good hotel room and that would

be fine. All she wanted was to see her husband and get a good night's sleep."

That sounded like Edie.

"And April?" Ali asked.

"She went to the hospital."

"Cedars-Sinai? They have a psych ward there?" Ali asked.

"I'm not sure about a psych ward," Officer Green returned. "I believe one of the EMTs said something about her going into labor."

Ali's heart constricted in her chest. "But I just told you. April Gaddis was holding both my mother and me at gunpoint. She's been waving a pistol around and threatening suicide. She should be on a suicide watch."

"I'm sure the EMTs who transported her conferred with the supervisor on the scene before they took her anywhere. Do you want me to call and check?"

Ali could imagine how long it would take Officer Green to navigate through any kind of bureaucratic roadblock.

"No, thanks," Ali said. "Don't bother. I'll find out for myself."

"The hospital?" Dave asked, following Ali out to where his car was parked directly behind hers.

"You don't have to come," Ali said.

"I'm coming," Dave declared.

"All right then," Ali agreed. "The hospital."

It was after two A.M. when both vehicles pulled into the hospital parking lot. The hospital was locked down tight. A security guard met them at the main door and led them to a lobby counter.

"We're here to see a patient," Ali said to the clerk seated in front of a computer screen. "She's on the maternity ward. Her name is April Gaddis."

The clerk typed something into her keyboard, then looked back at Ali with a frown. "Are you a relative?" she asked.

Clearly the clerk was less than prepared to hand out any information. And with the new federal privacy rules, Ali knew she was fighting an uphill battle. She tried to lighten the mood.

"Not a relative," Ali said breezily. "Just a good friend. I'm going to be the baby's godmother."

"Excuse me," the clerk said, rising. "If you'll just wait here. I need to check with a supervisor."

"Not good," Dave said under his breath. "When they have to go check with a supervisor, it's never a good sign."

A few minutes later a formidable black woman emerged from a closed door behind the desk. "I'm a supervisor, Audrey Barker. May I help you?" she asked.

"I came to see April Gaddis," Ali said. "She's a patient here—a maternity patient. She was brought here by ambulance a couple of hours ago."

"And what is your relationship to Ms. Gaddis?" Audrey Barker asked. "Are you a relative?"

"As I already told the other woman, I'm not a relative—just a good friend."

"Would you happen to know the names of any of Ms. Gaddis's relatives? She told us her mother is deceased."

"Monique Ragsdale *is* deceased," Ali answered. She

was starting to get a bad feeling from all the questions. Surely coming to visit a patient didn't usually result in the visitors being given this kind of third degree.

"Do you know of any others or how we could contact them?"

"I never met her father," Ali said. "And as far as I know, April is an only child. She used to have a step-brother, but not anymore. Why?"

"But you and she are good friends?"

"Yes," Ali said at once, carefully avoiding meeting Dave's eye as she said so. "Why?"

"Because," Audrey Barker said kindly, "I'm afraid I have some very bad news."

CUTLOOSEBLOG.COM
Monday, September 19, 2005

First of all, my mother is safe. She was found a few hours after I posted that last message. She was slightly hurt in the process but not enough that she required either treatment or hospitalization. Thanks so much to those of you who wrote to express your concern.

This has been a dreadful week. My husband is dead. So is his girlfriend and so is their unborn baby. My husband was found murdered late last week and I remain a "person of interest" in that homicide. April Gaddis, his girlfriend and the mother of his unborn child, committed suicide after being admitted to the maternity ward of Cedars-Sinai Hospital. I'm able to report her name here because April's next of kin, her long-estranged father, has now been located and notified.

Overwhelmed by events, April suffered some kind of breakdown. In the process she not only murdered her own mother, she ended up holding two other people at gunpoint. My mother was one of the two. I was the other. When officers finally arrived at the second scene, April was taken into custody and transported by ambulance to the hospital after convincing EMTs she was about to give birth. Once there, she went into the bathroom of her hospital room, supposedly to change clothes. Instead, she somehow managed to hang herself.

During my years in the news business, I remember using the words "senseless violence" on occasion. And the words apply here as well. A whole family has been wiped out—one that would have been my husband's second family. Four people are dead, including a baby who never had a chance to draw her first breath and a grandmother who never saw her granddaughter's face.

In the process, my own life has been threatened. So has my mother's. I've also been accused of murder. In the course of all the turmoil, things became so complicated that I was told to avoid blogging entirely for fear I might end up saying something in my commentary that would be considered self-incriminating. (As you can see by this post,

I'm not always good about taking advice from
attorneys—even when I'm paying them big
bucks to give me that selfsame advice.)

Putting all that together, you can probably
understand that when I came dragging back
to my hotel this morning at a little past four, I
was feeling more than a little shattered, to say
nothing of exhausted. To top it all off, my faith
in the human race was pretty much obliterated.
My mother, who had been missing, had been
found safe, but I was too tired to count that as
a blessing right then. She had been endangered
for no other reason than she is my mother, who
had come to L.A. to help me with my mounting
difficulties. I believe this can be filed under the
heading of "No Good Deed Goes Unpunished."

In other words, everything that had happened had been more than I could handle—and
then some. So once I finally made it back to my
hotel and dropped my car off with the valet, I
staggered into the lobby intent on going straight
up to my room to go to sleep. Halfway across
the lobby I was waylaid and greeted by name by
someone I knew but had never met in person.

She was an older lady with bright blue eyes
and a halo of thinning snow-white hair. She
was sitting on a couch just inside the entrance.
Parked next to her was a walker that sported
red, white, and blue tennis balls and a tiny
American flag. She stood up the moment she
saw me. "There you are, Babe," she said. "How's
your mom?"

Those of you who have been following cutloose for some time will recognize the name Velma T of Laguna. She had read my previous post, the one that said my mother was missing. She was so concerned about what was going on that she ended up doing some detective work of her own. She figured out where I must be staying, and came here—in a cab!!!! When I told her my mother was safe, she simply smiled and nodded. "I know," she said. "I've been praying for her all night."

I offered to give Velma T a ride back home, but she turned me down. "You look tired, honey," she said. "You'd better get some sleep. I got here under my own steam, and I'll get home the same way."

And so, with my faith in humanity restored by an eighty-eight-year-old bundle of goodwill, I came up here to my room, stripped off my clothes, and slept like a baby. Without moving a muscle. When I woke up late this morning and logged on to my computer, there were 87 messages in my in-box, almost all of them expressing concern for my mother. (Please pardon me if I don't respond to all of them.) A few of the ones from this morning were from people who had already learned from some other source that my mother had been found. I guess by now I should be accustomed to the amazing immediacy of the Internet community, but I'm still learning. And I'm still grateful.

I have no idea when bodies will be released for

burial or to whom, so I have no idea how long it
will take for funeral arrangements to be made. As
a consequence, I have no idea how much longer
I'll be in the area. But believe me, I'm more than
ready to go back home to Arizona. Sedona is
sounding pretty inviting to me about now.

Posted 11:43 A.M., September 19, 2005 by Babe

Ali had made arrangements to have brunch in the
hotel dining room with her parents and Chris. To get
there, she had to make her way through the lobby. Once
again there was a gaggle of camera- and microphone-
wielding reporters waiting for her.

"Ms. Reynolds, Ms. Reynolds," one of them shouted
as Ali exited the elevator. "Are you all right? Is your
mother okay?"

Ali started to walk past without answering, but
then, remembering they were only doing their jobs, she
relented and decided to get it over with. She stopped
and spoke directly into one of the cameras. "My mother
is fine," she said. "So am I."

"At the time April Gaddis was holding you and your
mother at gunpoint, did either of you suspect that she
intended to commit suicide?" another reporter wanted
to know.

"I did everything in my power to keep it from happening," Ali answered. "A troubled young woman died
unnecessarily. So did her baby. This is a very unfortunate situation for all concerned, including April Gaddis's
grieving family. I'd appreciate it if you'd all respect our
privacy. I have no further comment. Neither does my
mother."

"But—"

"No buts," Ali replied firmly and walked away, leaving a flurry of unanswered questions echoing behind her. She was relieved when she finally made it into the dining room, where the others were already gathered and where her father was perusing the menu.

Edie took one look at her daughter's face and was immediately on the alert. "What's wrong?"

"Nothing," Ali said. "Just that bunch of reporters outside."

Edie nodded. "Such pushy people," she said. "You didn't used to be like them, did you?"

"I hope not," Ali said, "but I probably was."

She sat down next to her father, who was still engrossed in the menu. "The prices here are higher than a cat's back," he announced. "This is highway robbery."

Bob's customary grousing was exactly what Ali needed right then. It took her mind off the reporters milling in the lobby.

"Don't worry about it, Dad," Ali said. "You're not paying."

"I don't care," her father returned. "It's the principle of the thing. The food better be top drawer, or I'm going to have a long chat with the manager."

As it turned out, the food was fine.

"So when can we go home?" Bob asked, settling in to mow his way through a plate of eggs Benedict that he pronounced almost as good as his.

"Mom won't be able to leave for a while," Ali told him. "The three of us—Mom, Dave, and I—are going to need to be available for the next several days while the investigation continues. And I still have to give my deposition for the wrongful dismissal suit."

"You don't need to hang around for any of that, Robert," Edie said. "Someone should be home minding the store. I don't like having the Sugar Loaf running on automatic with both of us out of town."

"You wouldn't mind if I went home?" Bob asked his wife. Then he turned to Ali. "And what about Paul's funeral? Won't you need me here for that?"

Ali was having a difficult time imagining how she was going to manage her estranged husband's funeral, but having to do it under the watchful eyes of both her parents would make it that much harder.

"You and Chris can go home, Dad," Ali told him. "Mom and I will be fine."

"I'm not going," Chris said. "Gramps and I already talked it over. I'll stay here for a couple more days and drive home with Grandma."

"Good," Edie said. "I'm glad that's settled, as long as you promise you won't drive the whole way without stopping to rest. You're not a spring chicken, you know, Bob."

During breakfast, Dave seemed far quieter than usual. At the café in Sedona, he and Bob teased each other constantly, but this morning Dave didn't participate in any of the hijinks. When Chris bugged out to go visit some friends and Bob and Edie went in search of the dessert buffet, Ali turned to Dave. "What's wrong?"

"I don't like being told to buzz off," Dave replied.

"Who told you that?" Ali asked.

"My good friend Easy. According to him, it's hands

off at the Pink Swan. He says the DEA is involved in some kind of complicated, long-term investigation going on over there. That means the Feds will take a very dim view of anything that upsets their apple cart."

"But if they're investigating the place, isn't there a possibility that they might have surveillance records that would show exactly what happened the night Paul disappeared?" Ali asked.

"They might," Dave agreed. "But good luck laying hands on them. The Feds aren't going to lift a finger to help anyone, including LAPD homicide, if they're running an undercover operation and helping out would tip their hand prematurely."

"How can that be?" Ali objected. "Paul was murdered. It makes no sense that the DEA won't help us."

"That's where you're wrong," Dave told her grimly. "The Feds don't have to make sense."

By then Bob and Edie were returning to the table with their dessert plates piled high. When Helga Myerhoff called a few minutes later, Ali excused herself. Avoiding the hotel lobby, she ducked into the nearest restroom to take the call.

"I heard all about what happened from Victor," Helga said. "Thank God you and your mother are okay."

Ali couldn't help wondering if Victor would be charging Ali for calling Helga and if Helga would be charging Ali for taking the call. As far as Ali could see, in this game the only ones coming out ahead were the lawyers.

"Yes," Ali agreed. "Thank God."

"As far as Roseanne Maxwell is concerned, I've been asking around," Helga continued. "If there's a divorce in the offing at the Maxwell household, nobody I know has heard word one about it. And nobody knows where Roseanne's disappeared to, either. That includes her best friend, who hasn't had a call from her. She says Roseanne isn't answering her phone and that her voice mail message box is full."

To Ali's way of thinking and with everything else that had happened, this sounded ominous. Especially for Roseanne.

"Jake told us she was in New York shopping for clothes."

"That doesn't compute," Helga replied. "The friend I just told you about—the one who complained about not hearing from Roseanne—is also the friend Roseanne usually does her NYC shopping junkets with. Since Jake hasn't done so, the friend is actually thinking of turning in a missing person's report."

"I hope she does," Ali said.

"Anything else you need from me right now?" Helga asked.

"You'll let me know if you hear anything?" Ali asked.

"Definitely."

Ali ended the call and returned to the dining room, where she discovered her father had managed to pay for brunch after all.

"Thanks, Dad," she told him.

"Thanks for letting me go home," he said. "L.A. isn't for me. It's too big, too crowded, and way too expensive."

"Too expensive is right," Edie agreed. "It doesn't

make a bit of sense for us to be staying at a place like this at whatever king's ransom they charge per night when a perfectly good house is sitting empty just a few miles away."

"The house on Robert Lane is still considered a crime scene," Dave pointed out.

"But for how long?" Edie wanted to know. "With April dead and Ali and me both safe, I don't see why that's necessary."

"It's a crime scene until LAPD releases it," Dave told her. "The detectives need to determine exactly what happened to Monique Ragsdale and also what happened to you."

"But April told us what happened to her mother," Edie objected. "That's what I told that first detective who interviewed me this morning. I'm sure it's what Ali told them as well."

"The problem," Dave pointed out, "is that you happen to be Ali's mother. As far as the investigators are concerned, one or both of you could be lying to protect the other. And until there's some forensic evidence to back up the story that April is the one who pushed Monique down the stairs . . ."

"What about the scratches I saw on April's arms?" Edie asked. "Can't they be matched up with scrapings taken from underneath Monique's fingernails?"

"They probably can," Dave agreed. "But it's going to take time."

"And probably a dozen more interviews," Edie said. "I've done enough police interviews in the last couple of days that I'm sick and tired of them." She glanced at her watch. "How about if they did something else for a change instead of just sitting around asking the same questions over and over?"

That was Ali's opinion as well. From what she could tell, police work seemed to involve a whole lot more talking than it did anything else.

When brunch was over, Bob and Edie went up to their room to help Bob get ready to head out. Once they left, Dave stood up as well. "If you don't need anything from me," he said, "I may drive over to Havasu and see the kids for a while. They're off school for the afternoon."

"Go ahead," Ali told him. "I think you've earned a little time off."

Upstairs, Ali was relieved that she now had a room to herself. Much as she liked her mother, Ali had spent months becoming accustomed to being on her own. And she liked it.

Opening her computer, she stretched out on the couch and logged on. The first message in her in-box came from a familiar address:

> Dear Babe,
> I guess I'm not as young as I used to be. I just now woke up. Well, a little while ago, I suppose. Long enough that I've had a cup of coffee and turned on my computer.
>   It was such a thrill to meet you last night—this morning really. Most people would have thought I was some kind of crazed stalker or something. Thank you for being so gracious

*to an old lady who happens to be a big fan of
yours.*

*Knowing from you some of what went on
yesterday, I wanted to check out what that jerk
at socalcopshop had to say. Sure enough. He's at
it again. Go ahead and read it, but it'll probably
make you mad. I don't know what LMB's
problem is.*

LOVE,
VELMA T

Unable to resist, Ali turned to socalcopshop.com,
and there it was.

ALISON REYNOLDS AND HER WEB OF EVIL

Alison Reynolds, the Black Widow of Robert
Lane, continues to spin her evil web from her
current base of operations, the posh Westwood
Hotel. This time her victim is April Gaddis, the
unfortunate young woman who was scheduled to
marry Ms. Reynolds's estranged husband on Saturday afternoon.

Overwhelmed by grief and run over by Ms.
Reynolds's army of high-powered attorneys, April
Gaddis committed suicide in a room on the
maternity ward of Cedars-Sinai Hospital early
Monday morning. Not only is Ms. Gaddis dead,
so is her unborn child. After finding the mother's
lifeless body, doctors attempted to save the baby
but were unable to do so.

Sources close to the investigation say that Ms. Gaddis spent the last several days of her life in the company of Alison Reynolds and her mother. Why would she have turned to her fiancé's former wife for consolation? Well, let's see. For one thing, Ms. Gaddis's mother, Monique Ragsdale, also perished over the weekend as a result of a nasty fall down a stairway in Ms. Reynolds's Robert Lane mansion. Coincidence? I don't think so, and neither do LAPD and Riverside County homicide investigators who are working this series of interrelated cases.

Alison Reynolds is the only common denominator in all of them. Who gave this Black Widow a license to kill and who's going to see to it that she pays for her crimes?

Posted 11:05 A.M., September 19, 2005 by LMB

So Lance-a-lot is at it again, Ali thought. When it came to spinning a web, Ali didn't hold a candle to April Gaddis, but she resisted the temptation to respond to LMB and tell him so directly. Posting anything on his Web site would only serve to add legitimacy to his claims about her. She sent a note to Velma instead.

Dear Velma,
Thanks for passing along the information about socalcopshop. The guy who writes it seems to have it in for me, and I don't know why.
Thanks, too, for what you did last night. Your loyal support meant more to me than you can possibly know.

> *If you have a weekend number for your*
> *nephew, you might ask him to give me a call. I*
> *believe I have information that might be helpful*
> *to his client.*

ALI

For the next hour or so, Ali sat at the computer sending as many thank-you notes as she could manage to the people who had written to express their concern over the fact that Edie Larson was missing or else their gratitude for her safe return. She posted some of the messages and simply answered the others. Good manners required individual replies wherever possible.

She had finally succeeded in clearing her mailbox and had closed her eyes for a brief nap when the "You've got mail" announcement sounded in her ear. The e-mail address, a series of numbers that were most likely a combination of birthdate and zip code, meant nothing to her, but that wasn't unusual. Most of the e-mail Ali Reynolds received at cutlooseblog.com came from strangers.

> *Dear Ali,*
> *I'm writing to you through a friend's e-mail*
> *account because I'm afraid my account is being*
> *monitored, and as you know, these are very*
> *dangerous people. I tried to call your old cell*
> *phone but it didn't work. If you have a new*
> *cell phone number please send it to me at this*
> *address. I need your help. Please don't tell anyone*

*that you've heard from me, and don't give anyone
this e-mail address, either.*

RM

Ali read through the message twice. RM? That could
only be Roseanne Maxwell. Had to be. And these dangerous people she mentioned? Dave had said much the
same thing about the drug traffickers—that they were
dangerous. Ali wrote back immediately, giving Roseanne her new Arizona-based cell phone number.

Then she waited. When her cell phone finally rang,
it was after four.

"Don't call me by name," the person said, although
Ali recognized Roseanne's breathy delivery as soon as
she spoke. "This is a throwaway phone. Don't bother
trying to trace it."

"What do you want then?" Ali asked. "Why are you
calling me?"

"Like I said," Roseanne told her. "I need your help.
I've got to disappear."

"As far as I can tell, you already have."

"This isn't a game," Roseanne Maxwell replied. "I
mean, I need to disappear for the rest of my life—for
whatever life I have left."

There was a desperate quality in Roseanne's voice,
one that convinced Ali that the woman wasn't kidding.

"What do you want me to do?" Ali asked.

"I'm staying with a friend up in Valencia," Roseanne
said. "Do you know where that is?"

"Of course," Ali said.

"Come to the Claim Jumper here in town," Roseanne said. "I'll meet you there at six. Be sure nobody follows you. We need to talk."

In the past several days, every time Ali had reached out to help someone, the effort had turned around to bite her in the butt. "Why should I?" she asked.

"Because you want to know what happened to Paul," Roseanne said. "You owe it to yourself, and you owe it to Paul."

I don't owe Paul Grayson a thing, Ali wanted to say. Instead she replied reluctantly, "All right. I'll be there."

{ CHAPTER 17 }

Ali picked up the phone and tried her mother's room, but the call went directly to voice mail. With her father already on his way to Sedona, it was likely Edie was taking a nap. After the previous night's misadventures, that was hardly surprising. Ali left a message that she was going to meet a friend at the Claim Jumper in Valencia and let it go at that. And she gave Chris a pass as well. She was glad he was off having fun with his friends. That was fine.

What about calling Dave? Ali wondered. With no strings other than friendship, the man had literally spent days helping Ali and her family at every turn. Now that he was taking some time and several hours to drive back over to Lake Havasu to spend time with his kids, Ali couldn't, in good conscience, involve him again—either by calling him or leaving a message. In fact, she was determined this was something she would handle on her own.

Besides, how dangerous could it be to meet up with Roseanne Maxwell in what would no doubt be the middle of a crowded restaurant? Still, remembering Roseanne's concern about Ali's possibly being followed, she did check the rearview mirror from time to time as she drove north on I-5 just to make sure there was no one suspicious behind her. In actual fact, Ali was far less worried about bad guys following her than she was about one of the stray reporting teams who were still camped out in and around the hotel.

As for Roseanne Maxwell herself? She wasn't what Ali would have considered to be a frightening proposition. For one thing, she was slight of build with the best curve enhancement and facial redefining money could buy. For Roseanne beauty wasn't skin deep—it was subcutaneous. For as long as Ali had known the woman, Roseanne had existed on a perpetual round of dieting and not dieting. That was why Roseanne's having set their meeting at an establishment known for its gigantic serving portions was a mystery in and of itself.

Ali had never been particularly close to Roseanne. Their husbands had been coworkers, competitors for the network job, and partners in the Sumo Sudoku scam. Ali and Roseanne had seen each other socially on occasion, but they definitely didn't qualify as good friends. Or even semi-friends. And why Roseanne would turn to Ali in a time of trouble was as much a mystery as where they were meeting.

It was six on the dot when Ali arrived at the Claim Jumper parking lot. The restaurant was jammed, and there was a crowd of people milling about outside, waiting for tables. Ali was about to walk inside and put her name on the list when a woman appeared at her side. Roseanne Maxwell was so changed that Ali barely recognized her.

The last time Ali had seen Roseanne had been at Paul's annual Christmas party the preceding year. She had been dressed to the nines with her hair piled on top of her head in a sophisticated platinum blond do, but the months since then had been anything but kind to Roseanne Maxwell. Her hair was brown now and cut short as well, shorn off in something that resembled chemo-patient chic. Ali barely recognized her.

The old Roseanne wouldn't have ventured out of the house without a complete assortment of high-end jewelry adorning her fingers, neck, and ears and a layer of full-armor-of-God makeup on her face. This new Roseanne wore no jewelry whatsoever, and her makeup consisted of a little lipstick and nothing else. Roseanne had stopped smoking years earlier. Without the ongoing attention of her cosmetic surgeon and artfully applied Botox, the telltale lines had reasserted themselves. In less than a year she had aged a good decade's worth.

Roseanne grabbed Ali's arm and hugged her close. "I know. I know," she whispered. "I look like hell. You don't have to tell me. Come on," she added. "I came early. I already have a table."

Ali allowed herself to be led through the crowded restaurant to a secluded table in the far back of the room.

"Nobody followed you, did they?" Roseanne asked nervously.

Taking her phone out of her pocket and turning the

ringer to "silent," Ali shook her head. "I don't think so," she said. "I checked."

"I hope you don't mind meeting me here. Carrie, the hostess, is a friend of mine. I met her in NA. I needed a place to stay, and she happened to have a spare bedroom in her house. So that's where I'm staying at the moment. And because I can't risk driving my own car right now, she gave me a lift when she came to work."

"NA?" Ali asked.

"Narcotics Anonymous," Roseanne returned. "I'm trying to get straight, if I can live long enough, that is." She patted her badly cut hair. "Good disguise, don't you think?"

"Very," Ali agreed. "Now what's going on?"

For an answer, Roseanne opened her purse and pushed a ziplock bag across the table. Ali picked it up and studied it. A collection of jewels and gold—diamond-studded rings, necklaces, earrings, and bracelets—winked back at her through the clear plastic.

"What's this?" Ali asked, handing the bag back across the table.

"My jewelry," Roseanne said. "I need to sell it—all of it. If I go to a pawnshop, I'll only get a fraction of what it's worth. Besides, I'm sure word of it would get back to Jake. Please buy them from me, Ali. I know you've got the money to do it, and it's my only chance to get away. Just give it to me in cash, and then I'll disappear. No one will ever find me. If they do, I'm dead anyway."

"Get away?" Ali asked. "From whom?"

"The people who ruined our lives," Roseanne replied, lowering her voice to a strained whisper. "The people who killed Paul."

"What people?" Ali demanded. "The drug dealers?"

"You know about them then?" Roseanne asked with a stricken look on her face.

Ali nodded. "A little," she said. "But not enough. You probably know way more. You should go to the cops and tell them what you know."

"I can't," Roseanne said in a hoarse whisper.

"Why not?"

"Because some of the cops are in on it. I've seen them."

Ali's first reaction was one of total disbelief. Obviously Roseanne was suffering some kind of paranoid delusion. If she was involved in drugs enough that she had turned to NA for help, maybe that wasn't too surprising.

"Look," Ali said placatingly. "I'm sure you have some reason to think so, but—"

"I'm afraid somebody tapped my phone," Roseanne said. "My old phone. I'm sure they were listening in on everything I said. Who else would have done that but the cops? That's why I got this new one—a disposable. They're much harder to trace than the other ones are."

Ali restrained herself from making a wry comment about conspiracy theories and people wearing tinfoil hats. Roseanne Maxwell was absolutely serious. Painfully so.

"It takes a lot of effort to tap telephones," Ali pointed out. "Cops can't do it just for the hell of it. They'd need judges, warrants, and everything."

"They already have those," Roseanne said.

"Who's doing this then?" Ali asked. "And why?"

At that precise moment, Ali's phone vibrated silently

in her pocket. With Roseanne already off the charts about people tapping telephones, Ali thought it best to ignore the call.

Roseanne sighed. "You know about the Pink Swan?"

"Some," Ali replied. "I know there's a lot more happening there than meets the eye."

Roseanne nodded. "When we first started going there, it seemed like it was all fun all the time. Jake always liked to gamble. It was a place where I could go along and do my thing while he was doing his. But eventually he got in over his head, and it got worse after the network cut him loose—a lot worse."

Ali managed to keep a straight face when Roseanne used the term "cut loose." It turned out there was a lot of that going around.

"That's how those people work," Roseanne continued. "They suck you in a little at a time. Like I said, at first it was just Jake's gambling and a few recreational drugs for me. It felt like a nice place, a safe place, because we had no idea what else was going on. By the time we figured out the rest of it, we were in way too deep. Jake said we either did what they said or else."

"So you moved from using drugs to transporting them?" Ali asked.

Roseanne looked at her sharply, then she nodded. "Yes," she admitted. "That's where Sumo Sudoku came in. It gave them a whole collection of RVs that they can use to run up and down the West Coast. That way, their loads come and go in plain sight with no questions asked. So far no one has ever suspected they're hauling anything but those damn rocks."

No one but Dave and me, Ali thought. "Paul was in on all of this?" she asked.

"No," Roseanne answered. "Even though April and Tracy McLaughlin were friends, Jake was the one who actually pitched the Sumo Sudoku idea to Paul. When it came time to put the deal together, Paul put up his money. I'm sure he thought we were putting up ours, too. But the money we used didn't really belong to us because we were broke by then, or we would have been."

"So the whole Sumo Sudoku thing is really nothing but a cover for moving drugs?" Ali asked.

"It's actually more than that," Roseanne admitted. "By involving Paul in the project, they ended up with what looks like a legitimate entity, and there was enough money in the deal for Jake that we were able to hang on to our house. They promised Jake even more—lots more—if he could get Sumo Sudoku some network exposure and have it go national."

No wonder they needed Paul, Ali thought. "What about the players?" she asked.

"The guys who drive the RVs?" Roseanne returned. "They all have their own particular vices, and the Pink Swan is a one-stop shop when it comes to that kind of thing. Tracy McLaughlin doesn't do any drugs other than cigarettes and beer. His big thing is gambling. That's how they hooked him in—gambling debts and forgiveness of same."

Ali realized this was more or less the same story Jake had told but with a few key differences.

"With so many illegal activities going on, how does the Pink Swan stay in business?" Ali asked.

"They pay off the right people," Roseanne responded. "I know for sure that several top dogs from LAPD are regulars at the gambling tables upstairs. I know them because I've seen them. The Pink Swan's management makes sure the club and its customers don't annoy the neighbors. The place is clean, it's quiet, and the club does a lot of strategic charitable giving. I hear they're big on putting playground equipment in local parks."

"What about the DEA?" Ali asked.

"What about them?" Roseanne asked with a shrug. "I don't know any people from the DEA personally, if that's what you mean, but they could be there. After all, if people from LAPD can be bought off, why couldn't people from the DEA? We're talking about astonishing amounts of money, Ali. Cops who play ball with them can make more money in a year than they'd make in a lifetime of pounding a beat somewhere."

A harried waitress veered in their direction, but Roseanne waved her away with a shake of her head while Ali thought about what Dave had said about the possibility of an ongoing undercover DEA investigation being conducted at the Pink Swan. Maybe there was something to what Roseanne was saying after all.

"You said you were going to tell me about Paul," Ali said.

Nodding, Roseanne took a deep breath. "I guess you know what it feels like to be cast aside," she said finally.

"I've met Amber, if that's what you mean," Ali said. She might have couched the comment a little more diplomatically. When Roseanne's eyes filled with tears, Ali was sorry she hadn't.

"She was at the house?" Roseanne asked. "At my house?"

Ali nodded.

"That didn't take long. I suppose I should have known she would be," Roseanne said. "There's a lot that goes over your head when you're screwed up on cocaine. I should have figured out what was happening, but by the time I noticed, it was too late. Amber already had her hooks in him."

Roseanne was right. For Ali Reynolds, the idea of an older wife being shoved aside in favor of a younger one was another all-too-familiar story.

"Amber was always there at the Pink Swan," Roseanne continued. "And why wouldn't she be? Her grandmother owns the place. It wasn't until I got in the program and started trying to straighten out my life that I could see what was what. It seemed to me that if I could just get rid of Amber, Jake and I might be all right. I mean, the two of us have a history together. Even if we lost everything else, I thought we'd at least have each other."

Why does she want him? Ali asked herself. *What's to hang on to?*

"But I didn't have nerve enough to go to the cops myself," Roseanne went on. "For one thing, I'm in it, too. So I blew the whistle to Paul instead. I told him everything I knew and everything I suspected about Jake and the others taking Paul for a ride."

"What happened?" Ali asked.

"At first I don't think Paul believed me, but he must have started looking into things on his own. Last Wednesday morning he called me and told me that maybe I was right about what was going on, but with everything coming up over the weekend—with both the divorce hearing and the wedding—he had decided not to do anything more about it until after he and April got back from their honeymoon.

"I begged him not to let anyone know I was the one who had told him," Roseanne continued. "He promised he wouldn't, but once I got off the phone with him, I got scared. I was afraid he might go to Jake instead. That's when I decided I needed to disappear. The next day, when Kimball was out getting groceries, I grabbed what I could from the house, then I took off and came here. When I heard Paul was dead, I knew I had been right. If I hadn't run away when I did, I'd be dead by now, too."

The waitress returned, more determined this time, with her order pad in hand. Neither Ali nor Roseanne had yet to glance at their menus.

"House salad," Ali said. "Ranch dressing and iced tea."

"I'll have the same," Roseanne said.

Clearly disappointed by their long delayed but paltry order, the waitress rolled her eyes and stomped off in the direction of the kitchen.

"But what makes you think your phone was tapped?" Ali asked, once the waitress was out of earshot.

"Paul's dead, isn't he?" Roseanne asked. "He didn't know anything about what was going on until I told him, and when I did, someone must have been listening in on my phone."

Or on Paul's, Ali thought. If Paul and Jake were partners, and if the authorities managed to get wiretapping warrants as a part of a drug-busting investigation, they'd have gotten warrants for the phones of all parties involved and perhaps even for their spouses' phones as well. At the time of Paul's death, Ali had still been his wife. Did that mean Ali's phone might have been tapped, too?

"That's why Paul's death is my fault," Roseanne continued as her eyes once more filled with tears. "If I hadn't told him what was going on, maybe he wouldn't be dead now."

"If the Pink Swan is a front for a major drug operation, I still think you should go to the cops," Ali said. "All of LAPD doesn't hang out around there. Surely there must be someone you could talk to?"

"But how am I supposed to know which ones are crooked and which ones aren't?" Roseanne returned. "As far as I can tell, they all are."

That's when Ali thought of Dave. He was, without a doubt, one of the world's straightest arrows.

"Look," Ali said. "I have a friend who's visiting right now, a cop from over in Arizona. He couldn't possibly be mixed up in any of this. Why don't you talk to him?"

"No," Roseanne said firmly. "No cops. Period. Why do you think they killed Paul? To let the rest of us know that even talking about going to the cops is a capital offense as far as they're concerned."

"What about talking to an attorney then?" Ali asked. "I know a top-drawer defense attorney. His name is Victor Angeleri. You're obviously involved in all this and you know what's really going on. Why don't you call him and let him see what kind of deal he could cut for you in terms of witness protection?"

"I don't believe in witness protection programs

any more than I believe in the Tooth Fairy," Roseanne returned. "That wouldn't stop them. If they killed Paul, they'll find me and kill me, too. Even if I get sent to jail, they'll still come after me. That's why I'm hoping you'll help me out. I don't need a lot of money. I have a place down in Mexico where I can live cheaply for a very long time. I just need some cash to make it work."

Roseanne pushed the jewel-laden ziplock bag back in Ali's direction. It lay there on the tabletop between them for the better part of a minute. Then, when the waitress reappeared with their salads and iced teas, Roseanne snatched the bag off the table and stuffed it back into her purse and out of sight.

Once again they waited until the waitress had walked away from their table.

"If these people are so all-powerful and all-knowing, who are they? You may have your suspicions that they're responsible for what happened to Paul, but do you have any proof?"

"I just know it," Roseanne said fervently. "I know it in my bones."

"That's not good enough."

"By the time I get proof, I'll be dead, too," Roseanne said.

Ali had to admit that was a pretty telling argument. She decided to change tactics. "So these people are all tied in with the Pink Swan," she said. "Tell me about that."

"The bottom floor is just your basic topless joint with a bar and nude dancing, and all the rest of it. That one is open to the public. Upstairs is private—an upscale gentlemen's club they call it. That's where the real action is—all kinds of action. You can go there and do whatever you want and nobody bothers you, especially no reporters. They don't come near the place."

"Who owns it?" Ali asked.

"A lady named Lucia Joaquin. At least, her name is the one on the liquor license. She's the widow of a major player in one of the Colombian drug cartels. Years ago when her husband was gunned down, she came here with her kids along with a ton of money, money she managed to invest in real estate all over L.A."

"Drug money?" Ali asked.

"I'm sure," Roseanne answered with a nod. "But just because she moved out of the country didn't mean she moved out of the drug business. She's kept her hand in the whole time she's been here. Her two sons may work for her, but even though she's been sick, Lucia is still the real brains behind the outfit. She's also the one who gave the Pink Swan its name. I've never met her, but I've been told she always wears pink—from head to toe."

"What about the sons?" Ali asked.

"Mario and Reynaldo," Roseanne replied. "They both went to school here in the States. One's an MBA type and the other's more of an engineer. Lucia's money comes rolling in from whatever source. The sons figure out ways to turn all that illicit cash into something more or less legitimate."

"Like Sumo Sudoku?" Ali asked.

Roseanne nodded. "Exactly."

"Which one of the sons is Amber's father?"

"Neither," Roseanne answered. "There was a third child—a daughter. I don't know her name. She died years ago. Lucia raised Amber and thinks she can do no wrong. Unfortunately, Amber doesn't have quite the same work ethic her grandmother has. But she's going to be loaded one of these days, so I can see why Jake might be interested in her. As for why Amber's interested in Jake?" Roseanne added. "I have no idea."

Having met the young woman in question the previous night, Ali could have told Roseanne that Amber came with her own set of problems, but she didn't.

"So will you help me or not?" Roseanne asked, going back once again to the jewelry.

Ali thought about it. Roseanne had brought her here under false pretenses. She had claimed to have information about Paul's death, but from Ali's point of view, what she had offered was little more than unsubstantiated suspicions—none of them enough to make Ali's trip worthwhile.

"I think my answer is not," Ali replied. "The only reason you brought me here was to unload your jewelry and get some cash."

"But—" Roseanne began.

Ali stood up. "If you decide you want to go to that lawyer or to the cops and tell them what's going on, call me again and we'll talk. In the meantime, Roseanne, I'm afraid you're on your own."

A despairing Roseanne watched as Ali flagged down the waitress. Roseanne was still seated at their table as Ali left. Enough time had passed that only a few stragglers still lingered outside, waiting for tables. Ali started through them and was headed for her car when someone called after her.

"Ms. Reynolds?"

Thinking it was someone who recognized her from her days on the news, Ali stopped and turned back to find the hostess hurrying after her. "Yes."

"There's a phone call for you at the hostess desk," Carrie said. "You can take it back inside. There's an extension on the wall there by the restrooms."

Why would someone be calling me here? Ali wondered. The only person who had known she was coming to Claim Jumper was her mother. That was probably the call she had ignored earlier.

"Thank you," Ali said, allowing herself to be led back into the restaurant. When she picked up the receiver, Ali was amazed to find Dave Holman on the phone.

"What's going on?" Ali wanted to know. "How did you know to call me here? Did you talk to Mom?"

"Listen to me for a minute," he said urgently. "Is Roseanne still there?"

"Yes, but—"

"Good," Dave Holman said, sounding relieved. "I'm glad I got here in time."

Ali glanced around the restaurant but didn't see him anywhere. "You're here? Where? I thought you were on your way to Lake Havasu."

"Things changed. Roxie had made other plans and didn't want me dropping in on the kids 'unannounced.' In the meantime, I'm in Valencia now. At a pay phone directly across the street from the Claim Jumper."

"You followed me here? Why? What's happening? And you still haven't told me why you didn't call on my cell."

"The last few days," he said, "with everything

that's been going on, I've managed to make friends with Bruno Cutler, the head of security at your hotel. Late this afternoon, someone came speeding into the hotel parking garage. He waved what was supposedly an LAPD badge at the garage attendant and said he was there to check on a stolen vehicle. The attendant didn't think that much about it at the time, but later on, when Bruno was reviewing the garage security tapes, he noticed someone messing around with your vehicle, and he called me."

"Someone was messing with my Cayenne?" Ali asked. "Who and why?"

"I've seen the tape now, too," Dave said. "And I'm pretty sure I know who it was. You do, too. He drives a Honda Element, and he's parked outside the restaurant right now. The Element is parked right next to your Porsche."

"Tracy McLaughlin followed me here?" Ali asked. "How could he? Roseanne was afraid someone might try to follow me, so I checked. There was no one anywhere near me."

"That's what I'm trying to tell you," Dave replied. "I think McLaughlin stuck a GPS tracking device under your rear bumper. If they were using one of those, there would have been no need to keep your vehicle in sight. The tape shows him taking something small out of his pocket and then reaching up toward the underside of your back bumper—right in the middle of it, straight down from the lock."

"I don't understand. Why would Tracy McLaughlin want to find me?" Ali asked.

"I think the people Tracy works for are looking for

Roseanne Maxwell. Tracy followed you in hopes you'd lead him to her."

Which I did, Ali thought with a sinking sensation in the pit of her stomach.

"But how could Tracy possibly know I was coming to see her?" Ali asked at last.

"Good question," Dave said. "That's why I'm calling you on the restaurant phone instead of your cell. It's why I'm not using my cell, either."

Ali stopped short, remembering Roseanne's concerns about the likelihood of her phone being tapped. Now Dave shared that worry.

"Are you saying someone may have been listening in on my cell phone calls?" Ali asked.

"Affirmative," Dave replied.

"What should I do then?" Ali returned.

"Where is Roseanne?"

"Still at our table. She rode here with a friend who works at the restaurant. I imagine she's planning on staying until the friend gets off work."

"Whatever you do, don't let her leave," Dave said urgently. "Did she tell you anything important?"

"She told me a little," Ali said. "But I thought she was delusional and making a lot of it up."

"I only wish that were the case."

"So you've found out more?"

"Lots more," Dave answered, "but let's not go into that right now. Just wait until I get there."

"You're coming in?"

"Yes," he said. "As soon as I can."

"What if Tracy spots you?"

"I'll wait until there's another fairly large group and

try to blend in with them," Dave said. "He's waiting for you to come out. With any kind of luck, he won't be paying that much attention to people going in."

"What are we going to do?" Ali asked. "Do you have a plan?"

"Not yet," Dave allowed. "When I come up with one, I'll let you know."

"I'll go back to the table and tell Roseanne to stay put. When you get here, talk to the hostess. Her name is Carrie, and she's Roseanne's friend. Carrie will be able to tell you where we are."

"Will do," Dave said, and hung up.

Still stunned by the idea that she'd been followed after all, Ali made her way back to the corner table. Roseanne didn't look up until Ali was standing directly over her.

"What happened?" she asked. "I thought you were leaving."

"So did I," Ali returned. "I changed my mind."

Roseanne brightened. "Does that mean you're going to buy my jewelry after all?"

"No," Ali replied grimly. "It means I'm going to try to save your butt."

{ CHAPTER 18 }

Looking alarmed, Roseanne half rose to her feet. "What's going on?" she demanded.

"Sit back down and don't make a scene," Ali ordered. "We can't afford it. Tracy McLaughlin evidently found out where I was going and followed me here," she added. "He's waiting outside in the parking lot."

Roseanne's face turned a pasty shade of white as she sank back into her chair. "He followed you?" she asked in a cracked whisper. "I thought you said you'd checked and that no one was there."

"I did check," Ali returned. "But we believe he put some kind of GPS tracking device on my vehicle. He knew exactly where I was without my being able to see him at all."

"But if they find me here . . ." With an almost physical jolt, Roseanne suddenly straightened in her chair. "Wait a minute. How did he know you were coming to see me? You must have told him."

"I didn't," Ali said. "At least not on purpose. You may be right, Roseanne. It's possible my phone is being tapped, just like you said yours was."

There was a long pause as Ali's news sank in. "What are we going to do then?" Roseanne asked finally.

"Dave Holman, that friend I told you about, the cop from Arizona, is on his way here right now," Ali told her. "Once he arrives, we'll figure out what to do."

Again, Roseanne attempted to rise to her feet. "I already told you I don't want to talk to any cops. I've got to get out of here. Now."

More time had passed than Ali realized. Now only two tables in that section of the restaurant were still occupied, but the people seated there seemed to be taking an inordinate interest in the ongoing drama between Ali and Roseanne.

"Sit," Ali hissed. "With Tracy out in the parking lot, leaving is exactly the wrong thing to do right now. He'll nail you the moment you step outside."

"What should I do then? Sit here and wait for him to come inside after me?"

"I don't know," Ali replied. "Be quiet and let me think."

Shaking her head, a trembling Roseanne slid back into her chair. Clearly the woman was petrified, and Ali didn't blame her. They needed a device that would take Roseanne out of harm's way without exposing her to whatever danger awaited her in the parking lot. Slowly a plan began to take shape in Ali's head. If Ali could somehow conceal Roseanne inside the restaurant while at the same time convincing Tracy that she had slipped away . . .

Before Ali could finish formulating a strategy, Carrie appeared, holding an armload of menus and leading Dave Holman directly to their corner table. Ali was thrilled to see him. Roseanne was not. As Dave took a seat, Roseanne shrank away from him, putting as much distance as possible between his chair and hers. Before the hostess could walk away again, Ali caught Carrie's arm.

"I guess you know we're having a bit of a problem here," she said. "That there are dangerous people actively looking for Roseanne?"

Carrie nodded. "She told me."

"One of them appears to be waiting for her outside in the parking lot."

"Oh, no!" Carrie exclaimed. "Should I call the cops?"

"Not just yet," Ali said. "But what about this? Would it be possible for you to hustle Roseanne into the kitchen and pass her off as part of the help long enough for us to decoy the bad guy away from here?"

Dave looked as though he was about to say something. Then he didn't.

Carrie seemed to consider. "That wouldn't be too hard," she answered. "I could put her in with the guy who washes dishes. He wouldn't mind having some extra help. I'll clear it with the kitchen. Let me know if you need anything else."

Carrie went away again, leaving Ali to make the introductions. Still huddled against the wall, Roseanne refused Dave's proffered handshake.

"Tracy's still out in the parking lot?" Ali asked.

Dave nodded. "Yup."

"Is he alone?"

"As far as I could tell."

Ali felt a surge of irritation with Dave. He was being uncommonly uncommunicative. She had expected him to arrive with some concrete ideas for solving their problem. Since he seemed to be fresh out of game plans, Ali continued to formulate her own.

"Do you have your cell phone with you?" Ali asked him.

"Yes. Of course."

"I'm going to call you on it," Ali said. "And I'm going to use my cell phone to do it. Since whoever may be listening in on my calls doesn't know we know about them, hopefully they'll take whatever I say as the gospel."

Roseanne let out a small moan. "But what about me?" she asked.

"What about you?" Ali returned. "You go to the kitchen and wash dishes like Carrie said until Dave or I come back to get you, but you need to know one thing, Roseanne. Dave and I aren't helping you out of the goodness of our hearts. This isn't a free ride."

"What do you mean?"

"I'm sure from what you said earlier that you'd like me to believe you're a mostly innocent bystander in all this," Ali returned. "If that were true, though, you wouldn't be so afraid of going to jail yourself. You claim to be a drug user and nothing more, but I'm guessing that by the time the cops finish investigating this case they'll be able to charge you with plenty, including conspiracy to distribute drugs if nothing else." Ali turned to Dave. "That's a felony, right?"

Dave nodded. "Yes, it is," he agreed.

"So," Ali continued, "your best bet for dodging jail time is for you to cooperate now. If Dave and I can manage to get you out of this alive, I want you to promise that you'll go to that attorney I told you about. Let Victor Angeleri see what kind of deal he can make for you in exchange for your testimony—your voluntary testimony—about the people at the Pink Swan and everything that goes on there, including your suspicions about who was really responsible for Paul's death."

"What if I say no?" Roseanne asked.

"That's easy," Ali returned. "Dave and I leave now,

and you can deal with Tracy and whatever's supposed to happen to you all on your own."

"You wouldn't do that, would you?" Roseanne pleaded. "You couldn't just leave me alone like that."

"Oh, couldn't I?" Ali said, reaching for her purse. "Watch me."

"No," Roseanne said, capitulating. "Please don't leave. I'll do whatever you say."

"Fine," Ali said. "Go to the kitchen. Stay there until you hear from us. Either Dave or I will come get you, or else we'll let you know that it's safe to go with whoever we send."

"All right," Roseanne agreed reluctantly. She stood up and headed for the swinging doors that led back to the kitchen. Ali glanced around. By then the customers at the other nearby tables had all left. Carrie had made sure that theirs was the only occupied table in that section of the restaurant.

A waitress—a different one this time—came over and took Dave's order.

"All right," Ali said once the waitress left. "Here's my plan. I'll call you and say that I met Roseanne here because she wanted me to buy some of her jewelry but that she slipped away while I was in the restroom. With any kind of luck whoever's listening in on my phone will believe she's gotten away from them, too. Then, later on, we'll be able to smuggle her out of here and get her to Victor."

Ali was talking to Dave but he didn't appear to be paying attention. He seemed to be focused on some distant part of the restaurant.

"Hello!" Ali said. "Are you even listening to me?"

Turning to follow his gaze, Ali saw two men standing talking to Carrie, who was listening carefully and nodding. Eventually they began making their way across the dining room. One was a tall, rangy black man Ali had never seen before. The other she recognized at once—Detective Montgomery Taylor with the Riverside Sheriff's Department Homicide Division, one of the two detectives who had interviewed Ali in the aftermath of Paul's death.

"Oh, no," Ali whispered under her breath. "What's he doing here? Don't tell me they're coming after me again."

The men walked directly to Ali and Dave's table. Without waiting for an invitation, they seated themselves. The man Ali didn't know nodded cordially in Dave's direction. The two of them shook hands.

"Good to see you, bro," the man said. "Where is Roseanne Maxwell?"

"In the kitchen," Dave responded. "Hiding out as a dishwasher. Are the takedown teams all in place?"

The stranger nodded. "Pretty much," he said. "We're just waiting for the restaurant to clear out some and for a couple more of my men to arrive on the scene."

"Roseanne's in the kitchen?" Detective Taylor asked. "I'll go make sure we don't lose her." With that, he got up and headed for the kitchen.

Feeling lost, Ali watched the detective's retreating figure. "What takedown teams?" she asked. "Who are these guys? What are they doing here? What's going on?"

"Sorry," Dave said. "I didn't have a chance to tell you, Ali. This is my friend Ezekiel Washington. We call him Easy. He's with the DEA. I believe you already know Detective Taylor." Dave waved in the direction of the swinging kitchen door where Taylor had disappeared.

"Glad to meet you," Easy said with an engaging grin calculated to match his name. "I remember seeing you on the news when you used to be on TV here. I guess you could say I was a fan."

"Thank you," Ali said stiffly. "I'm delighted to know that, I'm sure. But you still haven't told me what's going on here."

"We're in the process of rolling up a major drug operation," he answered. "We've been working on this case for months. We weren't quite ready to make our move, but with your husband dead and with the possibility of your stirring up the pot on your Web site, we're having to go ahead and stage our raids now after all. If we wait any longer, there's a good chance you may write something in your blog that will give away what we're doing. At this point in the investigation, we can't afford to have a loose cannon on deck."

"So now I'm a loose cannon?" an irate Ali demanded of Dave Holman. Then she turned back to Easy Washington.

"Sorry," Easy said. "I didn't mean that the way it sounded. What happened to your husband is terribly unfortunate. It was never our intention that he would be at risk, and believe me, we're doing everything we can to bring his killers to justice."

"Not your intention . . . ?" Ali began.

"Mr. Grayson had been working with us for some time, and that's what it takes to bring down a whole organization like this—time. If you move too fast, you just get pieces of the puzzle—small fry mostly—rather than the people in charge. And that's what we're trying to do here—bring down Lucia Joaquin's entire group, from top to bottom. Mr. Grayson came to us several months ago when he first started having concerns about what was going on with the Sumo Sudoku group. He agreed to do what he could to help, and he understood that it wouldn't happen overnight."

Ali could barely believe her ears. "Paul was working with you? Is that why he was killed?"

"Not exactly," Easy replied. "We've known for some time that our communications system had been compromised, so we were careful that our contacts with your husband were done in an untraceable fashion."

"You're telling me someone's been tapping your phones as well?" Ali asked.

Easy nodded.

"But you're the DEA."

"Exactly," Easy said. "And that's a big part of the problem here. We believe that someone from the Joaquin organization penetrated LEMO and installed a Trojan horse."

"LEMO?" Ali asked. "What's that? It sounds like a cartoon for kids."

"LEMO, not Elmo," Easy explained. "The Law Enforcement Monitoring Organization. Think of it as the wiretapping central office for all the law enforcement agencies in the western United States, and it happens to be located right here in L.A. If, as we suspect, someone was able to install a keystroke-logger inside the system, they automatically have access to all our passwords and communications. They know exactly who and what we've been listening in on and what we plan to do. They've been making a shambles of our operations for months. Evidently they've also been doing some unauthorized listening on their own."

"Including my phones?" Ali asked.

Easy nodded. "And the phones of anyone else whose activities interested them, including Roseanne Maxwell. And that's where we got in trouble. Your husband was already working for us when Roseanne called and asked him to come to us with what was going on."

"You're saying Paul was killed because it seemed like he was going to go to the authorities with what he knew, not because he was already doing so."

Easy Washington nodded again. "At first I was afraid someone on our side—someone who knew about his involvement with us—had betrayed him, that we had a mole in our midst. That's why it was so helpful to us initially that everyone thought you were responsible for Mr. Grayson's death. That took a lot of the pressure off us and gave us a chance to investigate the situation. Now, though, we're pretty sure that Roseanne's phone call is what set your husband's murder plot in motion."

Ali was struggling to comprehend what was being said. Was it possible Paul really had been actively at work behind the scenes to help out in a DEA investigation? Over time his actions toward her had led Ali to think of the man as an entirely contemptible human being. Easy Washington seemed to consider him to be some kind of hero. For Ali, that didn't quite compute. And what about April? Had she been with Paul in all this or against him?

"You're saying Paul was helping you."

"He was a huge help," Easy said. "I can't tell you how sorry I am that we weren't able to move fast enough to prevent this senseless tragedy."

Ali stood up.

"Where are you going?" Dave asked.

"Back to the hotel," Ali said. "This is a bit more than I can handle."

"You can't go back to the hotel," Dave said.

"Why not?"

"Because you're checked out," he answered. "With everything that's going on, Easy and I thought it would be best if you were moved to a different location. Your mom packed up your stuff. I've got it all in my car. Your mother and Chris have moved out, too. Chris is staying with friends. I got your mother a room at the Motel 6 just up the corridor from mine. Edie said you probably wouldn't like it, but there's a room there for you as well."

Ali was suddenly more than moderately annoyed. "You moved my stuff?" she demanded.

"Just for the time being," Easy said reassuringly. "Until we can stage our raids and have all the suspects in custody."

"You had no right to do that," Ali announced. "And my mother is right. I have zero intention of staying at the Motel 6. The Westwood is fine with me, thank you very much."

"Please don't go back there, Ms. Reynolds," Easy said. "Desperate people do desperate things. I wouldn't want to see you hurt. You don't know what the Joaquins are capable of."

"I know exactly what they're capable of," Ali said. "I'm the one who identified my husband's body, remember? I want my stuff, Mr. Washington. And I want it now. Not later, now."

With the possibility of a shooting war about to break out in the parking lot, Ali knew she was being unreasonable, but she was tired of being booted around by people—good intentioned or not—who were busy deciding what she would and wouldn't do.

"Ali, please—" Dave began.

"Give me your keys, Dave," Easy interjected, standing up and holding out his hand. "Tracy McLaughlin knows what you look like. I'll send someone to get her stuff. Where's your car?"

"Out back," Dave replied. "Next to the Dumpsters."

Ali barely waited for Easy to leave the table before she rounded on Dave. "How dare you . . ."

"Easy and I were worried about you."

"Like hell," Ali returned. "You just didn't want to let me in on what was going on."

"You can't go back to the Westwood," Dave insisted. "What if they send someone there after you?"

"Why would they?" Ali demanded. "Their only interest in me had to do with whether or not I'd lead them to Roseanne, which, sorry to say, I seem to have done unerringly. I led them to her, and I led your friend Easy to her as well. By the way, what about Roseanne? Is she under arrest or what?"

"Probably not at the moment," Dave answered. "More likely she'll be taken in for questioning."

"Will they give her a deal if she cooperates with the authorities?" Ali asked.

"That remains to be seen," Dave replied. "I know you mentioned to her that she might be able to work out some kind of a plea bargain, but those decisions are best left up to prosecutors."

"Not to loose-cannon bloggers, right?"

"I didn't say that," he returned. "I didn't say anything of the kind."

"Never mind," Ali put in. "You didn't have to."

Easy returned carrying Ali's two suitcases and the computer case as well. "Where do you want these?" he asked.

"In my car," Ali said. "I'm leaving."

"No, you're not," he answered, putting the luggage down next to the table. "Nobody's leaving right now. All my men are in place. We're waiting for the last two parties of diners to leave the restaurant. Once they're gone and are out of danger, we'll make our move. As soon as we have Mr. McLaughlin safely in custody, you'll be welcome to go anywhere you like. Until that time, though, I need you to stay here."

Time passed slowly. Gradually the restaurant cleared. Finally the door to the kitchen opened. Detective Taylor led Roseanne Maxwell into the room. She was in handcuffs and in tears. "They're going to take me to jail," she said accusingly to Ali. "I thought you told me that if I helped them I'd be able to make some kind of deal."

"I thought so, too," Ali said. "It turns out I was wrong."

"What about that attorney you told me about?" Roseanne asked. "What's his name again?"

"Victor Angeleri," Ali answered. "He may be more than you can afford right now."

"What about my jewelry?" Roseanne asked. "Do you think he might take some of that in trade?"

Months ago, Roseanne Maxwell would have been able to afford the best legal representation money could buy. Now she was one step away from selling her worldly possessions on eBay, and most likely she'd end up with a public defender.

"I don't know about that," Ali said. "You'll need to call Victor up and ask him yourself. Maybe you can work it out."

Easy held up his hand for quiet. Only then did Ali notice he was wearing an earpiece of some kind.

"Okay, people," he announced. "We've got a couple more vehicles to move into place, then it's a go. I'm going out through the kitchen. Everybody else get down on the floor. Keep your heads well below the level of the windowsills. Stay under tables if it's at all possible. Nobody steps outside the restaurant until I give the all-clear. Got it?"

Ali paused long enough to watch Detective Taylor help Roseanne to her knees. Then, with her own heart pounding in her throat, Ali dropped to the floor and scrambled under the table where they'd been sitting. She may have been mad as hell about what was going on right then, but she wasn't stubborn enough to risk her own life because of it.

Lying there on the dingy floor, Ali waited breathlessly to see what would happen next. When nothing did, she turned over far enough to peer up at the table above her. There, in plain view, were several pieces of dead and dying bubble gum, chunks of the stuff that thoughtless diners had unloaded by sticking them to the underside of the table.

For some unaccountable reason, seeing those messy

wads of bubble gum while at the same time anticipating the sound of gunfire struck Ali as a kind of grim joke. Unable to help herself, she began to giggle.

Moments later, she was jostled as someone else scrambled into the confined space under the table.

"What's so funny?" Dave asked. "Are you okay?"

Not quite able to explain it herself, Ali finally managed to stifle her fit of inappropriate laughter. When she did, she found she was still upset with him.

"What are you doing here?" she wanted to know. "I thought you'd be outside playing cops and robbers with your friend Easy."

"Come on, Ali," he returned. "I've told you before. This isn't my jurisdiction. I've got no more legal right to participate in a DEA operation than you do. And that's why, when Easy asked me to keep quiet about what was going on, I had to do just that—keep quiet."

His excuse didn't sit well with her. "Fine then," she said. "Here's an idea for you. How about if you keep on keeping quiet? It seems to me you've said enough for one day."

Dave's exasperated sigh wasn't lost on her. He didn't say, "Women!" but he could just as well have. Turning her back on him, Ali inched forward far enough so she could see the front of the restaurant. The remaining waitstaff had disappeared into the kitchen except for Carrie, who had taken shelter behind the hostess desk.

In the end, all of Easy Washington's advance preparations for a flawless takedown still weren't enough—at least not for the one in Valencia's Claim Jumper parking lot. Before Easy and the last of his officers could move into position, something must have alerted Tracy

McLaughlin to their presence. Ali didn't see the suspect slam his Element in gear and shoot forward across the parking lot, but she did hear the squeal of tires and brakes as the vehicle screeched to a stop just outside the restaurant's front door.

Seconds later, Tracy McLaughlin charged into the entryway lobby. Stifling a scream, Carrie tried to retreat farther into the restaurant, but he was too fast for her. As she attempted to dart away from the hostess stand, McLaughlin got one arm around the terrified woman's neck. With his other hand, he held a gun to her head.

Out of the corner of her eye, Ali saw Detective Taylor rise to his feet, weapon in hand. "Drop it," he ordered.

"You drop it," Tracy returned. "If you don't, this woman dies."

"Don't hurt me," Carrie wailed. "Please don't hurt me."

For a long moment, the three of them remained in a frozen tableau. Then, moving slowly and deliberately, Detective Taylor grasped the handle of his .38 with the thumb and forefinger of his left hand and carefully deposited the weapon on a nearby table.

"That's better," Tracy said. "Move away from the table."

Detective Taylor complied.

"Now," Tracy went on. "Do you have any way of communicating with those bozos outside? If so, I want you to tell them to stay put so nobody gets hurt."

Lying there, waiting for what she thought was an inevitable volley of shots, all Ali could think about was a pair of cold-blooded armed killers silently roaming the hallways and classrooms of Columbine High School, stalking their innocent victims. Determined to fight back, she unholstered her Glock.

"Stay here!" Dave whispered urgently in her direction, then he moved away from the spot under the table that had sheltered them both. Staying under the cover of intervening tables, he slithered across the floor of the darkened restaurant in a surprisingly rapid commando crawl.

"Not really," Detective Taylor replied. "They're Feds. I'm local. Our radios aren't compatible."

"Isn't that just great," Tracy muttered.

Anxious to provide a diversion from whatever action Dave was about to take, Ali surprised herself by finding her own voice.

"Let Carrie go, Tracy," she urged. "Haven't enough people been hurt already?"

"Who are you?" he demanded, glancing around the room, trying to fix her position. "Are you a cop?"

"You know me, Tracy," she answered. "I'm Ali Reynolds. I'm the woman you followed here, remember? And the whole place is surrounded by cops. You can't get away. Give it up. It's your only chance."

"No matter what, I'm not going back to the slammer," he declared. "So come out from wherever it is you're hiding. Show me your hands."

Attempting to estimate the distance Dave would have to cover to circumnavigate the dining room and how much time it would take for him to be within striking distance of the armed man, Ali tried to stall a little longer.

"Why should I?" she asked. "So you can shoot me, too?"

"Because if you don't come out where I can see you, I'm going to shoot her," Tracy returned ominously. "If that happens, this woman's blood will be on your hands as much as it is on mine."

Carrie moaned in protest. Somewhere in the restaurant, Roseanne Maxwell began to sob as well.

Hoping Detective Taylor saw her do it, Ali tucked the Glock into the back of the waistband of her jeans. Then, aware Tracy would have to peer through the gloom in order to observe her every move, Ali raised her hands and slowly rose to her feet. Once upright, Ali stepped forward until she was standing a foot or so in front of Montgomery Taylor and slightly to one side. The move left her Glock's exposed handle well within the detective's reach.

"What do you want?" Ali asked, willing Tracy to keep his attention focused on her. "What are you hoping to accomplish?"

At that instant, Dave materialized to the right of the front door. Without being observed, he had managed to work his way all around the restaurant. Now, coming from just outside Tracy's line of vision, Dave smashed into the two people locked in their life-and-death embrace. The unexpected blow propelled the couple apart, sending Carrie in one direction and Tracy and his weapon in the other.

Carrie screamed. A burst of gunfire pierced the air, but only for a moment, then it was over. In the sudden silence that followed, Detective Taylor grabbed Ali's Glock and charged forward to help Dave subdue Tracy.

Seconds later the room was filled to capacity as more officers raced in from outside.

"Is he dead?" Roseanne Maxwell's plaintive question came from two tables away. "Please tell me the son of a bitch is dead."

Ali walked over and helped Roseanne emerge from her hiding place beneath the table.

"I'm afraid not," Ali returned. "It looks to me as though he came through just fine."

"Damn," Roseanne muttered.

Easy Washington appeared. He seemed shaken. His dark skin had taken on a peculiarly ashen hue. "Is everyone all right?" he asked.

"I think so," Ali said. "I believe everyone's fine."

"Too bad," Roseanne added. "I was really hoping."

Dave showed up just then with concern written all over his face. He grasped Ali by the shoulders. "What in the world were you thinking, standing up like that?"

"I was trying to get him to look at me instead of you."

"Are you nuts? You don't even have on a Kevlar vest."

"Do you?" Ali returned.

Dave ignored her question. "Are you all right?" he asked.

"I'm fine," she said. "Perfectly fine."

And for some strange reason, right at that minute, she wasn't even mad at him anymore. In fact, she felt lighter than air.

{ CHAPTER 19 }

In the aftermath of the Claim Jumper incident, Ali found herself once again on the wrong side of the thin blue line. While Dave went off to confer with the other officers, Ali was interviewed in a cursory fashion by a pair of young uniformed cops who took her statement and then left. They made it clear that most of the team was focused on what had happened to Carrie and on the pivotal roles Dave Holman and Detective Taylor had played in effecting Carrie's rescue.

Ali was tempted to point out to one of the young cops, "Hey, I helped, too." Instead, she let it go. In the grand scheme of things the fact that Carrie was safe was all that mattered.

Because shots had been fired in the course of the incident, all weapons on the scene—including Ali's Glock—were collected by crime scene investigators, bagged, cataloged, and taken away for forensic examination. Ali's objections about losing possession of her Glock were duly noted and duly ignored. Nobody but Ali seemed to care much that her weapon was going away nor were they willing to say when, if ever, she'd be able to have it back.

The better part of an hour passed before Tracy McLaughlin and Roseanne Maxwell were loaded into separate patrol cars and carted off. For a long time after that, Ali sat drinking free Claim Jumper coffee and being pretty much ignored by all concerned while a small army of people hustled around the restaurant processing the scene. It was frustrating to be right there in

what was supposedly the middle of the action and still
have so little information about what was going on.

Finally, Ali reached for her computer case and her
computer. Minutes later she was logged on to a wire-
service news site. What she found wasn't much but it
was a lot more than anyone had bothered telling her.

> A joint task force made up of local and federal
> officers staged a series of coordinated raids at
> several locations late today targeting what is
> thought to be a major drug-distribution operation
> centered in the Los Angeles area. Several arrests
> were made, including a number of people—both
> customers and employees—at an exclusive area
> topless bar called the Pink Swan.
>
> Mason Louder, the Drug Enforcement Agen-
> cy's local public affairs officer, has announced
> that a press conference dealing with today's oper-
> ations is scheduled for 10 a.m. tomorrow morn-
> ing at the Federal Building.
>
> Two of those arrested at the Pink Swan
> location are thought to be Mario and Reynaldo
> Joaquin, sons of local real estate magnate Lucia
> Joaquin. According to sources close to the
> investigation, Ms. Joaquin, now in ill health and
> living in semi-retirement in Palm Springs, has
> long been suspected of maintaining close ties with
> Colombian drug cartels, in which her deceased
> husband, Anselmo, was once considered to be a
> major player.
>
> For years, Ms. Joaquin maintained a high-
> profile lifestyle and counted among her circle

of acquaintances many of Southern California's media elite, including television network executive Paul Grayson, whose grisly murder late last week as well as the subsequent deaths of both his fiancée and her mother are all thought to be connected to the case and may well be what sparked tonight's coordinated law enforcement action.

Mr. Grayson's widow, former L.A. news anchor Alison Reynolds, was originally suspected of having some involvement with his death. Ms. Reynolds's mother, Edie Larson, who is visiting from Arizona and was interviewed at her hotel late this evening, told reporters that she hoped that the cloud of suspicion lingering over her daughter's head would soon be lifted.

Ali reread that sentence. "Interviewed at her hotel . . ."

What hotel? Ali wondered. It sounded as though at least one reporter and probably more had managed to track Edie to her new location at the Motel 6. And yes, Paul's death was definitely related to the Joaquin organization, but Monique Ragsdale's death and April Gaddis's had nothing at all to do with it—at least not as far as Ali knew. That meant the so-called sources close to the investigation didn't have all their facts straight.

Unable to find any more information elsewhere, Ali turned to her cutlooseblog.com mailbox, where the "new mail" symbol told her she had forty-seven new messages. Daunted by the very thought of starting to mow through all of those, Ali turned instead to her personal mailbox, one she had set up in order to keep her blog life separate from everything else. There she had only three new messages.

The first one was from her father:

> Dear Ali,
> Back home but from what I hear—and don't hear—from your mother, obviously I shouldn't be. I should have stayed there instead. What in the world is going on? Call me.
>
> DAD

Ali didn't answer the message right then, and she didn't call, either. Her father was her mother's problem more than he was Ali's, and Edie was going to have to handle him on her own.

The second message was from her wrongful dismissal attorney, Marcella Johnson. Like Victor Angeleri and Helga Myerhoff, Marcella, too, worked for the firm Weldon, Davis, and Reed. Although sharing a sky-high hourly rate, the three attorneys had totally different areas of expertise. Despite their inarguable effectiveness, Ali had sometimes found herself wishing she'd hooked herself up with more of a general practitioner attorney rather than three separate and amazingly expensive specialists.

> Dear Ali,
> My God woman, what are you thinking? Your name has been everywhere this weekend—in the

*news, in the papers, on the radio. With our case
coming up next week, now would have been a
good time for you to keep a low profile, but since
you didn't ask my advice on that score, I guess I
won't give it.*

*When is your husband's funeral? We're due
to give depositions on Tuesday afternoon, but I'm
wondering if I should ask for a continuance. Also,
I'm getting a few hints here and there that opposing counsel may be ready to come forward with a
deal. Don't leave town without letting me know
and keep your cell phone handy in case I need to
reach you.*

MARCELLA

Does Valencia count as out of town? Ali wondered.

Dave turned up then, looking agitated. "I just talked
to your mother," he said. "I thought we'd managed to
ditch the reporters back at the other hotel, but now it
seems they've tracked her to the new one, too."

"I know," Ali said.

"You talked to Edie?" Dave asked.

"Not exactly," Ali replied. "I read it online."

"Online?" Dave asked. "Somebody put your mother's
whereabouts up on the Internet?"

She brought the article back up and pushed the
computer over so Dave could read it for himself.

"Geez!" he said, when he finished. "They're everywhere."

"So I guess Motel 6 is out?" Ali asked.

"Easy's already working the problem, and it's a good

thing, too. When I left him he was on the phone with LAPD, trying to clear it with them so you can go back to your own house tonight."

"On Robert Lane?" Ali asked.

Dave nodded. "We're thinking that's the last place anyone would expect you to be along about now."

Me included, Ali thought. But if Dave and Easy were still concerned about Ali's safety, did that mean some member of the Joaquin group had escaped law enforcement's coordinated dragnet?

"Who's still on the loose?" Ali asked.

"Jake Maxwell," Dave answered. "We're not sure how or where we missed him. Amber and Lucia are still unaccounted for as well. Easy thinks I should pick up your mother and then go to the house and keep an eye on both of you there until we know Jake and the others are in custody."

As if on cue, Easy sauntered into the room. "Done," he said to Dave. "LAPD Homicide has cleared the house on Robert Lane. You'll stay with them and keep an eye out?"

"Absolutely," Dave said.

Easy came over to where Ali was sitting. "Hold out your hand and close your eyes," he said.

Ali did as she was told. A moment later, something metallic and shaped like a silver dollar dropped into the palm of her hand. It was smooth on one side while the other side was tacky with the residue of some adhesive that could have been rubber cement.

"What's this?" she asked, staring down at the shiny disk.

Easy grinned. "A memento," he said, "just for you. Compliments of the DEA."

"But what is it?"

"A GPS tracking device Dave removed from the inside of your rear bumper."

"Don't you need it for evidence?" she asked.

Easy shook his head. "We have enough evidence, and I think you earned this. It turns out we've got several of them from several different vehicles. The warehouse complex out behind the Pink Swan is a veritable jungle of electronic tracking and wiretapping equipment complete with an armload of these. Not only have the Joaquins been keeping tabs on what we've been doing, they've also been running electronic surveillance on their competition. Our IT guys tell us that the place is an absolute gold mine of drug-dealing intelligence if we're able to move on it fast enough and before anyone else knows what we have."

Ali examined the device for a moment or so longer before stuffing it in the front pocket of her jeans. "Are you sure you should be saying all of this in front of a 'loose-cannon' blogger?" she asked.

"Sorry about that," Easy said apologetically. "I was out of line earlier. I think we can trust you. Dave told me what you did to help out in there, and I'm very grateful. He and Monty might not have managed without you. Clearly we were lucky to have you on the team tonight. Still, now that you mention it, it might be better if you didn't bring up any of the details of this operation in your blog until after tomorrow morning's news conference."

"Maybe you should take a look at what's out there on the Net right now," Dave said, nodding in the direction of Ali's computer screen. "Some of it's already showing up, and she didn't put it there, either."

Without a word, Ali turned the screen so Easy Washington could read it. "They don't have a lot of it straight," he observed when he finished reading. "Just enough to cause trouble." He turned back to Ali.

"Have Dave give you my numbers. Once the press conference is over, I may be able to give you an exclusive about all this."

He was offering Ali an exclusive story about a major drug bust that would appear first on cutlooseblog.com? Ali knew that would be a scoop that would drive her former cohorts in the media—friend and foe alike—utterly nuts. It would be especially galling to the people who were spending tonight doggedly tracking her mother's every move.

"Thank you," she said. "So in the meantime you and Dave think I should go back to the house?"

"Only if you want to," Easy said. "There's not much sense in your hanging around here. Going to the house makes sense because it's presumably a spot where no one would think to look for you. For one thing, it's still officially off-limits due to being a crime scene. But if you'd be more comfortable somewhere else, or if you'd like me to send some officers along to look out for you—"

"No," Ali said. "The house is fine, and sending extra officers along is unnecessary. The less fuss there is about it, the more likely it is that no one will notice we've gone anywhere. For another, Dave will be there. He's just going by the hotel long enough to pick up my mother. I'm sure you can make better use of your people here. We'll be fine on our own. Oh," she added. "Is it all right to use my phone now?"

Easy waggled his hands. "We *believe* so," he said. "We're hopeful that the Joaquins' entire electronics setup was centered in that one location. At this time, however, there's always a chance that they have backup equipment somewhere else that's still in operation."

"So it's possible someone else might still be listening in on whatever I say."

"For the time being, yes," Easy answered. "Possible but not likely."

Easy went back outside. Ali packed up her computer, and Dave helped carry that and her luggage out to her car. "Do you want me to come with you?" he asked.

"No. You go get Mom. I'm sure she's worried sick. Just make sure that no one follows you when you bring her to the house. Although," she added ruefully, patting the pocket of her jeans where she had stowed the GPS device Easy Washington had given her, "I now know that it's sometimes harder to know you're being fol- lowed than one would think."

"I'll be careful," Dave said. "Besides, I don't think the media routinely passes out GPS tracking devices."

"Let's hope," Ali said.

He opened the car door to let her inside and touched her shoulder tentatively as she did so. "Be careful," he said.

"I will."

By then it was late enough that, other than a long parade of slow-moving semis, traffic into the city was relatively light. Among all those trucks, the Cayenne might as well have been invisible.

Propped up by cup after cup of coffee, Ali was tired but nonetheless wide awake as she drove. As the miles sped by, she couldn't help thinking about Paul. Did the fact that he had been working with the authorities at the time of his death mean he was, in fact, some kind of hero?

During that fateful phone call from Roseanne, he had evidently told her that he would go to the authorities but only after both his wedding and honeymoon. That delay—most likely done out of deference for April—had given the Joaquins the ammunition they needed and the opportunity to take him out. The irony was that they had killed Paul because they suspected he might *possibly* go to the cops when in fact he had already done so. That wasn't lost on Ali, either. She knew those were facets of the story she would need to address when it came time to write Easy Washington's promised exclusive for cutlooseblog.com.

Most of the time what appeared in cutloose consisted of opinion—Ali's opinions and those of her readers. After months of using the blog to revile Paul Grayson for his two-timing treatment of her, it was difficult for Ali to think of him in any context other than worm. She wondered if she'd somehow be able to muster the necessary distance and evenhandedness to write the rest of the story and do justice to it. For that, Ali would have to revert to her old self and to her original training as a journalist—with one minor exception. Well, a major exception, actually. Most of the time reporters were expected to relate what happened without actually being involved. In this situation, Ali could hardly claim to be a disinterested bystander.

Lost in those complicated thoughts and driving on automatic pilot, Ali steered the Cayenne up the familiar steep curves of Robert Lane. When she arrived at the entrance, she was surprised to see that the broken gate had been repaired. It was standing open, but the broken post had been mended and the wrought-iron gate itself had been reattached to the hinges. Once inside the gate she rolled down her window and attempted to use the free-standing keypad to punch in what she remembered as the old gate-closing code. To her surprise, the gate swung shut.

She had decided on her way into town that it would probably be best if, for the time being, she and her mother stayed in the pool house. There were two bedrooms there and it would be better for her to stay in what had been Chris's apartment for the past several years rather than for them to venture into the house where April and Paul had been living together in her absence. Eventually Ali would have to deal with April's things and with Paul's, too, but not right now. Not tonight. Not with so much of what had happened to those people still far too fresh.

So, after rolling the window back up, Ali headed for the pool house with its attached carport. Even if it was locked, she knew Chris had always left an extra key in the utility cabinet at the front of the carport. As she drove through the yard, the motion-activated security lights came on. Passing the garage, she was surprised to see the garage doors standing open. Before she could react, though, a figure emerged from the garage doorway—a figure carrying a gun. Her first thought was simply, *No! Not again!*

She knew it was Jake Maxwell before she even saw

his face. And when he used the barrel of the gun to rap sharply on the window next to her head, she knew exactly what he wanted and did it at once. She put on the brakes and stopped.

Even though she couldn't hear him very well through the closed window and over the sound of the engine, it was easy enough to read his lips. "Roll down the window!" he ordered.

With a weapon trained at her head and with her own Glock packed away in some crime scene investigator's evidence storage locker, Ali had no choice but to comply. She rolled down her window.

"What are you doing here?" she asked.

Jake ignored the question. "I need your car," he said, "and I need it now. Get out."

There was a splotch of grease on the front of Jake's otherwise white shirt and grease on his shirtsleeves as well. He had been doing something in the garage, something mechanical. Or at least he'd been trying to. His face was drenched in sweat. He looked desperate. And scared.

In that moment Ali recognized something about the man that she had never known before. Jake Maxwell was a coward. Whatever crimes he may have participated in, it was unlikely he had ever done his own dirty work.

"No," she said simply. "I won't."

Jake was almost beside himself. "I've got a gun. What do you mean you won't?"

Just like in the restaurant, Ali was making calculations in her head. She had probably left the Claim Jumper several minutes before Dave had, although she wasn't sure by how much. And she had most likely driven faster than he had. When it came to power, his little Nissan didn't compare with the Cayenne's V-8. Maybe he had fudged the speed limit coming into town—Ali certainly had—but she doubted it. And once he got to the city, he would be going first to the Motel 6 to collect Edie. How much longer would that take him? Half an hour? Forty-five minutes? Could she stall Jake that long? Ali realized that her best bet was to engage him in conversation.

"What's going on, Jake?" she said as calmly as she could manage. "Why the gun? We've known each other for a long time. You don't mean this. You wouldn't hurt me."

"I'll hurt you if I have to," he insisted. "I need your car! Get out."

"Can't we talk about this?" she asked.

"There's nothing to talk about," Jake said. "The cops are after me. So are some other people. Either way, I'm a dead man. Give me your car."

Ali knew now that Jake was as frightened of the Joaquins as Roseanne had been.

"Surely it can't be as bad as all this," Ali said. "Get in. I'll take you wherever you need to go."

Much to Ali's amazement and without an additional word, he walked around the front of the car. There were a few short seconds when she might have jammed her foot on the gas pedal and run him down. That would have ended the confrontation there and then, but something—basic humanity, maybe?—held her back. She was betting the farm that he wouldn't gun her down in cold blood because she was someone he knew. The problem was, that was her situation as well. Ali couldn't kill Jake for the exact same reason—she knew him. They had once been friends—at least she had always thought they were.

Ali punched the "unlock" button on the car and let him inside.

"Where to?" she asked.

"Mexico," he said. "And not down the I-5, either. They'll be checking the border there. Head for Julian. Know where that is?"

Ali nodded. Julian was in the mountains east of Escondido. If you passed Julian and continued on over that particular range, you came out north of Brawley—and near what was considered to be more of a back-door entrance into Mexico through Calexico. But going that way was anything but direct. Ali suspected Jake was probably right in terms of people not thinking he'd attempt to go that way. There would be far more focus on the main I-5 corridor and far less on secondary routes.

She wondered how closely Jake had been following the situation on the ground as the takedowns happened and whether or not he had any idea that most of the Joaquin organization along with Tracy McLaughlin and Roseanne had all been taken into custody.

"Sounds like you're headed the same place Roseanne is," Ali ventured casually. "And considering she knows all about you and Amber, I doubt she'll be thrilled to see you when you show up."

"You know about Oaxaca?" Jake demanded. "How?"

Ali hadn't known where they were headed in Mexico exactly—but now she did. And she also knew from Jake's reaction that he had no idea Roseanne had been placed under arrest.

"Roseanne told me," Ali said, goading just to see how he'd react to the news. "She called me because she needed cash in a hurry and wanted to unload some of her jewelry. I took a few pieces off her hands."

"But she's still all right?"

"You mean have your friends the Joaquins caught up with her? Not yet."

From the dismayed look on Jake's face, Ali knew he was taken aback. "How do you know so much about all this?" he wanted to know.

Ali decided to choose a Joaquin—any Joaquin—to turn into a fall guy. "Reynaldo," Ali said. "He's made a deal with the Feds. From what I hear, he's giving them an earful and spilling his guts about everything that's been going on around here. By morning the whole organization will be in custody. You sure you want to be the last man standing?"

Once again Jake waved the gun in her direction. "Why are we still sitting here?" he demanded. "I told you to drive."

Ali's phone rang just then, startling them both. "Don't answer," Jake began, but Ali already had, hoping beyond hope the caller would be Dave and that she would somehow be able to let him know what was going on.

"Ms. Reynolds?" an unfamiliar male voice asked.

"Yes."

"I'm so sorry to disturb you at such a late hour. My name is Fred Macon. You know, with Three Palms, the mortuary?"

Ali struggled to conceal her disappointment. "What can I do for you, Mr. Macon?"

"Your husband's remains have just been transported to our facility here. There seems to be some confusion with the paperwork. I had been told that April Gaddis was the person to be consulted about services and so forth, but it's been brought to my attention that Ms. Gaddis is also deceased at this time, and since yours is the only other contact number available to us . . ."

"It's well after midnight, Mr. Macon," Ali pointed out. "Do we really need to have this discussion right now? Can't we plan my husband's funeral during daylight hours?"

"Well, yes, certainly," Fred Macon said quickly. "There's one check mark on the form that wasn't properly handled over in Riverside, however, and it would be a big help to all of us here if we could get that one straightened out as soon as possible."

"What check mark?" Ali asked.

"Embalming," Fred Macon said. "It would be helpful to us to know whether or not you intend to have Mr. Grayson's remains embalmed."

Paul had died on Thursday night. It was now edging toward dawn on Tuesday morning. That went a long way to explaining Mr. Macon's middle-of-the-night urgency. Embalming was probably long overdue.

"By all means," Ali said.

"Thank you," Fred said. "Thank you so much. So I can note on the file that you gave me a verbal authorization to do so over the phone?"

"Yes."

"And I can let the office know that you'll be in touch to finalize arrangements for the services tomorrow . . . later on today, actually?"

"That, too," Ali told him.

"And, if you'll pardon my asking. Our information about Ms. Gaddis didn't come through what you would call official channels. I just happened to see it on the news and made the connection. Will you be handling arrangements for her as well? If a joint service is required—"

"No," Ali said. "I believe someone else will be in charge of that."

"Oh," Fred said. He sounded disappointed, as though he had somehow missed the opportunity to drum up some extra night-shift business. Ali wondered if perhaps he actually made a commission. "All right then," he added. "Thanks so much, and again, I'm sorry to disturb you in the middle of the night."

"That's quite all right," Ali said.

She ended the call. "The mortuary," she explained to Jake. "Calling about Paul's services. You already knew he was dead when you came to court on Friday, didn't you?" she added.

"I said drive," Jake said, but she noted a lack of conviction in his voice, and that uncertainty gave her courage.

"No," she said suddenly. "We're not going anywhere. I think you know who the guilty party is. I want to know who killed Paul and why."

"Ali, I'm telling you," Jake said menacingly. "If I have to shoot you, I will. Don't make me do it."

The window on Ali's side of the car was still open. With a speed that surprised her and caught Jake totally flat-footed, Ali shut off the ignition, extracted the car key, and flung it out through the open window.

She welcomed the tiny whisper of a splash as the leather-topped key landed in the nearby swimming pool and sank to what she knew was the bottom of the diving end.

Jake heard it, too, and was outraged. "You bitch!" he screamed at her. "Are you nuts? What the hell are you thinking? Now we'll never get out of here."

That's the whole idea, Ali thought.

"Maybe it's time you thought about calling the cops and turning yourself in," she suggested.

"Goddamn it!" he roared furiously. "Get out! Get the hell out of this car! I was working trying to hot-wire Paul's Land Rover when you showed up. It's a lot harder than it looks, but I almost had it. Once I get it running, we'll take that instead. Go on! Move it. You're driving."

Ali did as she was told. She moved. She was headed for the Land Rover when a new set of headlights rounded the last curve on Robert Lane and stopped just outside the gate.

Ali's heart quickened within her. She was sure the new arrival had to be Dave, that once again he had somehow ridden to her rescue. Then she heard Chris's voice.

"Mom?" he called. "Is that you? The gate is closed, and I don't have a clicker. Come let me in."

Ali's insides lurched. It wasn't Dave at all. It was her son. Her baby.

Jake grabbed Ali's arm from behind. She felt the barrel of the gun press into her back. "We're coming to you," Jake called. "Stay right where you are. I have a gun, and I'm not afraid to use it. If you move or make so much as a sound, your mother dies. Understand?"

They came around the corner of the pool house to the spot where Ali could see Chris standing beside Edie's idling Olds.

She wanted to urge him to run. Or to tumble down the bank of lush pampas grass her neighbors had allowed to flourish on the steep hillside. But with the gun pressed against her spine, and with her arm twisted almost up to her shoulder, she said nothing. It would be bad enough if Jake shot her. The idea that he might hurt Chris was unthinkable.

At last they reached the gatepost. "Open it," Jake ordered, propelling her forward.

Ali punched the keypad, and the gate swung open.

"In," Jake said, waving his weapon in the direction of Chris's car. "You drive. Your mother and I will sit in back."

"Mom," Chris asked. "Did he hurt you? Are you all right?"

"Shut up," Jake said.

Chris did as he was told, too. He shut up and got back into the driver's seat while Jake heaved Ali into the car and across the backseat. He shoved her hard enough that her shoulder smashed painfully into the door on the far side.

Jake settled in behind her and slammed the door. "Thanks," he said to the back of Chris's head. "You couldn't have come at a better time. Now take us to the Ten and go east, and do it in a hell of a hurry."

That meant they weren't going to Julian.

{ CHAPTER 20 }

"Mom, who is this jerk?" Chris demanded. "If you hurt her, I swear I'll—"

"I said shut up and drive," Jake repeated. "And I meant it."

Ali rubbed her bruised shoulder. It hurt, but not nearly as much as her bruised ego. How had she allowed this calamity to happen? It seemed to her that somehow, in a week full of disasters, she should have seen this one coming and been able to prevent it.

"I'm all right, Chris," she said. "Do what he says so no one gets hurt."

Chris was outraged. "For God's sake, Mom. How can you say that? The man was holding a gun to your head!"

"And now I'm holding one to yours," Jake reminded him. "So you'd best pay attention. Turn the car around and get going."

Chris complied by slamming his foot on the accelerator. He backed away from the gate so fast that he came perilously close to the edge of the road. Then, after pulling a swift U-turn, the Alero sped back down Robert Lane.

"Have a ball," Chris declared. "Shoot away. Then we'll all see exactly how well Grandma's Olds drives with no one behind the wheel! I don't think this model comes equipped with a self-guidance system."

Ali knew that "Go ahead and shoot me" often qualify as famous last words. In fact, she suspected they had been included in the Darwin Awards as an often-quoted exit line.

For God's sake, don't antagonize him, Ali thought. "Chris," she cautioned. "Please."

"Slow down," Jake said as Chris raced through the stop sign at the bottom of the hill. "The last thing we need is for the cops to come after us because you ran a damned stop sign."

Chris slowed slightly. They traveled for the better part of a mile in silence.

"So what are you?" Chris asked finally, studying Jake's face in the rearview mirror. "Somebody who's just been profiled on *America's Most Wanted*? An escaped convict? What?"

"He's a friend of Paul's," Ali supplied. "Used to be a friend of Paul's."

"Some friend," Chris muttered.

Once on the 10 there was far more traffic than there had been on the surface streets, and more semis than cars, all headed east, trying to make as much distance as possible before the blinding sun came up. Ali wondered about the drivers of those various big rigs. How was it that they could tool along, blissfully unaware of the life-and-death drama playing out in Edie Lawson's innocuous-looking white Alero? Why was it none of them gave the speeding Oldsmobile a second glance?

Watching the lights of the not-quite-sleeping city speed past outside the window, Ali knew it was late but she didn't know how late. Somehow, in the course of the struggle on Robert Lane, her wristwatch had disappeared. Huddled too far in the corner of the backseat to be able to see the clock on the dash, Ali was damned if she'd ask Jake Maxwell for the time of day. Finally, as they sped through Ontario, she caught sight of a huge neon clock at a Ford dealership. It was 2:12 exactly. No wonder she was tired.

As they drove, Ali couldn't help being struck by the latest irony in her situation. Earlier that evening and without either her knowledge or permission, someone working for the Joaquin organization had followed her every move by using the very tracking device that, even now, was still in her pocket. Through the soft denim material, she could feel the presence of that smooth round disk. Fortunately—or unfortunately, depending on your point of view—the people who had been so vitally interested in her whereabouts earlier were now all under arrest. So even though it was technically possible for someone to track her, it seemed unlikely that anyone would do so.

With a sinking heart, Ali realized that all the high-tech GPS technology in the world wasn't going to save her and her son. When it came to being rescued, she and Chris were on their own.

Still maintaining an uneasy silence, they traveled eastbound for some time. As they approached the merge with the 60, Ali's hopes rose. Off to the right, she saw the lights of a phalanx of emergency vehicles sweeping onto I-10 ahead of them. When Ali first caught sight of them, she hardly dared breathe. She watched them for a few hopeful moments, praying that the lights were somehow related to what was happening to them, praying that Jake wouldn't notice. And he didn't. But by the time Chris negotiated the I-10/60 merge with its tangle of complicated traffic and disappearing lanes, the parade of cop cars or ambulances or whatever that Ali had put such hope in had shot on far ahead and completely out of sight.

Despairing, Ali closed her eyes and concentrated on some straightforward praying.

At last Chris spoke again. "Where are we going?"

"Don't worry," Jake replied. "Just stay on the Ten. I'll tell you where to turn. It won't be for a while yet."

"If we're going very far, we'll need to stop for gas."

Ali caught her breath as Jake leaned forward and peered over the front seat.

"All right," he said finally, having read the gauge for himself. "I guess you're right. We do need gas. Pull off at the next exit, but find a full-service pump. No one gets in or out of the vehicle while we're stopped, understand? No one!"

Somewhere in Beaumont they pulled off the freeway and stopped at a convenience mart. While the three of them sat in the car and waited for the slow-moving attendant to fill the tank, Ali was startled by the ringing of her phone. She looked at the readout.

"It's my mother," she said. "She was supposed to come by the house tonight. If she did, she's probably upset that I'm not there. She'll be worried. She might even call the cops."

"Answer it then," Jake said. "But put the phone on speaker first, and don't try anything funny. Understand?"

Ali understood all too well.

"Alison?" Edie said when she heard her daughter's voice. "Are you all right? Where are you?"

Sometime earlier—was it hours or days?—with an armed and unstable April Gaddis standing in the kitchen at Robert Lane, Ali had somehow managed to convey the gravity of the situation to Dave by speaking to him in a kind of code. Now, though, with Jake Maxwell's gun digging into her ribs and with him privy to both sides of the conversation, speaking to Edie in code simply wasn't possible.

"I'm fine, Mom," Ali said as reassuringly as possible. "I got called away from the house by an emergency with an old friend. There wasn't time to let you know. I'm sorry."

"You couldn't have called?"

"No. Calling just wasn't possible."

"Well," Edie said, sounding both perplexed and disgruntled, "the gate is shut. A cab brought me over, but I can't get inside. What am I supposed to do, stand around here all night?"

Ali could have given her the gate code, but she didn't. If something happened and Ali and Chris didn't survive, the parked Cayenne would be the only real evidence as to what had happened to them. Ali didn't want that evidence disturbed.

"Use the cab and find a hotel then," she said. "I won't be able to get back there before sometime tomorrow."

"What about Chris?" Edie asked. "Where is he?"

"Staying with friends," Ali said.

"It's just that it's not like you to be so irresponsible, Ali," Edie said. "You're sure you're all right?"

"I'm fine," Ali said quickly. "I've got to go now, Mom. Take care. I love you."

It hurt to think those might be the last words Edie Larson ever heard from her daughter, but they were the best Ali could do.

Seconds later they were back under way. "You still haven't said where we're going," Chris reminded Jake.

"That's because you still don't need to know."

"Mexico," Ali supplied. "Oaxaca. At least that's what he told me earlier."

"Shut up!" Jake said.

The barrel of his gun dug deeper into Ali's ribs, but she was grateful that it was pointed in her direction rather than in Chris's. He had his whole life ahead of him. As for hers? If she had to gamble her life to save her son's, that's exactly what she'd do.

Ali looked out across the darkened desert where mountains loomed black against a star-studded sky. They were only a few miles west of the Highway 111 turnoff and the place where the speeding train had plowed into a parked Camry—the place where Paul had died. Ali couldn't help wondering if maybe she and Chris were destined to die there as well—in much the same manner.

"I need to take a leak," Chris said from the front seat.

"Me, too," Ali added quickly. "I had way too much coffee earlier."

Jake immediately seemed to assume that their request for a pit stop was nothing but a ploy. And up to a point it was. Although Ali genuinely needed to use the facilities, it was also her sincere hope that in the process of getting in and out of the car, there would be an opportunity for Chris, at least, to get away.

"You'll just have to wait," Jake said. "You can hold it for a while."

Soon, though, and now that she was thinking about it, Ali really couldn't hold it any longer. She had drunk way too much coffee.

"I really do need to go," she said.

"I told you, we're not stopping."

"Fine," Ali said. "If you don't mind sitting in a puddle of urine, neither do I."

"There's a rest area coming up in a few minutes," Chris said. "Maybe we could stop there."

"Oh, for God's sake!" Jake exclaimed. "Stop then. By all means, but the two of you go in and out of the restroom one at a time, and your cell phone stays with me. Give it to me. Yours, too, if you've got one," Jake told Chris. "Hand it over."

As Chris signaled to merge onto the rest area exit ramp, Jake held out his hand to collect first Chris's phone and then Ali's. Chris passed his back. Involved in reluctantly handing over her own, Ali never saw exactly what happened. One moment they were slowing to exit the highway. The next the desert came alive with the flashing lights of a dozen police and emergency vehicles as the Alero gave a sudden violent lurch and veered to one side. Then it staggered forward on the rims of four instantly flattened tires.

"Nail strips!" Jake shouted in a panic. "Keep driving. Keep driving."

But Chris had already reached another conclusion and slammed on the brakes. As the vehicle slowed and came to a stop, Ali heard a voice she barely recognized as her own, screaming at her son.

"Get out," she screeched at him. "Go! Go! Go! I'm right behind you."

But that wasn't true. Before Ali could touch the door handle, Jake's fingers clamped down on her wrist. Ali may still have been trapped inside the car, but Chris was in motion before all the words had tumbled out of her mouth. She saw her son land and land hard, thrown forward by a combination of his own momentum and that of the vehicle. Then to her immense relief, he scrambled to his feet. Limping slightly, he raced to cover behind one of several waiting California Highway Patrol vehicles.

After that, in the middle of the chaos—accompanied by a cloud of swirling dust and the blinding flash of lights—there was a moment of utter silence followed by someone shouting, "All right, Maxwell. You're surrounded. Put down your weapon. Come out with your hands up."

Jake looked at Ali. "How do they know it's me? Who told them?"

Ali had no answer for that, but with Chris out of the car and out of danger, she found herself immersed in a well of complete calm—a place where Jake Maxwell's threats no longer held any sway with her. She was immune.

"It doesn't matter who told them, Jake," she said. "What matters is that they *do* know. It's over. You can't get away. Give it up."

"You have to believe me, Ali," he said, after a pause. "I had no idea she was going to kill him."

"Kill who?" Ali asked.

"Paul. I thought Lucia was just going to teach him a lesson. That's the way the Joaquins work, you see. They give people lessons, hard enough lessons so you know what they're capable of, and you don't need another one."

The comment came from so far out in left field that it took a moment for Ali to process it. "You mean you knew?" Ali demanded. "You son of a bitch, are you saying you did it?"

"I didn't. All I did was help get him drunk. I swear to you, I didn't know anything about Tracy and the rest of it. I never meant for Paul to die."

"You did mean it," Ali returned. "You meant it, and he did die. Why? Were you jealous because he got the job and you didn't? Was that it?"

With that Ali reached for the door handle.

"Wait, Ali," Jake said. "Don't leave me, please. I'll drop the gun if you stay. I promise. They won't shoot me as long as you're with me."

What Ali felt in that moment was a contempt and loathing so complete and all-consuming that there was no room left in her soul for anything else, especially not fear.

"Forget it," she told him. "You're on your own."

"But I have a gun."

"You may have a gun, buddy-boy," she told him, "but I know for a fact you don't have balls enough to use it."

With that, she opened the car door and stepped out into a world of flashing lights. And even there, in the middle of the sudden chill of the cold desert night, she knew that at least one or two of those flashing lights were bound to be cameras.

Blinded by them, she was startled when a pair of strong arms grabbed her and pulled her behind one of the waiting vehicles.

"Ali. Thank God!" Dave exclaimed. "Are you all right?" In the pulsing light she caught a glimpse of the relief on his worried face.

"I'm fine. Really."

"Come on, then," Dave said, leading her away. "It's too dangerous. Let's get out of here."

"How did you find us?" Ali asked. "How did you know where to look?"

Dave didn't answer. "Later," he said.

"Where's Chris?"

"Out of the line of fire. Where you need to be, too."

Someone shouting over what sounded like a bull-horn was still ordering Jake Maxwell out of the Alero as Dave led Ali to the far side of the concrete restroom complex. There she found Chris sitting on a picnic table with a paramedic applying ice to his ankle.

"The EMT grabbed me and wouldn't let me loose. It's just a little sprain, Mom," he said reassuringly. "It's nothing. How are you?"

Ali hurried over and hugged him. "I'm fine," she said. "I'm completely fine."

She turned back to Dave. "But how did you know . . ."

"Ask your son," Dave said. "Once he realized you were in trouble, he punched his phone's redial, and the last number dialed happened to be your folks' phone back in Sedona. Fortunately Bob was there and answered. Chris was wearing his Bluetooth mini ear-plug. That allowed Bob to overhear everything that was going on in the vehicle without Jake having any idea anyone was listening in. Bob immediately put another call through to us—a conference call—so we could all monitor the situation."

Ali remembered giving Chris a tough time when he had returned from a weekend skiing trip to Aspen with a telephone earpiece attached to his head. Now it appeared that an even smaller mini earplug might well have saved both their lives.

"And knowing what was up," Dave added, "Easy was able to get one of his electronic techs working the Pink Swan warehouse scene to reinitiate your GPS."

"So, from all that, you knew where we were the whole time," Ali said.

Dave nodded. "Pretty much," he said. "But none of that would have happened if Chris here hadn't used his head."

Flooded with relief and gratitude, Ali gave her son another hug. She and Chris had been in danger, all right, but not nearly as much as she had supposed.

"But you were here waiting for us," Ali said a moment later. "How did you do that? You and Easy were still in Valencia when I left. I thought you were going to pick up my mother."

"Fortunately, we were unavoidably delayed. And after that, it took some doing," Dave said. "And some pretty amazing police car driving on Easy Washington's part. Of course, it helps to have CHP cars clearing traffic ahead of us all along the way."

"So that was you?" Ali asked. "The flashing lights I saw merging off the Sixty onto the Ten just as we got there?"

Dave nodded. "Our first intention was to do this in

Beaumont when you stopped for gas. Then we decided there would be less risk to the general public if we did it here at a rest area instead, so we cleared out as many civilians as we could, and here we are. Which reminds me. You should probably give your dad a call and let him know you're okay."

But Ali's phone had bounced out of her hand the moment the tires had gone flat. She had no idea where it was now—none.

"Let me use yours, Chris," she said, holding out her hand.

He shook his head. "I was on the phone the whole way here," he said. "I'm out of battery."

"Oh, for Pete's sake," Dave said, taking out his own phone. "Here. Use mine."

Bob was overjoyed to hear his daughter's voice. "Does your mother know?" he asked. "She's been worried sick and on the phone to the restaurant the whole time."

Ali had reached Edie and was talking to her when Easy Washington came trotting around the corner of the building. "All clear," he said. "Maxwell is in custody. Is everyone here okay?"

"Just my ankle," Chris said, "but it's nothing serious."

"And you?" Easy asked Ali.

"I'm fine," she said. "One hundred percent."

"The Alero's going to have to be towed," Easy said. "And Dave's car is still at the Claim Jumper. I'll have one of my guys load you into a Suburban and take you back. The rest of us have one more stop before the evening is over."

"What stop?" Ali asked.

"In the Old Las Palmas area of Palm Springs," Easy replied. "That's where Lucia Joaquin lives. She and her granddaughter, Amber, are the only ones still at large. We've had Lucia's place under surveillance all night long. There's been no unusual activity, so we're hoping she has no idea we've managed to roll up her entire operation in the course of the last several hours. And now we're going to nail her."

"She's the one who ordered Paul's murder?" Ali asked.

Easy nodded. "I believe so."

"Then I want to go, too," Ali said. "I want to be there."

"You can't," Easy objected. "It's impossible. I'm not allowed to put civilians in danger. It's absolutely against regulations."

"I've been in danger all night," Ali pointed out. "So has Dave. So has Chris."

"Yes," Easy agreed. "But that wasn't my fault."

"Please," Ali said quietly. "After all we've been through tonight, shouldn't I be able to be there to see her taken into custody?"

Easy Washington shook his head. At first Ali was convinced he was turning her down, then he called over his shoulder to one of his men.

"Hey, Sal. Does anyone here have a couple of extra Kevlar vests? A small and a large. We've got someone here who's going to need one."

{ CHAPTER 21 }

The Kevlar jacket was bulkier than Ali could have imagined. And hotter, too. Minutes after donning it, she and Dave climbed into the backseat of Easy Washington's black Suburban.

In the rush of donning the vest Ali had lost track of her son.

"Where's Chris?" she asked. "I thought he was coming along."

"He's on his way to an ER in the ambulance," Dave answered. "The EMT insisted his ankle has to be X-rayed and refused to take no for an answer. By the way," Dave added, "did anyone ever tell you Chris is one hell of a kid? Really used his head tonight. He did a great job with your dad and us on the phone."

"Yes," Ali agreed. "He is one hell of a kid."

In the front seat, Easy was on the radio and cell phone both, coordinating his troops. At the rest area Ali had caught sight of several officers she had met in the course of the previous several days, cops she knew from L.A. and Riverside, in addition to Easy's own crew from the DEA. This was clearly a complicated, task-force-style operation with Ezekiel Washington calling the shots.

"I've never been to Palm Springs," Dave said, studying a map Easy had handed him. "We're going to a street called Via Hermosa."

Via Hermosa was a name-brand Palm Springs address, and Ali remembered visiting several of the venerable old mansions there years earlier as part of various charitable functions. She took the map from Dave long enough to point to the general area.

"Old Las Palmas is part of old Palm Springs," Ali explained. "Big houses. Big lots."

"Big bucks?" Dave asked.

"That, too, but I would guess Lucia Joaquin can afford pretty much anything she wants."

Ali thought about the other massive old places she had seen in old Las Palmas—the eight- or nine-bedroom luxury homes with their many-car garages, their lush furnishings and equally lush grounds. She didn't know which house Lucia lived in, but it had to be one like that.

And the more Ali thought about it, the more the whole idea of Lucia Joaquin offended her. She resented the idea that a woman, clad in pink from head to toe and closeted in absolute luxury, could sit at home in total comfort and safety while sending her minions off to do her bidding—up to and including committing acts of cold-blooded murder. While one of her worker bees had left a trussed and helpless Paul Grayson—who she merely suspected might go to the cops—to die on the train tracks, Lucia had been a few miles away, probably sleeping peacefully in her bed.

"Where do people like Lucia come from?" Ali asked Dave finally.

He shook his head. "They're vermin," he said. "They crawl out from under rocks."

They had turned off I-10 and onto Highway 111. As they sped through the night with the blue and red lights pulsing overhead but with no siren, Ali tried not to look at that particular part of the desert, but she couldn't help it. Her eyes were drawn to the black pool of unrelieved darkness where she knew the train track ran. What a desolate place it was—what an awful place to die.

Easy returned his radio to its holder. "Okay," he said, "here's the deal. We have yet to locate Amber, the granddaughter, but we're pretty sure Lucia is inside the Palm Springs house. It's possible she's there alone, but it's also possible there's a caregiver with her. The place sits on an acre and a half, and the whole thing is surrounded by a twelve-foot rock wall with only one gate. Since Lucia isn't in the best of health these days, she's not going to be climbing over that fence. As long as we control the gate—which we do—we also control access."

Dave nodded. Ali said nothing.

"I've got a trained tactical team in place and primed to do the heavy lifting," Easy continued. "These are guys who know what they're about and we're going to let them do it. I've put my second in command in charge. Since the two of you are here on my say-so, I'm not letting either one of you out of my sight for even so much as a minute. And you're not going any closer to the action than I say, got it?"

"Got it," Dave said at once.

"Ms. Reynolds?" Easy asked. "I don't believe I heard a response from you."

"Got it," Ali said.

"Good. I know you're anxious to see the takedown. Considering the circumstances, I can't say that I blame you, but you're not to go near that woman until my guys have the situation under control."

"Yes," Ali said. "I understand."

She looked at Dave. He sat there alert but seemingly at ease, with the palms of his hands resting squarely on his knees. If he was concerned about the coming confrontation, his impassive face betrayed none of it. But then, Ali realized, he was a Marine. Clearly he would be accustomed to going into potentially dangerous combat situations. She was not. Her heart pounded in her chest. Sweat dribbled down the back of her neck and soaked her shirt under the arms. Despite the fact that she had said she wanted to be here and see Lucia taken into custody, it was clear to Ali that she wasn't ready at all—and probably never would be. And she missed having her Glock, missed it more than she could have imagined.

"How long before it all starts?" she asked.

She had aimed her question at Dave, but Easy Washington was the one who answered. "Depends on how long it takes us to get there," he said.

Ali had always been under the impression that it took approximately forever to drive from the Palm Springs turnoff on I-10 into the city itself. Tonight it seemed to happen in the blink of an eye. Long before Ali had managed to prepare herself, Easy was already turning off Palm Canyon and headed toward Old Las Palmas. Ali closed her fists and let her fingernails dig into the flesh at the base of her palms. She may have been petrified about whatever was coming, but she sure as hell wasn't going to show it.

As they approached Via Hermosa, cop cars and roadblocks seemed to be everywhere—all kinds of cop cars from all kinds of jurisdictions. But Easy and his

Suburban had the secret code or maybe it was a magic charm. Every time the Suburban came close to stopping, they were waved on through the barricade.

When they finally came to a stop, it was on the far side of a wrought-iron gate with a massive wall on either side that seemed to stretch out of sight in both directions. The sky was starting to brighten almost imperceptibly on the far horizon while the view in through the gate was nothing short of idyllic. A lit fountain, spilling water, was the centerpiece of a bricked courtyard. Curtains of blooming bougainvillea framed a pillared front porch. The massive double doors, made of some kind of metal, gleamed in the light of equally massive sconces. It was an impressive entryway, one that made a statement. It also looked like a fortress.

Motioning for Dave and Ali to stay inside, Easy stepped out of the vehicle. Once again he had a phone clapped to one ear and an earpiece in the other. "Okay," Ali heard him say. "We're in place now. If everyone's ready, it's a go. On your say-so. Right."

What followed seemed to Ali like a moment of anticipatory silence. Then, as if on cue, all the officers standing outside the Suburban—all the ones she could see, Easy included—seemed to glance in the same direction at the same time, looking off over their shoulders, back toward downtown. And then, through the open car door, Ali heard the sound that had obviously captured their attention—the distinctive *rat-ta-tat-tat* of an approaching helicopter.

Ali's first assumption was that the aircraft was some kind of support vehicle brought in to serve as backup for the officers on the scene, but as it flew directly overhead, it laid down what sounded like a spray of automatic gunfire. At the sound of it, the officers on the ground all dove for cover.

"Holy shit!" Dave exclaimed. "We're taking fire."

The helicopter dropped to the ground on the far side of the gate, easing down beside the lighted fountain. Behind it, one of the massive double doors flew open and two women emerged—Amber and a white-haired woman, dressed all in pink and leaning on a cane. Amber hurried her forward. The two of them walked under the churning helicopter blades without ducking their heads, as though they were totally accustomed to them. As they approached the cockpit, Amber pulled herself inside and then reached back to help the older woman.

By then Easy's assault team was moving forward. Weapons at the ready, they crouched behind a growling Hummer that paused for only a moment before ripping the gate off its hinges and clearing the way for the team to spill inside the compound. As they surged forward, though, the helicopter had collected its passengers and was already lifting off. As it rose from the ground, another spray of bullets came through the craft's open door.

Instinctively, Ali and Dave ducked as bullets smashed into the front of the Suburban and whined past them in the empty air. The windshield splintered. And then there was another sound—an ugly, guttural groan of pain—the sound of someone hit and badly hurt. Outside the open front door, Easy Washington seemed to spin in place. Then, slowly, he fell backward.

Over the roar of the helicopter engine, Ali heard a group of shouted commands followed by yet another blast of gunfire, this one from the officers on the ground. At first it seemed as though it made no difference. For a time the helicopter continued to rise unimpeded. Then it seemed to hesitate slightly. The blades stopped spinning abruptly as the craft tilted drunkenly over to one side. Then, slowly to Ali's fear-fueled mind, it began to fall to earth.

Ali saw two somethings, one pink and one not, spill out onto the ground and land, like limp rag dolls, on the hard brick of the courtyard. And then the helicopter crashed down there as well—smashing almost silently and eerily in the exact same spot. Immediately it burst into flames.

As the flames rose in the air, Dave vaulted out of the Suburban with Ali right behind him. By the time Ali reached the ground, Dave was on his knees lifting his friend's dreadfully limp body. Already drenched in Easy's bright red blood, Dave was cradling the man and doing his best to apply pressure to a wound at the base of Easy's chin.

"Find a phone!" Dave yelled at Ali. "Call nine-one-one. Hurry!"

Without knowing how she found it, Ali's fingers closed around the telephone Easy Washington had dropped when he fell.

"Nine-one-one," the operator said. "What are you reporting?"

"A man's been shot," Ali shouted into the phone. "A man's been shot and there's been a helicopter crash."

"What is your location?" the woman wanted to know. "You're calling on a cell phone. I need the exact address."

"Somewhere on Via Hermosa in Palm Springs," Ali returned. "Right next to the burning helicopter."

Four people died last night and three DEA offi-cers were wounded, one critically, when gunfire erupted and a fleeing helicopter crashed in the normally quiet Old Las Palmas neighborhood of Palm Springs during a DEA-led task-force opera-tion targeting a highly sophisticated network of alleged drug traffickers.

After a monthlong investigation and after staging numerous arrests all over Southern California, officers turned their attention to the home of a longtime Palm Springs resident thought to be the ringleader of the group. Both the unidentified woman and her granddaughter along with their pilot and another crew mem-ber perished when the helicopter in which they were attempting to flee crashed during takeoff. One unidentified DEA officer is hospitalized at Eisenhower Memorial Hospital with what are thought to be life-threatening injuries.

The gun battle came at the end of a long day of stunning high-profile arrests that netted sev-eral members of L.A.'s media elite along with some people thought to be highly placed mem-bers in law enforcement circles. Much of the operation centered around a trendy Beverly Hills topless club known as the Pink Swan.

One suspect was arrested and two carjacking victims were rescued at the Morango rest area on I-10 when officers, alerted by one of the hostages over a cell phone, managed to throw down nail strips, which disabled the fleeing vehicle. One of the two victims, both of them Arizona residents visiting in California, was slightly injured during the operation. The other was released unharmed.

It was almost noon that same day when Ali looked up from reading the online news report and considered those words, the understated and dispassionate journalese that toned down the very real drama of the story.

"One was slightly injured." That would have been Chris and his sprained ankle. The one who was released "unharmed" was Ali herself. And the "critically injured" officer was Dave's friend Easy Washington, who had been struck in the neck by a stray bullet. The theory was that one of the bullets fired from the helicopter had ricocheted off the Suburban's engine block. It had glanced off Easy's Kevlar vest and had slammed into his inferior thyroid artery.

The other thing the words didn't do justice to was the frantic lifesaving effort that had ensued. Dave had been in the thick of the action and only his knowledgeable application of pressure to the wound had saved his gravely injured friend's life. Ali's last glimpse of a blood-spattered Dave had been as the EMTs helped him into the waiting ambulance along with Easy.

A little past noon Edie Larson emerged from the pool house. Carrying a cup of coffee, she set it on the patio table next to Ali's computer and then she sat down next to her daughter.

"How are things?" Edie asked. "Any word about Dave's friend?"

"No," Ali said. "At least they're not updating his condition anywhere here."

"And you haven't heard from Dave?"

"Not so far."

"You will," Edie said confidently.

Ali studied her mother. Edie's face looked far more worn than usual. "You never let on that you knew about the whole thing when I was talking to you on the phone," Ali observed.

"No, I didn't," Edie agreed. "I was afraid I might give something away. I knew Dave and the others were working hard with Dad and Chris to get the two of you out of there, but I wanted you to hear the sound of my voice. I wanted you to know that you weren't all alone out there."

Ali had pictured her mother standing outside the gate of Robert Lane during what she had thought might be their last-ever phone call. Now she knew that, in actual fact, Edie had placed the call from the safety of an LAPD squad car.

Ali reached out and covered her mother's hand. "Thank you," she said.

"You're welcome," Edie returned. "But knowing you were out there with all those bullets flying . . ." Edie shook her head. "Oh, my. I was terrified."

"So was I," Ali admitted. *And with good reason,* she thought.

Edie stood up. Her freshly poured cup of coffee was already gone. She could drink coffee hotter than anyone Ali knew.

"Is there any food in the house?" Edie asked, nodding toward the big house where none of them had stayed. "The pool house fridge has coffee and a bottle of ketchup but that's about it."

"Probably," Ali said, "but I don't know for sure."

"I'll go check," Edie said. "Chris was still asleep on the couch when I came through the living room, but I know we'll all feel better if we have a decent breakfast under our belts."

Vintage Edie Larson, Ali thought.

Once Edie was in the house, Ali continued scanning the various online news Web sites. There were three that included pictures of Dave dragging her away from the Alero during the rest area confrontation. The captions on two of those identified her as an "unidentified carjacking victim." In the third, the usual suspect and journalistic busybody LMB, the blogger at socalcopshop.com, identified her by name in the caption of a particularly unflattering photo. In it, Ali looked downright ghastly.

Knowing that some of her cutloose fans were bound to see the photo and worry, Ali decided it was time to face up to her blog and write something about what had been going on.

CUTLOOSEBLOG.COM
Tuesday, September 20, 2005

Years ago I remember reading a poem by Rudyard Kipling in which he said "the female of the species is more deadly than the male." In the last few days, I have seen this statement borne out on several different fronts.

In recent days I had the misfortune of seeing my former husband's fiancée choose to end her own life and that of her unborn child rather than face the consequences of her own murderous actions. April Gaddis took her mother's life. Then she threatened my life and my mother's as well. Days earlier, someone had referred to me as a "Black Widow." April Gaddis may not have been married prior to her death and she may not be directly responsible for Paul Grayson's murder, either, but I still believe the term applies—to her.

Yes, my husband, Paul Grayson, was murdered, and it turns out his death was merely the tip of the iceberg. Because there's been another Black Widow at work in Southern California for a very long time. Lucia Joaquin was in fact a widow—the widow of a known drug kingpin—and a successful drug trafficker in her own right. I'm not sure how Paul got caught in her web of evil, but he did. She's dead now, too, as is her only granddaughter. They both perished when the helicopter in which they were attempting to flee crashed and burst into flames.

I owe the fact that I am writing this today to the heroic efforts of a friend of mine, a guy named Dave Holman, who has come to my rescue more than once in the last few days. Dave is a police officer in Sedona, Arizona. He's also a member of the Marine Corps Reserves. Last night I watched him work frantically to save the life of a friend of his, a wounded DEA officer, who is also in the Marine Reserves. In the past I don't believe I've ever spent much time wondering about the Marine Corps motto *Semper fidelis*. Now I've seen it in action.

I've looked at my new e-mail list. It's stuffed to the gills. In fact, my server is probably rejecting e-mails as I write this, claiming my mailbox is full and my bandwidth is over its limit. As I've indicated, I've had my hands full for the last few days. I'll get around to answering the mail when I can. Please be patient.

Posted 1:05 P.M., September 20, 2005 by Babe

P.S. Amazing!! My attorney just called. My former employers have settled my wrongful dismissal suit! For an undisclosed sum. The terms of the settlement dictate that I'm not allowed to discuss the amount. What I can say, though, is that it's generous enough that I won't be having to look for a day job anytime soon. cutlooseblog.com will continue indefinitely.

Ali was starting to slog her way through the mail when Chris, still limping, ambled out onto the patio. His hair was standing on end. The way he looked reminded her so much of how he had looked as a child that it made her heart melt, and it took real effort on Ali's part to keep from leaping up and hugging him.

"Where's Grandma?" he wanted to know.

"Making breakfast," Ali answered.

"Great. I'm starved."

Chris stretched and headed for the kitchen. As soon

as he opened the back door, Ali caught a whiff of her mother's baking coffee cake wafting through the air. Ali followed her son's lead. Then, once she was inside the house, she heard the sound of a hair dryer coming from the living room, and she followed that as well.

Wielding a whining hair dryer, Edie stood over the bird's-eye maple credenza in the front entryway. Nearby, a mound of bulging black plastic bags lay stacked by the front door.

Ali spoke to her mother three times before Edie noticed her. She switched off the noisy hair dryer and then turned her hearing aids back on.

"What are you doing?" Ali asked again.

"I asked your father what to do about this water mark," Edie said. "Someone must have put a vase down without wiping off the bottom. Dad says to try the hair-dryer routine first. If this doesn't work, he says I should bring it home and he'll refinish the top for you there. Or else Kip will. Dad says he's pretty good with his hands."

As far as Ali could see, the ring wasn't getting much better, but she appreciated her mother's effort more than she could say.

"And I got rid of the old dead flowers," Edie added. "They were falling all to pieces, dropping petals everywhere, and stinking up a storm. Hope you don't mind."

Ali didn't mind at all. She was delighted to find that the bouquets that were to have marked Paul and April's wedding had been swept away in the flower-clearing operation along with all the condolence bouquets. The catering tables and chairs had been collected and stacked at one end of the living room.

"Your yard man," Edie said, nodding toward the chairs and tables. "He helped me with that. What's his name again?"

"Jesus."

"Yes, that's it. Jesus. He said he needed to finish doing something out front, but that as soon as he's done, he'll come collect the bags of dead flowers and put them on his compost heap."

Of course, Ali realized.

Jesus had come back to reclaim his job, just as she had asked. Crime scene tape aside, he must have been the one who had repaired and reassembled the broken gate.

"He said I should tell you that the lawyer you sent him to was very good."

Right then, with Marcella Johnson's big touchdown on the scoreboard, Ali was glad to hear that another of her many attorneys had turned out to be a positive for someone.

"Good," Ali said. "As much as I'm paying in legal fees at the moment, it's only fair that we end up with decent representation and a few wins on our side."

"Jesus and I were having a bit of a communication problem," Edie continued. "As you know, my Spanish isn't all that good and I had my hearing aids turned off because the hair dryer was so loud, but I think he said a friend of his is coming over a little later. He mentioned her name, but I didn't quite catch it. Olivia maybe?"

"Elvira?" Ali asked. "My old cook?"

"That could be it. I just didn't hear him properly."

They had finished their breakfast of cheese baked

eggs and coffee cake when the doorbell rang. When Ali went to answer it, she found that the bags filled with dead flowers had magically and quietly disappeared. She opened the door to find Elvira Jimenez standing nervously on the front porch.

"Why, Elvira," Ali exclaimed with pleasure. "How good to see you again. Come in."

Elvira hung back. Ali went out and gave her a welcoming hug.

"I should not have come," Elvira said.

"Of course you should have," Ali said. "Our other cook just left. If you're not working somewhere else, maybe you'd like your old job back."

Chris appeared in the doorway. When Elvira saw him, her face broke into a broad smile, and she allowed him to lead her into the house.

"You're too skinny," she told him, patting his belly affectionately. "Someone needs to give you more cookies. And tortillas."

Chris took her into the kitchen, where Elvira sniffed the air. Nodding appreciatively in the direction of the coffee cake, she held out her hand to Edie Larson.

"I believe I have met you other times when you were here," Elvira said.

"Yes," Edie agreed. "It's nice to see you again. Won't you sit down?"

Elvira looked uncomfortable. Her eyes slipped from one face to another, finally coming to rest on Ali. Elvira shook her head and remained standing.

"Jesus said I should come," she said at last. "And his niece. She said the same thing."

"I've spoken to Andrea," Ali said, hoping to find

some common ground that would ease Elvira's obvious discomfort. "She's a nice girl."

Elvira's dark eyes bored into Ali's. "A nice girl?" she asked.

"Of course," Ali said.

"Some people would not call her that—nice," Elvira ventured. "She got pregnant once when she wasn't married. She had to have an abortion."

Ali shrugged. "Those things happen," she said. "It's important to the girl it happens to and to her family, but it's not important to the rest of the world."

"But it is important," Elvira said urgently. "It's a sin— a mortal sin."

Ali saw at once that she had stepped into something. So did Edie.

"It's considered a mortal sin by some people," Edie said kindly. "And I, for one, happen to agree with you."

Elvira smiled wanly. Then she reached into her threadbare cloth bag and pulled out a worn leather wallet. From it she removed a photo—a wallet-sized photo—of a newborn baby with a knitted pink cap perched on top of her head. Elvira handed the photo to Ali, who studied it for a moment. The baby had dark hair and fair skin, but there was something striking about the eyes.

"My great-granddaughter," Elvira explained. "My granddaughter's daughter."

"Congratulations," Ali said, handing the photo on to Chris. "She's very pretty."

Of course, the baby wasn't pretty at all. She was in fact wrinkly and more than a little ugly, but there are times when white lies are not only acceptable, they're downright necessary.

Chris glanced briefly at the photo and then, in turn, handed it along to his grandmother. Edie took one look at it then settled heavily onto one of the kitchen chairs.

"Oh, forevermore," she breathed. "Not another one!"

"Another one?" Ali asked. "What do you mean?"

"Don't tell me you can't see it!" Edie exclaimed. "This child has her father's eyes. She looks exactly like Paul Grayson."

{ CHAPTER 22 }

The story came out gradually over the course of the next few days while Ali went about the job of handling Paul's funeral. It had to be done and since there was no one else to do it, Ali did. Fortunately, April's father came forward and insisted on handling April's final arrangements. Ali was relieved to learn that he wanted nothing at all to do with a joint service. That meant Ali didn't have to worry about giving Fred Macon of the Three Palms Mortuary any more business, either.

But Ali did have to worry about Jesus Sanchez, who finally came forward and told her what he knew—and far more than Ali wanted to hear. He told her about how his niece, without his knowledge, had come to a party at the pool house. Paul had served drinks to Andrea and several of her young friends and then had taken advantage of the situation when Andrea was too drunk to see straight. When Andrea had turned up pregnant, Paul had paid for her abortion and given her money over and above that as well. He had also promised her father, Jesus, that it would never happen again. But it had—as everyone now knew—with Elvira's young visiting granddaughter, Consuela.

Paul had tried the same program with Consuela that he had used successfully with Andrea. He had offered to pay for an abortion plus a five-thousand-dollar premium. Except Consuela wouldn't go for it because it turned out she was a good Catholic girl. The trait had skipped Consuela's own mother and had jumped a generation, going straight from Elvira to her granddaughter. The baby, Angelina, was now a month and a half old.

A few months earlier, Ali Reynolds would have taken some satisfaction in learning that Paul Grayson had been screwing around on April at the same time April had been maintaining her long-term cozy friendship with Tracy McLaughlin. But Ali's paradigms had inalterably shifted that night out there in the desert—the night when she and her son had almost died. What had been important to her before no longer seemed to matter.

Ali's concern now, knowing that Consuela's child existed—that Angelina Rojas existed—was seeing to it that Angelina was properly provided for. Once again she found herself huddling with attorneys, trying to sort out reasonable support arrangements for this baby who could by no means be called a "love" child but who nonetheless deserved to have a very real claim on her father's assets. And the fact that Ali was prepared to be more than fair—that she was determined, in fact, to be downright generous with her former husband's assets—made a complicated situation far easier to handle than it would have been otherwise.

The negotiations went forward in utmost secrecy. That was the one thing Ali insisted upon—for Angelina's sake, until she was old enough to choose for herself. Until she was old enough to ask her own questions and hear the answers.

Edie and Chris stayed until Friday, after the funeral on Thursday. Knowing Ali would most likely be listing and selling the house, they helped her sort and pack. Paul's clothing—the expensive suits that he had reveled in—went to Goodwill, with the exception of the blue pinstripe Hugo Boss, which Paul would wear in his casket. April's things were packed into boxes and taken to her father to do with as he saw fit.

Ali herself went through the house, sorting out what she wanted and what she didn't. Most of it she didn't. The art would go to an auction house. So would most of the furniture, dishes, and glassware, with the exception of the comfortable leather chair and sofa from the family room and the water-marred bird's-eye maple credenza from the entryway. Those and everything else Ali wanted, she stacked in the family room until such time as she was ready to call for a moving van. As for the wine cellar? Ali managed to locate a company that specialized in moving fine wines and made arrangements for Paul's entire collection, racks and all, to be moved to Sedona.

She talked to Dave on the phone from time to time during the course of that week and had offered to come over, but Dave said that wasn't necessary. He stayed on in Palm Springs at Easy's bedside, and since Ali wasn't Easy's friend, she thought it best not to intrude.

By Monday evening of the following week, Paul was buried and the house was more or less sorted out. Ali had blogged some but not much. She had done enough to let people know she was alive—enough to let them know she was okay. But everything that had happened had left her more traumatized than she would have thought possible, and she wasn't ready to talk about it just yet—not nearly.

She was sitting in the mostly packed family room, surveying the debris field and having a solo glass of wine, when the doorbell rang. Startled out of her solitude, Ali hurried to the front door, looked out through the peephole, and was delighted to find Dave Holman standing on her doorstep.

"Hello, stranger," she said, unlatching the security locks and opening the door wide. "What are you doing here?"

"I'm on my way back home to Sedona tomorrow," he said. "I wanted to stop by tonight and see how you were doing and if you needed anything."

"How's Easy?" Ali asked, leading Dave into and through the house.

Dave shrugged. "Out of the woods for now," he answered. "At least, he's out of the ICU. That's major progress."

"So he's going to make it?"

"His doctors seem to think so," Dave said. "And his wife thinks so, too. She says he's too damned stubborn to die, and maybe that's true."

Ali nodded.

"And I hear the grand jury has already started handing down indictments," Dave continued.

Ali nodded again, but without really knowing what was what. She had spent little time following the stories that had surfaced in the media in the aftermath of the Joaquin arrests at the Pink Swan and Amber's and Lucia's deaths in the Palm Springs shootout. Ali found she had scant interest and even less patience left over for people who had allowed themselves to be caught up in Lucia Joaquin's machinations.

Someone else might have been fooled by Ali's studied indifference to the subject at hand, but not Dave Holman. "What's going on with you?" he asked.

At the door of the cluttered family room, Dave paused long enough to survey the damage. Then he stepped forward and moved a stack of boxes off the leather couch, clearing himself a place to sit while Ali poured a glass of wine from one of Paul's most cherished bottles.

"According to Paul's complicated and computerized grading system," she said, handing him the glass, "this is a rare five-hundred-dollar-a-bottle Bordeaux. It's supposed to be top of the line."

Dave took a tentative sip and smacked his lips. "I don't think I've ever tasted five-hundred-dollar wine, but it's not bad. Not bad at all."

They sat for a minute or so in silence. "You still haven't answered my question," he reminded her.

"Have you ever read Ernest Hemingway?" Ali asked finally.

"Not my style of reading material," Dave said. "Why?"

You may not read Ernest Hemingway, Ali thought fondly, *but if you're not a character straight out of Hemingway, I don't know who is.*

"I keep remembering a story of his I read once," Ali continued aloud. "I'm not sure, but I think the title was something like 'The Short Happy Life of Francis Macomber.'"

Dave took another sip of his wine. "And?" he prodded.

"As I recall, Francis was a big-game hunter who took his bitch of a wife along with him on an African safari."

"Sounds like fun," Dave said. "Please tell me the story has a happy ending. Just say the bitchy wife dies."

"That's the whole problem," Ali said. "She doesn't die. She and her husband have a huge fight—or several of them, more like it. He finally tells her to go piss up a rope. Then he walks out into the bush to shoot his buffalo and his wife kills him."

"So he was happy between the end of the fight and the time his wife kills him?" Dave asked. "That's it? That's his short happy life?"

"Pretty much," Ali answered.

Dave helped himself to another sip of wine. "Does this story have a point?" he asked.

"Sort of," Ali said. "Here I was just getting used to the idea that maybe I was wrong about Paul. I was beginning to think that if he was helping Easy catch the bad guys, maybe Paul wasn't as bad as I thought. Then whammo. Out of the blue I find out he has a brand-new baby, a baby no one—including April Gaddis—knew anything about."

"All that means is what goes around comes around," Dave said. "I suppose that's fair."

"For everyone but the baby and her mother," Ali said.

"What are you going to do about it?"

Ali told him.

"You're doing all this without even the formality of a paternity test?"

"I don't need a paternity test," Ali said. "All you have to do is look at Angelina's eyes. She looks just like her daddy."

Dave shook his head. "Sorry," he said. "I never met the man. I guess I'll have to take your word for it."

Ali nodded. "I guess you will."

"And what are you going to do?" he asked.

Ali waved vaguely in the direction of the goods stacked haphazardly in the family room. "Call for a truck, have this stuff dragged back home to Sedona."

"You're not going to stay here?"

"Why would I?" Ali said. "I don't fit in here anymore."

"What are you going to do when you get home?"

"I don't know."

"What about cutloose?" Dave asked. "I've been checking your blog. There's nothing new on it—hasn't been for days."

"I haven't had that much to say," Ali said quietly. "For the first time in my life, I'm at a loss for words. I don't have a clue what I should say about any of this."

It was true. She had tried to respond to the avalanche of e-mail that had poured in, but her heart hadn't been in it. Not even when she was writing to people she knew, like Velma T in Laguna.

"Maybe you could try talking about how lucky you are," Dave suggested.

"Lucky?" Ali asked in dismay. "I'm supposed to be lucky?"

"Sure," Dave said with a grin. "My ex is still alive and giving me hell. Yours is giving you hell, but at least he's dead. So no matter what Paul Grayson has done so far, he won't be doing it anymore." Dave raised his glass. "So here's to cutloose," he said, "because you are cut loose—finally. And here's to your going back home and going to work. People are waiting to hear from you, Ali, Dave Holman included."

"Thank you," Ali said, raising her own glass in return. "Thank you very much."

An exclusive sneak peek at

Hand of Evil

Featuring Ali Reynolds

Available now

Preface

When the car door slammed shut on his hand, the universe came to a stop and nothing else mattered. Nothing. He dropped to his knees, howling in agony while a nearby coyote, startled by the sound, responded with a howl of its own. Rigid with pain, at first he couldn't even reach for the door handle. By the time he did, it was too late. The door lock inside the vehicle had already clicked home.

"Please," he begged. "For God's sake, open the door."

But the answer to that was no—an unequivocal no. The engine turned over and the car began to move.

"You can't do this," he screamed. "You can't!"

. By then the pavement was moving beneath him, slowly at first, then faster and faster. He held out his other hand, trying to brace himself or somehow pull himself back to his feet. For a moment that almost worked and he was close to upright, but then the speed of the car outdistanced his scrambling feet and he fell again, facedown this time, with the full weight of his body pulling on the exploding pain in his fingers.

As the speed of the vehicle increased, so did his agonized screams. The parking lot's layer of loose gravel scraped and tore at him, shredding his blue-and-white jogging suit; shredding his skin. By the time the hurtling car bounced over the first speed bump, he was no longer screaming. Plowing face first into the second one momentarily knocked him unconscious.

He came to when the car door opened. Once his trapped hand was released from the doorframe, he fell to the ground. He couldn't actually see the car or even the ground for that matter. He seemed to have been struck blind. Nor could he differentiate the pain in his crippled hand from the agony in the rest of his tortured body, but his ears still worked. He heard the car door slam shut again and felt the spray of gravel from the tires as it drove away into the night, leaving him in absolute darkness.

He lay there for a long time, knowing he was barely alive and feeling his life's blood seeping out through layers of damaged skin. He tried crawling, but he couldn't make that work.

"Help," he called weakly. "Somebody, please help me."

In the wilds of Phoenix's South Mountain

Preserve, only a single prowling coyote heard the dying man's final whispered plea for help. The coyote was on the trail of his dinner—an elusive bunny—and he paid no attention.

No one else did, either.

Sybil Harriman strode through the early morning chill and reveled in the sunlight and the clear crisp air. Across the valley, she could see the layer of smog settling in over the rest of the city, but here it was cold and clear—cold enough to see her breath and make her nose run and her eyes water, but not cold enough to scare her away from walking the full course of the park's Alta Trail and back to the parking lot along the Bajada.

She had been warned that Alta was "too difficult" for someone her age, and that she certainly shouldn't walk it alone. So she did so, at least twice a week. Because she could. And as she walked along, huffing and puffing a little, truth be known, she was also drinking in the view and the cactus and the birds—birds so different from the ones she'd grown up with back in Chicago—and she was also thinking about how wrong she'd been and wishing things had been different.

Herman had wanted to move here the moment he retired from working for Merck. She was the one who had fought it, saying they should stay where they were in order to be closer to the kids and grandkids, although a lot of good that had done. Finally, when Herm's arthritis had gotten so bad that he could barely walk, she had relented. Now she was sorry they hadn't come sooner, while Herman would have been able to reap some of the benefits of desert living.

His arthritis had improved so much once they were in Arizona it was unbelievable, but then the rest of it had happened. The dry climate could do nothing at all to stave off the ravages and gradual decline that was Alzheimer's. As for the kids? Once Herm died, it had been plain enough that what they wanted more than anything was to get their greedy little hands on their father's money. Well, thanks to the trust Herm had wisely insisted on setting up, they weren't getting any of that, not until Sybil was damned good and ready. And that was another reason she walked every single day. She was determined to live as long and as well as she could.

Let 'em wait, she told herself fiercely as she marched along. *They can wait until hell freezes over.*

When she returned to Chicago for Herm's funeral, her friends there hardly recognized her. They thought she had dropped the excess weight she had carried all those years in a fit of sudden grief. In actual fact, the process had been much less abrupt than that—and much more permanent. She had started by walking four miles each day on the flat but circular streets in their Awatukee neighborhood. Later she had forced herself up and down the steeper grades and gradually more and more difficult trails throughout Phoenix's South Mountain Preserve.

Sybil was one of the early birds this crisp January morning. She had seen not a soul on her morning walk—at least no other humans—in the course of her almost three solitary hours. There had been plenty of bunnies, however, and scads of other early birds—doves, quail, skittish roadrunners, breakfasting cactus wrens, finches, colorful hummingbirds, hawks, and even an ebony-feathered, red-eyed phainopepla. Now, as she approached the spot where the trail crossed San Juan Road, it was close to midmorning and the sun was high.

San Juan Road had been closed indefinitely for some strange reason, so there shouldn't have been any traffic. Still, Sybil was too much of a city girl to cross a road or a street without looking both ways. And that's when she saw it—what appeared to be a pile of rags or trash lying in the middle of the roadway some thirty or forty yards northeast of the now-abandoned San Juan parking lot.

Offended that someone would toss out a load of garbage and leave it there in the road, Sybil headed in that direction. She was determined to clean up the mess and haul it off to the nearest garbage containers. Ten yards or so away from the debris field, however, she saw the blood.

With a trembling hand, she pulled out her cell

phone and dialed 9–1–1. "Emergency operator. What are you reporting?"

Sybil was closer to the mess now—much too close—and wished she wasn't. There was blood everywhere. It was hard to tell that the flayed and bloody pulp inside the pile of shredded clothing was even human, but she knew it was.

"A body," she managed at last. "I've just found a human body lying here in the middle of the road."

She didn't hear the panic in her voice, but the operator evidently did. "Calm down," the operator advised her. "What is your name and your location?"

Sybil took a deep breath and forced herself to get a grip. "Sybil Harriman," she replied. "I'm in the park—South Mountain Preserve. The body is just to the east of the abandoned parking lot on San Juan Road."

"Units are on the way," the operator told her briskly. "Are you sure the person is dead? Did you check for a pulse?"

Sybil looked at the mound of bloody flesh, searching for wrists. One hand, virtually skinless, was little more than a bloody stump. The other hand contained a relatively recognizable thumb, but the four fingers seemed to have been mashed flat. Sybil knew at once there would be no pulse in either one of those two mangled wrists nor would there be any possibility of bringing the bloodied victim back to life.

"He's dead," she whispered to the operator. "Sorry. I've got to hang up now."

Sybil snapped the phone shut. Then, gagging, she staggered over to the edge of the road and promptly lost the single banana she had eaten for breakfast.

As she straightened up and waited, listening for approaching sirens, Sybil Harriman knew it was the last banana she would eat for a very long time.

Chapter 1

With her laptop asleep and perched virtually untouched on her crossed legs, Ali Reynolds stared into the flames of the burning gas log fireplace. She was supposed to be working on her blog, cutlooseblog.com, but on this chilly January morning she wasn't. Or maybe she was. She was trying to think of what to say in today's post, but her mind remained stubbornly blank—right along with her computer screen.

Ali had started cutloose in the aftermath of the sudden and almost simultaneous ends of both her television newscasting career and her marriage. Back then, fueled by anger, cutloose had been a tool for dealing with the unexpected bumps in her own life. To her surprise, what had happened to her was far more commonplace than she had known, and what she had written in cutloose had touched chords in the lives of countless other women.

Since the murder of Paul Grayson, Ali's not

quite but nearly ex-husband, cutloose had morphed into something else entirely. For weeks now it had focused on grief and grieving—on the pitfalls and setbacks that lie in wait for those attempting to recover from the loss of a loved one or even a not-so-loved one. Ali had learned enough from her readers that she could almost have declared herself an expert on the subject if it hadn't been for the inconvenient reality that she had zero perspective on the topic. She was still too deep in grief herself. As her mother, Edie Larson, would have said, drawing on her endless supply of platitudes: She couldn't see the forest for the trees.

Because Ali was back in her hometown of Sedona, Arizona, grieving. She grieved for a phantom of a marriage that had evidently never been what she had thought it was and for a job she had loved but which had come with zero job security and no reciprocal loyalty.

Having people write to her and tell her that "someday you'll be over it" or "it doesn't matter how long it takes" wasn't helping Ali Reynolds. She couldn't yet tell what she was supposed to be over. Was she supposed to be over Paul's death or over his many betrayals? How long would it take her to move beyond the shock of learning of the child—a little girl—her husband had fathered out of wedlock while he was still married to Ali? Ali hadn't even known of Angelina Rojas's existence until after Paul's death, and looking out for the financial welfare of the child and her mother had made tying up Paul's estate that much more complicated.

There were times Ali felt downright resentful when she heard from widows—real widows whose husbands had been faithful, honorable men—who were struggling with their own overwhelming sense of loss. It was all she could do sometimes to keep from writing back to them and saying, "Hey, you, don't you know how lucky you were? At least your dead husband's not driving you nuts from beyond the grave."

Sam, Ali's one-eyed, one-eared, sixteen-pound tabby cat, shifted uneasily on the back of the couch behind her and let one paw fall on Ali's shoulder. Sam had belonged to Matt and Julie Bernard, the children of Ali's murdered friend, Reenie Bernard. When the children had gone to live with their grandparents, Sam had been unable to join them and Ali had taken in Sam. Ali had never liked or particularly disliked cats. She had never thought about them much one way or the other—and Sam was anything but outgoing or sociable. But now, almost a year since Sam's unexpected arrival, Ali had started thinking of the animal in terms of "my cat" rather than "their cat."

Ali turned and scratched the seemingly permanent frown lines on Sam's ugly forehead. "How about if you do the blog this morning?" she asked.

Sam simply yawned, closed her one good eye, and went back to sleep. When the doorbell rang, Sam leaped to life. Spooked by newcomers of any kind, the cat scrambled off the couch and disappeared from view. Ali knew from past experience that it would probably be several hours before she'd be able to coax the wary feline back out of hiding.

Putting the laptop on the coffee table, Ali hurried to the door. She was expecting Kip Hogan, her parents' handyman, to drop off her refinished burled-maple credenza. That and the comfy leather sofa and chair were the three pieces of furniture she had brought to her mountaintop mobile home with her from her former digs in L.A. The top of the credenza had been damaged when someone had carelessly deposited a wet vase on it. Now, after careful sanding and varnishing, Ali's father assured her that the wood had been restored to its former glory.

Except, when Ali looked out the peephole, Kip Hogan was nowhere in sight. The man on Ali's front porch, a wizened but dapper looking elderly gentleman in a suit and tie, was holding a small envelope. He looked somewhat familiar, but she couldn't quite place him. In the old days, growing up in small-town Arizona, Ali wouldn't have hesitated at opening the door to a stranger, but times had changed in Sedona. More important, Ali had changed. She cautiously cracked the door open but only as far as the length of the security chain.

"May I help you?" she asked.

"Ms. Reynolds?" the man asked. He wore a brimmed leather cap that he tipped respectfully in Ali's direction.

"Yes."

"A message for you, madam," he said politely. Removing a soft leather driving glove, he proffered the envelope through the narrow opening. "From Miss Arabella Ashcroft."

Ali recognized the name at once. "Thank you." She took the envelope and started to close the door, but the man stopped her.

"If you'll forgive me, madam, I was directed to wait for an answer."

Using her finger, Ali tore open the creamy white envelope. It was made from expensive paper stock, as was the gold-bordered note card she found inside. Written across it, in spidery, old-fashioned script was the following: Dear Alison, Please join me for tea this afternoon if at all possible. 2:30. 113 Manzanita Hills Road. Miss Arabella Ashcroft.

A summons from Miss Arabella, one of Sedona's more formidable dowagers, was not to be taken lightly or ignored.

"Of course," Ali said at once. "Tell her I'll be there."

"Would you like me to come fetch you?" the messenger asked, gesturing over his shoulder at the venerable bright yellow Rolls-Royce Silver Cloud idling in Ali's driveway.

"Oh, no," Ali told him. "I can get there on my own. I know the way."

And she did, too, despite the fact that it had been twenty-five-plus years earlier when she had last had afternoon tea with Arabella Ashcroft and her equally daunting mother, Anna Lee, at the imposing Ashcroft home on Manzanita Hills Road.

Ali's visitor bowed slightly from the waist and backed away from the door. "Very well," he said. "I'll tell Miss Arabella she can expect you." He tipped his cap once again, turned on his heel, and marched away. Once he drove out of sight, Ali closed the door. Then, with both the note card and envelope in hand, she returned to the couch lost in a haze of memories.

On a Friday afternoon two weeks before Ali had been scheduled to graduate from Cottonwood's Mingus Mountain High School, she had bounded into her parents diner, Sedona's Sugarloaf Café, for her after-school shift. All through high school she had helped out by waiting tables after school and during Christmas and summer vacations. As she tied on her apron she spotted an envelope with her name on it propped up next to the cash register. There was no stamp or return address, so obviously it had been hand delivered.

"What's this?" she had asked Aunt Evie, her mother's twin sister and her parents' full partner in the restaurant venture.

"It's still sealed, isn't it?" Aunt Evie had asked. "How about if you open it and find out?"

Ali had opened the envelope on the spot.

Inside she had found a note card very similar to the one she had received just now: "Please join my daughter and me for tea, this coming Sunday, May 21, 2:30 P.M. at our home, 113 Manzanita Hills Road, Sedona, Arizona." The note had been signed Anna Lee Ashcroft, Arabella's mother.

"Tea!" Ali had exclaimed in disbelief. "I've been invited to tea?"

Taking the note from Ali's hand, Aunt Evie examined it and then handed it back. "That's the way it looks," she said.

"I've never been invited to tea in my life," Ali said. "And who all is going? Are you invited?"

Aunt Evie shook her head.

"Is anyone else I know invited, then?" Ali asked. "And why would someone my age want to go to tea with a bunch of old ladies in the first place?"

"You'll want to go if you know what's good for you," Aunt Evie had said severely. "But this doesn't give us much time."

"Time for what?" Ali had asked.

"To get down to Phoenix and find you something appropriate to wear," Aunt Evie had answered.

Ali's high school years had been tough ones for the owners and operators of the Sugarloaf Café. Things had been so lean during Ali's junior year that she had turned down an invitation to the prom rather than admit she didn't have a formal to wear and couldn't afford to buy one.

By the end of her senior year, things were only

marginally better, but she was astonished when Aunt Evie took the whole next day—a Saturday—off work. She drove Ali to Metrocenter, a shopping mall two hours away in Phoenix, where they spent the whole day at what Ali considered to be the very ritzy Goldwater's Department Store putting together a tea-appropriate outfit. Aunt Evie had charged the whole extravagant expense—a stylish linen suit, silk blouse, and shoes—to her personal account. The loan of Aunt Evie's fake pearls would complete the outfit.

At the time, Ali had been too naive to question her aunt's uncharacteristic behavior. Instead she had simply accepted Aunt Evie's kindness at face value.

The next week at school, Ali had held her breath hoping to hear that some of her classmates had also received invitations to the unprecedented Ashcroft tea, but no one had. No one mentioned it, not even Ali's best friend, Reenie Bernard, so Ali didn't mention it either.

Finally, on the appointed day, Ali had left her parents and Aunt Evie hard at work at the Sugarloaf doing Sunday afternoon clean-up and had driven herself to Anna Lee Ashcroft's Manzanita Hills place overlooking downtown Sedona. Compared to her parents' humble abode out behind the restaurant, the Ashcroft home was downright palatial.

Ali had driven up the steep, black-topped driveway and parked her mother's Dodge in front of a glass-walled architectural miracle with a spectacular view that encompassed the whole valley. Once out of the car, Ali, unaccustomed to wearing high heels, had tottered unsteadily up the wide flagstone walkway. By the time she stepped onto the spacious front porch shaded by a curtain of bloom-laden wisteria, her knees were still knocking but she was grateful not to have tripped and fallen.

Taking a deep, steadying breath, Ali rang the bell. The door was opened by a maid wearing a black-and-white uniform who led her into and through the house. The exquisite furniture, gleaming wood tables, and lush oriental rugs were marvelous to behold. She tried not to stare as she was escorted out to a screened porch overlooking an immense swimming pool. Her hostess, a frail and seemingly ancient woman confined to a wheel chair, her legs wrapped in a shawl, waited there while another somewhat younger woman hovered watchfully in the background.

Ali was shown to a chair next to a table set with an elaborate collection of delicate cups, saucers, plates, and silver as well as an amazing array of tiny, crustless sandwiches and sweets.

"So," the old woman said, peering across the table at Ali through a pair of bejeweled spectacles, "I'm Mrs. Ashcroft, and this is my daughter, Arabella. You must be Alison Larson. Let's have a look at you."

Feeling like a hapless worm being examined by some sharp-eyed, hungry robin, Ali had no choice but to endure the woman's silent scrutiny. At last she nodded as if satisfied with Ali's appearance. "I suppose you'll do," she said.

Do for what? Ali wondered.

"Your teachers all speak very highly of you," Anna Lee said.

Ali should have been delighted to hear that, but she couldn't help wondering why Anna Lee Ashcroft had been gossiping about her with Ali's teachers at Mingus Mountain High. As it was, all Ali could do was nod stupidly. "Thank you," she murmured.

"I understand you want to study journalism," Anna Lee continued.

Ali had discussed her long-held secret ambition once or twice with Mrs. Casey, her journalism teacher, but since going to college seemed like an impossible dream at the moment, Ali was trying to think about the future in somewhat more realistic terms—like maybe going to work for the phone company.

"I may have mentioned it," Ali managed.

"You've changed your mind then?" Anna Lee demanded sharply. "You're no longer interested in journalism?"

"It's not that," Ali said forlornly, "it's just . . ."

"Just what?"

"I still want to study journalism," Ali said at last, "but I'll probably have to work a couple of years to earn money before I can think about going to college." It was a painful admission.

"My parents really can't help out very much right now. I'll have to earn my own way."

"You're telling me you're poor then?" Anna Lee wanted to know.

Ali looked around the room. Even out on this screened patio, the elegant furnishings were far beyond anything Ali had ever seen even in her friend Reenie Bernard's more upscale surroundings. Ali had never thought of herself or of her family as poor, but now with something for comparison she realized they probably were.

"I suppose so," Ali said.

Without another word, Anna Lee Ashcroft grasped the handle of a small china bell and gave it a sharp ring. Almost immediately a man appeared bearing a tray—a silver tray with a silver tea service on it. Remembering the scene now, Ali couldn't help but wonder if that man and the sprite who had delivered that morning's envelope weren't one and the same albeit a few decades older.

The man had carefully placed the tea service on the table in front of Anna Lee. She had leaned forward and picked up a cup. "Sugar?" she asked, filling the cup to the brim and handing it over with a surprisingly steady hand.

Ali nodded.

"One lump or two?"

"Two, please."

"Milk?"

"No, thank you."

Arabella moved silently to the foreground and began deftly placing finger sandwiches and what Ali would later recognize as petit fours onto delicately patterned china plates. Mrs. Ashcroft said nothing more until the butler—at least that's what Ali assumed he was—had retreated back the way he had come, disappearing behind a pair of swinging doors into what Ali assumed must lead to a hallway or maybe the kitchen.

Ali juggled cup, saucer, napkin, and plate and hoped she wasn't doing something terribly gauche while Anna Lee Ashcroft poured two additional cups—one for her daughter and one for herself.

"I don't have a college education, either," Anna Lee said at last. "In my day young women of my social standing weren't encouraged to go off to college. When Arabella came along, her father sent her off to finishing school in Switzerland, but that was it. Furthering her education beyond that would have been unseemly."

No comment from Ali seemed called for, so she kept quiet and concentrated on not dribbling any tea down the front of her new silk blouse.

"But just because my daughter and I don't have the benefit of a higher education," Anna Lee continued, "that doesn't mean we think it's unimportant, right, Arabella?"

Arabella nodded but said nothing. Sipping her tea, she seemed content to let her mother do the bulk of the talking, but there was something in the daughter's wary silence that made Ali uneasy.

"You must be wondering why you've been asked to come here today," Anna Lee continued.

"Yes," Ali said. "I am."

"This is the first time I've done this," Anna Lee said, "so it may seem a bit awkward. I've been told that most of the time announcements of this nature are made at class night celebrations or at some other official occasion, but I wanted to do it this way. In private."

Ali was still mystified.

"I've decided to use some of my inheritance from my mother to establish a scholarship in her honor, the Amelia Dougherty Askins Scholarship, to benefit poor but smart girls from this area. You've been selected to be our first recipient—as long as you go on to school, that is."

Ali was stunned. "A scholarship?" she managed, still not sure she had heard correctly. "You're giving me a scholarship?"

Anna Lee Ashcroft nodded. "Not quite a 'full ride' as they say," she added dryly. "What you'll get from us is enough for tuition, books, room, and some board. If your parents really can't help, you may need to work part-time, but you shouldn't have to put off starting. In fact, you should be able to go off to school this fall right along with all your classmates."

And that's exactly what Ali had done. The

scholarship had made all the difference for her—it had made going on to college possible. And everything else in Ali's life had flowed from there.

So Alison Larson Reynolds owed the Ashcrofts—owed them big. If Arabella Ashcroft wanted to summon her to tea once again some twenty-five years later, Ali would be there—with bells on.

Experience
Ali Reynold's
spine-tingling
adventures
on audio!

New York Times bestselling author
J. A. Jance's "Ali Reynolds" audiobooks
include
Hand of Evil and *Web of Evil*.

Praise for J. A. Jance's audiobooks:

"Karen Ziemba's narration places listeners
right in the middle of a mystery with
her convincing characterization...Ziemba
threads emotions into her reading and weaves
interest with thumbnail portraits..."

—*AudioFile*, on *Web of Evil*

SIMON & SCHUSTER
AUDIO

POCKET BOOKS
A Division of Simon & Schuster
A CBS COMPANY

Listen to free excerpts of these and many other titles at
SimonSaysAudio.com

16663

Not sure what to read next?

Visit Pocket Books online at

www.simonsays.com

Reading suggestions for
you and your reading group
New release news
Author appearances
Online chats with your favorite writers
Special offers
Order books online
And much, much more!

POCKET BOOKS
A Division of Simon & Schuster
A CBS COMPANY

POCKET STAR BOOKS
A Division of Simon & Schuster
A CBS COMPANY

13456

Looking for a **thrill?**
Pick up a blockbuster thriller from Pocket Books!

A Thousand Bones
P.J. Parrish
A female cop...a haunting memory...
And a trail of murders from the past leading to a
vicious crime in the present.

Takedown
Brad Thor
For a terrorist mastermind, America is the land of
opportunity...and only one man can bring him down.

Counterplay
Robert K. Tanenbaum
Sometimes an eye for an eye isn't enough.

Twenty-Seven Bones
Jonathan Nasaw
There are twenty-seven bones in the human hand...and
twenty-seven trophies for a ruthless killer to covet.

Dead Line
Brian McGrory
A reporter's hunt for the truth becomes a race for survival...

Unholy Birth
Andrew Neiderman
Congratulations! It's a boy. But is he a blessing...or a curse?

POCKET BOOKS
A Division of Simon & Schuster
A CBS COMPANY

POCKET STAR BOOKS
A Division of Simon & Schuster
A CBS COMPANY

Available wherever books are sold
or at www.simonsays.com.

16825